Walt & Stumpy

Walt & Stumpy

Adventures of a Man and His Squirrel

Mark S. Haman

Mark S. Haman

Printed in the United States of America.

ISBN: 978-1-951568-24-5
Library of Congress Control Number: 2022907249

Cover and title page art by Lee Muir-Haman

Title page and chapter photo: iStock/FunkinsDesigns

Designed by Mary A. Wirth

493 South Pleasant Street
Amherst, Massachusetts 01002
413.230.3943
smallbatchbooks.com

To my parents,
Anne Marise Haman and Howard Haman Jr.,
and to Jerry Wooding and Jerry Boucher, loyal listeners
and even more loyal friends.

CONTENTS

INTRODUCTION

Meet Walt and Stumpy

WELCOME TO KIBBEE Pond, legendary abode of Walt Walthers, weather watcher, and his buddy Stumpy the Squirrel. A few words of explanation may be in order before you dive into this book. Salman Rushdie may posit a whole "sea of stories" from which a storyteller can draw inspiration, but this book offers something less formidable: a *pond* of stories, where you may not encounter any great waves of narrative sublimity or tides of intense emotion, but where you can expect some ripples of laughter and occasional splashes of amusement. Some of you—the three or four of you who happened to stumble onto my radio show a few years back—are already familiar with Walt and Stumpy, but the rest of you might like to know that Walt is an octogenarian who lives on the shore of a small pond in Townsend, Massachusetts, in a cabin he built mostly himself about twenty-five years ago; he, of course, likes to report his age as "eleventy-seven," and you'll soon see further evidence that he prides himself on being clever with language, inventive, and generally playful.

Walt, retired now from his previous employments, calls himself a weather watcher, a title that demonstrates what he considers pleasing alliteration (as well as assonance and consonance), especially when attached to his name. His "profession" consists of using a variety of resources to alert his clients to present and potential future meteorological conditions; some of those resources, of course, are technological and electronic, and he has plenty of equipment around the cabin to monitor online what's happening with weather around the world. However, his own powers of observation and his respect for the natural world are themselves resources of substantial value. Most people who subscribe to his service are as interested in his comments about wildlife and his own existence at the pond as they are in his meteorological predictions—although his prognostications have proven remarkably accurate over time.

In recent years I've spent a lot of time at Kibbee Pond myself, chatting with Walt and enjoying the company of Stumpy, a young gray squirrel who lost his tail in an accident a few years back and now spends most of his time with Walt. Stumpy tends to be more excitable than his philosophical human roommate, but the two share an appreciation of the seasonal cycle and the small wonders of the physical world. Both have attuned themselves to the shifting moods of the pond itself—to the songs the wind makes in the different kinds of trees around the cabin, the calls of frogs and birds and insects, the varied play of light on water or snow and ice, and all the mundane beauties that others might take for granted. I'd love to live at Kibbee Pond, but visiting there has helped me open myself to the simple beauties around my own home.

Just the other day, I asked Walt, over a glass of iced coffee and one of his peanut butter and chocolate chip muffins, if he ever felt the urge to travel. His answer sounded almost like a credo: "I did some traveling earlier in my life, especially during my stint in the Coast Guard during World War II, and seeing other parts of the world broadened my view and gave me a sense of the universal elements in human nature—you know, the things we share, despite the important differences. But I've always felt that my fulfillment comes from focusing on the place where I live, trying to know it and appreciate it through close observation of specific details, and from interacting respectfully with the animals and plants and other natural elements around me, as well as the people I encounter. I've always thought of myself as an animist, trying to stay open to the larger spirit that runs through everything and from which all things take life, so I have no problem talking to squirrels or trees or rocks or the wind; they all share that spirit, I think. The trick is to listen to them, too, and not just talk. I'm only one small element in this huge world, and I try not to overestimate my own importance, while still accepting responsibility for the consequences of what I say and do."

As you read these stories, you may wonder what audience I had in mind when I wrote them. I have trouble answering that question, but I think my best effort at a true response is that I wrote the stories for adults who haven't lost touch with the child inside them and who don't think themselves silly or irresponsible when they hunger for a simpler world, a place where people and animals treat each other well, with respect and compassion. That's the kind of place Kibbee Pond is—a "Peaceable Kingdom," where the Labrador retriever lies down with the squirrel, and a sprightly geezer leads them.

Let's go there now. Walt has a fresh batch of muffins about to come out of the oven—gluten-free blueberry-lemon, I think—and he's set up some extra chairs on the deck above the pond. Pour yourself some hot or iced coffee, and pull up a seat.

Note: You may notice that my writing in this book has a conversational tone. That's because I wrote the stories initially to read aloud, live on the air, during a radio show I hosted some years back. With any luck, you'll hear a real speaking voice as you read, a voice that blends sentimentality with a playful, gentle humor. The stories also reflect the weather of the years, seasons, and specific weeks when I wrote them. Thus, beneath the titles are the dates when I planned to read each story on the air.

Walt & Stumpy

1

Stumpy and the Snapper

JUNE 15, 2011

While most people around here have been having a quiet summer, Walt Walthers's cabin on Kibbee Pond over in Townsend was a veritable hotbed of social activity last week, at least by Walt's standards. After the excitement of a small thunderstorm-inspired waterspout, Walt, who supplements his retirement income with the proceeds from his weather-watching service, and Stumpy, his short-tailed pet gray squirrel, were hoping for some R and R, and they had settled back into their daily early-summer, early-morning routine. That routine, by the way, starts with them enjoying breakfast from seats on the deck overlooking the pond; it continues with them watering the garden and then the tomatoes on the deck before pulling weeds around the bean shoots, which are now sprouting through the openings in the black plastic Walt put down before planting on Memorial Day weekend. I should clarify that Walt is the one who actually holds the hose and carries the watering can, and he is also the one who pulls the weeds; Stumpy "supervises," as Walt puts it, which means hopping from row to row and watching while Walt works . . . or maybe even nibbling on a bit of grass or other greens that the human gardener has cast aside. After these duties, coffee is next on the agenda.

After their morning coffee—I say *their*, but Stumpy, of course, doesn't drink coffee; he just keeps Walt company out on the deck—anyway, after their morning coffee, Walt fires up the three-horsepower Johnson outboard on Nelly, his wooden rowboat, and takes Stumpy on a quiet ride around Kibbee Pond. Wearing his omnipresent porkpie hat, the man is careful also to put on his life vest, and though he doesn't have the exact equivalent for his buddy, he always throws a flotation cushion into the bow, where Stumpy likes to ride. I should point out that before they head down to the dock, Walt leaves a message for his weather-watcher clients on his answering machine, just in case one of them tries to contact him while he and the Stumpster are out on the water; he does, after all, pride himself on providing his clients with up-to-date and accurate information about the weather, even when he is attending to other responsibilities. Later in the day, he will send out emails and even leave a voice-mail message for his faithful followers.

In the aftermath of the waterspout that tore through during a violent thunderstorm earlier this month, the two crewmates have found the southwest corner of the pond particularly interesting, because a swath of broken trees, including one giant white pine that has tumbled into the water, shows where the twister burst out of the woods and onto the pond. "Definitely tornadic," Walt said on their first visit to the spot, referring to the kind of waterspout that is merely a continuation of a land tornado, as opposed to the fair-weather kind, which springs up over the ocean or large lakes. With its area of a mere two hundred acres, Kibbee Pond, it's fair to say, does not qualify as a large lake, let alone an ocean.

Some mornings, by the way, Walt also throws his fly rod in the boat, but he rarely fishes these days, content to watch for birds and other wildlife. One recent morning, in fact, the two crewmates watched a mink swim from one shore of the large pond to the other side, a distance of close to a quarter mile. Walt followed at a safe distance so as not to terrify the aquatic weasel, but he was ready to proffer an oar if it faltered and started to sink. "No real cause for worry, I guess," Walt said, marveling at the animal's stamina.

Other mornings, they have cruised close to shore, looking for turtles on branches or on rocks that stick out of the water or on the trunks of downed trees, which form convenient ramps for the painted turtles and stinkpots that like to crawl out for a nap in the sun. One morning last week as they putted past an unusually long row of shell-toting sunbathers, Walt chuckled and said, "I've often thought that I might have some turtle DNA, given my predilection for basking. I wonder if these guys put on their sunscreen this morning. Maybe they'll have to put up some beach umbrellas later in the day for a little relief from all those rays."

Another morning last week, as the Johnson eased them along, Walt noticed—well out from the shore—what at first looked like the tip of a thick tree branch sticking up from the surface of the pond thirty yards or so in front of the boat. He had learned from past experience that, despite appearances, what he was seeing was not likely to be driftwood, even in the aftermath of a big storm. Quietly, he said, "Watch this, Stump." He revved the motor slightly to move closer. When the boat was about five yards away, the branch disappeared, and the surface of the water roiled in a disc shape about two feet long. Walt laughed. "Snapper," he said, "and pretty big at that! But not as big as that one we see cruising off the end of the dock sometimes." Over the years, Walt has learned that snapping turtles enjoy cruising on the surface, catching the sun's warmth and surveying their domain, paddling serenely along like some royal barge in King George I's time, stroking slowly with each rear leg in sequence as if keeping time to the stately measures of Handel's *Water Music.*

After their boat ride, Walt and Stumpy often have "their" second cup of coffee out on the deck, where they can feel some of the breeze off the water. If the day is getting warm, Walt may move his chair to the southern end of the deck, where a midsize maple supplies some shade, but Stumpy likes to bask regardless of the temperature, sometimes even rolling over on his back on the deck rail. "You know, Stumpy," Walt has said more than once, "the way you love the sun, you, too, might just be part turtle. Maybe that's why your tail isn't any longer." Walt chuckles each time, but Stumpy's routine includes ignoring his human companion's jokes.

By the way, if you've been wondering how Stumpy lost his tail, the story is a bit embarrassing for Walt; consequently, he generally avoids telling it. Nevertheless, I can give you a brief synopsis now. About a year and a half ago, Walt was living alone and had been training the squadron of squirrels that lived in the vicinity of his cabin to take peanuts from his hand. One particularly rambunctious young rodent (he has since become only slightly less rambunctious) had taken to climbing the screen of Walt's kitchen door in his impatience and enthusiasm for his morning treat. This particular morning, the fur-faced creature now known as Stumpy had climbed up to the eaves, and when the squirrels' benefactor opened the door, the young rascal launched himself from the roof onto Walt's head. In his surprise, the gift-bearing geezer lost his balance and fell at the edge of the step, landing in part on Stumpy. The impact shattered the bone in his furred friend's caudal appendage, and after emergency veterinary surgery, Dr. Brad Schmidt could save only two inches or so of the once-gorgeous ensign. You might be tempted to say that that was not a banner day for Stumpy or Walt, but time has proven such a statement to be an oversimplification, for without that fortunate fall, that *felix culpa,* the deep connection and abiding friendship between man and squirrel that arose from Walt's patient nursing of the injured Stumpy might never have occurred. Walt's penance seems to have compensated for Stumpy's lost pennant.

But back to the more immediate present of our story. . . . On another morning last week, as the two voyagers were tying back up to the aluminum dock that projects from the beach below the cabin, Stumpy started chattering and twitching, and Walt realized his sidekick had spotted something on the shoreline. The young squirrel was out of the boat and up the dock, in full guard-dog mode, before Walt could object. Only after cleating the bowline was Walt able to turn his attention fully to what had galvanized his rodent buddy. "Uh-oh," he muttered as he clambered stiffly up onto the dock. "Stump!" he yelled. "Don't do anything stupid now. You don't want to mess with her."

At the crest of the sandy bank above the dock, Stumpy was facing off against a huge snapping turtle, with a shell closer to three feet long than two. Walt suspected that she was the big one he had seen on hot mornings for many years now swimming along on the surface of the pond. But if Stumpy was part turtle, he was also part canine, with a territoriality that may have had more to do with loyalty to Walt than with any possessiveness on the young squirrel's part. Right now, he was chirring and cursing in full rodent street vernacular, and while Walt couldn't make out any specifics, he understood the gist.

The turtle, on the other hand, was saying little, just giving off an occasional hiss, like air escaping a leaky tire valve . . . if tires ever had crusty shells and sharp reptilian beaks. She was also standing fully upright on all four legs so she could turn slowly and step toward Stumpy. Walt had crested the sandbank by now, and he approached the turtle from one side. "Stumpy," he said, "get over yourself. Come here." Then he slapped the side of his thigh—the signal for his friend to jump up, climb his pant leg, and perch on his shoulder. Stumpy, however, had enough of a bee in his bonnet that Walt had to deepen his voice and put a warning tone in it: "*Stumpy* . . ." This time, the squirrel complied, and in a couple of seconds he was nuzzling Walt's right ear.

Walt slowly backed away from the snapper. After a few more seconds, she turned back landward and lumbered a bit farther north through the sparse grass. The elderly man walked back toward the deck, where the squirrel hopped down, then commenced a wild, rollicking dash that took him back and forth over the deck and up and down over the railing five or six times before he finally stopped on the rail post next to Walt. There, he drew himself up into a sitting posture and nodded his head several times quickly at the man. Walt laughed. "Well, you certainly had a skeeter in *your* scooter! Pretty proud of yourself, aren't you?" He laughed again. "I may have to get you a collar and a rabies tag and then put up a sign reading 'Caution: Security Squirrel on Duty!' I don't think 'Beware of Dog' would be as intimidating." Stumpy eased down onto the rail and commenced cleaning himself. Maybe preening is a better word. Walt chuckled and went into the cabin.

When, after a few minutes, Walt looked out the cabin window, the snapping turtle was digging in the sand of the pond bank, but when he looked again an hour or so later, she was gone. He had always suspected that that area served as a nesting ground for turtles, but even though he had been lucky enough several years before to see two large adult snappers mating in the shallows nearby, he had never until now seen a female laying eggs. He hoped that the raccoons would not find and devour this clutch so that in a few months, he might be luckier still and see some of the young hatch out. He'd really like to see them march down to the water.

The bit of excitement I have just described occurred on Wednesday, and Walt assumed that things would quiet down again thereafter. On Thursday morning, however, they had another unexpected visitor. As the two friends were relaxing with Walt's second cup of coffee on the deck at about ten o'clock, an unfamiliar silver Volvo sedan pulled into the driveway and stopped next to the vinyl tent that serves as a garage for Walt's old pickup, Lulu. From a partly open rear window, the head of a huge yellow Labrador retriever protruded, its mouth open and its long, pink tongue hanging out nearly to the gravel. "Oh, brother," Walt muttered as Stumpy started to growl behind him on the deck rail. When the driver's door opened, a tall older woman with curly gray hair emerged and stood facing the deck.

"Walt?" she called softly.

Walt had already gotten out of his chair and stepped toward the edge of the deck. The woman laughed as Stumpy hopped off the rail, scooted to Walt's side, and climbed his pant leg to sit on his left shoulder like an oversize, furry earring.

"Arlene?" Walt responded after a moment.

"Yes," the woman said, starting forward, then pausing and turning back toward the car. "Big Bruno," she said, "you stay put and be good." The gigantic pink tongue flicked up and then lolled again, to the left side, sending a rivulet of drool down the car door.

The visitor was Arlene Tosh, and she and Walt had a history. Well, not a history exactly, but the two had dated briefly in high school. Walt, though, had been more interested in Arlene at the time than she was in him, so a romance had never progressed. Nevertheless, they had remained friendly and stayed in contact even after both had settled down to start their families with other partners. Walt and his wife, Annie, had even on occasion had dinner with Arlene and Bill, her husband. Walt hadn't seen Arlene in some time, however; he remembered sending her a card when Bill had passed away a few years back, but it had been ten years or more since they had conversed.

"What brings you out this way?" Walt asked.

"Well," Arlene answered, "I've been taking watercolor painting classes, and my teacher recommended an exhibit that includes some of his work up in Ashby at The Gallery in the Woods. I remembered that your place was not far out of the way, and I thought it had been awhile since I'd seen you. I took a chance you'd be around."

Walt chuckled. "Yes, here I am. I don't stray too far from the pond these days. Too much to see and do right here, especially this time of year. Afraid I might miss the mountain laurel blossoms opening out in the woods or the wood ducks hatching their brood up in the swamp."

Arlene nodded and smiled but said nothing.

"Come on up for a cup of coffee, if you like," Walt continued. "It *has* been awhile. But first, allow me to introduce his nibs, His Most Royal Highness Stumpy the Squirrel." Walt did an elaborate but somewhat stiff bow, so that his left shoulder extended toward the woman, with its gray-furred occupant balancing carefully.

The two caught up over coffee on the deck while Stumpy sat on the front deck rail and stared toward Arlene's car. Arlene talked about her daughter, who was a lab researcher in Minnesota, and Walt told her about his three sons, who were all in distant parts of the country, one of them even abroad in London. They talked also about how they spent their time: Arlene with her work in the DAR, her walks, her painting, and her daily training of Big Bruno; Walt with his weather watching, his work in the garden and on his two vehicles, his metal casting and woodworking, and his stewardship of Stumpy. Once, the dog in the Volvo woofed toward the humans on the deck, and Stumpy stiffened and twitched, resisting the urge to burst into full-voiced chatter.

Arlene, however, turned to Walt and asked, "Do you mind if I let him out for a bit? I brought him along in hopes that he might get a chance to swim. He loves the water, and I'm positive he'll leave Stumpy alone. He cares about only two things, really—food and B-A-L-L-S. I've seen squirrels and rabbits run right in front of his nose, and he hardly even notices. Besides, he likes kitties, and I can just tell him that Stumpy is a 'nice kitty.' Would it be an imposition to bring him out?"

Walt tipped back the porkpie and said, "I think we can give it a try." Then he turned to the watchful squirrel. "Stump, you just give Big Bruno a wide berth. Don't go looking for trouble. Why don't you come up here?" Walt slapped his leg, and soon his earring was back in place, this time on the right side.

When Arlene opened the car door, the tan retriever leaped down, put his nose to the ground, and started snaking back and forth, checking out the olfactory evidence in the driveway and around the deck, pausing at various bushes as if other dogs had been squirting territorial markers there, then thundering on a short distance before screeching to another halt to poke his schnoz into a small pile of leaves and scoff up something. "Probably some kind of poo," Arlene said. "He even eats his own, sometimes." When she took a yellow tennis ball out of her purse, though, Big Bruno looked back at her as if a telepathic connection existed between them. Maybe he had just heard her or smelled the ball, but in any case, his eyes riveted themselves on the chartreuse orb in her hand.

There followed five minutes of feverish aquatic fetch as Arlene threw the ball out into the pond and Big Bruno heaved his hundred-pound frame down the sandbank and flung himself into the water as if he had gills that were being corrupted by the oxygen he had been taking in. Each time, he brought the ball back up the bank, and most times, he spat it out at Arlene's feet, though occasionally he would drop it on purpose a few feet away, then lunge at it with both front feet simultaneously until it started to roll down the hill; at that point he would throw himself headfirst onto the sand and skid like an otter on its slide before picking the ball up again and bringing it back to the woman. He'd come up looking like a butter crunch ice-cream cone that some kid has dropped at the beach but is still trying to eat. Even Stumpy seemed impressed, however, with the big beast's energy and enthusiasm. After more than a dozen plunges, Arlene took the ball, led the dog back to the deck, and commanded him to lie down. At that point, Stumpy decided to come down off Walt's shoulder and approach the exhausted canine. Big Bruno lifted his massive head to sniff in the squirrel's direction, thumped his tail a few times, then rolled onto his side and seemed to pass out.

"He's not used to that much exercise," Arlene explained. "He's a bit overweight, and even though we walk every day, he needs a more strenuous workout on a regular basis."

The two human friends talked awhile longer, with Walt telling Arlene about the big female snapper. She responded with a turtle story of her own.

"When I was eight or nine, we lived in Derry, New Hampshire, and had a cottage on a lake there. I was something of a tomboy, and my best friend was a boy named Roger. He used to call me the Spider Lady because I had a collection of pet spiders and other bugs I would find. Just about every day, we got out our rods and fished from a little neck of land near our place. I always had to bait the hooks for both of us because Roger was squeamish, and if either of us caught anything, I had to take it off the hook. The one exception was if we caught a hornpout; I couldn't deal with the spines, so I'd go get Auntie Eunice, who was the best fisherperson in the family. She'd cook and eat anything we caught, too, even an eel I hooked one time. That thing was so slimy that once I'd touched it, I couldn't get the muck off my hands. It was even nastier than the slugs I used to feed to our ducks. Anyway, sometimes Roger and I fished with worms, but more often, we found freshwater clams and cracked them open.

"One time, we were using the big orange clams—not the smaller, white-fleshed ones—and I got a huge bite. When I reeled in the line, there at the end of it, with its jaws locked around the meat of the clam, was a good-sized snapping turtle. It must have been July 3, because I remember that I put the turtle in my bucket and took it home, where I left it overnight in the bathtub. I was all excited because the next day was the big Fourth of July turtle race for kids down at the pavilion.

"At noon the next day, I carefully lifted my turtle out of the tub by the back of the shell and put it in a brown paper bag. Roger came by, and we walked down to the pavilion, where all the contestants were supposed to put their turtles down under a big cardboard box in the middle of a circle about five feet in radius. Everybody else had a painted turtle much smaller than my snapper, so I figured I was going to win, no contest. When they lifted up the box, though, all the other turtles scuttled off as if their tails were on fire. Mine just sat there, with its legs and head drawn back inside its shell. I was so embarrassed that I stormed out and started home.

"Roger ran to catch up with me. 'Aren't you gonna bring your turtle back?' he asked.

"I shouted out, 'No!' and kept walking straight ahead. I refused to talk about the race for the rest of the summer."

Walt chuckled as the story ended. By that time, Stumpy had climbed up into his lap and was watching Arlene's hands move as she talked. The conversation meandered awhile longer like a small stream moving comfortably over a level landscape, until Walt discovered that he had lost track of time. It was almost noon.

Then Arlene looked at him and asked, "Do you get lonely out here?"

Walt started a bit and then turned to look into her eyes. After a moment he said, "I get lonely just about anywhere. It's just a fact of life. But here it's a bit better than anywhere else."

Arlene nodded. After a moment she said, "Well, Big Bruno, we should probably get going if we want to take in that art exhibit." The hairy leviathan pulled himself up like a bodybuilder struggling with an excessively heavy barbell and then shook one last time, flinging a spray of damp sand onto the other three. Stumpy hopped down from Walt's lap and slowly approached the wagging, droopy-faced dog. Big Bruno sniffed once or twice and then looked up at Arlene.

"Give the kitty a kiss," she said.

The gargantuan pink tongue lapped out and lightly brushed Stumpy's nose. The squirrel jumped back and let out a dismayed chirr. Still, he didn't climb back up Walt's leg.

"Come back if you like," Walt said as Arlene climbed into the Volvo.

"I will."

As the silver car disappeared again behind the hemlocks, Stumpy hopped back onto the deck rail. Walt looked over at his friend. "Well, Stump," he said, "I always used to say the best part about company was when they went home." The dapper duffer reached up and adjusted his porkpie, then cleared his throat before continuing. "All things considered, though, that was fun, and I wouldn't mind seeing them again." Time would tell if the kindly geezer's words were an empty wish or a prophecy.

2

Stumpy and the Squealing Squirrels

June 29, 2011

Ever since Arlene Tosh and her massive yellow Labrador retriever, Big Bruno, visited two weeks ago, Walt Walthers, the elderly weather watcher who lives out on Kibbee Pond in Townsend, has been trying to figure out how to get Stumpy to play ball. Stumpy is the young, tailless squirrel that Walt adopted a year and a half ago when an accident took off the little fellow's magnificent plumed caboose close to its base. During that recent visit with Arlene and Big Bruno, the diminutive rodent seemed fascinated by the dog's enthusiasm for throwing himself into the water or diving into the sand to chase the tennis ball that the woman repeatedly threw for him. Since then, however, nothing Walt has tried with an old tennis ball has sparked any reaction from Stumpy, who certainly shows no predilection for emulating Big Bruno's ardor for fetching.

Walt first brought out the tennis ball while the two were sitting on the deck with their—or, rather, Walt's—morning coffee. "Here, Stumpy! What do you think? Do you want to chase this?" Walt rolled the ball gently toward the far end of the deck, but Stumpy only hopped in the opposite direction to examine a pine cone that had dropped onto the planking during the night.

By the way, without the feathery, gray flag of a tail so typical of squirrels, Stumpy looks more like a short-eared bunny than anything else, and when he hops, the similarity becomes even more pronounced. Walt has sometimes considered another viable comparison: to a woodchuck, albeit an anorexic, prematurely graying one.

Pushing his omnipresent porkpie hat back up his forehead, Walt got slowly out of his chair, walked a bit stiffly down to where the ball had stopped, and bent down to pick it up. "Now, Stump. I don't expect you to *fetch* it back to me. I just thought you might like to *chase* it. Just to clarify my intention here. I didn't mean to insult you. Hey, what if I toss it gently *to* you? Maybe you could catch it with your paws or something. Let it bounce once or even twice, though, so it's not going too fast." Walt gently underhanded the ball toward the squirrel; it bounced once and was headed directly at Stumpy's head, but as the ball approached him, rather than show any interest, Stumpy simply turned his head and leaned enough to one side that the ball continued past him without making contact. He then turned back to his pine cone. Walt wasn't sure what else to try.

After fielding a couple of phone calls from weather-watcher clients, though, Walt thought that a change of venue might make a difference, particularly if he could take advantage of Big Bruno's example. Therefore, he headed over to the pond bank above the dock. He had often seen Stumpy and other gray squirrels tearing across the open stretch of sand under the pines there, chasing each other—changing direction suddenly, screeching to a halt, then dashing up tree trunks and back down—so he figured Stumpy might associate the spot with other kinds of playfulness besides the canine sort. Nevertheless, the squirrel showed no interest whatsoever in the ball, whether Walt tossed it into the sand, rolled it down the bank toward the pond, or balanced it up on a tree branch. Even if Stumpy did have the canine characteristic of territoriality that made him a good watch-"dog," he apparently clung to a squirrel's definition of play.

Walt was hopeful that his buddy would like playing ball because the old-timer has long been an avid fan of the local baseball team, the Squannacook Squealing Squirrels. As it turns out, even before Stumpy came into Walt's life, he was a Squirrel fan. Thus, every couple of weeks during the baseball season, the congenial codger enjoys driving over to home games at the playing field in West Groton, which is known as The Square. (By the way, the locals are vehement that no one should refer to it as a diamond; they're big fans of alliteration as well as baseball.)

The Squealing Squirrels play in the Rose Hip League, and their competition includes such squads as the Wachusett Wood Warblers, the Melrose Mute Swans, and the Taunton Toddlers (no one has ever explained adequately to Walt why any team would want as their mascot some middle-aged guy dressed up as a one-year-old baby in a huge cloth diaper and constantly sucking his thumb, but there the guy is at all the Toddlers' games). The perennial league champions are the Nashoba Tooth-Gnashers, named by the local orthodontist who is their primary sponsor.

As with any minor league baseball team, the main appeal of the Squealing Squirrels comes from the personalities involved, and boy, do the Squirrels have personality! Their manager is the legendary No-Tooth Newcomb, who has been the skipper of the team for as long as Walt or anyone else of his acquaintance can remember. People in the area are convinced that many of the sayings attributed to Yogi Berra, Leo Durocher, and Danny Ozark actually originated with No-Tooth, who earned that sobriquet as a young player when he ran into the outfield fence while chasing a long fly ball. He made the catch but lost all of his front teeth and has never gotten around to having them replaced, even in the offseason. Rumor places his age somewhere between ninety-one and one hundred and four.

The first baseman is Boss McAllister, a forty-four-year-old who spent all of two months in the Big Show with the old Montreal Expos about twenty years ago. Boss, five-foot-four and somewhere around 285 pounds, is, with his unique physique, a terrific power hitter, this season averaging a home run in every four at bats. However, that physique has some disadvantages, too, and Boss is not quick on the basepaths. In fact, he set a Rose Hip League record one week this past May with six ground outs . . . to the outfield.

The Squirrels' shortstop is Skillsaw Jenkins, another real character. His claim to fame is the precision with which he carves out a ninety-degree angle at each bag as he runs the bases. He never rounds the bases, and the fans at The Square enthusiastically applaud his geometrical accuracy, even if his approach does cost him time and does get him thrown out at the next base with frightening regularity. After all, how could you fail to love a player with that degree of spatial precision?

The big excitement at The Square this season, though, is the new pitcher, a local eighteen-year-old known as Ever-Ready Evans. His fastball consistently clocks in at ninety-eight miles per hour, and major league scouts have expressed interest in him, though they also have some substantial reservations about him as a prospect. You see, control is an issue for Ever-Ready. He, too, had set a Rose Hip League record by the end of this May, having already beaned six . . . *umpires.* In one game, he went all nine innings, chalking up twenty-six strikeouts out of the twenty-seven possible outs; unfortunately, he also walked sixteen, fourteen of them on four straight pitches, and he hit seven batters. The Squealing Squirrels lost 6-3, despite three solo shots by Boss McAllister.

As you can see, games at The Square are never boring. Besides, a Squirrels' home game is a good excuse for Walt to stop in at the Four Leaf Farm Store for one of their delicious Squannacookies as a snack—oatmeal chocolate chip cookies with pecans and dried cherries added to the batter; sometimes he even shares the cookie with Stumpy when he gets home. Walt sees a pleasant irony in the fact that he was a Squealing Squirrels fan well before Stumpy came into his life, but having Stumpy as an audience to whom he can recount each game when he gets home has only added to the fun.

Walt did try taking Stumpy to one of the games, but only with great trepidation, fearful that the plethora of new sights, sounds, and smells would overwhelm the little squirrel. He worried that his friend might panic and run away, and Walt realized that Stumpy might still be in the latency period for the form of rodent traumatic stress disorder through which Walt had patiently nursed him after the accident that claimed his tail. Therefore, with some yarn and fancy knotwork, Walt rigged a harness for Stumpy and designed a way to secure the harness to a wooden picnic basket that he brought along to the game; he had stuffed the basket with two of the woolen scarves his wife, Annie, had knitted for him many years before. His hope was that Stumpy would feel more secure if he had such a lair as his home base, so to speak.

For the first inning or so, the normally rambunctious rodent remained inside the basket, with the cover tilted back so he could peer out inconspicuously, but the colors of the uniforms and the movements of the players on the field fascinated the gray-furred onlooker, and as the visitors were batting in the top of the second inning, Stumpy crawled out of the basket and into Walt's lap, where he sat quietly, observing closely. By the top of the third, he was perched on Walt's shoulder, next to the ubiquitous porkpie hat, occasionally emitting an approving *chit!* as one of the players made contact with the ball or ran the basepaths. He seemed particularly intrigued by the gargantuan, barrel-shaped form of Boss McAllister, twitching and chattering several times as Boss came to the plate in the bottom of the third, as if the squirrel knew something exciting was about to happen.

Sure enough, the behemoth first baseman got hold of a 1-and-2 fastball and lifted it, not only over the centerfield fence, but also over the line of white pines beyond. Someone said later that the ball actually ended up in the river over by the RiverCourt retirement residence. As was the custom after each of the rotund player's homers, a pair of fans along the first-base line pulled out a banner, spread it out, and started waving it; it read, "West Gro-Town is Boss-Town!" In addition to celebrating Boss's formidable batting strength, the banner seemed intended as a dig against the big-city residents and fans in Boston, who thought that they and their major league team were better than anything Hicksville or Sticksborough could produce.

Boss's big blast was when the trouble started, though, and two events convinced Walt that bringing Stumpy to the games might not be such a good idea in the future. First, in the general excitement around the ballpark after that homer, Stumpy had begun chattering loudly on Walt's shoulder, standing up on his rear legs and then sitting down again as if he had seen fans in big stadiums doing the wave and he wanted to emulate them. Farther up in the bleachers behind them sat a loud and abrasive middle-aged man whose picnic basket held something different from Walt's and who had been dipping into that basket regularly throughout the game. Stumpy's excited celebration had caused the inebriated man's bleary eyes to focus on the dancing squirrel, and the booze-besotted man slid down across two more steps of the bleachers to get a closer look. "Hey!" the rummy shouted. "What's that thing, some kind of (moimbly, moimbly) stinkin' rat?" He, of course, didn't say "moimbly, moimbly" or "stinkin'," but this is, after all, designed to be a family-friendly story, so you'll have to use your imagination.

Walt turned to look at the speaker, recognizing his condition from the slurring of his speech and from Walt's own observations of him earlier in the game. As Walt turned, Stumpy, still on his shoulder, began quietly to growl. Walt, well aware of the squirrel's territorial and protective instincts, tried to hush his friend with a few quiet words from the corner of his mouth before speaking to his interlocutor.

"Whoa there, pardner," Walt said, after that brief pause. "I see you have been tippling from Bacchus's blissful barrel. Beautiful day for a ball game, isn't it?" Walt studied Latin in high school and still enjoys working references to classical mythology into conversations, especially when he can use them with comic and ironic effect. Stumpy's aggression, however, was escalating, as Walt could tell from the deepening of his growl and the greater intensity of his twitching. He'd seen his diminutive friend confront skunks, large dogs, and a monster snapping turtle, and he knew the man's bulk would be no deterrent.

"Whazzat?" the man responded. "I ast you what izzat thing on your shoulder, some kinda tailless rat or . . . *burp!* . . . f-f-ferret?"

Walt tipped his cap and said, "No, my good sir, that is *Sciurus carolinensis*"—which is, of course, the Latin, scientific name for the gray squirrel—"and I must ask you, please, to return to your seat if you don't want him to become *Furious carolinensis* or even *Sciurus furioso*! Maybe you could just scurry off before he gets too scary. It's no fun to fool with his furry fury." Walt has always been quick with words in a crisis.

The drunk laughed, amused at the sound of such a lot of alliteration, but then he was finally able to focus, at least for a moment, on Stumpy's twitching form and the two large incisor teeth that the bellicose rodent was baring. Even after a half-pint of peppermint schnapps, the bleacher jockey decided he might still manage a tad of discretion, and he lightened his abrasive tone. "Hey, that's kinda funny: a scurrilous, furry puss-o, or whatever you said. . . ." Then he dragged himself a couple of rows higher in the bleachers, back to his original seat.

Breathing a sigh of relief, Walt gave Stumpy the traditional understated acknowledgment used by generations of rodent trainers throughout the world when their charges perform well: "That'll do, squirrel."

Stumpy had stopped his growling and was ready to turn his attention back to the game. Still, the encounter left the elderly and somewhat reclusive Walt a bit shaken. He had never liked calling attention to himself, and he realized that he had ignored one dangerous reality in bringing Stumpy to the game: His friend was—literally—a squirrel, and as a squirrel attending a Squannacook Squealing Squirrels game, Stumpy's presence was bound eventually to draw a lot of attention, and maybe even serious questions about why Stumpy shouldn't become the team mascot. Walt wasn't sure that Stumpy, or he himself, would handle *that* situation particularly well.

The second event and the determining factor in Walt's decision to leave Stumpy home for future Squealing Squirrels games came in the bottom of the fifth inning, when tradition called for all the Squannacook players batting or running the bases to don, for that half inning only, three-foot-long simulated gray squirrel tails. The tradition was a crowd-pleaser, with the fans all indulging in several rounds of the Squannacook Squeal, their special battle cry that actually sounds more like something emitted by a stuck pig than any sound that Stumpy or his brethren would ever have uttered. Walt hadn't thought about the implications for Stumpy until he saw his friend's crestfallen look when Shanklin "The Shark" Sharkey, the third baseman, led off the inning with a line-drive single to left and then flashed down the line to round the bag with his fake tail streaming behind him. Stumpy was clearly experiencing the loss of his own tail afresh, and Walt decided then that leaving his friend home for future games was probably advisable on humanitarian grounds. Before the inning ended, he coaxed Stumpy back into the picnic basket and headed back to the pond. In fact, at the same time, he decided to give up his regular attendance at Squealing Squirrels games; he knew he would feel guilty about having fun without Stumpy.

Walt was therefore pleased this week when he got a call from Jeremy Beauchemin, the former college roommate of Walt's second son, Larkin. Jeremy was inviting Walt to join him in the big city of Manchester, New Hampshire, to take in a baseball game between the New Hampshire Fisher Cats, the Double-A affiliate of the Toronto Blue Jays, and the Richmond Flying Squirrels, a San

Francisco Giants farm club. Especially given the name of the Richmond team, it was an offer that Walt couldn't refuse.

Jeremy is a single, middle-aged man who teaches English at a private school in southern New Hampshire. Walt has always enjoyed his puns and wit. Jeremy had lost his dad several years back and his mom the past winter, and Walt understood that the younger man might have been seeking his company as a way of compensating for his own loss but was also kindly filling in for his buddy Larkin, who lives too far away to see Walt regularly. The plan was for Walt to drive his 1960 Chevy pickup truck, Lulu, up to Jeremy's school and park on campus; Jeremy would drive them from there up to Northeast Delta Dental Stadium in the revitalized section of Manchester along the Merrimack River, where the brick buildings that had once been woolen mills now house several successful businesses as well as the campus of UNH Manchester.

Walt put on his newest plaid flannel shirt for the occasion, along with a clean pair of chinos, his red suspenders, and the omnipresent porkpie hat. Jeremy joshed him a bit about the hat. "You know, Walt, we *are* going to a baseball game. You *could* get in the spirit and wear a baseball cap. We can even pick up a Fisher Cats cap at the team shop on the way in."

"Thanks," Walt replied, "but I have an odd-sized head to fit, and these fellas are the only comfortable kind of headgear I've found . . . except for the wool hats Annie used to knit me. Besides, I wouldn't look good in anything flashy."

The game was scheduled to start at 7:15, so Walt had tucked Stumpy in at the cabin with a special treat of five shell-on peanuts. Walt didn't leave the young squirrel alone too often and didn't want to put him outside with darkness bound to fall before the ball game was over. He suspected that Stumpy would settle in and just snooze the time away.

At the stadium, Walt was struck immediately not only by the size of the structure and the number of fans but also by the variety of food vendors who had booths in the enclosed area above the main seating area. Jeremy treated him to a warm ham-and-cheese sandwich on pretzel bread and an iced tea; Walt turned down the younger man's additional offer of a bowl of chili, nervous about the potential gastrointestinal consequences. The two of them settled into their seats just under the overhang of the main stadium roof on the third-base side. The ranks of lights on either side of the outfield intensified the green of the playing field, and Walt chuckled at the big screen out in center field that flashed shots of young children and their parents in the crowd.

As they finished their sandwiches, a parade of a hundred or more motorcycles processed from center field to left field and then up the third-base line and around to the first-base line, part of some fundraiser whose purpose got muffled over the PA system. Jeremy, with his usual sarcastic wit, leaned over and jokingly asked, "How many laps do they have to complete in *this* race?" As the PA announcer was announcing the starting lineups, Jeremy excused himself, saying, "I've got to go to the little boys' room." He was back well before the opening pitch, however, easing himself back into his seat and saying conspiratorially, "Whew! I had to take a Wikipedia!" Jeremy likes jokes with technological references.

As Walt drank in his surroundings, he kept comparing how procedures back at The Square measured up to the big time at the Fisher Cats game, and he found much that amused him and held his attention even between innings at the big stadium. For instance, a couple of staff members came out after the second inning and fired T-shirts into the crowd from a big elastic band they stretched between them. After the third inning, three young children were called out of the stands and each was positioned on a base; then they raced the Fisher Cat mascot, who was in his bulky costume and looked like an otter on steroids. The mascot started from home plate and had to make it all the way around before the kids finished; the kids, of course, beat him and won coupons for free pizza. Before the bottom of the fifth, a guy in a hot dog costume came out with the slingshot catapult again to lob thermal-wrapped frankfurters into the stands. "Who does he think he is?" Jeremy asked. "Anthony Weiner?" He was referring to the disgraced New York State congressman who had sent lewd pictures of himself to women via email. Jeremy likes topical, political jokes as well.

A similar crowd-pleasing diversion happened in each inning, and during the seventh-inning stretch, the crowd joined in to sing the traditional "Take Me Out to the Ballgame." As they were about to start, Jeremy leaned over to Walt and asked, "Do you suppose at

Blue Jays games in Toronto they sing 'Take Me *Oot* to the Ballgame'?" Jeremy even likes jokes about Canada! Walt could only chuckle.

Walt decided by the end of the game that his favorite part of the experience had probably come in the bottom of the first, when Ollie the Bat Dog retrieved the Fisher Cats players' bats after they made a trip to the plate. Walt found himself wondering if Arlene could ever train Big Bruno to do something like that. Ollie, in fact, looked a lot like Big Bruno except that Ollie's hair was longer since he was a golden retriever and not a Lab. Walt also enjoyed watching a red-tailed hawk that, in the early part of the evening, would fly from one light tower to another or soar out over the street behind the outfield wall.

The game itself was entertaining, though, too, with some dazzling catches in the outfield and a couple of double plays that the infielders turned almost before Walt could focus on what was happening. The skill level here was definitely higher than at the Squealing Squirrels games, though nobody seemed to hit the ball farther than Boss McAllister could. The outcome was satisfying in that the Fisher Cats staged a late rally, scoring three in the bottom of the eighth to take a one-run lead into the top of the ninth, when their reliever gave up a lead-off double. The next batter worked the count to 3-and-2 and then sent a foul ball arcing back over the opposing dugout along the third-base line.

"Oh my God," blurted Jeremy, "that's headed right our way! Look out, Walt!" But before Walt could even think about ducking, another reflex kicked in: He snatched the porkpie off his head and stuck it out, feeling the ball snag in the crown of the hat. Somehow, he maintained his grip on the narrow brim. The crowd cheered as he reached in and pulled out a hardly scuffed baseball and held it up. "Wow!" was all Jeremy could say.

The Cats' reliever struck out that batter on the next pitch and retired the next two Flying Squirrels to end the game. Walt and Jeremy stayed a few more minutes for the fireworks show over the outfield, something else Walt enjoyed and looked forward to telling Stumpy about the next day.

The octogenarian fan was tired by the time he got back to the cabin on Kibbee Pond, but Stumpy was still awake and waiting for him, and Walt had brought his friend a special memento. The little squirrel, for the first time, seemed enthused about having a ball of his own, though Walt found out over the next couple of days that Stumpy still would not chase, let alone *fetch*, even this special ball. Nevertheless, the little guy has, since that first night, insisted on sleeping with his feet wrapped around the baseball Walt brought him. Walt says he still won't let it out of his grip during the night.

By the way, yesterday's Squealing Squirrels game didn't end well for the home team over at The Square. They were facing the reigning Rose Hip League champions, the Nashoba Tooth-Gnashers, and hung close, trailing 4-3 as the game went into the bottom of the ninth. Skillsaw Jenkins led off with a bloop single to right, and Willie "Wheels" Williams followed, beating out an infield single on a slow roller to third. With men at first and second and nobody out, Boss McAllister hit a towering fly to right that was sure to advance the runners, but he got a bit under the ball, sending it higher rather than farther. We might even be justified in calling his effort a "thundering blast," because as the Tooth-Gnashers' right fielder positioned himself under the ball, the orb broke into the firmament and provoked a brief shower of rain that blinded the player for a moment; as a result, the ball fell at his helpless feet.

When Skillsaw realized what had happened, he did what he does best: began plotting his precise course for third and calculating the needed angle to make the turn for home with the tying run. When Wheels realized what had happened, he put his head down and ran like a graceful deer, as only he can do. Unfortunately, as also only he can do, he rounded second and passed the still-calculating Skillsaw, arriving at third before his teammate, and the umpire quickly signaled out number one. Pulling into the station a moment later, Skillsaw looked up from his calculations; seeing Wheels already there, he froze momentarily, like a doe in the headlights, and then in his confusion started back toward second. With the throw-in from the right fielder now in the shortstop's glove, it was easy to tag the hapless Skillsaw for the second out. Meanwhile, Boss McAllister had seen the ball he had hit headed for the heavens, assumed he had hit a game-winning walk-off home run, and had gone into his home run trot, which might be better called a home run waddle. The shortstop was waiting when Boss minced into second, and he tagged the big man for the final out. As a result, the game ended in a triple play for the Tooth-Gnashers. Fortunately for the Squealing Squirrels, no one was shooting video yesterday, or their folly might have gone viral. But was it folly, or was it just misfortune? The Tooth-Gnashers improved their season record to 24-8; the Squealing Squirrels are at 9-22. Sometimes fate and lovable incompetence are hard to tell apart.

3

Stumpy and the Bluegills

JULY 6, 2011

After Walt's trip last week up to the big city of Manchester, New Hampshire, where he watched the New Hampshire Fisher Cats play the Richmond Flying Squirrels in a Double-A minor league baseball game, the elderly weather watcher was hoping he would not become discontented with his daily routines, what with his recent exposure to the bright lights and the urban atmosphere. The truth is, however, he loves no place better than Kibbee Pond here in Townsend, Massachusetts, and he finds no one's company more enjoyable than that of Stumpy, the gray squirrel he adopted a year and a half ago after an unfortunate accident had taken off the adolescent rodent's tail near its base. As soon as he got home from the Fisher Cats game, Walt gave his buddy a baseball he had caught in the porkpie hat he always wears; a foul ball had looped his way in the top of the ninth inning, and without thinking, he had removed his hat, held it out, and snagged a souvenir. When he got home, he presented the ball to Stumpy, who has shown surprising enthusiasm for the gift despite his previous reluctance to fetch or even play with a tennis ball. Of course, Stumpy still will not employ the baseball in any conventional way; instead, he has insisted every night since the game on sleeping with his legs wrapped around the cowhide sphere. That fact, however, pleases Walt more than he cares to admit. He has always respected those who can find unconventional uses for common objects.

The morning after the game, the two friends arose at 6:00, as usual, and began a typical day, with Walt checking the weather forecast for the area from a variety of sources and Stumpy waiting at the door until Walt could let him out onto the deck. By the time the tailless squirrel scooted out the door, the sun was already dazzling above the far shore of the pond, and Stumpy scouted around for any pine cones or other sources of a tasty snack that could tide him over until Walt had readied his regular meal inside. He also kept his eyes open for any of the other neighborhood squirrels who might have dropped by. He frequently romps with two other young squirrels who Walt theorizes might actually be his siblings; Walt calls them Burwell and Lansdowne, for no particular reason. This morning, though, all Stumpy saw, heard, or smelled were the handful of chipmunks who also populate the vicinity. When Walt came to the screen door and spoke his name, the gray-furred rodent hopped across the deck, back into the house, and up onto the counter, where he sampled the contents of his dish, which Walt had just replenished with some savory hamster kibbles he had bought at a pet store.

When Walt had finished his own oatmeal (he had left a small pile of uncooked oats on the counter as an extra treat for Stumpy), he called the squirrel and took his coffee out to the deck, where he claimed his all-weather, cushioned chair and Stumpy claimed *his* usual spot on the deck rail, from which he could watch both the driveway and the pond. "Well, Stump," Walt said, "I was thinking that this morning might be a good time to feed the fish and then take a little jaunt in Nelly." Nelly is Walt's ten-foot wooden rowboat, and she is equipped with a three-horsepower Johnson outboard motor whose purr is only a little bit louder than Stumpy's when Walt is giving him a one-fingered face rub.

Most mornings when they go out in Nelly, the two mariners simply cruise the shoreline, but once in a while, Walt will load his fishing rod, and he will either troll with the line behind the boat or go in close to shore, shut down the motor, and cast a few times to try his luck. When he does manage to catch something, Walt always wets his hands, removes the hook carefully, and releases the fish back into the pond. He knows how easily a dry hand can damage the mucus that protects a fish's body, so he is conscientious about the care with which he handles his catches; he worries so much, in fact, that he has cut back on the frequency of his fishing over the years. Still, the urge is strong from time to time, and he can't always resist;

after all, what lies beneath the surface always exercises a pull of some power on most of us. Besides, his memories of fishing span many years and include many friends now gone, including his wife, Annie. Sometimes, he feels her presence when he is fishing since she accompanied him regularly in the early years of their marriage. Even though she has been gone many years now, it still amuses . . . and irks . . . him to remember that *she* always seemed to hook the most impressive catches.

What Walt calls "feeding the fish" is an occasional prelude to the morning boat trips and involves taking some stale bread down to the dock, tearing off small bits, and dropping the crumbs into the water below; in response, the local colony of bluegill sunfish dart to the surface to claim their share of the treasure. Walt is frugal and lives on somewhat limited means, so he doesn't feed the fish every day, but he usually has enough homemade bread crumbs in the freezer, and he enjoys sharing his bounty with the bluegills and pumpkinseeds whose nests hollow and honeycomb the sand beneath the shallow stretches of shoreline.

On that morning after the Fisher Cats game, Walt left a detailed message on his answering machine in case any of his weather-watcher clients should call while Stumpy and he were down on the dock or out on the water. Then he reached into a plastic bag on the counter, extracted the heel from a loaf of bread, tore it in two, and replaced one half in the bag. As the two friends made their way down to the dock, the sun was getting well up in the sky, and the angle was right so that they could look down into the water and glimpse the sunfish streaking closer from the complex of nests around the little cove.

The fish have been conditioned to associate Walt's footsteps on the wooden dock with the feast that sometimes follows, and they are not shy about congregating and saying a hasty grace before the feeding frenzy begins. They are not quite sharks or piranhas, but the bluegills are serious about their snacks, so serious that they will strike at Walt's fingers if he puts them into the water, even without holding any of the bread. The bigger ones, of course, have the advantage in any scuffles, though the smaller ones can be surprisingly aggressive and daring in their attempts to outmaneuver their larger rivals; sometimes, in fact, speed and mobility triumph over the cocksure arrogance of bulk. Occasionally, Walt will kneel and hold a bit of bread two or three inches above the water; the fish come to the surface and hover with their mouths open to see if Walt will drop the bread right in. Sometimes he does, but other times, he waits, and eventually, one or more of the sunfish will launch themselves partway out of the water, like dolphins or orcas at SeaWorld, to grab the morsel from his hand. Once members of the group start jumping, some individuals launch themselves while Walt's hand is still a foot or so above the surface; only rarely, though, do they rise entirely out of the water.

While the show was going on that morning, Stumpy sat at the edge of the dock, watching and occasionally begging Walt for a scrap of bread to eat himself. When a particularly ambitious bluegill would thrust its head beyond the surface, the squirrel would chatter in excitement, but mostly, he watched in quiet fascination. Sometimes, after sampling one or two bits of the bread, he would take another small piece in his mouth, lean over the edge of the dock, and drop the morsel into the water, bobbing his head excitedly as a scaly beneficiary claimed his doughy charity. Walt hoped that one day Stumpy might figure out some way to lean close enough to the surface that a bluegill would jump and take the tidbit from his mouth. That day, however, has not yet come.

That particular morning, Walt was noticing the size differential among the piscine participants in the feeding frenzy. Many of the fish were only three or four inches in length, but a number of them were substantially larger, eight inches or maybe even more.

"Hey, Stump," Walt said, pitching a bit of crust out away from the dock and then watching as six different dark streaks headed toward it. Almost immediately, the water roiled, and tails and dorsal fins flashed above the surface as the bread disappeared. Walt paused dramatically. "Did I ever tell you about the huge bluegills that are supposed to have lived in Kibbee Pond over the years? No? Back in the forties, there was this one fella they called Count Bouillabasie—get it? Count Bouillabasie, like the orchestra leader *and* the fish soup? Anyway, this fish was said to be an unusual color—a lemon yellow, some said, though others claimed he was more like burnished gold—and he would cruise close to the surface so that folks'd sometimes see his dorsal fin and several inches of his scaled back hump up out of the water and flash in the sun like an idol made of the purest gold. The legend went that he was four feet long and would leap out of the water to pluck birds or even chipmunks and . . . squirrels . . . off overhanging branches. One story had him following a swimming mink and then coming up behind it and sucking it in like a strand of spaghetti." Walt looked at Stumpy, but his furry friend was watching the sunfish slipping in and out of the shadow of the dock, as if he weren't even listening. It is hard, even for me, to tell whether Walt is inventing a story or actually speaking the truth, and I've known him for several decades; sometimes Walt himself seems to believe in stories he has clearly made up.

"Anyway," Walt continued, "there was this other fish they talked about when I first moved here in the eighties, though they said they hadn't sighted him in a while then. They said something about a thirty- or forty-year life cycle for these huge fish and how the pond could only support one at a time. . . . I guess I wasn't really listening closely, but there have been times when I know I've seen something really big moving beneath the surface, slipping out away from the shore like a living shadow drifting over and under the pond simultaneously. Back when I was still kayaking regularly, I was resting out in the middle of the pond one morning, dangling my hands over each side to cool off, and something came up and bit the tip off my pinkie. Did I ever show you that?" He held up his left hand, and—sure enough—the end of his little finger was missing, scar tissue beveling back from his nail almost to the first knuckle. "I made a vow then that someday I'd get the fish that took my finger.

"By the way," Walt continued, "the name they gave this latest leviathan was Old Smokey, apparently because he's gray like smoke, and he's there one moment but gone the next, also like smoke. People used to argue about which one was bigger, Count Bouillabasie or Old Smokey. I don't like fishing for our friends here by the dock—not much challenge in it, and besides, they *are* like friends now—but wouldn't it be something to land Old Smokey? I mean, especially after what he did to my finger? Maybe I'll just bring along my rod more regularly and try my luck. What d'you think?"

Stumpy was now cleaning his paws and seemed determined not to look up despite Walt's interrogative tone.

With feeding time over, Walt climbed carefully into Nelly, put on his life preserver, and then patted the middle seat to encourage

Stumpy. The squirrel hopped in easily and darted to the bow, where Walt leaves a buoyancy cushion in the bilge so Stumpy will have protection in an emergency; the gray-furred first mate likes to ride with his front paws up on the gunwale and his tailless bottom on the cushion, but sometimes, before Walt notices and discourages him, the daring deck mate will clamber up onto the bow with all four feet, carried away by the breeze blowing in his face. His human companion worries that the squirrel might end up overboard, and he doubts that Stumpy will prove a confident or even competent swimmer, despite his fearlessness and bravado.

Just then, an osprey dropped out of a white pine they were passing, and then, after regaining altitude, it soared out over the open water. "You know, buddy," Walt said as the Johnson purred and Nelly putted around a bend in the shoreline, "the best thing about having a boat is a lot like the best thing about having a car to drive: You get to decide where you want to go and then take yourself there. The handle on this motor and the steering wheel in a truck or car are like symbols of mobility and choice and freedom. If I want to, I can just pull my arm this way and follow that fish hawk wherever he goes. Well, within reason, since I can't fly and Nelly isn't an airplane. Just the same, I've always liked being able to determine my own course, take responsibility for my own fate, and steer my way toward whatever awaits. Especially on a beautiful morning like this."

The two friends continued their early-morning routine for most of the week in that fashion, with Walt once or twice taking some time for a few casts with his fishing rod. However, some welcome variety came with the arrival of the weekend and its lead-up to the Fourth of July. In years when the weather is good around the Fourth, Walt likes to take Nelly the length of the pond and then maneuver through a relatively narrow channel that connects Kibbee Pond to the larger and more populated Beech Tree Lake. Each year, the residents at the larger lake stage a Fourth of July boat parade, and Walt looks forward to the occasion as the highlight of his Independence Day celebration. This year, the parade was taking place on Saturday, July 2, starting at noon, so Walt packed a sandwich, popcorn, and some homemade iced tea. Stumpy, of course, was coming, too.

To get to the channel, Walt motored down the length of his side of Kibbee Pond, which is actually horseshoe-shaped. Walt's twenty acres of land is located along one tip of the shoe, and Stumpy and he had to voyage down to the curve at the south end of the pond and then back up almost to the other shoe tip to reach the channel.

This year's boat parade was, as always, entertaining. Walt has a friend, Prof Harris, who lives in a cottage on Beech Tree Lake, and Prof, a retired English professor who still teaches evening writing courses at Fitchburg State University, has given Walt a standing invitation to come ashore or moor under his maples for the annual occasion. From that shaded spot this year, Walt and Stumpy were able to watch the line of decorated boats pass along the far shore and then circle back in front of them.

Walt counted twenty-seven boats in the procession, and some of the people had outdone themselves this year. The vast majority of the craft in the parade were pontoon "party boats," and many of the participants had built wooden scaffolds and frames to support elaborate "costumes" for their boats. First in line was a Mississippi River steamboat, with paddle wheels that actually turned and smokestacks that belched smoke; the skipper wore a derby hat and a red vest and had his sleeves tied up like a dealer in a casino, and the passengers all sat around a table, playing cards. Another party boat was outfitted with banners and cutouts of the characters from the *SpongeBob SquarePants* television show, while yet another had thirty or more balloons tied to the railings, and all of its crew were dressed as clowns. Among Walt's favorites was a pontoon boat fitted with a curved wood-like hull, shields along the gunwales, and even a mast so that the whole thing looked like a shortened version of a Viking longboat; the people on board wore fake orange beards and plastic helmets with curved horns on either side. Also impressive was an old Camaro that somebody had somehow gotten onto two pontoons; a guy at the automobile's steering wheel actually turned the wheel to direct the boat. Toward the end of the parade came a party boat with an awning fitted to the back to look like a shark's open-mouthed head swallowing the stern.

"Whoa!" said Walt. "That's like something out of *Jaws* or *Moby Dick*! Or maybe that's Old Smokey the bluegill, and he's gotten out into this lake through that connecting channel!"

The parade continued past Walt and Stumpy's vantage point and across the mouth of a small neighboring cove, from which, all of a sudden, yet another craft emerged, this one a small aluminum rowboat powered by an outboard motor. It was decorated to look like a vintage World War II German U-boat, and the two college students on board wove it in and out among the other craft as if they were lining up and firing torpedoes to sink an Allied convoy. Walt thought it was a clever idea but suspected that the boys had had a few too many beers.

The next morning, Sunday the 3rd, brought more beautiful weather, with bright sunshine but comfortable temperatures. Walt and Stumpy set out on their morning Kibbee Pond cruise a bit earlier than usual because Walt wanted to try fishing a stretch of the pond down along the base of the horseshoe. In the stillness of a placid morning, with only occasional birdcalls and the lapping of water against the hull to break the silence, Walt suddenly got a strike on the line that bent his rod down to the water's surface. Stumpy had been dozing in the sun, turtle-like, up in the bow, but when his human friend gave out a startled, wordless cry, the quick-to-react rodent sat up immediately. He saw the elderly man standing in the stern, bracing himself and gripping the rod firmly, and the next thing either crew member knew, Nelly was being pulled, very slowly, through the water. "Yikes, Stumpy!" Walt called out. "I think we're on a Nantucket sleigh ride! This thing is so big, we may have to use a harpoon!"

Stumpy had put all four feet up on the starboard gunwale to try to make out what was happening, when, in an instant, the pressure on the fishing line released, and the rod snapped back, twanging into the young squirrel and knocking him overboard. When Walt glanced over the port bow, he saw Stumpy in the water, doing a very amateurish and squirrelly version of the dog paddle; later on, he would say that this was one situation in which losing his tail may have been an advantage for Stumpy, since a soggy squirrel tail might just have dragged him under and certainly would have slowed even more his advance toward the boat.

When Walt looked back to starboard, however, what he saw raised the hackles on his neck. A large gray fin had emerged from the water some twenty yards away and was headed for where Stumpy was struggling toward the boat. In that instant, the aged angler had the presence of mind to toss his fishing rod overboard before kneeling over the gunwale and calling out, "Just look at me, Stump, and swim toward me *as fast as you can.*" Walt kept his voice low but gave the last words special emphasis.

With his fur soaked through, Stumpy looked tiny in the water, little more than a morsel for one of the big bluegills around the dock, let alone for Old Smokey, if that was in fact what was swimming toward him. Fortunately, though, all his skylarking with Burwell and Lansdowne has kept the squirrel's legs strong, and he was making good progress, even in a foreign medium like the pond water. Walt was able to lean over and scoop Stumpy up and into the rowboat with several seconds to spare before whatever it was dipped beneath the surface and passed right under Nelly's hull. Walt wondered if it was still dragging his fishing rod along behind it.

Heart pounding, Walt unbuttoned his flannel shirt and tucked his trembling, diminutive friend inside, using the shirt as a simultaneous towel and blanket. "Wow, Stump, I had visions of something out of the Bible story of Jonah and the whale, except that I was pretty sure you wouldn't pop out of Old Smokey's belly after forty days! I was a little worried, too, that I might end up like Captain Ahab, tangled up in my own line and dragged down to the bottom by a giant aquatic creature. I guess we were both lucky."

Stumpy now poked his head out from under Walt's shirt. He clearly had recovered his equanimity, because he hopped off Walt's lap and onto the middle seat, putting his front paws up on the port gunwale, staring off toward where the big fin had disappeared and growling in vociferous defiance. Walt laughed and said, "You know, old buddy, I thought that a squirrel's first instinct when confronted with danger was to freeze and that his second instinct was to run away. Looks like you got your genetic wires crossed somehow!"

As they slowly motored back toward their end of the pond, Walt started calling Stumpy Queequeg; he even made some jokes about how maybe the rodent should get some tattoos so he could look like a South Seas squirrel. Those jokes continued for the next few days. In keeping with his self-deprecating style, however, Walt also directed some jokes his own way, saying that maybe he should look into having his friend Nancy France, the woodworker, carve him a wooden fingertip so he could have a "pegfinger." "Maybe they'll even start calling me Long Walt Silver," he commented more than once.

After the excitement of that "voyage," the two friends were content to have some quiet time on Monday, the actual Fourth of July. That evening, though, they did get to watch some distant fireworks, apparently from Lunenburg, burst and billow over the south shore of the pond. Though man and squirrel were both fond of watching the stars from the deck on clear nights, the fireworks made for a pleasant variation on their routine, and they slept well afterward, Stumpy with his feet, of course, still hugging his souvenir baseball.

4

Stumpy and Timmy

JULY 13, 2011

After last week's Fourth of July boat parade on nearby Beech Tree Lake and an alleged encounter with Old Smokey, the legendary four-foot monster bluegill of Kibbee Pond, Walt Walthers and his rodent roommate, Stumpy, thought they needed some time for rest and recuperation. As a consequence, they made no big plans for the ensuing days. Instead, Stumpy, the tailless, young gray squirrel whom Walt had adopted some time ago after an accident cost the little fellow his proud plume, followed his human friend around as Walt watered and weeded the garden, mowed what little lawn lies between the cabin and the driveway, and tended to his duties as the local weather watcher. Those duties involve monitoring the computer, radio, and television and then sending out a group phone message or email and answering any phone calls from clients; Walt likes to give those clients the most up-to-date meteorological information for the surrounding area. After seeing to those duties, the two roommates spent a good deal of time sitting on the deck and enjoying the sunshine, which Stumpy loves almost as much as do the tanning-addicted turtles of Kibbee Pond. In short, the duo kept up most of their usual routines, with one exception: They were a bit reluctant to get back out on the pond in Nelly, Walt's wooden rowboat with the three-horsepower Johnson outboard motor attached to its stern. The stress of Stumpy's time overboard with the hungry, finned predator bearing down on him had left the usually fearless rodent slightly shaken, and Walt didn't want to rush or pressure his buddy in any way.

As things turned out, though, fate did not respect their desire for a long stretch of quiet recovery time. On the second day after their epic duel with the lacustrine leviathan, Walt opened the screen door so Stumpy could hop out onto the deck and wait while the silver-haired octogenarian put cream into his morning coffee. By the time Walt got back to the door with cup in hand, however, he could hear the little squirrel emitting a series of single *chits* with the tone and rhythm that usually indicated a warning of some sort.

"What is it, Stump? Is it something about Timmy and the old, abandoned mine shaft?" Walt had enjoyed the old *Lassie* television series and still likes to make joking allusions to it. "Or is it that big mama snapping turtle? Is she back again?" He was being serious this time.

Walt held the screen door open and peered out but couldn't see anything immediately. Stumpy, however, continued his chattering, so Walt stepped out on the deck and set his coffee mug down on the rail next to his cushioned chair. The stub-tailed rodent was facing west from the deck and away from the pond's shoreline, looking across the yard toward the hemlocks that conceal the stretch of rutted dirt driveway connecting with Kibbee Pond Road; he remained agitated, bobbing his head and glancing every few seconds back at his human friend while his voice rattled in his throat.

"Something out by the road, buddy? Shall we take a look?" Walt stepped off the deck and walked slowly across the driveway. With that incentive, Stumpy followed, moving with his usual hop-hop-pause-hop-again stride but quickly catching up to the elderly man. From the other side of the hemlocks, both could hear swishing, as if someone were lashing a stick through the air or even beating something on the ground with it, and when they drew parallel with the tree line, they saw that their ears had not deceived them. Another ten yards down the dirt driveway stood a young boy, between three and four feet tall. He had something slung over his left shoulder and some kind of figurine in that hand, but with his right hand he was holding a slender, whip-like tree branch and slashing at some tufts of tall grass with it. He wore a faded blue T-shirt, some nondescript shorts, and battered red sneakers, and when he looked up at them, Walt could see that his face was dirty, his hand having at some point rubbed his runny nose and then smeared his cheek in passing.

"Hi," said Walt. "Whatcha doin'?"

The boy, who had paused in his ministrations, commenced swinging the branch again as he replied, "Whacking. Mommy says I'm good at it."

"I can see that," the elderly man said, a smile starting to draw at his lips as he continued to walk toward the diminutive trespasser. He could also see now, from closer up, that the object over the boy's shoulder was some kind of makeshift bow for shooting arrows, though he could see no quiver and—thankfully, he thought—no arrows. Judging from the way the sealing strip from a large plastic bucket was looped over both ends of the curved wooden stick, though, this bow would never have enough bounce in its bungee to fire any kind of projectile. "My name's Walt. What's *your* name?"

Turning slightly and now swinging his whacker back and forth across the front of his body, the boy mumbled something that seemed to start with a *T*.

"Timmy?" said Walt, knowing that his ears weren't working as well as they used to. The boy didn't reply.

"Well, Timmy, where do you live? Somewhere close?" Walt knew that the nearest house was about an eighth of a mile down Kibbee Pond Road, but also that that house had been vacant for several months.

"Over there," the boy replied, with a vague thrust of his left shoulder. Then he looked up, seeming to notice Stumpy for the first time. "Hey, whazzat, a bunny rabbit?"

"No," Walt said, "that's my buddy Stumpy. He's a gray squirrel."

"How come he dun't have a tail?"

"Well, he did have one, but he lost it in an accident."

"I don't *have* accidents anymore because *I'm* a *big* boy."

"Oh," said Walt, "it wasn't *that* kind of accident."

"Well then," the boy replied, "what kinda accident did he have?"

"Well, that's a long story. . . ." Walt began.

"Did you ever see a toad that got runned over?" Timmy interrupted. "There's one out on the road."

"Yeah, kinda disgusting, huh?"

"Do you have any juice? I'm getting thirsty," the boy said.

Wow! Walt thought. Talk about a short attention span! "Well, Timmy," he said instead, "does your mom know where you are? I don't want you to get in trouble with her, and I'm sure she'd worry if she didn't know where you'd gone."

"Yeah, she knows," the boy said. "I told her I was coming to visit you guys."

Walt noted the absence of logic in that statement but also suspected that Timmy didn't even know he was reshaping the facts to suit his own wishes. "Well," he said, "I'd like to meet her. Where did you say you lived again, Timmy?"

"Why do you keep calling me Timmy?" the boy asked. "My name is *Tony.*"

"Oh-h-h," Walt laughed. "Sorry about that, but my ears don't work as well as they used to. You sure you wouldn't rather be called Timmy? I've always liked that name. . . ."

"But my name's TONY!" the besmirched urchin replied.

"Okay, okay, I get it. I'll only call you Timmy on special occasions then, all right?"

Throughout the conversation, Stumpy had hung back a bit, standing behind Walt's right leg and leaning out from time to time to look at the boy. While Stumpy was used to Walt's sense of humor, he may have had doubts about whether the boy could tell that the geezer was joshing him. Tony noticed the squirrel again now and asked, "Hey, does he do any tricks? I see some squirrels on TV that rode bicycles."

Before Walt could answer, Tony changed the subject again. "Hey, why does he keep looking at me like that? First he goes to one side, and then he goes to the other . . . and *now* he's disappeared!" The boy was giggling now. Stumpy seemed to be hiding behind Walt's leg, but then he leaned out again. It was pretty clear to Walt that Stumpy knew what he was doing.

"Well, Tim . . . uh, Tony, I think he's playing hide-and-seek or peekaboo with you."

Tony started laughing outright as he stepped closer and tried to peer around Walt's leg. Stumpy hopped a few steps away, stopped, and stood up on his hind legs, looking back over his shoulder at the boy.

Tony laughed again and said, "What's he doing now?"

"I'm not sure," Walt answered, "but I think he's playing some kind of game with you."

When the boy stepped behind Walt to get a better look, Stumpy hopped around in front of the man and looked back through Walt's legs at his giggling pursuer. He bobbed his head twice.

"Can I play with him?" the boy asked as he started back around to Walt's front while Stumpy immediately scampered back behind his silver-haired companion.

"I think you already are," Walt answered as Tony ran behind him and Stumpy scooted up Walt's leg to his shoulder and then even onto the porkpie hat that always crowned the weather watcher's head.

"Now, Timmy . . . I mean Tony, before we go any further, I need to make sure you're not gonna get in trouble by being here." The boy was laughing up at Stumpy, who was repeatedly bobbing his head down at his would-be pursuer. "And Stump," Walt continued, "you just stay put for a minute up there, will you? Okay, Tony, do I have your attention? Are you listening? First of all, how old are you?"

"I'm five, Mr. Walt. Do you know what I got for my birthday? It's a—"

"Now hold on there, pardner," Walt interrupted, chuckling. "I need some answers before we can go any further. Do you live near here?"

"Uh huh."

"Whereabouts?" Walt asked.

"Over there," the boy replied, wiping his nose again. His arm gesture was suitably vague. "The window in my bedroom has a crack in it, and the—"

"Okay," Walt said, "you're gonna have to take me to your house because I need to be sure your mom knows where you are and doesn't mind your being with us. Come on. Let's walk there together."

As Walt had suspected, Tony trudged to the end of the driveway, turned left on Kibbee Pond Road, and headed toward the once-empty house at the bottom of the incline. Stumpy had moved down to Walt's right shoulder, where balancing was easier for him as the man walked along the washboard surface of the road.

"See? There's that toad," Tony said as they passed the hardly recognizable flattened form.

"Gee," Walt said, "maybe I should scrape it up and save it for my supper. I don't get meat that fresh very often."

Tony looked up, goggle-eyed. "You wouldn't *really* eat it, would you, Mr. Walt? That'd be yucky."

"You never ate a toad before?" Walt replied. "Tastes like chicken." When he saw the boy's face vacillate between disgust and mystification, Walt continued. "Oh, I'm just kidding you, Tony. I don't really eat toads, you know."

"You don't?" the boy said wonderingly.

"Well, not without my special sweet pickle relish anyway," Walt responded. "Oh, just kidding again, pal," he had to say as the boy's face started to fall for a second time. "Hey," he hastily added to change the subject, "do you know what's brown and sticky?"

"No," Tony said.

"A stick!" Walt said in triumph.

Tony hesitated a moment and then started to giggle. "You're funny, Mr. Walt."

By this time, they were approaching the small gray Cape, which was tucked in behind a line of young chestnut trees. A nondescript navy blue compact car sat in the pull off that served as a driveway next to the wooden deck extending from what Walt assumed was the kitchen door. From inside the house, a woman's voice rang out: "Anthony? *An*thony?"

"Who's this 'Anthony' guy?" Walt asked, trying to keep a straight face.

"That's what my mommy calls me," the boy replied.

"So hold on," Walt said. "How come *she* gets to call you what she likes, and *I* have to call you Tony?"

"She's my mom," the boy replied.

"Well, it doesn't seem fair," Walt said. "Why can't *I* call you Timmy, then?"

But Tony, or Anthony, was already running toward the house, and he slowed only slightly as he clambered up the deck before disappearing through the door. Walt waited by the edge of the road, with Stumpy still on his shoulder, wondering how the boy's mother would react.

A few moments later, a young woman stepped out the door and onto the deck, with Tony right behind her. "See? There's Stumpy," he said, pointing.

"Hello, ma'am," Walt said, tipping the porkpie as the squirrel on his shoulder wobbled slightly with the unanticipated shift of position. "I'm Walt Walthers, and it looks as though we're neighbors. I live in the cabin just up the road."

"I'm Amy Riggetti," the woman responded. "Would you like to come up?" Walt estimated her age at twenty-five or younger, and he noted approvingly that she stood as straight and slim as the saplings that lined the road beside the house, though her hair was light brown rather than chestnut in color.

"Well, ma'am, I wouldn't want to impose, and I really came down to make sure you knew where your boy was. He's welcome to visit, but I didn't want anyone worrying about him, and I figured I'd better make sure you didn't object to his being with me."

"We just moved in two days ago," the woman said, "and in my chasing around to get unpacked, I told him he could explore the woods around the house if he didn't go too far. I didn't know he had gone all the way up to your place. I'm sorry if he was a bother. He hasn't met any other kids yet, and he gets restless sometimes. I should have kept a closer eye—"

"Well now," Walt interrupted, sensing that the woman had already been worn out with the stress of moving and was now on the verge of tears, "he's not been any trouble, and he deals pretty well with my joshing, so he's welcome to stop by if he likes. Stumpy here seems to like him, and the two of them have about the same amount of energy; maybe they can tire each other out. Let me give you my phone number, and if you don't mind, I'll take yours, too, so we don't have to be traipsing up and down the road if we want to check on what's going on. By the way, does Tony know how to swim? We're right on the pond there, and we've got a dock and a small boat with a motor. You could both come for a putt around the shore sometime. And maybe your husband would like to join us. . . ."

"My husband's in Afghanistan," Amy said, her voice cracking slightly.

"Oh," said Walt. "So you're here by yourselves, the two of you?"

"Yes," she said, "at least for another few months. We were living in Worcester, but I grew up in the country in New Hampshire, and I didn't want Anthony to miss out on having the woods to explore. My husband knows the owner of this place, who said it was vacant and was glad to have someone move in for reasonable rent just to keep an eye on it, so we finally got things arranged last week, and we moved up. I've got a job lined up two days a week at a hair salon in Ayer, and my boss says Anthony can come to the shop with me if need be, so . . . we're off on this adventure together."

"Well, I think you'll like it here," Walt said, "as long as you like quiet. No place *I'd* rather be, but then again, I've been here a long time already. Of course, the neighbors can be kind of wild. . . ."

"What do you mean?" Amy asked, her brow knitting.

"Oh," Walt answered, "I mean *literally.* We've got more wild animals than people around here . . . skunks, porcupines, raccoon, muskrat, coyotes, beavers, otters, deer, even the occasional bear or two . . . and, of course, chipmunks, red squirrels, and the *Sciurus carolinensis* here." He pointed to Stumpy. "He's got a whole extended family around the neighborhood, though he spends most of his time with me now. Nothing to be worried about. Just take any bird feeders you have in at night so you don't encourage the bears to raid them. And you'll probably see deer almost every day if you're out at the right times; they have a path down to the pond just up the hill from your driveway."

The conversation continued awhile longer, and Walt exchanged phone numbers with Amy. Then he invited Tony to come up a little later to help him feed the fish from the dock and told him that the blueberries were ripening up so that they might want to go picking in the woods sometime soon. "I make good blueberry muffins and a bread I invented called blue ban-apple bread, with bananas, apples, and blueberries in it. I like it for breakfast, and I had a piece of it this morning just before Stumpy heard you out in the driveway. What do *you* like for breakfast, Tony?"

Tony mumbled something from the deck, and what Walt heard was "fresh roast squirrel."

"Whoa, now, old buddy!" Walt responded. "With Stumpy around, it's not the nicest thing to say that you like to eat fresh roast squirrel! You might hurt his feelings or even scare him off saying that."

Amy was already fighting back a giggle when Tony, looking a bit miffed, said, "I didn't say *that*!" He disappeared back into the house and almost immediately reemerged carrying a plastic bag of prepackaged bread; then he hopped off the deck and trotted down, holding up the bag so Walt could read the label.

"Well, what do you know?" Walt said, chuckling. He read the name of the product aloud: "French Toast Swirl! So you don't want to eat Stumpy after all. Then again, you never know: He might taste like chicken too!"

Amy was giggling openly by that point, and Walt continued to chuckle.

"As I said before, we can go blueberry picking in the woods sometime, and if it's okay with your mom, we can take my boat, Nelly, out and do some blueberry picking around the islands sometime too. That's where I *really* enjoy picking: out on the water with the sun and the breeze. Lots of birds to see too. You ever seen a cormorant, Tim . . . uh, Tony? Funny-looking bird with a skinny, hooked bill. They love to swim on the surface and then dive under to hunt for fish. Japanese fishermen tie strings around their necks and use them to catch fish. . . . Oh, but I've never tried that," Walt said, chuckling. "One of the ones on the pond has a big white spot on his breast. I call him Whitey Bibble because he looks like he's put on a white bib in preparation for his seafood dinner in a fancy restaurant."

Stumpy had long since hopped down from Walt's shoulder and had been nosing around under the chestnut trees, as if he could smell the previous season's nuts there. Tony had been watching the squirrel, and now he walked closer. Soon, he was turning over small rocks, looking for insects, and Stumpy, always curious, joined him, chattering excitedly and bobbing his head when Tony found a red eft salamander.

"Those probably taste like chicken too," Walt said and then winked at Tony and glanced back up at his mom. "We've got a standing joke going already," he said, somewhat apologetically. "Come to think of it, we've probably got three or four!"

And that's how Walt and Stumpy met Timmy, I mean Tommy, I mean Tony. Or is it Anthony?

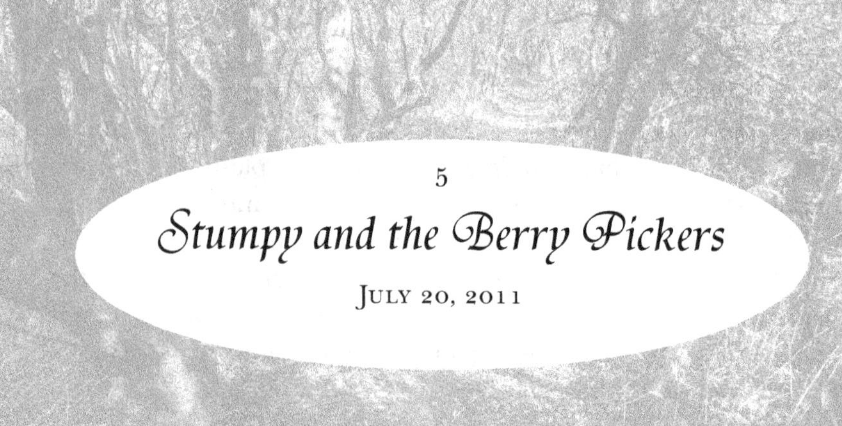

5

Stumpy and the Berry Pickers

JULY 20, 2011

Last week, Walt Walthers and his friend Stumpy the tailless squirrel made the acquaintance of Tony Riggetti, the five-year-old who had just moved into the long-deserted house a short way down the hill from Walt's cabin on Kibbee Pond in Townsend. Soon thereafter, Walt proved true to his word and issued an invitation for Tony to join him on a blueberry-picking excursion into the nearby woods. Tony's mom, Amy, had taken Tony with her for her first day of work at the hair salon in Ayer, euphonically named Ayer Hair, but Walt thought that he might help her by offering to look after Tony at his place the next day she was scheduled to go in. Since Amy was working only two days a week, Walt was thinking about offering his child-watching services on a regular basis, but he figured he'd better see how things went before he got carried away.

The arrangement was for Amy to drop Tony off on her way to work. Walt and Stumpy had already finished their morning coffee and were sitting on the deck when the dark blue Hyundai emerged from behind the screen of hemlocks. I say "*their* morning coffee," but of course, Stumpy shows little interest in Walt's java. On the rare occasions, however, when Walt has a can of beer in the evening, Stumpy will haunt his elderly caretaker, putting his front paws up on the rim of the can and sniffing its contents through the opening, until Walt gets a small saucer and pours out one or two teaspoons of the stuff for his buddy to imbibe. One time, when he had finished his own portion, set the can down, and then left the sitting area for a moment, Walt had returned to find Stumpy on his back on the rug, his rear legs elevating the bottom of the can so the remaining drips could trickle out into his mouth. That sight—and concern that finding a twelve-step program for rodents might prove difficult—led Walt to reconsider his own need for an evening tipple; subsequently, he has cut back considerably on what had once been a pretty regular part of his evening relaxation regimen . . . if a person can have a regimen for relaxation.

Anyway, Walt rose from his cushioned chair and stepped off the deck as the car stopped, with a crunching of gravel beneath its tires. After the preliminary growls that his self-imposed status as watch-squirrel seemed to require, Stumpy relaxed enough to hop along behind Walt with his characteristic halting stride: two hops forward, a hesitation, then a hop again. Amy laughed as she got out of the car: "You're right, Walt! He does look like a short-eared rabbit when he hops." Then she walked around to the passenger side and opened the door for Tony, who was unfastening the restraints on his booster seat. Although his mom had put a clean T-shirt on the boy a half hour before, some smears of grease and dirt had already appeared down its front. "What am I gonna do with you, buddy?" she asked, laughing again. "I just can't seem to keep you clean."

"Don't worry," Walt said. "Look at Stumpy. I gave him a bath this morning in spring water and rose petals, and just look at him now. Kids these days!" he said, shaking his head.

As usual, the young squirrel simply ignored Walt's barb.

Tony didn't answer his mother either; he was in too big a rush to get around the car and start his adventure with his new friends. "Hey, Mr. Walt!" he shouted as he charged around the front of the car. "Where's Stumpy? Can we go down on the dock and feed the fish?"

"Sure," Walt said, "but don't you think we ought to say goodbye to your mom first? She has to go off and work."

Having spied his mammalian pal beside Walt, Tony turned back, gave Amy a quick hug, and then said, "C'mon, Stumpy!" before trotting down the hill toward the dock. The squirrel started to follow the boy with his characteristic gait but had to move quickly to catch up; such was not the case when he was keeping pace with the substantially older Walt. Tony did turn back again to wave quickly, but almost immediately the adults could see him bending down next to the dock, rolling over a rock that promised to conceal some kind of living creature.

"He'll be fine," the white-haired man said, "but call anytime if you feel the urge."

"Thanks," said Amy. "I really appreciate this. Maybe you can join us for dinner tomorrow or the next day."

"Great!" Walt replied. "Just please don't make some kind of roadkill toad casserole. I'm not as fond of cooked amphibian as I've led Tony to believe."

After the detour to the dock to give the bluegill sunfish of Kibbee Pond a morning treat of bread crusts, Walt showed Tony his weather-watcher equipment inside the cabin: his thermometers, barometer, television, computer, radios, and telephone system. Earlier, he had recorded the latest weather predictions on his answering machine, also instructing any clients who might call back to leave a message so he could contact them as soon as he returned. (The forecast, by the way, called for sunshine and moderate humidity, with high temperatures in the low eighties.) Then the man and the boy got ready for their planned morning outing, with Walt packing a thermos of coffee, a couple of juice boxes, and some graham crackers in his pack; he also included a stack of empty plastic margarine containers he kept handy for food storage and an old plastic children's beach bucket he had dug out of the basement. He figured a bucket with a handle would be easier for Tony to hold. Before fastening the pack flap, Walt made sure he had the right number of covers for the containers since he would be putting any berries they picked back into the pack to carry them to the cabin, and he didn't want the waste or mess of spillage.

"Let me put some of this bug spray on you," Walt said. "The mosquitoes around here are so ferocious, they not only bite a chunk out of you, they also try to carry you off like take-out Chinese food to eat later. Plus, the deerflies are out now, and they find humans just as tasty as they find deer."

Stumpy had watched most of their activity from the rafter over the woodstove, but he could tell the time had come to go out again, so he jumped to the kitchen counter and scooted to the screen door, where he waited, twitching excitedly.

Walt's plan was to walk out into the woods on a path that he strolled along for exercise nearly every day. It ran through a mixed forest for three-quarters of a mile before opening into a big field that a local farmer used for hay. There was plenty to look at along the way, at least for people who looked closely and who knew where to look. He figured he could show Tony some wildflowers and mushrooms at the very least, and if they were lucky, some sort of wildlife would appear at some point—maybe turkeys in the field or even a deer in the woods. The berry bushes popped up at several points in open areas along the path. He didn't know how soon Tony would get tired or bored or both, but they could always turn back and try something else. Amy had given him permission to take the boy out on the pond in Nelly, his rowboat with the three-horse Johnson outboard motor.

"All right, Timmy Spaghetti, it's time to go!" Walt announced as he lifted the pack to his shoulder.

"That's not my name!" Tony replied. "It's Tony Riggetti! You know that, Mr. Walt."

"Oh yeah," the white-haired man said, eyes twinkling. "I keep forgetting. It's just that I like pasta so much . . . and, somehow, you look like a Timmy to me. Did I ever tell you about my friend Timmy MacDonald? He woke up one morning with a Tootsie Roll up his nose. Never knew how it got there . . . but he said his brother might have snuck it in while he was sleeping."

Stumpy's routine during Walt's daily walks was to romp on his own, climbing trees as the mood hit, thundering down the leaf-strewn and root-crossed path to provoke the chirps of the resident chipmunks, sometimes even romping with the neighborhood gray squirrels, especially the two that Walt thought might be his littermates and that Walt had nicknamed Burwell and Lansdowne. Sometimes, the rodent rapscallion would scamper back and dash up Walt's leg to ride awhile on his shoulder and nuzzle at his friend's ear. This day, however, Stumpy was a bit conservative to start with, sticking close to Tony, who sometimes held Walt's hand and sometimes wandered a little ways off the path to look at something that caught his eye. Eventually, though, the young squirrel must have satisfied himself that Tony was content, because suddenly, he took off down the path at full bore. The next thing either human knew, a gray-furred whirlwind was chattering at them and bobbing his whole body from a tree limb that arced above their heads and crossed the trail a few yards ahead of them.

"Well," said Walt, "I guess he's got a skeeter in *his* scooter! You ever get that way?" Tony laughed. Before either one of them could do or say anything else, however, Stumpy was off again, and he did the same dash-climb-and-babble routine from four different trees and tree branches before rejoining them on the ground and hopping more placidly beside them.

Walt did find some mushrooms to show the boy since the *Russula* and boletes were popping up at various points. One time, Walt stopped to show Tony the green-and-white patterned tracery on the leaves of several clumps of rattlesnake plantain; the flower stalks stood upright, but the blossoms had not formed yet. "I think the leaves look a little bit like turtle shells," he said.

Tony knelt down to look more closely. "Can we find a turtle to look at too?"

"Well," Walt said, laughing, "we probably need to be closer to the pond for that! Then again, a bit earlier in the year, the male Blanding's turtles might have been on the move through these very woods, looking for mates. I think we're a little late to spot one of them now, though."

After twenty or so minutes of slow-paced walking, the friends came upon a small glade with the first clump of blueberry bushes, and Walt stopped, lowering the pack from his back to remove the bucket and one of the margarine containers. "Now, Tony, you can put the berries in here so you have some to take home, but you can also eat them if you like. Do you know how to tell when they're ripe?"

Tony shook his head.

"It's pretty easy," Walt said. "If they're green or red or white, don't pick them yet. Leave them to get darker and ripen more, and we can come back for them in a few days. They need to be really blue or dark purple or even just about black to be ready to eat. Let me show you." The elderly man pointed out the different shades of color and degrees of ripeness and then added, "As long as they have *some* color, though, you can put them in your pot. If you leave them on your kitchen counter for a day or two, they'll ripen up on their own. They'll just be tangy if you try to eat them too soon.

"Now, we can practice picking right here, side by side. You can take the ones you can reach down lower, and I'll concentrate on the ones higher up. That's teamwork. Sometimes you have to move the branches aside with your hand to see ripe berries that are hiding behind the leaves and behind the unripe ones. Like this, see? You'll get your eyes trained to it after a little while."

Tony laughed as the first few berries plopped into his bucket, and soon, he was saying things like, "Ooh, Mr. Walt, look at this big one!"

Walt had always enjoyed berry picking, too, and he tried to explain what made it special for him.

"One thing I love about berry picking, Tony, is that it's like part of a big game of hide-and-seek with the world. The berries are there, like lots of other things, but they're not always easy to see. You have to believe that they're there in the first place and then move branches a little bit and look closely. Or sometimes the opposite is true; you don't expect to see any in a particular place, or at least for them to be ripe yet, and then they're there anyway, looking perfect, and you find them and feel lucky! It's like getting a surprise gift from the world around you, as if you were being rewarded for something you didn't even know you were doing right. Does that make any sense to you?"

"I like surprises, and I like it when I get presents."

"That's it," said Walt. "Think of berry picking as gathering up free gifts from the world. Once you know where the bushes are and when the berries are likely to be ripe, you just invest a little time and effort, and you come home with a bucket full of free gifts!"

"I couldn't ever fill my bucket up full, Mr. Walt," the five-year-old commented.

"Well, one reason for that is that you're eating better than half of what you pick! Which is okay . . . that's part of the fun too. You get to decide whether you want to eat the berries now or later. You just can't have your berries and eat them too."

"Whazzat mean?" the little shaver said, sounding mystified.

"Yeah, I know," Walt said. "I always thought they should say that differently. Usually, people say, 'You can't have your *cake* and eat it too,' which sounds silly. It just means that you have to choose: You can't eat your cake, or your berries, now and still have them to keep for later. Sometimes, people complain because they want more than they can have. Other times, everything seems just right, and they don't want anything to change, so they complain when it does. But things always change, and you have to accept change eventually. You can't always have things the way you want them, and sometimes, different *is* better."

But Tony was no longer listening. He had noticed a snake on the side of the path and was bent over, looking closely as the creature scooted off through last year's brown leaves.

"That's a garter snake," Walt said. "See the black and yellow stripes along its body?"

"Can I pick it up?" the boy asked.

Walt caught the snake and told Tony to stroke its back so he could see that the skin was dry and textured rather than slimy. "See?" he said. "Just like tooled leather." Then he showed Tony how to grip the creature just behind its head, looping its body over Tony's left arm for better balance. All the while, the snake was darting out its tongue, and occasionally it gave a squirm with its whole body. "Okay," Walt said, "why don't you just set him down gently on the ground and then let go of his head? He'll take off where he wants to go. He's got every bit as much a right to be here as we do."

All this while, Stumpy had been helping himself to ripe berries from the lower branches, sometimes grasping a branch and pulling it down with one front paw while easing a dark, sweet orb off with his teeth. However, when the humans finished their experiment in snake charming and Walt had stowed their containers and berries back in the pack, the squirrel was also ready to move on to the next prime picking location. Strolling—or hopping—farther into the woods, the trio quickly came upon one of the richest sections of berry bushes, so Walt again took the bucket out of his pack, along with an empty margarine container. "One for you, and one for me," he said to Tony.

Stumpy must have had his fill of berries for the time being because he climbed up in an oak tree whose branches hung over the big bush from which Walt and Tony were picking. "Nap time?" Walt asked jokingly when he saw his furred friend stretching out on a branch that ran parallel to the ground about eight feet up. He knew Stumpy always liked spots that were good vantage points, but he suspected that his friend was also experiencing postprandial repletion.

"Anyway, Tony, as I was saying before, I guess I like berry picking for a number of reasons," Walt said, continuing his earlier lecture. "First, you get these free gifts from the world, and you don't have to plant the bushes or weed them or tend them; all you have to do is pick the berries yourself. You can pick as many or as few as you feel like; you can pick as fast or as slow as you feel like.

"And when I'm picking berries, I always feel like I'm doing something really basic to human nature, gathering the bounty of the earth like the early human beings did or like Adam and Eve did in the Garden of Eden before they messed with the wrong tree. It's like turning back the clock to a simpler time and a simpler way of living."

He rattled on for a while longer, but eventually he realized that Tony wasn't saying anything in response. The self-deprecating old-timer chuckled to himself as he wondered if Tony, like Stumpy, had already learned just to turn Walt's voice off when he started in on one of his "sermons." That's what he had called his philosophical ramblings when his own boys were little. Since Tony and he had been picking from the same large bush, though, Walt also wondered if the boy might have wandered around toward the far side and gone out of hearing range.

"Hey, Tony!" Walt said in a much louder voice, almost a shout. He got two responses. From his left he heard Tony's voice say, "What?" but from closer by to the right, he heard a loud, surprised, deep-pitched "*Woof!*"

Oh no! Walt thought. Immediately, he said in a moderated but insistent tone, "Tony, I need you to come back to where we were picking together a moment ago, and don't be scared if I start making a lot of noise in just a moment."

"Why?" Tony asked.

"I can't tell you now," Walt said calmly. "Just come back here, please, and stay behind me."

Staring at Walt over the blueberry bush from about fifteen feet away was a black bear, not the biggest he had ever seen, but big enough. Furthermore, he realized that its relatively small size might be cause for even greater concern, because mother bears often roam the area with their offspring in June and July. The tan snout with its tip like a huge blackberry, the tiny dark eyes, the ears erected toward him . . . these were all unmistakable facial characteristics of an ursine interloper. Walt knew that the recommended way of dealing with a bear was to make oneself as large as possible and produce a lot of noise, so he was starting to remove his porkpie hat as a prelude to waving his arms and shouting, when something else happened.

Walt had forgotten that Stumpy had retreated to the oak tree for an apparent snooze; he had also forgotten that Stumpy's instincts tend toward constant surveillance of his surroundings. Later on, the man would realize that he should have known the squirrel had been aware of the bear's approach. Just as Walt heard Tony step up behind him and gasp, he also heard chattering from the tree overhead and saw a gray-and-white ball of fur plunge down on top of the bear's head.

The bruin spun around in confusion, but the squirrel had already vaulted back up onto the oak branch. When the bewildered bear turned back toward Walt and Tony, the squirrel launched himself downward again, kamikaze-like, his throat rattling with his chatter. Briefly he seemed to run in place on his hind legs between the bear's ears before leaping up again to the safety of the boughs overhead.

In that split second, Walt found himself thinking odd thoughts, his mind swirling with vague associations; he was somehow remembering images from the Greek myth of Theseus battling the Minotaur in the palace at Knossos and recalling photos of archaeological artifacts that depicted the bull dancers of ancient Crete. In ancient times, those young men and women displayed the combined skills of matadors and gymnasts, leaping onto and vaulting over charging bulls. Later, the amateur historian and classicist would have time to understand the associations his mind was making in those moments, and he would make a joke about his acrobatic roommate: "Stumpy may not be a Cretan bull dancer," he would say, "but he certainly is a Townsend bear bouncer!" And the techniques involved were remarkably similar. The elderly man's imagination may have carried him away, but Walt could have sworn (and would frequently afterward contend) that following the squirrel's second leap onto the beleaguered bear, Stumpy had actually turned a somersault before landing back on his chosen branch.

Walt was about to tell Tony to back slowly away in the direction from which they had come when the hirsute ursine decided it had had enough of invisible airborne predators. With another snort, it threw itself down on all fours and galloped away into the depths of the woods. Walt could see the leaves and bushes shake as the bear vamoosed, sometimes even crashing into the trunks of small saplings in its panic. Meanwhile, the tailless rodent warrior did a victory dance along the oak branch, chattering vociferously as he watched his foe disappear in the distance.

Walt could feel Tony's hand tugging at his, and he looked down. "Wazzat a bear?" the five-year-old asked.

"Yes, Tony, it was," Walt answered. "Were you scared?"

"No," Tony said, "but I didn't get a good look. Do you think you could get it to come back?"

Walt laughed. "I don't think that bear wants to be anywhere near Stumpy, and I'm just as glad. Sorry to disappoint you."

"Were you scared, Mr. Walt?"

"No, Tony. How could I be scared when I have you and Stumpy the Bear Bouncer to look after me? Though I have to say I *am* a little scared of what your mom will say when she hears our story. . . ."

Fortunately, though, Amy was more understanding than Walt expected, and although she put the kibosh on any more picking expeditions into bear territory in the near future, she was impressed with Stumpy's prowess and insisted on giving him one of the one-fingered face rubs that Walt had told her his friend likes. "Well, Stumpy," she said, gently stroking upward between the eyes of her knight in furry armor, "these guys make you sound like a real swashbuckler!" Stumpy started to purr.

Walt chuckled and said, "He's not your run-of-the-treadmill squirrel, that's for sure!"

Amy reached into her purse and presented the bucktoothed hero with a bag of honey-roasted cashews she had bought as a snack for herself. During the next week, he would enjoy a few of them several mornings running while Walt was savoring his morning coffee on the deck.

Before Amy took her son home for dinner, Walt addressed his

diminutive protégé: "Well, Tony, I guess we won't be going that far into the woods for a while, but we can always make a trip out in Nelly and pick berries around the islands. Even Old Smokey is less scary than a bear."

"Who's Old Smokey?" Tony asked.

"Oh," Walt replied, "didn't I ever tell you about Old Smokey? You know the bluegills that we feed from the dock? Well, for years and years, people have been saying that there's a giant bluegill that lives in Kibbee Pond, and a while ago, Stumpy and I had a run-in with him. . . ."

But I'll interrupt Walt here because you've already heard that story, and I wouldn't want anyone to be offended if his details don't exactly match the ones he gave before; each version he tells of one of his stories does tend to stretch the truth a bit further than the previous incarnation. As the eloquent codger himself says, "My tales evolve every time I tell them, taking on a sometimes mythic dimension." I'll leave you to figure out what that means.

6

Stumpy and the Chimney Sweep

August 17, 2011

The last few weeks at the height of summer have been busy for the folks out at Kibbee Pond. Among other exciting events in the recent past, Walt Walthers, the kindhearted octogenarian who lives in a comfortable pondside cabin, and his roommate and partner in crime, Stumpy the stub-tailed gray squirrel, took their neighbor, five-year-old Tony Riggetti, on a blueberry-picking tour of the pond's shoreline and islands. On that jaunt in Walt's skiff, Nelly, the genial geezer pointed out turtles as well as birds, including cormorants, herons, and an osprey, though Tony, whose mom works in a beauty parlor, naturally insisted on calling that fish hawk a "hair spray." The week after, in part as a thank-you for that outing, Tony's mom, Amy, invited Stumpy for his first sleepover at the little house down the road from the cabin. Stumpy livened up the festivities there by panicking during a thunderstorm and diving into Amy's open flour bin while she was preparing supper; otherwise intrepid, our fur-faced hero does suffer from one unshakable fear: astraphobia. Clad in white as he emerged moments later from his baptism in the glass container, he looked like a neophyte wearing the robes of some kind of religious conversion . . . or like a creature who was undergoing either an unsuccessful fashion makeover or a metamorphosis to albinism.

Rounding out the recent excitement, about a week ago, the rarely daunted rodent made a heroic Hail Mary catch, though without a football helmet or stickum on his paws. His new friend, the teacher and biologist Michael Swift, who is pursuing his summer research on insect migration, had nevertheless failed to net the green darner dragonfly he wished to fit with a tiny radio tag; coming to his rescue, Stumpy made an acrobatic leap in the tall grass along the shore to snag the escaping insect so that Michael could attach the tiny transmitter and then release the unharmed creature for later tracking.

Ever since that escapade, the rambunctious rodent has been acting rather full of himself. Walt is not surprised, because he himself is proud of the furry fellow; still, the easily entertained elder finds amusing the regularity with which Stumpy will jump into the air at odd moments or throw his body sideways into tall grass, then pause as if hearing in his head some rousing theme music or thunderous applause. Of course, The Catch itself (and even Walt has been thinking of that exploit in capital letters, as part of a newly established legend) made a good story for Walt to tell to Tony when the youngster next visited them; Stumpy's pretentious behavior after his triumph has made that story even better.

"You should have seen it, Tony! Michael said that he stretched out just like one of the wide receivers for the Patriots, then gently cradled the insect in his paws as he landed."

"Gee whiz, Mr. Walt! I wish I'd been here!"

Although Tony had missed The Catch itself, the boy has in the past few days gotten to witness something comparable. You see, Stumpy has discovered the large short-horned grasshoppers that congregate on the sunny gravel of the cabin's driveway; the insects let a human or squirrel get within a foot or so and then *P-YANG!* into the air as if shot from a catapult, landing a yard or more away. Never one to ignore a challenge, the tailless squirrel has taken to stalking the locust-like hoppers and, when they leap into the air, launching himself in pursuit, stretching his body out and extending his front paws in a recurring effort to pluck his prey in mid-flight. The hoppers, however, have some evolutionary tricks up their sleeves, so to speak; as they take off, their hind wings—in a potentially startling way—flash black with a yellowish ring, but as they reach the apex of their leaps, the hoppers draw those wings back in under a gravel-colored covering so that their whole bodies virtually disappear against the camouflaging backdrop of the driveway. With some practice, however, Stumpy has been able to anticipate the flight patterns and snag several of the creatures in midair, turning over and landing on his back to protect his treasures from harm. Then he lets them go and begins stalking others in adjacent areas of the drive. As Walt told Tony, "I taught him to be a catch-and-release kind of guy."

Usually, Stumpy conducts these football practice sessions in the midmorning, when Walt is on his second cup of coffee. Tony often shows up about that time and chortles, giggles, and guffaws as the gray-furred acrobat goes through his antics. The second morning Tony got to watch, he even insisted on phoning his mother, Amy, and inviting her up to join Stumpy's other "fans" in rooting him on. Amy *oohed* and *aahed* as the squirrel threw himself up and twisted his body around, and she laughed as he tumbled into some of his landings and, especially, when he seemed to strike poses after making a "reception." They all jokingly agreed that Stumpy deserved an NFL tryout.

One morning while Walt and his diminutive neighbor were enjoying their furry buddy's gyrations and gymnastic skills, a strange pickup truck pulled into the driveway from behind the screen of hemlocks and rolled to a stop. So caught up in his own performance that the intrusion surprised him, Stumpy unceremoniously flopped out of the air, scooted over to the deck, and scrambled up Walt's leg, stopping only when he reached his accustomed perch on the elderly man's right shoulder.

From the light-blue cab emerged a large, jovial-looking man with a ruddy complexion, a balding pink dome, and a short, reddish-blond mustache. His belly protruded slightly over his beltline under a yellow T-shirt that read, in black letters, "Squirrel . . . It's What's for Dinner!"

"Hi, folks," he called, grinning. "Is one of you Walt Walthers?"

By this time, Walt was out of his chair and headed down the stairs to greet their visitor, Stumpy still riding his shoulder. "That would be me," he said. "Or, to be fully grammatical, that would be *I*."

"I'm Jim Barack," the smiling man replied, extending his right hand. "I understand you're the local squirrel expert."

"I don't know about that," said the ever-modest weather watcher, accepting the handshake, "but as you can see, I do have some experience with a rodent roommate. Now, I take it your T-shirt is a joke rather than a serious statement of intent."

Jim laughed. "Yeah, I just like to stir things up whenever I can. You can ask my ex-wives!"

"Ouch!" Walt said. "I don't dare ask how many. You said your name was 'Barack'? Like the president?"

Jim laughed again. "Spelled the same but pronounced a bit differently. No relation, though."

Walt chuckled. "Well, Mr. Not Quite President, what can I do for you?"

"Actually," Jim said, "I'm a college professor, and I'm doing some research into melanism in squirrels—you know, melanistic squirrels are the ones whose pigmentation is darker than most members of the species. Sort of like the opposite of albinism."

"Wow!" Walt interjected. "The moon must be full! You're our second biological researcher in the last two weeks."

Jim laughed yet again, something he seemed accustomed to doing almost constantly. "Better get out the garlic, crucifixes, and wooden stakes!" he said, pretending to look around suspiciously.

Walt pushed back his porkpie hat and chuckled. He was beginning to like this guy.

"Anyway," Jim continued, "I've heard reports of some colonies of gray squirrels around Townsend that show signs of melanism, and I was wondering if you knew any good spots to look for subjects for my study. Does this fella have any dark-furred concubines or compatriots?"

"Can't say as I've ever seen any melanistic squirrels around here," the cordial codger replied, "but why not have a cup of coffee with us, and I'll search my memory banks. You haven't seen any especially dark-furred squirrels around, have you, Tony?"

"No sirree!" the little shaver said.

Long story short, both Walt and Tony enjoyed Jim's company, and even Stumpy warmed to him despite the T-shirt and despite Jim's having taken the spotlight away from the stub-tailed rodent for the time being. Unfortunately, the only locations Walt could remember seeing dark-furred squirrels were in Michigan when he was growing up. Nevertheless, when Jim left, he gave Walt his cell number and email address in case the pond dwellers should spot anything unusual.

As Jim's pickup crunched out of the driveway, a whistled cry of

SKREE! SKREE! resounded from above, and Walt looked up to see a big hawk circling high overhead. "Well, Stumpy, I don't think Jim is any threat to turn you into dinner, but I suspect that fella would like to!"

"What is it, Mr. Walt?" asked Tony.

"Well, it's some kind of big raptor, but I'm not sure exactly what kind. . . ." he said, shielding his eyes from the sun. Tony had started quietly giggling as the older man spoke. "What's so funny?" Walt wanted to know.

"You're joshing me again, aren't you, Mr. Walt? You said that it was a raptor, but it doesn't look anything like a dinosaur . . . and I know a lot about dinosaurs. Mommy got me some books for Christmas."

"It's an interesting point you bring up," the cabin-dwelling Renaissance man replied. "Some kinds of dinosaurs were called raptors, but when I said, 'raptor,' I was using the word in a different way. It also identifies a bird of prey—in other words, any kind of bird that catches other animals to eat, but especially eagles, hawks, and owls. This looks like a red-tailed hawk, and given the size of the bird, I'd say it's a female. Among the hawks, females do tend to be bigger than males. But the other interesting thing is that scientists see many direct links between the dinosaurs of eons ago and today's birds. In fact, some scientists even say that birds *are* dinosaurs. Do you know the archaeopteryx?" Tony nodded. "Well," Walt continued, "it was an early dinosaur-hyphen-bird. Hard to say whether it was more one than the other."

As Walt and Tony were talking, Stumpy had positioned himself close to Walt's legs and in his shadow, clearly trying to keep himself out of the predator's keen sight. When the soaring bird turned at the appropriate angle to the sun, Walt said, "Yes, indeed, that's a redtail! If you look up at the way the tail fans out and wait a minute, she'll fly back around to where the sun will let you see the orange-ish color of her tail feathers." The bird called again, and Walt said, "Stumpy, old buddy, you'd best be on your toes while she's around. You don't want to end up as rodent fricassee!"

The string of last week's visitors—human, avian, and otherwise—continued on Wednesday, when Walt had made an appointment to have Nathan, the chimney sweep from Milford, New Hampshire, come down to do the annual cleaning of the cabin's stovepipe and chimney. Not all that long ago, Walt was still cleaning his own chimney, but he has never been fond of heights, and for four or five years, he has been relying on Nathan to keep him creosote-free for a safe season of fires in the woodstove. All three of Walt's sons, though they all live far away, have made it clear that working on the roof is one of the activities they want their father to avoid, and in this case, Walt is glad to comply.

Since Tony had never seen a chimney sweep at work, Walt made sure he was there when Nathan arrived at about ten o'clock in his white Chevy van with the black "Stevenson's Stoves" lettering on the side. Stumpy seemed to recognize the vehicle since he didn't even growl when it pulled into the driveway; instead, he sat on the deck rail, chattering excitedly. "What kind of a watchdog are you if you just welcome the intruders?" Walt asked jokingly.

Nathan, though muscular, is not tall; in fact, Walt noticed that the man's height seems to fall almost exactly halfway between his own six feet and Tony's four. Nathan was wearing black jeans, a black T-shirt, black work boots, and a battered Red Sox cap, and he smiled at Walt through his goatee as the two shook hands. "Didn't get lost this time, I see," Walt commented.

Nathan laughed. "Walt, I got a bit turned around the first time I came here, and you won't let me forget it. You know, I'll bet you went out that day and switched some of the road signs just so you could ride me for the rest of my life. How long ago was that, anyway? Had to be five years, I'd say. You'd think I'd earned a little respect by getting here without incident the last several times."

"Well," said Walt, "how do I know that you didn't leave Milford at 6:00 a.m. this morning? You could have been driving around northern Massachusetts for four hours, for all I know."

"Okay, okay," Nathan chuckled. "I can see I'm not gonna win this argument. Are you gonna tell me how to do my job too?"

"Nah," Walt replied. "I'll just let you screw up on your own. By the way, this is my faithful sidekick, Tony Riggetti, from down the road. He thinks he might like to be a sweep when he grows up, so he'll be keeping an eagle eye on you. Make sure you do everything right, 'cause Tony'll be taking notes. You know Stumpy from past years; I suspect he'll be keeping an even closer eye on you since he can go up on the roof, and Tony and I can't."

"I told you last time," Nathan quipped, "that Stumpy might work even better than my brush if we just tied a string to him and dropped him down the pipe. I could pull him up and down four or five times and save wear and tear on my own equipment. What do you think, Stumpy?"

After living with Walt for a while, the gray-furred bandit recognized a bantering tone when he heard one, so he just bobbed his head a couple of times from his perch on the deck rail. He continued to watch with interest as Nathan walked back to the van and unloaded an aluminum ladder.

"You just want the cleaning and inspection this year, Walt, or would you also like me to install one of those big, barn-size rooster weather vanes while I'm up there?" Nathan was warming to the battle of wits.

"Nope," Walt fired back, "you're the only dumb cluck I want on my roof today, thank you kindly."

"All right," the younger man said, throwing up his hands. "I give up! I can't win with you any more than I can with my wife."

"Are you saying you're *hen*pecked?" Walt asked, raising his eyebrows.

"O-o-oh!" Nathan laughed. "You better just let me get to work."

"Mr. Nathan," Tony said, "what's that picture on your arm?"

"Oh this?" the chimney sweep replied. "That's a tattoo."

"I know," the boy responded. "My daddy has one, too, but his is my mommy's name. Yours is a picture."

"Oh, well, it's a picture, sort of a cartoon, I guess, of a chimney sweep holding a big broom and smiling," Nathan said, pulling his sleeve up a little and leaning toward the youngster so he could see better. "Actually, we don't use regular brooms like that one. We have brushes and rods and other equipment I can show you as I get things ready."

Nathan did take several minutes to show Tony what was on and in the van, explaining how things worked. "Today should be pretty straightforward, though," he said. "I just have to take off the chimney cap and clean the stovepipes from the roof, then go in and vacuum out the stove and inspect the flue in the basement. Walt has what we call a multi-flue stainless steel cap, because he's got both an oil furnace and a woodstove, so he needs two pipes. See how the cap's screened around up there to keep out squirrels like Stumpy and birds and other critters? Otherwise, they could slip in and start nesting or fall down into one of the flues; if that happened, they might not be able to get out again."

Walt and Tony lugged their chairs out into the driveway so they could have the best view possible as Nathan set up his ladder and then carried his equipment bag up to the roof. Stumpy was already up there, waiting. Walt hadn't seen whether the squirrel had climbed the screen door and then shinnied up the shingles of the cabin or whether he had jumped down from one of the pine limbs that hung over the roof. Nevertheless, the gray-furred apprentice sweep wandered back and forth along the ridgepole and down along the slant of the roof to wherever the view seemed best at the moment. Of course, he acted more like a supervisor than an apprentice, and Nathan conversed with his companion, pretending to ask his advice as he set about his work. When the black-clad expert removed the chimney cap and laid it down, Stumpy had to sniff it from several angles before sitting back to observe the rest of the operation.

At one point, Nathan had to return to the van for some piece of equipment, and the gray-furred sun lover reclined along the roof ridge, flopping on his back while waiting for his work "crew" to return and looking ready both to soak up some rays and to catch some z's. It was probably a good thing, however, that he chose to lie on his back, because that position left his eyes to the sky and gave him a split second to react, saving him from what might otherwise have happened next.

Walt had no time even to cry out as the big hawk's shadow crossed the deck and the redtail thunderbolted down at Stumpy. The squirrel must have caught a glimpse of something coming at him and may also have felt a sudden shift in air pressure or employed some other sense that humans lack; in any case, he rolled off the ridge and down the near side of the roof just as the feathered storm cloud struck but missed. The squirrel scrambled up quickly and darted first in one direction and then in another as the rapacious predator recovered her balance in the air and turned back for another pass. Tony was yelling, "Run, Stumpy, run!"

This time, Stumpy did not waste another moment. Like a sprinter in the forty-yard dash, he raced for the chimney and threw himself up and then down into one of the aluminum-piped flues. The baffled bird landed on the chimney and looked about like a diner in a restaurant who confronts a mysteriously emptied plate that only moments before held a perfectly cooked filet mignon.

Walt had, of course, risen from his chair and was now waving his arms and yelling, "Ya! You, get outa here. Go on, you big bag of feathers!"

The redtail looked calmly down at the gesticulating man, then glanced about disinterestedly before lifting off and winging away over the pond.

Walt, Nathan, and Tony all hurried into the cabin and across to the woodstove, where they could hear a scrabbling from inside the metal pipe. "I'll get the flue open," Nathan said, reaching for the lever. In the meantime, Walt knelt down and grabbed the handle of the stove door, bracing himself for what he would see when he opened it. No sooner did he swing the door open, however, than a soot-covered Stumpy darted out onto the braided rug, in one piece but sneezing and shaking himself . . . and black from his head to his nub of a tail.

"Look at that!" Nathan said. "Kinda like a ride down a water-slide, but not quite as cleansing . . . or refreshing!"

"You okay, Stump?" Walt asked as the squirrel continued to inspect himself and then tentatively began trying to clean off the clinging ash, soot, and creosote only to sneeze again and make hocking and spitting noises. He looked up at Walt with the miserable expression of a cat that has fallen into a full bathtub.

"Gee, Mr. Walt," Tony asked, "is this what Jim Barack was looking for when he asked about the dark-furred, melon-eating squirrels?"

Walt laughed. "Not quite, T-man. He was looking for melanistic squirrels, ones that are *naturally* darker than other squirrels. Stumpy's coloration here is a bit . . . artificial. Still, Jim would probably enjoy the story, so maybe I should call him after all."

Walt turned back to his bedraggled and begrimed buddy and said, "You don't mind if I tell Jim, do you, Stump?" Then the good-spirited geezer paused a moment before quipping, "You know, you may look melanistic at the moment, but I suspect you feel melan*choly*!"

Turning back to the young human, Walt said, "Now, I should make something clear to you, Tony. You saw Stumpy turn white after he dove into that flour bin, and now you've seen him turn black from diving down the chimney. Nevertheless, he's not an albino, and he's not melanistic. He's just a unique and wonderful *gray* squirrel!"

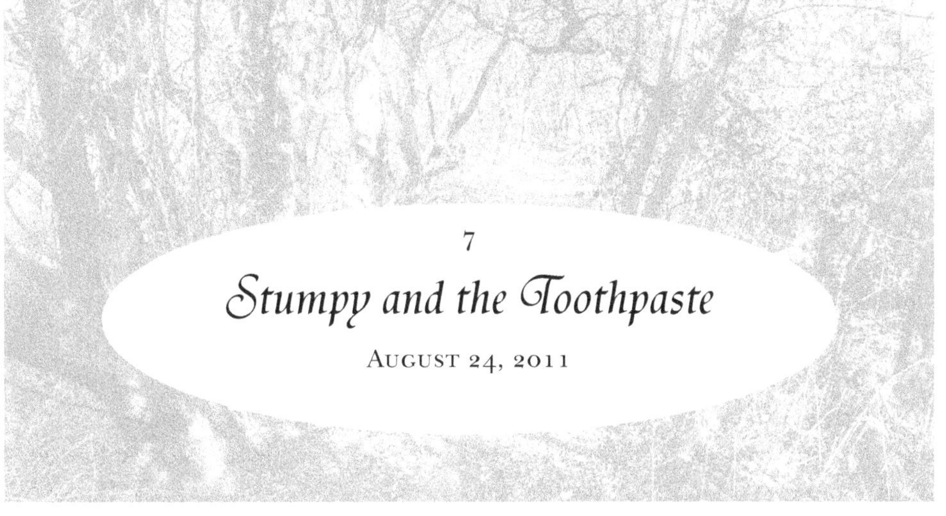

7

Stumpy and the Toothpaste

August 24, 2011

After the excitement last week that resulted from three visitors—Nathan the chimney sweep, Jim Barack the naturalist researching melanism in squirrels, *and* an unnamed red-tailed hawk—Walt Walthers, the elderly weather watcher who lives in a cabin out on Kibbee Pond in Townsend, and Stumpy, the stub-tailed gray squirrel who has become Walt's constant companion, were hoping for a quieter week, especially with summer winding down toward fall and the start of school. Of course, they still looked forward to their regular visits from five-year-old Tony Riggetti, who lives just down the road with his mom, Amy, and who always manages to bring some excitement with him. In addition, for Walt, a particular nostalgia had arisen since he had learned that Tony would be starting pre-kindergarten at the end of the month and thus would subsequently be out of the picture, at least on weekday mornings.

Tony was apt to show up anytime in the morning or afternoon, sometimes banging on the screen door even before Walt had completed his "morning ablutions," as the kindly geezer calls his leisurely procedure of washing his face, shaving, brushing his teeth, and otherwise preparing for the day ahead. From the moment of Stumpy's arrival almost two years ago now, the curious rodent has been fascinated with Walt's deliberate preparations, perching on the window next to the sink to watch as Walt guides the electric razor over his cheeks with the precision of a systematic farmer cutting his hayfield with a tractor. Walt is especially patient in shaving his throat around his Adam's apple, and the squirrel sometimes nods his head with excitement as the man leans his own head back to create a smoother plane for the blades.

Even more interesting to the squirrel are the toothbrush and toothpaste when the time comes for Walt to clean his teeth; Stumpy never tires of all that spitting, and he has always been mesmerized by water coming out of a faucet, so the dental cleaning is a highlight of his mornings. Because he often wrinkles his nose when Walt opens the tube of toothpaste, his friend on occasion will hold it up to his face so he can get a good whiff. The furry rascal enjoys sniffing the aftershave bottle, too, and even Walt's deodorant stick, but nothing interests him as much as the tube of gel that Walt squeezes onto his toothbrush two and sometimes three times a day.

A week or so ago, Walt had just unscrewed the tube cap when he heard Tony rapping on the screen door in the kitchen, and the half-groomed oldster stepped out to greet his other partner in crime, leaving the toothpaste sitting open on the bathroom counter and Stumpy perched on the windowsill.

"Well, if it's not Timmy Spaghetti!" the white-haired mischief-maker said as he waved his protégé into the kitchen.

"Mr. Walt!" the half-pint protested. "You know what my real name is!"

"Yes, I do, Anthony, but sometimes I just can't help myself. I still say you *look* like a Timmy . . . oh, but I'll try to control myself. Say, don't you have a birthday coming up soon?"

"Mommy says it's less than a month away now, Septober 27!"

"Really?" the playful codger replied, fighting back a smile. "How old you gonna be, eleventy-seven?"

"No, Mr. Walt. I'll be six."

"Hmm-m-m. Did you know that *my* birthday is two days later, Septober 29? I might actually be eleventy-seven this year myself. . . . So, you're gonna be six? Is that old enough to get your driver's license?"

"No, Mr. Walt. I'm not big enough for that yet."

"Well, even so, we're gonna have to find a way to celebrate the momentous occasion. Does your mom have plans?"

"I don't know," Tony said.

"Well, maybe we can take a trip to the dump or something."

"Mr. Walt, I don't want to go to the dump!"

"Well, how do you know? You ever been? They've got some great stuff there, just waiting for folks to snap it up. I saw a two-wheeled tricycle there once and an old toilet bowl. . . . Just 'cause people throw stuff out doesn't mean it can't be perfectly usable. . . ." (Now he noticed Tony's lip curling and knew his teasing was going a little too far.) "Oh, but I don't really mean to take you to the dump for your birthday, buddy. We'll just have to work on a plan for something fun. . . . You think about it, and we'll consult your mom too. Hey, maybe we can go to the snail races at the town hall if they have them that week!"

Although Tony had started to giggle, Walt noticed that, suddenly, his face fell again as he looked behind the elderly man at the floor outside the bathroom door.

"Is . . . is Stumpy all right?" the boy asked.

Walt turned to see his furry roommate skulking across the rug, his mouth foaming whitely, and Walt's own jaw dropped momentarily until his mind put the puzzle pieces together. Then he laughed. "Why, you little sneak! Didn't I tell you you couldn't have any toothpaste? Now you look like some kind of rabid rabbit! Oh, say *that* five times fast!"

Subsequent observation confirmed Walt's theory about what had happened: As soon as the man had left the bathroom to greet Tony, the curious rodent had dropped to the countertop and pounced on the toothpaste tube, pressing down with his front paws until a snake of Colgate lay coiled next to the sink. After a quick sniff of the irresistible minty sweetness, Stumpy had sampled a little and then scoffed two or three mouthfuls, until—apparently—the taste had proven overpowering. Then he had tried sneaking out of the bathroom, in hopes of evading Walt's watchful eye.

"Come here, you bandit," Walt said, and the frothy-mouthed squirrel complied, advancing slowly with his head down. "Let's get a good look at you," the man said, bending over to pick up his mammalian friend. Holding Stumpy out from his body, Walt turned toward Tony so the boy could see the bubbles and cream smeared around the squirrel's muzzle. "Looks like he's got hydrophobia," Walt commented.

"Whazzat?" Tony asked.

"Well," Walt answered, "it's another name for rabies. That's a contagious viral infection that can damage an animal's nervous system and make it aggressive toward other critters it would usually avoid, like people. Sometimes you hear people talk about a 'mad dog,' and they usually mean a dog with rabies, or hydrophobia. Hydrophobia means 'fear of water,' which is one of the symptoms in advanced human cases; the victim has trouble swallowing, can't quench his thirst, and panics when given something to drink. Sometimes around here, we get rabid raccoons, and they'll walk right up to people. If you ever see a wild animal acting funny, be sure to stay away, and let a grown-up know. If a rabid animal bites a human, he can get the infection, too, and the results can be really bad."

"But Stumpy's okay?" Tony wanted to know.

"Oh yeah," Walt assured him. "He may have a tummy ache from eating too much of that sweet stuff, but I don't think we have to worry even about that. Hey, it could even be a good thing, especially if it makes his choppers whiter and his breath sweeter!"

The next day, Tony's arrival produced turmoil of a different sort. The tyke was already snuffling when he came through the door, and it took a while before Walt could assemble the bits and pieces into something like the full story. Walt led Tony to the couch and sat with his arm around his young friend while the soon-to-be six-year-old coughed out a phrase here and a word there between sobs. Stumpy had followed them and sat on the back of the couch, nodding his head at his little friend, who continued trying to squeeze out his tale: "B-b-big boys . . . (muffle, snuffle) . . . bikes . . . (snuffle, snuffle) . . . called me . . . (sniff) . . . 'baby' cuz . . . cuz I . . . still play . . . (sniff, sniff) . . . with . . . (snuffle) . . . *trucks* . . . (snuffle, snuff) . . . ran over . . . (uh, uh) . . . my new road . . . WA-A-A-A-H-H-H!"

Walt knew that at the house down the road, Tony had turned a sandy stretch along the edge of the pull-in driveway into his favorite play area. With a toy grader and bulldozer, he spent some time there every day building new roads, driveways, and parking lots for his Matchbox cars. Apparently, some older boys had come along on bikes and picked on him, but only when Amy knocked on the door of the cabin and then joined them inside did Walt get a fuller picture. According to the young mother, three boys—she thought nine or ten years old—had ridden up while she was still getting ready for work. She had seen the boys ride by once or twice in the past, but they had never stopped before. From the window she could see they were saying something to Tony, who soon stood up with his fists clenched and shouted back at them. By the time she got out to the front deck to ask what was going on, the boys had ridden off down the road in the opposite direction from Walt's cabin. Tony had run up to the house, crying, and had thrown his arms around her legs; apparently, as the boys rode off, the bike tires of one of them had gouged a track through the road Tony had been building, but Amy wasn't sure the damage was intentional. Nevertheless, she was not happy.

"So," Walt said, turning to Tony, "what exactly did these big boys say to you, pardner?"

By now, Tony had regained much of his composure, and he said, almost without any stammering, "They said I was a . . . baby . . . for still playing with toy trucks." Now his jaw was set, and he seemed to have gotten past his tears.

"Well, now, buddy, you're not a baby. You know *I* still like to play with trucks, and I'm not a baby, am I? They were just trying to rattle your cage and get you worked up. Best way to deal with somebody like that is to ignore them or laugh at what they say."

"I wanted to *punch* them," Tony replied firmly.

"I understand that," Walt said, "but if they're bigger and older than you, you'll just get yourself hurt. And violence isn't a good solution even if you're bigger than the other people. There are other ways to be tough and earn respect, and the best ways usually involve controlling your anger and using your brain. I know you've got a good one of *those*, and maybe we can put our heads together and figure something out. Your mom has to go to work, so why don't we take Stumpy the Wonder Rodent out for a boat ride? Maybe we can talk him into trying to water-ski! Grab the life preservers, and give your mom a smacker. We'll talk more about this later."

The bigger boys came back the next day, and at first Tony did pretty well at ignoring them. They tossed out the word "baby" one too many times, however, and from inside the house, Amy could hear Tony shouting, "I am not!" as she rushed to open the slider to the deck. Once again, though, the trio was gone before she could corral them. That pattern continued for the next couple of days, with Walt and Amy getting almost as frustrated as the five-year-old.

Thursday morning, Walt sat down on his couch again with Tony, saying, "What we need is some way to show them that you deserve their respect, that you can do something they can't but would like to.

"When I was about your age, I lived on a small farm out in the country, and I had to go to church in town every Sunday. Afterward, in the Christian spirit of generosity, my mother expected me to bring back one of the boys from town for lunch at our house, but the boys from town and we boys from the outlying farms saw each other as rivals, and the townies always thought they were better than we were. So I had to figure out a way to impress them, show them that I could do something they couldn't or didn't dare to. Sometimes it was enough to blindfold myself and walk across the holding area near the barn; there was a lot of cow manure out there, and the trick was to get across without stepping in any of it. Extensive practice meant that I could do it fine, but any of my guests who dared to try ended up with disgusting, stinky muck on their sneakers. Not everyone is able to perform such a delicate manure . . . I mean, such a delicate ma*neu*ver!

"Sometimes, though, that trick wasn't impressive enough. Well, we had an electric fence at our place to keep the cows in their pasture. Do you know what those are? No? They're just electric wires connected to a transformer, and if someone—cow or human—brushes up against them, he gets a shock; the cows don't like getting zapped, so they usually stay where they're supposed to once they get the idea. Now, I knew how to short out the fence by leaning a bunch of tall grass up against it so the charge would run into the ground; that way, I could touch the fence without getting a shock. When I had a Sunday guest who wasn't impressed by my manure maneuver, I'd take him out there and dare him to grab the wire. Of course, no one wanted to do that, but I'd distract them for a second and get the grass in position, then grab the wire myself and—*ZZZZZT!*—*pretend* that I was getting shocked. I'd shake and shudder, clench my jaw and throw my eyes wide, make my teeth chatter, and hold on for ten seconds or so before releasing my grip, wiping my forehead, and saying something like, 'Wow! That was invigorating. Sure *you* don't want to try it?' After that, my guest would usually be staring at me in admiration, and for the rest of the visit, he'd treat me with respect.

"Once in a while, though, I'd run into somebody skeptical, and

I'd have to kneel down, stick out my tongue, and touch *it* to the wire. Of course, I'd go through similar antics and contortions as if a million volts were passing through my entire body. When I was done, even that guy would be looking at me with awe.

"But when I was going into seventh grade, my mother realized that I had never brought home this one kid who was the toughest and least gullible of all the town boys. I'd been avoiding him and hoping she wouldn't notice, but somehow, she caught on (as moms always seem to do), and she insisted that I bring him with me the next Sunday. I worried and worried, because I was sure that Taylor Dillingham wasn't going to fall for my grabbing the wire with my hands, and he probably wouldn't even be impressed with my putting my tongue on the line. I wasn't sure what I *could* do to impress him.

"Well, the day came, and my fears were justified. I grabbed the supposedly live wire with my hands, and Taylor just laughed. I put my tongue on it, and he only let out a 'Humph!' I couldn't see any other way, so I gathered my courage, unzipped my pants, and used another part of my body."

Tony's eyes went wide.

"And that," said Walt, "is how I got my nickname. After that, everybody called me Lightning Loins!" Walt looked at Tony, whose jaw was hanging down. "Now we just have to come up with a similar plan for you. But don't worry: It won't involve an electric fence!"

Inspiration didn't strike right away, but that night, shortly after turning out the light, Walt sat up again in bed. "Stumpy," he said, "I think I've got it . . . as long as you cooperate." The squirrel lay on the bed beside him, legs wrapped around the souvenir baseball Walt had brought him earlier in the summer; he didn't answer, however, because he was already sound asleep . . . and also, of course, because squirrels can't talk. Walt, however, got out of bed and, because it was only ten o'clock, called Amy to let her in on his plan.

The next morning, when the three big boys pulled up on their bikes, Tony was out at his construction site, making *V-ROOM!* and *putt-putt* noises as he pushed his trucks and other vehicles around the highways he had carved out. Amy was watching from inside and quietly opened the side door to let Stumpy out.

"Hey! Look at the baby with his toys!" sneered a chunky boy with a crew cut.

"Yeah," said a second boy, this one a blond with a bowl cut and an Atlanta Falcons jersey, "little Bubba Boo-Boo's prob'ly gonna cry!"

Tony played on without looking up.

The third boy, a gangly redhead with glasses, joined in: "Don't you know only babies play with toy cars? I bet you still ride a tricycle!"

Tony kept on making *V-ROOM! V-ROOM!* noises and smiling to himself.

Before any of the big boys could say anything else, the blond with the football jersey blurted, "Whoa! What's that?" and they all looked up to see a tailless squirrel with white foam around its mouth staggering down the dirt road toward them. Every couple of steps, it would emit a loud, growling, gargling noise, and it seemed to be headed right for the bike riders.

"Better stay back," said Tony, jumping to his feet and interposing himself between them and the apparent threat. "It looks like one of those rapid squirrels! He must have hyperfoamia, and you don't want to let him bite you, or you'll get the gravies too!" Tony now walked toward Stumpy, making soothing noises in his throat.

"What are you *do*ing?" asked the boy with the crew cut. "Are you crazy?"

"No," Tony answered. "I think I can calm him down so you guys can get away." Still crooning, he reached out his right hand toward the squirrel, which stopped and then sat up on its haunches, its growl transformed to a contented sound like a cat's purr. The five-year-old stroked its head with one finger, then closed his fist and held out his forearm; the squirrel scrambled up his arm to his shoulder and sat quietly, looking at the three older boys.

"It's safe now," Tony said. "You can leave."

"What are you," said the blond boy, his jaw hanging, "some kind of squirrel whisperer?"

"I guess so," Tony said. "I'm good at taming wild animals. You got to be calm and patient."

"What are you gonna do now? Aren't you scared?" the redhead with glasses asked.

"I'm gonna take him up the road to my friend Mr. Walt, who knows everything about squirrels and other animals. He'll know what to do."

The three bigger boys continued to stare, wide-eyed.

"You better get on your way before this guy gets upset again," Tony urged. "You can come back later if you want, and I'll tell you what happened."

The three, somewhat reluctantly, pedaled off down the hill on their bikes, each looking back occasionally over his shoulder at the five-year-old standing in the road. When they were out of sight, Tony waved at his mother, lowered Stumpy to the ground, and then scampered up the road to the cabin to tell Walt what had happened.

Although the four conspirators couldn't be sure of the outcome at that moment, the three boys did come back that afternoon. Amy went out and oversaw introductions all around before Tony led the other boys up the hill to meet Walt and Stumpy and to explain the plot they had all concocted. How could anyone have foreseen at the time that Stumpy's fascination with Walt's morning ablutions would result in Tony establishing a lasting friendship with the three older boys? As future installments will demonstrate, however, that's how things turned out.

That night, as Walt and Stumpy settled down on the bed to sleep, the elderly man chuckled and said, "Well, I guess we've discovered yet another reason why dental hygiene is so essential." Turning toward the squirrel with his lips pursed, he continued, "Now, did you want to give me a goodnight smacker with that sweet, minty breath of yours?" With his usual forbearance, however, Stumpy just turned over in silence, back to Walt, and pulled his baseball closer with all four feet.

"No?" the bright-eyed geezer said. "Well, I guess I just have to keep a close eye on you so you don't get addicted to sucking down the Colgate! On my fixed income, I don't have sufficient funds to support a rapid rodent's toothpaste habit!"

8

Stumpy and the Bareback Rider

August 31, 2011

The last ten days or so have been pretty eventful out at Kibbee Pond in Townsend, where Walt Walthers, the octogenarian weather watcher, and his rascally rodent companion, Stumpy the squirrel, have weathered both a mild earthquake and the remnants of Hurricane Irma, not to mention a number of human visitors.

The earthquake occurred a little before two o'clock on Tuesday of last week, shortly after Walt's old high school friend Arlene Tosh had pulled into the driveway at his cabin for a visit. She had, naturally, brought along her one-hundred-pound yellow Lab, Big Bruno, with whom Stumpy had struck up an acquaintance earlier in the summer. As Arlene pulled into Walt's gravel driveway, the dog's gargantuan head protruded from the rear window of her silver Volvo sedan. His tongue lolling almost to the gravel, Big Bruno panted happily in greeting—no small feat given the tennis ball that Walt could also see tucked back in his cheek like a plug of fluorescent yellow chewing tobacco.

"What's the story, Arlene?" Walt asked innocently, nodding at the tawny mega-mutt. "Do you have to get that thing surgically removed every night?"

Arlene had just climbed out from behind the wheel, and she turned to look at her pet. "Now, Walt, you know how much he loves his ball, and you also know that all you have to do to get him to spit it out is offer to throw it for him."

"That's one offer you're not likely to see me making!" Walt laughed. "Slimy dog drool is not my favorite commodity."

Just at that moment, Stumpy, who had been sitting upright at Walt's feet and staring happily at his huge-headed, pink-tongued blond friend, emitted a slight yip and scooted up the right leg of the man's chinos, ending wide-eyed on Walt's right shoulder. Walt only had time to mutter, "Now what's gotten into . . . ?" before he felt a trembling under his feet. He staggered slightly in order to keep his balance, and he looked at Arlene, who also had a quizzical look on her face.

"Could that have been an earthquake?" she asked.

"Maybe," Walt replied, grinning, "but didn't you once tell me that men were always claiming the earth moved when you came into the room? Why would pulling into my driveway be any different?"

"That was my Bill's joke, the sweet, silly thing. He used to say that he couldn't tell whether I had just walked onto the scene or if he was coming down with Parkinson's. But seriously, I felt something. Didn't you?"

"Yes, definitely," Walt replied. "And Stumpy seemed to know ahead of time that something was about to happen. We can check on the television or computer inside if you like."

Arlene released the giant canine from the back seat of the Volvo, and Stumpy slipped down from Walt's shoulder to approach the dog. "Be a good boy," the woman said. "You remember the nice kitty, don't you?"

Ball in cheek, Big Bruno turned into a wagging machine as he stood in place, head slightly turned aside so as not to make direct eye contact with the much smaller animal. Clearly, he was deferring to the squirrel and letting Stumpy dictate the pace and extent of their interaction.

"Is he always that respectful?" Walt asked. "He's not afraid, is he? All he'd have to do is sit on Stumpy, and the little guy would be smooshed."

"Well," the woman replied, "he's used to cats—really loves them, in fact—and he's learned from one in particular not to be overly enthusiastic or he'll get swatted. My daughter's cat Willow will run up to him and rub against his legs, but if he shows any interest, she hauls off and biffs him in the nose. I assume Bruno thinks Stumpy is a cat, since that's what I've been calling him, so he's just being cautious. Besides, he doesn't have a mean bone in his body."

As the humans watched, Big Bruno slowly turned his face toward the squirrel, lowered his block-like head, and spat out the ball in such a way that it rolled slowly toward Stumpy. The squirrel leaned down to sniff the slobber-covered orb, but instead of turning away in disgust as Walt had anticipated, he looked the staring dog in the face and gently swatted the ball with one paw back toward the pooch, who happily picked it up again and started wagging with even greater vigor while looking at his owner.

"What a good boy you are, Big Big!" she said. "And what a nice kitty Stumpy is! Do you want to give the kitty a kiss?"

Big Bruno, however, had other ideas and didn't seem interested in relinquishing the ball again. He looked toward the pond, then back at Arlene, then back at the pond. "Oh, we'll have a swim a bit later, but we have to go inside first. Come, Big Bruno!" the woman commanded.

As the humans were turning toward the cabin to go inside, however, Tony Riggetti, the almost six-year-old from down the road, came charging up the driveway, yelling, "Mr. Walt! Mr. Walt! Did you feel it? Did you feel it?"

Walt laughed and said, "What's happening, Chicken Little? Is the sky falling?"

"No!" the wide-eyed youngster shouted. "It's a earthquake! Mommy says there could be after-shops!"

"Well, big guy," Walt said, "let's go in and see what the TV has to say about that." As he spoke, Stumpy scrambled up Tony's leg and perched on his shoulder, nuzzling his right ear. "But first," Walt continued, "let's have some introductions. Arlene, this is Tony Riggetti, my faithful sidekick and world-renowned squirrel whisperer. Tony, this is Ms. Arlene, my longtime friend and the former Miss America of 1946."

With a dismissive glance at Walt, Arlene smiled at the boy, held out her hand, and said, "Did you say, 'Timmy Spaghetti'? What a great name! It's nice to meet you, Timmy."

As he took her hand, the boy turned his bewildered glance toward Walt but said nothing, so the elderly jokester, with a twinkle in his eye, corrected her. "No, Arlene, that's TONY, not Timmy."

"Huh," she replied, leaning over to gaze at his face. "How come he looks like a Timmy, then?"

Tony looked again at Walt and said, "Mr. Walt, are you joshing me again? You told Ms. Lurlene to say that, didn't you?"

Chuckling, his white-haired friend said, "Good work, T-man! I may have coached her a little on the phone."

Tony grinned proudly, and Stumpy bobbed his head.

Once they got inside the cabin, the television news report confirmed that a moderate earthquake, 5.8 on the Richter scale and centered in Virginia, had caused tremors as far north as Maine but had produced no significant damage in the region. The chances were slim that significant aftershocks would affect any part of New England.

With that issue resolved, the quintet went back outside. A wagging Big Bruno led the way toward the sandy stretch of shoreline near the dock, where Nelly the rowboat was tied.

"Do you want to throw the ball for Big Bruno?" Arlene asked Tony.

"Yes, please!" he answered.

"Put it down! Put down!" she said firmly. The tan bear of a dog spat the ball out with a *p-tooey!* and then dropped onto his elbows, hind end still up and gyrating as the tree branch of a tail whipped back and forth, seemingly of its own volition. Sand coated the surface of the ball immediately, but Tony picked it up and tossed it into the water a few feet away from shore, and Big Bruno spun around, thundered four steps toward the pond, and went airborne, hanging in the air for a second or two, before shattering the calm surface with his descending bulk.

"Gee whiz," Walt quipped, "that news report didn't say anything about a tsunami, did it?"

After a few dog-paddled strokes, the Lab came upon the ball, now yellow again as it floated in front of him, and with a lunge engulfed it with his huge mouth before spinning back toward the shore. Big Bruno emerged like a canine waterfall and stood momentarily dripping at the water's edge before shaking off a minor tropical storm of moisture. Then he was up the beach again and at Tony's feet, the ball *p-tooing* again, its sandy coating quickly adhering once more. Stumpy was chattering happily at Walt's feet, apparently in approval of his canine friend's effort.

Alight with giggles, the youngster continued to throw the ball, and a delighted Big Bruno continued to fetch it until Arlene, after ten or so fetches, said, "Let's give Big Big a break to catch his breath. Otherwise, he'll keep going until he collapses."

"What say we go up to the deck for some iced tea and cookies, Tony?" Walt said. "I made my variation on Squannacookies—chocolate chippers with some oatmeal thrown in as well as cashews and chopped apricots." Walt had never seen the little fellow move so fast, and Stumpy was right behind him. A now sand-covered Big Bruno caught on and joined the race.

Stumpy had gotten up on the glass-topped table on the deck where Walt had put the plate of cookies; there, the kindly codger handed the squirrel his own special cookie, heavy on the cashews and light on the chocolate. Each human had a chair, and the elders caught up in conversation while Tony fed the begging squirrel bits of his second cookie. Big Bruno, struck by the waterlog fatigue well known to swimmers of all sorts, had collapsed on the wooden surface of the deck, his deep breaths occasionally rending themselves into snores. Walt had stocked a few dog biscuits, knowing that Arlene was coming to visit, and had given the tawny beast one when he brought the rest of the snacks out. Stumpy had insisted on trying a bit of the biscuit, having sampled such fare before, but he preferred the cookies, as his begging showed.

As the humans chatted over their snack, Stumpy had hopped down onto the wood of the deck, and now he approached the sleeping dog where the brontosaurus-sized beast lay on his right side. The nosy rodent sniffed at Big Bruno's nose, and the dog's bloodshot left eye opened. The creature lifted his humongous head and gave one slight flip of his tail so that the thud reverberated over the deck. Then Stumpy walked up Big Bruno's side and perched on his shoulder, looking up at Walt where he sat at the table.

"You settling in for a snooze or trying to get a horseback ride?" Walt asked his furry friend. "Too bad you don't have some spurs, or you could enter a barrel-riding competition."

"Isn't that cute!" Arlene exclaimed. "I'll bet Big Bruno would let Stumpy have a ride if he wants one." With that, she stood up and said, "Now, hang on, Stumpy, and you may just qualify for the title of Buckaroo before we're done." She paused and then said, "Get up, Big Big, and give the kitty a ride."

At first, Stumpy grabbed on to the fur around Big Bruno's withers with both front paws, hind legs splayed behind him, but as Arlene led his Brobdingnagian nag around the deck, the rodent slowly relaxed his grip and stood up on the Lab's broad back. Soon, he was walking from shoulders to hips, standing upright on his hind legs, and doing just about anything he could think of to show off, including a forward roll. Big Bruno wagged and grinned as he followed his owner's directions. Then Arlene commanded him to sit, and Stumpy slid down his back as if it were a huge playground slide, whereupon the big dog turned around and swiped the squirrel's face with his massive pink tongue.

"Oh, nice kitty!" Arlene said. "And what a *good* boy Big Big is!"

Clearly awake again now, Big Bruno wagged and walked to the pondside steps, where he turned back and looked at his master. "You want another swim?" Arlene said. "Well, good boys deserve to get what they want. Okay!"

The tennis ball, of course, had been in the dog's mouth ever since he had woken up, even apparently during his slurping of Stumpy's cheek, and Walt suspected that it had been there even while Big Bruno was sleeping, tucked up into some cavern inside the dog's barn-sized cheeks. Now the beast ran to the sandy crest above the dock, turned, and spat the ball onto the ground, looking back and forth from the ball to Arlene to the ball to Tony to the ball to Arlene and so on. "Notice that he doesn't even *look* at me," Walt observed.

"Let's try something new," Arlene said, stooping to pick up the ball. "Bruno, fetch!" So saying, she tossed the ball out so that it bounced in the middle of the aluminum dock and then continued with two more increasingly lower hops and rolled right off the end. Big Bruno was in motion as soon as the woman's arm started forward, and he dashed along the dock, hesitating only slightly before leaping off the end and plunging into the water. Three big doggy paddle strokes, and he lunged at the ball, mouthed it, spun, and swam back to shore.

"Want to try it, Tony?" Arlene asked.

The boy nodded and picked up the sandy ball from where the dog had dropped it, his tail frantically wiping windshields behind him. Big Bruno again followed the throw off the end of the dock and retrieved the ball. "Wow!" said Walt. "I think even the Russian judge would have given that dive a ten! But does he do anything more sophisticated than a belly flop?"

Arlene simply raised an eyebrow at the teasing geezer.

Stumpy had followed the group to the shoreline and seemed a bit irked that his massive canine comrade was getting all the attention now. He chattered at Walt's feet and then dashed a circle around Tony as the boy was bending to pick up the ball again. Then the squirrel approached the wagging, dripping dog and bobbed his head three times. Big Bruno good-naturedly glanced at him, gave him a relaxed wag, then refocused on the ball and fed a bit more fuel into the motors that power his tail.

Miffed at his canine friend's apparent rejection, Stumpy jumped onto the dog's back to demand more attention just as Tony picked up the ball and wound up to throw it. Oblivious to the added weight when his beloved orb was about to be launched into flight, Big Bruno spun toward the water and thundered down the bank like a ski jumper accelerating down the ramp. Arlene's sharp "No!" came too late to have any effect. The squirrel had little choice but to grab the fur of the dog's back with his front paws and try to grip farther back with his thighs like a competitor in an equestrian event; Walt couldn't see for sure, but Stumpy may even have tried using his rodent incisors to grasp some of the dog's loose shoulder skin.

As Big Bruno launched himself from the end of the dock, Stumpy's rear legs flapped free behind him as if the dog were carrying some kind of gray pennant that was whipping in the wind. The upward explosion of water when Big Bruno struck the surface was more like the impact of ten cannonballs than that of one, but as the human trio held their breath, the broad tan back rose above the surface with a soggy gray squirrel still clinging to those canine shoulders, though Stumpy's rear feet had slipped off to the port side. As his aquatic conveyance neared the shore, however, the soaked squirrel managed to right himself, and his body was aligned with Big Bruno's spine when the dog walked out of the pond and onto the shore.

Simultaneously, the three onlookers realized what was about to happen next, and all three shouted at once, "NO-O-O-O!" Big Bruno shot them a puzzled look and paused for a split second as his backbone started to dip, but then, as if shrugging off their concern as well as the water, the dripping brute shook. Stumpy had presumably been breathing a sigh of relief, both literally and figuratively, and he had not realized what was coming. Like a giant dun-colored water droplet, he was thrown head over heels to the dog's left, going face-first into the sand and rolling over. When he lifted his head, sand clung to nearly every inch of his dampened body. He, too, shook himself then and tried to look nonchalant as he sat down to groom his fur.

"Ooh," said Walt, "some days, you stick the landing, and some days, the landing sticks you. And *some* days, the landing sticks *to* you. You okay, buddy?"

The squirrel ignored his human roommate, but Arlene walked over to him and picked him up, cradling his soggy body against her breast. "Poor Stumpy!" she said. "We were worried about you." She stroked his nose with one finger, and Stumpy settled on his back into the crook of her arm like a human infant, looking contented, even blissful. In a few more seconds, he was starting to purr. "Listen to that!" Arlene said.

Walt interrupted with a grin. "I still say you got to work on that dismount if you're gonna make it to the Olympics. You know how much time Nadia Comaneci put into training as a gymnast? You can't expect to get it right the first time. But if you keep practicing, maybe we can give you an Eastern European name like Vasilli the Squilli and get you on the Romanian team."

Stumpy stared balefully at the man, then pulled himself upright, gave Arlene's nose a nuzzle, and hopped to the ground. With a determined swing to his hips, he strode over to a wagging Big Bruno, who was once again staring from the ball to Arlene to the ball to Tony and so on, apparently ad infinitum if no one chose to indulge him. The squirrel bobbed his head and emitted three short *chits*; then he vaulted onto the dog's back, turned to make sure the humans were still looking, and bobbed his head at Tony.

The boy picked up the sandy ball and turned to his silver-haired mentor. "Okay, Mr. Walt?"

Walt shrugged and replied, "There'll be no living with him if we don't try again. Go ahead."

With his buckteeth bared, Stumpy was scooching down onto the dog's back and working his feet for the best grip possible. Tony wound up and bounced the tennis ball with one high hop off the metal of the dock. Big Bruno spun again and gunned his engines down the bank. Two more strides took him to the end of the dock, where he lifted off like a jetliner from a runway. Afterward, Walt would have sworn that the tawny creature hung in the air for a preternaturally long time, as if he really were taking off. Eventually, however, the *kersploosh* had to come, and this time, as Big Bruno paddled to shore, the squirrel pulled himself upright and walked along his own broad, fur-covered runway. As the gigantic Lab stepped onto the shore, Stumpy crouched again and took his grip, anticipating the first shake; when it came, the determined rodent hardly moved, and Big Bruno stopped in mid-shake, confused because the soggy squirrel's weight had not shifted. When the beast's second shake came, Stumpy was once again prepared, and he launched himself into the air, tucking his body into a forward rotation—once, then twice around—before landing on his hind feet in the sand. When the humans burst into spontaneous cheers, Big Bruno gave a startled bark and then turned to his rodent partner with another slurping, congratulatory kiss.

"Well," said Walt, "now I don't know whether to contact Béla Károlyi or go out and buy you some chaps, some cowboy boots, and a Stetson. Maybe I should do both. You know, the international bull-riding championship circuit has a stop at the Centrum in Worcester this year. You could scoop up the championship belt there and still have time to go into training for the Olympics as a gymnast. What do you think, Comrade Buckaroo?"

9

Stumpy and the River Shoes

September 21, 2011

Some new wrinkles have emerged in the daily routine of Walt Walthers and Stumpy, the stub-tailed gray squirrel who has become Walt's near-constant companion over the last couple of years. Walt, of course, has for some time been living at Kibbee Pond in Townsend as a self-employed weather watcher, relaying up-to-the-minute meteorological conditions to his clients by telephone or email in exchange for a small monthly fee, while also providing information to television and radio stations in the Boston area. This summer, however, his world expanded when Amy Riggetti, a young woman whose husband is serving in Afghanistan, moved in down the road with her then five-year-old son, Tony. Since that time, Walt has spent a great deal of time with his new "family," especially with Tony, who enjoys visiting "the two dapper gents up the road," as Walt sometimes refers to Stumpy and himself. Thus, while Walt, as an octogenarian, is no stranger to literal wrinkles, some new figurative ones have appeared in his life.

The newest wrinkle on top of a new wrinkle, as it were, is Tony's enrollment in kindergarten, which has necessitated his riding the large yellow school bus to and from Spaulding Memorial School in Townsend center for morning sessions five days a week. Ellie Wentworth, the bus driver, is an old acquaintance of Walt; the daughter of one of his grade school friends, she is herself now retired after thirty years of teaching second grade and uses the bus driving to supplement her retirement account. For Tony's first day of school, right before Labor Day, Walt and Stumpy walked—well, in all fairness, Walt shuffled a bit with stiffness, and Stumpy employed his characteristic hop-hop-pause-hop-again stride—down the hill to the turnoff that functions as the Riggettis' driveway. There, they had waited, with Amy and their diminutive buddy, for Ellie's arrival.

"Just remember," Walt had told Tony, "don't eat the chewing gum you find under the seats in the classroom. It's already used." Stumpy had chattered in seeming agreement and bobbed his head.

"Mr. Walt," Tony had replied, "I'm no dummy."

"Well then," Walt had countered, "be sure not to put any tacks in the teacher's chair."

"Mr. Walt!" the little guy protested.

"And don't dip anybody's pigtails in the inkwell!" Walt urged.

"You know, Walt," a laughing Amy had jumped in, "schools don't have inkwells anymore. They didn't have them even when I was a student."

"Humph!" Walt exclaimed, pretending to be flustered. "All these modern improvements! I just can't keep up."

A low rumble from the north signaled the impending arrival of the bus, and soon, the four could hear the clattering as Ellie negotiated some of the ruts just the other side of Walt's cabin. Stumpy scrambled up Tony's pant leg to nuzzle his ear before leaping down and scampering over to one of the oaks that border the road. As the bus appeared over the crest of the hill, the gray-furred rascal launched himself up the trunk and scooted out onto the branch with the best view of the road, where he perched, bobbing his head as he usually did when anticipating an exciting prospect.

"Look!" said Amy. "Stumpy's gone up to wave goodbye to you."

The bus pulled up next to the pull-off, its engine loud but steady as a heartbeat, and a wave of heat poured from the engine compartment, sweeping over the three humans. The double doors squeaked a bit as they swung open, and Ellie's smiling face, surrounded by graying curls, beamed down at them. "*Mister* Walthers," she said in a mock-serious voice, "are you properly dressed for school today? Aren't plaid flannel shirts and red suspenders a violation of the dress code?"

"Gee, Ms. Wentworth," Walt replied, doing his best impression of fake contrition, "the last time I checked the dress code, it said nothing about suspenders being a violation."

"Yes, but admit it, young man. That was in 1938, and you haven't read the code since!"

"Well, you got me there!" Walt laughed, and Ellie's face also collapsed into giggles. "Say, Ellie, this is my buddy Tony Riggetti, and he's gonna be riding down to Spaulding with you each morning."

"Hel-lo, Tony!" Ellie said while the little shaver looked at his feet. "No need to be shy or nervous. I'm in control of this yellow monster, and it eats right out of my hand."

"And this," Walt continued, "is Tony's mom, Amy, whom I have supplied with a surfeit of lies about what a slow and careful driver you are. You can thank me later for my generosity in that regard. On the other hand, I warned Tony that I taught you how to drive way back when, before you became a NASCAR champion, so he's expecting you to get him back home from school in seven minutes flat. I also mentioned to him your philosophy of driving: that a school bus should rarely have more than two wheels on the pavement at any one time."

"Well, it is true that Walt taught me to drive," Ellie said, "but Amy, you needn't worry, either, even if you've ridden in that hot rod he has disguised as a pickup truck. I rejected that two-wheel rule long ago, as soon as I got my license and was out from under the tutelage of old Leadfoot there." Walt threw up his hands, as if outraged at the epithet. Ellie continued, "The kids on this route are pretty nice, too, especially this early-morning, younger group, so Tony should be able to relax and enjoy the trip. Sit right up front today, Tony, so we can get acquainted. Later on, though, you may want to try the back. If you're riding back there when we go over bumps, sometimes ol' Bertha here will toss you right to the ceiling. It's quite a thrill!"

"Is Bertha the bus's name?" Tony asked, now looking at Ellie. "Walt's truck is Lulu, and his boat is Nelly."

"Yup," Ellie said. "I do a lot of the maintenance work on her myself, and I think of her as a faithful friend."

"I must admit," Walt chimed in, "that she is purring like a kitten today . . . or maybe, given her size, like a lion. You've done well."

"You taught me that, too, if you remember," Ellie said with obvious affection.

"Aw, shucks!" Walt said. "You're gonna give me a swelled head if you're not careful."

"*Give* you a swelled head?" Ellie chortled. "I'm pretty sure you were *born* with that! Now, Amy, the turnaround is about two hundred yards down the road, at the Lunenburg town line, so we'll be right back up in a minute or so if you want to wave. You're the last stop on the route."

"I hope we're not inconveniencing you," Amy said, "by making you come all the way out here."

"Nah," Ellie replied. "I've always thought it was pretty down here, even if I do have to pass the dreaded Walthers residence. In fact, since Tony will be the last one I drop off in the afternoon, I'll have an excuse to stop in on the old geezer on occasion and force him to make me a cup of coffee; that way, maybe I can stay awake while he tells me one of his stories. Has he tortured you with any of his anecdotes yet?"

"Oh, I *like* Walt's stories," Amy laughed. "So does Tony. Maybe we'll have to know him another week or two before we turn completely against him."

"Ouch!" said Walt. "Thanks, Ellie, for making my only human friends go sour on me! Boo-hoo-hoo! Well, at least I still have Stumpy."

"Yeah, where is that bandit?" Ellie laughed.

"He saw you coming, and he ran up the stoutest, tallest tree he could find, for safety's sake. Wait a minute! I refused to take him to the nut factory yesterday. He may be planning to hop onto your roof, climb in a window, and hijack the bus! Oh my gosh, you guys may be going on a field trip on the first day of school!"

"Okay, Mr. Walthers," Ellie said, shaking her head, "I've wasted enough time on you for one day. I've got to get these kids to school! Get out your bugle and blow a charge on it, will you please?"

Walt held his right thumb to his mouth and simulated a bugle call: "Ta-da-da-duh-dadah!" Then he gave Tony a high five, and after a quick hug from Amy, the almost six-year-old walked smiling up the stairs and popped into the vacant seat immediately behind Ellie.

"Bye, Mommy!" he called, waving out the door. "Bye, Mr. Walt! And bye, Stumpy!" Ellie shut the doors, and the bus pulled away down the road.

As Ellie had promised, the gargantuan yellow vehicle came rolling back up the hill a couple of minutes later. Tony could see Walt and his mom waving, and he returned the gesture. Then he also noticed Stumpy on the oak limb, standing upright on his hind legs and turning somersaults, first to the left and then to the right. Tony didn't realize then that Stumpy would be perched and waiting on the same limb when the bus dropped him off again around noontime. Even so, Walt and Amy's last glimpse of the boy was of his grinning face.

Amy sniffed once and wiped her right eye. "Walt," she said, "can I interest you in a cup of coffee?"

"You bet," the white-haired man replied.

Since that first morning, that post–school bus cup of coffee has become a daily routine for Amy and Walt. Stumpy joins them inside for a few honey-roasted cashews, which Amy has kept in stock ever since the gallant gray squirrel frightened off a black bear earlier in the summer while Tony and Walt were picking blueberries. As a curious creature, the stub-tailed rodent also enjoys exploring the small Cape house while the two humans chat, and sometimes he curls up for a nap inside one of the baskets that Amy has hung from the kitchen rafter. Although she works twice a week at a hair salon in Ayer, she has some breathing time even on those days between Tony's early bus and her nine o'clock start. When she is working, *both* Walt and Stumpy walk down the hill to greet the returning bus at 12:15 when Tony gets home. The three then have the afternoon together until Amy returns from the shop around six.

The two adults became close quickly after Amy and Tony arrived earlier in the summer, and what had cemented their bond was probably the daylong picnic trip Walt had suggested back in mid-August. He had made some sour cream and mustard potato salad and chocolate-raspberry brownies, and Amy had cooked some barbecued chicken. Then the quartet, three humans and their bucktoothed mammalian mascot, had climbed into the cab of Lulu, Walt's green 1960 Chevy pickup. They headed then to a stretch of the Souhegan River along Route 31 in Greenville, New Hampshire, where they could pull off the road under the tall pines and enjoy both sunshine and shade. Having thrown into Lulu's bed two inflated inner tubes, a couple of folding chairs, the cooler of food and drinks, and his portable cassette player, Walt had helped Amy and Tony find their seat belts and had reminded Stumpy that he needed to share the seat space—a new wrinkle for the mischievous squirrel, who was used to having his run of the cab. Nevertheless, Stumpy quickly learned that he liked the extra company, and he tried all the options—Tony's lap, Amy's lap, Tony's shoulder, Amy's shoulder, even climbing into the glove compartment when it was open—before settling on the spot between Amy and Tony up on the back of the bench seat. There, they could both pat him, and he could see well, out the rear window and, of course, out the windshield.

Walt's idea was, in part, to re-create some family trips from the time when his oldest sons, Ross and Larkin, were about the same age as Tony. He and Annie, his wife, who succumbed to cancer some twenty-five years ago, had, in those earlier days, packed comparable picnics, as well as their boys and whichever dogs were currently living with them, and they had made a day of it, sometimes three or four times in a summer. Walt would explore the shallows with the boys and dogs, sometimes leading one or both of his sons by the hand across the silt-covered and slippery rocks to the other shore, sometimes carrying one on his shoulders, while Annie picked wildflowers for dried arrangements or basked in the sun. The rounded stones of the river bottom were negotiable in bare feet, but Annie and Walt had taken to leaving in the station wagon at all times a pair of old sneakers for each family member. That way, wherever they were driving—by the ocean along the New Hampshire coast in Rye or at one of the local rivers like the Souhegan or the Piscataquog in New Boston, another favorite spot—they'd be prepared and could break out their "river shoes," as they called them. The rubber soles helped a bit with traction and at least softened the impact with rocks and submerged sticks. Knowing the river shoes were there made them feel ready for any adventure they might encounter.

Some stretches of the river in Greenville were good for leisurely tube runs, and Walt would cradle Larkin in his lap while Ross, the older boy, commanded his own craft down through the maze of rocks in the calm-running current. Sometimes, Annie would join them on their odysseys downstream, and other times, the family would find a quiet pool wide enough so they could just float side by side, all four of them in the two tubes, with their hands and feet dangling over the sides and the dogs splashing nearby. One stretch they liked on the river had a deeper pool that extended up under the roots of a big oak, and there they could all sit neck deep while small trout fry and even some larger fish swam nearby. Annie would laugh as the tiniest fish came up to nibble the fine hairs on her legs. Sometimes, a scolding cry would sound overhead, and a kingfisher would flash past, disturbed by the usurpers inhabiting what he considered his own kingdom. By mid-August, the reddish purple blossoms of joe-pye weed signaled the height of summer, and the bright red blooms of cardinal flower would fill Walt with a vague longing that had something to do with another year passing away. One family game that evolved was a contest to see who would spot the year's first cardinal flower blooms. Somehow, it always seemed to be Larkin who shouted out "cardinal flower!" before anyone else could. He even turned it into a joke so that when they passed a river on their Thanksgiving or Christmas trips to visit relatives, he would shout out "cardinal flower!" even though all blossoms and all green growth were obviously done for another year.

This August, when Walt pulled Lulu off onto the shoulder, he felt a dizzying duality, as if he were inhabiting two times simultaneously. The light sifted through the pine boughs onto the rust-colored needles below at the same angle he remembered from nearly fifty years before, and beyond the truck windows, the river made its familiar hushing sounds, sounds he had once loved but now had almost forgotten. The sensation was like what he felt every time he revisited the New Hampshire shoreline, realizing anew how much he loved and had unconsciously been missing the ocean. When he said, "Here we are!" and glanced across at Tony and Amy, he thought for a moment that he saw Annie's smiling eyes transposed onto the young mother's face, and his loss washed over him anew. As Amy and Tony slid off the high seat and hopped laughing to the ground, however, Stumpy remained on the back of the seat and took a tentative step toward his elderly friend, as if he sensed what Walt was feeling. He gently crawled onto the man's shoulder and poked his nose under the brim of the omnipresent porkpie hat to nibble gently at Walt's ear.

"I'm okay now, buddy," Walt said quietly as he pulled down on the door handle and swung his legs to the left. The squirrel gripped the man's shirt collar with his front paws as the two roommates slid to the ground together. "All right," Walt said loudly, "who's going to help me carry this stuff?" Stumpy hopped to the ground as Amy and Tony walked to the back of the truck to start unloading.

The rest of the day was memorable for all four of the companions. Before leaving the cabin at Kibbee Pond, Walt had warned the others to bring their river shoes even though he could no longer trust his balance on the slippery rocks, with or without sneakers. Thus, while mother and son explored the pools and channels and poked under rocks, Walt busied himself with setting up the folding chairs and laying out the food so they could eat when the others had built up an appetite. Then he sat down, took off his work boots and socks, and put his feet in the cool water of the shallows as Stumpy hopped from rock to rock behind Tony and Amy, occasionally chirring at them to get their attention. Dragonflies darted past the adventurous squirrel, and back on shore, Walt laughed because he could tell that his buddy was weighing the odds: Could he re-create a moment of glory from earlier in the summer when his skillful leap had snagged a much-desired dragonfly specimen for his entomologist friend Michael Swift? Walt chuckled again as Stumpy turned away, opting for discretion rather than valor, but the next rock the squirrel had to negotiate in order to continue following Tony and Amy was a bit farther away than he calculated. His front claws scrabbled at the pitted but unyielding granite as he slid slowly into the drink; when, immediately, he thrust with his hind legs in hopes of pushing himself back up onto the rock, he could get no traction and slid back into the shallow water. "See, Stumpy?" Walt called from his chair. "I told you you should bring your river shoes!"

It was, however, a baking-hot day, so despite the indignity, the splash had a welcome cooling effect. Besides, it gave Stumpy an excuse to clamber up and sprawl on the sun-warmed surface of the same rock to dry off, showing once again his propensity for turtle-like basking. "Ooh, you furry Adonis," Amy said to him, as Tony and she returned hand in hand from their first round of explorations, "I intend to try some sunbathing myself before the day is done. But can you really be working on your tan? Isn't it more like working on your gray?"

Twenty or more months in Walt's joking company had given Stumpy plenty of opportunities to practice and master a deadpan look, and now he shot one of those in Amy's direction.

"Come and get it, or I'll slop it to the haw-awgs!" Walt called from the shore, where he had just inserted four D batteries into his battered boom box and was now popping in one of his Duke Ellington tapes, having promised to initiate Amy into the joys of the music of his era. The strains of "Do Nothing Till You Hear from Me" were floating above the steady rush of the river as the young people worked their way back to the grassy shore.

"Oh, this is nice," Amy said quietly as she sipped some minted iced tea and "In a Sentimental Mood" started up on the cassette player. "And is that bacon in the potato salad? Yummy!"

"Glad you like the music!" Walt replied. "The old Duke was really something, if you ask me."

"Actually," the young mother answered, "I recognize most of these tunes. I guess I had just forgotten how much I liked them."

"Well, you'll have to introduce Anthony Sr. to them when he gets back home. You can come up to my place and dance to them on my deck some moonlit night."

"It's a deal," Amy said quietly.

After lunch, mother and son, in the bathing suits they wore beneath their clothes, tried out the inner tubes on one of the bigger pools, and Stumpy emulated them by draping himself over a tree branch he found floating in an eddy. With the sun toasting him, however, he once again fell asleep and didn't notice when the branch drifted into the swifter currents, which swept him quickly downstream. When the branch jolted into a clump of reeds, however, he awoke suddenly and found himself face-to-face with a muskrat that had been nosing about in an inshore channel. Stumpy's startled *chirr!* sent the muskrat whisking away even farther downstream, whereupon the squirrel set out to work his way back up the shoreline to his human friends.

Stumpy arrived back at the picnic site as Amy and Tony were coming ashore from their outing in the tubes. Walt was dozing in his chair with "Sophisticated Lady" playing on the tape deck, dancing in his dream with his wife in a field of Queen Anne's lace while the moon laid out a set of golden steps across the ocean beside them. When he awoke, Amy was smiling at him, and again, he needed a few moments to distinguish between the dream and the reality.

"Sorry," he said sheepishly. "I guess I can't get away with claiming that I was only resting my eyes, can I?"

"No need to," Amy replied. "Care for some iced tea?"

As the older two sipped their tea in the shade, Tony and his squirrel buddy played cars in the sand along the water's edge, with Stumpy digging tunnels and fetching sticks to serve as telephone poles, then helping Tony to pat flat the walls of his sand towers. The sun was taking on the slant of late afternoon when the adults began to pack up.

"On the way back, if you like," Walt said, "I can tell you the story of The Golden Tree. It's about a king who misjudges his queen and then has to travel long and far to win her back."

Amy smiled as she said, "I think I'd like that one."

10

Stumpy and the Kindergarten Class

SEPTEMBER 28, 2011

Walt Walthers, the elderly weather watcher who lives in a cabin out at Kibbee Pond in Townsend with his rambunctious rodent buddy, Stumpy the squirrel, recently discovered a possibility for a new supplementary career. The seed was planted back in August, before Tropical Storm Irma came through; Walt and Stumpy had invited their neighbors from down the road, the almost six-year-old Tony Riggetti and his mother, Amy, on what the dapper old codger called "a river shoes picnic." They loaded Walt's green 1960 Chevrolet pickup with food, two inflated truck inner tubes, and an old pair of sneakers each so they could protect their feet while exploring the Souhegan River in southern New Hampshire. Then they set out for a day of sun, water, and relaxation—not to mention music, since Walt also packed his cassette deck and several Duke Ellington tapes. On the way home, Walt realized that his guests were both missing Tony's dad and Amy's husband, Anthony Sr., a soldier serving in Afghanistan. Consequently, the silver-haired codger was preparing to tell mother, son, and a not-always-awake squirrel an old story from India called "The Golden Tree."

Walt had pulled Lulu the pickup back out onto Route 31 and was headed south, with the still waterlogged and exhausted Stumpy curled up in Tony's lap. The young lad, sitting in the middle of the big bench seat, was leaning his head against his mother's shoulder. "Gee, Mr. Walt," he said for the second time, "why do we have to leave? Couldn't we just stay there forever?"

Walt laughed and replied, "Well, pal, that's just the way things work; all good things, eventually, have to come to an end. As my dad used to say, 'That's just the way the pickle wrinkles.' If you and your mom like, we can go back again sometime, and maybe next summer, we can even bring your dad along when he gets back from the service."

"It really was a wonderful day," Amy said, "and I loved the Duke Ellington music."

"Well," Walt said, "I'm glad, and maybe we can play some of it again next time we get together."

After Walt had put Lulu into third, pulling back on the long shift rod where it rose from the central transmission hump, the truck's engine had settled into a contented-sounding rumble. Then, with the sun peering over the top of the tree line that bordered the road, the silver-haired driver settled into his tale.

"Long, long ago in a country far to the east of us, a prosperous king ruled. He lived in a huge castle with his beautiful young wife and more counselors and servants than he could shake a stick at . . . and at the time he was the world's stick-shaking champion, so you know he had a lot of people waiting on him and giving him advice. That sort of situation can make a person feel more important and wise than he really is and can make him think he has something to prove . . . which maybe he does. I guess I mean to say that he thinks he has to prove the *wrong* thing: namely that he *is* important and better than other people, or at least held to higher standards than others might be. You can see it's easy to get confused when you have that much power and influence, and you can easily do things that you will regret.

"Well, that's essentially what happens in this story: The king, who was at heart a good man, started to worry about what people were saying about his wife, whom he loved very much. You see, everyone wanted the king to have an heir, someone who would be in line to take over the throne if anything happened to the king, and his wife had, so far, produced no child. Some of the counselors started whispering, 'She is barren and will never produce an heir,' and others went even further, claiming, 'She is the daughter of a demon and is draining our sovereign of all his strength and good judgment!' For a long time, the king resisted his counselors, but eventually, they wore him down. Against his better judgment, he finally agreed to banish his beloved queen, sending her out into the wilderness alone, without any gold or jewels or even food."

Tony interrupted at this point. "How could he do that, Mr. Walt? You said he was a good man."

"I know, Tony. It's hard to believe, but even good men make mistakes, especially when other people they should be able to trust give them bad advice or false information. We'll leave the king behind for a minute, though, and see what happens to the innocent queen as she journeys into the forest.

"The young woman went on alone, so ashamed that she hardly looked up as she left the palace and the city, and she wandered a whole day without food or even a dribble of water. When nighttime came, she found herself at the edge of a great forest, and because she didn't have someone like Stumpy around to protect her, she quickly grew terrified of wild animals and other things whose shapes she could hardly begin to imagine. As darkness descended with its oppressive weight, she climbed a tall tree, where she spent the night, exhausted but unable to sleep. With the first light of morning, she climbed back down again, but she felt so weak and sick that she could struggle on for only an hour before she collapsed beneath another tree. When she heard the rustling of some bushes nearby, panic overtook her, but she was too enervated even to get to her feet.

"Then from the bushes emerged a silver-haired and very handsome elderly man, wearing a plaid flannel shirt, Sears work boots, red suspenders, and a battered porkpie hat. He said, 'Don't be afraid. I won't—'"

"Mr. Walt!" Tony protested. "That sounds like you! You can't be in the story and tell it at the same time!"

"Wait a minute. You assume this guy is me just because he's wearing a porkpie hat? Let me tell you that porkpie hats have been very popular down through the centuries and in various cultures. I think the pharaohs of ancient Egypt even wore them when they were inspecting the pyramids back in the days when those wonders were still under construction."

"I don't know," said Tony. "What about the plaid shirt and red suspenders, then?" Amy was quietly giggling next to the passenger-side window.

"Hmm-m," Walt answered. "I guess you got me there. Do you really want me not to be in the story?"

Tony was quiet for a moment and then said, "You can be in it if you want. Are you gonna be the hero?"

"Not exactly, though I did pick a flattering role for myself. I'm the wise and kind old man of the forest—a role I wouldn't mind playing in real life. Anyway, the queen instinctively trusts the man and goes back to his cabin on the pond—I mean, hut in the woods—where he provides her with food and drink and a secure place to sleep. That night, she dreams of a beautiful golden tree growing from a pool in an enclosed garden, and as she gazes on the tree, an old man, this time dressed in white robes—though she recognizes him as the same man she is staying with—comes close to her and hands her a golden chain with a golden dingly-dangly thing—what do you call them?"

"An amulet?" Amy offered.

"That's it," Walt said, "a golden amulet in the shape of the tree she saw. In her dream, the old man hangs the amulet around her neck, and then she wakes up. The strangest thing, however, is that when she wakes up, the golden tree is still hanging from her neck!"

"Wow!" Tony said quietly, and even a sleepy Stumpy sat up in the boy's lap as if to listen more carefully. Walt continued to tell of the kindness of the old man, whom the queen now knew had been sent to aid her and to whom she told her story of the counselors' resentment and her own banishment. She explained that her banishment was horribly ironic because all the signs suggested that she was going to have a baby after all.

The queen agreed to stay with the old man, who said that the king would see his mistake eventually, and she began to help the man with his work, which was to create beautiful things out of the gold and precious stones that he dug from an old mine nearby, purified, and then cast into various shapes. The most beautiful were always shaped like the golden tree the queen had seen in her dream and now wore around her neck. The old man refused to sell his creations and thus remained poor; instead, when he finished them, he would melt them down and start over again. "The act of creation," he said, "is what truly matters."

After some time, the queen, with great joy, gave birth to a son, and on that night, the king, back in his castle, had his first dream of a golden tree, beneath which he saw the banished queen weeping. Tormented each night by the same dream, he sought advice from his counselors. Some said the dream meant he should send servants to search for his lost wife; others said he should find a craftsman to create a golden tree of his own; still others said he must set out alone to find the golden tree himself if he wanted release from the dream. The king realized now that he still loved his queen, but no servants could find her, and although he hired a famous goldsmith and had all his gold melted down, none of the craftsman's attempts matched the tree in the dream. Finally, the king appointed his steward to rule in his place and set out alone in search of the golden tree.

After many months of wandering and stumbling ever closer to despair, the king met an old man in the forest. "Oddly enough," Walt said, "the old man was wearing . . . a porkpie hat." This time, Amy and Tony both giggled. The sun was well down below the tree line now, and dusk was starting to pool as they drove along.

Walt's story continued with the king accepting food and a place to rest with the old man at his hut. There, he saw a veiled woman with a young child, but he did not recognize her even though she did recognize him. The old man sent the king deep into the forest to a river, whose boiling waters originated in a spring that bubbled up from far down in the earth; within that spring, surrounded by the seething water, he would find the golden tree, but he could approach it safely only if he was wearing the old man's shoes—as Walt put it, a pair of magic "river shoes." If he failed to return the shoes to the old man afterward, he would, of course, once again lose the precious tree.

The king found the river, the fountain, and the tree, and the shoes buoyed him through the roiling water, but he learned that the tree was itself a fountain made of molten gold. Nevertheless, he trusted his intuition, reached out, and grasped the trunk of the tree, which did not burn him and instead turned solid at his touch so that he could break it off and float away safely on its trunk. When he looked back from the shore, he saw that the fountain went on creating and re-creating the golden tree every second, and that while each shape was different, the essential form remained the same. His tree became heavy once he was away from the river, but he persisted in carrying it back to the old man's hut, where he confessed to his host, admitting his horrible mistake in banishing his queen, and professed his continuing love for her.

"Of course," Walt concluded, "that was when the handsome old fogy removed the young woman's veil and revealed who she was. The repentant king fell all over himself apologizing and promising to do better, which for some women wouldn't have been enough, but the queen was not just some woman. Smiling with forgiveness, she chose that moment to introduce him to his son. Next morning, the three of them bade farewell to the old craftsman, who was currently working on what promised to be his greatest creation—a golden tailless squirrel—and they made their way safely home. Which is where we are, too, by the way," he said, having just made the turn onto Kibbee Pond Road.

"Walt," Amy said as Lulu pulled into the turnoff that served as her driveway, "did you ever think about becoming a professional storyteller? You could go around to schools and festivals."

"Huh! I'll have to give that some thought," said the old man with the plaid shirt, red suspenders, Sears work boots, and magic porkpie hat.

That was how Walt last week found himself shaking hands with the kindergarten teacher, Ms. Aristea, as he entered Tony's classroom. Well, some other factors also encouraged Walt along the way to his new hobby, starting with his regular after-school sessions with Tony and Tony's older friends, the three ten-year-olds Mac, Shel, and Hammy; the garrulous geezer had found himself regularly telling stories, both remembered and invented, to that quartet in recent weeks. Some of you might be surprised to hear Shel, Mac, and Hammy described as Tony's "friends," since the youngster met the trio under unpleasant circumstances; however, to the older boys' credit, they had apologized to Tony for their initial teasing of him and had acknowledged that they deserved the prank Tony and his coconspirators had played on them. As you might remember, at Walt's suggestion and with the aid of Stumpy's Oscar-worthy performance, Tony had earned the sobriquet "Squirrel Whisperer" from the older boys by pretending to tame that apparently rabid rodent, the froth around whose mouth was in actuality only the foam from toothpaste. Through that prank and subsequent visits, the older boys had found that Tony and his buddies Walt and Stumpy were fun to be around.

But back to Walt's visit to Tony's classroom! Another important factor in the generous geriatric's decision to tell some stories there was the unending enthusiasm Tony showed for his new teacher in the first weeks of school.

"Mommy! Mr. Walt! Stumpy!" he had shouted as he disembarked from the bus after his first day. "You should meet my teacher! She's awesome! She likes bugs and poetry! And I told her about Stumpy, and she said he could come visit some day!"

"Whoa!" Walt said. "What's this wonder woman's name?"

"I'm not sure," Tony answered. "It's kind of weird. It's something like Ms. Hair-a-Sprayer."

"Not exactly, pal," Amy said. "It's Ms. Aristea. It's a Greek name meaning 'the best of all.' She sent a letter home a week or so ago to introduce herself to parents."

"Well," Tony said, "all I know is that she's really smart, and she has pet spiders at home that live in her basement, and she has a bunch of tanks and animals in the classroom, like permit crabs and a Monarch butterfly pupil that's in its crystalized phrase! And she's really smart and pretty!"

"So," Walt asked with fake puzzlement, "you're saying you don't like her?"

"Mr. Walt!"

"Okay, okay. Even I can see you like her a lot. You know how I like to josh you."

Tony's enthusiasm for his teacher did not wane over the next two weeks, and each day he came home with a new account of her wonderfulness.

"Today, Ms. Aristea told us about how mosquitoes hatch and about the diseases they can carry."

"Today, she read us a poem about a woodpecker digging bugs out of a tree."

"Today, she read us a Greek myth about this guy named They See Us, or something like that, and this monster that was half man and half bull—the top half—and it lived in this lab-o-rinth-tory that had all these confusing passingways that you couldn't get out of, and the They See Us guy used a ball of string that some girl gave him and unrolled it behind him so he could get out after he killed the Miniature Tor, which is what they called the monster. The story was scary for a while, but I really liked it. It shows that brains are better than prawns."

"Hmm-m-m," Walt had replied. "This They See Us guy wasn't a real shrimp, was he?"

"No," Tony had blurted, "he was just young, but he must have been strong to kill the bull-man thing."

"You know, Walt," Amy had said then, "do you remember what I said about how you could become a storyteller if you wanted to? Why don't you let me ask Ms. Aristea if she'd like you to come in and tell some stories to the children?"

"What do *you* think, T?" Walt had asked then, and Tony had started jumping up and down and yelling, "Please! Please! Please! And bring Stumpy too!"

"Okay, okay, buddy," Walt said. "I guess I'll have to start practicing. I'm not used to big audiences."

"It's only nineteen kids," Amy had said, "and I'll bet they'll be very enthusiastic listeners. I'm sure Stumpy will be welcome, too, but I'll ask to make sure."

Thus, Walt had found himself over the next day or two writing out some outlines for stories he remembered reading or telling to his own sons, and he also had started thinking about how he could turn some of his adventures with Stumpy, the Gray-Furred Marvel, into tales he could use. And before he knew it, he was turning the key in Lulu's ignition one morning with his rodent sidekick beside him on the seat and then making the drive down to the Spaulding School. Stumpy rode on his shoulder as he checked in at the office and then walked down the corridor to Ms. Aristea's kindergarten room. Along the way, children peered out of the doorways of other classrooms with their mouths hanging open. Some adults passed them in the corridor, too, smiling and often laughing like much younger people when they saw Stumpy.

"Mr. Walthers, it's so nice to meet you," Ms. Aristea had said, taking his hand, when Walt arrived. Walt saw that she was Amy's age or even younger, with long, straight brown hair that hung to her waist or below, hair that the sun had honeyed with tones of gold. Her eyes twinkled above her smile, and Walt felt dumbfounded, as he had the first time he saw Ingrid Bergman on the movie screen, in *Casablanca.* A Greek goddess alive and well in the twenty-first century! Walt thought.

"And who is that handsome rapscallion on your shoulder?" Ms. Aristea had asked then. She held her hands up to her chin and turned her head to one side, feigning coyness in Stumpy's direction, as she spoke.

"Why, ma'am," Walt had replied in a cowboy accent, "that thar is the orneriest varmint ever to tread the sands of the Monument Valley, the meanest, nastiest, stinkin'est polecat in the whole West: first name Stumpy, middle name The, last name Squirrel. Approach that rodent bandit at your own risk!"

However, Stumpy was bobbing up and down on Walt's shoulder, chattering with excitement as he looked past the young teacher at the classroom full of children. When he heard Tony call out his name from the back corner of the room, he leaped to the floor and then, suddenly shy, performed an almost slow-motion version of his characteristic hop-hop-pause-hop-again maneuver as he approached the closest student, sniffing at the hand the little girl held out toward him before dashing off to his down-the-road buddy and climbing to Tony's shoulder. The children were almost delirious with laughter as Stumpy climbed farther to the top of the boy's head and then bobbed and chirred at his fans.

At that point, the gray-furred rascal noticed the fish tank nearby and hopped from Tony's head to the table on which the tank sat. He went from the front to the side, peering in and finally spotting the large brown catfish that flapped its ventral fins and climbed the tank wall next to him, as if expecting the squirrel to toss in some food. "Well, children," Ms. Aristea said, "it looks as though Sloppy Joe likes Stumpy too!"

When the initial mania had finally quieted a bit, and Stumpy had made the rounds in a more sedate manner, introducing himself to each of the students, Walt settled into a rocking chair at one end of the big room, and the children settled in a semicircle on the floor in front of him, all but one girl in a wheelchair who seemed unable to straighten the angle of her head and clearly could not leave her chair. When Walt asked Stumpy where he was going to sit for the stories, the squirrel had looked at Tony but then had hopped to the floor near that girl's chair and quietly climbed up onto the chair arm; when the girl had smiled back at him, he had stepped down and curled his body into the crook of her arm, where he looked quite comfortable.

"Oh, Madeline, isn't that nice?" Ms. Aristea had said, and Walt had added, "Yes, Madeline, but if he starts snoring, will you give him a nudge, please?"

Walt had started with his version of "Why Dogs Hate Cats."

"Any of you ever noticed that whenever a dog sees a cat, he's more likely to chase it than shake its paw and ask it how it's doing? Well, here's a story that explains why dogs and cats don't generally get along.

"In the old days, the dog and the cat were the best of friends, and they did everything together: They went to the movies together; they took horseback riding lessons together; they even played video games together. But the thing they most liked to do together was eat, and they had the same favorite food: They both *lo-o-oved* ham! Whenever one of them had a little money, he would go to the store and buy a piece of ham.

"Well, one day, the dog was craving a piece of ham, but he didn't have enough money to buy any by himself, so he asked the cat if the cat wanted to pool their money and share a piece of ham. The cat agreed, and they went off to the store and bought a nice big chunk of ham.

"As they walked home, they took turns carrying the meat, and whenever the dog carried it, he sang a little song, almost howling in his excitement, as dogs sometimes do: 'Ou-u-u-u-ur ham! Ou-u-u u-ur ham!' But when it was the cat's turn to carry the ham, he sang a different song, mewing and almost yowling, as cats sometimes do: 'Mee-y-y-y-y ham! Mee-y-y-y-y ham!' They went on like that, taking turns, but finally the dog said, 'Mr. Cat, every time *I* carry the ham, I sing, "Ou-u-u-ur ham!" But every time *you* carry it, you sing, "M-y y-y-y ham!" Why do you do that?'

"Well, the cat was carrying the ham at the time, and all he did at first was crook his tail into a question mark the way cats do. But when he got close to a big hickory tree, he took off as if he had a skeeter in his scooter and scampered up the tree and out onto a big branch well above the ground. And there he ate up every last bit of the ham!

"Well, the dog was furious, and he snarled and barked and jumped up at the trunk of the tree, but of course, dogs can't climb trees, so finally, there was nothing he could do. Before he went home alone, however, he made a vow: 'Mr. Cat, if I ever see you again, I will chase you until I catch you or until I drop!' And that's why dogs chase cats. They still remember that time the cat stole all the ham."

The children laughed and applauded, and Stumpy's facial expression suggested that *he* would never have fallen for any trick that a stupid old cat could come up with. Walt went on to tell several more stories, but the children seemed especially spellbound when he told them "Stumpy and the Sneezing Skunk," a true story that even the radio audience hasn't yet heard. Maybe you'll get to hear that one, too, sometime soon.

11

Stumpy and the Birthday Celebration

October 5, 2011

Last week, Walt Walthers, the elderly weather watcher who lives in a cabin out on Kibbee Pond in Townsend, took his first step toward a new career as a storyteller. Walt's roommate and faithful sidekick, Stumpy, a gray squirrel who lost most of his tail in a bizarre accident nearly two years ago and has since lived with Walt, rode with the silver-haired gentleman down to Spaulding Memorial School for a tale-telling session with the kindergarten class of their nearest neighbor, Tony Riggetti. The children and their teacher, Ms. Aristea, loved Walt's stories and Stumpy's antics, so that everyone viewed the visit as a success.

At the time, Tony was just about to celebrate his sixth birthday, which fell on, as he had been calling it, "Septober 27." Interestingly enough, Walt's birthday fell two days later, on what he took to calling "Septober 29." That coincidence led to Walt's plan, in collaboration with Tony's mother, Amy, to turn the entire week into a series of special events to commemorate the twin occasions. Walt called the whole shindig their "Festive Birthweek Celebration." To anyone who asked him his age, Walt, of course, continued to claim that he would be turning eleventy-seven years old to Tony's six.

In the meantime, despite some unseasonably warm temperatures, the leaves were showing signs of turning color, and Walt braced himself for the autumn spectacle of city-dwelling leaf peepers creeping at turtle-like speeds along the back roads of the town. Kibbee Pond Road, of course, runs through a picturesque area, and to the fall visitors who stumble upon it, Walt's cabin above the pond's shore seems especially quaint. Cars drive past it at a crawl, and Walt waits for the inevitable: another person who will stop and ask to snap some photos of him standing in front of his place. Whenever it happens, he cooperates but does make a joke about how he doesn't want the photographer to try to pass off his or her shots as long-lost pictures of the poet Robert Frost, whom Walt does, in fact, resemble a little. One year, on the rear bumper of Lulu, his green 1960 Chevy pickup, he put a sticker that read: "They call it tourist *season*, so why can't we just shoot them?" Funny as he found the slogan, however, it didn't really reflect his sentiments, and he scraped the sticker off after a few days.

Part of him enjoys the prospect of a serendipitous meeting with someone interesting, and besides, he realizes how fortunate he is to live where he does. He dwells in a location that he loves, a place where he can track the turning of the season and catalog the dates when certain kinds of trees have changed color over the years; furthermore, he lives in a spot where he can watch overhead when the annual hawk migration begins, bringing some unusual raptor visitors to the area. He loves the place he lives even when the first frost comes, though he feels real ambivalence about that event and all it portends. This year, as usual, the ashes, hickories, and birches were among the first trees to turn, and though only a handful of swamp maples around the lake had gone red by last week, plenty of yellows were impinging upon summer's verdancy.

On Monday last week, the day before Tony's actual "natal anniversary," as Walt was referring to it, Walt and Amy arranged the First Annual Kibbee Pond Highland Games, to which they invited the birthday boy's three older friends, the ten-year-olds Mac, Shel, and Hammy. As luck would have it, Stumpy "invited" two of his squirrel friends as well, the two gray-furred bandits that Walt theorizes are Stumpy's siblings, probably even his littermates. Walt calls them Burwell and Lansdowne, and the two frequently show up in the pines around the cabin when Walt and Stumpy are outside; although they never approach any of the humans, they are happy to romp through the branches and even scuttle across the needle-covered ground while people are around. Walt marvels that even though Stumpy has lost his tail and must have acquired all kinds of strange and unnatural-seeming smells from his time inside a human dwelling, his rodent relatives nevertheless accept him without ostracism.

The Kibbee Pond Highland Games, as Amy and Walt conceived them, were an adaptation of the traditional Highland Games that Scots immigrants brought with them from Caledonia's fair shore; such events are popular throughout the United States and Canada and feature feats of strength, speed, and skill such as foot races and the caber toss, which usually involves lifting and throwing a tree trunk about the size of a telephone pole. The traditional caber comes from a larch tree and is just under twenty feet long, weighing about 175 pounds, and the object is to throw it not for distance but rather for accuracy so that it lands in a straight line from the thrower with what was the top end now closer to the thrower than the end he held. Legend has it that the event evolved from the need in the Scottish Highlands to create bridges by throwing tree trunks across abysses. Walt was able to find a birch sapling that he cut to an appropriate size for his young competitors.

The goal for both the old-timer and the young mother was to find a way to mimic the adult games and encourage friendly competition without leaving any of the competitors feeling crushed. The contestants in the adult versions, of course, always wear kilts, but although both Walt and Amy have high percentages of Scots blood, and although Amy's skills as a seamstress are certainly good enough for her to manufacture four tartan garments, Walt's wisdom prevailed: He was sure the older boys in particular would embrace their culture's definition of "macho" behavior and object to wearing what they would see as skirts.

The three-legged race came first, shortly after the older boys arrived from their full day of school. Tony was teamed with Mac, a natural athlete with blond hair and a bowl haircut who always seems to be wearing a different professional or college football team's jersey and who is probably the fastest of the boys; Shel, a redhead with glasses and a Red Sox cap worn backwards, paired up with Hammy, a heavyset youngster with a crew cut who regularly pauses in whatever he is doing to hike up his shorts. After Amy supervised each pair in tying their near legs together with strips from an old sheet, and after she had allowed each pair a minute or so to practice together, Walt directed them to the starting line, which was near the kitchen deck, and pointed out the finish line, which was on the far side of the gravel driveway, about fifteen yards away. Walt was wearing a whistle on a lanyard around his neck—a remnant of his days of coaching youth soccer and basketball when his own sons were young. Once the contestants were at the line, he tweeted them on their way—using the whistle, of course, not a cell phone, something he does not in fact own; service is unreliable at best around the pond, and he relies on his land line for his weather-watching service.

Shel and Hammy grabbed the lead but soon overreached themselves, achieving a velocity they simply could not sustain; they toppled to the ground halfway across the driveway. As the quick-tempered Shel tried to scramble to his feet but fell down a second time, he blurted, "Crap!"

"I don't do that on command!" Walt replied, with eyebrows raised.

"Sorry!" the embarrassed redhead replied.

Mac and Tony, despite their disparity in height, fared better than the fallen pair, having adopted a reliable tortoise-like discipline to counter the other racers' hare-like haste. With his Patriots cap turned backwards on his head and his tongue in the corner of his mouth, Mac counted out "One, two, one, two . . ." until they passed between the two kitchen chairs that served as the finish line. Walt and Amy shared a satisfied glance during the ensuing round of high fives between the victors; their concern had been that the younger Tony might not garner any of the blue ribbons Amy had cut and sewn for first place in all the contests, and they had hoped that pairing him right away with the thoughtful and strategy-minded Mac might redress any developmental imbalance.

The next event was the horseshoe-pitching contest, but the rules Walt had devised were different from conventional ones, as no one should be surprised to hear. Instead of proving how far they could throw the heavy metal objects or how close they could get the shoes to a post, the boys had to stand eight feet away from a big pine tree (or six feet, in Tony's case) and ricochet the shoes off its trunk; the one who, after five tosses, got the most shoes to land with the opening facing directly back toward the thrower would win. Walt was trying to inject an element of chance into this contest, and his plan worked, with Shel's score of four nipping Tony's three for the blue ribbon.

With all the shrieking and laughter produced by the first two events, the three squirrels had retired to the lower branches of a big pine that overlooked both the driveway and the pond side of the cabin, where the horseshoe toss took place. Burwell and Lansdowne flicked and whisked their tails in nervous excitement (something Stumpy, of course, couldn't do, or at least not so obviously), and all three chirred and scolded when the volume rose particularly high. The humans, however, were too caught up in their own activities to concern themselves with rodent disapproval. Besides, the festive spirit was catching, and it was only a matter of time before the furred threesome would devise some games of their own.

Knowing that the young boys would need a conventional race in which to stretch their legs at some point, Walt and Amy had planned a cross-country course and actually had staked it out. The route would take the runners into the pine woods and force them to jump or climb over a number of obstacles, including fallen logs that blocked the path and even a big boulder, where the grown-ups had directed the course in order to necessitate some climbing. At one point where the path intersected a small stream, Walt had been able to tie a knotted rope to a tree limb so that the boys needed to swing across as part of the competition. In a bizarre twist, the finish required them to run out onto Walt's aluminum dock and clamber into Nelly the rowboat.

Mac went out quickly at the start of the event and sustained a lead over Shel through the woods all the way to the boulder, but there, something about the soles of his sneakers caused him to slip in climbing, and Shel took a two-step lead as they made the turn to head back toward the cabin. Hammy and Tony, who had been trailing, gained some ground, and Tony actually moved into third place when the somewhat heavy Hammy had to slow down to hitch up his shorts, something his husky build required him to do regularly. All four were close together because the leaders had to slow a bit down the hill to the narrow dock, and when Mac and Shel bumped hips as their feet reached for the aluminum decking, both lost their balance and plunged into the shallows. The diminutive Tony swept past them and nimbly slipped into Nelly's stern, a huge grin spreading across his face.

After a quick change into dry clothing for Mac and Shel, the caber toss came next, and it was Hammy's turn to shine. Not only was he strong enough to lift the birch trunk easily, but he also proved nimble enough to get the proper English on the caber so that it landed the way he wanted it to. Each of his three throws left the caber within two or three minutes of twelve o'clock, the desired angle.

As Amy awarded the blue ribbons on the deck, the squirrel sibs began their own impromptu version of the games. However, their cross-country course seemed to take them up, down, and around . . . and around . . . and around again . . . and up and down again a whole series of the big pines that lined the pond near Walt's cabin; no real pattern seemed apparent to the human onlookers, who laughed and pointed, but the squirrels seemed to know where they were going and how long the race would last, because, finally, they ended up back in that original tree, chirring and bobbing heads at each other as if arguing about the outcome. Once their tempers cooled a little, they engaged in what seemed to be *their* version of the caber toss, climbing to the top of the pine tree to gather cones and then taking turns dropping those cones to the dirt below. Dashing down the trunk, they then gathered to inspect where their cones had landed and once again burst into apparent argument over who had "won." Walt went into the cabin and came back out with a handful of shelled peanuts, which he then tossed into the middle of the querulous rodents; his tactic worked, as the gray-furred rascals hushed their gab to gather their booty, which they may well have considered the equivalent of the boys' blue ribbons.

"Goobers for the goobers!" Walt laughed as he led the boys back to the cabin for some celebratory peppermint stick ice cream with homemade fudge sauce.

The Festive Birthweek Celebration continued the next day, Septober 27, which happened to be Tony's actual birthday. In his desire to do something special to mark the occasion, Walt, that silver-haired fox, had experienced a brainstorm a week or two before. He had been watching Stumpy, Burwell, and Lansdowne, the squirrel siblings, cavorting through the trees, across the pine needle–carpeted forest floor, and over the deck. As he admired the nimbleness of the three squirrels in following each other through a serpentine and convoluted sequence of direction changes, he had remembered that one of the local vegetable farms had this year put in a corn maze. Walt himself had a fondness for mazes and labyrinths of all sorts and had decided that a trip to the Flat Hill Maze would make a good birthday surprise for his now six-year-old friend. The squirrels' labyrinthine cross-country course the previous day during their version of the Highland Games had seemed to Walt a further sign that the maze expedition was a good idea.

Thus, on Tuesday last week, when Ellie Wentworth, the smiling driver of the 12:15 school bus, dropped Tony off from kindergarten, Walt was waiting with Amy and Stumpy in the pull-off that serves as the Riggettis' driveway, and in the spirit of the occasion, he had a further surprise for his young friend: They would make their drive to Flat Hill in Spot the Volkswagen. Walt had kept Spot after his wife, Annie, died many years earlier, and he took pride in maintaining the vehicle as carefully as he had done in the days when Annie drove it every day to the hospital where she worked as a registered nurse. He saw his efforts as a labor of love that helped him preserve his sweetheart's memory. Once a month or so, he made sure to start up the sky-blue Bug, pull it out of the small wooden shed next to Lulu the pickup's vinyl tent, and let it run awhile. Occasionally, he also took Spot out for a short jaunt. On this occasion, since he did keep the registration up to date, he could legally make the short trip to Lunenburg that they had planned and offer Tony another dimension to his birthday treat.

"All right," Walt said as he opened the passenger side door and tilted the front seat forward, "hop in, pint-size! Let's split this clambake and burn some rubber!" Giggling, Tony *clam*bered—appropriately enough—into the back, and Walt whistled for Stumpy, who had been inspecting acorns around the base of the oak tree in which he perched every day while waiting for Tony's bus to bring his young friend home. The gray-furred forager scuttled across the leaves on the ground, where they had just begun to fall, and up over the doorsill into the back with his buddy. Still holding the door open, Walt turned and offered Amy his hand. "Your turn, m'lady," he said with a half bow, and she stepped forward and climbed into the front.

Once Walt was in the driver's seat and they were on the road, he started his lecture for the day, this time about the merits of labyrinths and mazes. "When I was a kid your age, Tony, that story about Theseus and the Minotaur that Ms. Aristea told you was my favorite. As you remember, Theseus heroically volunteered himself to go to King Minos's palace on the island of Crete as part of the tribute that the people of Athens had to send every year: a hundred of their young men and women, to be sacrificed to the Minotaur, that monster that was half human and half bull . . . kinda like some of those NFL football players that Mac likes so much! And of course, along the way, Theseus was so gallant and brave that the king's daughter, Ariadne, fell in love with him and taught him the trick of how to get out of the labyrinth. Getting *in* was not difficult, but when you tried to get out again, all the twists and turns and possible wrong choices could make a fella's head spin, if he managed to keep the Minotaur from ripping it off in the first place. Well, Theseus never worried about whether he could handle the monster or not, and he was right not to worry, because the battle was all over in a Minotaur two, *ahem*. You get it? A Minotaur two? And then, because he had listened to Ariadne and unrolled a ball of twine behind him as he went into the labyrinth, he could just follow that trail back out. I still think conquering the labyrinth is the ultimate hero's task, even though what Theseus did to Ariadne when he left her behind was not very classy. Dumping somebody who's taught you how to solve the labyrinth seems pretty low, in fact. You never know about these hero characters in myths.

"Still, he wasn't afraid to risk getting lost, which is what labyrinths are all about—twists and turns that disorient you and leave you confused about where exactly you are. Getting lost isn't always a bad thing, though, because it forces you to look closely at what's around you and to think about where you really are. What was it Henry David Thoreau used to say? 'Not till we are lost . . . do we begin to find ourselves, and realize where we are and the infinite extent of our relations.' Or something like that."

Amy laughed at this point and said, "Gee, Walt, you really are excited about this, aren't you? I didn't realize you were so interested in labyrinths."

"Hey, did you know," Walt continued, "that there are actually two different kinds of labyrinths? The one most people think of is called 'multicursal' because it involves a series of choices of which path to take; you could always choose wrong and just go deeper and deeper into the labyrinth in the wrong direction, away from the center or the way out again. You're always reaching crossroads, where you have to go one way or the other, and it's easy to get confused and frustrated. You look one way and then the other, and you figure it's half of one, six dozen of the other . . . is that how that expression goes, half of one, six dozen of the other? I think so, because if you choose wrong, you could make a *gross* error, and without a guide or signs or clues like Ariadne's twine, you might never get out. Scary, huh? I think that's the kind of labyrinth they have at Flat Hill. Many people call the multicursal ones mazes. I guess that's where our word 'amazed' comes from; it used to mean 'bewildered' or 'perplexed,' the way you'd feel if you were trapped in a maze, though now it's less specific and means something like 'filled with wonder.'

"Then there's the second kind, the 'unicursal' labyrinth. 'Uni-' meaning 'one,' because you never really have a choice, except for whether to keep going or to turn back. It's one long path that twists and turns like crazy but has no dead ends or crossroads and requires no choices on the part of the person inside. If you're patient and persistent enough, though, it will take you where it's going. It leads you itself but always keeps reversing direction so you can get confused about exactly where you are at any one moment. Though you may be confused and frustrated, though, you're never truly lost because you can just keep following the path. Some medieval cathedrals actually had labyrinths laid out on their floors so people could walk through them as an act of devotion, and these days, some people even build them in their yards so they can walk them whenever they want to as a kind of meditation. When I used to walk in the woods every day, I sometimes thought about the path there as a kind of labyrinth that twisted and turned and sometimes left me confused about exactly where I was; still, I knew that if I followed the path out and back, I'd get home safely."

By this time, Spot had putted along well into Lunenburg, and Walt turned up the incline that would soon become Flat Hill, with its several farms along the spine of the hill. Stumpy had started out by exploring the back seat of the Volkswagen, climbing into the pockets under each of the side windows to see how well they fit him and clambering up onto the window ledge behind Tony to peer out backwards at everything moving away from him. He had just climbed back down into Tony's lap and seemed about to settle down at last when Walt turned into the long dirt driveway of the farm with the corn maze.

"Hey!" said Walt as the foursome got out of the Beetle. "I just thought of the perfect name for this place. 'Maize' is another word for corn, right? So why couldn't we call this The Amazing Maize Maze? I suppose it could also be The Laborious Liberating Labyrinth . . ."

"Okay, Walt!" Amy laughed. "I'm getting dizzy just listening to you. Let's go see if they'll let us try it out."

As it turned out, the quartet had picked a quiet time to explore the maze, with no one there except for the farm's owner and some workers who were picking pumpkins and apples. The owner introduced himself and smiled at Stumpy, who was perched on the elderly man's shoulder. Then he asked, "Did you bring that fella along as your guide? I can offer you our sheet of Maze Wanderers Tips, but somehow I suspect you'd like to try it on your own."

Walt immediately replied, with a touch of mystery and hubris, "Oh, I think we've got it covered, thanks."

"Are you sure?" Amy asked.

"Of course," Walt said. "I've got an infallible sense of direction."

"That's what Anthony Sr. says, too, so he never uses a map or GPS and absolutely refuses to ask directions. We've had some *long* car trips as a result."

"Well," Walt replied, "not to denigrate your husband's skills, but I've been around a long while, and I have an uncanny ability to pick the right path. Besides, I have a cunning plan. Tony, do you still have that packet of saltines I gave you?"

Sure enough, the birthday boy proffered a wax paper–wrapped package of soda crackers, and Walt eased it open along the seam. "We may not have Ariadne's clew in the form of string, but this should work just fine."

Walt might very well have paused then to explain that the word "clew," a somewhat archaic term which means a literal ball of twine and usually appears in association with the Theseus myth, took a different form over time: the more figurative "clue," familiar from detective stories, which means a piece of evidence or information that guides someone to the solution of a crime or mystery. He might even have quoted—in the original Middle English—Chaucer's description of the Cretan labyrinth and its "solution" from *The Legend of Good Women*:

> And for the hous is krynkeled to and fro,
> And hath so queynte weyes for to go—
> For it is shapen as the mase is wrought—
> Therto have I a remedye in my thought,
> That, by ***a clewe of twyn***, as he
> ["he" being Theseus, of course] hath gon,
> The same weye he may returne anon,
> Folwynge alwey the thred, as he hath come.

Then Walt might have supplied a translation into more modern English, something like:

And because that structure is crinkled and crisscrossed with back-and-forth turns and winding passages and contains such crafty, cunning paths on which to pass (because it is shaped just as a maze is contrived), I have therefore a solution in mind: that by unrolling a ball of twine, and always following that strand as he goes, he can soon return the same way he has come.

But enough of these linguistic tangles. Walt didn't make those particular pedantic additions, and I'd best get back to the main narrative before I lose the thread of the plot; otherwise, I might be left without a clue about how to continue.

After his mention of Ariadne's alternative to a Global Positioning System, the porkpie-hatted adventurer demonstrated his own, breaking a cracker in two and tossing a piece down in the pathway beside them. "We'll just mark each turn clearly, and that way, if we get stuck, we can trace our way back, just like Theseus, or Hansel and Gretel. And if we get hungry, we can nibble on a few of these babies and still have a plentiful supply of trail markers. Easy solution, with no strings attached, and never the twine shall meet!" The genial geezer chuckled at his own wordplay.

The theory was sound, but, as you might have suspected, the execution left something to be desired. Stumpy had hopped down to explore on his own while the humans pressed forward, and at the first few junctures, they seemed to choose well and were able to proceed through the ten-foot-high tunnel of cornstalks without obstruction. Walt kept dropping crackers at key points, but about twenty minutes into the maze, they finally ran into a dead end.

"That last *bivium* must have screwed me up," Walt said. "*Bivium* is the Latin word for any place where you have two choices, like in Robert Frost's poem 'The Road Not Taken': 'Two roads diverged in a yellow wood. . . .' You know that one, don't you, Amy? I guess we just have to retrace our steps. . . ."

However, as he turned around, his eyes fell on Stumpy, who had just hopped up behind them and was obviously chewing something. While Walt was peering at his rodent friend, a few cracker crumbs fell out of the squirrel's mouth onto the dirt of the path. "Oh boy . . . ," Walt muttered. "There goes that plan."

Fortunately, though, Stumpy saved the day by slipping out through the densely packed cornstalks and chattering from the outside to direct them back to one of the key turns; from there, Walt's instincts proved more reliable. Stumpy squeezed back into the maze with his friends, and in another ten minutes, they had found their way through the puzzling structure, with Walt occasionally pausing to hold his gray-furred friend up high over his head for a glance over the green and gold wall when he was feeling uncertain. "Times like this, Stump, I kinda wish you were a crow so you could fly up above and see the whole pattern. A change of perspective, especially that detached view from on high, is often the best way to defeat a maze."

Walt was a bit quieter on the ride home than he had been on the way over, clearly chastened, but also aware that everyone had had a good time regardless of his own overly confident approach. He realized that more celebrating lay ahead, with Amy planning a dinner for that evening. Besides, his own eleventy-seventh birthday was just two days away, and he now has good friends to celebrate *that* occasion with too.

12

Stumpy and the Bike Rider

October 12, 2011

Last week, I told you about how Walt Walthers, the elderly weather watcher who lives in a cabin out on Kibbee Pond in Townsend, planned what he called a "Festive Birthweek Celebration" for his now six-year-old neighbor and himself, their birthdays being only two days apart. Tony Riggetti was turning six, of course, but Walt was turning "eleventy-seven," the same age, by the way, that he turns every year. I told you about how Tony's mother, Amy, and Walt planned the First Annual Kibbee Pond Highland Games for Tony and his three ten-year-old friends Mac, Shel, and Hammy and about how Stumpy, the stub-tailed squirrel that lives with Walt, and his two long-tailed wild siblings, Burwell and Lansdowne, spontaneously devised their own version of the games. I also told you how Walt, on Tony's actual birthday, drove mother, son, and squirrel sidekick to explore a corn maze at a nearby farm and how that silver-haired schemer laid down a trail of crackers so they could find their way back out of the maze; unfortunately, I also had to tell you how Stumpy ate the crackers, inadvertently demolishing their version of Ariadne's clew that our own Theseus in a porkpie hat had trailed behind him. I also told you, however, about how Stumpy helped the group reorient themselves and find their way back out of the maze.

The Festive Birthweek Celebration did not end with "Septober 27," as Tony had referred to his birthdate, actually continuing through Walt's birthday, on "Septober 29," and even beyond. But since I spent so much time last week talking about the first couple of days, I *won't* tell you tonight about how, the day before his own birthday, Walt took Stumpy and the five humans to a nearby orchard or about how they all had a grand time, first looking at all the pumpkins, which ranged from the conventional orange sugar pumpkins to more exotic varieties, like the round, white Luminas; the squat orange Long Island cheese pumpkins; the warty Knuckle Heads; the beautiful Tondos, with their dark green stripes and yellow ridges; the reddish-orange Cinderella pumpkins, which look as though they could easily be turned into carriages; the big, deep-ribbed Fairytale pumpkins; the dark blue-green Marina di Chioggia pumpkins with their bumpy surfaces; even the multicolored green-to-red-to-white turban squashes and the subtle-colored dusty-blue Hokkaido squashes; the peanut pumpkins and the Silver Moon squashes; and the gourds—oh, the gourds!—with their twisted necks and all their shapes and shades. Walt would have liked to buy a dozen or more to arrange on his deck, but I won't tell you about how instead he told the boys to each pick out a pumpkin so they could carve jack-o'-lanterns closer to Halloween. Nor will I tell you about how they all walked out into the orchard together with bags to pick their own apples and how, even though other people had claimed the easy-to-reach ones, Stumpy proved of invaluable help by scurrying up and out the branches to where some big beauties still remained, too high to reach without some kind of ladder . . . or a nimble squirrel assistant. Nor will I tell you about how Walt waited below, porkpie at the ready in his hands, and maneuvered under the falling Cortlands and McIntoshes as Stumpy bit through their stems. Even though the Major League Baseball playoffs are currently taking place, I won't tell you about the skill Walt showed in snagging some of the falling fruit, nor about how he mimicked Willie Mays with at least one over-the-shoulder catch when Stumpy got a bit exuberant.

No, I won't bore you either with an account of how they went back afterward to Amy and Tony's little house down the road and all pitched in to peel the apples and gather the other ingredients for an apple pie, including the cinnamon, nutmeg, and allspice, and how Amy rolled out the homemade crust and how then they actually baked the pie and how, almost before it had cooled sufficiently, each ate a piece with a small scoop of vanilla ice cream melting on top and a chunk of cheddar cheese on the side. If I told you all that, you'd probably get as hungry as I am now *not* telling you about how delicious that warm apple pie was.

Nor had I better tell you about Walt's actual birthday celebration and how, in a big metal tub that Walt set up on his deck, the boys all bobbed for apples they had picked the day before, laughing and splashing as they dipped their heads and tried to open their mouths wide enough to get a grip with their teeth on the apple of their choice. And I certainly can't tell you about the game of Pin the Tail on the Donkey they played inside amidst shrieks of laughter because I wouldn't want to make you too envious of the fun they had. Suffice it to say, however, that Hammy, the slightly plump ten-year-old who always seems to be hitching his pants up, got so spun around and dizzy during his turn that he actually tried to pin the tail on Walt's behind! I wouldn't dream of mentioning that, meanwhile, out on the porch, Stumpy—copycat and fun-lover that he is—was trying his hand . . . or paw . . . or buckteeth, actually—at bobbing for apples, too, and that he, naturally, lost his balance and fell into the tub of water. Nor will I tell you that when the folks inside heard the splash, they all ran out to find Stumpy pulling himself back up over the rim of the tub and that Walt said, "Stump, if I'd known you wanted to take a bath, I woulda gotten out the special patchouli-scented body bath I bought my wife, Annie, all those years ago, and you coulda soaked in a warm tub and come out smelling real pretty!" I also don't think it fitting to tell you that the humans all dissolved in laughter again when Walt suggested that maybe they should throw some honey-roasted cashews into the tub, then supply Stumpy with a straw to use as a snorkel, and watch him do his best impression of a South Seas pearl diver probing the depths in search of treasure.

And I won't tell you how, despite the humorous remarks Walt was often sending his way, Stumpy was so deep-down devoted to the fun-loving old geezer that, after he dried off, he went out to the vinyl tent where Walt keeps his old Chevy truck, Lulu, and selected from his own neatly squirreled away winter cache of nuts three beautiful beechnuts or how he stuck them in his mouth one at a time and snuck them into the cabin so that while the humans were busy with their festivities, he could, unbeknownst to Amy, decorate the special birthday cake she had made from scratch for his elderly roommate. And I definitely don't want to tell you how that affectionate rascal put his special presents right on top of the boiled frosting Amy had so laboriously prepared and so carefully swirled on top or how he came away with a white beard and gummy feet or how Walt, when he spotted his friend's sugary facial accretion, blurted out, "Wow! Christmas in Septober, and here's old Santy now!" I am, however, tempted to tell you about Amy's reaction to Stumpy's cake-decorating efforts, mainly because it speaks so clearly to her forbearance and understanding, since despite her initial shocked intake of breath, she regained her equanimity, smiled, and said, "Awww, look, Walt! Stumpy must be a Renaissance squirrel. Not only is he brave enough to scare off a black bear and nimble enough to ride a bucking yellow Labrador retriever, but he also has a highly developed aesthetic sense!" And if I'm not going to tell you about that, then why would I need to tell you that Walt was so touched by his buddy's gift that he lifted the still slightly damp rodent up and gave him a big smacker of a kiss right on his frosting-covered nose, saying, "Thanks, pal, and, Amy, that frosting tastes so delicious that I think we'd better get to cutting that cake and eating it right now"? And I won't tell you that that's exactly what they did!

You see, what I really want to tell you about is a visitor who arrived at Walt's cabin last Sunday morning. The weather watcher and his rodent buddy were expecting a quiet day, with Amy and Tony on their way up to New Hampshire on a visit to Amy's parents' house, where they would spend the night before the Columbus Day holiday. Walt was carrying his second cup of coffee out onto the deck, Stumpy hopping languidly behind him, when they both simultaneously noticed a man in cycling gear standing next to his bicycle in their driveway. The squirrel, who prided himself on being a good watchdog, must have felt a bit embarrassed at letting a potential intruder sneak up on them, so he mustered no convincing ferocity in the growl he attempted; I suspect he was feeling more sheepish than canine, more sheepish even than rodent-like. The man had been gazing out toward the pond, but when he noticed the two companions on the deck, he raised a hand in greeting and called, "Beautiful morning, isn't it? I hope you don't mind that I pulled in. I thought I might get a better look at the pond that way. I think I may have taken a wrong turn somewhere, though I doubt I could have found a spot more pretty than this."

"No problem," Walt replied. "It must be nearly perfect weather for a bike ride, though I understand it might warm up uncomfortably before the day is done. Can I offer you a cup of coffee, or is it against the Tour de France training guidelines?"

"Sounds great," the man said, chuckling. As he approached, Walt could see that he was tall, fair-complexioned, and well into middle age; his blond mustache was silvering, and his eyes smiled behind his wire-rimmed glasses as he extended his hand. "Jerry Woodley," he said, "and though I may have taken a wrong turn, I think I know now where I am. Aren't you Walt Walthers? And that fellow"—he was pointing to the gray-furred bandit at Walt's side—"could only be the legendary Stumpy the squirrel."

"Nice try, but you've failed to see through our clever disguises," Walt said, laughing. "Actually, *he's* Walt, and *I'm* Stumpy . . . though if you like, we can resume our true forms now."

Conversation continued over coffee and honey-roasted cashews, with Jerry keeping a keen eye and ear turned toward the pond, sensitive, as it turned out, to even the slightest hint of avian presences. "I'm pretty sure I saw an osprey pass over just before I noticed you guys on the deck."

"Well," said Walt, "that's probably old Pandion, who passes through every year about this time. I named him after the mythological character whose daughters got turned into birds, plus that's the first part of the osprey's scientific name, *Pandion haliaetus,* the last part of which means 'sea eagle.' I suppose I could have called him Bone-Breaker, since that's what the Latin word *ossifragus* means, and that's where 'osprey' comes from."

Jerry let out a low whistle. "Impressive," he said, smiling and nodding.

Walt continued, "Now, I got the sense you were about to tell us why you know who we are when we don't yet know you. Frankly, you've got me a little curious, though I don't know about the Stumpmeister there. He can be downright inscrutable at times." Stumpy, however, had moved closer to Jerry and was looking up at him, as if awaiting his answer.

"Well," Jerry said, "I heard about you from my colleague at Laurel Academy, Michael Swift. He's the head of the science department, and I teach chemistry and ornithology there."

"Sure," Walt said, smiling anew. Michael Swift was, of course, the entomologist who had come by back in early August and cruised the lake with the cabin-dwelling pair. Stumpy had helped him with his research into dragonfly migration by making an acrobatic catch of a passing green darner, reminding Michael of Julian Edelman. Michael had joked about buying Stumpy a number eleven Patriots jersey in gratitude. Walt told Jerry his version of that day's events while Jerry's eyes continued to scan the surroundings for birds.

"Sure is pretty out here," Jerry commented in a quiet moment as the sun warmed their shoulders and the breeze off the water cooled their faces.

"Not much color yet in the leaves," Walt said. "As I understand it, without cold nights and bright sunshine during the daytime, the colors can be disappointing. We haven't had a hard frost yet, and we got so much rain through August and September that I don't think we've met the solar requirements either."

"You're right about the basic principles," Jerry said. "You sure you're not a science teacher in exile, or something romantic like that? As I understand it, the whole leaf-shedding process is caused by the trees' need to protect against losing water in the winter, when it's scarce. Hardwoods have less wax on their leaves, so the water escapes through the leaf surfaces, something that doesn't happen with the evergreens. Cold weather triggers the hardwood trees' production of a layer of corklike material where the leaf stems connect to the branches, and that layer keeps water and nutrients from passing to the leaves. With the interruption of photosynthesis, no chlorophyll gets to the leaves, so other pigments come out that have been covered up before: xanthophylls to produce yellows and carotenoids to produce reds, oranges, and yellows. Some reds and even purples come from the anthocyanins, which the trees produce in the autumn if crisp nights and sunny days come in the right combination."

Walt said, "There was a lovely old ash grove near the house where I grew up, and I remember the blend of green and yellow and purple when the leaves turned. My wife always said she wanted to weave a fabric that would capture that blend of colors. I've heard a lovely old-time tune called 'The Ash Grove' too. Always makes me think of my childhood and those gorgeous purple-tinged trees."

Just then, Jerry sat up straight in his chair and then stood, eyes riveted on a witch hazel bush back toward the tree line. "I think that may be a warbler over there. Have you ever *pished* birds?"

"Well," Walt giggled, "I may have once or twice when I had a few too many beers, but I'm afraid I don't really remember."

Jerry gave him a funny look and then said, "I said *pish* . . . not what you're thinking. Here, come along with me." He led the way toward the tree line. Stumpy hopped curiously behind the men with his characteristic stop-and-go gait, or more accurately, his hop-and-hesitate gait. Suddenly, Jerry emitted a strange sound: "*Ps-s-s-sh! Ps-s-s-sh! Ps-s-s-sh!*" He continued making the noise at regular intervals for almost a minute, pausing only occasionally to take a breath.

Some bird noises emerged from the bushes and trees in front of them: *feeemping* and *chuck-chucking*, and soon, Walt could see several birds coming closer. He could see a white-breasted nuthatch hopping closer along a low tree branch and a red-bellied woodpecker peeking out from behind another branch. Finally, a chickadee landed with a little inquisitive buzz of a chirp on a branch inches away from the two men's faces. "Humph," Jerry said in a disappointed tone, "no warblers in there that I could see."

"Wow!" Walt said. "I've never seen anyone do that before! Does it always work?"

"Not always," Jerry said, "and a lot of birders think that *pishing* is cheap, a kind of trick that you shouldn't have to use to spot birds. Still, I like to use it when I'm out with my students, just to make sure they get to see *something*."

"I suppose you have to be careful about it on a breezy day," Walt said, a smile playing about the corners of his mouth.

"What do you mean?" Jerry asked.

"Well," the porkpie-hatted trickster said, "you wouldn't want to *pish* into the wind!"

"You know, Walt," Jerry said, "this could be the start of a beautiful friendship."

And it was.

13

Stumpy and the Love Affair

November 16, 2011

Walt Walthers, the elderly weather watcher who lives out on Kibbee Pond in Townsend with his rambunctious rodent roommate, Stumpy the stub-tailed gray squirrel, won't soon forget the past several days. After all, this was the week he realized that Stumpy was in love.

In his focus on preparing for the late-October snowstorm two weekends ago and then in the busyness of the post-storm cleanup and the rescheduling of Halloween, Walt must have missed some of the signals Stumpy inevitably put forth. Walt *had* noticed a sluggishness in his friend, which he put down to a variation of early-onset seasonal affective disorder, and—to excuse Walt further—Stumpy did recover much of his energy around Halloween, what with the excitement of wearing a costume and acting a role in Walt's plot to get back at the three ten-year-olds who had toilet-papered his deck. Furthermore, the always-stimulating company of Tony Riggetti, the six-year-old who lives just down the road with his mom, Amy, had also kept the squirrel busy during the week that kindergarten was out because of the power failure. However, over the last couple of days, Walt was finally able to recognize that his buddy had made a romantic attachment. Unfortunately, the concerned geezer feared that Stumpy's feelings were not fully requited and that the gray-furred bandit might be headed for heartbreak.

Walt's commitment to regular exercise was at least partially responsible for Stumpy's infatuation. As a much younger man with three young sons, Walt had run the backcountry roads regularly after work and on weekends, if only two or three miles at a time, and he had played weekly pickup basketball games at the town courts, especially when his sons were around to join him. Aging had brought the need to adjust his regimen, however, and he shifted in his late fifties to running one day and walking the next in order to ease the strain on his knees and hips; somewhere along the line, he had also taken up kayaking, the activity that had first brought him to Kibbee Pond. Still later, after the death of his wife, Annie, he had sold the family home and invested in the twenty acres he now owns at the northwest end of the pond, where he soon built the cabin he has lived in since then. As time passed, however, he had needed to make further adjustments to his exercise plans, since lugging the kayak to the water and getting in and out of it without incident posed challenges; he had also had to acknowledge his sons' fears that kayaking alone was dangerous, so he had reluctantly put away his paddle.

Nevertheless, he does not feel right without exercising and remains committed to walking regularly, at least when snow and ice do not make conditions too slippery. Thus, virtually every day, Walt walks up Kibbee Pond Road to the north, where it joins Gold Crest Road, the most direct route to Lunenburg, and he continues up that road a ways farther; his turnaround there is a bit more than a mile away from the cabin, and that distance is enough to help loosen his joints and to leave him pleasantly tired and aerated when he sits down again at home.

Walt is flexible about his walking time each day, but with Tony in kindergarten on weekday mornings, the fitness-concerned codger usually tries to go out around seven thirty or eight o'clock so he can have the rest of the morning open for chores and other necessary activities. Stumpy almost always accompanies him on these outings, hopping along the edge of the woods, nosing about the mast underneath the oaks in search of tasty morsels, sometimes climbing up into the branches overhead as if in search of an undefined something, then scurrying to catch up with his human friend. When the exceedingly rare vehicle appears on the road ahead, the squirrel usually scampers up Walt's pantleg and perches on his shoulder until the intruder has passed; then he climbs down to resume his wandering and foraging.

Only two houses stand along Gold Crest Road, the first a small place that was once the area's one-room schoolhouse. Walt's acquaintance Byron Ford, a painter, had bought the place back in the seventies and renovated it so that he had small but comfortable living quarters in the original building, onto which he had added a spacious studio. Over the woodstove in his own cabin, Walt has hung one of Byron's paintings, what he considers a gorgeous depiction of an autumn stream tumbling over a partially collapsed stonewall; the work had been a gift for a favor performed many years before, and Walt remains amazed at Byron's generosity in offering up a piece of himself so readily, even though the painter had claimed the work was flawed.

The second house on Gold Crest Road is a more recent structure but also modest in size; it is painted tan with white trim and has a small front porch facing the road, with just a bit of gingerbread adorning the peak of the porch. Two rocking chairs have long sat neatly on that porch, and in season, tasteful flowerpots sit on either side of the front steps so that the house always looks inviting. Walt has a passing acquaintance with the woman who lives there, Marguerite Kearney, an elderly widow, though still appreciably younger than Walt. They have exchanged waves and pleasantries many times over the past few years but have never spoken at greater length.

Walt had come to take Marguerite's presence for granted, so he was not expecting to encounter new residents a few weeks back, but encounter new residents, albeit temporary ones, he did. The first hint of the change was a soft "Woof!" that greeted him as he strode past the place one early morning back in the second week of October. During their time together, Stumpy has always enjoyed hopping over to the steps of the house and even weaving his way in and out of the openings in the porch railing, much to Walt's consternation given the codger's deeply ingrained respect for others' property. This particular morning, however, before he had even gotten close to the porch, Stumpy had heard the foreign sound and bolted for Walt's leg, scrambling up to his secure post next to his friend's right ear. Together, they turned to see, standing at the top of the stairs, a red-eyed, floppy-eared canine beauty, a vision of loveliness in tan, black, and white—in short, a gorgeous female basset hound, staring at them with her tail gently wagging behind her. In that moment, Walt realized that her bark had held no threat whatsoever but was merely an attention-getter, the dog's way of ensuring that the man would not walk past without noticing her.

"Hel-*lo*, beauty!" he had answered her, with a slight bow. She continued to hold the eye contact she had established with him, tail swinging deliberately back and forth. "Well, gorgeous," he continued, "you certainly put the 'cur' in 'curvaceous'!" As he spoke, the basset stepped down two of the stairs, paused, resumed wagging, and drew Walt's eyes to hers once again.

"You can come see us, beauty, as long as you don't hurt my buddy here," Walt said, and the dog stepped down two more stairs before pausing again for more wagging and eye contact.

At that moment, an attractive dark-haired woman had stepped out the front door, saying, "Chloe? What are you up to?" and then, having caught sight of Walt, "Oh, hello there."

Walt had tipped his always-present porkpie hat and replied, "Good morning, ma'am. We were just admiring your remarkably pulchritudinous pooch. I don't think I've ever seen a more beautiful basset, and I've been a fan of the breed for many years."

"Thank you," the woman replied. "I wish I got as many compliments as she does, but she's just as sweet as she is pretty, so I guess I can't hold it against her. That's a remarkable companion you have *there* too. I didn't realize that people could keep squirrels as pets."

"On that score," Walt said, laughing, "he probably thinks of me as *his* pet. I usually refer to him as my roommate or companion to avoid any presumption on my part. By the way, my name is Walt Walthers, and I live out on Kibbee Pond. This dapper fellow is Stumpy the squirrel. I don't believe we've seen you here before, and we walk by nearly every day. May I ask if you're visiting Marguerite?"

The woman laughed and said, "Not exactly. Aunt Marguerite has gone to Italy for a month, and I'm house-sitting for her. I'm Nerissa Logan. Okay, Chloe, you may go say hello if you like."

Thus released, the basset finished her deliberate descent of the stairs and then advanced, still slowly wagging and still seeking Walt's gaze. Stumpy sat silently on the man's shoulder, staring at the dog, who seemed to have eyes, literally and figuratively, for only Walt.

When Chloe got close enough, Walt bent over to stroke her large, velvety ears while she continued wagging happily and peeping gleefully into *his* peepers. Meanwhile, Stumpy retained a firm grip on the collar of Walt's parka to avoid toppling off, as he might otherwise have done because of Walt's shifting posture and the strength with which Cupid's dart had struck him. Walt, of course, could not see his friend but could only feel where he was perched; had he been able to see the amorous expression on the smitten rodent's face, he might have recognized right then what was happening. Instead, he continued to pay tribute to the incarnation of canine loveliness that still held his gaze from the ground below him. "Aren't you a vision, you brown-eyed goddess?' the geezer gushed.

"Now, Mr. Walthers," the woman said, laughing, "don't get carried away! She already has a high enough opinion of herself."

"Please call me Walt," the porkpied duffer replied, "and I'm sorry if I'm getting carried away, but bassets have always had a way of making me feel that they are looking right into my soul. There's a divinity in their doghood for me."

"Well, call *me* Nissa," she said, laughing again, "but don't you dare go on to say that 'dog' spelled backwards is 'God.' Chloe already takes that statement literally."

Walt laughed, too, as he straightened up and took his eyes off the object of his worship to look at the dog's owner, realizing then how striking she was herself. Stumpy, however, continued to lean off his carrier's shoulder, attempting to keep *his* eyes fixed on Chloe.

"When I told my sister I was thinking about getting a dog," Nissa said, the laughter still in her voice, "she asked me if I was drunk. She was talking about the time and expense, I guess, and I think she thought I was lonely and seeking a surrogate for human companionship. Maybe she was right. In any case, I didn't realize then that an animal could be a bigger narcissist than a human. Still, Chloe's good company, and she gives me lots of opportunities to make new friends . . . though sometimes I think people like me for my dog more than my own delightful personality."

"Well," Walt responded, "I'm beginning to think that *that* mistake would be impossible to make for long." He looked shyly away.

The conversation continued for several minutes more, with Walt learning that Nissa was an English teacher at Laurel Academy and well acquainted with his friends Michael Swift and Jerry Woodley, both of whom taught in the science department at the same school. Shortly thereafter, she excused herself to leave for work, but in the following days, Walt began timing his morning walk to take the two cabin dwellers past the little house early enough to say hello almost every day. In his own admiration of the attractive teacher, Walt never realized the torment his gray-furred friend was enduring because of these daily contacts with the object of *his* affection. While Chloe seemed to hunger for Walt's attention, and Nissa expressed fascination with the apparently shy and well-behaved Stumpy, the smitten rodent seemed stump-like in his indifference to the woman's attentions, and while Walt glowed with his old man's crush on Nissa and became increasingly talkative with each encounter, the poor squirrel suffered his pangs without acknowledgment, either from his oblivious canine ladylove or from his human roommate, who would have sympathized had he woken up to the situation. Had he been seeing with clear eyes, Walt might also have recognized comic similarities with Shakespeare's *A Midsummer Night's Dream.*

As time passed and the morning walks continued, the suffering rodent would climb down off Walt's shoulder and approach the freckled legs of the basset, craving even a deprecatory glance from her, but for all the attention Chloe would grant him, he might not even have existed. Even Walt, in the midst of his own flirtations, noticed that the dog was ignoring Stumpy. "Whatever happened to the good old days," he said at one point, "when self-respecting dogs knew enough to *chase* squirrels?" Stumpy's devotion to Chloe would come into clear focus for the equally infatuated Walt only later, with an intrusion from the natural world.

Even as this star-crossed love quadrangle continued, autumn was advancing despite some warmer than usual temperatures; out on the pond, a persistent wind blew, even on sunny days, and now fallen oak leaves would spiral across the deck, leaping up like sparrows startled from feeding, then tumbling back down. Walt had noticed that Stumpy would often sit in the window watching the leaves blow about, but he assumed that his friend was feeling his own apprehension about the approach of true winter and the threat of more snow, snow of the persistent and lasting sort.

One afternoon last week, when Amy had stopped in to pick up Tony after his post-kindergarten visit, Walt pointed across the driveway and said, "Look at the prickle-pig!" A large porcupine had ambled into view and now waddled, without apparent concern, toward the stand of young hemlocks set back among the oaks and sassafras trees. Stumpy had come out of his leaf-watching reverie long enough to growl a little in the intruder's direction.

"Can I go look at him, Mr. Walt?" the six-year-old asked.

"Sure," said Walt, "though he'll probably just walk off at his own pace, grumbling. Better not try to pick him up, though." He winked at Tony as he said those words.

"Aw, Mr. Walt," the little shaver replied, "I didn't just fall off the turnip truck this morning!"

"Hmm," Walt said to Amy as her son trotted toward the slow-moving rodent, "he may have been hanging around me too much if he's using archaic expressions like that."

"It's all part of your charm," Amy replied, laughing. "What's with the porcupines? I saw one down our way yesterday afternoon when I got back from work. You think it was the same one?"

"Well," Walt said, "it might have been, but this is their breeding season, just like it's the rut for deer. Sometimes in October or November, you'll see two or three males trailing after a female in estrus. I actually saw two porcupines mating once a few years ago."

Amy said, "I know the old joke—you know, how do porcupines make love . . . very carefully—but it must be something to actually see."

"It was," Walt said. "I once saw two huge snapping turtles mating in the shallows here at the pond, and that was almost as memorable, but it was also very different. There was a lumbering sense of power and inevitability about that, something . . . reptilian, I guess. But the porkies were almost courtly in their behavior. The male stood up on his hind legs and tail and did a delicate little dance of invitation; then the female stood up, too, and danced, and then the two came close together, made some guttural love sounds, and rubbed noses before engaging in what almost looked like a brief boxing match, batting each other with their front paws. Then she backed up toward him and moved her tail to one side, and he leaned in on one elbow, and . . . they were together. I've heard scientists say that the male sprays the female with urine before mating, but I didn't see that happen."

"How romantic!" Amy said sardonically.

"Well," Walt responded, "that's why daddy porcupines tell their sons to mind their Ps and quills." Amy only groaned.

Tony had reached the prickly creature, which turned in the opposite direction and headed for a nearby oak. "Hey, Mr. Walt," the youngster called, "I think he clicked his teeth at me!"

"They'll do that," Walt called back. "Is he talking to you too?"

"Yeah," came the laughing reply. "He sounds *really* crabby!"

"He's probably going to climb that tree to get away from you. Just don't get close to his tail. They can't throw their quills, but they can swing with their tails and drive them into you."

When the porky had climbed straight up the small oak like a telephone worker going up a pole, it perched itself in the crotch of a branch about ten feet up. Tony came reluctantly back.

Walt said, "You know, I always think they sound like grouchy old hermits, muttering and swearing under their breath. *Fn-n-n-rn-n-n-f-n-n-nh. Fn-n-n-nf-n-f-n-n-nh. Fn-n-n-nf-n-f-n-n-nh. Why don't you just leave me alone?*" Both Tony and Amy laughed.

"When I was a dog owner," the gregarious geezer continued, "I chased porcupines out of my backyard with a garden hose more than once. They didn't like getting sprayed with water. They didn't move very fast, but they sure cussed me out good. I'm glad I don't understand porcupine 'cause I don't think I want to know what names they called me.

"Still, I didn't want them around because those quills can do awful damage to a dog, and some dogs just never learn to leave those pesky pincushions alone. One particular dog of mine I must have taken to the vet six times he'd get so many quills stuck in him."

All this while, Stumpy had been sitting disconsolately on the deck rail. He had watched Tony approach the porcupine but now had returned to staring at the windblown oak leaves.

Amy leaned toward Walt. "Is anything wrong with our friend?"

"You know," Walt answered, "I had been thinking it was just the turning of the seasons, but now that I compare his symptoms to my own, I think he may have developed a bit of a crush."

"Is there some lady squirrel around that I haven't met?" Amy asked.

Walt shook his head. "I'm afraid he's got an interspecies romance going on, but I also fear it's a little one-sided. He's been making goo-goo eyes at the pretty basset hound that's staying out on Gold Crest Road."

"Stumpy's fallen for a dog? But what were you saying about your *own* symptoms?" Amy persisted.

After a pause, Walt replied, "Well, the dog's owner is quite a stunner herself, and I find myself wishing I was forty or fifty years younger. But I know better," he added before Amy could say anything.

Sunday of this week, the lovelorn gents' morning walk gave them another chance to chat with Nissa and Chloe, but they received some unanticipated news. Walt casually asked what Nissa would be teaching over the next few days, and she had answered, "Oh, we're going to be looking at some of Shakespeare's sonnets." Stumpy was sitting upright on the ground staring at Chloe, who, oblivious to the suffering squirrel, was wagging energetically and trying to draw Walt's eyes away from her mistress.

"Oh-h-h," Walt exclaimed just before he started reciting.

> That time of year thou may'st in me behold
> When yellow leaves, or none, or few do hang
> Upon those boughs that shake against the cold,
> Bare, ruin'd choirs where late the sweet birds sang.

"Oh, you know that one?" Nissa laughed and joined in.

> In me thou see'st the twilight of such day
> As after sunset fadeth in the west,
> Which by and by black night doth take away,
> Death's second self that seals up all in rest.

"Okay," Walt said, drawing a breath before continuing.

> In me thou see'st the glowing of such fire
> That on the ashes of his youth doth lie
> As the deathbed whereon it must expire,
> Consumed with that which it was nourished by.

Together, then, they spoke the closing couplet.

> This thou perceiv'st, which makes thy love more strong,
> To love that well which thou must leave ere long.

"I'm impressed," Nissa said then. "I didn't realize that you were so literary. But I'm afraid *I'm* the one who must leave 'ere long.' My aunt comes home tomorrow, and Chloe and I will be moving back to our apartment on campus tonight."

Walt tried to mask his disappointment by muttering, "Oh . . . well, I'm sure it will be nice not to have to drive back and forth to school every day."

But just at that moment, the normally placid Chloe gave three sharp woofs, her large and sensitive nose having caught an unfamiliar scent, and she spun toward the tree line at the back of the little house. There, Walt saw a large porcupine shuffling casually across the grass as if carrying a beach towel and book bag toward a chaise longue on the first day of his vacation. At that instant, however, Chloe was galvanized into uncharacteristic action, and her short legs began churning; her baying cry ululated across the lawn as she gathered headway toward the prickly invader.

Even much later, Walt was never sure how, with the dog's head start, Stumpy had been able to get between Chloe and the porcupine. He *had* heard that love could fly quicker than the wings of thought but had always thought the line was figurative and hyperbolic. Somehow, though, the doughty squirrel literally covered the distance, and when he saw that Chloe had no intention of stopping, he interposed himself between her and her target, throwing himself backwards onto the other rodent's lashing tail so that his ladylove would be spared. As if noticing Stumpy for the first time, the dog stopped baying and pulled up short of her prickly target. As Stumpy came back down onto all four feet and collapsed limply on the grass, Walt could see, even across the yard, that his friend's back had become a pincushion, with twenty or more quills protruding where it had made contact with the porcupine's tail. Walt knew removing those spears of hair would be painful for his chivalrous roommate.

Nevertheless, as Stumpy's spiny assailant grumbled its way back toward the safety of the trees, something happened that Walt was sure would prove a satisfying consolation for the squirrel. Chloe sniffed at him where he lay apparently lifeless, whined once, and then gave his dark-eyed rodent face a concerned and grateful lick with her long, pink tongue. Stumpy had sat up then and, despite the swordlike shafts impaling him, seemed to take on a glow even as he gritted his teeth.

Later that morning, back at the cabin, Walt removed the quills one by one as gently as he could. "Maybe this is what Ovid meant by 'the flames and arrows of love,'" Walt said, pliers in hand, as he dropped another quill into the pile that was growing on the table. "But you know what, buddy? At least you ended on a high note and made a positive impression." He paused a moment and then continued, "Come to think of it, maybe I did too. You know, we may be unlucky in our amorous endeavors, but with your heroic gesture and my sonnet recitation, at least this time we both went out in style."

14

Stumpy and the Pie-Baking Contest

November 23, 2011

After their amatory adventures of last week, Walt Walthers, the elderly weather watcher who lives in a cabin out on Kibbee Pond in Townsend, and Stumpy, the tailless gray squirrel who has been Walt's roommate for almost two years now, have been trying to put their romantic disappointments behind them and focus on the annual joys of Thanksgiving. For Walt, in particular, those joys include preparing for the pie-baking competition sponsored by the Church of Our Savior Lurks in West Groton, a contest that has been part of his holiday tradition for a dozen years or so. Walt has been a devoted baker since the days when his sons were little whippersnappers and when cooking breakfast for them on the weekends and desserts at least once a week was part of his definition of good fatherhood. For the past decade or more, Walt has spent a good chunk of his time in the weeks before Thanksgiving trying out new recipes and polishing old favorites, and although only a handful of other males have even signed up to participate during Walt's tenure in the contest, he has managed to win three times, including last year. This year, with Stumpy still pining after the departure of Chloe, the basset hound of whom he had become enamored, Walt thought that he might be able to distract his friend with the hectic activity that baking always seems to involve. He also thought that Stumpy might be open to the traditional remedy for the lovelorn: eating, especially eating sweets.

Walt got his annual call last week from Edith Bagshaw, who has been coordinating the competition since before Walt became part of it. Though Edith always puts signs up at the church and at the

Four Leaf Farm Store in the middle of West Groton, most of the competitors are veteran participants, and Edith does them the courtesy of a reminder phone call . . . as if any of them need it. For several years, the real heat of the competition has involved three people: Maureen Ripley, a three-time widow who is famous for the flakiness of her crust and the steeliness of her stare; Louise Barnes, a one-time widow whose meringue is her claim to fame; and Walt, who has developed a reputation for daring flavor combinations. This year, Walt has felt the heat of the competition all the more because he has for some time been under the impression that both of his main competitors consider themselves rivals as well for his affections, despite his decided indifference to either in that regard. Being the defending champion has upped the ante for him too.

For this year's competition, Walt decided he would take advantage of his newest friends to help him refine his recipes and therefore arranged for Amy Riggetti, the young mother who lives with her six-year-old son, Tony, just down Kibbee Pond Road from the cabin, to be his taste tester. For good measure and in the spirit of neighborliness, he also invited Tony and his three ten-year-old friends, Mac, Shel, and Hammy, to join the sampling crew. His plan was to bake a pie a day, Monday through Thursday, and much would go to waste without more mouths to sample his culinary skill. Thus, the arrangement was for the five tasters to arrive at about 3:30 each day last week after the older boys had gotten out of school. Amy has been working mornings recently at the beauty parlor, Ayer Hair, so that her schedule would complement Tony's morning kindergarten classes; thus, she was free for the pie-sampling times as well. On Thursday, the baker would poll his tasters to see which of his four creations was most popular, and on Friday, he would bake a second version of their favorite for the contest Saturday morning.

Monday, Walt spent the early afternoon rolling out the piecrust and slicing the apples for his first effort: a crumble-top apple-and-red-raspberry pie with gouts of cream cheese just beneath the topping; the secret ingredient was a quarter cup of applejack brandy he poured across the apples before adding the cinnamon and brown sugar topping. The smell of the pie baking had the desired effect on Stumpy, who had been mooning by the window but seemed drawn magnetically toward the oven; thus, when the timer went off at 2:15, the squirrel was perched on the top of the stove among the dormant burners. Walt remembered the old cartoons in which a beckoning finger of aroma would emerge from a cookstove and tantalize the characters closer. When the elderly kitchen master removed his creation from the oven, Stumpy was sitting upright in the posture Walt associated with begging dogs.

"You're just going to have to wait, old buddy," the man told the ravenous rodent. "I don't want you burning your mouth, and besides, it wouldn't be polite to let you dig in before the rest of the gang even arrives. Plus, part of the effect is to let everybody *see* the finished product before I cut into it. As Chaucer says, 'Patience is a high virtue.'" Walt was, of course, secretly glad to see that his roommate was breaking out of his love-induced lethargy. "Let's step outside for a few minutes and let that thing cool. You can keep me company while I rake up some of those oak leaves into a pile in case Tony and the guys want to jump into them. You can even test the leaf pile out ahead of time if you like."

An hour or so later, everyone's reaction to the first bite of the pie was a collective moan of "Mm-mm-m-m-m-m!" Amy got a little more specific: "Oh, Walt, that crust is delicious. How do you make it?"

"Well," the oven admiral replied, "I start with all whole-wheat flour and add a bit of cider vinegar as I'm forming it. Annie taught me that years ago, when we were first married, and I've always stuck to it. The crust is never as flaky as one made with white flour, but I think the flavor is more than adequate compensation."

"I'd have to agree," Amy said.

Tuesday brought equal enthusiasm for Walt's peanut butter meringue pie, a recipe he had adapted from a card in his mother's ancient wooden file box. The beautiful browning of the meringue itself brought *oohs* and *aahs* from the appreciative audience as soon as he lifted the cover off the cake box he had placed the pie inside; better still, the flavor disappointed no one. Stumpy, who also received a small slice of each pie, seemed especially enthusiastic about the filling of this one, even smacking his lips and making a contented noise somewhere between a chatter and a purr.

Wednesday morning, as Walt was thumbing through his recipes and contemplating some improvisations on the one he had selected for that day, he got a phone call from Arlene Tosh, his classmate from their long-distant high school days who had rekindled their friendship earlier in the summer. Walt had extended an open invitation to Arlene and her ginormous yellow Labrador retriever, Big Bruno, to stop by anytime. Now, having just returned from a visit to her daughter in Minnesota, Arlene asked if her canine companion and she might come by for coffee on Friday, and Walt was happy to say that he was free as soon as he got his pie baked for the next day's competition. He knew that Stumpy, too, would welcome a visit from the woman and especially her galumphing goofball of a dog, with whom, for the squirrel, familiarity had eventually bred affection rather than contempt.

In the meantime, though, Walt had a Shaker vanilla pie to bake, a variation on what many call a shoofly pie, with buttery crumbs and molasses filling being two of the recipe's central elements. He set to work a little before lunchtime so the pie would still be slightly warm when the tasting crew arrived. This time, the four boys were less enthusiastic about the results than they had been the previous days, but Amy gushed with praise: "Oh, Walt, I just *love* molasses, and the flavor comes through beautifully in this. And the crumb topping is so short and delicious. I don't think the boys are so keen, though, because it's not as sweet as the others."

Thursday's pie was Walt's own invention, and he was proud of it. He had saved it for last, expecting to wow his tasters; he hadn't forgotten the dislike of nuts from which many young folks suffer, but he somewhat hubristically assumed that the sweetness of this recipe and its unusual combination of flavors would win them over. He called it the Stumpster Special in honor of his rodent roommate, and it was in essence a pecan pie, with cashews replacing the pecans and with coffee added to the corn syrup, egg, and brown sugar mixture that gelled around the nuts; cinnamon further highlighted the creation's unique flavor. When his guinea pigs proved as pleased as he had predicted, Walt laughed and said, "I *knew* you'd like it. After all, it's just like me: nutty on the outside, exquisitely sweet on the inside." Stumpy did something Walt had never seen his friend do before: He begged for a second slice, sitting up on his haunches and bobbing his paws while batting his eyes. The whole crew accorded on their suggestion: that Walt should make another Stumpster Special for the contest on Saturday.

Thus, Friday morning, Walt rose earlier than usual, feeling an anticipation similar to that he still remembered from childhood Christmas Eves. He made himself go through his typical routine, including his "morning ablutions," as he called his washing and shaving and toothbrushing. After breakfast and his daily walk with Stumpy, he got down to business, assembling and rolling out two separate piecrusts, which he then positioned in pie plates before crimping their edges. If he had a weakness as a piemaker, he felt it was his crimping, something at which his wife, Annie, had excelled; try as he might, he had always felt his results were inferior to hers, and even now, as a veteran contest winner, he always joked nervously about his perceived limitation, saying, "I have to style my crimps so they don't cramp my style." This particular morning, though, both crusts looked terrific, even to Walt's hypercritical eye, so he wrapped and froze one, then set about preparing the filling for the second. He had the preternatural sense that he was in the baking zone that day and could do no wrong.

By the time Arlene's silver Volvo pulled into the driveway around 11:00, the Stumpster Special was cooling on top of the stove and filling the cabin with its delectable aroma. Stumpy was sitting on the kitchen counter right next to the stove, staring longingly at the pie until he heard the crunching of gravel; then, after a quick glance out the window, he leaped to the floor and raced to the door, where he jumped up and down in place. With a laugh, Walt swung the door open, and his stub-tailed buddy dashed toward the Volvo, within which Walt could see the behemoth head and mile-long pink tongue of Big Bruno behind a rear window that he had systematically besmeared with slobber. Stumpy had recommenced his pogo stick–like jumping next to the Volvo's driver side, and Arlene was already laughing as she opened the front door and spryly climbed out. "Stumpy! Why don't you ever get enthusiastic when we come to visit? You make us think you don't like us."

Arlene opened the back door, and the leviathan bulk of Big Bruno squeezed out, a flash of yellow showing from beneath one cheek where he had a tennis ball tucked away like a chaw of tobacco. Tail a-wag, he leaned forward toward the squirrel, who now stood somewhat shyly in front of his friend. "You remember the nice kitty, don't you, Big Big? Give the kitty a kiss." The pink tongue slathered gently across the rodent's cheek, galvanizing Stumpy into action again; he launched himself up onto the dog's shoulders, where he spun around and then skittered down the dog's back to the base of the swinging tail and then back up as if he were a fighter plane readying for takeoff from the flight deck of an aircraft carrier. Big Bruno looked up at his mistress, who said, "It's okay, good boy. Give the kitty a nice ride." Thus, the humongous pooch shifted himself into forward motion, lumbering ahead like a diesel eighteen-wheeler gaining momentum with the squirrel clutching fistfuls of tan fur. The dog made a loop around the Volvo and then cantered up onto the deck, where he stood wagging back at his mistress as she and Walt smilingly followed.

The four friends entered the cabin, where the proud baker got to show off his creation, which seemed to him as close to perfection as any pie he had ever made. Arlene exclaimed over the fragrance, the artistic crimping of the crust, and the exquisitely browned nut-studded surface. "Oh, Walt," she continued, "I can't imagine Maureen, Louise, or anyone else matching this one in appearance or smell. Are you sure you can't think of any way for me to taste it as well? Would a bribe help?" she said, batting her eyes at him and then breaking down in giggles.

"Thanks, Arlene, but I have to admit my legendary sense of humor is a bit strained, what with the pressure of the contest. It's not easy being a defending champion, especially with tigresses like Mesdames Ripley and Barnes snarling in pursuit."

"That reminds me, Walt," his remarkably youthful octogenarian companion replied. "I forgot that I have something in the car for you, as a good luck present."

Ever the gentleman, Walt stepped out onto the deck again with Arlene, who removed a brightly wrapped package from the front passenger seat.

I should pause here to say that one of the central traits of the Labrador retriever as a breed is its eagerness to please the important humans in its life . . . and often even humans it has never met before. Along with that positive trait goes its tendency to be the easiest of all breeds to shame, if an owner is inclined to that tactic, and sometimes even if he or she isn't; the Lab feels very strongly the weight of human disapproval, at least for a short while. A less savory—in all senses of the word—characteristic of the Lab, however, is its voluminous appetite, its willingness to eat just about anything at any time; I say "voluminous" in part because Labs have been known to eat old books, especially if the books' owner has been unfortunate enough to spill even a smidgen of soup on their covers. Walt knew that fact from experience. Of course, the *dog*'s sense of what is savory rarely overlaps with human tastes and often contravenes its owner's sense of decency, with droppings of all sorts, including its own, ranking—and again I use that word purposefully—high on its list of favorites. All that said, Walt and Arlene made a serious mistake when they stepped back outside without remembering that Big Bruno was still inside. He had already done a round of what Arlene calls "vacuuming," big nose to the floor and working his way from one spot to another in the main room of the cabin, finding plenty of tasty—to him—tidbits that Walt's *electric* vacuum cleaner had apparently missed.

If Arlene had found the pie's aroma enticing, you might imagine how irresistible her dog found it. As soon as the humans left the room, the barn-sized beast walked determinedly toward the stove, snoot in the air and sniffing, as if a casting fisherman had hooked and was reeling in a rhinoceros-sized trout. Labs simply don't have consciences when their owners are not in the room. Before Stumpy could dissuade his canine compatriot from rash action, the mammoth mammal had extended his massive head over the stove top, hooked his incisors over the edge of the pie plate, and tugged his prize onto the floor. By the time the door opened and the humans returned, less than ninety seconds after exiting, the dog had wolfed down the entire pie, not even thinking to share with his squirrel buddy.

To Stumpy's credit, he positioned himself between Big Bruno and Walt immediately. Somehow, the pie plate had not broken in the fall to the floor, and Walt saw the empty Pyrex dish as soon as he stepped back into the cabin. His jaw also fell, possibly even farther than the pie plate had done. Arlene could only stammer, "Oh, W-Walt!"

To Walt's credit, however, he surprised himself by breaking out in laughter as he looked at the hangdog expression on Big Bruno's face, even as the dog continued to smack his lips. "I should have known better than to count my chickens when I hadn't even finished collecting the eggs. Those two women make me so nervous that I find it easy to forget what's really important. Count on this greedy Gargantua to reopen my blinkered eyes." He stepped forward to pat the big dog on the head. "Here I thought it was a pie-*baking* contest when it was really a pie-*eating* contest." As Walt and Arlene both chuckled together, Stumpy hopped over to his silver-haired friend and slipped quickly up his pantleg to his shoulder, where he nuzzled Walt's ear.

Arlene and Big Bruno stayed for lunch, and after the king-sized canine had had some time to start digesting the Stumpster Special, the foursome walked down to the water so the big brute could indulge another of his appetites: for swimming. Walt wore, in place of his habitual porkpie, the chef's hat that Arlene had brought as his present. Given the now-chilly temperature of the water, Stumpy eschewed the bareback bronco riding he had mastered on Big Bruno's broad shoulders back in August; instead, he chattered and bobbed his head from the dock as the tan dog cavorted and floundered like an unusually furry manatee.

Once the visitors had left, Walt took the other piecrust out of the freezer and reassembled the ingredients for the filling of the Stumpster Special. This time, though, he could feel that the magic had temporarily drained from his recipe. The next morning, he drove Lulu, his forest green '60 Chevy pickup, to the church in West Groton and stoically awaited his fate. Stumpy went with him, as had been the case last year as well, and the gregarious mammal enjoyed the gushing greetings and complimentary pie samples he received.

When the announcement came that Louise Barnes was this year's champion, receiving the blue ribbon for her chocolate-peppermint ice-cream surprise pie, Walt shook her hand with a smile. The squirrel, however, quietly demonstrated his dissent by helping himself to another of the small wedges of Walt's pie that remained for those present to sample. Walt appreciated the affectionate gesture, and as they drove back home, the grateful geezer said, "You know, Stump, only Big Bruno knows for sure just how good that other pie of mine was, but I had a strong intuition that it was a winner. We'll never know now, but I'm proud of myself for being able to laugh it off. Besides, the guilty expression on that poor dog's face was priceless." He laughed again remembering the moment, and as he turned onto Kibbee Pond Road, he started to whistle one of his favorite tunes, "They Can't Take That Away From Me."

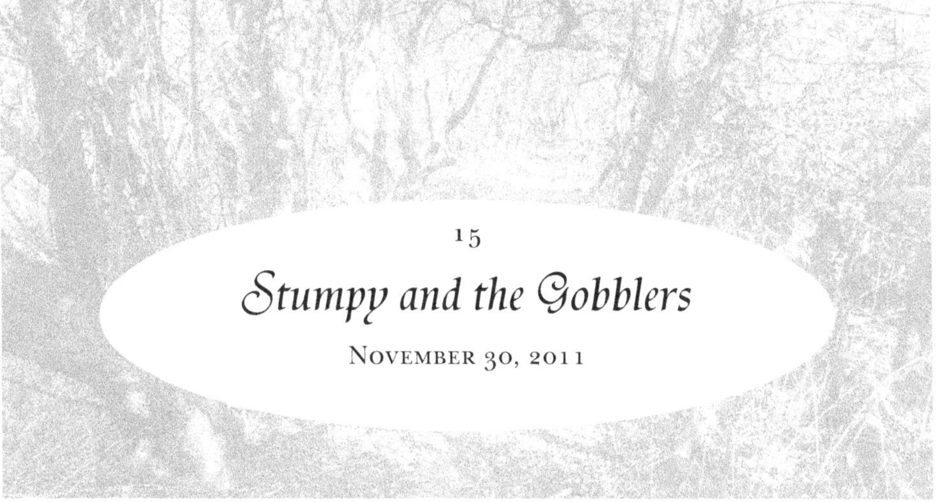

15

Stumpy and the Gobblers

November 30, 2011

Some weeks are busier than others for Walt Walthers, the elderly weather watcher who lives in a cabin out on Kibbee Pond in Townsend with his sidekick and confidante, Stumpy the squirrel, the stub-tailed rodent who lost his magnificent gray plume in an unfortunate accident two years ago, just about this time of year. For the two of them, the week leading up to Thanksgiving had been packed full of socializing, what with the annual pie-baking competition at the Church of Our Savior Lurks in West Groton, a contest that Walt has actually won three times in the dozen or so years he has been participating. Unfortunately, he did not come home with the blue ribbon this year, primarily because a visit from his longtime friend Arlene Tosh had provided Arlene's preternaturally large yellow Lab, Big Bruno, with just the window of opportunity he needed to wolf down the potential prize-winning coffee-cashew pie that Walt had unwisely left cooling on his stove. The early part of that week had seen daily visits from his five-person pie-tasting committee, who had voted among four different options from four different days to choose which recipe Walt would enter in this year's contest. That committee had included, of course, Walt's neighbor down the road, Amy Riggetti, a young mother whose husband is serving in Afghanistan, and her six-year-old son, Tony, who has become a particular favorite of both the silver-haired geezer and his rodent roommate; for good measure, Walt had also invited Mac, Shel, and Hammy, the three ten-year-olds who have also joined his entourage in recent months, to loan to the selection process their considerable skill and experience at eating desserts.

Walt had been able to approach his disappointment philosophically, laughing off the loss of his pie and shrugging off his second-place finish in the competition for the replacement he had hastily assembled. After all, he has always looked forward to Thanksgiving as a special time of year, poignant and bittersweet in its ambivalent anticipations, on the one hand a threshold into the cold and darkness of winter, but on the other a prelude to the lights and eternal hopefulness of the Christmas season; above all, though, he sees the holiday as an opportunity to remind himself of all the things for which he is thankful, and there are many. Certainly, his new group of young friends and his mischievous gray-furred mammalian sidekick head that list.

All the pie tasting had left Walt and Stumpy surfeited on rich foods, and Walt was glad to curtail his baking in the days immediately before Thanksgiving. He knew that in the wild, most animals were working hard to build up a layer of protective fat that would help them get through the lean winter months ahead, but he figured he already had sufficient flab, and he knew that exercising regularly became harder in the cold weather: No need for him, then, to pile on the pounds. Stumpy had finally recovered from his lover's lethargy and had returned to gathering acorns and other mast for storage in the shed where Walt parked the old Volkswagen Beetle, Spot, that had belonged to his wife, Annie. Although the squirrel had fallen hard for a beautiful basset hound that had been sojourning in the neighborhood the previous month, the visit from that goofy behemoth, the yellow Lab Big Bruno, had broken the spell of amatory thralldom and allowed the normally optimistic scamp/scamperer to return to his natural pursuits.

Amy and Tony were planning to spend Thanksgiving with Amy's parents up in New Hampshire, but she had insisted on inviting the "two dapper gents from up the road," as Walt sometimes refers to Stumpy and himself, down for a pre-Thanksgiving supper on Tuesday night. That meal—turkey cutlets à la Normande, with the white meat braised in apples, onions, and cream and served on a bed of noodles, along with baked carrots with balsamic vinegar and a corn bread–and-corn casserole—reminded Walt of how difficult it could be to stick to diets and resolutions, but it also gave him a chance to invent some Thanksgiving mythology for his buddy Tony.

"So, Tony," Walt said between bites of the succulent meal, "I suppose you're getting pretty excited about the arrival of Father Harvest on Wednesday night. Have you got the apple and cracked corn ready yet?"

Tony, usually on top of his manners, could only stare blankly at Walt and say, "Huh?"

The conniving codger elaborated, "You know, have you got things ready for the arrival of the Great Gobbler?"

The little shaver still could manage only a blank look and a stammered, "Mr. Walt, I-I don't know what you mean."

"Wait a minute. Amy, do you mean to say that you've never told your son about Father Harvest and the Thanksgiving Chariot? Don't tell me you've been derelict in your duties as a mother! *Every* young person should know that story. Where does he think the stuffing for the Thanksgiving turkey comes from?"

"Oh, Walt," Amy said, having learned to play along, "I've been so busy. It must have slipped my mind. Maybe *you* should tell him, right now, while we have the chance."

"Well, I guess I had better. You see, Tony, every Thanksgiving Eve, a special visitor flies out of the deep woods, bringing gifts to all the people who are truly thankful for the good things in their lives, and we need to welcome him by putting out chopped apples and cracked corn. Father Harvest dresses all in rusty brown, the color of the oak leaves this time of year, even wearing a garland of oak leaves and witch hazel flowers on his head. He has a long brown beard, tinged with gray, and he wears the ends of his mustache turned up like the handlebars on a bicycle so a little gray junco bird can perch on each side. He calls a dozen wild turkeys from the depths of the forest, the same twelve every year, and he hitches them up to his chariot in pairs. At the front are Foghorn and Drumstick, the leaders. Foghorn has a deep, booming voice, which works well on stormy and foggy nights to let others know they need to clear the way for the Great Gobbler, as Father Harvest is also called. Drumstick is like the coxswain in a rowing scull; he makes a clicking or clucking sound in his throat that provides the rhythm for all the turkeys' wing strokes. What a sight it is to see those birds flying in unison and in formation, each one looking a bit like a big feathery football that some quarter-back has arced high in the air toward the end zone!

"You must at least know that Father Harvest visits every house on Thanksgiving Eve. You don't? Well, down the chimneys of those who have been truly grateful, he tosses a plastic bag of stuffing for the Thanksgiving turkey. For those who have taken everything for granted and *not* expressed their gratitude, he drops a whole raw turnip down the chimney instead. Sometimes, if you listen carefully on Thanksgiving Eve, you can hear the Great Gobbler's team of turkeys going *wooble-ble-ble-ble-ble!* as they fly, and if you're lucky, as they get closer to your house, you'll hear Father Harvest call out, 'Come and get it!' which is what he always says when he tosses out a package of his special corn bread and sausage stuffing. If he gives you the turnip, though, he just shouts, 'Bomb's away!' Sometimes, he has to stop and get out on the roof if his throw misses the chimney on the first try, and then you can hear the turkeys' claws scrabbling away, trying to get a grip. And that's why it's good luck to find turkey feathers, especially on Thanksgiving morning . . . and even better luck to find them on your fireplace hearth."

Tony could only say, "Wow!" his eyes as big as serving platters.

"I'd love to see some turkeys in the wild," Amy said. "My folks say they have a flock that comes around their house, but I've never been there to see them. I do occasionally spot turkeys from a distance."

Walt replied, "They're around, but they're usually wary critters. I sometimes put cracked corn out for them in the winter, but I don't see them around here much except in the colder weather. I read that their vision is six times as good as humans', and that, of course, makes them tough to sneak up on. My Annie loved seeing turkeys, and I always kept an eye out for them when I was walking in the woods near our old house. Sometimes I'd see a flock walking out single file into the big field I visited regularly, but if they noticed me, as they always seemed to do, they'd head right back for cover. When they need to, they can go about twenty-five miles an hour on the ground, taking four-foot strides. Talk about track-and-field athletes! From time to time in those days, I'd find one or more turkey feathers lying on the ground, and I'd take them back to Annie, who kept a collection sticking out of a coffee can. I always talked about them as my version of the Firebird's feather."

"What's a Firebird?" Tony asked.

Walt laughed and said, "It's a creature that some say is mythical, and it appears in a number of Russian folk tales. Did I ever tell you about the huntsman and Princess Vasilissa?"

"No," Tony said. "Could you please tell us now?"

"Since you asked so nicely," the kindly codger replied, "I think I can. The story goes something like this: One day while riding his faithful horse, a huntsman sees lying on the ground the golden feather of the Firebird, that legendary and much-sought creature of Russian mythology. When the huntsman dismounts, however, the horse utters a dire warning: 'Gee whiz, Boss, don't be a Numb Noodle! If you pick up that feather, you'll find out what real trouble is!' Nevertheless, blinded by his dream of glory, the huntsman grabs the feather and carries that treasure to the king, expecting praise and congratulations . . . and maybe even a cushy position at court as the royal wine taster or the royal mattress tester. The king, however, immediately says, 'Good Lord, old chap, if you've found one feather, you should be able to capture the whole blinking fowl, eh what, what? Fetch me the Firebird, or I'll chop off your head!'

"That isn't the response the feather finder was expecting, but when he stops blubbering for a moment and reveals his task to his trusty steed, the horse downplays the immediate difficulties, raising one hairy eyebrow and saying, 'Calm down, Boss! This is no big deal. The real trouble is yet to come. For now, just get his royal pomposity to have a barrel of corn spread in a clearing in the forest, and then borrow Jerry Woodley's birding scope.' (You remember my friend Jerry Woodley, don't you, Tony? The guy with the bike who teaches a course about birds at Laurel Academy?)

"Well, anyway, that night, when the Firebird flies down to feast on the corn, the horse spies her through the scope and then steps on her wing so she can't escape. The huntsman then gathers up his prize. Boy, Tone, don't you wish *you* had a horse like that?"

Tony giggled and nodded his head.

Walt continued his tale. "No sooner does the king take possession of the pyrotechnic partridge, however, than his avaricious, lustful heart recalls another of his deepest desires. 'I say, chappy, you promise to be a most useful blighter. What say you go now and procure for me a princess . . . and not just any princess! Bring me the Princess Vasilissa, who lives by the sea at the far end of the world.

I saw the photos of her winning the Royal Tropic Surfing Contest, and I fancy a lifetime of tumbling in her well-tanned arms, don't you know.'"

"Walt!" Amy exclaimed, mock-seriously.

"Sorry!" Walt blurted. "Sometimes I forget what audience I'm working with! Yes, well, despite the king's impossible command, the horse, once again, calmly reassures his master: 'No worries, Exalted Boss and Master.' (The clever equine's sarcastic side is coming out more and more.) 'This is nothing, but remember, I'm warning you: More trouble, even worse trouble, still lies ahead. Those Firebird feathers bring just as many trials and tribulations as they do treasures!'

"Under the horse's instruction, our hero assembles a golden tent with matching beach umbrella, also laying out an array of Little Debbie snack foods and a selection of fine foreign wines. He is waiting for Princess Vasilissa on the beach as soon as she disembarks from her daily bronzing-and-tubing expedition on her father's cabin cruiser, ready for a late-afternoon nibble. When she falls asleep after a little too much of the Chardonnay, the huntsman throws her across his saddle and rides back to the king.

"When the princess awakens, however, she insists that she cannot marry the king without the family heirloom wedding gown that lies under a great stone at the bottom of the sea . . . back at the far end of the world. Once again, however, the horse maintains his stiff upper lip (which, after all, isn't that hard for a horse to do), saying, 'Pshaw! You call this trouble?' and soon both charger and chargee stand on the beach, where the horse puts his hoof this time on the shell of a huge crab, who then promises to fetch the gown. The coerced crustacean calls up an army of relatives who quickly execute a pincer movement (composed of several thousand smaller pincer movements), and they recover the dress.

"This time, however, when they get back to the palace, the peeved princess insists that she will marry the king only after the huntsman is punished for his impudence by being thrown in a tub of boiling water. 'I say,' cries the sadistic king, 'this sounds like a ripping good show! Really hot stuff!'

"The huntsman, despairing of his life but having learned where to turn when all hope seems to have, ahem, evaporated, asks permission to kiss his horse goodbye. Despite the sniffling and moaning of the huntsman, the horse is once again optimistic: 'Don't sweat it, Boss! No need for both of us to have long faces. You may be in a bit of hot water, but you'll survive.'

"The faithful animal then speaks a charm, far too difficult for me to pronounce correctly, and almost immediately, the huntsman emerges from the boiling water safe and sound, as well as cleaner and more handsome than he went in. Boy, I *really* wish I had a horse, or even a water heater, like that! Anyway, the king, never satisfied and now brainlessly desiring a similar transformation in personal pulchritude, hops in the tub. Before he has a chance to recognize his predicament, let alone to stew about it, he dies. The people proclaim the huntsman their new king, and Princess Vasilissa, who recognizes that a man is only as good as the stallion he rides, and impressed now with how nicely the huntsman has cleaned up, marries the saddle-sore but still-exultant sovereign, and they spend the rest of their days in love and concord and regal splendor, with the horse as their chief counselor.

"So, remember, Tony, don't walk past any feathers you see on the ground, 'cause they might be Firebird feathers. 'Course, then again, you might not be up for the challenge of a Firebird feather unless you find a horse like the huntsman's to help out. Oh, but then again again, maybe Stumpy would be willing to go along on the quest instead. I'm at the stage in my life, though, where I'd be just as happy to find a *turkey* feather, especially on Thanksgiving morning, with all the good luck it will bring."

Walt didn't think much about it when Stumpy wanted to spend more time than usual outside Wednesday morning. He hoped his buddy was recovering from his broken heart and had thrown himself into his species' annual search for food to store for the winter. What he didn't know was that Stumpy was wandering farther out into the woods around the cabin, on a somewhat different quest. The gray-furred rascal returned around lunchtime but then disappeared again for a good portion of the afternoon. Walt was attending to some bills and other paperwork, and he also used the afternoon to catch up on some reading. When Stumpy returned around four o'clock as the sun was dipping toward the horizon, he was clearly tired, and he curled up in a corner of the couch.

Walt's plan for Thanksgiving morning was to drive to the middle school playing fields to watch the ten-year-olds Shel, Mac, and Hammy in an informal pickup Turkey Bowl football game with some of their friends. He planned to return to the cabin by noon, when traditionally each of his three sons would call, in sequence over the next couple of hours, with holiday greetings from various distant parts of the country. When he went out to the tent around nine o'clock, however, to fire up Lulu the pickup, Stumpy had not yet returned from his morning jaunt. Walt had been planning on taking the gregarious rodent along to watch and visit with his three young friends.

The elderly rodent trainer had long ago mastered the three-noted, two-fingered whistle that Roy Rogers used to employ in calling his palomino stallion, Trigger, and he used that whistle now, hoping to summon Stumpy back from his rambles. He scanned the pine trees around the cabin and looked out toward the line of sassafras saplings along the forest edge, and finally, into view came the familiar gray-and-white figure, looking without a tail like some sort of short-eared rabbit. As Stumpy neared, Walt could tell that he carried something in his mouth, and when he was only a dozen feet away, the squirrel slowed his pace to his characteristic hop-hop-pause-hop gait, as if he were feeling shy.

"What's that you've got, old buddy?" the porkpie-hatted codger asked, just before Stumpy dropped at his feet a big, beautiful wing feather from a turkey. At first, Walt was too stunned to speak, but then he managed to say, "That's a beauty, pal. Did you bring it for me?"

The gray-furred sentimentalist sat up on his haunches and bobbed his head as Walt bent to pick up the feather. "I'm touched," he said, slapping his leg so that the bucktoothed rapscallion vaulted quickly to his shoulder, where he nuzzled the elderly gentleman's ear. "Maybe that myth will prove true, and this feather will bring us both good luck for the next year." Holding the feather in his left hand, he reached up with his right to scratch under Stumpy's chin.

"Say," Walt continued, "I wonder if that luck will rub off on our friends as well. Let's go watch some of Shel, Mac, and Hammy's game, and see if the feather works its magic for them!" Stumpy hopped down and raced to the truck.

16

Stumpy and the Christmas Celebrations

DECEMBER 28, 2011

Christmas has finally passed at Kibbee Pond in Townsend, where Walt Walthers, the elderly weather watcher, lives with his rascally roommate, Stumpy the stub-tailed gray squirrel. As New Year's Eve approaches, the two friends are anticipating a quiet commemoration of the annual restart to the calendar, especially with the wintry temperatures that have finally begun settling in after a warm fall. Looking back at all their planned and unplanned activities in preparation for the holiday, the two friends see that Christmas itself proved a satisfying combination of public and private celebration.

The two cabin dwellers spent a festive Christmas Eve down the road at the little Cape where Amy Riggetti, the spirited young mother, and her six-year-old son, Tony, are living while waiting for Anthony Sr. to finish his tour of duty in Afghanistan and return home. Amy had the day off from her work at Ayer Hair, the beauty parlor, and she spent much of the day cleaning and preparing for the dinner, which consisted of maple-glazed pork tenderloin, oven-browned potatoes in Dijon mustard, apples slices baked with a touch of molasses, and green peas with pearl onions. The homemade squash rolls demand mention as well. With some spare time earlier in the week, she had also set about her annual cookie baking, starting with a batch of cinnamon shortbread (her own adaptation of an old family recipe) and moving on to peppermint puffs (which had crushed peppermint candies mixed into a vanilla dough and which were dipped into whipped egg whites and then sugar and had a chocolate chip pressed on top of each before they went into the oven) and even rugelach (a dry, cream cheese–based dough enclosing a walnut, chocolate, and raisin filling). Whether cleaning or cooking, she had sung Christmas carols and holiday songs as she worked. In fact, she was in the habit throughout the year of humming and singing outright while she did household chores. Although much of the time Amy was not even aware that she was singing, Tony would always remember the clear, unselfconscious flow of his mother's music as the element that most convincingly defined home for him.

Around four thirty, as darkness was starting to descend, Walt and Stumpy sauntered down the hill from their cabin, but Amy had the Christmas lights turned on already, including a string of multicolored ones along the rail of the deck that ran the length of the house's front. Even more striking, however, was the very large inflatable plastic snowman that stood just below the deck, with one arm waving and the other clutching a bundle of brightly wrapped packages. At first, Stumpy, who had been hopping happily along beside Walt, had frozen in mid-stride when he spotted the giant airbag. After all, how could he have anticipated the wobbling bulk of the top-hatted monster apparently cutting them off from their goal? Even Walt hadn't realized that Amy's taste in decoration ran in such garish directions, though time would reveal that the snowman did not, after all, reveal *her* taste. When Stumpy had recovered from his initial shock, his courage returned, and a growl rattled low in his throat.

"Easy there, buddy," Walt said, reaching down with his arm so the squirrel could clamber to his shoulder. "It's not really alive, and it's not really even a snowman. It scares me a little, though, too. Looks too much like the Stay Puft marshmallow man in that *Ghostbusters* movie, as if its smile could dissolve into a set of fangs opening up to suck us in."

At that moment, Tony called from the kitchen door that opened onto the deck. "Hey, Mr. Walt! Hey, Stumpy! How do you like our snowman?"

"I don't know," replied Walt. "Is it safe to walk past that thing?"

"Gee whiz, Mr. Walt. Does it scare you too?" the six-year-old said.

"It did give us both a bit of a jolt when we first saw it, but I think we've recovered now. Where did Godzilla come from?"

Amy had stepped onto the deck in time to hear Walt's question, and her musical laugh rang out in the crisp air. "My parents had it sent down because they thought Tony would enjoy having a huge snowman in his yard even if we don't get any snow for Christmas. But I'm not sure either one of us was completely prepared for it either."

"I guess that's one of the prerogatives of being grandparents, though," Walt said, "indulging your whims in gifts for the grandkids without worrying about all the implications. I fear I was the same way."

Amy laughed again, and Walt was reminded how much he admired the young woman's capacity for maintaining a positive attitude; he knew she had much to worry about, including her husband's welfare far away in a war zone, but her smiles and laughter came freely and naturally, and she spared no time for self-pity. She said, "Well, my parents' taste and mine don't always coincide, and in this case, I'm not sure how long I can pretend they do. If Tony liked the thing more, I'd be fine with it, but he says that its smile is creepy."

"I'd have to agree," Walt said.

By this time, Walt had skirted the inflatable monstrosity and was climbing the steps to the deck. Stumpy's head had swiveled slowly as they passed the snowman, his eyes fixed to the carrot-nosed, coal-eyed face as if some Cyclops were threatening a gray-furred Odysseus as the wily warrior made his escape on board his steadily moving craft. The growl continued to rattle from low in his throat.

Once inside the little house, though, the two guests reveled in the warmth—literal and figurative—that they found. Amy's holiday decorations were more extensive than Walt's, and some of them were familiar. Arranged on the coffee table in front of her battered old paisley couch were the buildings and figurines of the Christmas village Walt had dug out of his basement and loaned his friends; his wife, Annie, had collected the items gradually over the years, and their three sons had looked forward to the village's appearance every year, as had *their* children; Walt had imagined that he would pass the village on to his great-grandchildren if and when they arrived, but he wondered now if the town had found its way to an appropriate home already.

Amy had covered the tabletop with white paper to simulate snow and had added some small pocket mirrors to simulate ponds and a river; then, with Tony's counsel and involvement, she had set out the houses and other structures around a main street and a central commons. The village included a blacksmith's shop, a bank, a general store, and even a boat-builder's shop, along with a number of cottages and more imposing residences. After Walt removed his coat, the trio sat down in the family room that opened to the kitchen in one large space and fantasized about which of them would live in which house in the village. Tony picked a big house near an open field that he took to be a playground—that way, his ten-year-old buddies Shel, Mac, and Hammy could play baseball and football with him when they came to visit, and Walt and Stumpy could have their own guest room so they'd feel at home anytime. Amy chose a snug little bungalow on the outskirts of the village, which she said looked as though it nestled below a mountain with a forest nearby. "It reminds me of the house where I grew up," she explained. Walt picked a big farmhouse that, paradoxically, sat in the center of town near the common. "I like that gazebo in the square," he said. "I imagine the town brass band would come and play there on summer evenings, and we could sit out on the front porch and hear the music just fine: Sousa marches and maybe some Ellington or even Django Reinhardt. I imagine a village like that would have a café or ice-cream stand somewhere, too, that would be easy to get to. I wouldn't mind a spot to hang out and chat with folks or get a cup of coffee and a muffin."

While the humans were sharing their imaginative visions, Stumpy had divided his time between listening to their conversation and admiring the Christmas tree that Walt and he had helped the Riggettis fetch from the woods. The warm white lights and brightly colored ornaments revealed a stronger aesthetic purpose than did the more haphazard decorations on the tree Walt had set up for Stumpy back at the cabin. After the conversation had continued for several minutes, however, the squirrel had suffered the onset of a burst of energy, and as was his wont when he visited his friends, he suddenly exploded with a scrabbling of his tree-climber's claws and tore off around the central staircase, making three or four high-speed circles before abruptly stopping, back hunched, to stare wide-eyed at his human friends, who were all convulsed in laughter at the rascal's antics.

"Well, Tony," Walt said, "it looks as if our friend there has got a skeeter in his scooter once again. Maybe you should take him outside for some exercise before he tears your mother's house down."

As soon as Amy got Tony bundled into his parka, scarf, mittens, and wool hat, the two youngsters stormed out the door to see what inspiration would hit them. Before they went, Walt said jokingly, "Watch out for that snowman, Stump! He gave us a chilly reception when we arrived, and I don't think he finds squirrels as charming as we all do. Don't do anything to get him angry. I'm pretty sure he's already got an inflated notion of his importance, and you wouldn't want to burst his bubble!"

"Let's play Lewis and Clark," Tony said when the two youthful friends were off the deck and along the edge of the woods; he'd seen a program about the Lewis and Clark expedition on the History Channel at his grandparents' house recently. As their play evolved, the two explorers peered out from behind trees—or in Stumpy's case, down from their branches—and snuck up on the Native American settlement they had discovered. They lurked just at the edge of the circle of light that surrounded the house, but soon, carried away by the excitement of Tony's scenario, the squirrel made a bold move, defying the malevolent snowman standing guard outside the settlement; the gray-furred scout dashed up the telephone pole at the edge of the pull-off that serves as Amy's driveway and then shinnied along the cable that runs from there to the corner of the Cape's roof. Now in full swashbuckling mode, Stumpy became even bolder and leaped from the cable toward the string of Christmas lights along the deck rail, successfully grasping the wire at the far end of the deck.

Unfortunately, as secure as his grip was, the lights themselves were merely wrapped around a single small nail at that end, and the daring marauder's weight was just enough to dislodge the brightly blinking strand from its anchor. Inevitably, like a pirate swinging from the rigging of his ship toward the deck of some Spanish galleon, Stumpy found himself swooping directly toward the dreaded snowman guard. When he struck the middle section of the snowman's body, the impact knocked the breath out of the squirrel, and he let go of the lights, bouncing once more off the broader base of the tripartite sculpture on his way to the ground. Although Tony had gasped with concern as Stumpy had swung toward the air-filled

Polyphemus, he couldn't help laughing now at the slapstick effects of the rodent gymnast's exertions. "Have you been watching that TV show *Wipeout?*" he asked, nearly cackling with laughter. The snowman stood, rocking slightly, but essentially unaffected by the impact.

Now, however, Stumpy's dander was up. He dashed up one of the wooden uprights supporting the deck, scooted along the rail, and launched himself, intentionally this time, at the snowman, which stood there, smug in its mocking silence. The mammalian ninja landed, teeth bared and tiny claws gripping, on the crown of the snowman's top hat, and from the ground below, Tony could hear the pop and hiss as the plastic tore open and the air began its escape. This time, Stumpy's descent was less precipitous, and he rode the slowly collapsing monster all the way to the ground. He stepped calmly away from the ignominiously crumpled snowman while Tony stared, openmouthed.

When the adults heard the story and surveyed the carnage, Walt apologized, but Amy's attempt to hide her giggles quickly failed, and she managed to sputter, between gasps, "That's one problem solved!" Soon, all three humans were laughing together, and Stumpy was looking even prouder of himself than he had been in the immediate aftermath of his triumph . . . if that is possible. They went back inside to savor their Christmas Eve dinner and share presents.

Christmas morning, Walt and Stumpy were up early enough to watch the sun brightening the eastern horizon through breaks in the clouds, but Walt, as a professional weather watcher, knew that the overcast would settle in before long. Since the roommates were expecting Amy and Tony for a Christmas brunch later in the morning, Walt wanted to take advantage of whatever glimpses of sun he could get. Putting on his parka, a scarf, a fur-lined hat with earflaps, and his lined leather mittens, he called his roommate to the door and headed out to peruse the shoreline. The overnight low had been nine degrees, and although the pond had thawed around the shore during the warm days in the middle of the previous week, the ice had formed once again. Near the shore, the surface was still essentially transparent, but farther out, the pond had whitened to opacity, except for some open patches well out to the south and east. He thought he could make out the dark shapes of mallard ducks on the ice near those openings. "We'll have to leave some corn out for those guys this afternoon," he said to Stumpy. "Another cold night should close things over completely."

Walt glanced back toward the tree line, where Nelly, his rowboat, lay, inverted and covered with a tarp. "I'm glad Shel, Mac, and Hammy came by to help me get Nelly and the dock out last week." (The dock is an aluminum affair with trailer tires that allow it to roll in and out of the water with relative ease.) Walt continued, "I was afraid I was waiting too long, but we didn't get the freezing weather early in the month the way we usually do. And I just didn't want to let go of the dream of summer; that season held particular joy for me this year." As the two headed back up the slope toward the cabin, Stumpy veered off toward the shed where Lulu the pickup truck was parked. "You staying out longer?" Walt asked. "Don't forget we've got a bit of Christmas celebrating to do." Stumpy spun around mid-stride and sat up, facing Walt and bobbing his head. "All right," Walt said in response, "I can see you've got important business to take care of. Let me know when you want to come in."

As Walt was brewing coffee a moment later, he heard a scratch at the door and opened it to a blur of gray fur that darted across the room to the Christmas tree where it stood by the bathroom door. Before Walt could say anything, Stumpy had flown up the tree and into the cardboard shoebox Walt had perched there the week before to serve as his roommate's "swinging bachelor's loft." A moment later, Stumpy emerged again, ignoring Walt's laugh and seeming to feign obliviousness to anything out of the ordinary in his actions.

"Well, I do have a couple presents for you, old friend," the kindly geezer said, walking to the kitchen closet, opening the door, and reaching inside to pull out a large red cloth bag with a string of small bells attached. "Wanna take a look?" He set the bag down in his recliner, and Stumpy was out of the tree and up in the chair in almost the same instant, poking at the tie that held the bag shut.

"Here, let me loosen that for you," Walt said, and as soon as he had released the string, the squirrel's head and upper body disappeared into the bag, the stump tail twitching excitedly as the rodent rooted for his gift. "Actually, there are two things in there. Why don't you bring out the round one on top first?"

Stumpy pulled back out of the bag, drawing something toward him with his paws until the round object rolled into the hollow in front of the seat back. As Walt chuckled, the squirrel looked from the cranberry-colored object up at his friend and then back again, chittering quietly as he did so.

"Do you know what that is?" Walt asked. "It's a pomegranate! It's a kind of fruit Annie used to get during the holidays when the boys were young. Sometimes she cut them in half and decorated wreaths with them, but she always kept at least one for us to sample, and I thought you might want to try an exotic fruit for Christmas this year. The seeds are dark red and tasty—sort of tangy but also pleasantly sweet. Let me get the peel off for you."

Soon, Stumpy was smacking away as Walt handed him the individual seeds, although the old-timer also reserved a few to pop into his own mouth. "All right. Now that I've started it for you, I'll bet you can get the seeds out for yourself. But don't you want to see what else is in there? I should probably help you getting it out."

The rambunctious rodent dove back into the bag while Walt opened its cloth mouth wide to make extricating the gift more easy. "Here. I've got it," Walt said, pulling out a rectangular package about a foot long by six inches wide, wrapped in newspaper. Stumpy was still partially inside the bag, peeking out. "Hey, you look a little like Little Red Riding Hood in there!" Walt said, chuckling. "Come on out now, though. Maybe we can use your new present for a trip to Grandma's house a bit later." The squirrel climbed out onto the arm of the chair and looked up at the man as if for an explanation.

"Well, here! Peel back the newspaper so you can see what it is!" the man said, anxious to see his friend's reaction. "I made it for you. I had to sneak in some time down in the basement on several occasions while you were out gallivanting with your crazy siblings Burwell and Lansdowne. And keeping it hidden once it was done was a challenge, too, given how much you like poking your nose into all sorts of nooks and crannies! I won't tell you where it was; that way, maybe I'll have a secure spot to hide future surprises."

Stumpy struggled at first with the tape that held the newspaper in place, but Walt used the time-honored holiday phrase: "Oh, just go ahead and rip it!" And that's what the excited squirrel did, using teeth and paws together to uncover a wooden object on runners, with a loop of cord attached to the curved front of each of those runners. The gray-furred rascal seemed to recognize the tiny sled almost immediately, jumping on the wood-stained pine platform and chattering far too quickly for Walt to attempt a translation, though the human grasped the gist of the rodent babble.

"Yes, I can see you want to try it out right away, but I don't think it'll work as well on pine needles as it will when we finally get some snow. Besides, I've got one more gift. This one's for both of us," Walt said, walking to his bureau and pulling a small, brightly wrapped package from one of the drawers. "Wanna take the paper off this too?" he asked as he set the gift down on the kitchen table.

Practice on the sled's wrapping made Stumpy efficient at stripping the green and gold wrapping paper off this package, and when he was done, Walt opened the cardboard box inside and removed from it a music box about five inches square. Beneath the glass cover was a miniature winter scene with three skaters on a small pond and a bench, a bridge, and some sheds nearby. When Walt lifted the cover, the tune "I'll Be Home for Christmas" began to play. He smiled at Stumpy and said, "That was always one of Annie's favorites. She used to sing it around the house at the holidays while she was cooking or cleaning. Tony says that his mom always sings when she works too. No wonder I like her so much." As the song played, the skating figures circled the pond, and when that song ended, another began. Though Stumpy had been revving his engines as if for takeoff a few moments before, he now seemed mesmerized as he watched the spiraling ice dancers.

When the roommates had listened to several more songs and had watched the skaters circle the pond an already-uncountable number of times, Walt looked up and out the window. "Oh, look at that," he said quietly. Outside, a few large snowflakes were falling, and the sight drew him to the window as ineluctably as the skating figures on the music box had drawn Stumpy.

After a minute or more of watching the hovering flakes, Walt turned back to the room before him just in time to see that Stumpy had shaken himself from *his* reverie, had climbed up into the Christmas tree, and was now emerging from his cardboard bachelor's loft with something in his mouth. The squirrel clambered down the tree, hopped over to the man, and set a foil package on the floor before him, then looked up at him expectantly.

"Is that for me?" Walt asked. He bent down and came back up

with the packet in his hands, noting that it was covered with a dusting of debris that seemed a combination of dirt and woody organic matter. “Oh, honey-roasted cashews!” Walt said, smiling. “I’ll bet you had these hidden in your stash of acorns and such out in the shed. Wherever did you get them? Hey, maybe this is the sort of present we should share the way we’ve been sharing the music box. What do you think?”

In answer, Stumpy jumped up to the back of Walt’s recliner and tipped his head toward the seat.

“You think we should sit down and have a snack? I guess I can answer that for you myself,” the man laughed. Then he sat down in the chair, opened the packet, and shook out a handful of nuts, handing one to Stumpy, who had hopped down to the chair arm, before popping one into his own mouth.

After three more nuts apiece, however, Walt shifted in his chair to peer out the window again. The snowflakes were still falling, though so slowly that they seemed suspended in the air or, perhaps, suspended in a moment that had itself been suspended in time. Walt thought immediately of the snow globe he had hung in the Christmas tree for Stumpy as an ornament, but the snow inside that swirled when he shook it, only gradually and momentarily achieving the deceptive stasis of these real flakes. As he watched more closely, of course, each flake did settle lower at an almost imperceptible rate, but for those instants, he felt as if he had stepped out of time.

“What do you say to another trip outside?” the silver-haired dreamer said to the squirrel. “You never know what could happen at moments like this, when time and motion seem like illusions. I remember snowfalls like this one from when I was a kid. I used to go out and try to catch the snowflakes on my tongue. You wanna give that a try?”

Stumpy was at the door almost before the words finished coming out of Walt’s mouth.

“And after that,” Walt said, “there might even be enough snow on the ground to try out your new sled. Merry Christmas, my dear friend.”

17

Stumpy and the Return to School

JANUARY 11, 2012

The elderly man pushed the porkpie hat back from his forehead and let his eyes pass from right to left over the children's faces before him. His gaze hovered briefly on the smiling visage of a dark-haired six-year-old whose left cheek was smudged with something that looked like peanut butter. "Well," the man said, adjusting his red suspenders and leaning forward in the wooden rocking chair beneath the classroom's big whiteboard, "even though you all live in Townsend, I'll bet you don't realize all of the strange things that have gone on around here over the years. I'm going to tell you right now about something that happened a long time ago out near Kibbee Pond, where Stumpy and I live now." He glanced back directly in front of him, where a little blond girl, her head twisted slightly to one side, sat in a wheelchair with a stump-tailed gray squirrel tucked in the crook of her left arm. The man thought he could hear a sound halfway between a purr and a snore coming from the animal.

Of course, you all know by now that the man was Walt Walthers, the octogenarian weather watcher who lives in a cabin out on that pond in the southern part of Townsend, and you also know that the recumbent rodent was Stumpy the Squirrel, Walt's often rambunctious roommate, who has been with him now for over two years. What you might not know is that the peanut butter–covered lad was Tony Riggetti, who lives with his mom, Amy, just down the road from the "two swinging bachelors," as Walt sometimes refers to Stumpy and himself. You might also not realize that the little girl with whom Stumpy was snuggling was Madeline Clough, whom he had met on a previous storytelling odyssey to the kindergarten class taught by Ms. Aristea. Walt remains convinced that Ms. Aristea looks more like a Greek goddess than a mundane, garden-variety human being, and her students hold her in similar reverence.

With the turn of the New Year and the reopening of schools, Walt had accepted an invitation to return to the classroom in which he had started his still-young second career as a storyteller. Just as visiting young people was a good way for him to avoid the winter doldrums, so having a storyteller visit was a good way for teachers to vary the daily routine as winter was starting to drag its heels; for the next three months or longer, Walt had weekly tale-telling sessions scheduled, with Ms. Aristea and also in other classrooms around the town and in neighboring towns as well. He also had a plan to test out a workshop in which he could teach students how to tell stories on their own, and the arresting Ms. Aristea would not rest or stay until Walt had agreed that her students would be the first beneficiaries of his expert advice in that workshop.

Right now, however, the white-haired story weaver was in the midst of sharing a tall tale with his youthful audience. He continued.

"It seems that back in the late 1800s, a young fellow by the name of Jack lived with his elderly mother, a poor widow, out on Warren Road, about a mile and a half from the Cooperage. Although it's now an antiques place, in those days the Cooperage was a barrel-making establishment. That's what coopers are: barrel makers, and in those days wooden barrels were one of the most important forms of container for shipping all sorts of stuff: pickled roosters and peppermint-coated pickaxes, zucchini underwear, bear traps made out of whispers, ferrets trained to hang out laundry . . . anything they *could* ship in a wooden barrel, they would. Anyway, Jack was sweet-hearted but a little slow at getting his thoughts in order. If I weren't concerned about maintaining my reputation for kindness and compassion, I might say he wasn't the brightest bulb in the closet, except that in those days, they didn't have light bulbs or electricity yet. I might say instead that he had the IQ of a bathtub, except they didn't have a way yet to measure IQs . . . though I'm pretty sure they *did* have bathtubs, whether they used them regularly or not. Anyway, Jack had never had a job and didn't seem particularly well suited for anything . . . except maybe basking in the sun like a turtle in warm weather and curling up like a cat near the hearth in cold weather. He and his mother had an old cow and a few chickens and scraped by on what she could make sewing clothes to order for other people.

"Unfortunately, times were hard for everybody, and the orders for clothing stopped coming in. On top of that, the cow went dry, and the hens stopped laying eggs. Soon, the widow had no choice. 'Jack,' she said (and now Walt shifted into a pinched and crabby old woman's voice), 'you're not good for much, and you never even look for a job. I'm telling you now that I can't support you anymore. I work my fingers to the bone while you do nothing. I end up with bony fingers, and my clothes are so old and tattered that they're falling off me, but you don't seem to care. You'll have to take the old cow to town tomorrow and sell her; that's our last chance for any money. And then you'll have to find a way to support yourself because I don't have the means to keep you here anymore.'

"I'll say this much for Jack," Walt continued. "He was always positive in his outlook and never gave up hope even though he sounded a bit like Mortimer Snerd. He said, 'Yes, Mother, I'll take the old cow to town and sell her and then bring the money back to you. Yup, yup! Maybe something else will happen along the way so I won't have to leave you after all.'

"'You're a good boy at heart, Jack,' the widow said, 'even if you're not the hard worker your father was. He never sat around doing nothing and staring into space the way you do, but then again, he was too tired at the end of the day to be much company for me. If you sell the cow, would you use some of the money to buy me a piece of decent cloth? With that, at least I can sew myself a new smock so I don't have to go around half-naked the way I do now. It makes me ashamed to wear rags like these all the time.'

"'Sure, Mother, I could do that. Yup, yup,' Jack replied, and then he curled up next to the fire and dozed off.

"The next morning, Jack attached a rope to the old cow, Dandelion, and led her down to the center of Townsend Harbor, where the market was going on. Eventually, he found his way to a dealer who specialized in worn-out creatures and bony old bovines like Dandelion and who offered him a few coins for the aged beast.

Once he had the money, Jack—very pleased with himself for having sold the cow as his mother ordered and for finally proving himself responsible—remembered his mother's request for cloth. He found a merchant who sold him a piece of brightly colored gingham, which Jack thought was truly beautiful and would please his mother, and after picking up a few other items the old widow had requested, he sat down on a bench in the sun to rest before the walk back home.

"The bench, however, was right outside the Conant Tavern, and as Jack dozed off, some of the town jokesters noticed him. Knowing his reputation as a gullible dunderhead and a gawky numbskull, two of them approached him and convinced him to enter the tavern with them.

"'Oh,' said the one, 'it's the custom around here for a young man who's just sold a cow or any other kind of livestock to have a drink of whiskey and to treat his townsmen to one as well.'

"'Yes,' said the other, 'you don't want to seem like a green farmer from the sticks, do you? This is the way to prove you're just as well-mannered and sophisticated as us town folks!'

"Well, as you can imagine, poor Jack was just like putty in their hands, and they could get him to do whatever they wanted. By the time he came out of the tavern several hours later, it was getting dark, all his money was gone, and he was feeling a little tipsy from drink. Nevertheless, he still clung to the packet of fabric for his mother's new dress, and he set out for the farmstead, weaving along the path as he walked. And he didn't give up hope. He said, 'Well, I've got no money left, and I don't know what I'll do or where I'll go tomorrow morning, but at least I kept my word, yup, yup, and I've got the cloth for Mother.'

"As his unsteady steps carried Jack away from the tavern, however, the darkness deepened, and a wind came up that seemed to push against him. Jack had never seen anything wrong with talking to trees and animals and storms and rocks, so he found himself talking now to the wind. 'Why are you blowing against me?' he asked. 'Wasn't I a good boy? Yup, yup. Didn't I do what Mother asked, and didn't I do what those men said I should do? Yup, yup. Wasn't I generous in buying everyone drinks? Yup, yup. You should get around behind me, Wind, and help blow me home, where I'm trying to go, instead of working against me. Yup, yup.'

"The wind, however, paid no attention to the silly boy and continued to push against him, sneaking in under his collar and poking into his eyes. Though his steps were unsteady and his vision was blurry, Jack soon realized he had come to the edge of a wooded area he had to cross in order to get home. In among the trees were pricker bushes that snagged on his clothes as if they, too, were trying to hold him back, and finally, he came to a thorn tree that had two stalks almost like legs; it was quaking and squeaking in the wind. At this point the silly-headed and somewhat tipsy Jack made a mistake, but the kind of mistake that only a kindhearted person would make.

"'Oh,' Jack said, addressing the thorn tree, which was a little shorter than he, 'you poor old woman, what are you doing out in this windy night? You should be indoors next to a warm fire instead of letting the wind blow the cold ache into all your bones. Yup, yup. Can I do anything to help you on your way? Are you lost?'

"But all the tree said was, 'Squeaky-squeaky-squeak-squeak.'

"'What's that you say?' Jack asked. 'You must be from New Hampshire because I can't understand your accent.'

"'Squeaky-squeaky-squeak-squeak-squeak,' the tree replied.

"'Nope. Didn't get it that time either,' the kindhearted nincompoop said. 'Why don't you try talking slower?'

"But the thorn tree wasn't listening to his suggestion. 'Squeaky-squeaky-squeaky-squeak-squeak-squeak.'

"'Poor old woman,' Jack continued. 'It feels like rain is on the way, and someone your age shouldn't be left out here alone in a storm. Why don't you come home with me to my old mum? Yup, yup. We can give you shelter for the night and a warm spot in front of the fire. What do you say?'

"But you already know what the tree said: 'Squeaky-squeaky . . . squeak.'

"'Why must you be so stubborn?' Jack asked. 'I'm only trying to help. Yup, yup. I can't carry you, you know, but if you don't come along, I'm afraid you won't make it through the night, what with the cold and the wet that seems to be coming. Won't you come along now?'

"But even now the tree didn't answer in a form Jack could understand. Still, the generous young man couldn't leave a fellow creature to face the night unprotected. (You see, he still didn't know it was a little tree and not an old woman.)

"'Dad-gummit!' Jack cried. 'I can't leave you to die of cold!' And he unwrapped the packet of cloth he had bought for his mother to replace her worn-out clothes and began draping it over the thorn tree, going around and around. 'There,' he said. 'That's the best I can do. Yup, yup. I'll come back in the morning to check on you and see if you're still alive, and I'll take my cloth back then. Yup, yup.' With that he turned into the wind once more and resumed his journey.

"When Jack reached home, the cold rain had started falling, but his mother had a warm fire burning, and he brought out the bacon and cheese he had bought before being lured into the tavern.

"'Oh, Jack,' his mother said. 'Did you get me that cloth I asked you for so I can get out of these rags?'

"'Yup, yup,' the lovable dunderhead replied. 'I got you a beautiful piece of cloth, but I don't have it with me right now.'

"'What do you mean?' the old woman asked.

"'Well, I was coming up to the edge of the forest on my way home, yup, yup, and I came upon this old woman sitting out in the wind with the rain and sleet threatening. She must have been deaf, yup, yup, because I kept yelling at her, but she wouldn't say anything back. No, she wouldn't. I got to feeling sorry for her, and she made me think of you, yup, yup, and I knew I wouldn't want *you* sitting out in a storm all alone without anything to keep you warm, so I wrapped your piece of cloth around her to try to warm her through the night. I'll go back for it in the morning, yup, yup.'

"'You're a good boy, Jack, to think of your old mum and be kind to strangers. You get to bed now, and you can go back first thing tomorrow.'

"Well, tired though he was, Jack got up at dawn and was soon on his way back to fetch the cloth. He whistled as he walked, happy that the storm was over and that the sun was coming up behind him. You can imagine, however, what had happened to his mother's beautiful cloth since he had wrapped it around a prickly old thorn tree with a heavy wind blowing and sleety rain falling all night. It had flapped and fluttered and flipped and flared for hours, and by the time he got back to the site, that fabric was torn to ribbons and of no use whatsoever.

"'Wait a minute!' Jack exclaimed. 'You were a prickly old thorn tree all along, and I thought you were a helpless old woman? I wrapped my mother's good cloth around you, and this is the thanks I get? You've tattered it and torn it and trashed it worthless? Wait *another* minute! Maybe you're not a tree at all but a witch who can change her shape, and you did this just to torment me, yup, yup. Well, you're not going to get away with it! I'll teach you to be mean to somebody who's trying to be kind to you, yup, yup! I'm going home for a shovel, and then I'm coming back, yup, yup, and I'll dig you up, and you'll never pull a dirty trick like this on anybody again!'

"Jack stormed off for his mother's place, snatched a shovel from the shed, and went charging back. He dug all around the tree, cut its roots, pulled it out of the ground, and heaved it a good ten feet away from the hole. When he glanced back down into the hole, however, he saw something glinting through the sand and dirt. And when he scraped more dirt away with the shovel, he found a big metal box with a padlock on it. And when he had pulled the box out and broken the padlock with the shovel, he lifted the lid to find . . . a thousand or more gold coins!

"Well, Jack did a little dance all around the box, and then he lifted it up on his back and carried it home, where his mother couldn't believe their good fortune. 'Oh, Jack,' she said, 'we've got all the money we'll ever need now!'

"Suddenly, though, the kindhearted Jack's smile faded, and he said, 'Oh, Mother, *we* may be set for life, yup, yup, but what about that poor little tree? Without it, we'd still be poor, and I went and dug it up and threw it away! Now I feel terrible! I've got to go back and put things right, yup, yup!'

"So Jack filled a bucket with water at the hand pump, grabbed the shovel, and went back . . . again. He lifted the little tree up gently, gave it a little kiss despite the thorns, spread out its roots, placed it carefully back in the hole, filled in the dirt again, and poured out the water. And he made a promise: 'Little tree,' he said, 'I'll come back every day and give you a drink of water until you get your feet on the ground again, yup, yup. Wait a minute! A bush doesn't have feet! I'll come back every day and give you a drink until you sprout new green leaves and grow a foot! Well, not *that* kind of foot! You know what I mean: until you grow a foot *taller*!'

"And Jack—good boy that he was—kept his word. He went back and watered the tree every day until it had grown *two* feet . . . I mean, two feet *taller*, and by the next year, that little tree had blossoms on it. Jack and his mother, of course, lived very happily with the money from under the tree, and if you ever go past the woods out there off Warren Road, be on the lookout, because you just might see Jack as he carries his bucket of water out to his thorny friend."

Walt leaned back in his chair and looked around at the rapt expressions on the faces of his listeners, who were quiet for a moment before they began to clap their hands. Stumpy woke up at the noise, climbed up to give Madeline's cheek a quick nuzzle, and then jumped down and hopped over to Walt's chair so he could share in the adulation that the silver-haired tale spinner was receiving.

"Oh, Mr. Walthers," Ms. Aristea said with a laugh, "you do have a way of making a story your own!"

"Thank you, ma'am," Walt replied in his cowboy voice, "the gray-furred varmint and I aim to please, and we're grateful for an attentive audience like these here polite young people. I tip my Stetson to them . . . well, actually, it's a porkpie, isn't it? Hm-mm."

Walt asked if the kindergarteners had any questions for him, and they had plenty, about stories and storytelling but also about Stumpy and squirrel behavior in general. One boy wanted to know if the loss of his tail had handicapped Stumpy in any way.

"I suspect it has its disadvantages," Walt answered, "especially since squirrels use their tails to communicate with each other. For instance, they flip them up over their backs when they're agitated. And I suspect the tail is helpful with balance in running along branches and jumping. But Stumpy seems to get by just fine, and he still hangs out sometimes with his siblings Burwell and Lansdowne, who seem to accept him and understand him and certainly romp with him. And I think he may even have developed some special communication skills of his own as compensation for his loss, abilities other squirrels don't have. For instance, I've never heard any other squirrel purr the way he does when he cuddles . . . like with Madeline when he listens to stories with her here in the classroom. Plus, he may be a better swimmer than most squirrels because he doesn't have a tail to slow him down and drag soggily behind him."

The questions continued for a while, and the students wanted Walt to look at the projects they had completed recently: structures made with all natural materials, including the fairy house Tony had assembled with moss and bark and sticks that Walt had helped him and his mom, Amy, find in the woods near the pond. Stumpy was anxious as well to renew his acquaintance with Sloppy Joe, the big brown catfish that Ms. Aristea keeps in a ten-gallon aquarium with some other, smaller kinds of catfish. When Stumpy approached the tank and peered in, Sloppy scooted up and down along the glass in front of him, as if he expected the squirrel to toss in some sort of tasty treat. After bobbing his head in greeting, the gray-furred rascal turned to the other tanks and pens in which the ambitious young teacher keeps her menagerie of critters, from horseshoe crabs to chameleons to mice to a large tan rabbit named Butterscut.

At last, though, Walt knew that he and the gregarious squirrel had to leave. Still, they couldn't get out the door without promising to return the next week to tell at least one more story. "Ms. Aristea," Walt said with a bow, "we'll be looking forward to pestering you folks again next Tuesday then, but right now, we need to hurry home. There's one pricker bush out behind the cabin that I've been meaning to check underneath, and I want to get my shovel out before the ground freezes up solid. If I find a metal box full of gold coins, I'll split my winnings with you, and we can take all your students with us on a trip to Las Vegas." And with those words, Walt and Stumpy were out the door and on their way back down the hallway. They knew that Lulu the pickup truck was waiting for them out in the parking lot, ready to carry them back home to the little cabin out on Kibbee Pond.

18

Stumpy, the Seawitch, and the Hag

JANUARY 18, 2012

The old man's voice rang with a husky sweetness, his words slowing as he neared the end of his tale. "The coyote galloped away toward the deeper woods, his tail tucked between his legs as if he were a pet dog caught raiding garbage cans. I looked up, and there, hanging safely from a branch by his hind legs, was Stumpy. The rascal . . . had gotten away . . . after all." With those final words the man pointed toward the stub-tailed gray squirrel that was sitting on the lap of a smiling ten-year-old girl in the back row of the classroom. Taking his cue, Stumpy sat upright on his haunches and bobbed his head several times in quick succession.

As the twenty or so fourth graders commenced clapping, Walt Walthers, the professional weather watcher who now doubles as a storyteller, removed his porkpie hat briefly and bowed at his audience. His busy post–New Year schedule had brought him to a classroom at Spaulding Memorial School in Townsend, where his audience included three acquaintances from the summer who had become regular visitors out at the cabin on Kibbee Pond where Walt and Stumpy keep their abode together. Shel, Mac, and Hammy, sports-loving and sometimes mischievous young fellows, had heard many stories from Walt before in the more intimate atmosphere out at the pond.

"Well, I've got one more story to tell today, and it's a long one, so I hope I haven't bored you already," Walt said, looking around. Twenty or so heads immediately shook no, and the storyteller knew it was safe to continue. "This is an old tale from Scotland that I used to tell my three sons when they were younger, and it involves three brothers that make me think a little bit of my three buddies out here in the audience." Shel, Mac, and Hammy beamed proudly at the acknowledgment. "By the way," Walt added, "the story is called 'The Seawitch and the Hag.'

"Many miles ago and many years away," Walt continued, "an old fisherman lived beside the ocean, but he was having a run of bad luck, and only an occasional fish swam into his nets. One day, he rowed his boat far out on the water, desperate for his luck to change. Suddenly, the water roiled, and up next to him rose a seawitch. I can't begin to describe that horrible creature, but suffice it to say, she was a truly hideous ten on a one-to-ten scale of true hideousness, and she was all the more terrifying for her snakelike voice when she said, 'S-s-s-so, what will you giff me, s-sir, if I s-s-send s-s-shoals of fis-s-sh to s-s-settle in your nets-s-s?'

"When the old fisherman said he had next to nothing to offer, the seawitch shook her snaky hair and tightened the grip of her tentacles on the boat's side before saying, 'Will you giff me your firs-s-st s-s-son if I s-send you fis-sh aplenty?'

"'I would give you my son, but I have none,' the fisherman replied, 'and now my wife and I are too old. I have only an old mare, an old dog, my wife, and myself.'

"'Ah, yes-s-s,' said the seawitch, 'then take these s-s-seeds. Here are three s-s-seeds to give your wife, three s-s-seeds to give your hors-s-se, three s-s-seeds to give your dog, and three more s-s-seeds to plant behind your cottage. In time your wif-f-fe will bear three s-s-sons, your mare will bear three f-f-foals, your dog three pups-s-s, and three trees will grow behind your hous-s-se. When one of your s-s-sons dies, one of the trees will wither as a s-s-sign. Go home now, and bring me your first s-s-son when he is-s-s three years old. Forget it not.' And with that the seawitch sank back into the sea.

"Well, the fisherman followed his instructions, and all happened as the seawitch had foretold. The fisherman's wife bore him three sons, and the other seeds proved viable, too, and for three years, the fisherman prospered, his nets always full. However, as the time of reckoning approached, he realized how much he loved, not just his first son, but all three of his sons. On the appointed day, he went out to fish, but he went alone. The seawitch rose beside his boat. 'Where is-s-s your s-s-son?'

"'Oh, drat!' the fisherman said. 'I did not bring him with me. I forgot what day it was.'

"'Yes-s-s, yes-s-s, s-s-so you did,' the seawitch whispered. 'Then you shall have four more years with him, and s-s-see if s-s-saying farewell *then* will be any eas-s-s-ier. Forget it not.'

"And although the fisherman rejoiced to have four more years with his son, he found, when the time was up, that he could not bear to part from the boy, so he went back to fish without him on the appointed day.

"'Where is-s-s your s-s-son?' the seawitch asked when she rose.

"Oh, was I supposed to bring him? Darn, I forgot all about that! I must be getting forgetful in my old age. Wait, what did I just say?"

But the seawitch showed no anger and calmly granted the fisherman seven more years before she would return to repeat her claim. Again, the father rejoiced, but again, the years flew by, his nets always full with flounder and cod and hake and halibut, until at last, the new date approached. Then he found he could not sleep, and he sighed and moaned until his son asked him what was troubling him. When the father told the boy the truth, his son said, 'Let me go to the seawitch. I will not be a source of trouble for you.' When the father refused, his son said, 'Then, if you won't let me face my destiny at sea, you must get the blacksmith to make me a mighty sword, and I will go in the opposite direction, inland and even to the ends of the earth, to find what fortune awaits me.' Boy, doesn't that sound just like something a real hero would say?" Walt raised his eyebrows, and everyone in the audience nodded their heads in agreement.

"The first sword the blacksmith cast and a second one even bigger and twice as heavy both fell apart when the son waved them in the air, he was so strong and brave. When the smith brought the third sword, he said to the son, '*This* is the sword for a true hero, and this is the sword for you. The arm that wields this blade must be mighty indeed.'

"As soon as the boy lifted the sword, he knew it was meant for him, and he said, 'This *is* the blade for me, and now I will respect my father's wishes and go as far from the sea as I can go.' He saddled one of the black horses that his father's mare had borne and set off with his black dog, one of the three pups, beside him.

"When he had ridden only a short way, the boy came upon the carcass of a large salmon in the road, over which a wolf, an otter, and a falcon were fighting. He dismounted, intervened, and divided the fish among the three animals so that each got a fair portion.

"'For your assistance,' the wolf said, 'I thank you.'" Walt paused. "You see, they were all really polite and classy animals despite their disagreement, which must have been caused by their hunger. You know how crabby we all get when we're hungry, right?" The children all nodded vigorously again. Walt continued the story, and the wolf continued his expression of gratitude by making a vow: "'If swift-running feet and razor teeth can ever help you, just think of me, and I shall be with you.'

"Then the otter said, 'If swift-swimming feet can ever help you, just think of me, and I shall be with you.'

"Not to be outdone, the falcon said, 'If swift-beating wings and piercing claws can ever help you, just think of me, and I shall be with you.'

"With no destination in mind, the boy, the horse, and the dog traveled onward, and the fisherman's son eventually took work as a cowherd at the castle of a king, where he would be paid according to how much milk the cows in his care produced each day. However, because the cattle had already stripped the grasses nearby, our hero quickly realized that each day, he would have to take them farther and farther away from the castle to find suitable grazing. After all, it wasn't a good sign that after the first day, he received only a few brussels sprouts and a mug of dirty water in exchange for the quarter pail of milk Bossie, Flossie, Nutmeg, and the rest of the girls had produced; he felt like an udder failure. Therefore, on the second day, he led the bevy of bovine beauties much farther, until they discovered a rich green meadow.

"The cattle gorged themselves, but when the time came for the boy to lead them home, he heard an odd sound—*crish! crush*—like little stones crunching and great grains of gravel flying up, and suddenly, a sword-carrying giant was rushing toward him. 'HOO! HAR-R-R! HAWGAROO!' the giant bellowed. 'My teeth clamor for the meat of your bones! You have fed your cattle on my meadow; now they belong to me, and you are a carcass to cook over my fire!'

"The boy laughed and said, 'Talk costs nothing. Deeds alone

yield rewards.' That was a slogan that he had just invented for himself, and he thought it sounded suitably heroic. The two went to battling, and as they came together, the black dog leaped on the giant's back, and before the dust had even flown up, the boy's sword had severed the head from the giant. Then the fisherman's son rode off to investigate the giant's house, which proved full of wealth of all sorts, but the boy left all as it was, taking nothing. After all, true heroes care more about honor and altruism than about financial gain. That night, after their rich grazing, Dandelion, Murgatroyd, Strathspey, and the rest of the herd produced so much milk that the king had to send for the carpenters to build more wooden milk pails. The boy got all the food and drink he wanted, even whoopee pies for dessert.

"The next day, our hero had to lead the cows even farther afield and on past the first giant's land. That's right, the *first* giant, because no sooner had he found another beautiful green pasture and loosed his heifers to chow down on the tender shoots than a second giant, even more savage than the first, came charging toward him—*crish! crush!*—like little stones crunching and great grains of gravel flying up, with a 'HOO! HAR-R-R! HAWGAROO! I shall fill my goblet with your blood and pick my teeth with your bones!'

"And of course, the boy replied, 'Talk costs nothing. Deeds alone yield rewards.' He had decided that he really liked that slogan. And the dog leaped, and the head was off that giant before the dust could even fly up. The boy was exhausted when he got home that night, but the milk flowed like . . . well, like milk from cows that have had plenty of delicious grass to eat and thus are healthy and happy. And so they continued for some time.

"One night, however, the fisherman's son returned to the castle to find everyone wailing in lamentation, and he learned only then of the three-headed water creature that lived in the nearby loch—a *loch* is what the Scots call a lake. Every year, that monstrous beast expected to be fed with the flesh of a young, healthy human being in exchange for leaving the people alone the rest of the year, and the time for this year's feeding was at hand. Even worse, the lot had fallen this year to the king's own daughter, and she was to be surrendered to the creature the next day. Some hope remained, however, because a suitor—a cross-eyed, carrot-haired cook—had promised to save the girl in exchange for her hand in marriage—well, not just her hand, you know, but all of her.

"The next morning, the king's daughter and the cross-eyed, carrot-haired cook went out to the loch to meet the water creature. When they reached the cliffside above the deepest part of the loch, they saw some ripples stirring on the water's surface, and before he could even be sure the monster was rising, the cross-eyed, carrot-haired—and cowardly—cook was sprinting for cover. The girl stood alone to face the monster until suddenly she saw the fisherman's son, her father's cowherd, riding up on his black horse with the black dog at his side.

"'Good morning, lassie. Whatever are you doing out here in such a lonely spot so early in the morning?' You see, he was pretending not to know what was happening.

"'I won't be lonely for long,' the girl replied. 'The flesh-eating water creature is coming to lunch soon, and I'm the only item on the menu.' Somehow the boy's calm demeanor had transferred itself to her.

"'Perhaps I'll keep you company for a while, if you wouldn't mind combing my hair. I got some burrs in it while tending to the cattle, and I can't get them out by myself.' He lay down with his head in her lap.

"'If you fall asleep, how will I wake you?' she asked, thinking ahead to the monster's arrival and admiring the boy's shiny sword.

"'Just take that ring off your finger and put it on my little finger. You have very delicate hands, you know,' he replied. Then he went to sleep.

"Soon, the girl saw black clouds rising over the loch, and for a moment a waterspout spun above the waves that swelled and boiled on the surface. Inside the stormy squall, the three-headed water creature was spewing spit and spray, and the king's daughter decided to wait no longer to wake her companion. When she slipped her ring onto his little finger, he awoke and strode forward with his sword and dog to confront the vehement behemoth.

"The fell opponents closed with each other, and the boy wasted no breath on words until he had swept one of the heads from the creature. 'Well,' said the monster, with a philosophical tone and an unexpected lisp, 'even if you've taken *one* of my headth, I ththill have two otherth,' and it raised huge waves in its wake as it disappeared into the depths of the loch.

"'Well done,' the girl said, 'but until the other two heads are gone, the beast will return each day to claim its due, which, I'm afraid, is me.' The cowherd scooped up the beast's head, strung it on a cord of twine, and gave it to the girl before waving goodbye in silence and riding away.

"On her way home, the cross-eyed, carrot-haired, cowardly cook slunk out, snatched the head from her hand, and said he would kill her if she did not report that *he* had performed the decapitation. 'Well,' she said, 'and who else but a hero like you *could* have done the deed?' She had, over her short life, already honed her skills at sarcasm and rhetorical questions.

"The next day, the king's daughter and the cross-eyed, carrot-haired, cowardly cook returned to the loch, and again that Judas goat slunk away, and the cowherd rode up to take his place. 'This time,' the cowherd said, 'you can awaken me by putting the ring from your right ear onto my right ear. I had my ear pierced last night just in case an occasion like this came up.' When the lake-dwelling leviathan arrived, the boy and dog faced it and claimed a second head before the beast fled, hissing and lisping and sloshing. Again, however, the cross-eyed, carrot-haired, cowardly cook took credit for facing the beast.

"On the third day, all happened as before, except that the cowherd asked the king's daughter to awaken him with the earring from her left ear, and when the water creature arrived, the fighting was more intense than before, with groaning and grunting, and grunting and groaning. When the two combatants paused to draw breath, the monster said, 'With justht a thmall drink of water, I could betht you yet,' and the boy replied, 'With just a small drink of wine, I could claim your last head.' Fortunately, the king's daughter had packed a picnic lunch that morning, with cucumber sandwiches and a tasty Chablis, and she ran to the boy with some of the wine in a long-stemmed glass. 'Thank you, dear,' he said just before sweeping the third and final head from the water creature's trunk. Immediately, the monster's body was gone, and only a puddle of water and a pile of sand remained. The boy strung the third head, like the others, on a cord of twine and gave it to the girl.

"Once again, however, the cross-eyed, carrot-haired, cowardly cook threatened the girl's life if she contradicted his lies, and when they returned to the castle, the king congratulated the cowardly cook and promised to hold the wedding the next day. 'First,' he said, however, 'take the heads off the cords of twine without cutting the cords. No one but the hero who put them there will be able to take them off.' But of course, the cross-eyed, carrot-haired, cowardly, crassly corrupt, and coercive cook could not do so, nor could anyone else at court, until someone thought to send for the cowherd boy. When he arrived, the king's daughter said, 'The man who took off the creature's heads has my three rings,' and when the smiling fisherman's son threw the rings down on the table, she said, 'You are the man for me,' batting her eyelashes at him with only a slight bit of irony. The king, of course, wasn't thrilled to have to marry his daughter to a cowherd, but he couldn't go back on his word. The ceremony took place the next day, and they lived very happily together."

Walt paused and raised his eyebrows as if ending the story, but he saw puzzled expressions on the faces of most of the third graders. "What? Did I leave something out?"

From his left came the voice of the heavyset Hammy, who, had he not been sitting down already, probably would have been hitching up his pants. "But Mr. Walt, what about the seawitch? Is she ever going to catch up with the fisherman's son?"

"Hm-m-m," Walt replied, "I guess I could make something up if you want. . . ."

"Oh, Mr. Walt, you know you weren't done yet," Hammy said, laughing. "There are too many loose ends you haven't tied up."

"All right, then," Walt said. "Let me see, then. Oh yes. One day, the king's daughter, who really did love picnics, got her new husband to take her to the oceanside for more of those cucumber sandwiches and that Chablis, but while they were looking for lobster buoys to take home as souvenirs, the seawitch slung her tentacles ashore, dragged the boy into the depths, and gulped him down in one mouthful.

"Nearly blind with grief, the king's daughter wandered the shoreline until she met an old blacksmith, who advised her to bring all her most beautiful jewels and spread them out on the shore. When the girl had done so, the seawitch rose up again above the waves and said, 'Luffly are your jewels-s-s, o king's-s-s daughter!'

"'Lovelier still is the jewel you have taken from me,' the girl replied grimly. 'Grant me one glimpse of my husband, and you may pick any one jewel you like.' The seawitch urped the boy up into her mouth so that his head stuck out, and the king's daughter said, 'Give him back to me completely, and you may take all you see here on the shore.' So the seawitch flung the boy ashore and took all the jewels, but she also swallowed the king's daughter, leaving the fisherman's son desolate, desperate, and bereft on the beach.

"The old blacksmith appeared then and told the distraught young husband, 'You have only one way to kill the seawitch and reclaim your beloved. On an island in the middle of the sea lives a slender-legged, white-ankled deer; if you can catch that fleet-footed flier, she will turn into a raven. If you can catch the raven, it will turn into a trout. Inside the trout's mouth is an egg, and inside the egg is the seawitch's breath, and if the egg breaks, she will die. You can use no boat to get to the island, though, for the seawitch will sink it and devour you.'

"'That's easy enough, then,' the boy said. 'I won't need a boat.' And he called his horse and dog, climbed into the saddle, and held on as both of the animals gathered themselves and cleared the distance from shore to island in one mighty bound. Once there, he sent the dog after the slender-legged, white-ankled deer, but that creature proved too swift even for the black dog.

"Oh, thought the boy, if only the salmon-eating wolf were here! and immediately the wolf was with him. The wolf quickly overtook the deer, which turned into a raven. 'Oh,' said the boy, 'it's time now for the falcon,' and immediately, the bird was there with him and took the raven out of the sky, but then the black bird turned into a trout that leaped into the sea. 'Oh, if only the otter were here!' and the otter was with him and after the trout, and when the otter brought the fish to the beach, an egg fell from its mouth. When the boy put his foot on top of the egg, the seawitch rose from the water and begged for mercy: 'S-s-spare my life, o fisherman's s-s-son, and rec-c-ceive all you s-s-seek!'

"'Then give back my wife!' the fisherman's son cried out, and immediately the king's daughter was at his side, and when he grasped her hand in his, he crushed the egg with his foot. And they went home and lived together with great joy."

Walt paused and once again looked around the room. "Can I stop now?"

Again, Hammy spoke up. "Mr. Walt, didn't you say the king wasn't happy that his daughter had married a cowherd?"

"Right you are, Hammy! I love having an audience that is paying attention. Well, the king's daughter insisted that her husband and she go on a celebratory picnic, and the cunning king suggested a particular spot for them to visit at the western border of his demesne. When they arrived and were sipping more Chablis and nibbling more of those delicious cucumber sandwiches, the fisherman's son noticed a black castle off in the distance. 'What castle is that?' he asked, with a true hero's curiosity, but his wife said she didn't know.

"That night, the fisherman's son asked his father-in-law about the black castle. 'Oh,' said the king, 'you don't want to go anywhere near *that* place. No one who has gone there has ever returned, even the greatest heroes.' You see, the king knew that his brave son-in-law could never resist the implied challenge, and he hoped the cowherd would never return. Of course, the next morning, despite his wife's pleas, the boy set off for the black castle.

"When the boy knocked at the front door of the castle, a tiny old woman, a wrinkled old hag with a wheedling voice, opened it. 'O-o-o-o-oh,' she said in her wheedling voice, 'beauty of all beauties, treasure of all treasures, where have you come from, my darling, my own?' Because she seemed harmless and gentle, the boy went in, but she had lulled and gulled him. Before he even had a chance to look around, she struck him on the head with a magic club that turned him into a pillar of stone. And that, it would seem, was the end of our hero and the end of our story."

But this time, none of the third graders were having any of Walt's foolishness, and they all shouted out, "No! Keep going!" One or two even thought to add, "Please!"

"All right," Walt said. "Remember that the fisherman's son had two brothers back at home and that three trees in the yard were linked to their lives? Well, when one of the trees withered, the fisherman's hut was just as mournful as the king's castle was when the king's daughter's new husband did not return. Nevertheless, the fisherman's second son mounted *his* horse and called *his* dog and set off to find out what had happened to his brother. His father had given him a fish bone that turned into an ivory-hilted sword, and the sword gave him understanding beyond his youthful age. He rode until he came to the king's castle, and because he looked exactly like his brother, the king's daughter rejoiced at her husband's return. To avoid spending the night in her bedchamber, however, he told her that he had made a sacred vow not to sleep at all that night. The next day, the king's daughter invited the second son on one of her picnics, and over a glass of the Chablis, the second son noticed the black castle in the distance. 'What is that place?' he asked, and the wife replied, 'Didn't you ask me that just the other day, and didn't I answer that I didn't know? I *knew* you weren't listening! You never listen to me!'

"'Oh,' he answered, 'I'm sure I didn't ask about the castle before now,' and—of course—he wasn't lying. Soon, he was on his way to the castle door, where the hag welcomed him, only to strike him with her club and turn him, too, into a pillar of stone. This time, I won't even ask you if you want me to continue.

"Back at the fisherman's cottage, another tree withered and wilted, and the youngest brother set out with his horse and dog to see what he could see about the fate of his brothers. He, too, carried an ivory-hilted sword that gave him understanding beyond his years, and he, too, came to the king's castle, where the first brother's wife greeted him as if he were her beloved. 'If you slept away from me the other night, you won't deprive me of your company tonight. I might think you didn't love me after all,' she said, batting her eyelashes—something she was becoming quite good at—and he replied, 'Many men have business that must take them from their beds on occasion, though they regret their absence deeply.' With that comment, they entered the chamber and lay down, but he placed a cold sword between them.

"The next morning, where did the wife want to go but on a picnic, and as the third brother bit into a cucumber sandwich, he saw the black castle in the distance and inquired about it. 'Didn't I tell you about that castle the last two days?' the king's daughter asked, but he simply said, 'No,' and set off toward it with his horse and dog.

"When the wheedling little hag met him at the door, she said, 'O-o-o-o-oh, come in, joy of all joys, love of all loves, and tell me what makes you happy.' The third son, however, with the sword-given understanding, was suitably suspicious, and before the tiny, wrinkled crone could swing her club, he struck off her head. The sword fell from his grasp, however, and the crone picked up her head with both hands and returned it to her shoulders. When the dog leaped at her, she struck the valiant animal with the magic club, and he fell to the ground, but the third son grabbed the club from her and gave her a taste of her own . . . well, would we call it medicine? Anyway, he bopped her one on the bippy, and she stiffened more quickly than Han Solo when he was frozen in carbonite. Then the third son saw his brothers standing stonelike side by side; when he touched them and his faithful dog with the club, they all three came back to life.

"With the hag's keys, they explored the castle, finding gold and silver and beautiful clothing and an entire room full of men who had been turned to stone. After restoring all those victims to life, the three brothers returned to the king's castle, where the remorseful king realized he had misjudged his son-in-law and could not afford to anger him, or his two strapping brothers, any further. The old king renounced the throne and gave his crown to the first son, who ruled wisely. The two brothers extended their visit for a year but then returned home with the crone's gold and silver and became contestants on a television dating show called *Who Wants to Marry a Fisherman's Son?* They became as famous as they were rich, and if they have not died in the meantime, they are all living still."

The students didn't need Walt to tell them that the story was truly over this time, and they responded with enthusiastic applause. "Thank you all," Walt said, "but now Stumpy and I have to get back home to the little cabin out on Kibbee Pond. We have some Chablis and cucumber sandwiches waiting for us. We'll be back soon, though." Waving, and with Stumpy perched on his shoulder, Walt strode off down the hallway, feeling like a much younger man and ready for whatever lay ahead, whether it was a seawitch or a hag or an afternoon nap.

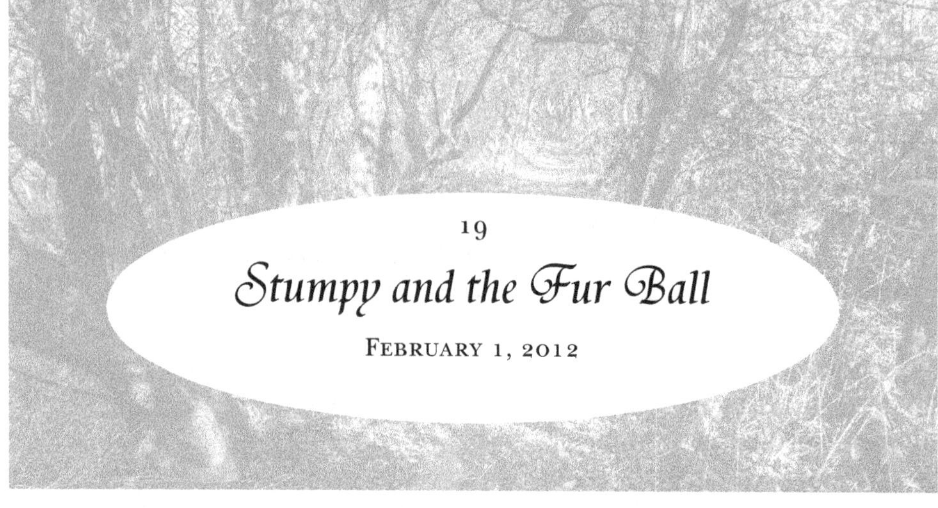

19

Stumpy and the Fur Ball

FEBRUARY 1, 2012

A stub-tailed gray squirrel lay sprawled out on the right thigh of the elderly man, who was running a wooden-handled cat brush through the animal's fur while a sound not unlike the purr of a contented feline emanated from the general vicinity of the little creature's mouth. A small boy with a smudge of peanut butter on his cheek sat on a wooden chair next to the man's recliner, smiling as he watched, and soon the besmirched urchin spoke.

"Why do you do that, Mr. Walt?" (Because, of course, the man with the brush was Walt Walthers, the professional weather watcher and storyteller who lives in his cozy cabin out on Kibbee Pond in Townsend.) "And why is Stumpy purring so loud?"

"Well, Tony," Walt replied (because, of course, the boy was Tony Riggetti, the six-year-old who lives down the road from Walt with his mom, Amy), "I have two main reasons for brushing the ol' Stumpster. First, the scoundrel seems to like it. And by the way, that's the reason he's purring: It feels good. My other reason, though, is that I want to keep his coat healthy, and I don't want him to get any fur balls." Tony giggled slightly, and Walt raised his eyebrows as he looked at the boy. "What's so funny about fur balls?"

"I don't know what they are," Tony answered, "and they sound funny. What *are* fur balls?"

"Well," the white-haired coot replied, pushing back the porkpie hat that sat on his head even inside the cabin, "people usually associate fur balls with cats, especially long-haired ones. When they groom themselves with their tongues, cats often swallow the hair that comes out, and some of it stays in their stomachs; because they can't digest the hair, though, they eventually urp the clump of hair back up, and what you end up with is a fur ball . . . or a hair ball, as some people call them. I guess I don't really think Stumpy will get a fur ball, but he likes the brushing, and I enjoy doing something nice for him. After all . . ." At that moment, Walt gave a small cough, cleared his throat, and said, "Excuse me! I guess I've got a frog in my throat."

Tony broke out in guffaws of laughter at that remark, and Walt smiled while raising his eyebrows once again. "Don't tell me you've never heard anybody say he had a frog in his throat before? You must have had a deprived childhood!"

"How big is the frog?" Tony asked. "Is it jumping around? Does it feel slimy?" He continued to laugh, though the questions sounded sincere.

"Hold on there, half-pint!" the kindly geezer said, chuckling himself. "First of all, the frog in my throat is not a real, literal frog. Sometimes you get some phlegm or gunk stuck back there, so you have to clear your throat to try to get it out. That's what people mean when they talk about having a frog in their throat, though now that I think about your questions, I suppose it may feel a little like an actual slimy frog moving around in the back of your throat near your uvula. A pretty small frog, though." Tony was, again and suddenly, convulsed with laughter. "So *now* what's so funny?" Walt asked.

Tony regained control long enough to sputter, "Yule-view-la," before the tide of hilarity rolled over him again.

"Oh, for heaven's sake," Walt said, unable to keep himself from laughing too. Stumpy had sat upright on Walt's leg and was watching man and boy as if they had finally surrendered to the insanity he had always suspected was lurking beneath their surfaces, but also as if he were not at all surprised.

Walt managed to regain some control and said, "It's *uvula,* the little piece of flesh that hangs down from the roof of your mouth in back where your throat begins. It helps keep food out of your nose, and it also helps people make certain sounds that go into speaking. I suppose you've never heard the word 'ululate' either? The uvula can help you ululate." With that comment, Tony continued to cackle, the laughter gurgling in the back of his throat.

"Gee whiz," Walt said, "you're almost ululating now yourself! But actually, you sound more like an old chicken cackling away. I used to laugh like that, too, when I was your age or younger. Did I ever tell you what my dad did to me in the bathtub one night?"

Still giggling but a bit quieter now, Tony shook his head.

"Well," Walt said, "I must have been about four at the time, and I really loved my nightly bath. Both my parents would come in while I was in the tub and talk to me, and my dad could always get me laughing, making up words or telling me silly stories. I would laugh hard, way back in my throat the way you've been doing, and Dad started saying, almost every night, 'Walter, you laugh like an old chicken. You keep cackling like that'—cackling is the noise chickens make—'and you're going to lay an egg.' Well, that just made me laugh harder, and every night, I would wait for him to say that and cackle all the harder when he did.

"One night—and I don't remember how long the routine had been going on at that point, maybe a few weeks—I was in the middle of my bath, with the bar of soap and the washcloth and a wooden boat floating beside me and my parents sitting next to the tub—it was one of those big, tall ones that stand on four legs, clawfoot tubs, have you seen those old-timers? Anyway, I was cackling away as usual when something brushed my leg. I looked down, and there, floating next to me, was a chicken egg! My parents said that my jaw dropped, and I just stared at the egg in silence. I can remember trying to recall if I had felt any unusual sensations in my nether regions as I was laughing. I don't remember now if my parents told me right away or if they waited and let me work it out for myself, but Dad had hidden the egg in the bathroom earlier so he could drop it in the tub when I was laughing and not paying attention. At that moment, though, I *was* a little scared that I might be turning into a chicken."

Tony was laughing again, but not so hysterically. "Mr. Walt," he managed to say, "did you ever have any *frogs* in your bathtub?"

"You're right," Walt answered, chuckling. "It seems more logical to have a frog in the tub than in your throat, and most people would be more likely to swallow eggs, at least cooked ones, and thus have them in their throats than in their tubs. I guess I'm just weird!" He raised his eyebrows, shrugged his shoulders, and shook his head.

"Wait a minute!" he then said. "I *am* weird! My nose runs, and my feet smell. Shouldn't it be the other way around?"

Stumpy had continued to watch the two humans, as if in disbelief that they could actually be talking about such bizarre subjects, but now, he hopped off Walt's leg to the floor, took a bound toward the kitchen, and then stopped, sitting up on his haunches as he stared toward the laundry basket that sat next to the kitchen table.

"Oh no you don't, you rascal!" Walt called out. "No more socks for you! Pretty soon I won't have any left if you keep stealing them." The alert codger turned to the boy to explain. "You see, Stumpy has developed a passion for my socks. When I do a wash in the basement and then bring the basket up, I've learned I have to be watchful. I usually put two socks together and then pull the elasticized opening of one of them over both so they stay together in one cylinder-like cocoon. Your mom probably does the same with *your* socks. It's easier to store them that way and to avoid losing one. If I'm not careful when I bring the clean laundry up, though, Stumpy will sneak over, grab a pair, and run off with them, almost as if they were nuts he was taking to a secret cache. He's done it several times in the last month or so, and I haven't figured out where he's got them socked away, so to speak, or even if he's putting them all in the same place. Twice, I *have* caught him later on carrying a pair around, as if he was constantly moving the location of his stash. I have to keep reminding myself to put clean clothes—or at least my socks—into their drawer right away."

"What do you think he wants them for, Mr. Walt?"

"I'm not sure," the silver-haired oldster replied with a laugh. "I've known a lot of dogs, though, who liked stuffed toys, so maybe it's something like that: a toy to carry around and show off or something to cuddle with. Come to think of it, I've known a couple dogs who liked to steal rolled-up socks and carry them around, too, and my son Larkin told me once about his cat Calliope; he has trouble laying out his clothes for the next day because that cat will steal his socks and drop them in different parts of the house. Sometimes she even walks into the living room carrying his underwear! Sounds like an epidemic of clothes-stealing!"

Tony was laughing again. "You don't think Stumpy is *eating* them, do you, Mr. Walt?"

"Whoa!" said Walt, laughing with him. "That would be worse than a fur ball, for sure! Now, what time is your mom due to get back from work?"

"Five o'clock," the boy replied.

"Hm-m-m," Walt said, "that should give us enough time for me to tell you a story, and I just remembered one that has a frog in it . . . and a fur ball!"

"Oh good!" Tony answered.

"Did I ever tell you," Walt continued, "that I have a prejudice in favor of frogs and against toads? For some reason, I associate frogs and their hopping with positive energy, in contrast with the more sedate and sedentary toad, which can hop around but is more likely to sit quietly, waiting for its prey. In folktales, frogs are often tricksters, and that doesn't surprise me. In one Chinese tale, a quick-witted frog triumphs over a hungry tiger. Sometimes, the story is called 'One Hair Ball.'

"A starving tiger sneaks up on a frog along the banks of a river. The frog, who has been watching his shadow and admiring himself as he practices jumping as high as he can, notices the prowling tiger too late to flee; in an instant, he sees that he'll have to rely on quickness of another sort. 'I beg your pardon!' he exclaims in a haughty voice. 'And just who do you think you are to disturb me in my much-cherished privacy? You seem rather a bedraggled, scruffy creature, though I presume you are some sort of cat. Is it possible that a cat of any sort can look so . . . so *ratty*?'

"In embarrassment that the insult may be justified, the tiger looks down, shuffles his feet, and apologizes. 'I really am frightfully sorry to intrude, and I wouldn't *dream* of being so rude unless the circumstances were *really* extraordinary, but I am afraid . . . that they are. You see, I've had nothing to eat for several days, and even though my dear old mother taught me always to be polite, hunger has driven me to the extremity of appetite and to this horrifying breach of etiquette. With your permission, I'd like to eat you so I can regain the strength I need to pursue bigger, more savory game. Normally, something as inconsequential and ill-tasting as a puddle-paddling frog I simply wouldn't bother with, but I'm afraid the desperate nature of my circumstances has made me less finicky than usual. I do hope you'll forgive me for any inconvenience I may cause you, but it will all be over in a few moments . . . as long as I can conquer my gag reflex.' You see, at heart, this tiger really is a well-mannered creature.

"The frog, again thinking fast, replies, 'Oh, I see. You are a *tiger*, aren't you? It's hard to be certain given the dreadful state of your grooming and hygiene, but I believe I read once that tigers sported striped coats rather like yours. Well, *I* don't generally concern myself with such puny beings as tigers. Perhaps your hunger has kept you from recognizing me. I am the King of All Frogs. I'll forgive you for your mistake, but I can assure you that no jungle-bred bumpkin of a feline could ever be a match for my regal, even divinely mandated grandeur or my extraordinary abilities. Nevertheless, since you *are* so obviously in need of food—I can count all your ribs, you know—I'll give you a sporting chance to earn me as your next meal and to realize—through direct experience—that I am, contrary to your current belief, the most appetizing entrée on the menu, today or any other day. I propose a leaping contest. If you *are* such hot stuff as you claim, then you should be able to leap farther than I can up the riverbank opposite us. If you can go farther than I go, I'll surrender myself for your culinary delight.'

"Wasting only a moment or two for a boast about the inevitability of his victory, the tiger tenses, tail twitching, and jumps. Just at the instant of take-off, however, the frog—behind the tiger's visual range—bites onto the tip of that striped tail, then nimbly times the release of his grip so that he lands farther up the sandy shore than does the tiger. When the tiger turns back toward the river to boast about his awe-inspiring, record-setting performance, he sees no frog.

"Then his amphibian adversary clears his throat *behind* the hungry beast. 'Ahem. I say, well leaped, Tiger! I never thought a feeble fur-wearer like you would be capable of jumping almost half as far as The Ruler of All Water and Land, but you've done quite well for someone from inferior stock. You see, they don't call me "Your Highness" for nothing!'

"Unfortunately, however, the angry and still ravenous tiger steps, growling, toward the frog, his patience and manners almost completely unraveled. Recognizing that he may have gone too far, the web-footed wise guy quickly proposes—in the spirit of fairness, according to him—another contest. 'I say there, chap, perhaps it *was* unfair to expect a malnourished and malodorous mammal like you to best me at jumping, which is, after all, my forte. They don't call us "hop frogs" for nothing, you know. Why don't we try something more your style and give you a fighting chance? I propose . . . a spitting-up contest! After all,' the trickster says, 'your stomach must have at least ten times the capacity of mine. You should be able to spit up *much* more than a puny "puddle paddler" like me! On with our new contest! All you have to do this time is regurgitate more than I! Go ahead. You may make the first attempt.'

"The tiger sticks a clawed finger down his throat but can produce only a meager strand of bile and saliva. After all, he hasn't eaten in almost a week. The frog, however, coughs slightly and immediately produces a small orange-and-black hair ball, apparently tucked carefully into his cheek after the jumping contest. 'Oh, pfff-t,' he exclaims, 'that *is* disappointing! But it has been nearly a whole day since I last ate. Now that I think of it, it was just about this time yesterday afternoon that another tiger, though a rather better-groomed and physically fit one, showed up while I was doing my daily martial arts leaps along the shore. I'm afraid I wasn't very hospitable, but I was *so* hungry after my workout that . . . well, you see how it is. Let's just say that I have never been a *strict* vegetarian. This hair ball is all that's left of that other fellow, I fear.' The tiger hesitates only a moment before fleeing back into the jungle.

"There, in the jungle, the panicked tiger, in full flight, crashes into his friend the fox, who asks what has so frightened him. The gasping tiger manages to blurt out something about the terrifying King of All Frogs, at which point the fox dissolves in laughter. 'You? Afraid of a mere frog? Terrified of a hopping, croaking nothing? Take me to him. I haven't had lunch today.'

"'No, you don't understand,' the tiger pants. 'You, too, will run when you encounter this regal carnivore, this royal, destroy-all warrior king, and you'll leave me behind to fall prey to the monster!'

"'Oh, come on,' says the fox. 'Do you want the word to get out that you're afraid of a puny pond paddler?'

"'*Don't call him that!*' the tiger roars. 'He's not puny; he's G-R-R-R-E-A-T!' And then the tiger falls into a trembling fit. When the fox continues to laugh at him, the tiger musters *some* courage.

'Well . . .' he says, 'maybe I can go back . . . if we tie our tails together for greater strength. And that way, I'll know you can't run away without me.'

"Hiding his mirth, the fox assents, and the tiger, who learned knot tying from a Boy Scout he once ate, ties their tails tightly together. However, as they approach the river, they find the frog calmly waiting on the bank. Once again, the bulging-eyed leaper seems unperturbed in the face of hungry predators.

"The frog waits only a few moments before speaking. 'Hey!' the web-footed deceiver shouts. 'Where have you been, you sleazebag fox? I told you to bring my tribute *immediately*, and that was three hours ago! I only let you live because you promised to bring me something bigger than yourself to eat. And what is this ratty, mange-ridden morsel you've brought for my dinner today? It looks like a tiger, only puny and pitiful.' You can appreciate now, Tony, just how quick a thinker that frog is, pretending that the fox is working for him!

"Well, at the frog's clever words, the tiger no longer has to choose between fight and flight; he simply turns and bolts again for the jungle. How could I have been so stupid as to step right into the perfidious fox's snare? he thinks. No way I'm going to wait around to end up as one more hair ball!

"When the tiger stops running, he is far out in the jungle, and only as he drops to the ground, breathing ragged and heart nearly shattered with the effort, does he realize that his tail is still tied to that of the fox, who has been battered to unconsciousness along the jungle path. Untying the knot, the tiger vows never again to go anywhere near the territory of the King of All Frogs."

Tony was smiling when Walt finished, and the aged tale-spinner asked, "So what did you think?"

Walt could see the twinkle in Tony's eyes as the boy said, "I really liked the story, and I'm glad that tiger didn't end up with a frog in *his* throat."

"Oh, good one!" Walt said, letting out an almost tiger-like roar of laughter. The two of them were still chortling a minute or two later when they heard a knock on the door just before Amy, Tony's mom, opened it and stepped through.

"What's going on here?" Amy said, grinning broadly. "It sounds as though a boatload of pirates were *yo-ho-ho*-ing over a couple kegs of rum."

"Oh no," Walt said, assuming an expression of disingenuous innocence, "there ain't nobody here but us chickens!"

Gales of laughter swept over Tony again. Walt shook his head and, chuckling himself, said, "Here he goes again! Never heard *that* one either?"

"What have you boys been up to, anyway?" Amy said, trying to resist the storm of hilarity that was spinning around her son and her elderly neighbor.

"Not that much," Walt replied. "Really. We had a conversation about etymology, and then I told him a story or two."

"Yeah," Tony piped in, "Mr. Walt said he was going to teach me to ovulate."

"Well, no, not exactly," Walt objected. "The word is *ululate,* you bandit!"

Now Amy was laughing as hard as the others had been, but just then Walt glanced toward the kitchen. Then he was shouting, "Hey, you flop-eared varmint, get *away* from my socks!" At that instant, Stumpy streaked past the three humans with something in his mouth.

20

Stumpy and the Magic of Kibbee Pond

February 8, 2012

Amy Riggetti had long suspected that something about Kibbee Pond was magic, and although she wasn't certain what that something was, she suspected that it had a lot to do with her nearest neighbor, Walt Walthers, and with Stumpy, the stub-tailed gray squirrel that lives with him. Those two make their abode in the cabin just up the road from the little Cape that Amy rents and lives in with her six-year-old son, Tony, and although Walt claims to be in his eighties, he seems, rather than slowing down, to have become more spry and youthful in the six months that Amy has known him. His mind is agile and quick, always twisting words and their meanings in new directions, punning and playing with sound and with sense as if he were an Olympic athlete in training for verbal rather than physical events. He laughs so frequently, and makes others laugh so frequently, that she has begun to wonder if joy and good humor have special healing or at least time-defying powers.

With her husband, Anthony, serving in Afghanistan and with her parents an hour and a half away in central New Hampshire, Amy feels especial gratitude for the close proximity of her warm-hearted neighbor, so generous with his time and so patient with both mother and son. And of course, his rambunctious rodent roommate is a constant source of camaraderie and entertainment as well. If her six-year-old is content to spend nearly all his free time with the grandfatherly man and the mischievous squirrel, she is herself occasionally envious that she isn't involved in more of the threesome's adventures. Still, her part-time work at the spa and salon Ayer Hair helps to ensure that they eat well, and she can imagine no more reliable babysitter or gently effective educator than Walt has proven in their time as neighbors.

Besides providing for Tony, Amy's other major concern is being available for the unpredictable phone calls from her husband on the other side of the world. To that end, she carries her cell phone with her at all times. She never knows if Anthony will be able to call once in a month or after only two weeks, or if she might have to wait even longer; she also can never be certain at what time of day the call will come. She understands intellectually the importance of military security and tries never to complain, but she has broken down once or twice, though only briefly, in Walt's company. She remembers how the first time that had happened, over morning coffee after the bus had picked Tony up for kindergarten, Stumpy had leaped into her lap, put his front feet on her breastbone, and gently nipped her left cheek, as if he couldn't stand seeing her unhappy and felt compelled to distract her; she could only smile and laugh at the furry rascal's concern, even though Walt had been appalled, and she had heard him speak harshly to Stumpy for the first time.

"It's all right, Walt," she had said, laughing. "See? His tactic worked!" Walt had risen then and quietly taken four honey-roasted cashews from the kitchen cupboard; as he fed them one at a time to the no-longer-crestfallen squirrel, the elderly man had apologized and stroked Stumpy's nose with one finger, the way the tawny rascal best likes.

"Neither of us likes to see you down," Walt had said quietly to Amy.

Amy was not surprised when she dreamed about Walt one night last week. With the intuitive sense that she had been following the elderly man in clandestine fashion for some time, she found herself watching from behind one of a grove of white pines along the pond's shoreline as Walt slowly approached the threshold between snowy beach and ice. As he stood there in his winter coat and porkpie hat, he lifted both arms and spread them as he faced east, and then he spoke; though Amy could not make out his actual words, he seemed to be addressing the absent sun, lost in the grayness of what seemed an early morning sky. Removing first his porkpie hat and then his gloves, the man slowly knelt and touched his fingers to the ice at the very edge of the shoreline. Before Amy could register what was happening or had happened, the ice and snow were gone; at her feet lowbush blueberries had leafed out, and all up and down the shore birdsong was trickling into the now-warm air. When she looked back at the man on the shore, he was unzipping his coat, and as he opened it, a dazzling glare of sunlight exploded from the east, blinding her for a moment. After several seconds of blinking to clear her vision, she again looked at the shore, where the coat lay in a crumpled heap and where, instead of a man, a fur-covered, bewhiskered critter frisked at the edge of the sand. In Amy's dream, the otter turned toward her and held her gaze for several seconds before springing into the water, back humping and powerful tail lashing the surface once. Then the animal disappeared beneath the wind-stirred, light-spangled surface. She tried looking out across the water to where she anticipated the otter's head emerging when the animal needed to take a breath of air; although she had to look almost directly into the rising sun, she thought certain she saw not one but two bewhiskered faces emerge with a spiraling and tussling of serpentine bodies before the wind was again all that altered the surface.

In Amy's dream, she remained standing with her hands pressed against the grooved pine bark for what must have been several minutes but seemed only moments. Then a rhythmic, quiet splashing caught her attention, and she saw a human swimmer approaching who proved, as he emerged from the pond, to be a young, beautiful, and very naked man. As water poured from his smooth torso, he reached down to the crumpled winter coat, lifted it, and draped it around his shoulders before turning once again toward Amy and holding her gaze. Then he turned back, letting his motion carry him into a spin, taking first the shape of a waterspout at the pond's edge, but then exploding into a storm of gray-blue feathers that resolved itself into a long-legged avian shape. That yellow-eyed, hoary-chinned, black-crested heron again turned toward the concealed Amy and held her gaze before flexing his stilt-like legs and lifting off the sand, wings slowly rowing in their oarlock sockets as he gained altitude and continued his deliberate strokes toward the northeast. Then Amy saw another huge bird sculling from the east on a course to intercept the first bird over the swamp, and in almost the same instant, as is the way of dreams, she saw the two birds together, the newcomer swooping up over the first bird, which rolled over on his back in midair and then peeled away to one side before righting himself and reaching out with his beak to tweak the tailfeathers of the other heron. The other—almost certainly a female, Amy believed—gave out an unmusical *SKRONK!* before settling in next to the first bird, the two now wing-stroking together toward the green trees on the northeast horizon.

The cell phone on the bedside table beside her shrilled Amy awake, but for a few moments, she could not remember where she was, what the phone's ring meant, or what she was supposed to say when answering a ringing phone. She managed a husky "Yes?" though she continued to wonder if such a response would bring down ridicule from the caller; she was so disoriented from her dream, however, that she might not even have been able to tell the caller what her own name was. Fortunately, she didn't have to.

At first as the male voice came through on the other end of the line, all she could say was, "Oh . . . Anthony! Oh . . . " and then she registered that her husband's voice was racing excitedly through something about *coming home, Sugar Babe*! And then she was finally and fully awake, though the dream hovered in the background, feeling linked umbilically to these waking moments. Despite the happy news, or perhaps because of it and her recognition of the still uncertain and difficult interim, Amy found herself sobbing after the call. It had ended, as their calls always did, with Anthony beginning the chorus of a Johnny Cash song: "Flesh and blood needs flesh and blood," and with Amy finishing it: "And you're the one I need."

The next day, Amy had the chance to tell Walt her news: that Anthony would be coming home in May. She had of course told Tony at breakfast, but after she saw him onto the yellow school bus driven by Walt's friend and former driver's ed student Ellie Wentworth, Amy had again walked up the hill and turned into the gravel of Walt's driveway. She paused as she stepped up onto the deck and looked out over the surface of Kibbee Pond, but it was firmly frozen despite the events of her dream.

Over coffee and with Stumpy doing his non-species-specific purr as he dozed in her lap, Amy told Walt of Anthony's scheduled return.

"You must be excited," Walt said, his eyes smiling at her over the rim of his mug.

"I am," she said, looking down for a moment before again raising her eyes to his, "but I'm also a bit apprehensive. We've been apart a long time, and I don't know how that place and his work may have changed him."

"Well," Walt said, "and you also may not be fully aware of how *you* have changed in the meantime. It'll take some work on the part of both of you . . . but you can do it. You have to give yourselves and each other the time to rediscover who you are and what your relationship means. Of course, even couples who are together every day have to do the same. We're never static even when little seems to be changing in our lives. Sometimes, though, in the times of the greatest upheaval and difficulty, you get to see the *really* essential things that stay the same, and those are what you build on. I find I say things best with stories these days. You mind if I tell you one now?"

Amy smiled back at the soft-spoken elder. "Please do."

"Well, I guess this one is a little like the one I told you back at the end of summer when we had our river-shoes expedition and picnic along Route 31. This one, though, comes from the far north and the Inuit people. I hope *you'll* get Inuit, too, if you see what I mean." Amy giggled.

"It's a myth, and like all myths, as you know, it takes place in the time before time really began, when the forms of things were still fluid, and both animals and humans could change their shapes. A great hunter named Qivioq lived on a lonely plain beside a silent lake, where one summer day, he heard the unexpected sound of laughter and saw six lovely girls bathing in the water. Qivioq sat in silent joy and watched them, but suddenly, the sky darkened, and a raven, black as nothingness, darted from above to grab one of the six white-feather cloaks that lay along the shoreline. As it carried the cloak away in its beak, the girls dashed out of the water, frantically crying, 'Hira! Hira! Hira!' Five of them threw on their feather coats, turned into snow geese, and flew away, but one remained on the shore, calling mournfully after them, 'Hira! Hira! Hira! Hira! Hira!'

"Have you ever seen a snow goose?" Walt asked, and Amy shook her head. "Beautiful birds," he continued, "smaller than Canada geese, and many are almost pure white. I saw them up close one winter out on the Hudson River, near where my sister lived. My list of favorite birds is very long, but snow geese have to be in the top ten. But back to the story!

"Qivioq slowly approached the trembling girl on the shore, saying, 'Let me help,' and holding out his fur sleeping skin for her. After a moment, she allowed him to drape it over her quivering form, and over the next weeks, Qivioq's patience and gentleness gradually won over the girl. He called her Hira because she spoke only in her snow goose language for their first weeks together. Nevertheless, as winter approached, Hira agreed to be his wife and sewed warm clothing and a kayak cover for Qivioq; when the snows settled in, they built an igloo together. In the spring she bore him a son, whom they named Hiro, and the next year brought a daughter, Hirola.

"Seven years passed happily, but one spring, an ominous thunder-and-lightning storm descended on the plain beside the silent lake, and the evil raven returned just as the snow geese were flying over and calling, 'Hira! Hiro! Hirola!' to their sister and her children. That bird as black as nothingness lurked behind the flock, concealing himself under the pure-white purloined feather cloak and crooning a magic spell to Qivioq's beloved wife, who went mad with her instinctive desire to fly again. She gathered white feathers that had fallen from her sisters and placed them between the fingers and along the arms of her children and herself. Calling out, 'Hira! Hiro! Hirola!' she ran along the lake shore and launched herself into the air, turning into a sleek snow goose as her children joined her in flight. Although they called out to Qivioq, he could do nothing to join them, and their tears fell on him like warm rain as they banked to follow their other relatives to the south.

"The silent lake and lonely plain were more silent and lonely than ever, and after only a short span of days, Qivioq rolled up his fur sleeping skin and set out to the south, calling, 'Hira! Hiro! Hirola!' For countless days, he battled over mountains of ice and endured snow slides, calling out in the bitter cold until his very words froze and shattered like thin ice at the edge of a pond. He walked on and on. After a hundred days, Qivioq descended the last mountain toward the sea as the air warmed around him.

"On the shore of the sea, Qivioq found the kind giant Inuqpuq carving the ivory of a walrus tusk. Exhausted and unafraid, Qivioq stood beside him and watched as the giant struck curving chips of ivory from the tusk with his jade ax. The chips tumbled into the cold brine and immediately turned into silver salmon as Qivioq watched in awe. When he asked the giant if he had seen three beautiful snow geese fly past, Inuqpuq boomed out a question of his own: 'WOULD THEY HAVE BEEN CRYING, "HIRA! HIRO! HIROLA!"?'

"'Yes,' Qivioq managed to say as he fought back bitter tears.

"'They flew south, weeks ago,' the kindly giant said, in a gentler voice, 'over the great sea. Their tears fell on me like warm rain.'

"'I have no kayak, but I must follow them. Can you help me?' Qivioq asked.

"'HO, HO, THAT I CAN!' Inuqpuq rumbled with his customary volume, and he knelt down on the shore of the sea and touched his fingertips to the edge of the tide line, then spoke a spell in words as soft as a rustling breeze, which Qivioq nevertheless heard. Almost immediately, the surface of the water began to ripple and then roil, and then Inuqpuq shouted out in excitement, 'DIVE IN AND JOIN QAQAQ, THE GRANDFATHER OF ALL SALMON. RIDE ON HIS BACK, AND HE WILL CARRY YOU WHERE YOU NEED TO GO.'

"Though the water was freezing, Qivioq plunged into the depths and swam among the myriad of fishes, who swirled and then drew apart in concert to reveal their monarch. 'Take hold of my dorsal fin,' the huge fish said, 'and breathe from the bubbles of air we pass through,' and they were in motion before Qivioq could reply, the whole mass of fish flashing through the depths like a flood of molten silver. Past whales and seawitches and nameless monsters they swam for day after day, though beneath the sea, the heroic human saw neither sun nor moon nor constellations and thus had no way to judge the passage of time. Eventually, however, Qaqaq dashed to the surface, and Qivioq viewed for the first time the warm southern world he had never seen before and had hardly even dreamed of. With thanks to the generous salmon, he waded ashore and searched until he found a path up into the mountains.

"Although Qivioq did not know where he was going, he determined to follow that path and see where it would lead him. On the cliffs at the crest of the mountain, he spotted an opening in the wall of rock, and beyond, he could see a green valley and smell the freshness of flowing streams and flowering plants. As he tried to step through the opening, however, the thieving raven met him, a black shadow between Qivioq and the springtime valley, a pool of nothingness waiting to suck Qivioq in. Still holding Hira's white-feather cloak, the raven grew in an instant to the size of a polar bear.

"Undaunted, Qivioq said, 'Where is my wife? Where is my son? Where is my daughter?' and he closed with the black-feathered fiend. They wrestled for one hour, and then they wrestled for two; they wrestled while the sun rose in the morning and while it hovered overhead at noontime and while it dipped down toward its rest, and they wrestled all through the hours of the night. As morning came again, however, Qivioq gathered all his strength and threw his evil opponent over the cliff; the ocean claimed the raven, swallowing his emptiness into its depths, and it never gave him back.

"Carrying his wife's feather cloak, Qivioq descended into the green valley, at the far side of which he saw a tent. He broke into a run when he saw his two children in their human forms, and they ran to greet him. His wife, Hira, stood by the entrance to the tent, a faraway look in her eyes until she turned and saw her husband. He stepped slowly toward her, proffering the white-feather cloak. 'This is your birthright,' he said quietly.

"'And I will use it to return to my home, which will always be by your side,' she said, looking into his eyes. 'Let us leave now. We have been too long away.'

"They left the valley and descended from the cliffs to the shore of the sea, where Qivioq knelt and touched his fingertips to the tide line, then spoke the words of the spell he had learned from Inuqpuq. Qaqaq, the grandfather of all salmon, returned, and each member of Qivioq's family grasped the fin of one of the fish for the voyage back home. When they reached the northern shoreline, all the salmon leaped into the air and, before they struck the ground at Inuqpuq the giant's feet, turned back into chips of walrus ivory.

"Inuqpuq bellowed, 'I AM HAPPY FOR YOU, FRIEND QIVIOQ, AND YOU HAVE PROVEN YOUR WORTH IN RECLAIMING YOUR FAMILY. I'M AFRAID, HOWEVER, THAT YOU HAVE A LONG WALK AHEAD OF YOU, OVER THE FROZEN MOUNTAINS.'

"'Perhaps not,' said a smiling Hira, who put on her feather cloak and laid some white feathers along her children's arms. As the mother called out, 'Hira! Hiro! Hirola!' the three metamorphosed into snow geese and lifted into the air. Then they descended again, with the mother taking Qivioq's hands and each child gripping one of his feet. All called out 'Thank you' to Inuqpuq as six wings stroked in unison and carried Qivioq over the mountains and on toward the lonely plain and the silent lake. Landing in laughter, the three snow geese became humans again.

"Qivioq's beautiful wife, Hira, held her feather cloak in her hand, then whirled it around and around over her head before releasing it into the air, where it assumed its goose shape and flew away, never to return. 'I will not leave you again,' Hira said. From that time on, the plain was no longer lonely, and the lake was no longer silent, with the family's laughter and loving words echoing all around them. Some say that they live there still, unchanged by the passage of time."

Walt and Amy sat quietly when he finished, and both could hear Stumpy snoring in Amy's lap. Finally, Amy broke the silence. "Have you ever seen snow geese around here?"

"No," Walt said, "I haven't . . . although swans do sometimes put in an appearance here on the pond . . . sometimes stick around for a few days, too, like huge white pond lilies floating off in the distance. To see them come in and land, too, is breathtaking . . . or to see them take off again from the surface, for that matter. Some cultures have stories about swan maidens, like the goose girls in that story I just told you. The human steals the feathered coat, hides it away, and forces the swan maiden to stay with him. Those stories don't always end happily, though, as you can imagine. The husband and wife don't always stay together."

"And why did you tell me that Qivioq story?" Amy asked.

"Traditional stories often have the man setting off in quest of his lost wife, but there are lots of ways of getting lost, and in real life, the genders may prove interchangeable. Anthony has been away for some time, but even after he gets back, it may take a while for him to get truly home, and you may have to go out after him, figuratively, more than once. He may keep slipping on his feather cloak and flying away. He may need you to be strong and patient and persistent, like Qivioq in the story. Sometimes the journey back is even longer than the journey out."

Both were quiet for a few moments, and they could hear Stumpy quietly sawing wood. Then Amy said, "I know there's a lot that he hasn't told me, a lot that he's seen over there that he doesn't want to burden me with."

Walt said, "I was the same with Annie, when I came home from the Pacific in 1946. I didn't want her to have to carry the images around with her too. It took some time for me to feel that this life was real and not a fantasy I would wake up from. Now that she's gone, sometimes I do talk to her about what I saw, what we had to do over there all those years ago . . . but I also tell her about lots of other things, happier things, more recent things, like the old Stumpster there, and about Tony and you. She would have liked all three of you, though she would have complained about *his* snoring, and I doubt she would have let him on the furniture."

Stumpy had rolled over on his back, legs splayed, and, still unconscious, he continued to produce a soft rumble from his throat. Amy smiled, and as she had been doing earlier to his nose and forehead, she stroked the white hair of his belly with one finger.

"Pretty soon," Walt continued, "he'll wake up and ask me to start up the music box I got us for Christmas, the one with the skaters pirouetting across the frozen pond inside the cover. Then pretty soon after that, he'll be at the door, begging to go out on the ice himself. I go out with him almost every day now that the pond's surface is frozen firmly, though I stay off it myself. He likes to get up a head of steam and skid along on his belly, and he likes to try to stand up and test out all kinds of spins. I was thinking that sometime soon we'll have to get Shel, Mac, and Hammy to come over for a broom hockey game with Tony and Squirrel Nutkin here. You can join 'em, too, if you like."

The young woman nodded and said, "It sounds like fun." After a moment, she said, "Walt, do you believe in magic?"

"Do I believe in magic?" the white-haired man repeated. "I guess I wouldn't still live here at the pond if I didn't. This place transforms itself almost every second—a breath of wind riffling the surface of the water, lonely snowflakes skittering down as a storm thinks about starting, otters tussling and then lifting their whiskered faces to stare before disappearing beneath the surface, a heron lifting off the sand and creaking away on those huge wings. Wouldn't *you* call all that magic, *natural* magic? That little fellow snoozing in your lap is pretty magical too. And there's human magic here as well: You and your boy have certainly cast a spell on this place and me. These days, I feel as if I'm young again."

Amy nodded. "I hope that when Anthony gets home, we can all help him feel that magic too."

21

Stumpy and the Valentine's Day Date

FEBRUARY 15, 2012

Valentine's Day is not a holiday to which Walt Walthers has given much thought over the last couple of decades, living as he does out on Kibbee Pond in Townsend in relative isolation. He lost his wife, Annie, almost thirty years ago, and romance has rarely crossed his mind since, despite the occasional old man's crush to which he has been subject. Besides, in the last two years or so, his stub-tailed gray squirrel roommate, Stumpy, has monopolized most of his attention, and the two bachelors have stuck together. Given Walt's octogenarian status, virtually all the women he knows are younger than he, including Amy Riggetti, the young mother who lives down the hill from the bachelors' cabin with her six-year-old son, Tony. With her husband away serving in Afghanistan, Amy has inspired paternal and grandfatherly feelings in her silver-haired neighbor, although their time together has resulted as well in an ever-deepening friendship that is transcending their appreciable age difference. Nor has Walt viewed any of his female acquaintances as serious or even potential love interests. Despite the occasional old man's crush, his wrinkled skin has proven impervious to Cupid's darts for some time now.

Still, Walt has maintained contact with an old flame whom he had dated briefly before he met Annie. Arlene Tosh has visited the cabin several times over the past few months, always bringing with her the elephantine yellow Labrador retriever Big Bruno, who has become a buddy and playfellow to Stumpy. In the summer the two creatures seemed ready for a career as circus performers. Inadvertently at first, and then with conscious, danger-defying intention,

Stumpy had found himself aboard Big Bruno's back when the gigantic canine was leaping from Walt's dock in pursuit of a tennis ball. These days, the unlikely friends always greet each other with enthusiasm when their human companions get together. A widow, Arlene nevertheless has kept busy with her children and grandchildren, with her friends, and with her activities, such as her membership in and role as secretary of her local chapter of the Daughters of the American Revolution. Thus, her visits to Kibbee Pond have been irregular. Although she lives across the state line in New Hampshire, however, the distance to Kibbee Pond is not prohibitive because Townsend itself is nestled along the Massachusetts border; therefore, when Arlene gets the urge to visit her old friend, she gives him a call, and they set a time. Though closer to Walt's age than most of his female acquaintances, Arlene, as one of his high school classmates, is still a few months younger.

Last week, Arlene phoned again, and the tone of her call had Walt shaking his head and talking to himself . . . or to Stumpy . . . for several days. "I don't get women," he muttered over his morning coffee the next day. "Sixty-five years ago, she told me she wasn't interested in a romantic relationship with me and then went off and married Bill. Now, she's saying things like, 'Don't you think it's time we had another date? It's almost Valentine's Day, and we girls can do crazy things when Cupid's arrow strikes.' What is *that* supposed to mean?"

Stumpy just stared back at him while nibbling a kibble from his dish on the kitchen counter.

"What am I doing now," Walt continued, his eyes widened, "asking for romantic advice from a squirrel?" Then he laughed. "Hey, maybe you could start your own syndicated column, "Dear Stumpy," and give Ann Landers and "Ask Heloise" both a run for their money. I can just see a photo of you at the head of the column, maybe with some eyeglasses on and with a pencil in one paw! How's that old song go: 'Love and rodents, love and rodents, go together like a cop and doughnuts'? Maybe not, but we could work on it."

Stumpy selected another kibble from the bowl and nibbled tiny bits from it, turning it around in his paws while watching his human roommate ranting. He rarely saw Walt display any degree of agitation.

"She said we should take in a movie matinee and maybe have some lunch, but I don't know what her real agenda is. Maybe you should come along as a chaperone."

Stumpy continued munching and selected his next morsel. Walt continued babbling and pacing on the kitchen rug, a bit like a restless dog tied out by a doghouse.

Still, another phone call that day solidified their plans: lunch at a Thai restaurant in Lunenburg Monday, followed by a movie at the mall in Fitchburg. "You'd better come along in case she tries any funny business," Walt said to his furry confidante. "You can pull me out if I get in over my head. We can smuggle you into the theater somehow."

Late Monday morning, Arlene pulled into the driveway in her silver Volvo, Big Bruno slavering happily at the rear driver's side window, obviously aware of where they had arrived. Walt thought that he could hear the sound of the big dog's tail thwacking the car seats as he manifested his enthusiasm through that appendage.

Arlene hopped spryly out of the car and opened the rear door for her rhinoceros-sized pet, who vaulted onto the gravel, threatening any trees in the vicinity with toppling should his tail get within striking distance. Because Stumpy had already raced over to the car, the two animals now stood nose to nose getting reacquainted, but soon, Stumpy was running figure eights beneath the behemoth's chest and around his four massive legs while the dog turned his head from one side to the other and watched his gray streak of a friend between the two Doric columns that doubled as his front legs.

"Arlene," Walt called as he stepped down from the deck, "you may want to keep that diminutive canine of yours close at hand. I'm nervous that if he gets out on the ice, where Stumpy is apt to lead him, last week's warm weather may have thawed things enough to make it unreliable. He's not exactly a featherweight ballerina, you know."

"Oh, Walt," the attractive elderly woman said, walking toward him, placing a hand on each of his elbows, and then raising herself on tiptoes to kiss him on the cheek, "he won't go far, not when we've just arrived and everyone is getting reacquainted." She had tucked her right forearm in the crook of his left arm and was steering him back toward the deck. She glanced back over her shoulder at the two mammalian playmates and called, "Come along, Big Big. The nice kitty will come inside too." Walt decided any further warning was unnecessary for the moment.

The two human friends had a chance to catch up as they sat inside, giving each other the latest news of their children and grandchildren and even, in Arlene's case, a new great-grandchild. "It's amazing how much he looks like Bill already," she said.

In the meantime, Big Bruno had revealed that, as always, he had a tennis ball tucked away in one cheek like a wad of chewing tobacco; now he spat it, along with a healthy portion of drool, onto the kitchen rug, where Stumpy and he began an impromptu game of nudge and roll. Big Bruno would nudge the ball with his nose so that it rolled toward his rodent buddy; then the dog would roll onto his back and, with his front legs held stiffly together, wave those massive pedestals up and down while Stumpy wrapped his four limbs around the tennis ball and dug at it with his hind feet before releasing his grip, butting the ball with his head, and sending it back to his gargantuan playmate. "Oh, look," Arlene said, "I love it when Big Big does his calisthenics!"

Soon, however, it was time to leave for lunch, and Arlene asked if leaving Big Bruno inside while they were gone was all right with Walt. "He likes it here, and I'm sure he'll be perfectly content with Stumpy to keep him company."

"Well-l-l," Walt said, "I more or less promised the Stumpster that he could ride along with us. Plus, what happens if it turns out like those paintings in bars where all the dogs are sitting around playing poker, smoking cigars, and drinking booze, except in this case one of the dogs is a squirrel? Big Bruno could probably sock away a lot of my cognac if Stumpy were here to show him where it is. Besides, more seriously, the little guy and I haven't gotten out much together lately, and he seems to have a touch of cabin fever. Big Bruno can stay here by himself, can't he? I promised Stumpy some real theater popcorn, and I thought it would be fun to bring him into the theater with us—you know, hide him inside my coat or in your purse or something like that."

Arlene looked at the silver-haired man and smiled. "Well, Walter Walthers, I think you're afraid I'm going to take you up into the back row and try to make out with you! What kind of a girl do you think I am?" She laughed as she spoke.

"Oh no," Walt said, sputtering a bit, "it's nothing like that. I mean, I didn't mean . . . oh, blast it! I just thought it would be a change of pace for him, too, to . . . you know . . . do something a little different. I'll bring along the yarn harness I use when I take him to the Squealing Squirrels baseball games in West Groton, so he doesn't get into any trouble."

Arlene laughed. "I'm not going to force you into anything you don't want to do or out of something you have your heart set on. Besides, it's a little exciting . . . to be flouting the law like that. I mean, I suspect it's illegal to bring an animal into the theater. But ladies do love outlaws, you know. I always wondered if you were really a bad boy at heart, my own Clyde Barrow." She arched her eyebrows at him.

Walt wasn't sure that the direction the conversation had taken now was one he cared to pursue further, but he seemed to have won his point, and he simply replied, "Maybe we'd better get going." He filled an aluminum bowl with water for the dog and set it on the floor. Arlene laughed and said, "Thanks, but he's likely just to drink from the toilet. It's a habit I've tried to break him of at home, but he doesn't see the logic, I'm afraid."

Then they were out the door, with Stumpy—though a bit reluctant to leave his canine chum behind—scampering beside them. Soon they were climbing into Lulu, Walt's green 1960 Chevy pickup, where she sat in the vinyl tent that served as Walt's primary garage. As they pulled onto Kibbee Pond Road, Arlene said, "There certainly wouldn't have been room for Big Bruno to come along in *here*. This way, though, I can slide over next to you if the heater isn't working properly."

Walt gave her a sickly smile in response, and the woman laughed good-naturedly. "Oh, Walt, relax! You're acting as if you think I'm trying to seduce you, and I promise, my intentions are entirely honorable. I just enjoy your company, and I wouldn't mind seeing you more often."

"Thank you," Walt said, swallowing. "I'm just a bit set in my ways, and I tend to forget until I see you how much fun we have together. I'm fond of your pet woolly mammoth too." After a quiet moment, he continued, "Now, I've never tried this restaurant we're going to, but you suggested Thai food, and it's right on the way to the movie theater."

"You see?" Arlene replied. "It's already a bit of an adventure, and I like to shake up my routine every once in a while."

Soon, they were turning into the parking lot for Bangkok Gardens, a small, well-kept-up wooden structure that looked more like someone's home than a place of business. "Now, old buddy," Walt said to the gray squirrel perched on the back of the bench seat and obviously anxious to get out of the truck and on to the next phase of their outing, "we're going to have to leave you here for a few minutes. This isn't like the old Brookside Restaurant, where Brian and Regina used to welcome you inside with open arms. These people probably have to worry about the health inspector. I'll crack the window so you have plenty of fresh air, and I'll peek out at you once in a while to make sure you're not chewing the upholstery or flashing the lights or anything like that. Okay?" Stumpy turned his back on Walt to stare out the cab's back window. "Oh boy," Walt said.

As they stepped inside, the homey impression the exterior had given continued, because the main dining area was hardly bigger than the interior of Walt's cabin, with only about a dozen tables, and small ones at that. Only one other couple was seated, but the check was already on their table, and they got up to leave as the hostess walked toward Arlene and Walt. She was a smiling Thai woman, middle-aged but aglow with a younger person's energy. "You can sit where you like," she said. "I'll bring menus." She stepped to the register counter, which stood under a portrait of a handsome Thai man decked out in regalia and medals; after inquiring later, Walt learned that he was the current king of Thailand. The woman stepped back with the menus before returning to the register to accept payment from the departing customers, but soon she returned to smile sunshine at Arlene and Walt. From the twinkle in her eye, Walt realized that their hostess was, as Annie would have said, "a live wire."

"Your first time?" the smiling woman asked.

"Well, yes, ma'am," Walt said. "We've not been in your establishment before. It is an intriguing layout, though, and the smells from the kitchen are delicious."

The woman turned to Arlene, her eyebrows raised. "Good manners, this one. You should keep him."

Arlene laughed easily. "I was thinking the same thing."

"Oh no," Walt said, blushing a little, "I'm in trouble now."

Laughing along with Arlene, the woman extended her hand toward Walt. "I'm Fai," she said. "Who are you?"

Walt stood to shake the proffered hand. "I'm fine, too, thank you," he said, his bewilderment raising a bit of a blush in his cheeks.

The woman laughed again. "No, my name is Fai. And you are?"

"Oh, excuse me," Walt said, returning the laugh. "Must be my hearing! I'm Walt, and this is Arlene. Very nice to meet you."

"You like Thai food? Know what to order?" Fai asked.

"I do," Arlene said, "but Walt may not be sure."

"Do you like things spicy hot?" Fai said, turning to Walt.

Now feeling more in the spirit of things, Walt replied, "Isn't that a rather personal question?"

Fai turned to Arlene in mock exasperation. "Ah, a dirty old man! I'm not sure you should keep him after all!" All three laughed.

With counseling from Fai, Walt decided on the chicken with cashew nuts, but Arlene had already had her heart set on some pad prik king, with both chicken and shrimp. While Fai took the order back to the kitchen, Walt stood and walked to the window to check on Stumpy. When the squirrel saw him, he set his rear feet on the passenger's side window ledge and extended his body up to grip the top of the window frame with his front paws, sticking his nose through the narrow gap where Walt had lowered the window slightly. "Uh-oh," Walt said back over his shoulder to Arlene, "looks like we might have a riot on our hands in cell block nine! Might even be an attempt at a prison break!"

Arlene joined him at the window and soon was giggling at Stumpy's thespian skills. "He does know how to ham things up, doesn't he?" she said as Fai stepped back from the kitchen.

"What do you see?" she asked, coming to the window.

"Oh, it's just my pet squirrel, Stumpy. We brought him along for the ride, but he thinks he should be able to come inside with us, and now he's trying to get nominated for an Academy Award. Best Performance by a Rodent Suffering in a Supporting Role."

"It's a quiet time," Fai said. "Bring him in."

"We don't want to get you in trouble with the health inspector," Walt said.

"It's a quiet time," Fai insisted. "He can hide in your purse if anyone comes."

And that is how Stumpy came to enjoy a complimentary spring roll on a chair between Walt and Arlene. As they were leaving for the movie theater, Walt and Arlene promised Fai they would return soon at what they hoped would be another quiet time.

Stumpy sat up on his haunches and bobbed his head at Fai. When she reached out her hand toward him, the furry charmer set his tiny clawed right front paw on her finger.

"Very polite," Fai said. "Just like the dirty old man."

All went well at the movies too. Arlene suggested that Stumpy climb into her bag, which proved capacious and comfortable, and they cruised into the lobby with their precious cargo safely stowed away. Walt bought a big tub of popcorn and two bottles of water, and they found their way to the proper theater for *Extremely Loud and Incredibly Close*, which they had chosen even though they agreed that Stumpy would probably have enjoyed *Star Wars: The Phantom Menace* more—3D, however, just wasn't Walt's thing.

They made their way to the back row, where they thought Stumpy would be less likely to call attention to himself. Although Walt arranged their coats as a barrier for further privacy, the theater never filled up, and Stumpy was able to sit on a chair arm and watch the previews and the opening of the movie without being obtrusive. Initially, too, the tawny-faced rascal was preoccupied with begging for popcorn, causing Walt to comment, "Good thing we got a big tub!" However, after only a few minutes of the movie, Stumpy found his way into Arlene's lap, where he curled up and soon was snoring quietly. If Arlene had had any designs on compromising Walt's honor, the squirrel's presence brought out her maternal side instead. Besides, Walt was pretty sure she just liked to tease him. She did, however, reach out and squeeze the white-haired geezer's hand at several points in the film. If you were wondering, by the way, Walt did remove his porkpie hat in the restaurant and at the theater; he is, as Arlene and Fai would tell you, an exceptional gentleman, and in a league by himself.

Stumpy slipped back into Arlene's bag when the show was done, and they walked back to Lulu. Walt helped Arlene negotiate the high seat of the truck, then went around to the driver's side. As he settled in behind the wheel, Arlene said, "Thank you, Walt. It was a lovely day, and I'm grateful that you agreed to be my Valentine. I knew way back in school that you were special, and your quiet, kind strength hasn't changed."

Walt smiled back. "I keep wondering how we can be so much older, when you still look the same to me as you did back then. Oh, you know, there are obvious differences, but I still see and hear that young girl in how you look and talk now. Annie always said I had a good imagination, and I always told her that I see with my heart as well as my eyes. Does that make sense?"

"Yes, and it's a very nice compliment," Arlene said quietly, reaching again to pat his arm. The truck was cold after their time indoors, so Stumpy was happy to huddle up and cuddle into Arlene's lap as Lulu made her way back toward Kibbee Pond.

"I'm just set in my ways and a bit prickly," the amenable duffer said.

"You're the least prickly person I know," Arlene scoffed. "If you're prickly, then I certainly am too. That makes us a prickly pair, and we'll just have to let people call us the Cactus Twins."

Walt chuckled. "Fair enough."

Stumpy was out of the truck as quickly as was humanly—or, rather, squirrelly—possible, and he flew like a gray-furred arrow to the kitchen door, through the window of which Big Bruno's gigantic head showed, with enough of a side-by-side motion to indicate that his huge tail was thrashing behind him. As soon as Walt unlocked and opened the door, the monstrous mutt exploded outside, spun around once or twice excitedly on the deck, then launched himself off the east side and thundered toward the partially frozen lake.

"Oh no!" Walt said, and Arlene shrieked, "Big Big, come! Big Big, come!" The dog, however, was already out on the marbleized surface, skidding and changing direction in his excitement but ignoring the humans calling from the shore. Stumpy had followed the huge hound to the edge of the pond, and he was chattering loudly when the three of them heard a crack. All of Big Bruno except his massive head disappeared beneath the ice about thirty yards from shore, and Walt and Arlene could see and hear the splashes as the dog flailed with his front paws at the edge of the pool, trying to get a grip to pull himself up and out but always sliding back again.

"Stay here and talk to him," Walt said. "Try to keep him calm. I'll get a rope." He headed toward the vinyl tent where Lulu was parked and returned within a minute with a coil of blue plastic line that he used on Nelly the rowboat. "I can't throw it that far, but I also can't see going out on the ice myself. I'll just break through before I get to him. Stumpy, do you think you could take this end of the rope out to your friend? If he'll grip it with his mouth, maybe we can help him up out of the water."

The squirrel seemed to understand because he gripped the line with his teeth and began making his way deliberately across the ice. Walt kept feeding out slack, and within seconds Stumpy was near the opening in the surface, where the hippopotamus-like canine continued to thrash.

"Don't get too close and fall in yourself!" Walt called. "Try to feed the line to him from a few feet away. Then get back once he has it in his mouth. Stand behind me, Arlene," he said to his human companion, who stood in silence now.

Miraculously, the big dog took the rope into his mouth, and Walt tested the slack, then instructed Arlene to grab onto the line behind him, with two hands as he was doing. The two planted their feet and leaned back against the rope while the dog continued to scrabble against the ice. Then, in an instant, his gigantic form emerged from the water and, not pausing even to shake, raced toward them across the ice. Stumpy followed at a slower pace. When the line had gone slack with Big Bruno's emergence, both Walt and Arlene had tumbled backwards, and now, as the relieved canine danced about them and twice shook freezing water on his three rescuers, Arlene laughed and said, "Walt Walthers, I think I just fell for you all over again." And that was the climactic event of the big Valentine's date.

22

Stumpy and the History Lesson

(A.K.A. THE TWO STUMPYS)

FEBRUARY 22, 2012

Before this past weekend, rumors of a possible nor'easter had swept through Kibbee Pond and its environs—and, for that matter, all of New England—but Walt Walthers, as an experienced professional weather watcher, knows better than to place too much credence in weather patterns forming on the West Coast and possessing the "potential" to become a big storm. Even with modern electronic meteorological methods and equipment, forecasting is still an inexact science, and Walt examines the evidence carefully before projecting gloom and doom onto his clientele.

Stumpy, the stub-tailed gray squirrel who has been Walt's roommate and near-constant companion for the last two years, has absorbed some of Walt's predictive skill and has two methods of his own for anticipating major weather events. The first is his natural rodent's sixth or eleventh or fifteenth sense—after all, do we really know how many senses we humans have, let alone wild animals who are significantly more attuned to the natural world than we and who have to be to persist through horrible conditions? Anyway, Stumpy's second method of predicting significant meteorological events is simply to observe Walt's increased activity around the computer and the other equipment inside their cabin at the pond. Nevertheless, despite Walt's greater focus last week on gathering data about the possible storm, the gray-furred bandito remained calm, and his lack of concern reinforced Walt's sense that the projected storm would fizzle out. It did, bringing only a dusting of snow overnight Saturday into Sunday; bright sunshine and an almost springlike feel persisted as temperatures gradually rose out of the thirties.

Saturday morning, Amy and Tony Riggetti had showed up in time for Walt's second cup of coffee, and the two visitors suggested that the foursome retire to the sunny, wind-sheltered corner of the deck for a few minutes to enjoy the season's smile even if that smile proved brief. Walt fixed coffee for the young mother, Amy, and hot chocolate for six-year-old Tony, but he also grabbed a handful of honey-roasted cashews for Stumpy and some sour cream and cinnamon muffins he had baked earlier for the humans. He knew full well that the bucktoothed pirate who lives with him would beg for a share of the baked goods as well, and *that* prediction certainly proved true. Scanning the pond from their chairs, the four friends shared the feeling that spring might not be such a distant promise; something in the air already had them thinking about unfurling ferns and sun-thirsty crocuses, though Walt certainly knew how long a month March often proves, with its tendency to dump large amounts of snow just when people are starting to feel secure about the return of pleasant weather.

Still, as the quartet sat there, looking out over the pond, they could see many open stretches where the ice had already melted, and Tony asked, "Mr. Walt, how soon do you think you'll be able to put Nelly back in the water?" Nelly is Walt's rowboat, which he fits out with an ancient three-horsepower Johnson outboard motor and uses in good weather for his daily cruise around the pond.

"Well, Tony," the silver-haired fogy said, "I usually wait until the ice is completely gone so I don't inadvertently ram into some and damage the hull. That usually means sometime later in March, but this year, I don't know. We could get lucky and start the boating season early if the weather stays this warm."

"Is it me," Amy asked, "or have I been hearing more birdsong lately?"

"You're not imagining it," Walt said. "I've been hearing the finches for some time now, and more recently, the robins have been singing. Stumpy and I took a bit of a stroll out into the woods the other day, now that the snow and ice are gone from the path, and in one of the clearings out there, we spotted a number of bluebirds. Of course, flocks of them do stick around here throughout the winter, but seeing them at this time of year always gets my spirits and hopes up. At my age, I can't afford to wish any more of my life away, but this is about the time when I do start to yearn for the sights and sounds and scents of spring. The change of light does it every year. On top of that, I've been catching little whiffs of those good earthy smells at odd moments this week, and my old man's heart rears up in my chest like a young colt anxious to get out in the pasture."

"Does Stumpy act different in the spring?" Amy asked.

"He's like me in some regards," Walt said. "When I get it into my head that spring is approaching, I find staying inside is difficult, and this last week, he's been asking to spend more and more time outdoors. I'm not sure how far he wanders, but I suspect he keeps at least half an eye open for fellow gray squirrels of the female persuasion, if you know what I mean."

"Part of the reason I ask," Amy continued, "is that he was down around our house yesterday acting a little strange."

"Strange how?" Walt asked.

"Well, I heard a pattering up on the roof and went out on the deck, and there he was, hopping around near the chimney. When he saw me, he ducked over and back down the far side of the ridgepole, and I'm not sure where he ended up. Later, I heard some chewing noises while I was up in the bedroom, and when I slipped outside, he seemed to be nosing around the vent plate to the attic, as if he was trying to get inside there. When I called to him, he disappeared again, up and over to the far side of the roof."

"Yeah," Tony added, "I was out playing trucks in the sand, and I saw him under one of the trees, but he ignored me when I invited him over, so I got up and walked over to him, but he ran up the tree, and then he kept going around and around to stay out of sight, and I kept running around the tree to try to see him, but I couldn't catch up with him. I thought he was playing a game with me at first, but then he never let me even see him. I don't know where he went either; he just disappeared."

"That *is* strange," Walt said. "I hope he didn't do any damage. I know a lot of people complain about wild squirrels that chew their way into the attic and then bite through wires and commit all sorts of mayhem. That just doesn't sound like Stumpy's modus operandi, though. Maybe I'd better try to keep him closer to home."

"What have you been up to, little buddy?" Walt said then to Stumpy, who had just climbed from Tony's lap to the boy's left shoulder, from which he was leaning forward in hopes that his young friend might hand him a bit more muffin. At Walt's comment, the squirrel looked over at the elderly man and cocked his head quizzically. Then he wrapped his upper body around Tony's neck and twisted onto his back so that he could toboggan down the little fellow's chest and into his lap, where he lay on his back with his legs splayed, waiting for his friend to give him a one-fingered belly rub.

"Whoa!" Walt said. "The old Slinky move! I haven't seen you do that one before. Something else that's new. If I could just find a traveling circus that wanted a trained squirrel, I could probably make a bundle!" Noting the six-year-old's puzzled look, Walt paused. "You know what a Slinky is, Tony?"

"No, Mr. Walt. What is it?"

"Well," the knowledgeable codger said with a smile, "it's a toy made out of one long piece of wire that circles around and around into a flexible, accordion-like tube. If you put one end down on the top step of a set of stairs and then flop the other end over, the Slinky will walk down the stairs, slinking up and over, up and over, up and over." Tony laughed.

They sat in silence for a minute, looking out at the pond. Then Walt spoke again. "That really doesn't sound like Stumpy, but then again, a couple of days ago, I went outside to fill the bird feeders, and I saw him on top of the plastic trash can. When he saw me, he took off like the long-tailed cat who happened into the rocking chair store, and at first, I thought he just had a skeeter in his scooter and was teasing me—you know, he was feeling frisky and playful and was trying to get me to chase him or pay attention or something like that . . . but he didn't come back, at least not until later in the afternoon, when he scratched at the kitchen window screen as he sometimes does. I checked out the trash can after he ran off and discovered that he'd been chewing at it as if he wanted to get at what was inside. He had gnawed a hole right through the handle, which left me thinking he'd probably been using those buckteeth on it more than once."

After another short silence, Walt continued, "I hope you guys will keep your eyes open and report back to me if you see the ol' Stumpster doing anything strange or inappropriate. I could always take him in to Dr. Brad for behavior modification therapy. At least

I'm pretty sure Brad does that sort of thing for dogs, though he claims not to be as much of an expert on squirrel behavior as he is on domesticated critters. Have you met Brad Schmidt, Amy?"

"Was he the one you introduced us to playing fiddle at the contra dance?" the young woman asked. "How could I forget a fiddle-playing veterinarian?"

"Yup, that's the one," Walt said. "Something of a Renaissance man, I'd say."

Amy glanced back over at the ice on the pond and then consciously changed the subject. "Walt," she said, "I've been wondering. Does the pond have a long history? Someone told me that it hasn't always been here."

"They were right," Walt said. "Oh, Vulpine Brook has always been here—they called it Vulpine Brook after all the foxes in the area; *Vulpes* is Latin for 'fox'—or at least it's been here since the last ice age. It probably would swell up pretty big in the spring, but in the old days, the local farmers used to graze their cattle around here. You might have looked out from this deck, if it had been here a hundred years ago, and seen old Bossie and Cowslip chewing their cuds right there where the deep water is now. This was the summer pasture back then, and the farmers would drive their herds out here to the rich green grass and leave them until the fall since they had easy access to both food and water.

"Hey," Walt said, "do you know why it's called Kibbee Pond?" He chuckled to himself as he asked the question.

Amy said, "I always assumed that it was named after all the kibbies—all the sunfish—that live in it."

"Yeah," Tony chimed in, "you said that some people called them bluegills or pumpkinseeds, but the real old-time local folkals called them kibbies."

"I did say all that," Walt said, "but I *didn't* tell you the pond was named after the fish. In fact, it was named after Henry Symberley Kibbee, something of a legend around here. I guess I never told you his story, then."

"I guess you never did," Amy said with a somewhat suspicious smile. "Are you going to tell us now?"

"Well . . . yeah!" Walt said, laughing. "As long as you want to hear it."

"Yes, please," Tony said.

"Well," Walt said, "Henry Symberley Kibbee made a lot of money in the railroad business back in the early decades of the twentieth century. Since he had originally come from the Leominster area, he decided that he wanted to have a summer home near that bustling metropolis. He didn't want to share a lake with anyone else, but he wanted to have some waterfront property, so he decided to create a waterfront for himself. He bought up this big plot of pastureland and hired men in the summer of 1925 to come in and cut trees, pull out stumps, and build a dike out of dirt so the water from Vulpine Brook would pool up. When the ground froze in the winter, he had teams of big Percheron horses brought in to haul the logs off to the sawmills at Townsend Harbor and to bring in loads of cow manure to help secure the dike. After that, he spent another bundle to bring in hydroelectric engineers to design and oversee construction of the dam. By the spring of 1926, the trickle of Vulpine Brook had expanded into the Kibbee Reservoir, one of the largest privately owned ponds or lakes in the Commonwealth.

"Henry Symberley Kibbee loved fishing, so he stocked the new pond with all sorts of game fish, most notably largemouth bass, pickerel, and even pike, though some claimed the pond was too small to sustain fish as big and ferocious as pike. Henry Symberley Kibbee also hired gamekeepers to patrol the water's surface and the surrounding land to ensure that no one else could fish in his pond, because he was as jealous of his creation and its piscatory wealth as an elderly geezer would be of a beautiful young wife. Some even told stories of him wandering around the shores of the pond at night and whispering blandishments to the pond itself, calling it 'my beauty' and saying strange things like 'Oh, my love, when will you fill me up as I have filled you up?' The gamekeepers knew when to stay away from him, and they knew better than to disturb him when he was in one of his moods. Some people claimed that all the coal smoke he had inhaled from the steam engines in Worcester, where the railroad's main office was, had made him loopy, but I suspect our modern psychotherapists would have all sorts of alternative theories and explanations for why his train had, so to speak, jumped the tracks."

"Grown-ups are weird," Tony commented.

"They *can* be," Walt continued, "and Henry Symberley Kibbee certainly was. With the passage of time, he became obsessed with catching a huge pike he called His Lordship, which may or may not have actually existed, and he spent money on all kinds of fishing gear, from rods and reels of various sizes and weights to throwing nets of different styles and even a solid-gold trident spear, like the ones you see in paintings of the Greek sea god Poseidon, even though everyone knew the metal was too malleable to pierce the scaly side of a fish, especially a Leviathan like the one he imagined as his quarry. Even in the depths of winter, he would have his gamekeepers drill and saw substantial holes in the ice so he could sit nearby on his stool, trident in hand, in case His Lordship surfaced. In the better weather, he continued his solo nocturnal patrols along the water's edge, but in the daytime he insisted that a full crew of eight oarsmen pull him from shore to shore across the pond in a Nantucket whaleboat he had bought for that purpose; Henry Symberley Kibbee sat in the bow with his trident poised and ready as if it were a whaler's harpoon.

"And then one night, the unthinkable happened. Long before, Henry Symberley Kibbee had abandoned his habit of whispering passionate phrases and self-composed love sonnets to the pond itself and had instead begun speaking to His Lordship, the gigantic fish that most people thought was simply a creation of his mad imagination; he was apparently trying to lure his archenemy close to shore so he could grapple with the demonic denizen of the depths. His nightly rambles would start with him speaking softly and calling out, 'Here, fishy, fishy, fishy,' but his frustration at the lack of response would build, and his tone would change until he was shouting curses and raging against the cowardice of this monstrous creature that was too fearful to meet him face-to-face.

"Later, a gamekeeper would reveal that on one fateful night, his employer had waded into the water not far from the spot where Vulpine Brook enters the pond at the northeast corner, apparently convinced that His Lordship had, at last, accepted his challenge and was waiting for him a bit farther out. Then, in waist-deep water, Henry Symberley Kibbee stepped into a jagged-jawed beaver trap his own men had set to keep the lake clear of mammalian dam builders. Convinced that he was in the jaws of His Lordship, the deranged man thrashed away, trying to pull his leg out of the metallic mouth that gripped it around his ankle while he simultaneously drove his trident down toward his feet. He succeeded, of course, only in further wounding himself, and that soft metal spear did not so much pierce his leg as rub it raw. Regardless, his leg was mangled so badly that the local doctors had to amputate it just below the knee once the gamekeepers had raced out to release their employer from the trap and save him from the drowning that would otherwise have proven inevitable.

"Henry Symberley Kibbee was never the same after his accident. As he lay in his hospital bed in Leominster recovering from the loss of his limb, he became obsessed with the idea of producing a wooden leg that would restore the same level of mobility and utility of which his living appendage had been capable before the incident. Because he remained convinced that His Lordship was real and had taken his leg as a punishment for the shady railroad dealings that had brought him his fortune, Henry Symberley Kibbee sold his remaining shares in the Kibbee Central Line, vowed never to return to Kibbee Reservoir, and then devoted all his wealth to research and development of sophisticated wooden prosthetics. He assembled a coterie of medical scientists, lumberjacks, and wood-carvers so that he would have the personnel necessary for what he saw as the three stages of the process: determining scientifically the appropriate form and composition for the artificial appendages; finding and cutting the most appropriate trees for the lumber necessary; and whittling and shaping that lumber into flexible and versatile fake limbs to provide the models on which mass production would be based. Unfortunately, his chain of factories started up only a short while before others took advantage of rubber, lightweight metals, and the new plastics to fabricate more efficient and ultimately less expensive prosthetics.

"Thus, within a few short years, the factories had shut down, driven into foreclosure, and the Kibbee fortune evaporated. Henry Symberley Kibbee himself became a recluse, living in a derelict railroad warehouse in Fitchburg, where he was rumored to come outside only after dark. Then, the stories went, he would stump up and down the alleys of the downtown area on one of several ornately carved wooden legs, each rumored to be made of a different kind of wood, each the prototype of a different design that the Kibbee factories had planned to produce en masse before bankruptcy left them, proverbially, without a leg to stand on. When Henry Symberley Kibbee died in 1957, his last will and testament specified that his twenty-three prototypes be donated to the Fitchburg Art Museum, where they remain locked in a special room in the basement, available for viewing if you provide sufficient advance warning to the museum staff. I've never gone to see if they really exist."

Walt paused and looked at Amy and then Tony. Stumpy was now sprawled on his back atop the deck rail, taking the sun full onto his belly. Walt continued his story. "As part of the bankruptcy proceedings, a group of investors purchased the property rights to Kibbee Reservoir and the surrounding land, changing the name to Kibbee Pond and subdividing the waterfront acreage in the belief that such property would prove marketable for summer homes. Somehow, though, the Fitchburg-Leominster area simply lacked the cachet to attract the clientele the owners hoped for, and much of the land sat on the market for several years. In the eighties, after Annie died, I was able to use the money from selling our house to buy my twenty acres and build this cabin, but relatively few people have built here, and I suspect most of the land will remain undeveloped for the near future. Anyway, that's the story of where the name Kibbee Pond comes from." His audience sat in silence.

"Anybody interested in a ride over the state line into New Hampshire?" Walt asked after a moment. "I've got a hankering for some maple syrup, and I understand the first-run syrup is available now, earlier than usual with the warm days and cool nights this month and last. I always say the flavor is much richer in the first-run stuff. You know, you might even be able to talk me into making a batch of my famous cornmeal blueberry pancakes for lunch when we get back. What do you say?"

The next day brought the solution to the mystery of Stumpy's strange behavior. Late in the afternoon, Walt went out to bring in the bird feeders for the night, something he did regularly as soon as he thought the black bears might be ready to come out of hibernation; over the years, bears had destroyed several of his feeders, and he had learned that being proactive was wise. Stumpy had been out for an hour or so, and Walt had lost track of his roommate's whereabouts while he was himself reading through some folktale anthologies, looking for good stories to tell during his now-weekly visits to local schools. The aging tale spinner was feeling a bit guilty because shortly before the squirrel had gone out, Walt had scolded him for doing further damage to the trash can, which now sported a chewed hole that looked just wide enough for a *Sciurus carolinensis* to squeeze through. As he crossed the deck to gather up the feeders, the elderly man heard a noise coming from the trash can, which sat beside the three-step stairway down to the driveway, and there, perched on top, was the stub-tailed rodent, bent over and gnawing frantically at his excavation project.

"Hey, you bandit!" Walt called out. "What is your problem?"

The stub-tailed marauder looked up at him and then sat up on his haunches with his ears laid back. Walt was about to begin an angry lecture when a motion caught his eye from the railing on the opposite side of the deck. There, popping over the edge to sit upright and stare toward the trash can, was another tailless gray squirrel! Walt looked back and forth between the two creatures, almost identical in size and coloration, and then noticed that the one on the trash can had a slight notch torn into the rounded bud of his left ear, a blemish he had never seen on Stumpy. Suddenly, the evidence of strange behavior on Stumpy's part made sense. Walt's Stumpy had not chewed up his trash can, nor had he tried to break into Amy's attic; the other Stumpy had. There were two Stumpys!

"Aha!" Walt said quietly. "One face, one voice, one habit, and two persons / A natural perspective, that is and is not . . ." The knowledgeable codger was, of course, quoting from Shakespeare's *Twelfth Night*, the scene in which the characters realize that they have been interacting with not one person, but with twins.

The two gray-furred rodents continued to eye each other, the stranger on the trash can emitting an occasional *chuck* as he tapped with his left front paw on the plastic cover he stood on; though his tail was as short as Stumpy's, the stub seemed to vibrate or even shiver as he continued to stare at the cabin's rightful resident. The original Stumpy's reaction was different. He sat upright like a boxer, the hair standing up along his back; with his ears pinned back, he began to chatter with his teeth, and *his* tail, or what little was left of it, twitched at regular intervals. Walt could tell that if his friend had retained his original plume, that flag would have been flicking back and forth above his spine. Then Stumpy charged off the rail and halfway across the deck before applying the brakes; nevertheless, his effort was enough to send the intruder packing. The stranger leaped from the trash can and motored toward the edge of the woods without looking back. Since then, neither Walt nor Amy and Tony have seen any sign of the faux Stumpy.

The real one has been acting pretty lordly, though, as if he has reclaimed his kingdom from a usurper and his good reputation from an encroaching maligner. His roommate has taken to calling the squirrel His Lordship, in honor of Henry Symberley Kibbee. Walt has been feeling a little silly, too, and apologetic about his false accusations against his sidekick, but the occasional extra portion of honey-roasted cashews seems to have taken Stumpy's mind off any injustice. Besides, Walt has never known him to hold a grudge.

"You know, old buddy," Walt told him, "for a while there, I was afraid you might be manifesting a split personality . . . like Dr. Jekyll and Mr. Hyde or, in your case, not so much Mr. *Hide* as Mr. Fur or Mr. Pelt. In any case, I'm glad I don't have to deal with a schizophrenic squirrel!"

23

Stumpy, the Meat Wagon, and Squiffy the Trout

MARCH 14, 2012

If anyone would be on top of a winter storm lumbering into New England, Walt Walthers would be, and he certainly was on top of the one that drifted into town two Wednesdays ago and then hung around into Thursday evening. After all, Walt is a professional weather watcher, and he has all the equipment he needs to track approaching weather events right there in the main living area of his cabin on Kibbee Pond in Townsend. He spent some time Tuesday night and Wednesday making courtesy calls to his regular customers to warn them of the impending precipitation. As he likes to say, "We can't do anything to change the weather, but we can get ready for what's coming." Fortunately, although the storm lingered like an unemployed college graduate at his parents' house, the snow it produced did not accumulate in massive amounts. As Walt pointed out to Stumpy, the stub-tailed gray squirrel who is his roommate and near-constant companion, "Those guys who plow driveways for a living have to feel relieved at the prospect of at least a little income. It's been a lean year for them."

One of those snowplow drivers is their good friend Todd Jormonen, who also shovels Walt's deck after storms and, at other times of year, is happy to take on all kinds of handiwork. As is his wont, Todd did the rest of his first round of plowing early Thursday morning, before making a pass at Walt's driveway and coming in for the late breakfast he knew Walt would be putting together for him. As soon as Stumpy heard the scrape and rumble of the metal plowshare on the surface of the driveway, he jumped to the kitchen counter and was standing at the window, chattering and scratching the glass with his front paws in a matter of seconds. The two bachelor roommates had seen their buddy the week before on a darts-and-dinner night out at Ayer Pool and Billiards, but Stumpy seemed as excited as if Todd were returning from a six-month cruise around the world.

With his usual efficiency, Todd needed only about two minutes to make a few passes, adjusting his plow blade once or twice along the way, and thus clearing Walt's driveway and leaving the snow neatly tamped around the outside of an almost perfectly squared rectangle. Like his friend the squirrel, the jovial plowman was in an especially good mood when he came in the door. Walt can always tell by the number of insults Todd hurls at Stumpy.

"Well, you snaggletoothed, mange-ridden son of a putrid polecat! Aren't you gonna greet your uncle Todd?" Stumpy was on the man's shoulder before the verbal wave had even crested, so the last words were half-spoken, half-sputtered through laughter, because Stumpy had already placed his front feet on the man's jaw and was nibbling gently at his cheeks. In almost the same instant, however, the furred marauder was sliding down Todd's chest and into the capacious pocket of his coat, which the man always leaves unbuttoned for this purpose and in which he always manages to keep some sort of treat for his mammalian playmate as part of their snow-day routine. On this occasion, when Stumpy's head emerged from the pocket, he was stuffing a dried cherry into his mouth with both front paws.

"What do you think of that, you verminous reprobate . . . oh, wait! I've been working on something! Okay . . ." Todd cleared his throat. "Get thee gone, thou brazen, muddy-mettled clodpole! Aroint thee, thou queasy, onion-eyed rabbit-sucker! Away with thee, thou saucy, shag-eared nuthook!" As he pulled off his watch cap, the middle-aged man smiled over at Walt inquiringly.

"What have you been doing, reading Shakespeare again?" Walt asked.

"Well, sort of," his friend replied. "I went online and found a site that lets you create your own Shakespearean insults from three columns of different possibilities. I figured I was running out of synonyms for 'rat' and 'vermin,' so where better to go than to one of the masters of the English language?"

"Do you still have that speech from *King Lear* memorized?" Walt asked.

"You mean Kent's speech to Oswald, the sleazy servant? Sure. Oswald has just pulled a fast one, cutting Kent off to deliver a message before him when Kent has already been waiting for an hour to deliver *his* message, and in his righteous indignation Kent calls Oswald . . . let me see if I've got this right: 'A knave; a rascal; an eater of broken meats; a base, proud, shallow, beggarly, three-suited, hundred-pound, filthy, worsted-stocking knave; a lily-livered, action-taking knave; a whoreson, glass-gazing, super-serviceable, finical rogue; one-trunk-inheriting slave; one that wouldst be a bawd in way of good service, and art nothing but the composition of a knave, beggar, coward, pander, and the son and heir of a mongrel . . . *ahem!* . . . squirrel, one whom I will beat into clamorous whining if thou deniest the least syllable of thy addition.' I did a little editing there, what scholars might call bowdlerizing, but I'll bet you can guess which word was my substitution. I would never call Stumpy anything *too* rude! Besides, he knows I'm just kidding around. Don't you, you cheeky, fur-faced varmint?" Stumpy dove back down into Todd's pocket and came up with another cherry, at which he smacked away.

"Well, what delicacies have you prepared for the breakfast of your hardworking minion this morning?" Todd asked as he pulled off his coat and hung it carefully on the back of a kitchen chair . . . with Stumpy still rooting around in the pocket.

Walt handed his friend a mug of steaming coffee as he answered. "We've got mouse-dropping pancakes with Pine-Sol syrup as the main course. Suit your tastes?"

"Gee, I liked the motor oil you put on the griddle cakes the last time. Got any more of that? And didn't you put tufts of squirrel hair in the batter, too, for extra protein?" Todd said.

Both men laughed, and Todd sat down at the table as Walt turned back to the stove. In the meantime, Stumpy had extricated himself from the coat pocket and hopped to the table—no small feat since the chair had been a bit tippy. Actually, a squirrel does have small feet, but I meant the kind of "feat" that has an *a* in it—you know, an exploit or act of skill or daring.

Anyway, the real menu included fresh fried potatoes, baked

beans cooked with a little maple syrup, homemade chicken-and-apple sausages, onion-and-cheddar omelets (no squirrel hair this time), and toast made with Walt's notorious anadama bread. To go on the toast, he had put out some of the wild grape jelly that he had made back in September with Tony Riggetti, the six-year-old who lives down the road. As Walt served each dish, Todd's eyes widened more and more. "Wow!" he said. "Lynn never makes me a spread like this, not even on my birthday. You're gonna make somebody a good wife someday, old-timer!"

"Naw!" Walt replied. "The only men I get interested in always seem to be married already. How bad's this snow to move with the plow?"

"Well, it's pretty wet and heavy, with the temperature around freezing as it is, but there's not so much of it that ol' Bessie can't handle it." Bessie is Todd's 2004 midnight-black Ford F-250. "It's just a pain because the storm is supposed to continue on into the evening."

"And maybe on into the early morning, according to my calculations," Walt said.

As the men ate, Stumpy plunked himself down in the middle of the kitchen table. His eyes glued themselves to the fork as it went from Todd's plate to his mouth. "You, my velvet-pelted plush toy, are a scrounge!" the smiling man said to the squirrel, who turned his glance nonchalantly away and seemed now to be looking at the kitchen cabinets. "I had a Labrador retriever once who used to do that: stare at your food until you looked him in the eye, and then he'd look away, all innocence. You sure your pet rat here isn't part Lab?"

"He does have his doglike traits," Walt said.

"Say," Todd said, "you seen any sign of bear yet? I suspect that some males are out and about after hibernation now even if the females are still tending cubs in their lairs. One guy across town told me he had seen a bear out around Willard Brook during the warm spell last week. The experts say they could be early this year with the abnormally high temperatures."

Walt said, "I haven't seen any yet, and they do come down to the pond to drink here when they wake up. I just take my bird feeders in at night throughout the year now, even when the bears are certain to be hibernating; it's part of my daily ritual, and I don't want to forget to refill them with seed and suet, especially during the winter months that are so lean for the birds."

Todd nodded.

"Hey," Walt said, "did I ever tell you about the bear I encountered back when I was in high school?"

Todd shook his head as he took another bite of omelet.

"It's an amazing story," Walt said, raising his eyebrows and nodding meaningfully at his younger friend. "You might even find parts of it . . . well, hard to believe."

"Oh boy," Todd said, lowering his fork for the moment. "I guess I'd better fasten my seat belt 'cause, if I know you, we could be in for a bumpy flight on our way to the Land of Make Believe."

"Oh, ye of little faith!" Walt replied, feigning a look of innocence. "Would I tell you a story that wasn't 100 percent true?"

"Oh boy," was all Todd had to say.

"Well," Walt continued, "this was back in Michigan, where I grew up . . . a little town called Three Oaks, named after the most striking arboreal features in the town center. We lived out on a side road on a small farm my parents ran, though my dad also worked when he could at Warren Featherbone, the factory in town that made stay material to go in women's corsets. We had an old horse named Euphemia and a buckboard wagon, and Mom kept a cow and several chickens, but we were always looking for ways to supplement our income or to come up with additional food. We had a big garden, and of course, we did some hunting and fishing. Mom also busied herself through the late summer and fall with putting up canned goods." As Walt settled into his narrative, Stumpy curled up on the table next to Todd's plate and went to sleep, as if he had heard it all before.

Walt continued, "We had a family friend named Ernst Kruger, who lived a couple of miles away on the other side of town, and every November, he would butcher his hogs, a messy and tiring task. By the time I was in the tenth grade, I was in the pattern of helping him each year, in exchange for which we would receive a portion of the meat. Since Ernie had twenty or thirty hogs, the job took all day or longer, and some years, we had to spread it over two weekends.

"Well, the year I was in eleventh grade, I drove over to Ernie's early one morning and worked all day until 4:30, when we finally finished up. I got my share of the meat loaded on the back of the wagon pretty quickly and was preparing to climb up into the seat when Ernie said, 'Do you have a gun, Walter?'

"'No,' I said. 'Do you think I'll need one?'

"'Well,' he said, 'there's bound to be some hungry critters out, and it gets dark early these days.'

"'Nah!' I said. 'I'll be just fine. Don't worry about me. I'll get home before nightfall. Ol' Euphemia can still move along pretty good.' And then I set off.

"Things went fine for the first stretch, where the road ran beside some open fields. The moon had come up already and was throwing some extra light even as dusk came on. I was feeling pretty good, headed home with a wagon full of meat, until I came to this one stretch where the road dipped down into a swamp and ran along with water on one side. Down there among the trees and bushes, everything seemed a lot darker than out in the open.

"Even though something ominous settled into the pit of my stomach like a murder of crows landing in a tree, I pressed on down the hill, but I hadn't gone very far into the shadowy unknown when I heard a strange sound, somewhere between a growl and a grunt, with even a touch of a hoot about it: '*Huunhhh*!' There, on the side of the road just behind me, was the biggest black bear I had ever seen, the size of my uncle Westy's prize bull, Duke, and from the way he was sniffing the air, I knew that my meat wagon and its delicious aroma had captured his full attention. I grabbed for my whip, which I had never used on Euphemia before, but she needed no urging from me once she caught the rank odor of that ursine monster. The bear was just gathering himself to leap into the wagon and start scoffing all that pig meat, when the horse lunged forward, and the bear's claws barely scraped the tailgate. Already now, the wagon was flying along that narrow swamp-side road.

"Poor Euphemia, however, wasn't as young as she used to be, and the bear had adequate motivation for determined pursuit, so soon, his slavering jaws were just inches behind the wagon. I reached back and grabbed a hog's head with one hand and flung it out behind, and that bear turned back to gobble it up. The lead we gained of a few yards, though, evaporated almost immediately, and

I had to toss out a big joint of meat. Again, the beast turned back, and we gained only scant ground, so soon I was tossing another hunk of pork out; this time, however, the bear snagged it out of the air like a center fielder, gulped it down, and hardly broke stride. I knew I had to do something more drastic.

"I looped the reins of Euphemia's harness around the side post and climbed into the back of the wagon. That horse needed no further motivation from me to keep running for home, and I thought if I got all the rest of the meat out, I could maybe delay that hirsute harrier long enough for us to get up the coming rise and thunder the last mile or so home. I was slinging pork out of that buckboard faster than an Irish bartender serves out whiskeys on Saint Patrick's Day, but the pile of meat dwindled quickly, and the bear showed no signs of losing interest or appetite; I might just as well have been doling out thimblefuls of birdseed for all the signs of surfeiting that creature showed.

"My terror had risen into my throat, paralyzing my vocal cords so I couldn't even scream by the time I had thrown the last piece of meat out. Maybe I should have faced my death square on, but I just couldn't do it. Instead, I lay facedown in the back of the wagon and threw my hands over my head. The last thing I saw before I closed my eyes was that mountainous beast licking his lips as he accelerated toward the tailgate, then gathered himself to leap on the wagon and make me his dessert. Every prayer I knew was running through my head, and I braced myself for those teeth tearing into my youthful flesh, but somehow he never touched me. I realized in that split second that he must have miscalculated and jumped right over the wagon and onto poor Euphemia. I heard a thud and groan from up ahead of me, and then the wagon stopped. Next thing I heard was a lot of chomping and smacking and crunching, but overcome by fear, I just froze in place. I knew I had no chance if I tried to square off against that insatiable bear, but I couldn't find the strength to try running away either. I stayed hunched over in the back of the buckboard, unable above all to face the nightmare of what he must be doing to Euphemia. Don't hold it against me; I was young and didn't have the gumption I developed later.

"Well, I lay there helplessly, having acquiesced to my fate at the jaws of that big-bellied ravener, when, to my surprise, the wagon started to move forward again. Soon, it was moving even faster, and eventually, I gathered the courage to sit up and turn around. What I saw made me first gasp and then laugh. That bear *had* jumped right over the wagon and landed on Euphemia . . . and he had eaten the poor horse up. However, in doing so, he had also eaten his way right into her harness, and now he was galloping down the road, pulling the wagon along smartly behind him!

"Well, I just gave him his head and let him run straight home, and by the time we pulled into the farmyard, he was as tame as a kitten and as well mannered as a girl at her first formal dance. Since Euphemia was gone, my dad let me keep that bear, and I drove him to school every day from then until graduation. When I went off to Kalamazoo College before the war broke out, Mom and Dad kept him on the farm as their main means of locomotion. He got really popular in town, and when the folks'd take him down to Ed Dreyer's sausage shop on Saturdays to buy their weekly supply of ring bologna, the kids would all feed him apples or carrots or sugar lumps, and they'd scratch him between the eyes. Mom and Dad didn't even get their first car until after the war, when Orsino died. Didn't need it. Man, do I miss ol' Orsino! That's what we called him, after the character in Shakespeare's *Twelfth Night.*"

Todd simply nodded at the end of the tale, as if registering disbelief would be admitting defeat. He chewed a bite of anadama toast slowly, stroked the lightly snoring squirrel lying next to his plate, and then said, "Did I ever tell you that my dad had an unusual pet too?"

Walt leveled his gaze back upon his friend and said quietly, "No, I don't think you ever did."

"Well, yeah," Todd said, "it's true. You may even have heard of him, Squiffy the trout? He was a legend around here."

"Squiffy the trout, eh?" Walt said. "Doesn't sound familiar. I guess you'll be wanting to tell me about him, though."

"Sure, if you'd like to hear . . ." But Todd had already launched into his story before Walt could answer one way or the other.

"My dad always loved fishing, and for as long as I can remember, whenever he had free time, he'd be off to our lot on Beech Tree Lake and out in his skiff with the little trolling motor. Sometimes he'd take me or one of my siblings, but fishing was Dad's release from the pressures of running the lumberyard, and often, he'd just go out by himself.

"Well, back on the thirtieth of June in 1969 (a landmark date in our family history), he had putted up into one of the coves at the northeast end of the lake and was drifting by this tiny island no more than ten feet on a side—I know the spot and go back there myself sometimes even now—it's got a big white pine that grows straight up out of the middle of the island, real pretty, especially when there's a fog on the water and the tree seems to be rising up right out of a cloud. Well, anyway, Dad had just dropped his line next to this one lily pad that was a trifle more purply than the others; he said it had a tear-shaped tear in it too. And by the way, you know, that darned thing was still there the last time I went out to fish! Anyway, right there, under that lily pad, he hooked this beautiful little six-inch trout, too small to keep for eating. Something about it, though, caught Dad's attention, and he looked at it more closely. It was a beautiful little thing, with evenly spaced freckles, a lofty brow, and intelligence radiating from its sleek little face. When Dad took that fish in his hands to unhook it, it held his gaze without squirming and patiently waited for him to release it. The little thing was so friendly that even after Dad dropped it back into the lake, it kept coming up to the surface to look out at him, in a sort of melancholy way, and then it started jumping up at the side of the boat, as if it was trying to get aboard and rejoin him. He said it made him think of a puppy that just wouldn't leave a person alone until it got some affection.

"Well, Dad had a bucket with him, and he scooped it full of water, set it on the transom, and then reached in, cupping his hands so that little fellow could swim right into them; then he lifted the fish out and put him in the bucket and turned back for shore. Now Dad had heard about people training trout, and he knew from what the experts said that you had to get a trout at just the right age, or they'd be too hardheaded and set in their ways to take to a human. This little fellow was so eager and bright and friendly that Dad figured he had the perfect specimen for proving what a great pet and companion a fish could be.

"Back at our camp, Dad had a tub, which was actually a big old barrel he had sawed in two. He drilled a hole at the bottom edge of that barrel and fitted a cork plug into it. Then he set that barrel up in a quiet corner of the place and filled it with water so the trout could feel at home. Every night, after the fish had gone to sleep, Dad would climb into the tub, reach down, jimmy the plug, and let out a little bit of the water until, eventually, after a couple of weeks, no water at all was left. The little guy would haul himself across the bottom of that tub on his fins—*fash! fash! fash!*—as if he were swimming along through the lake water. The trout had just gradually adapted to breathing and living in air, never even suspecting that anything was different and proving just how accommodating that finny little rascal was.

"Now, once Dad had had a chance to examine the little fish closely, he realized that his right pectoral fin was just a bit shorter than his left, and when the little guy would crawl around in that tub, happy as a clam—if crustaceans really do experience emotion—the trout'd kind of list to the right, a bit like a drunken man trying to find his way home. That's how Dad came up with the name Squiffy for him, and that's what Dad called him thereafter.

"Once Squiffy had adapted to breathing air, Dad knew he was ready for training, and he took the little fellow outside and let him crawl around on the pine needles and sand. By then, of course, Squiffy was feeding out of Dad's hand, and Dad could encourage him to try new things by dangling a worm in front of his nose. He got Squiffy to scuttle up a little ramp and then slide down the other side and to vault nose-first over stones he would set in the path. Wherever Dad went, Squiffy was sure to follow, though Dad did sometimes have to clear a path for him through the brush when it got too thick. They got to be such good friends that Squiffy wanted to follow Dad everywhere, even into the bathroom. Dad was, however, careful never to let him near the bathtub; after all the hard work that had gone into training his piscine compadre, he didn't want all their efforts to go down the drain, so to speak.

"Well, Dad remained addicted to his fishing, and since Squiffy insisted on being with him, the old man figured his friend wouldn't be happy unless he took *him* on the boat, too, though he claimed later to have had a premonition about doing so. They started going out together in the skiff, every morning and sometimes in the evening, too, cruising around the weeds and lily pads and trying out all the good spots. Squiffy had an instinct for where the big fish would be, and he'd perch up on the bow seat, adjusting the position of his body to point in the desired direction so Dad could steer the boat accordingly. And it wasn't just trout whose hiding spots Squiffy knew; he led Dad to some of the biggest bass and pickerel ever caught in New England too.

"The problem was that Squiffy would get really agitated when he was on to a good spot because he wanted to please Dad, and he'd start flopping up and down on his seat. Dad thought his antics were cute and would occasionally tease the little fish by purposely pointing the prow in a direction different from the one Squiffy had indicated. One day he did just that as they were passing that little pine island where the two buddies had first met, and Squiffy got *so* animated in his protests that he flipped himself up and over in a somersault that took him right out of the boat. He landed *kerplop* in the water right where that purply lily pad with the tear-shaped tear was, right where Dad had first hooked him. Dad tried to reverse that trolling motor, but by the time he got back around . . . that little trout . . . had drowned.

"Dad was heartbroken, of course, losing his best friend like that. Though he'd been a dog man all his life, he once told me that he'd never known a dog that was as good company as Squiffy was. We suggested that he fish for a replacement since he had proven what a good trout trainer he was, but Dad just gave us a mournful look as though we couldn't possibly understand what the experience had meant to him. He blamed himself for what had happened to his finny soul mate, and he never went fishing again. He buried the little tyke in the flower bed and used a hammer and chisel to carve out the word 'SQUIFFY' on a small rock he placed over the grave.

"Now, Walt," the snowplow driver said quietly, "if you'd like to see firsthand once the summer weather gets here, I can take you out to that very torn and purply lily pad where Dad both met and lost his best friend, Squiffy the trout."

Walt glanced at Todd quickly, then reached for the coffeepot, which sat next to the still-dozing Stumpy. "Yes, I'm sure you could," the silver-haired man said, still fighting back a grin. "So, your father was an accomplished animal trainer, was he?"

"Oh, sure," Todd replied, "didn't I ever tell you that his very first job was as a zookeeper?"

"No, you never did," Walt said dryly.

"Yeah. He had to quit though," the younger man continued, straight-faced. "He couldn't take the smell. His main job was, three times a day, to clean out the pen of that zoo's big attraction, what they referred to as 'The Lynx That Stinks.'"

"Okay," Walt said, "you win. This is what I get for telling the wrong person a shaggy dog story."

"A shaggy *dog* story?" Todd answered. "I thought your story was about a *bear*."

24

Stumpy and the Mosquitoes

March 28, 2012

Although it's been pretty chilly the last couple of days, you may remember that this time last week, we were enjoying temperatures in the seventies. The warm weather continued for several days out at Kibbee Pond in Townsend, where Walt Walthers, the elderly weather watcher, lives in that cozy cabin with his rambunctious rodent roommate, Stumpy the stub-tailed gray squirrel. Neither of them would have been sad to say goodbye to winter completely, but Walt certainly has had sufficient experience to know that nature sometimes likes to snake back around and nip us all on our posteriors. Even though the temperatures hovered around eighty for a couple of days near the official first day of spring, Walt and Stumpy did not engage in any premature celebrations (and the recent weather has proven them wise); instead, they simply tried to savor the foretaste of spring and summer that the baking sun brought them. Stumpy, in fact, spent quite a bit of time tanning on the deck; well, it's not accurate to call his sunbathing "tanning" since the sun has no effect on the color of his fur and since his face and some other parts of his body already have a tawny tone. Nevertheless, toward the tail end of last week, he often sprawled on the rail of the deck in his quest to soak up the rays, usually with his white belly turned up. Of course, he always seemed to keep at least one eye open because of the skirling cries of the pair of broad-winged hawks that nests each year in the tall pines along the pond's southern shore; those feathered predators have been especially active this year already, almost as if the unseasonable weather has made them feel they missed some vital early part of the mating and nesting process.

Walt has busied himself lately with some shoreline cleanup, since the winter—and especially that late-October snowstorm—left a fair amount of debris, including fallen pine branches. The pond has tossed up some flotsam as well, so Walt sometimes gets out his old aluminum wheelbarrow to haul the driftwood and the oak leaves he has raked from the pond edge back to the brush pile just inside the tree line of the woods. Stumpy likes to supervise from the boulder beneath the trio of white pines next to the dock or from one of the branches slightly higher than Walt's porkpie hat. Occasionally, a pine cone will fly down and land next to Walt where he is raking, but the kindly geezer enjoys pretending he hasn't noticed that he is being bombarded. His lack of reaction is sometimes frustrating enough to the mischievous tree hugger that the gray-furred rascal will burst out in some overhead scolding, just to be sure he can still get Walt's attention. "Quiet down, you pie-*rat*!" Walt will respond. (Note the pronunciation.) "You're gonna wake up the whole neighborhood." Such comments just make the squirrel chatter more, which in turn makes Walt chuckle at having maintained the upper hand, something he isn't always able to do with his rascally roommate.

Late one weekday afternoon, the two swinging bachelors—as Walt likes to call Stumpy and himself—welcomed to the cabin their favorite neighbors, Amy Riggetti and her six-year-old son, Tony, who live just down Kibbee Pond Road in a little Cape that had been empty for several years before they moved in last summer. Amy had brought some oatmeal raisin cookies as payback for all the snacks Tony and she have enjoyed at the cabin; of course, I should mention that Walt and Stumpy have a standing dinner invitation at the Riggettis' every Wednesday evening, and they always eat well on those visits. The folks who live out at Kibbee Pond don't go in for freeloading of any sort.

"Well," Walt said, "it's getting close to suppertime, but I can't turn down homemade cookies, and neither can the ol' Stumperama here. In fact, he might be willing to sell his squirrelly soul for an oatmeal raisin cookie! Shall we get some drinks and head out to the deck to enjoy some of those balmy breezes?"

"Say, Mr. Walt," Tony said after they had gone outside and settled in at the deck table, "now that the dock is in, have you had a chance to take Miss Nelly out for one of your pond cruises?"

Walt laughed. "Your buddies Shel, Mac, and Hammy were just here yesterday to lug Nelly down to the water and fetch the three-horse Johnson motor from the shed. But I haven't taken her out yet, even though I did turn the motor over. I figured you and your mom might want to join me for that first outing."

"Oh, please!" Tony answered.

"Well," Walt said, "let's enjoy our cookies for a bit, and then—if your mom is okay with the idea and it doesn't cut into your supper plans—we can take a short spin and make sure that everything is still where it's supposed to be. You okay with that, Amy?"

The young woman's blue eyes twinkled as she said, "We don't need ulterior motives to visit you, Walt, but the idea of a nautical jaunt had already crossed both our minds."

At that moment, Amy slapped at her leg and said, "Oh no!" and simultaneously, Walt heard a high-pitched whining in his ears. Soon, all three humans were swatting the air around them, and even Stumpy was sitting up on the deck rail and darting out one front paw at a time in his attempts to grab the insect invaders that had started to swarm around the group.

"Well," Walt said, "*there's* one downside to an early spring: The mosquitoes come out earlier too. These guys have that just-hatched desperation to them as well. Maybe we can get away from them out on the pond where the breeze is steady. Tony, you grab the life vests and meet us down at the dock. I'll get ready to cast Nelly off. Come on, Stump! You don't want us to leave you behind to face these vicious predators by yourself." Stumpy had just snatched another mosquito out of the air and was stuffing it into his mouth, but at his friend's words, he leaped off the rail and scooted down toward the pond. "Now he's literally got a skeeter in his scooter!" Walt laughed.

Walt had the Johnson purring before Amy and Tony settled into their seats. Amy took the middle spot, giving an occasional swing of her arm or outright swat at the swarming insects that had followed them from the deck. Tony went up into the bow, which was usually Stumpy's prerogative; the squirrel, however, was happy to assume a mariner's stance on the six-year-old's right shoulder, facing forward and into the breeze even though Tony had to face the stern.

"Oh, that's better already," Amy said when Nelly had advanced only twenty yards or so out into the open water.

"Yeah," Walt said, "those vampiric flyboys don't like to leave their tree cover for long." They were putting past one of the little islands ringed with blueberry bushes, and from the lower branches of a solitary pine tree, a song sparrow was releasing its simultaneously reedy and liquid song. The last phrase ended with a rising note like a question, and Walt said, "That song sparrow sounds hopeful, doesn't he? That's what a taste of spring will do to you. See that dark spot in the center of his chest? It's a pretty distinctive marking for that species, but the song is recognizable, too, and one of the prettiest ones I know."

"Mr. Walt?" Tony said, turning his head back toward his elderly friend.

"Sir?" Walt answered.

"Mr. Walt, do you know why we have to have mosquitoes? They're one of the only bad things about spring."

"I agree with you on that point," the skipper said, pushing his porkpie hat back on his forehead and throttling the motor down so that Nelly barely glided along. "I don't much care for the bloodthirsty monsters myself. I believe that every creature in this world has some sort of useful function to perform, though, and I'm never quick to assume that eliminating even a tiny, pesky organism is a good idea. Scientists say that mosquito larvae supply food for all kinds of fish and migratory birds while they also process decaying leaves and organic matter and microorganisms in the water; in addition, adult mosquitoes are on the menu for frogs, salamanders, lizards, snakes, insects, spiders, bats, and birds of all sorts, and they also pollinate many kinds of plants, so they do have some useful functions. On the other hand, some scientists argue now that other organisms could step in to fill their niches without much disruption and that eliminating mosquitoes would have a huge benefit because of the decrease in the diseases they can transmit from one person to another. Perhaps one of their original functions was to keep human and animal populations down so that overcrowding wouldn't occur.

"Of course, then again, if I was prone to facetiousness, I might say that mosquitoes exist for two main purposes."

"Mr. Walt, what's feces-ness?" Tony asked.

"Fa-*ce*-tiousness," Walt said, "is being a wise guy, being flippant, making a joke about something that other people are being serious about."

"What are the two feces-tious purposes of mosquitoes, then, Mr. Walt?" the little shaver asked.

"First of all," the silver-haired jokester replied, "they teach us to accept unpleasantness with patience, and second, they help us build up our foot speed and stamina for when we just can't take it anymore and have to run away."

They were cruising slowly along a spit of white pines that sticks out perpendicularly from the biggest island in the pond when Walt pointed to a dead tree at the end of the spit, where a white-bellied, cigar-shaped bird perched in the sun, chittering quietly. "Look!" he said. "There's the first tree swallow of the year. Swallows are one of the signs of spring I most look forward to." The chittering vocalizations continued as the boat passed around the tip of the spit.

"Do you know any stories about mosquitoes?" Tony asked.

"As a matter of fact," Walt said," there's a Native American story I like about how mosquitoes came to be. Let's see. How does it go? Oh yeah . . . long ago, in the time before time really began, before everything had taken on the form and shape it has now, a horrible, bloodthirsty monster was preying on the people. This monstrous giant liked to lie in wait for them, jump out, and then chomp down their flesh and guzzle their blood. You know the Cookie Monster on *Sesame Street*? This creature looked a lot like the Cookie Monster, just more scary. I imagine it might even have talked like the Cookie Monster. Anyway, the people were terrified and soon became desperate as they lost more and more of their tribe; before long, they called a council to try to choose a course of action. One young man stood up in front of the others and said, 'I can rid us of this monster if you will let me try,' and the elders agreed, without even hearing his plan.

"The next day, the young man went to the last place where anyone had seen the monster and lay down in the path there, pretending to be dead. Along came the bloodthirsty fiend, and when it saw the man lying there, it said—let me see if I can do my Cookie Monster voice—'Oh, now these people are making it too easy for me. I don't even have to chase these human cookies. They just fall down and die, they're so scared of me! Ooh, this one is still nice and warm! Om, nom, nom, nom! He will taste delicious, just like a chocolate chip cookie!'

"The monster threw the young man over its shoulder, head down like a bag of grain, and carried him back to its lair, where it threw him down near the fireplace. When it saw that all the firewood was gone, it went back out to fetch some.

"As soon as the giant went out, the young man arose and grabbed the monster's huge knife from a nearby table, which was a good thing, because almost immediately the giant's son entered the lair. The young man grabbed the giant's son, who was not fully grown yet, put the knife blade to his throat, and said, 'Tell me where your father's heart is, or I'll cut you wide open!'

"The giant's little son said, 'Oh no, please don't hurt me. I'll tell you whatever you want, you delicious-looking human. My father's heart is in the heel of his left foot.'

"At that moment, the father's gigantic foot appeared in the entryway, and the young man stabbed the left heel with the knife as the giant's son fled outside. The giant collapsed and died. Mission accomplished! A moment later, however, the giant-slaying hero heard the monster's disembodied voice making a vow: 'Though you have slain me, I will come back from the dead and keep eating you human cookies until the end of time.'

"'Oh no you won't!' the hero replied, and he cut the giant's body into pieces and burned them all to ashes in the fire. Then he cast all the ashes into the wind and watched them blow away.

"As they blew away, however, each bit of ash turned into a mosquito, and those ashen mosquitoes all came together into a big swarm, which hovered over the young man's head. From the swarm came the giant's voice again: 'I will never stop eating human cookie flesh and drinking human cookie blood!' Then the hero felt first one burning sting, then another, and yet another, as the mosquitoes started drinking his blood. And all he could do about it was swat at them and scratch himself."

"Holy cow, Mr. Walt!" Tony said. "Did that really happen?"

"What do *you* think?" Walt said. "I wasn't around back then to be an eyewitness either. I heard the story much later."

"Wow!" Tony said. "I hadn't really thought before that mosquitoes were actually eating us, but I guess they are."

"Now," Walt said as Nelly continued along the shoreline and as Stumpy climbed down off Tony's shoulder and up into Amy's lap on the middle seat, "not all mosquito stories are scary. Some are actually funny."

"Like what?" Amy said in mischievous challenge as she stroked Stumpy's nose and forehead with one finger.

"Well, there's the one about the three noodleheads who had just arrived in Boston by boat from Europe, thinking they could become rich quick. Together, they bought a big piece of land in Lunenburg, sight unseen, from a sleazy real estate agent there, and they were so anxious to get to work clearing it and planting it that they set out on their own without any kind of guidance—no maps, no directions, no compass, no GPS. They wandered around for most of one day, looking for landmarks and getting so lost that they eventually realized they were traipsing around in circles.

"'Sacrebleu!' said one of them, the one from France. 'Zis ees *très* discouraging, zis walking around and around and getting us nowhere to go!' (He was new in this country, and his English wasn't very good.)

"'*Si, señor,*' said the second numbskull, who happened to be from Spain. 'In Espain, we have not this confusion kind of pathway. All roads go in lines of straightness.'

"'*Jawohl,*' said the third nincompoop, this one from Germany. 'Ve vill do vell to look for shelter for *die nacht.*'

"They settled down under some hemlocks along the edge of a swamp, but before they even closed their eyes, they heard a humming and then a high-pitched whining, and then suddenly, they started slapping at their faces and arms. 'Oh! Oh! Oh!' shouted the Frenchman, 'somesing ees sinking ze hot needles into me!'

"'Vass iss das?' the German shouted. 'Ooh! Ooh!'

"The Spaniard shrieked, '*Porque* do she stab me? I do nothing wrong!'

"They all huddled down and tried to cover up as well as they could, but they spent the night swearing in their own languages at the tiny demons that continued to attack them. In the morning their faces were swollen, and their arms and legs were covered with red welts; in the light of dawn, they at last were able to see what had been plaguing them. However, they didn't know what to call their insect tormenters because no one had ever warned them about mosquitoes.

"In desperation they set off to seek some shelter or a way out of the trackless swamp in which they were now lost, but they continued to wander in circles. Finally, as dusk was again falling, they came upon an abandoned shack, and they went inside, believing that its windows and doorways would protect them from the bloodthirsty marauders that had attacked them the previous night. Hungry and exhausted, they collapsed on the floorboards.

"'Ve haff nussink now to fear,' the German said. 'Zose hell-hunds cannot bite us here!' Soon they all fell asleep despite their grumbling stomachs.

"In the middle of the night, however, the snoring of the Spaniard woke up the Frenchman, who saw little lights winking on and off around the room. 'Ah, *mon Dieu*!' he cried. '*Allez*! *Allez*! We must to go! Ze devils are back to be sucking of our blood! Zis time, zey will kill us! Zey have brought with zem ze lantern lights so zey can see in ze dark to suck out all of our bloods!'

"In their panic, the three nutjobs ran right through the door without even opening it, and they were so desperate that, this time, they ran in a straight line right back to the docks in Boston, where each boarded a ship bound back to his home country. You see, not only had they never heard of mosquitoes, but they had also never heard of fireflies, and they had no way of knowing that those glow-in-the-dark night fliers were absolutely harmless."

Nelly had nearly completed her circuit of the pond, and as they approached the dock again, Walt said, "Now, as soon as we pull in, you two should head up to the cabin with Stumpy so ze demon insects do not stick zeir hot-needle poke-airs into ze tender flesh. I'll be up as soon as I get Nelly tied up. I've got one more mosquito story for when we get inside."

Amy was sitting on the couch with Tony leaning comfortably

against her when Walt started his final story; Stumpy was munching on some honey-roasted cashews Amy had produced from her bag.

"Well," Walt said, "this is a story about the time Stumpy went courting Mr. Coyote's daughter." The full-cheeked squirrel looked up at the mention of his name. "Mr. Coyote wasn't much to look at," Walt continued, "but his daughter was absolutely gorgeous, a real fox. Well, not a fox literally, you know, but a foxy lady, in a figurative sense, and she certainly did have a fine . . . figure. In any case, all the male animals in the neighborhood were eager to pay their respects and try to win her favor.

"Farnsworth Fox was the first to call on her, and Mr. Coyote let them sit out on the front porch together on the glider couch. Unfortunately for Farnsworth Fox, however, Mr. Coyote's house was down low in the swamp, and as soon as they plunked down on the glider, mosquitoes the size of stealth bombers came zooming in. Poor Farnsworth started swatting away at them, all in a panic, like he couldn't help himself. Mr. Coyote yelled out the window, 'Get out of here, you rust-colored rag mop! No man is gonna court my daughter if he can't stand a few little skeeter pokes!'

"Next up was Carlton Coon, but he didn't even get his bee-hind set down on that glider before he lost his composure and started flailing away at those winged bloodsuckers. 'Get your striped petunia back home!' Mr. Coyote yelled out the window, and Carlton hightailed it out of there, so to speak.

"Same thing happened with Malcolm Mink and Reginald Rabbit and a whole host of other critters till the ol' Stumpster here heard about the fair young female. He bought some chocolates, picked some flowers, and even wrote a love poem called 'To His Coyote Mistress' and then set off for Mr. Coyote's place down there in the swamp.

"Now Carmela Coyote had heard about Stumpy too. You know, his reputation always precedes him, and ever since third grade, she'd heard he was the cutest and cleverest critter in the county, so she set about making herself as pretty and fetching as could be, what with rouge on her cheeks and strawberry-scented deodorant, with mascara and depilatory cream, with breath freshener and toenail paint. That's not to mention the sequined halter top and the jeans about three sizes too small that she squeezed that foxy figure into. When Stumpy saw her, he swallowed once in disbelief and then stepped up onto that porch. He's always ready for a challenge, amatory or otherwise." The Stumpy outside the story had long since stopped chewing and was now leaning back against Amy's stomach, listening intently.

"Now, Mr. Coyote knew about the ol' Stumperoo's reputation as a lady's man, so he was not about to leave the two of them alone together, especially with Carmela dressed up the way she was. He pulled up his own rocking chair and joined them there on the porch just as the first squadron of kamikaze mosquitoes was zeroing in on the redoubtable squirrel. *ZROWM! ZROWM! ZROWM!* Stumpy stayed cool, though.

"'Lovely spot you picked for your home, Mr. Coyote,' Stumpy said. *ZROWM! ZROWM! ZROWM!* He had to fight the impulse to take a swing at the aerial invaders, but unlike some animals, he has preternatural self-control.

"'Well,' Mr. Coyote replied, 'some claim we're too close to the swamp.'

"'Naw! Really?' the stub-tailed boy toy replied calmly. *ZROWM! ZROWM! ZROWM!* 'That's hard to believe. Say, you know what I saw down in Townsend center today? A spotted horse! Never saw one of those before.' *ZROWM! ZROWM! ZROWM!*

"'I never saw one my own self,' Mr. Coyote said. 'Tell me about it.'

"'I'm yours if you want me,' Carmela whispered. 'You're my hero.' I guess she'd never ever seen a spotted horse either. Like every other female, she had fallen hard for the rodent Casanova's gray-furred charm.

"'Well,' the Stumpilator said, 'that old horse had one spot right *here*!' He slapped his left biceps, where a mosquito with a proboscis about three inches long was preparing to sink it into the flesh beneath his luxuriant gray fur. *SPLAT!* 'No kidding,' he continued, 'and that horse had another spot right *here*!' He splatted another insect that had perched expectantly right between his black button eyes.

"'Your eyes are *so* cute!' Carmela panted under her breath.

"'You don't say!' Mr. Coyote said. 'Where else did that equine oddity wear his spots?'

"'Well, right here on his leg.' *SPLAT!* 'And between his shoulder blades.' *SPLAT!* 'And on his left buttock!' *SPLAT!* 'And on his right calf.' *SPLAT!* And that rascally rodent kept on slapping the mosquitoes that were bugging him, and he kept on describing that horse's beauty marks until he had made mosquitoes just about extinct in the entire state of Massachusetts. By the time Stumpy was done swatting, Mr. Coyote had dozed off out of boredom; after all, nobody could be *that* interested in a pinto pony's paint job.

"That was the moment when Carmela lost control of her passion and dragged Stumpy out behind the bushes . . . but I'd better stop the story there because I don't want to get an R rating." Walt drew a deep breath. Stumpy had turned his head to one side where he sat in Amy's lap; Walt could have sworn that his tawny cheeks had flushed slightly redder.

"What's an R rating, Mr. Walt?" Tony asked.

"That's what moviemakers give to a movie that grown-ups might appreciate but kids would find boring," Amy answered for the mischievous geezer. "It was a good story, though, wasn't it, Tony?"

"Yes, ma'am," the tyke said, nodding energetically. "I'm not sure which mosquito story I liked best."

"I'm pretty sure I know which one Stumpy liked best," Walt said, chuckling.

Perched on Amy's left leg, the gray-furred stud muffin took that opportunity to nod energetically himself.

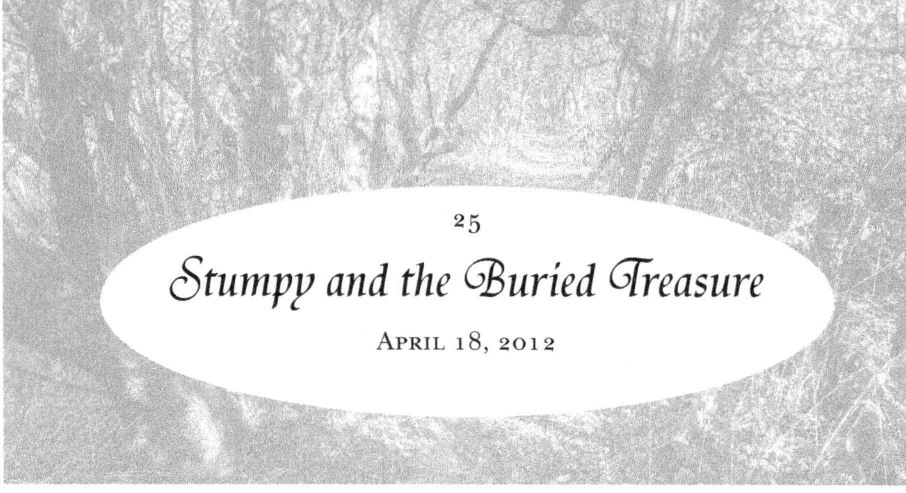

25

Stumpy and the Buried Treasure

April 18, 2012

April *can* be a cruel month. Just ask Walt Walthers, the elderly weather watcher who lives in a cabin out on Kibbee Pond in Townsend; he's been through more than eighty Aprils. He knows that unseasonable warmth in late winter can coax out blossoms and green shoots that a sudden April freeze can then decimate, and he knows that April snow can drag down and tear off many branches from trees and bushes because of the newly opened foliage. He knows best of all that human spirits soar at the prospects of spring but that April can be teasing us with the prospect of warm sun and pleasant breezes, only to taunt us with the realities of chilly rain and biting winds, making spring seem an impossible fantasy. As a longtime follower of the Boston Red Sox, he also knows from this year—and others—that April can disappoint the hopes of overly optimistic fans and minimize the rejuvenating impact of spring. He was nonetheless relieved when the home-opening series against the Devil Rays went well (he likes to call them the Devil Rays still despite their official name change a while back; he figures the people in Tampa may *think* they're more pious and righteous than they really are). Nevertheless, the baseball season is long and invariably includes many ups and downs, as veteran Red Sox fans have learned. Walt knows not to let his hopes get too high, but even at his advanced age, he still likes to cultivate a few impossible dreams.

Walt's roommate and constant companion, Stumpy, a gray squirrel who lost his magnificent tail in a freak accident more than two years ago, is not as philosophical as his human friend. He is, in fact, indifferent to the fate of the Red Sox, and he pretty much lives every day as it comes, taking whatever weather comes with it. If it's rainy and raw, Stumpy is happy for the excuse to stay inside and snooze on the back of Walt's recliner; if it's sunny and pleasant, he is glad to grab the opportunity for some sunbathing, sprawling on his back outside on the deck rail. Regardless of the weather, he's always ready for a ride in Lulu, the green '60 Chevy pickup, or Nelly, Walt's ten-foot rowboat, with her three-horse Johnson outboard. And he always savors mealtimes when they arrive. Maybe he is both a stoic and an epicurean after all.

Walt decided during the first week of April that a special event commemorating the real start of spring could be fun, and he figured he would revive an old family tradition, from the days when his sons were small: He would put together a treasure hunt for his friend and neighbor Tony Riggetti and enlist the help of the six-year-old's mom, Amy, as official clue reader. When he broached the topic, Tony was still recovering from the excitement of the egg hunt his neighbor had staged Easter morning, but as always, he was game to try one of Walt's suggestions. Amy, however, was curious. "Why another hunt so soon after the egg hunt? That really was a wonderful occasion, and Tony hasn't stopped talking about it."

"Well," Walt answered, "this one is different enough in purpose and procedure that I don't think it'll prove too repetitious, and it's a good excuse for us all to get outside together in this pleasant weather. This one will involve some written clues, so you can help Tony make sense of them. Besides, the idea is central to my personal philosophy: Something unexpected and wonder-filled is always right under our noses, but we're not always open enough to the possibilities to see those things. Sometimes we need to direct our looking to find the best treasures, and other times, we need to open up so we can find unexpected treasures while we think we're looking for something very different. What is it that Thorin the dwarf says in Tolkien's *The Hobbit*? 'There is nothing like looking, if you want to find something. . . . You certainly usually find something, if you look, but it is not always quite the something you were after.'

"I always say that spring is one of the best times for looking because something about the season makes us more open to seeing what's really there, maybe because we're expecting wonder-filled things after the cold and dark of winter. I like the way some of the old stories start, sending their heroes and heroines off in a state of *not* knowing so they have to accept their own limitations and put themselves in the hands of other guides and forces they can't control. There's one Russian folktale that starts with the character receiving a command: 'Go—not knowing where; bring—not knowing what; the path is long, the way unknown; the hero knows not how to arrive there by himself.' There's another one in which the king orders the hero to find a place called 'I know not where' and bring back a thing called 'I know not what.' When Stumpy and I go out for our daily walk in the woods, I often repeat a line that comes up again and again in traditional stories: 'I will go, and we shall see what we shall see.' When we go out, we don't know what we'll see. But—you know?—we always see *something*."

"Okay," Amy laughed, "I just didn't want you to put yourself out again so soon after the other occasion. We'd love to be part of the treasure hunt. Just let us know what we should do."

Thus it was that on Saturday morning, with sun warming the deck and a light breeze breathing off the pond, Amy and Tony knocked on the cabin door. Walt quickly opened it, and his friends stepped inside. As Stumpy scooted up Tony's leg to his shoulder, put his paws on the boy's cheek, and sniffed at his ear, Amy laughed. Then she said, "Here we are, and we brought open minds and open eyes!"

Even in his plaid flannel shirt, red suspenders, and battered porkpie hat, Walt sounded a bit like a mystical shaman or prophet when he replied, "What is it Jesus says in the book of Matthew? 'Ask, and it shall be given you; seek, and ye shall find; knock, and it shall be opened unto you: For everyone that asketh receiveth; he that seeketh findeth; and to him that knocketh, it shall be opened.' Sort of like how I opened the door just now!"

Tony asked then, "What kind of treasure are we looking for, Mr. Walt?"

"Good question!" the smiling codger replied. "That'll depend a bit on you guys. The philosopher Meno used to ask, 'How will you go about finding that thing the nature of which is totally unknown to you?' You see, I can't really tell you what the treasures are; that's one of the things I want you to figure out for yourselves. The figuring out itself might turn out to be one of the treasures."

"I don't think I understand, Mr. Walt," the boy replied.

"There are lots of things we don't understand, Tony," the silver-haired mentor said, "and sometimes we don't even realize what we don't understand. But that's okay; the first step is to realize we don't know everything and that we want to know more. Something is always missing from our lives, and sometimes realizing that we are missing something is our chance to retrieve it or find it for the first time. But enough said! I don't want to confuse you more by talking gibberish. Here's how this'll work.

"I'll give you a written clue, and with luck you and your mom'll figure out what it's talking about and where to go to find that particular treasure. Once you get there, you'll find another clue, and that'll take you somewhere else. Remember that *I* wrote the clues, so it's as if I'm there with you, trying to show you the way without showing you too much. And the Stumpster would probably like to go along literally and help out if he can."

"Oh yes," Tony said. "I bet he'll be a big help."

"Okay," Walt said, "if you guys are ready, here's your first clue." He handed Amy a folded piece of paper.

"I'm surprised you didn't make an origami shape with this to aid our understanding," she said.

"Ooh, I'll have to try that next time," the elderly guide said, "or maybe I could draw you a map."

"I like treasure maps!" Tony said.

"Well then, maybe you can think of the clues as a kind of map, just made out of words instead of pictures," Walt said. "Your mom can be the map expert who helps you read the map and get the pictures straight in your head."

"Here goes!" Amy said. Then she unfolded the paper and read the first clue: "'I am the sentinel of the swamp; come and touch my gnarled skin.'"

"What's a 'centennial'?" Tony asked.

"'Sentinel,'" Amy said. "A sentinel is a watchman or lookout, someone who watches over someplace and keeps an eye out for whatever might be coming."

"What's 'snarled'?" the youngster asked. "Is that like what happens to people's hair sometimes?"

"That is what 'snarled' means," Amy said, "but this word is

'gnarled,' and it means full of knots or bumps, the way tree bark is bumpy and rough? Older people's skin can be gnarled or rough instead of smooth."

"Oh," Tony said, "but isn't a tree's bark like its skin? So couldn't it mean a tree of some sort? And couldn't a big tree be like a sentimental?"

"Very good," Amy said, "but the word is 'sentinel.'"

"Well," the boy said, his voice rising, "couldn't that big pine at this side of the swamp be the . . . scent-tunnel then?"

"Makes sense to me," Amy said, then turned to Walt. "I don't suppose you can tell us if we're hot or cold . . . ?"

Walt just laughed and shook his head. "I'll be inside doing some weather watching, and I'll leave the three of you to your quest. I've put out ten clues, counting this one, but I think you'll know when you're done anyway."

"Come on, Mommy," Tony said, tugging at Amy's hand. Stumpy skittered down the boy's arm and hopped to the pine needle–covered ground, then looked up to see what the humans would do next. They set out hand in hand along a path through the trees along the pond shore, and soon the squirrel was scampering ahead of them.

Five minutes' walk took them to the base of an eighty-foot-tall white pine at the tip of a neck of land that extended into the swamp at the pond's northwest corner. "See, Mommy? It *does* look out over the whole swamp, and feel its skin; it *is* all bumpy and rough."

"Look at the patterns in the bark, too, these grooves and channels," Amy answered. They had found another folded paper at the base of the trunk, but absorbed now in the tree, they noticed, too, how its bark wasn't just one color but instead was red and brown and gray and even blue-green with its patches of lichen. They noticed, too, how all the lower branches of the sentinel pine were missing or dead, with just jagged stubs sticking out until the healthy branches with green needles started, more than halfway up the trunk. As they examined the tree, Stumpy clambered up the gnarled surface and gave them some perspective on just how far up the living branches started. He sat on one of the dead stubs and chattered happily down to his friends. "Look how much at home he is up there!" Amy said.

Tony put his hand on the roughness of the bark. "Mommy, do you suppose the pine tree gets lonely out here?"

Amy smiled at her son and said, “It does have the other trees and bushes for company, but—I don’t know—maybe it could. Sometimes I feel lonely even when other people are around. Not when you’re with me, though,” she added quickly, putting her hand on her son’s shoulder. “Shall we look at this other clue?” she asked.

Tony, however, had stepped away from the pine and toward the swamp; he was gesturing for her to come closer. “Look!” he whispered. Amy edged her way closer, trying to look where he was looking, and Stumpy eased himself quietly down the trunk, just as curious about what Tony was seeing; when he reached his young friend, the squirrel scooted up to his shoulder again. Tony pointed, and the others saw then: On a floating log about thirty feet off shore, twelve or more turtles were lined up, all facing in the same direction, all with their necks outstretched as they enjoyed the spring sun, though their sizes varied dramatically.

“Painted turtles,” Amy said. The trio walked slowly closer, but as they did so, the turtles, one by one, in exact sequence from right to left, plopped off the log and disappeared under the water. “We’ll have to tell Walt about that.”

And that’s the way the rest of the afternoon went, with Amy reading the clues and the pair figuring them out together and Stumpy tagging along to provide comic relief from the intensity of the search with his antics and clowning. For the clue “I am fruitful but cranky,” Tony quickly blurted, “It must be that crabby apple tree that Mr. Walt hung the Easter eggs from,” and when they arrived at the spot, they not only saw the incipient blossoms on the tree but also heard maniacal avian laughter from the pine forest beyond. Soon thereafter, a huge black-and-white bird levered its way through the air past them, lifting and then dipping as its wings rowed the air. “Oh, look!” Amy said. “It’s a pileated woodpecker. Walt says they nest back in there. I wonder if we can be patient enough to wait for that one to return and then figure out which tree the nest is in. Shall we try?” Tony nodded his head vigorously, and they found a comfortable, moss-covered rock near a line of big trees and waited there.

As they sat, Tony spotted some mayflowers peeking out from the dried leaves on the forest floor, and though he didn’t know what the pink-tinged white blossoms were, his mother did. Together, they knelt down to inhale the faint but intense sweetness. As they noticed more of the flowers peeping out in other locations, they walked on their knees, laughing, from one clump to another, bending over at each to sniff and arguing playfully about which clump was most fragrant. They had lost track of the time when, suddenly, they heard again the cackling call of the pileated. They managed to look up quickly enough to see it land in a particular pine. "We'll have to tell Walt about that too," Amy said.

Another clue, "I purr like a kitten, but unlike a kitten, I like to swim," took them to Walt's dock and to Nelly, with her outboard motor. There, they watched a spider stringing a web under the stern seat, and they found a plastic bag containing two pieces of stale bread that Walt had left for them along with the final clue. Remembering Walt's stories and their own experiences the previous summer, they broke the bread into bits, giving a few to Stumpy but using most to lure the bluegill and pumpkinseed sunfish out from under the dock. Amy and Tony laughed at the feeding frenzy that ensued, though Stumpy seemed a bit miffed that the humans would waste so much tasty snack food on creatures with gills instead of lungs and scales instead of fur. Even the greedy squirrel, though, was impressed when Amy held the bread bits in her fingers a couple of inches above the water's surface and started coaxing the kibbies to jump out after their treats. Some even leaped all the way out of the water.

When they finally got around to reading the last clue, it said, "I am the best place in the world at the end of the day." They looked at each other, laughed, and—with Stumpy hopping and skittering behind—silently headed for their house, just down the hill from the cabin. There, they found Walt waiting on the deck in a chair; he closed his Patrick O'Brian novel and said, "I guess you figured out that last clue okay. Journeys are best when they take you to new places and show you new things but also when they bring you home again. I cooked up a pot of chili at my place and brought it down here, along with some garlic bread."

Amy looked at her watch then. "Oh my," she laughed. "I had no idea it was this late."

Walt laughed too. "Now you have to tell me what treasures you found on your quest, and then I'll tell you a story or two while we're eating." Stumpy had climbed into the man's lap and seemed ready to start snoring even before he finished curling up there.

Once Walt had picked up the sleeping squirrel, and they had all retired inside to the warmth and comfort of the little house, Amy and Tony told the porkpie-hatted gent about the day's treasures: the turtles and the mayflowers and the pileated woodpecker nest and the spider's web and the sunfish circus and dozens of other wonders they had witnessed in the course of the afternoon. They realized as they talked that some of what they had seen Walt had intended them to see, but also that putting themselves in the path of the unexpected had brought them some other treasures that even their elderly guide could not have anticipated.

After ladling out the chili and passing around the garlic bread, Walt settled back in his chair and started his story. Stumpy was sprawled on the back of the couch across the room. "Many years ago, back before the Civil War, a fellow named Luke Flinders lived here in Townsend, eking out a living from a starve-acre farm he had inherited from his father. The farm was called Tumblers Bottom. Luke had no money to spare and seven hungry children to raise, and his wife always seemed to be reminding him of something else they didn't have but needed. Even when he tried to sleep, his dreams would bring him back to his failure to provide adequately for his family.

"One night, however, the nature of Luke Flinders's dreams shifted; instead of nightmares about dragons devouring his cattle or county officials coming to take away his loved ones to the poor farm, he had a vision of an elderly man in a white robe, who urged him to travel west to Williamstown and seek a treasure there, buried under a bridge over the Green River. For two nights, he wondered about the dream but ignored its import, even though the bearded man seemed insistent. The third night's repetition of the dream, however, was too much for Luke, who rose early the next day and, with only minimal explanation to his wife, departed for the western part of the state, carrying a bundle of clothes on his back and only a few coins in his pocket.

"When he arrived in Williamstown, he found the Green River and the bridge but could see no logical place to begin digging. Besides, the traffic over the bridge was so regular that he was reluctant to expose himself to inquiries from passersby and, especially, the police. Luke lingered nearby for three days, at night sleeping back in the woods and during the daylight hours hoping for further clues or an opportunity to begin digging.

"A house stood not far from the bridge, and a middle-aged man who lived there noticed Luke haunting the spot. On the third day, that ruddy-faced man walked closer and inquired why the shabby visitor was lurking on the bridge. Luke answered, 'I am mortified to admit my folly, but I dreamed three times of an old man who told me of a treasure beneath this bridge, and I figured that if I came to Williamstown, I could go home a wealthy man. Now I realize that I don't even know how to begin my search.'

"The ruddy-faced owner of the house laughed, though not cruelly. 'I laugh,' he said, 'because if I had your naive faith in dreams, I might have wasted my time just as foolishly as you have yours. *I* once had a similar dream, but mine told of a treasure buried way back east in a town called Townsend at the bottom of a well on a run-down old farm called, of all things, Tumblers Bottom. Seeing you makes me all the more glad I didn't give in to the temptation to chase that dream! Come across, and let me give you some warm food.'

"'No, thank you,' said Luke, having absorbed already the implications of the other man's story. 'I'd better be on my way. I've already left my family alone too long.' Two days' traveling brought Luke back to his farm. To his wife's shock and confusion, he began immediately to dig up the old well that had long since ceased to yield water. Her shock, however, turned to joy when Luke's shovel pinged on the outside of a metal-lined box, and he opened it to reveal a mound of gold coins and more wealth than the family had ever dreamed possible.

"When Luke and his wife examined the box more closely, they found an inscription in Latin on the outside of the cover. Neither of them read Latin, but they copied the words onto paper and gave the sheet to their oldest son, who took it to the local school with him and asked the kindly old Latin teacher there to help him pronounce the words. 'Oh, I can help you pronounce them,' the teacher said, 'but do you know what they mean? I can tell you that too.' He studied the words a moment and then said, 'It seems a sort of riddle: "Like what lies beneath this cover, under this you'll find another."

Very mysterious.' But the son knew right away what the riddle meant, and he rushed home and told his father to grab the shovel again. They dug farther into the well and found another box full of gold, this one even bigger than the first. With some of their newfound wealth, Luke and his family paid to restore the old church on the common, which a fire had nearly consumed two years before. The rest they parceled out carefully to provide for improvements to the farm and to establish a fund so the children could attend college. One daughter eventually became a noted psychologist whose specialty was the interpretation of dreams."

As Walt finished, his listeners could hear Stumpy's even snoring from across the room. "Of course," Walt continued, "there's another similar story, a French tale, about a dying farmer who makes his sons promise never to sell his land. He tells them that a treasure is hidden somewhere in the soil, and though he doesn't know the exact location, they will eventually find the right place if they throw themselves into their work and look carefully. After telling them to dig, plow, and plant every bit of the land, the father dies, and the sons, who have always loved their father deeply, work that ground and turn all the soil over, in keeping with his dying wish. Though the sons never find a literal treasure buried there, the fields become ever richer in their yield of grains and vegetables, and the brothers' bond grows ever stronger as they labor side by side. Thus, the father's wisdom comes out clearly: He was showing them that work itself can be the hidden treasure.

"You see," the silver-haired tale weaver said, "it's like your treasure hunt. What was important and brought you joy was not what you first thought, not some objects you carried home, but the search itself, the time you had together, the unexpected glimpses and wonders you shared and will remember together now. And although you covered a fair amount of ground in your wanderings today, you didn't have to travel the entire world to find what is precious to you: It was right here all along, right here at home. And now you know how to look for it again . . . though the treasure will never be quite the same, because you'll never be quite the same yourselves."

Amy and Tony were holding hands across the table, and the young mother said, "Thank you, Walt." Tony got up then, climbed into the elderly man's lap, and threw his arms around his friend's neck, his face pressed against the plaid flannel of Walt's shirt. "Thank you, Mr. Walt."

The smiling mentor said, "You, my dear friends, are more than welcome."

26

Stumpy and the Swan

May 2, 2012

In the last two weeks out at Kibbee Pond, Walt Walthers and Stumpy the squirrel have experienced a veritable smorgasbord of weather, a wide range of meteorological conditions that any lover of spring in New England would find palatable, from hot, dry spells to rainy stretches, from quiet days when the pond surface was like a mirror to wild and windy times when blasts from the southeast caused the water to lap the shoreline almost as loudly as the ocean gnaws at Cape Ann. As you know, Walt is a professional weather watcher, so you won't be surprised when I tell you that he has delighted in that variety. He is a fan of the unpredictable uniqueness of each year; in his eighty-plus springs, he says he has rarely seen the leaves and blossoms emerge as early as they have this year, and he rather likes the way the world can keep us guessing about what will last and what will come next. He has even assigned a new name to this mercurial, amorphous season we are passing through: He calls it May-pril. He told his buddy Todd Jormonen the other day that he's not sure if that name will carry over into the next month as well; perhaps it will if the temperatures stay cool and the winds continue to make things feel like *early* spring. Of course, if things warm up unnaturally, he may have to coin a new name, like Majune or Jumay or even Sprummer. The kindly codger likes to play with words as much as he likes watching the weather. And, of course, Walt, ever the optimist, remembers that Maypril is a much more lively and enjoyable time than the preceding period of Marchuary, the stretch of time from January to April that many consider the very tomb of winter and the deadest part of the year, when only red geraniums in kitchen windows and paper white bulbs on adjacent sills keep hope glowing and green.

His buddy and constant companion, Stumpy the tailless gray squirrel, has been equally content with the meteorological ebb and flow. If things get too chilly, he can always go inside the cabin and pick a cozy spot for a nap, and if the sun is out, even on windy days, the Stumpster can stretch out on the rail of the deck to soak up some rays. Recently, he has also reconnected with two other young gray squirrels that Walt calls Lansdowne and Burwell; Walt has long theorized that they are Stumpy's littermates and siblings, and the three provide entertainment with the games of tag and chattering contests they perform in the big pines that line the shore near the cabin. Walt can sit on the deck with a Patrick O'Brian novel if temperatures allow and listen to the rascally rodents making mayhem; occasionally, a furry blur will flash across the pressure-treated floorboards, soon to be followed by another and then another, as the smoke-colored bandits frisk and romp. He sometimes chuckles and calls them "a whole scurry of squirrels with skeeters in their scooters."

A few moments ago, I mentioned that Todd Jormonen had stopped by earlier in the week. Todd plows Walt's drive and shovels his deck in winter and performs odd jobs at other times of year now that Walt is a bit less spry than he used to be. Of course, Todd is a great deal more than hired help to both Walt and Stumpy, and his visits are occasions for much high-spirited frivolity. The gray squirrel actually climbs into Todd's coat pockets when he's wearing a coat to see what treat he has concealed there, and in the warmer weather, when Todd goes coatless, the squirrel's unofficial godfather nevertheless will have peanuts or honey-roasted cashews or hamster kibble or even dog biscuits tucked away somewhere on his person; thus, the ritual at his arrival involves Stumpy skittering up one pant leg and across his shirtfront, then over his shoulder and down past his back pockets, back up and over again, and often even up onto Todd's battered Red Sox cap, inside which the jovial trickster more than once has hidden something tasty, like a fresh-baked Squanna-cookie from the Four Leaf Farm Store in West Groton.

Todd usually brings along his Martin D-20 acoustic guitar or his well-seasoned Gibson mandolin so he can play the latest old blues or gospel tune he has taught himself. Walt still remembers the first time Todd brought the mandolin; when he started playing Sleepy John Estes's tune "Goin' to Brownsville," Stumpy dropped the peanut he had been shelling and sat up on Walt's lap to listen. Ever since then, the aesthetically sensitive rodent has gone quiet and settled down with rapt attention whenever Todd has brought out the Gibson—sort of like the woodland animals responding to the banished wild man's harp in the Middle English romance *Sir Orfeo* that Walt likes to tell at schools when he has one of his storytelling gigs. Oh, and I should mention that Walt has inspired Todd to do some storytelling of his own, with the two on occasion engaging in tale-weaving contests, each trying to one-up the other.

This Sunday when Todd stopped by, the plan was for him to join Walt and Stumpy for the trio's annual early-spring tour of the pond, a tradition now in its third year. They call these occasions the Voyages of Exploration and Discovery, in emulation of Lewis and Clark and other adventurers of the early days of the American republic. Although the wind was a bit rambunctious Sunday, the sky was endlessly blue and cloudless, and temperatures in the mid-fifties meant that conditions for the ride would be brisk but pleasant.

Walt had had the chance to attach his homemade pulpit to the bow of Nelly, his ten-foot rowboat with the ancient three-horsepower Johnson motor on the back. Last summer, he had built the wooden structure, emulating the projecting platforms on the bows of Atlantic lobster boats, so that Stumpy could climb out over the water into the breeze . . . or what small breeze the headway accomplished by the little outboard motor could produce. Walt had lined the sides of the pulpit, from railing to ramp, with chicken wire to help ensure that the squirrel would not topple overboard, as he had done on more than one occasion before the advent of the pulpit; you see, the little fellow was apt to climb up on the gunwale and, in his enthusiasm, lean a bit too far over the unprotected bow.

Earlier that morning, Walt had cooked up a batch of his famous ground-turkey sloppy joes for lunch, knowing the crew would be hungry when they returned to shore. He was putting the pan on a back burner when Todd arrived. As usual, Todd burst through the door with an affectionately insulting greeting: "Hey, hey, you crotchety old grouse! How are you?" He had also, of course, prepared a rude salutation for his furry godson: "Where's that mangy little weasel you try to pass off as a squirrel? Is he off somewhere hiding your socks again?" Todd was referring to a passing fancy that Stumpy had exhibited a few months earlier for stealing Walt's socks and then squirreling them away—oh, is that where that expression comes from?—uh, anyway, squirreling them away in all sorts of bizarre locations. Walt had thought the tendency might have had something to do with a repressed nesting urge, but he had no way of testing his theory now that Stumpy had abandoned the behavior in question. Of course, before all the words were out of Todd's mouth, Stumpy was scampering up over his buddy's shoulder. When the Sox cap fell to the floor and the Squannacookie tumbled out of it, all the amiable visitor could do was laugh heartily.

When he had had a chance to catch his breath, Todd announced that he had brought four bottles of brown ale made by his son Merle to go along with lunch. "Merle calls it Old Lady Nutjob," Todd said, "supposedly after his mother, though fortunately, Lynn takes it as a joke; she even seems to think it's riotously funny. Sons can get away with stuff that husbands would never dare even try. I sure wouldn't want to risk calling her anything like that, even if I had just invented a delicious new beer!" Todd and Lynn had named Merle after two of Todd's favorite guitarists, Merle Travis and Merle Watson. Since Doc Watson had been his big inspiration to pick up the guitar in the first place, Todd had always been particularly pleased to have emulated that master flat-picker in choosing his son's name.

After Walt picked up the several remaining pieces of Stumpy's Squannacookie and wrapped them in cellophane for later, the three adventurers headed out the door, with the two humans zipping on their life vests. With Todd taking the middle seat and Walt stationed in the stern to man the motor, they prepared to cast off for their voyage. Stumpy lost no time in clambering out onto his pulpit, where he stood facing forward with his front paws up on the railing, at least until he realized that Walt had not yet even set the choke or pulled the starter cord; then the gray-pelted rapscallion turned to glare impatiently back at his roommate. When Todd laughed at his gruff expression, Stumpy let out a cranky *chit!* which only inspired more chortles from the good-natured crew member. "Looks like Queequeg the squirrel—or should I say Squeequeg the squirrel?—may start tossing his harpoons at someone other than the great white whale if we don't get underway soon! Avast, me hearties! Let's boogie!" Todd was not exactly on top of his Nantucket whaling lingo, but like Stumpy, he was caught up in the excitement of the moment.

Once Walt had Nelly's motor purring, they did pull away from the dock. The elderly skipper takes great pride in keeping the motor well tuned so that it always runs smoothly and quietly, making little more noise with its purr than Stumpy does with his when Walt or Amy, their next-door neighbor, gives him a one-fingered nose rub on a rainy afternoon. The boat eased on down the west shore of the pond, and the three shipmates watched five or six tree swallows darting in the wind down toward the water's surface and then back up again. All along the near and far shores, the travelers could see new leaves at various points in the process of opening, and the range of colors in the foliage was almost as great as during the peak season of the fall, except that the colors were a bit more subtle; still, reds and oranges and yellows and tans, even some blues, mingled with colors that were the more obvious and expected shades of green.

"So," Walt asked as he steered Nelly down toward the south end of the pond, "are you and Merle still working up some tunes for that show at the VFW next month?"

"Yeah," Todd replied, "but we were wishing we had a good female singer to take some lead vocals and give us three-part harmonies. Unfortunately, my daughter has just started a new job out around Pittsfield, so she's not available. We've got a mix of stuff, from John Hurt to John Hiatt, from the Carter Family to Duke Ellington—some blues, some bluegrass, some swing, some traditional tunes."

"You know," Walt said, "you should talk to Amy Riggetti down the road. You know Amy and Tony, her six-year-old, don't you? Nice folks, and I've heard her singing while she does the housework. Nice clear alto voice with a sweet ache to it—sometimes her singing carries all the way up to the cabin when the windows are open. Frankly, she makes me feel like Odysseus listening to the Sirens or Stumpy listening to your old Gibson—moved and calmed at the same time. Talk to her. You might be surprised, like stumbling onto a treasure you weren't aware existed."

"Sounds like a good idea—" Todd started to reply, but then he interrupted himself. "Hey, what's that up ahead?" He pointed into a small cove they were putting past, and Walt shut down the engine almost immediately, his eyes focusing on a large white shape drifting among the lily pads that were just beginning to peek up from beneath the water's surface. His first thought was that somehow one of the pond lilies had opened early and had kept expanding magically until it had reached the size of a small raft. Almost immediately, though, that impression gave way to the equally wondrous reality: A mute swan had found the pond and was refreshing itself before moving on again. The large bird moved slowly, as if savoring the quiet and seclusion just as the three voyagers had been doing. As the trio on the boat watched, the swan's long, elegant neck arced slowly backward, and its dark-billed head emerged from the shallow water close to the shore. Walt felt it was a little like watching a cloud that had descended from the sky take on the more defined shape of the swan; he wondered when that piece of the sky would abandon its illusion of solidity and re-ascend to the heavens. The three voyagers watched in silence for several minutes as the bird calmly swam and fed, and even Stumpy seemed charmed by the graceful creature. The offshore breeze kept Nelly from drifting closer, and the swan showed no signs of discomfort at their presence. Walt wondered if the others felt themselves slowly but steadily filling with joy as he was doing.

Finally, Walt decided to break the spell, feeling they'd been fortunate so far not to disturb the blossom-like visitor with their presence. The moment seemed a holy gift to him, and he wished above all not to blaspheme by gawking and overstaying his welcome. When he gently pulled the cord to restart the motor, neither Todd nor Stumpy protested, and as Walt completed their circuit of the pond over the next ten minutes and then turned for home, all remained silent. Reverence seemed in order.

Later, as the two men savored their sloppy joes and sampled their Old Lady Nutjob ales, they recovered something of their earlier boisterousness, but even Stumpy retained some of the calm, almost sacred glow from their encounter with the petal-feathered heaven traveler. The men had given the squirrel two teaspoons of the ale in a bowl, and he had lapped it up enthusiastically, but he showed no signs whatsoever of tipsiness. Nevertheless, Walt suspected that his rodent roommate might need a nap a bit later in the afternoon.

The humans decided to savor their libations. After taking one mouthful of ale, Todd held the liquid on his tongue, trying to analyze its component flavors. When he swallowed, he shook his head and said, "I guess I just don't have as sensitive a palate as Merle does, but I agree with his assessment of the flavor of this brew. He said it had a 'caramel and coffee, roasty and toasty' flavor, like sweet bread.'"

"M-m-m," Walt replied. "I just call it delicious. I'm glad you brought us two apiece."

"Wait a minute," Todd said, his brow furrowing. "I brought one for you and three for me. Don't get any inflated notions of my sense of equity and generosity here!" The two men laughed together; then Todd continued, "You know, our encounter today reminds me of a story, and I'm gonna turn the tables on you and be the one who tells a tale now. This is one I heard from the Scottish storyteller Duncan Williamson, though I'll dress it up a bit to make it suit me.

"It seems that many years ago in a town not far from here, a cabin stood next to a small pond in the forest, tucked in among the tall pines. In that cabin lived a kind man who craved his solitude because of the unfortunate treatment he received at the hands of his fellow humans. You see, he had been born with visible differences from the people around him: His right shoulder was hunched, and his lower back twisted to the left side so that he leaned and staggered as he walked. His head and face, too, were different: His forehead bulged above his brow ridges, and his mouth suffered a constant grimace. Besides his visible deformities, the man was also unable to speak. But as grotesque as he appeared on the outside, he was full of love on the inside. He made a meager living for himself by gathering firewood in the forest, tying it in bundles, and carrying it the two miles to the nearest village, where he sold it to the residents, who scorned him to his face but relied on his wood to warm their houses and cook their meals. He would have been satisfied with one kind word, but instead, the people called him Hunchy; they gave him a few pennies for the wood, then laughed and sang out mocking chants as he shuffled back down the central road. 'Hunchy, Hunchy, bring your wood in a bunchy. . . .' The tears would mingle on his cheeks with dust from the road as he walked back home.

"But Hunchy would not let the love inside him go to waste, even if no human could see the beauty of his soul. He used the pennies he earned from selling the wood to buy flour and the other ingredients he needed to make bread, and then he shared his bread and what little other food he could afford with the wild creatures of the woods—the birds and the squirrels and the chipmunks and the mice. Every morning, the creatures would gather outside his door and wait for Hunchy to come out to them, and after he had shared out his bites and crumbs, they would come close and climb onto his legs and lap and shoulders and sometimes even onto his poor twisted head. For that short time, Hunchy would smile.

"As much as Hunchy loved his forest companions, however, he loved someone else even more. There, on the pond which his cabin overlooked, lived a beautiful mute swan, and every day, he sat by the water's edge and watched her floating quietly through the pond lilies, her long and graceful neck arcing and straightening and bending to the water and straightening again as she glided along. On the days when the wind and water were still and the blue sky was full of fair-weather clouds, the water's surface reflected back those clouds, and the swan seemed to be one of them that had taken on a special grace to descend, like a glorious star come to live among the benighted multitude below.

"Each day, after sharing his meal with the little animals, Hunchy would take a portion of the bread that he had saved and approach the shoreline. Then he would throw the pieces of bread as far out into the pond as he could, hoping that the swan would come closer to investigate. The swan, however, never showed any interest, ignoring him as if he were invisible, and each day, he would walk back to his cabin, sit down there, and—sighing—watch her from his doorway. Although all the other animals loved him and gathered around him, the one he cared for most would not even acknowledge his existence.

"The summer wore on, and each day, Hunchy fed his animal friends and carried sticks to the village; then he would stumble to the shoreline and cast his bread upon the water and wait patiently, but the swan would never come closer. His heart swelled with love and with the pain of unrequited affection. Then, one day, the wind across the water had a sharper edge, and Hunchy knew that October had come, with winter peering over its shoulder and edging nearer. The animals knew it, too, and they began their preparations for the cold season. The mice and chipmunks and squirrels gathered seeds where they could find them and built up their larders in hidden places, and the birds—the downy woodpeckers and nuthatches and chickadees and finches and wrens—felt the season turning as well. And still, each day, the twisted little man walked to the shore and made his wheaten offering to the beautiful white bird that would not even look in his direction.

"One morning, however, everything changed. The people in the village realized that they had not seen the kindly, misshapen man who brought them the fuel to keep their hearth and cooking fires going. 'Hunchy, where are you?' they called forlornly, but Hunchy never came. He never appeared back at the lake, either, where his furred and feathered friends missed his loving looks and touches even more than they missed the bread he gave them. Though often jealous of each other and reluctant to share their friend with one another, now the animals gathered outside the cabin and talked quietly among themselves, trying to understand what had happened to their dear friend. By the third day, even the rabbits and the deer joined the conference, but none of them knew what to do. Out on the lake, the swan turned in gentle circles as if she, too, had noticed the man's absence, as if she had always wanted to come closer but couldn't, for reasons even she did not understand.

"Finally, the wren spoke up and addressed the whole group outside the cabin: 'Comrades and companions, we must find out what is wrong with our friend.'

"The squirrel was next to speak: 'How *can* we find out? The cabin is shut, the windows are closed, and no smoke is coming from the chimney. Something must be wrong, but what can we do?'

"The swallow spoke then: 'I know what's wrong. We all do. And there is only one thing to do: We must ask the swan to visit him. I will fly out to the elegant creature on the lake and tell her how she is hurting us all with her unkindness to the kindest creature we have ever known.'

"The swallow swooped out over the lake, soaring high over the pond lilies and then dipping down to circle around the graceful white bird. He told her that the animals all knew that their friend had fallen ill and that she was the only one who could help him. She was the only one. Then the swallow circled back to the cabin.

"All the animals watched as the swan hesitated for only a few moments and then swam steadily to the sandy shore; she walked out of the water and up to the cabin door, which she nudged open with her beak. The chickadee flew up to the top of the window frame and perched there, peering through the window upside down.

"'Well, what's happening?' the other animals all clamored, for they couldn't see from where they were, in a circle on the ground.

"'She's walking to the bed, and he is lying there with his eyes closed,' the chickadee said.

"'What's she doing now?' the animals asked.

"'She's standing next to him and looking at him. His face is pale with pain, and he looks deathly ill, with his eyes closed, as if they may never open again.'

"Inside the cabin, the swan was looking at the man, and she thought, Why was I afraid of him? He would never hurt me. He knows only kindness in his heart. And she stretched out her long, graceful neck to rest her cheek on the poor man's cheek, at which he opened his eyes and saw her close to him. He reached up his hand to touch her lightly on the neck.

"'What's happening *now*?' the animals all called to the chickadee, and the chickadee said, 'She has returned his love at last, and they are snuggled together!'

"'They're snuggling! They're snuggling!' the animals all cried.

"Inside the cabin, the man sat up and spoke for the first and only time: 'My love.' Then the swan drew a feather from her wing with her beak and gently pierced the man's deformed shoulder with it. Suddenly, his twisted body transformed into the beautiful, white-feathered form of a second swan. This time, when the animals called to the chickadee, that kindhearted bird was so moved that he could say nothing. Nevertheless, the other animals soon saw for themselves as two swans walked out the cabin door and down to the water's edge. There, they paused for one glance back before drifting away like the sails of a pair of boats or like two white blossoms on the water. Back by the cabin, the chickadee finally found his voice again: 'They have found each other at long last.'"

Todd leaned back in his chair and looked at Walt.

"Good story," Walt said.

"Glad you liked it," his friend replied. "You didn't ever have a love affair with a swan, did you?"

"Well," Walt answered, "my wife, Annie, did have lovely white skin and a graceful neck, but she wasn't big on flying. I *have* told a few stories about swan maidens, though. Hey, what say we open those other two bottles of Old Lady Nutjob and toast our guest out on Kibbee Pond? I suspect she'll be gone by tomorrow."

After Walt poured another thimbleful of ale into Stumpy's bowl, the two friends raised their glasses to their swan sojourner, and though Walt's prediction proved correct, no one was deeply disappointed that the beautiful bird had departed. After all, the three adventurers had had another memorable Voyage of Exploration and Discovery.

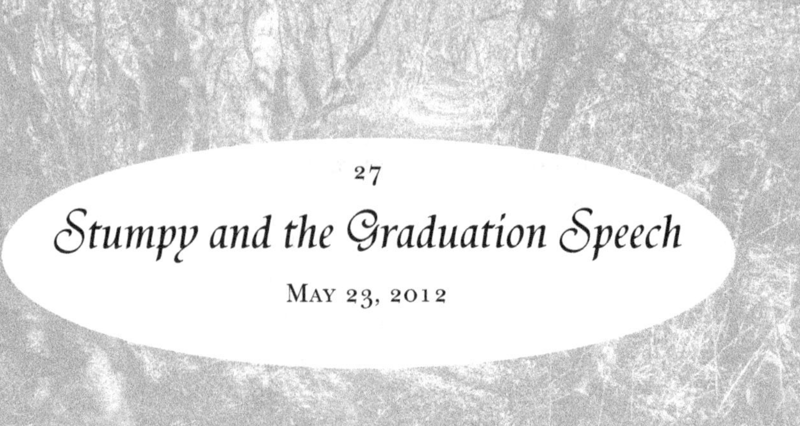

27

Stumpy and the Graduation Speech

May 23, 2012

Out on Kibbee Pond, the yellow pond lilies are starting to bloom up in the swamp, just north of the cabin where Walt Walthers, the octogenarian weather watcher, and his rambunctious rodent roommate, Stumpy the stub-tailed gray squirrel, make their abode. The advent of crisp, dry weather was a source of delight last weekend for the two bachelor gentlemen, because it gave them a chance to get back to their beach cleanup in the mornings, and that activity justified some *late*-morning lounging around on the sun-washed deck. Sunday also brought a visit from their nearest neighbor, Tony Riggetti, who lives with his mom, Amy, in a little Cape just down the incline of Kibbee Pond Road from Walt's cabin.

As was his custom, Tony burst through the cabin door after a knock too quick to be answered; it was about 8:15, but Walt and Stumpy had already been up a couple of hours. On these beautiful late-spring mornings, Walt enjoys watching the sun first peek over the treetops along the eastern side of the pond and then throw a rush of brightness onto the deck as it leaps higher. Even if he has to put on a cardigan, Walt wants his first cup of coffee out in the open air so he can watch the show, which also includes the wind patterning and, with the sun's help, spangling the water's surface. That early, Stumpy is full of a young mammal's energy, and he often launches himself up the trunk of one of the grand old pines along the waterfront and out on a spar-like upper limb for a squirrel's-eye view of the sunrise over the pond. It is also a likely time for him to meet up with one or more of his siblings Burwell and Lansdowne for some high-level and high-caliber cavorting. Thus, by the time Tony arrived on Sunday, the gray-furred vandal had already had a chance both to get his exercise and to recover from his outing by napping on the deck rail, and Walt had even had time to bake some maple-raisin muffins to offer Tony, along with a glass of orange juice.

"Mr. Walt! Mr. Walt!" Tony called as he stood panting next to the stove.

"Whoa there, pardner!" Walt laughed from a few feet away. "I'm right here, and so is the Stumpster! What's got you so fired up?"

"My daddy's coming home next week!" the little shaver blurted. "He'll be here before the weekend, my mommy says!"

"Holy mackerel!" Walt answered, though Amy had already filled him in on the details. "You must be pretty excited to see him again."

"I sure am," Tony said. "He's coming all the way from Afterghanistand! But he won't be here in time for my graduation sermonery, Mommy says." Walt previously had noticed Tony's tendency, when agitated, to fall into malapropisms and spoonerisms, although the youngster was usually remarkably well-spoken for someone his age. Walt had always assumed that Amy's insistence on reading to her boy every night had already paid off in the overall sophistication of his vocabulary and sentence structure.

"Well, it's too bad he won't be here to see your graduation," Walt said. "I'll bet he'll be very proud of you, though, and you'll get to see him a couple days later."

"Yeah, but, Mr. Walt, that's the other thing," the talkative tyke continued. "Ms. Aristea wants me to ask you for a favor. We all talked it over, and we want you to be our gradulation speaker!"

"My goodness!" Walt said, a bit taken aback. "That's a big honor. Your mom has already invited me to go along, so I was planning to be at the ceremony, but I wasn't expecting this! I guess I should talk to Ms. Aristea."

"Ms. Aristea said she would call you later today, but she wanted me to be the class speaksman and ask you first," the wide-eyed laddie replied.

And so it was that after Walt and Stumpy did some frog hunting with Tony along the pond's shoreline and then walked him home, the kindly duffer and his squirrel sidekick returned to their own abode to a phone call from Ms. Aristea, the bright, young bug-loving kindergarten teacher whom he often likens to a Greek goddess.

"Walt," the young woman said, "I hope you don't feel pressured into doing this if you don't want to. It's just that the children were so excited at the idea. Madeline was the one who proposed it." Madeline Clough is confined to a wheelchair with spina bifida, and whenever Walt has visited the class (and he has been back to tell stories at least six times this year), Stumpy has cuddled up on Madeline's lap while everyone is listening.

"I'm happy to speak to them, but I don't know whether what I say will be a conventional graduation speech," Walt said. "I certainly want it to be special for their sake. Do you think it will be all right if I tell a story or two as part of the address?"

Ms. Aristea laughed. "I think that's what the children are hoping, but I'm sure they'll listen carefully to whatever you say."

Thus, a soggy Wednesday morning found Walt pulling up to Spaulding Memorial School in Lulu, his green 1960 Chevy pickup, at a few minutes before eleven. Stumpy, of course, was with him, having spent part of the ten-minute ride on the back of the truck's bench seat, part on the seat itself, and part with his front paws up on the window ledge as he tried to peer out at the side of the road. The furry bandit seemed a bit more restless than usual, perhaps picking up on Walt's nerves, as animal companions so often do with their human housemates. The graduation speaker had dressed for the occasion by donning a plain red flannel shirt with a black-and-silver Western string tie, some tan leather suspenders, freshly pressed khaki pants, and a brand new porkpie hat that matched his pants. He had decided that Clifford, as he called his everyday porkpie, was a bit too worn and dirty for the ceremony. Still, as Walt climbed out of the cab and invited Stumpy onto his shoulder for the walk into the school, he said, "I don't know, Stump. This is a little different for me. I'm not big on formal occasions."

However, a kindergarten graduation is not a fancy shindig on the order of, say, graduation at a prestigious private high school like Laurel Academy, and as soon as the two friends started down the hallway to Ms. Aristea's classroom, they began to relax. By the time they actually entered that magical room, the familiar, enthusiastic faces reassured them that only love and receptivity awaited them.

Ms. Aristea met them at the door. "We're all so excited to have you here, Walt . . . and of course, you, too, Stumpy." She addressed her next comment to the squirrel. "I think Sloppy Joe is waiting for you to say hello, and I know the children all are."

Those words were Stumpy's cue to skedaddle over to one of the many tanks that lined one wall of the classroom, inside of which a large brown catfish was scooting up and down along the front corner. When Stumpy hopped up onto the table and scooched down so he could look through the glass, the catfish stopped his antics to hover on the other side, body undulating as he faced the squirrel. After a few moments of communing with his finny acquaintance, Stumpy darted back across the room to make his preliminary rounds of all the students.

In the meantime, Ms. Aristea was introducing Walt to some of the parents who were attending the ceremony, and of course, Tony was eager to accompany his neighbor as his official honorary guide—a mostly unnecessary function since Walt had visited the class many times. Nevertheless, Tony led the classroom celebrity to a special pair of chairs, where they could sit side by side while waiting for the festivities to begin, as happened promptly at eleven o'clock. In honor of Stumpy, Ms. Aristea led the class in a spirited version of the traditional fiddle tune "A Squirrel Is a Pretty Thing," with simple lyrics that the clever teacher had added herself. The squirrel in question had already assumed his seat on Madeline's lap in her wheelchair and shrank back at first when all eyes turned his way, but soon he was bobbing his head up and down in rhythm. Walt had often said that his rodent roommate seemed canine for his eagerness to play the watchdog role and feline for his quickness in purring if anyone gave him a one- or two-fingered nose rub, but now the graduation speaker leaned over to Tony and said that Stumpy might even be part pig because he was hamming it up so much.

When the song was done, Ms. Aristea introduced Walt, and the aged tale weaver left his seat next to Tony for a rocking chair placed centrally so that all the students' seats faced it.

Walt cleared his throat and began. "In preparing to speak to you today, I tried to remember what it was like to be six years old myself, but that was so long ago that my memories are a bit blurry." Everyone laughed. "Nevertheless, I do remember my pet dinosaur" (more laughter) "and my first teacher, Mrs. Gillingham. She oversaw the one-room schoolhouse where I attended the first four grades back in Three Oaks, Michigan, the town in which I grew up. She used to say to me, 'Walter, if that story you're telling Billy Faber is so funny, maybe you should tell it to the whole class'" (more laughter) "but while she didn't expect me to do so that first time, I took her up on the offer, and after that, she continued to encourage me to tell stories. For that reason, I mention her today, to show you that you might not recognize a lifelong interest when you first encounter it, and you might not realize that what you're doing now, in the present moment, can be steering you toward something important in your future. That's why I always try to keep my mind open to new possibilities. If I hadn't done that when Tony's mom suggested that I take up storytelling last summer, I wouldn't be with you today. However, the first seed for my new career was planted many years ago, when I was just about your age.

"You've all just finished your first year of school, and you've had a chance to see how exciting learning can be, especially with a teacher like Ms. Aristea. I'm not very good at lecturing people or giving advice, so now I just want to tell you a story about some other young people who valued learning. The story comes from the other side of the world—specifically, Morocco, in North Africa." He looked around the room, smiling into the eyes of each student, and started his tale.

"Many years ago, a king ruled over a vast kingdom, and he had a daughter, an only child, who was curious about everything and valued learning above anything else. She wanted to know why the sky is blue and how deep the ocean is and why caterpillars turn into butterflies; she wanted to know why the seasons come in the order they do and why some people are born to wealth and privilege while others are born to poverty and labor and suffering. Her father, the king, was very proud of his daughter's desire to learn, and when she said she wanted to learn from someone truly wise, he inquired for someone suitable to teach his daughter. When he learned of an aged wise man who knew how to read the stars, he sent for that man. Of course, because the wise man could read the stars, he knew the messenger was coming and, when that messenger arrived, was already packed for the trip back in the king's golden carriage.

"When the wise man came before his host, the king said, 'If you will teach my daughter how to read the stars, I will build you the finest observatory the world has ever seen so you can study the stars even more closely,' and the old man could not refuse. He did, however, establish one condition: 'I must teach your daughter without anyone else present.' The princess listened carefully and learned quickly, so that, within a year, she knew all that her teacher knew about the stars. When he returned home, the wise old man found his observatory ready for use.

"The princess read the stars each day and soon was able to use her knowledge of the heavens to foresee an invasion; when she warned her father, he was able to foil the evil neighboring king who was plotting against him and thus keep his kingdom safe. Thereafter, he made his daughter his chief counselor.

"As the princess continued her studies on her own, she read in the stars of a fabulous mountain which held a treasure of gold; she also learned, however, that only one person knew how to enter that golden mountain. Fortunately for the princess, that person was her former teacher, the wise man. When the king once again fetched that venerable person in his golden carriage, the wise man was deeply concerned about the dangers in the endeavor and warned both the king and the princess that they must follow his instructions with precision. Reluctant as he was to put the princess at risk, he relented when he learned that the king would reward him with a telescope that could magnify the stars a thousand times.

"The girl and the old man traveled together in the king's golden carriage to the mountain, which they had to reach before midnight, the precise moment when they must utter the magic spell that would move the large stone blocking the entrance to the cave that held the treasure. The old man said, 'Remember: This threshold will remain open for only a half hour, after which the stone will inexorably slip back into place, and anyone inside will be trapped.'

"Once inside the mountain, the princess marveled at the wonders she saw: spiders made of diamonds that seemed to come to life in the lantern light, a tree that reshaped itself constantly from the pool of molten gold in which it grew, silver snowflakes that fell and rose again over and over. So fascinated was she with the wonders of the cave that she would have forgotten to leave on time if her mentor had not been present to remind her. As they hurried through the opening, the rock slid back into place right behind them.

"The wise old man departed with his treasured telescope and one final admonition to the princess not to lose track of time when she returned to the golden mountain. Because one of the treasures she had seen—a perfectly formed golden seashell—haunted her memory, she determined to go back the very next night. She arrived—alone—just before midnight and recited the spell to draw back the stone, but as she entered, she brushed against a thorn bush, which tore a single gold thread from her dress.

"Her excitement was so great that she was lightheaded and short of breath, but she found the golden seashell quickly and picked it up. Thinking that she might be able to hear the sea, she held the shell to her ear, discovering only then that the shell was magic; instead of the ocean waves, she heard voices speaking, and when she moved the shell a little, she could hear other voices. In that way she soon recognized that just by adjusting its position, she could use the shell to hear anything that anyone was speaking anywhere in the world. So engrossed did she become in her discovery that time slipped away, and she came back to herself only when she heard the rumble of the stone rolling back into place. Now she was trapped inside the mountain.

"When the king learned his daughter was missing, he knew instinctively where she had gone, and he ordered his soldiers to dig their way into the mountain to rescue her. Their efforts, however, were fruitless. The king then sent for the wise old man, confident that he would be able to say the spell to open the doorway into the mountain, but that star-reading wise man had died, leaving no one outside the cave who knew how to gain entrance. All the king could do was offer a reward to anyone who could rescue the princess; that reward was half the kingdom and the princess's hand in marriage, but whereas many came to try their luck with spells and stratagems, nothing worked, and the princess remained enclosed in the vast treasure chamber.

"At first, she tried reciting the spell from inside the cave, but that technique did not work, so she used the magic seashell to listen to her would-be rescuers. In that way she discovered that they had failed and that her father had promised her hand in marriage to anyone who rescued her. She wasn't sure she liked that idea, but she had no way to object.

"Exploring the cave, she found a spring of water, which nourished a nearby carob tree; thus, she had both food and drink. Because she had not lost her love of learning even in her frightening situation, the princess used the seashell to listen to lectures by the most learned men and women around the world as the months of her imprisonment passed."

Walt paused and scanned the faces in the room. Each of the students was listening openmouthed, the parents were poised in their chairs, and even Stumpy sat alertly on Madeline's lap, staring back at him. The silver-haired word weaver smiled at Ms. Aristea and continued.

"In an alley of the kingdom's largest city lived a clever boy named Mahmoud. His family was poor, but Mahmoud prided himself on finding ways to keep his siblings and parents from starving, and one day, he heard an old woman calling out in the marketplace that she had an oud for sale, a stringed instrument a bit like a guitar. When others looked at the battered and stringless instrument, they simply laughed at the woman and mocked its worthlessness, but when Mahmoud saw its pear-shaped wooden body, graceful as a beautiful woman, all his instincts told him that he must buy the oud. The boy had always loved music, and he believed that someday he could distinguish himself as a musician and make enough money playing the oud to support his family. 'I could at least polish and restore it, and then one day when I have more money, I could buy strings for it.'

"In his pocket Mahmoud found only three copper coins, but when he offered them to the old woman, she accepted and told him, 'You have made a wise purchase, for this is a magic oud. For its magic to work, however, you must outfit it with golden strings. Don't worry, for you will not regret your purchase.' Before Mahmoud could ask her how the magic worked, the woman had disappeared into the crowded bazaar like mist melting into the morning air. He stood there, holding the worn and silent instrument in his hands.

"Like many others, Mahmoud had heard the story of the trapped princess, and he fantasized about rescuing her. Without any conscious plan, he traveled to the golden mountain, having bid farewell to his parents and siblings and taking with him only the oud. During the day he hung back from the crowds of curious people who had come to the site, but that night, after the thrill seekers had gone home again, he moved closer. Something gleamed in the moonlight, and when he investigated further, he discovered a long thread of gold dangling from a thorn bush. Not knowing that the thread had come from the princess's dress, he nevertheless plucked it from the thorns and in that instant had a further inspiration: He would attempt to string the magic oud with this golden thread. Perhaps it would meet the old woman's specifications.

"As Mahmoud began to string the oud, he found that the thread was exactly long enough to supply all the needed strings. He finished his work just at midnight, and when he plucked the strings for the first time, the oud sang out in words that sounded like a magic spell. The mountain itself began to rumble, almost as if it were singing, too, and the rock rolled back. A surprised Mahmoud was soon embracing the grateful princess, who had, through the seashell, heard the oud sing its spell and had run out to thank her rescuer.

"A royal wedding followed, for the king was a man of his word, and he was filled with joy to learn that his daughter had escaped her imprisonment. Because Mahmoud was not only naturally clever but also loved to learn as much as the princess did, the two were well matched as wife and husband, and the princess forgot her earlier reservations about her father's promise. Because the two were also willing to learn from each other, they were well matched as queen and king when they came to share the throne. They established schools throughout the kingdom and hired the wisest men and women in the world to share their knowledge with young students from all sorts of backgrounds, and in that way they spread their love of learning among their people.

"I chose to tell that story today," Walt said, "because this graduation ceremony means that all of you have started walking down the path of learning, and that is a road you can continue exploring your whole life long. I'm still on that path myself, and I learn more things, about the world and about myself, every day. My hope for you is that, like me, you can enjoy keeping your minds open; I hope you can enjoy learning on your own but also in company with other people, just the way that Mahmoud and the princess do in the story. Thank you again for inviting me to speak today and for listening so attentively, and congratulations to you all, graduates and parents alike."

The audience applauded, and Ms. Aristea stepped forward to take both of Walt's hands. "As usual," she said, "you found the perfect story! Thank you so much." She planted a kiss on Walt's cheek, making him blush as she turned back to the room of people. "Now, everyone," she said, "I will hand out the certificates, and after that, our party can begin."

As it turned out, Walt and Stumpy's duties were not quite over. At the request of the students, they agreed to add their "signatures" to that of the principal on the documents, so the two roommates took their places at Ms. Aristea's desk. The honey-haired, doe-eyed teacher produced a fountain pen for Walt and a stamp pad of ink for Stumpy. Walt would sign one certificate, then set it down in front of the squirrel, who would press his front paw onto the ink pad and then onto the paper, leaving his footprint next to Walt's John Hancock. Lots of hugs followed for Walt from the students, and lots of cuddles and pats kept Stumpy feeling appreciated too. In fact, on the way home in Lulu, even with the rain still falling, Walt found himself humming. When he asked Stumpy if he had enjoyed himself, the squirrel gave a quiet *chit*, leaned back against the truck seat, and nodded his head three times.

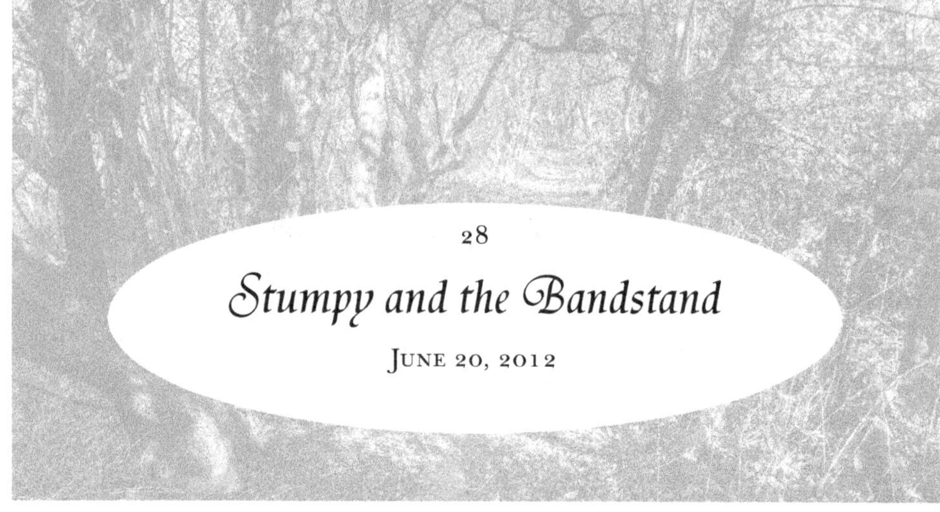

28
Stumpy and the Bandstand

June 20, 2012

The approach of the summer solstice has always lifted the spirits of Walt Walthers, the octogenarian weather watcher who lives beside Kibbee Pond in his compact cabin, but never more than in the last couple of years, since the arrival of his now-permanent roommate, Stumpy the squirrel, that caboose-lacking freight train of a rambunctious rodent. Although Stumpy possesses a high level of energy throughout the year, something in the air of early summer infects him with a contagious surge of enthusiasm for living. Of course, he had experienced a setback a couple of weeks ago after his annual checkup at the vet's office, when Dr. Brad Schmidt, the veterinarian, had suggested that the furry snack enthusiast was inhaling a few too many sweet treats, like the honey-roasted cashews and the many varieties of muffins that Walt likes to share with his roommate. Not that Stumpy should change his name to Plumpy or that he was developing love handles just yet, but Dr. Brad did express concern about the unhealthy effects that overindulgence in sugar would have on the rascal's teeth. In an uncharacteristic burst of levity, the doctor even quipped that he'd hate to see Stumpy have to order "rodentures." The squirrel's immediate reaction to being put on a diet was to go into a record-setting three-day pout. Thus, in more recent days, the kindly geezer was especially grateful to see the return of his friend's high spirits.

When Walt's wife, Annie, had been alive and when their three sons had lived within accessible distance, the family had always celebrated the summer solstice with a feast, a practice Walt had revived last year for the young squirrel's benefit. This year, he hoped to share the celebration with the two roommates' good friends down the road, six-year-old Tony Riggetti, his mom, Amy, and his dad, Anthony, newly returned from service in Afghanistan. To that end, he had phoned the Riggettis last week.

In accepting Walt's proposal, Amy had a counter-invitation of her own. "We'd love to come," Amy said, "but we all also were hoping that you and Stumpy could find a way to join us for the concert next Monday night at the bandstand in Lunenburg center. It's part of the Lunenburg Turtle Time celebration, and it's one of the band's first truly public gigs. A lot of fun things will be going on throughout the week, but we could use your moral support Monday night. I think Todd mentioned it to you already."

Todd is Todd Jormonen, Walt's good friend who also happens to plow his drive in winter and perform various handyman's tasks at the cabin throughout the year. Todd and his son Merle have long been playing music together but have only recently organized a band, with the idea of performing at local events and clubs. More recently still, they have added Amy to the band as a lead and harmony vocalist—a role that proved a pleasant distraction in the last difficult weeks as she impatiently awaited her husband's return from across the world. Todd often brings his guitar or mandolin with him to the cabin to play for the "two swinging bachelors," as Walt sometimes refers to Stumpy and himself, and they have often heard Amy singing as she does housework at the little Cape house down the hill from the cabin; in fact, those overheard bits of song were what had inspired Walt to mention Amy to Todd as a possible addition to the band. The roommates had not yet, however, heard their friends playing and singing together.

"How can we pass that up?" Walt had said to Amy on the phone. "I do get a little nervous bringing Stumpy into crowds of people, because he's not used to a carnival atmosphere or to having so many unfamiliar faces around. When I took him to a Squannacook Squealing Squirrels baseball game over in West Groton, things didn't go so smoothly; he does sometimes attract attention from the wrong kind of people. Of course, he's done really well at schools and my other storytelling jobs over the last year, so maybe we'll luck out this time. I know he wants to hear you guys as much as I do."

"You can come early," Amy said, "and hang out while we get set up if you like. Anthony and Tony will be there, checking out the booths and displays that are part of Turtle Time every year."

"It's a date," Walt said.

The next day, Tony, as is his wont, wandered up to the cabin for a visit. As he was helping Walt load his wheelbarrow with oak leaves, pine needles, and other detritus from his raking along the beach, the tyke said, "Mr. Walt, what do you call a person who lives in Lunenburg?"

"You know, Tony," Walt replied, "I've heard a couple of different answers to that one. Some say 'Lunenburgites' and others say 'Lunenburgers,' but I've always thought the latter sounds like something you should put in a bun and eat with condiments. I've never been able to mustard up the energy to do more research, and I don't relish the idea of having to catsup on all the quirks of life in the neighboring towns. 'Residents of Lunenburg' does sound too formal, though."

"Maybe we could just call them Loonies," Tony suggested.

Walt looked at the little fellow to see if he was being serious, but Tony was smirking and trying to keep from smiling. "Oh-h-h, good one, you Skeezix!" the elderly trickster said. "We'll make a punster of you yet!"

Tony dumped another rake full of pine needles into the wheelbarrow; Walt had dug out a child-size leaf rake from the basement, something his grandchildren had used a few years before. "Mr. Walt, do you know much about the Loonie-burg Turtle Time? I mean, how it got started and stuff like that? I know it's got booths and music and all, and it sounds like fun, but I'm curious about why people call it Turtle Time."

"Well," Walt said, leaning on his rake, "you know that the summer solstice is coming up, right? The longest day of the year and the shortest night? Part of the idea of Turtle Time is to celebrate the arrival of summer at the solstice. This time of year, though, also happens to be a time when turtles are particularly active, especially the females of different species looking for places to lay their eggs. You've probably seen turtles along the side of the road lately or even out in the road, right? Besides the egg laying, both males and females like to seek out heat because they are cold-blooded, so sometimes they'll get out on the tarred road where the black pavement soaks up even more of the sun's warmth and retains it even after the sun goes down."

"What's 'cold-blooded' mean?" Tony asked.

"Well," Walt replied, "I probably should have called turtles 'ectothermic' since scientists prefer that term. It means, though, that like other reptiles, they're animals that rely on things outside their bodies to regulate their body temperatures. Mammals, like humans or squirrels, for example, have pretty complicated mechanisms *inside* their bodies that help them stay warm even without outside heat sources. Turtles and such depend more on the sun in particular, and maybe because the days are longer in early summer, they are out and visible more often then."

"But," Tony said, "I still don't get what the sol-stitch has to do with turtles and Lunenburg in particular." Tony was having a little trouble concentrating on Walt's explanation, because while the two humans were raking, Stumpy had been rampaging through the big pines overhead, engaged in a rollicking game of chase-and-be-chased with his siblings Burwell and Lansdowne, both of whom have full-blown and fully intact tails. For the last minute or so, however, the three *furred* loonies had been scampering along the shoreline and between the man and boy, continuing their game on the sand and interrupting the humans' work—or so they would have done if Walt and Tony hadn't already paused to converse.

"You're right," Walt said, stepping back slightly to avoid three silver bullets, or at least gray bullets, that had rumbled like miniature freight trains right over his work boots. "I haven't explained that connection, though I was trying to get to it. I guess it's all just a coincidence, though, so it doesn't really have an explanation. The solstice falls around June 21 every year, and turtles are out and about frequently during that time, too, so somebody thought it would be fun to put the two together, probably someone like me who likes turtles. People seem to have a need deep inside to connect to animals. You know how schools often have animals as mascots, like the Hopkinton High Hawks or the Groton School Zebras? Well, at Turtle Time, the whole town of Lunenburg identifies with turtles. People wear turtle masks and hats, and at the festival, people sell

T-shirts with paintings of different kinds of turtles on the front and long-sleeved T-shirts decorated to look like turtle shells with turtle legs sticking out. They even call for a town-wide Turtle Patrol."

"What's that?" the curious little guy asked.

"Turtle Patrol means," Walt said, "that everybody is especially conscious of turtles along the roads, and if anybody sees one in the road or along the shoulder, then they do something to get the turtle out of harm's way, like carry it to the other side or put it into a nearby body of water. The town officials also keep an unofficial count of how many turtles people have helped out of the roads and post the number on a big sign outside the post office. Some people even carry gloves, cardboard boxes, and hockey sticks in their cars so they can pick the turtles up or nudge them across the road."

"Do they whack them with the hockey sticks?" Tony asked.

"No," Walt said, "but some people aren't comfortable picking up snapping turtles, especially the big ones, because they have a nasty bite. Those people can use the hockey stick to scooch the snappers along across the pavement or even tumble them over to the edge of the road if need be."

"Wow!" Tony said.

Walt laughed. "My Annie used to be a big-time turtle patroller, even when our boys were little. She'd hop out and pick up a snapper by the back of its shell so the beak couldn't reach her and then lug it over to the shoulder. Well, sometimes, she'd carry it back to the car first, to show the boys. She always tried to figure out what direction the turtle was headed in and take it to the side of the road it wanted to be on so it wouldn't just double back into the road again. At first, the boys liked us to bring the turtles in the car and carry them to a pond near our house and release them there, but then we read that turtles have complicated internal navigation systems that tell them where to go, and if you take them away from the area they know, they end up confused and unhappy and, well, lost. After that, we just tried to put them in a safer place close to what seemed to be their desired destination."

"Why do people like turtles if they bite?"

Walt laughed again. "Most turtles don't bite," he said. "Even snappers don't bite except when they feel threatened, like when they're out on land. When they're in the water, they know they can get away and don't bother you at all. Most turtles are far more scared of humans than you could ever be of them."

"Mr. Walt," Tony asked, "do you like turtles?" The three frisking squirrels had now retired back into the pines, where each stretched out along a limb high enough to give a good view of their surroundings.

"Yes, Tony, turtles are among my favorite animals. I identify with them because they take their time and they don't rush; they savor what's around them, and I like to do that too. Plus, they like to bask in the sun, and—in case you haven't noticed—I like the occasional nap in the sun too. On top of all that, they have cool patterns on their shells. Say, did I ever tell you about how I got my Native American name?"

"No, you didn't," Tony said. "Do you really have a Native American name?"

"Not exactly," the chuckling codger said, "but I like to think I earned one through my exploits with turtles. There was this movie called *Dances With Wolves* about a cavalry soldier who got stuck at an outpost by himself and befriended a wild wolf; the Native American tribe that eventually adopted the soldier gave him the name Dances With Wolves because they had seen him playing with that wolf. I gave myself a similar name back in my younger days when I still kayaked on the pond regularly. I saw it as a challenge to glide up to a turtle resting on a rock or log and grab it, and the first time I succeeded, I started calling myself Snatches Up Turtles, mostly as a joke. But I was also kind of proud of myself. I did it several times, just to prove to myself I could. Stinkpots, the musk turtles, aren't too hard because they fall asleep in the sun, but painted turtles are a real challenge because they're so wary.

"One time, I had paddled up into the stream to the north that feeds the pond, and there, on a big log along the edge right where the stream comes into the swamp, was a painted turtle, sunning itself. I paddled fairly close, but the turtle slid off into the water. I could see it in the shallows, though, calmly stroking along underwater and coming up for a breath of air near the kayak's bow. I paddled so the turtle was along the right side of the bow, about a foot and a half back, but when I got to where I could consider reaching out with my hand, the turtle curled off to the right farther, so I had to spin the boat around and go back after it. When I got up alongside it again, it veered to the right once more, and I had to do another one-eighty. I must have changed directions like that eight or nine times at least, until I finally got smart . . . or probably just lucky. This time, when I pulled up next to the turtle, I swung the bow at the last second so that the swimming reptile was on the left instead of the right, and it stayed just close enough to the kayak that I could reach down six inches into the water with my left hand and close my fingers around the outside of its shell. I brought it into the boat but then apologized for frightening it and put it back into the water almost immediately so it could swim away. I felt a little bad about disturbing it . . . but also a little proud about having been able to catch a swimming painted turtle."

"Wow!" Tony said. "Maybe *I* should call you Mr. Snatches Up Turtles . . . and maybe I can get Mommy and Daddy to take me on Turtle Patrol too."

When Monday night rolled around, Walt and Stumpy climbed into Lulu, Walt's '60 Chevy pickup, and drove the Green Streak, as Walt sometimes calls Lulu, over to the center of Lunenburg. Lots of parked cars lined the side streets, particularly along Lancaster Avenue and Leominster Road, because the bandstand is located on an island between them and because various booths had been set up in that vicinity too. The town police were out directing traffic, and when Walt pulled Lulu in behind a car on the northbound side of Lancaster Avenue, a tall, large-bellied officer with glasses approached the truck. "I'm sorry, sir," the officer said, "but you'll need to try it again. Regulations say that all four of your wheels must be completely off the pavement. You need to pull all the way onto the grass."

"Fair enough," Walt said, smiling. "Should be an easy maneuver." And it was, in fact; he simply backed Lulu up a few feet, then pulled forward again, a little farther over to the right this time.

"Thank you, sir," the officer said, tipping his cap. "We try to do things by the book." At that moment, he caught sight of Stumpy on the bench seat beside Walt. "Oh, and, sir," he continued, "you'll need to keep your Chi-hoo-a-hoo-a on a lead at all times here at the festival. We don't want to get involved in any dogfights or other kinds of brouhaha."

Walt suppressed a smile at the officious policeman's mispronunciation of the Spanish word for the dog breed. "Yes, sir, I've got a twine harness on him that I made when I used to take him to the Squealing Squirrels games over in West Groton. He's not used to crowds, even though he likes people. Officer, allow me to introduce the inimitable Stumpy"—at that moment, the gray-furred bandit stood up on the truck seat, front paws together, and nodded at the tall, uniformed man—"and I'm Walt Walthers. We live out at Kibbee Pond, just across the town line in Townsend."

The officer shook Walt's outstretched hand, saying, "Pleased to meet you. I'm Officer Irv Stickler—Stickler by name, stickler by nature. Watch out for that big pothole there when you cross the street, and I'm sure you've brought a plastic baggie in case you need to clean up after that little fella at some point. Oh, excuse me now . . ." and he turned away to caution another driver whose parking job was not up to snuff.

As Walt extended his right arm so Stumpy could clamber to his shoulder, he said quietly, "Interesting fellow, but he may be a bit too literal-minded about his duties. Now you stay up there, Stump, at least until we find Tony and the crew. And stick close, in any case. This is unfamiliar territory, and there could be some dogs around that think squirrels are food, not friends."

The two roommates took a few minutes to walk along the stalls set up on the lawns and sidewalks, where baked goods and various craft items were for sale, along with all kinds of turtle-related paraphernalia. Included were books, hats, puzzles and games, wood carvings, paintings, prints, jewelry, cookies and cakes baked in the shape of turtles, and, of course, the shirts Walt had mentioned to Tony. Nearly everyone was wearing clothing commemorating the occasion and celebrating our chelonian friends, members of that ancient, ancient zoological order.

Other activities were going on around the center of town, including a pet costume contest to determine the non-turtle pet dolled up to most closely resemble the real thing. Several dogs were among the entries, in shells sewn from cloth or shaped from papier-mâché and other materials, but the winner, eventually, was a hamster, the surface of whose shell was made from bottle caps attached to an old bathing cap, which in turn was supported by a balsa wood frame made from old model airplanes. Walt admired the ingenuity of that outfit and assumed that the judges did too. He was pretty sure, however, that the hamster didn't appreciate any part of the costume or the contest. "Gee, Stump," the elderly jokester said to his shoulder-riding companion, "if I'd known you were eligible, I bet I could have whipped up something really impressive for you to wear!" The squirrel registered his reaction by standing up, grabbing the brim of Walt's omnipresent porkpie hat with his front paws and his mouth, and pulling the fedora down over his roommate's eyes. Walt chuckled for the next block or two.

The other big event was the turtle race, for kids twelve and under, and when the roommates arrived at the race "course," the preliminary heats were just finishing up. Unbeknownst to Walt, Anthony had managed to catch a painted turtle for Tony to enter, and that creature—Tony had named him Crawler . . . or Cruller . . . Walt wasn't exactly sure because Tony was so excited when he saw his friends from the pond that he spoke extra fast, running his words together. In any case, moments earlier, Tony's turtle had qualified for the finals.

"Whoa, Mr. Walt, wait till you see 'im! Boy, Stumpy, he can really go!" the six-year-old blurted out. He held a medium-sized turtle in his hands, with beautiful yellow stripes on its face and legs. Anthony was grinning, too, and Walt was glad to see no sign of the shadow that sometimes crossed the returned soldier's face. Some time remained before Todd and Amy's concert would commence, so Walt saw no conflict of interest in staying there for the championship round.

The race "course" was a huge piece of paper on which someone had drawn a circle with a six-foot radius. In the center of that circle was another circle with about a foot-and-a-half radius. When race time came, the turtle handlers would place their charges (or char*gers*, they hoped) within that circle, and the race officials would place over the contestants a cardboard box suspended from a string. When the starter blew her whistle, she would also pull on the string, raising the box and releasing the turtles.

When the box came up during the finals, three of the six contestants failed to move at all, as if frozen in place; two were painted turtles slightly bigger than Crawler, and the other was a snapper substantially larger than any of the others, which simply blinked its fathomless eyes once or twice but held its ground. Two of the other contestants, including one musk turtle with a thin layer of algae still on its shell, made a few tentative steps out of the inner circle but then began meandering and even doubling back on themselves. Despite the encouraging calls of all the handlers, Crawler was the only one who simply started crawling in a relatively straight line and didn't stop until he passed over the big circle's circumference.

After Tony and Crawler's victory, the group of five made their way to the bandstand for the concert, with Walt hoisting the victorious athlete waist-high in the cardboard box that served as his garage or stable or locker room, depending on your perspective, and with the winning turtle handler hoisted onto his father's shoulders.

"On the way home," Tony said, "we're going to drop him off at the swamp where we found him yesterday."

"Good for you guys!" Walt said.

The concert turned out to be a great success as well, despite one small incident, as you'll hear shortly.

Walt was surprised to hear that neither Anthony nor Tony had heard Amy sing with the band before. "She's a little shy and easy to embarrass," Anthony said, "even though she did have solos with the chorus in high school. With my being away so long, though, this is a side of her I haven't really seen, and she didn't want us going to rehearsals."

Amy, nonetheless, had an impressive stage presence and a lovely alto voice, and the audience, mostly seated on lawn chairs or reclining on blankets on the grass, were receptive on the cool summer night. Walt had forgotten that, along with Amy on vocals and Todd and Merle on guitars and mandolins, his veterinarian friend, Dr. Brad Schmidt, played fiddle with the band. The electric bass player was actually a selectman in a neighboring town; in his youth, Stuie had played bass for Jonathan Edwards for several years, even on his big Top Forty hit, "Sunshine." The music this night was a blend of blues and bluegrass tunes, with some jazz, classic country,

R&B, and swing thrown in, including a brief set of Duke Ellington songs and instrumentals. A big Ellington fan himself, Walt was especially satisfied knowing that he had reintroduced Amy to the Duke the previous summer and that her love for those songs had led her to explore as well other elements of the Great American Songbook. When she sang "Do Nothin' Till You Hear From Me," she even dedicated it to "my dear friend and the best neighbor in the world, Mr. Walt Walthers." Walt thought he might never stop glowing after that moment.

Just as the band was launching into Patsy Cline's "Imagine That," however, the unfortunate incident mentioned above occurred. Many of you will remember that Stumpy, atypically brave as he is for a squirrel, does retain one insurmountable phobia: a fear of thunder-and-lightning storms. Walt had first learned of that fear almost exactly a year ago, when a waterspout touched down in Kibbee Pond and Stumpy went berserk; Amy had seen firsthand the same trepidity during the amiable young mammal's first overnight with Tony, when a clap of thunder had sent that furry missile diving into his hostess's flour jar, from which he had emerged nearly transformed into albinism. Not that the weather suddenly turned stormy Monday night; in fact, it was a glorious early summer evening, if I haven't already made that fact clear. Nevertheless, trouble did arrive suddenly when a huge dump truck loaded with loam drove up toward the traffic lights along Lancaster Avenue; the driver didn't see the big pothole near Lulu, and he clanged into that hole with a rumble every bit as loud as a blast of thunder almost directly overhead. Tony was holding the end of Stumpy's twine harness at that point, with both of the youngsters standing and swaying to the music, but when the crash came, Stumpy's irrational panic kicked in, and he bolted, snatching the cord from his friend's hand. Before anyone knew what had happened, the squirrel had launched himself up the side of the bandstand and across the shingles of the roof all the way to the cupola at the peak. There, he huddled, trembling and as unmoving as Crawler's competition in the turtle race.

Like true troopers, the members of the band pressed on with their number, and Amy had never sounded better despite the potential distractions. Walt was shaken but not deeply upset because he could see his rodent pal and had faith that a solution would present itself. He reassured Tony, who was upset that Stumpy's leash had been in his hands at the time of the truck's descent into the infernal pothole.

The solution did present itself, and almost immediately, in the somewhat unlikely form of Officer Irv Stickler. Officer Irv had witnessed Stumpy's flight, and as surprised as he had been to see a tiny dog dash up onto the gazebo's roof, he also imagined that any critter from Mexico would by definition prove unpredictable when transported to New England. For all his shortcomings as an expert on canine breeds, however, the policeman was a good man and calm in a crisis. He walked to a nearby house and borrowed an aluminum extension ladder, and then, while Todd and the band launched unfalteringly into Mississippi John Hurt's "Trouble, I've Had It All My Days," the good-hearted policeman climbed up the ladder, crawled on hands and knees up to the cupola, coaxed Stumpy into his arms, and then eased them both back to the ground.

A grateful Walt met him at the base of the ladder and accepted a somewhat sheepish Stumpy from his arms. "Thank you, Officer Stickler," he said. "This guy does get himself into some fixes."

"You're welcome, Mr. Walthers," Officer Irv replied.

"Please call me Walt," the elderly rodent owner said. "After all, you did just rescue my Chihuahua."

Officer Irv looked skeptical. "Are you sure the pet store people didn't trick you? I'm not convinced now that this guy is a dog after all."

In response, Stumpy let out a very un-canine-like chattering noise. Walt laughed. "He may be only part dog, but I still love him. Maybe you should join us at the pond for lunch sometime as a thank you. I make a mean grilled cheese sandwich, and you can get to know this fur-faced scamp a little better."

"I'll do that, Walt," Officer Irv said, with a broad smile, "but right now, I need to get this ladder back to its owner. You know me: Stickler on detail, Stickler on duty."

29

Stumpy and the First Night of Summer

June 27, 2012

After last week's excitement at the Turtle Time festival in Lunenburg, Walt Walthers, the elderly weather watcher, and his constant companion, Stumpy the squirrel, had only a day or so to recover before the next big event. That would be the celebration of the summer solstice and the first official night of summer, to which the two bachelor roommates had invited their nearest and dearest neighbors, the Riggettis, who live just down the hill from Walt's comfortable cabin on Kibbee Pond Road. If sidekick is the right word for Stumpy's relationship to Walt, sidekick is also probably the right word for six-year-old Tony Riggetti's relationship to both Walt *and* Stumpy, though Tony can never seem to remember the term correctly, often referring to himself as the dangerous duo's "sideswipe" instead. Walt rather likes the change in phrasing and sometimes uses the term himself, as when he says something like, "Well, my faithful juvenescent sideswipe, what say we take a trip to the dump this morning?" He also enjoys coining other combinations, as in, "Well, my sempervirent fledgling, weren't we going to take Nelly out for a cruise this morning to survey the boundaries of my demesne?" Sometimes Tony asks him what his fancy words mean, but at other times, he follows Stumpy's example and simply pretends he knows what Walt is talking about.

Of course, Walt and Stumpy have not been seeing quite as much of Tony or his mom, Amy, these days as had been the case over the previous months, because Tony's dad, Anthony, has recently returned from service in Afghanistan, and—understandably—Tony has wanted to spend all the time he can with his father. Amy is also delighted to have her husband back, and Walt has been working consciously to respect the family's privacy. Fortunately, Anthony appreciates the care with which Walt watched over the young mother and son during his own absence, and despite the emotional difficulties that his return from the war has occasionally brought down upon him, Anthony understands and respects the bond of mutual fondness that grew in his absence. Walt has already proven a support to him, too, having lined him up with part-time work at the car repair shop of Walt's friend Andy Martin in Groton. Thus, all three of the Riggettis were looking forward to starting the summer right on the solstice by reveling and jubilating as a fivesome with the elderly weather watcher and the rodent rapscallion.

Monday night's outdoor concert at the bandstand in the center of Lunenburg had been a big success for Amy and Todd Jormonen's band; they had performed as part of Lunenburg's summer solstice festival, known as Turtle Time for its celebration of the aquatic reptiles so active at this time of year. Of course, Stumpy had provided some unexpected excitement when, panicking after a dump truck had hit a pothole with a crash like the thunder the young squirrel so fears, he had fled to the top of the gazebo within which Amy and Todd's band was playing. Fortunately, Officer Irv Stickler of the Lunenburg Police Department had climbed up to rescue the still-trembling squirrel and reunite him with his human friends. Though his dignity had been somewhat compromised and his pride slightly wounded, Stumpy had recovered quickly from his trauma, undoubtedly because of all the concern and affection that his human friends showed him in the aftermath. The following morning, the bandy-legged bandit was once again scampering with his two favorite siblings, the effervescent Burwell and Lansdowne, through the big pines and along the beach at Walt's lot on Kibbee Pond.

Tuesday of last week was a cool and overcast day, perfect for Walt to do some cooking in preparation for the solstice celebration the following evening, especially with the weather patterns and forecasts calling for the arrival of three hot, humid days on the cusp of summer. The first, easy steps in Walt's culinary preparations were to make a batch of his wife, Annie's barbecue sauce for the chicken he planned to grill outside and to whip up his own version of potato salad, in which the key ingredients for its unique effect include

Dijon mustard, sour cream, chopped dill pickles, chunked sharp cheddar cheese, and bits of freshly browned bacon. After those preparations were complete, Walt would turn to some more complicated tasks: He would assemble and roll out the crust for a shoofly pie; then he would prepare the filling and topping, combine all the elements, and pop the pie in the oven. He could shuck the store-bought corn on the cob and make the salad the next day. He did, however, still have one important item to make ahead of time.

When Annie had been alive and when their three sons had lived within accessible distance, the family had always celebrated the summer solstice with a feast, the model for what the silver-haired chef was planning. Last year, Walt had decided to re-create that solstice feast and had made, among other things, the old family favorite Destiny Cakes—prepared from raspberry jam mixed into doughnut batter, then deep-fried in random shapes, and finally drizzled with honey. The idea was to choose one of these confections from a cloth-covered plate—without looking—and then to predict something about the coming year from whatever the shape suggested. Of course, this year, with Stumpy's newly imposed diet, Walt had doubts about the appropriateness of building the solstice celebration around too many sweets, but the Destiny Cakes still seemed a good idea, especially because the plan was to share them with Anthony, Amy, and particularly Tony. Walt wasn't sure the six-year-old would go for the molasses-based shoofly pie, but he had no doubt the tyke would enthusiastically accept the cakes as his personal destiny, so to speak.

The plan for Wednesday evening called for a cookout, followed by a bonfire and candle boats, another of the old family customs Walt had resurrected last summer for Stumpy's benefit. On the sandy hillcrest above his dock, the elderly Renaissance man had many years before built a brick fireplace, and not far away from it, he had also constructed a rock-lined firepit, which he had used for bonfires with some regularity twenty years or so earlier, when his sons and their young families were closer at hand. Both structures were still functional even though he had rarely used them in recent years. Thus, two tasks for the previous weekend had been to clean up the grill and firepit and to assemble some fuel for the bonfire, easy enough to do with the driftwood and fallen limbs Walt had been collecting and stacking in several spots around the property.

The candle boats had busied Walt for the last three evenings. Last summer, for Stumpy's celebration of the solstice, Walt had dug through the basement and found a wooden boat he had made for his sons decades before, and now he wanted to make three more. Because he had a system of floodlights trained upon the waterfront and also upon the deck, he had been able to do some cutting and shaping with his skill saw and jigsaw after supper. As dusk had turned to darkness each night, moths had begun circling the various light bulbs, and a barred owl had initiated its "Who cooks for you?" call from back in the pinewoods; thus, Walt had extra company, even beyond the Stumpster, who joined him on the deck, nosing through the sawdust and eventually curling up to snooze amongst the tools stacked on the table. The design of the boats was simple, with a rectangular base cut into a triangular point at the prow, a shorter second piece for the cabin, and a square pilothouse as the third level; behind the pilothouse Walt also drilled a hole large enough to hold a half-inch-diameter candle, which they would light before releasing each boat on the pond at dusk. The idea was that each boat "captain" would make a wish, and if that candle boat made it to the opposite shore, that captain would get his or her wish.

When the pieces were assembled and each of the boats was sanded sufficiently, Walt painted the craft in contrasting colors, adding initials to the stern of each. The red, yellow, and white boat bore a *T* on its stern; the blue, silver, and white one bore a *W*; and the forest green, sky blue, and white one had even more inscribed on its stern: *A & A*. Stumpy's older model was already painted a moss green with silver and white trim, but Walt added an *S* to its stern so Stumpy wouldn't feel left out.

Late Wednesday afternoon, once Amy had returned home from her part-time job at the salon Ayer Hair, the three Riggettis walked up the hill to the cabin of the Dos Amigos, as Walt had taken to calling Stumpy and himself. He had recently watched Jon Landis's film *The Three Amigos*, and he was working on perfecting some of the lines from the movie: "Wherever there is injustice, you'll find us. Wherever there is suffering, we'll be there. Wherever liberty is threatened, you will find . . . the Dos Amigos!" Walt didn't use the line when Tony and his parents arrived, though; he figured he'd wait for the right moment, maybe even practice the line some more first. He led his company down to the flat plain above the shoreline, where he had some briquettes piled in his metal charcoal starter on the grill awaiting a match; in the firepit he had also arranged some of the wood he had gathered so it was ready to light later, when dusk came. Walt had also set up a blue canvas awning, under which stood a card table and four outdoor chairs, their dining area for the evening. The tall pines along the side of the pond always provide late-afternoon shade, especially welcome now after a day with temperatures in the high nineties; air stirring on the pond, however, was already aiding in the cooling process.

Next, from a cooler, Walt brought out several bottles of ale made by his friend Todd Jormonen's son Merle, who played in the band with his father and Amy but was also a budding brewer. Merle had named this brew Old Lady Nutjob, after his mother, Lynn, Todd's wife, or so the young man had jokingly claimed; when Walt had sampled it before, he had found it delicious, and now he wanted his adult friends to try it, too, so he had convinced Merle to sell him a few bottles. "If you don't enjoy this stuff," Walt told the young wife and husband, "then I will have to admit to serious doubts about both your taste and your judgment!" For Tony, Walt had bought two bottles of Piscataquog brand maple cream soda, which the old connoisseur claimed was the most delicious soda he had ever tasted even though it was manufactured by a small local company; the six-year-old, despite his more limited exposure to carbonated beverages, would soon concur with his elderly friend's verdict.

Next, Walt brought out some tortilla chips and black-bean-and-corn salsa as well as some cheese-stuffed celery sticks to serve as appetizers. After sampling some of both, Tony and Stumpy moved closer to the shoreline to build a sandcastle with some plastic buckets, shovels, and rakes that Walt had stored in the basement after his grandchildren had outgrown them. While Tony lectured the squirrel about his vision for their project, Stumpy sat upright and nodded his head, as if he agreed with the six-year-old's plan to construct a condominium where the squirrel could live with his siblings Burwell and Lansdowne. As the planning phase shifted to actual construction, Tony seemed to be doing the bulk of the manual labor—filling pails with sand, dumping them into place, and shaping the slightly damp material with his shovel blade to establish the outer wall—with the squirrel functioning in a primarily supervisory function, hopping over the wall here to survey it from a different angle, standing up on his haunches there as if concerned about keeping the height of the wall uniform at all points, chittering and chattering everywhere as if offering suggestions for engineering improvements.

In the meantime, the adults relaxed in the shade, with Amy and Anthony *oohing* and *aahing* about the ale. The conversation was relaxed and comfortable, as Anthony had now come to accept his neighbors as part of his extended family even if he was, technically, still getting to know them. When they'd all had time to savor their ale, Walt and Anthony went up to the cabin to bring down the green salad and potato salad as well as the chicken and barbecue sauce for charcoaling. Walt had already shucked the corn, washed it, and put the ears in some water on the stove in the kitchen; the butter-and-sugar variety had come from southwestern Massachusetts, some of the earliest of the season, and he hoped it would prove palatable. While the menfolk were readying the cooking materials, Amy joined Tony and Stumpy in their construction endeavors, encouraging her son to describe the various rooms and their functions in the rodent mansion he envisioned.

Supper itself proved a great success. Walt had resurrected the corn-holding device he had designed the previous summer so Stumpy could enjoy an ear of his own; the invention was a wooden tray with three nails protruding from the base so Walt could impale a piece of corn and Stumpy could nibble at it without the ear rolling away. When Stumpy finished the top side, Walt simply turned the ear over, and his roommate started on what had been the bottom. Tony, who has never been a finicky eater, was just as effusive in his praise of the meal as his parents were, but the Destiny Cakes, as dessert, were clearly his favorite part.

"Gee whiz, Mr. Walt, so I just reach under the towel and pull one out without looking?" the boy asked.

"That's right," Walt said, "and then you tell us what the shape looks like to you and make a prediction for the next year based on that shape. Do you want me to go first and show you?"

Tony nodded his head vigorously.

Walt reached under the towel and pulled out a lopsided cake, rounded on one side with a narrow projecting piece from the other side. "Well," he laughed, "this looks to me like a wild turkey, with the big, rounded tail and the skinny neck. Maybe it means I'll get a close look this year at Lord Lurkey, the gigantic tom turkey that I've glimpsed at a distance in the big open field at the Townsend-Shirley-Lunenburg border. Look! There's even a little bit of dough that hangs down like his wattles."

Tony drew next and claimed that his cake looked like a dog. "So maybe you guys'll get me a puppy!"

Amy laughed and said, "I'll bet any of these cakes would have looked like a puppy to you!"

Under the pines on the pond's western shore, the dusk came on earlier than out on the water itself, and at around 7:30, Walt lit the bonfire. "You know," he said, "bonfires on Midsummer's Eve are a long-standing tradition throughout Europe. Originally, people may have been using them as magic to aid the sun and encourage crops to grow. I think of them, too, as a means of combating darkness with light, and besides, it's just pleasant to sit outside in early summer and watch a fire burn. We'll probably see plenty of fireflies adding their fires, too, but now I think it's time for us to send out our candle boats."

A first sight of Walt's wooden creations brought further exclamations from the three guests, and all three were reluctant to release their boats for fear that they would get lost on the pond and prove irrecoverable. Walt said, "Oh, we can always take Nelly out tomorrow and track them down. They're certainly not going to sink!" He produced some wooden matches and lit the candles on each boat; then he pushed Stumpy's boat gently away from the shore before doing the same to his own. Anthony and Tony knelt side by side and launched the other two. With only a faint offshore breeze to affect them, the candle boats continued to drift slowly away while the humans watched from the shore, with Stumpy up on Walt's shoulder now.

"How about I tell you a Midsummer's Eve story while we're letting the elements carry our craft on their way?" Walt suggested.

"Yes, please," Tony said.

"Well," Walt said, "this one should interest your parents as well as you. It's an old English folktale called 'Diccon and Elfrida,' and it's about a young goatherd, Diccon, who falls asleep one Midsummer's Eve—just like tonight—and dreams of a voice calling his name. When he awakens, he wanders out of his cottage just at dusk, almost exactly this time of night, and notices that at the top of the nearby hills is a line of dark forest trees that he has never noticed before. Mystified, he climbs the hill and finds that, instead of being an optical illusion caused by a formation of clouds, the trees are real, the edge of a large forest which simply did not exist before. A mysterious, unearthly music draws him on until he comes to a clearing, where he sees figures dancing while the moon casts its light down upon them. Somehow, the music is full of joy and sadness at the same time, pulling him ever closer, until the fairies invite Diccon to join them in their dance.

"Among the fairy dancers is a beautiful maiden with long, golden hair and eyes as green as new leaves, and Diccon wishes that *his* eyes could never lose sight of her. Soon, her cool hand is on his arm, and she draws him away until he is lying with his head in her lap, and she is stroking his hair and singing to him."

Tony's head was already nodding, and Amy said, "That sounds like a good idea, Tony. Let's sit on the sand, and you can rest your head in *my* lap."

Walt continued his story once they were settled. "Lying there, looking into the maiden's green eyes, Diccon knows that he never wants to leave her, but she tells him that he can stay only until dawn and that dawn is fast approaching. She kisses him once and tells him that her name is Elfrida, but when he repeats that he cannot leave her, she says, 'You do not understand, Diccon. My people are sometimes cold and cruel, and they care not if they harm a human. I *do* care about you, though, and I could not bear to see you hurt. Please go! You can only regret staying here.' However, when Diccon sees that he cannot stay, he begs Elfrida to go with him, and with a rooster crowing to signal the sunrise, she reluctantly takes his hand and urges him to flee through the forest, which dissipates around them as the sky fills with light.

"For a year they live in great happiness together, but as Midsummer's Eve arrives again, Elfrida warns Diccon that the fairies will come to reclaim her that night and that he must bar them out with branches from a rowan tree and his iron scythe. All night long, the fairies cry out for Elfrida, but the couple remains still until dawn, when the voices cease.

"The next year, the lovers again bar out the fairies, but on the third Midsummer's Eve, the fairies trick Diccon by calling out in his beloved Elfrida's voice; when he opens the door, the fairy king steps in and says, 'Human, you have defied me, but you have no power to keep what does not belong to you. For your presumption, I will turn you into a dried autumn leaf and blow you away from here forever.'

"Elfrida intercedes, however, saying, 'The blame is mine, and so should be the punishment. I will go with you if you will spare my love.' Then, turning to Diccon, she says, 'I will love you forever, and I will come back to you. But look carefully for me, for I may not be the same as you see me now.'"

As Walt paused to draw breath, Anthony joined his wife on the sand, taking their now-sleeping son into his arms as Walt continued. "Back in his realm, the fairy king shows some pity, sentencing Elfrida to live in exile and to change her shape every seven years but giving her one small hope: If Diccon ever recognizes her as Elfrida while she is in another form, she will regain her original appearance, though she will lose her immortality.

"Over the next many years, however, Diccon fails to recognize Elfrida although she tries to choose forms that will allow her to watch over him. She becomes first a thrush—like that one you can hear singing back in the woods right now—and she sings to him from the cherry tree outside his cottage for a year, but in his despair Diccon pays little attention, and assuming that she has forgotten him, he decides to sell his flock and go to war. He works as an apprentice to a smith to earn his armor, receiving a sword after six years of labor. The sword is Elfrida. After seven years, she becomes a shield; then a bag of gold that helps him buy a house, marry, and start a family; then a watchdog that after seven years of devotion dies protecting him from a robber; then a young boy who becomes his trusted servant; then a golden ring he purchases from a peddler and wears on his finger. Diccon never forgets Elfrida, but he never recognizes her either.

"Only on his deathbed, as a very old man, and after he has lost his prized ring, does he finally see Elfrida in her transformed state, this time as a white cat who slips into the room and jumps onto his bed. Something familiar about her green eyes causes him to say, 'Elfrida, have you come back to me?' Immediately, she is herself again, in all her youthful beauty, and she explains to Diccon that in all these years he has never been alone, revealing all the forms in which he failed to see her. He dies, embracing her, and her heart breaks; they are buried side by side."

Walt paused, darkness awash around the fire, in whose flickering light Tony lay in his father's lap, breathing deeply. Stumpy had climbed into Amy's lap and was snoring softly. The young husband and wife were listening intently to Walt. "It's a sad story," Walt continued, "about not being able to see what's right in front of your eyes. But I have a second one, an antidote to the first, this time from the Maori people of New Zealand.

"A fisherman named Ruarangi had a wife so lovely that the fairies talked about her constantly, their voices ringing like birdsong in the trees. The fairy king, invisible to humans, heard the rumors and, taking on the form of a bird, flew off to see the woman for himself. This first viewing immediately filled him with desire for her.

"As soon as Ruarangi next put to sea, the fairy king approached the house and lingered nearby, calling in the sweet voice of the lute-wing bird to entice the young wife. When she came outside to search the garden, her eyes filling with tears from the beauty of the song, the king flew to her, embracing her gently but inextricably and carrying the enraptured woman ever higher until the old world was distant and her old life forgotten. Then he spirited her to his kingdom, where the king's mesmeric voice, constant in her ear, wrapped her in a cocoon of song. Thus, she forgot her husband and their life together, believing the king when he told her that his palace and garden were her home and always had been.

"When Ruarangi returned from fishing to find his wife missing, he ran nearly mad, searching the shoreline and the forests and streams nearby, calling on his neighbors to help, and finally turning to the tohunga, the village priest, who knew about magic and could see what others could not.

"The tohunga cast out the vast nets of his mystical sight and drew back in a vision of the fairy king carrying off the wife; he knew that the king had ensnared her soul as well as her body. When he told Ruarangi what he had seen, the husband cried out, 'Then I have lost her forever!' But the tohunga replied, '*Forever* is a word too final for me to grasp. Few things are lost forever. What does your wife most love to do?'

"After long and deep thought, Ruarangi said, 'She loves listening to the birds and can recognize and even mimic the songs of them all.'

"Smiling, the tohunga said, 'Then certainly she will know this song.' And he began a chant that fluttered and trilled like the song of the tulura, the Maori lovebird. That spell song took off on wings like those of the bird itself, passing over highlands and lowlands until it landed in a tree in the fairy king's garden, where, among the marvelous, ever-ripe fruit, Ruarangi's wife was walking.

"For a year the fairy king's beautiful singing had entangled the wife in its melodic web, locking her away inside herself, but when she heard the tulura's call, she paused, for it was simultaneously fresh and familiar, tickling her memory and slowly clearing her ears and eyes. Gradually that birdsong unlocked her remembrance of a whispered voice and a pair of smiling eyes, and, finally, it brought back the name of her husband: Ruarangi. In that moment she remembered him and longed for him more than for anything ever before in her life. She spoke his name—'Ruarangi!'—and in doing so severed the final strands of the fairy king's control over her. She looked around at her suddenly unfamiliar surroundings, then walked through the garden and into the open fields beyond. There she saw, in the distance, something now dear to her once more: her husband, Ruarangi, who had traveled long and far from the village, following the tulura's song, to arrive at the fairy king's palace. He ran to her when she called, wrapping her exhausted and shivering body in his cloak and leading her home, where he cooked for her and fed her with his own hands until she was warm and whole again. At last her eyes smiled back into his smiling eyes, and her whispers answered his.

"The fairy king had followed, hungering for revenge, but the tohunga was waiting for him and could see the king, even if others could not. Recognizing the king's great strength, the priest chanted another spell song, drawing on love, the greatest power that mortals know: He sang of a man and woman who would work side by side and, after their work, would repose side by side, a man and woman whose love would bring children into the world. He sang of joys and powers the immortal fairies could only envy. Threatened with ensnarement in that spell song, the fairy king could do nothing but forget the young wife and retreat to his palace, alone."

In the stillness of the falling dark, the three adults could hear Tony's rhythmic breathing and Stumpy's snoring. After a moment, Walt said, "I guess those two stories are about the difficulty of truly seeing your partner. On the one hand, Diccon can't see Elfrida in her transformations even though she is with him almost constantly. On the other hand, Ruarangi sees his wife most clearly when he seems to have lost her, but his ability to recognize what she truly loves allows him to reclaim her, with the tohunga's help. Maybe the fairy king is another side of Ruarangi himself, that part of any spouse that wants to turn the loved one into a possession, to imprison her or him in a desired image instead of accepting the other's real identity and doing the hard work of understanding that otherness."

The fireflies were flickering at the edges of the trees above the shore, as if they were sparks that had drifted away from the now-dying bonfire. "I've got a blanket right here," the silver-haired pond dweller said. "Why don't we let the youngsters keep snoozing on top of it while you two take Nelly out for a putt around the pond. Even with night gathering here under the trees, there's still some light out on the water, and besides, I keep a flashlight in the watertight box by the motor if you should need it. We won't get more than a sliver of moon tonight, but there might be enough to add to a romantic atmosphere out there. Go slowly, though; there's no need to rush. You can check on the progress of the candle boats if you like. Remember what I said? If any of them make it to the other shore, those people get their wish. I suspect Stumpy's counting on some honey-roasted cashews despite his diet, and I've noticed that Tony keeps talking about a puppy. I suspect you two have wishes of your own as well."

Anthony wordlessly put his hand on Walt's shoulder as he and Amy stood up; Amy kissed the geezer's cheek before husband and wife stepped toward the dock, where Nelly awaited. Anthony turned back briefly to say, "We'll just head out for a little while, tohunga, and see what we can see."

30

Stumpy and the Rodent Regatta

JULY 4, 2012

Never one to turn down a formal opportunity to celebrate but always one to find cause for joy in everyday events as well as special occasions, Walt Walthers, the elderly weather watcher who lives out on Kibbee Pond with his rambunctious rodent sidekick Stumpy the tailless gray squirrel, was delighted to discover that late June and early July brought much to celebrate, in both the sense of formal holidays and that of more personal, private occasions. First had come the summer solstice, which this year had included an outing to the Lunenburg Turtle Time festival and a smaller gathering with his favorite neighbors, the Riggettis; the latter occurred on the actual evening of June 20, the first day of summer and the longest day of the year. Next would come the Fourth of July, and because the actual date fell midweek this year, Walt and Stumpy had a chance for a preliminary celebration the previous Saturday, June 30, when they attended the annual Fourth of July Boat Parade at nearby Beech Tree Lake, where Walt's friend Prof Harris has a comfortable year-round home. The timing of that event also left them free for other Independence Day–related occasions closer to the day itself. On top of the national holiday, however, Walt had learned that July 11 was the birthday of Amy Riggetti, the young wife and mother who has become like a daughter—or maybe even a granddaughter—to him in the last year. In that time, Amy's six-year-old son, Tony, has become a near-constant sidekick to both Walt and Stumpy—or as Tony would say, a "sideswipe." Even Amy's husband, Anthony, since his recent return from service in Afghanistan, has also quickly become dear to the "swinging bachelors of

Kibbee Pond," as Walt sometimes labels his squirrelly companion and himself.

"A bonanza of festivity!" Walt exclaimed to his furry housemate one morning last week as they sat sunning themselves on the deck. "Almost like the way Thanksgiving, Christmas, and New Year's all come in close proximity at the end of the year. Still, some quiet time here around the ol' ranch is also welcome, especially on a gorgeous morning like this one!" The cordial codger leaned back in his chair and closed his eyes for a moment, not unlike his figurative kin, the turtles, when they soak up the rays on rocks and fallen trees around the pond. When he reopened his eyes, however, he exclaimed quietly, "Hey, little guy, do you know where you are and who you're with?" He was addressing a small chipmunk that had frozen on the wooden planks of the deck right at Walt's feet, much as a human hiker might do if he were striding confidently past the base of a mountain that suddenly shifted position and spoke to him. "I'd say you're welcome to the Ponderosa and can relax, except that the Stumpster here has sometimes shown animosity to striped rascals of the chipmunk persuasion. I'm guessing it's a territorial thing mostly, but it may be a species-related prejudice too. Solid colors versus stripes, that sort of thing."

The invader remained frozen in place, as if trying to calculate from which direction the avalanche would come when the mountain did completely collapse. He was probably as tense as a stretched elastic band, but he didn't move except to blink his eyes, and Walt wondered if talking to the little creature could also be having a mesmeric effect on the striped marauder. Stumpy, uncharacteristically, had not slipped into his guardian's routine of growling, doglike, at animal trespassers, but out of the corner of his eye, Walt could see that the larger rodent was alert, if calm; he assumed that the tone of his own voice had suggested to Stumpy that no aggression was required or desirable at the moment.

The chipmunk seemed to have come to a decision as well, and he resumed his explorations of the planks, as if he expected some hoard of seeds to materialize magically in the cracks between the boards. The little guy was prone to sudden changes of direction as he sniffed for treasure and to quick spurts of movement, but those alternated with moments of utter stillness, with only a tail twitch or two to distinguish him from a porcelain statue. Having advanced all the way to Walt's work boots, the rust-colored varmint sniffed at the laces as if they presented unexpected culinary delights for an epicure of his tastes, but then he changed direction again and scuttled to the driveway-side steps before disappearing down them.

Walt chuckled. "Well, Stump, it looks as though we have a new neighbor, *Tamias striatus.* You know, he might even have designs on moving in as the third roommate. Hey! Maybe we could upgrade the *Dos* Amigos to the *Three* Amigos and go back to the original slogan from the movie: 'Wherever there is injustice, you'll find us! Wherever there is suffering, we'll be there. Wherever liberty is threatened, you will find . . . the Three Amigos!' What do you think?"

Stumpy had settled back down on the deck rail and seemed intent on soaking up as much sun as possible before the events of the day would interpose and interrupt his hard-earned rest. Besides, he is not an effusive animal and seems to have learned that the best way to cope with Walt's satiric jabs and thrusts is simply to ignore them. Of course, Stumpy's apparent indifference never completely deters Walt, either, from his good-natured joking. As his beloved wife, Annie, used to say when she was still alive, "You certainly can tickle yourself, can't you?"

Now, as if demonstrating that principle in action, Walt chuckled again and said, "But if he is going to join our fraternity, he'll need a name, and I'm going to call him . . . Ge-e-e-o-o-rge! After the imaginary friend I never had when I was a kid. No, actually, after somebody else. You see, my dad used to tease one of the neighborhood kids back in Michigan by pretending to remember his name wrong; he'd call him George, and the kid would get peevish and say, 'My name's not Ge-e-e-o-o-orge!' The really funny thing was that whenever Dad told the story later in life, he couldn't remember the kid's *real* name. Thus, he lives on in our family history as simply Ge-e-e-o-o-orge."

Stumpy didn't move, apparently not impressed with the humor quotient in this story either. "Ah, well," Walt continued, "I guess we'll wait and see if ol' George wants to hang out regularly. He's finding enough acorns and seeds around here. . . . I must say, though, he doesn't seem to be the brightest bulb in the drawer. Slow but nevertheless cute . . . not a bad combination . . . 'cause it's just like me!" At this comment, Stumpy shifted slightly away from his human friend but never opened his eyes to register a more pointed reaction to Walt's frivolity.

Over the next couple of days, George made increasingly regular appearances on the deck, going about his business whether the two cabin residents were outdoors or not, but seeming to welcome their company when they did make an appearance. George would calmly pass across the deck as Walt was watering his potted cherry tomatoes at the south end, with the striped youngster coming within an inch or so of Walt's boots before continuing across the expanse of boards and disappearing temporarily down the steps toward the pond; a minute or two later, he would reappear and pass without panic back in the opposite direction, often with his cheeks puffed out, sure evidence that he was transporting some tasty treat—or likely several tasty treats—for concealment in a stash nearby. "Just don't get any ideas about using my tomato pots as the vaults of your food bank!" Walt said good-naturedly as George passed him yet again in his focused, businesslike manner.

Although Stumpy often resents animal intruders and occasionally defends his territory more vociferously than Walt would prefer, the squirrel continued to show no animosity toward the busy young chipmunk, and on the third day of George's sojourn in Stumpyland, the gray-furred homesteader actually slipped off his deck rail perch and, anticipating the smaller rodent's southward course, hop-hop-pause-hopped over to intercept him. Although George applied his brakes a foot or so before he reached Stumpy and stood with his tail erect but horizontal behind him, he didn't change direction; he simply stopped and stayed still as Stumpy hopped closer. The two distant cousins sniffed noses, but when Stumpy maneuvered to investigate further in the vicinity of George's hindquarters, the smaller critter simply resumed his purposeful journey toward the tomato pots and beyond. After a predictable few seconds had gone by, he reappeared and passed, unruffled, back toward the lake. I say "unruffled," but of course neither chipmunks nor squirrels dress so formally that they would ever be ruffled. Stumpy does have a fashionably white breast, but that's natural and composed of fur, not of some elegant fabric like chiffon or tulle that ruffles are usually made of; he does not wear a waistcoat or breeches, either, in case you wondered. *His* beauty is entirely a matter of his natural endowments and not at all of artificial accoutrements! Similarly, George wears only what nature has provided for *him.* Ah, if only humans were so unaffected and accepting of their own, unvarnished appearances! I should add as well that Stumpy and George never have to use varnish of any sort.

When George next appeared from the pondside stairs, however, he altered course, steering his quick steps toward the squirrel, where Stumpy now sat under the table. From inside his cheek pouches, George produced an acorn, which he then laid at the tailless bandit's feet before getting back to his work and journeying on; apparently, he had room in his cheeks for other items that he needed to secure in his safe-deposit box, wherever it was located. "Wow!" Walt said, having seen the whole encounter. "Those cheeks must be more capacious than they look. He hid that acorn as convincingly as Big Bruno conceals his tennis ball." Big Bruno is the gigantic yellow Labrador retriever belonging to Walt's longtime friend and onetime sweetheart Arlene Tosh; the tennis ball is like Big Bruno's version of the American Express card: He doesn't leave home without it—in fact, he rarely leaves anywhere without it—always tucking it into one or the other of his huge cheeks, under a flap of skin about the size of an elephant's ear. However, it does seem harder for Big Bruno to share his tennis ball than it was for George on this particular day to share his acorn.

Never one to be rude or to ignore another creature's kind gesture, Stumpy picked up the acorn in both his front paws, sat back, and sampled his gift with a quick nibble. The results must have pleased him, because he then hoed in to his snack, having nearly finished it by the time George reemerged from behind the tomato pots. At that moment, the squirrel seemed to decide that George was all right after all, and Stumpy began to follow the smaller animal around as he continued his quest for edible—and storable—foodstuffs. The stub-tailed mimic could sustain George's pace for only a few minutes, however, before he became either too tired or too bored to continue. "Well," Walt laughed when Stumpy once again stretched out on the rail of the deck, "good old Ge-e-e-o-o-orge must make you feel a bit like the grasshopper in the old story of the grasshopper and the ant! Good thing *you* don't have to store up for the winter, although he's more industrious than most chipmunks I know to get started this early. Well, I suppose I should give you more credit, too, though; you do have your caches of nuts and such in both the sheds, so you're not a complete layabout. So, Stump, what do you think of old George?"

At that moment the striped creature emerged yet again from behind the tomato pots and continued across the deck at his deliberate pace, a bit like a roadster with black-and-white racing stripes cruising straight down a country lane bumpy enough to keep the car at a moderate but deliberate speed. When Stumpy took two playful hops toward him, however, George froze, and the squirrel stepped forward and sniffed at the parallel black-and-white stripes that ran down his side.

"Hey," Walt said, "I know a Native American story about how the chipmunk got its stripes. Why don't we let old George finish up his freight hauling for the day while I tell you what the Iroquois people said about his ancestor?" Resignedly, Stumpy sidled back over to the table and climbed into Walt's lap.

"Well, Stumpster," Walt said, "you've had some experience with bears, so you might be able to understand that the Iroquois thought those big bruins had a pretty high opinion of themselves. You know, as massive, powerful animals, bears think they can do anything. Now, back in the days before everything was locked into the way it is now, back when the animals could still talk, a bear was moving through the woods, overturning logs in his search for something tasty to scavenge. He was repeating the bear *mantra*: 'I can do anything. Look at me. I can do anything.'

"Suddenly, however, the bear heard a voice say, 'Oh, really?' When he looked down, he saw the tiny face of a tiny chipmunk peering out at him from the tiny hole of its tiny burrow.

"'Yes!' the bear replied. 'Watch this!' With his huge paw, he lifted a fallen tree next to the chipmunk hole and flung it across the forest floor. 'See that?' he continued. 'I can do anything. I am the strongest creature in the forest, probably the world, maybe even the universe! All animals live in terror of me. I am one *major Ursus*! And . . . you know what? I can do anything.'

"'Harrumph!' the chipmunk said. 'Can you stop the sunrise?'

"'I never considered trying that before, but, yes, I can do that! I can do anything. I am Bear!'

"'Really?' the chipmunk said, concealing a giggle.

"'Yes,' the bear roared, 'tomorrow, there will be no sunrise!' and he sat down and waited through the night, repeating this chant, 'Tomorrow, there will be no sunrise,' while the chipmunk curled up in his homey nest, laughing at the bear's arrogance and blind stupidity.

"Hours later, as the sky began to brighten in the east, the bear was still chanting, 'There will be no sunrise!' but the sun wasn't convinced and rose anyway, as the chipmunk had known it would. The little rodent came out of his burrow with the sun climbing the sky, and he laughed at the bear out loud, so amused that he kept repeating things like, 'Oops! Where did the sun go? Is it an eclipse?' and 'It's so dark, I can't see a thing. Can anyone tell me what time it is?' Then he abandoned irony and scoffed openly: 'I thought you said you could do anything, but you can't even stop the silly old sunrise! Ha, ha, ha!'

"If the chipmunk was amused, the bear wasn't, and as the little animal danced around in glee and finally fell on his back in uncontrollable laughter, the cranky carnivore flashed out his paw like a bolt of lightning and pinned his tormenter to the ground. 'I may not have stopped the sunrise, but I certainly can stop your heart!' he growled. 'Enjoy your last breath.'

"'Oh, come on,' the chipmunk said, thinking fast, 'I know you're the strongest creature in the universe. I was just having a little fun with you.' The bear, however, did not let up his terrible pressure, and soon, the smaller creature was trying another approach. 'Oh, Bear, you're right. For scoffing at someone as awe-inspiring as you, I deserve to die. Please, though, let me say one last prayer before I go home to meet my Maker and my ancestors.'

"'Go ahead,' the bear grumbled, 'but make it quick. It's time for you to go to that Great Nut Cache in the sky!'

"'Oh,' the chipmunk said, 'but to pray, I need to draw a breath, and you are pressing so hard on my chest that I won't be able to say a single word. Please let up just a little so I can pray to the Maker who created the mighty, mighty Bear and the unworthy, imbecilic Chipmunk.' Inflated with his triumph, the bear let up just the slightest bit, and in that instant, the chipmunk squirted out from beneath the bear's paw and flew to the safety of his hole. The bear swatted at the fleet little varmint with one massive paw but couldn't catch him. Nevertheless, his claws raked their way down the chipmunk's back, leaving the black-and-white scars that he still bears today. And that's how the chipmunk got its stripes." Walt drew breath himself and sat back in his chair.

Over the next couple of days, the relationship between the two rodents established itself on comfortable, informal terms. Walt was still rationing Stumpy's daily allotment of honey-roasted cashews because of the diet Dr. Brad the veterinarian had put him on, but one morning, the gray-furred charmer made a point of dropping one of his apportioned treats on the deck in the middle of the path that George invariably traversed as he went about his business. The chipmunk stopped, and, this time, instead of tucking the nut into his cheek and carrying it off to his leguminous treasury, he sat up on his haunches, then nibbled his way into and through his present. When Walt later offered him a crust of bread from his morning anadama toast, George showed his first signs of a willingness to deviate from the straight-and-narrow path, both literal and figurative, that he had been following. Thereafter, he joined the duo for their morning snack, sometimes sitting on the deck near Walt's feet but gradually daring to work his way up an empty chair to sit on the table opposite the porkpie-hatted octogenarian. Stumpy usually joined George on the table as well, even though the deck rail is his customary perch. After a few minutes of leisure, though, the sedulous George would go back to work, never able to relinquish his industrious side completely.

Back on the summer solstice, Walt had constructed three new wooden boats so his dear friends the Riggettis, down the road, could participate in his long-standing family tradition of candle boats; he had made one such craft for Stumpy the previous summer. Each boat was about sixteen inches long, with a flat, rectangular base as the hull; a second, smaller rectangle as the cabin; and a taller, square block as the pilothouse. Behind the pilothouse he had drilled a hole big enough to hold a half-inch candle securely. The idea was to light the candles, make a wish, and then launch the boats onto the pond. If one made it to the other shore, the wish its "captain" had made was supposed to come true. The following day, June 21, Walt and Stumpy had taken their usual morning cruise in Nelly, the ten-foot rowboat with the three-horse Johnson outboard motor attached, and had collected all four of the candle boats from the shrubs and blueberry bushes along the pond's farther, eastern shore, with Walt exclaiming, "Wow, Stump! It looks as though we all get our wishes!" When the tour of their watery domain was done that morning, Walt had left the four boats down by the cabin's shoreline, knowing that Tony and his parents were likely to come by for a swim in the hot weather; he figured that Tony in particular would not only enjoy knowing that the craft had all made it to the other shore and come back safely, but would also appreciate having the chance to play with them more by the water's edge.

Also on solstice eve, Tony and Stumpy had collaborated on a sandcastle that the young human intended as a condominium for Stumpy and his squirrel siblings Burwell and Lansdowne. Unlike the ocean, whose tides have a tendency to swallow and reclaim even sandcastles built well up from the water, Kibbee Pond is less volatile and voracious in its workings, so Tony's condo castle was still standing last Monday, when Stumpy led his young, striped colleague down to the shore. Stumpy showed George how to go through the arched entryway of the castle, which was a less tight fit for the slimmer animal, and gave him a tour of the various chambers that Tony had designed. As far as I know, Stumpy couldn't explain the specific functions of those different rooms, but George seemed to enjoy exploring, possibly convinced that an acorn storeroom would appear somewhere in the elaborate structure. To that end, he often pressed on ahead of his tailless host.

When their exploration of the sandcastle was done, George wandered out onto the dock, surveying Nelly as if she might have a hold laden with rich, durable foodstuffs. When he and Stumpy hopped aboard, the young chipmunk was less concerned with admiring the pulpit off the bow that Walt had built for Stumpy than he was with searching under the seats and beneath the bailing can for secret stashes of nuts and seeds. Finding nothing appetizing, George went ashore once again and worked his way down the beach to the stack of candle boats, now minus their candles, resting on the sand just above where the water lapped.

Whether Stumpy was trying to demonstrate the boats' function by reenacting their solstice launching we'll probably never know for certain, since Walt was off watering his main vegetable garden and no one else was present to witness the proceedings. Nevertheless, the mischievous squirrel managed to nudge one of the boats into the water, then started chattering excitedly to his striped friend. Somehow, George misunderstood Stumpy's intention and leaped onto the now-floating boat, which tipped and shifted enough under his weight that the little fellow panicked and could only cling desperately to the cabin and pilothouse as the chipmunk's momentum carried the craft farther offshore. A steady breeze out of the north was just strong enough to push the craft and its discomfited occupant even farther away from dry land. George huddled helplessly (and Stumpy watched just as helplessly) as the boat's distance from the shoreline increased from two feet to six to ten to twenty.

If Stumpy had been Lassie the wonder dog, he might have thought to run up the hill and around the cabin to bark—or in the squirrel's case, chatter—at Walt so that the elderly man would drop the hose and follow him back to the dock, there to figure out a way to save the day. Stumpy, however, is and never has been Lassie, for all his doglike traits, so nothing of the sort occurred to him. Instead, desperate not to abandon his new friend, who may have felt more like a younger brother to the squirrel than anything else, the would-be lifeguard pushed another of the candle boats into the water and clambered aboard it himself. Stumpy has proven himself a capable swimmer in the past, but he is not fond of such natatorial exploits, having last summer almost fallen prey to the legendary Old Smokey, the four-foot bluegill sunfish who apparently splits his time between Kibbee Pond and the larger Beech Tree Lake, which are connected by a narrow channel. Still, the squirrel, who is as foolhardy in his bravery at one moment as he is craven in his cowardice in the next, would not abandon George to a watery grave. Of course, Stumpy had no way to propel his boat, and George's craft had a substantial head start on the loyal gray fur's boat, so that doughty mariner could do little but sink his claws into the wood and bob along, praying that he would not get seasick.

By the time Walt had finished watering the garden and had come down to the shore in search of his rodent roommate, the candle boats had drifted about a hundred yards out into the pond; nevertheless, they were still visible from the dock. Walt wasn't sure how much the humor of the situation counterbalanced his concern, but he couldn't help chuckling a little as he eased himself into Nelly. In a matter of moments, he had the Johnson purring, and *his* boat was advancing on the fur-bearing flotilla. Somehow in the intervening time, Stumpy's candle boat had gotten closer to George's, and Walt circled around the two castaway rodents, then cut his engine so both candle boats would drift with the wind toward him. First, the nimble geezer reached into the water and grasped George's boat, lifting it and the chipmunk out of the pond and over the gunwale into Nelly. Next, he stretched his arm out toward Stumpy so the squirrel could walk up to his shoulder; a moment later, Walt was able also to bring Stumpy's boat aboard as well.

When they got back to the dock, with both the rodents remarkably dry and apparently none the worse for wear, Walt felt comfortable making a joke at his old and new friends' expense: "Well," he said, "maybe the lake association over at Beech Tree Lake will want to make this an annual event, part of the Fourth of July celebration along with the Boat Parade. Just think! They could call it the Rodent Regatta!" Walt chuckled, but no one else was laughing.

31

Stumpy and the Vulpine Thief

July 11, 2012

Late one morning last week, those two pond dwellers, Walt Walthers and Stumpy the tailless gray squirrel, left their cabin on Kibbee Pond to visit Walt's friend and former driver's ed student, Ellie Wentworth, at her farm across town at what she calls Justaplain Island on the Nashua River. In addition to her long-standing friendship with Walt, Ellie is also the school bus driver for Walt and Stumpy's neighbor six-year-old Tony Riggetti; at least she is when school is in session. Now that summer vacation is underway, Walt has a standing invitation to stop in for coffee, especially since Ellie lost her longtime companion, Barney Hood, about two years ago. The amenable codger always enjoys visiting with Ellie and with her menagerie, which includes the usual domestic critters: two dogs, Peggie and Claude, both border collie crosses; several cats; and two horses, the white behemoth Snowball and the elegant, trim bay mare Clarissa. However, several less-standard animals are also part of Ellie's coterie, including the once-orphaned mallard hen Doodle, whom Ellie and Barney hatched from an egg and raised and who has been returning to the barn each spring for over seven years to lay a clutch of eggs and then take her ducklings to the river once *they* hatch. In addition, living on her property and dining on the rich greenness of her lawn and pastures is a colony of escaped domestic rabbits, intended by a farmer down the road for the meat market; that colony, however, continues to proliferate, feral generation after feral generation, and Ellie continues to feel an emotional attachment, nearly as much as if they were her actual pets. Of course, the area also has its share—or more than its share, given its verdancy and seclusion—of wild denizens: ospreys and even bald eagles along the river; herons in the swamp on the other side of the property; songbirds of all sorts; turtles; frogs; snakes; and the usual array of mammals, including squirrels, chipmunks, raccoons, woodchucks, beavers, skunks, otters, bears, and foxes, just to name some of the temporary guests and sojourners Ellie has reported to Walt in recent times.

Snowball and Clarissa stepped out of their shed's shade and into the sunlit pasture as soon as they heard Walt's '60 Chevy pickup, Lulu, turn onto the tree-lined lane that leads to Ellie's house, with its stable on the ground floor and unique living space on the second. The two horses started walking down the field toward the main building as if they had been expecting visitors and were the official welcoming committee. However, the dogs, Peggie and Claude, apparently thought they had won that official role as well, because they were waiting near the house, barking and wagging as the truck pulled up. Fortunately, they were so accustomed to Ellie's expectations that they not chase her cats or rabbits that they had readily accepted Stumpy during earlier visits, as if he were in fact part kitty, part bunny, and part dog, as Walt sometimes claims he is. Still, on this day, the gray-furred bandit stayed up on Walt's shoulder for the bulk of their initial tour, even when Ellie emerged from the downstairs stable and the group started their meandering stroll around the premises; he did, though, hop up into the rafters of the pole barn and explore on his own near the barn swallows' nests while the humans paused to give the horses a carrot and a scratch on their equine necks. For some reason, he remained wary about the farm dogs' intentions, and Walt was glad that his roommate was, for once, practicing discretion.

Ellie has a wooden deck of her own out along the river, and as noon approached, she brought out some sandwiches and iced tea for a light lunch out there, where the basswoods provided shade and the breeze off the water was a pleasant complement to the warmth of the sun. The dogs stayed inside so Stumpy could explore the trees, inspect the zinnia garden, and reacquaint himself with the resident rabbits without feeling uncomfortable. "I've had some foxes around lately," Ellie said as they sat down to eat, with Ellie supplying some carrot curls and shelled peanuts for the squirrel's delectation. "They make me nervous about the cats, the rabbits, and Doodle's ducklings, especially because these rust-colored scavengers look scrawny and very hungry. They're brazen, too, stopping out in the pasture to stare at me, as if daring me to try to chase them off. Yesterday morning, something even more unsettling happened."

"What was that?" Walt asked.

"About 5:15, I woke up out of a dream . . . you know that feeling of swimming up from the depths, gradually getting closer to consciousness with a growing awareness of sound? Well, at first I thought I was hearing a car horn blaring over and over again, but after a few moments I came to the realization that I was waking to something else: the frantic, repeated cawing of a crow, which seemed to be right outside the bedroom window. As I came further awake, I realized that not just one crow was calling; when I swung my legs out of bed to see what was going on, I was pretty sure that at least three crow voices were blending together in one loud and repeated squawling noise, all the birds timing their calls perfectly into one harsh, brassy blast. I thought perhaps they had mobbed an owl or even an eagle and driven it to take refuge in one of the trees around the house, but as I went from window to window, I just couldn't see where the birds were. I went back to the window that looks out on the alley from the pole barn up to the pasture shed, and suddenly, a ratty-looking fox trotted out from behind the barn and headed up the alley, a dead crow hanging from its mouth. I could hear the birds then, calling individually, and could see one or two following the fox, flitting from treetop to treetop, until the mangy-looking thing cut across toward the tree line along the edge of the swamp and disappeared into the bushes. How the fox caught the crow I don't know; I have to wonder if it was a young crow that was down in the grass and just wasn't wary enough, but foxes have the reputation for being crafty, so the story may be more complicated."

"You never know with foxes," Walt said, "how much is cleverness and how much luck. Of course, crows are a lot smarter than most other birds, so I agree with your last idea: that flea-bitten rascal may well have hatched some elaborate plot to get himself some lunch."

"It's upsetting in part," Ellie said, "because my late mother was so devoted to crows. She used to buy a loaf of bread each week and put slices out for the neighborhood murder of crows. They knew the times she was most likely to be putting out their treats and would come in once or twice a day to check out the buffet. If she was late, they would sit in the top of the big ash and call to her until she came out and tossed them their slices; she'd talk back and had developed a convincing *caw!* of her own. One morning, she looked out to see that a big hawk had just struck one of her crows on the ground, and she was out the door immediately, clad only in her nightgown and yelling at the top of her lungs. The hawk fled, and the crow flew off, rescued by a shrieking septuagenarian." Ellie laughed.

Out on the river, a mother mallard was leading a pack of seven ducklings toward the shore, announcing their presence with a loud *WA-A-A-ACK*! "That has to be Doodle," Walt said, adjusting the brim of his porkpie hat so he could see better against the sun glinting off the water. After another couple of minutes, the flock waddled out of the water and up onto the riverbank, with Doodle leading them to a ceramic bowl filled with layer pellets. Having noticed the new arrivals, Stumpy hopped over from the portion of the lawn where his distant cousins, the rabbits, had been grazing; clearly curious, he hop-hop-pause-hopped to within ten feet of the feathery free-loaders, but he must have gotten just too close for Doodle's liking, because she put her head down and extended her bill as she darted toward the squirrel with another, decidedly less-cordial *WA-A-A- CK*! Stumpy ended up on the lowest branch of a nearby maple.

"Well," Walt laughed, "sometimes, our feathered friends *can* get the upper hand on the mammals of this world! Makes me think of 'The Nun's Priest's Tale' from Chaucer's *Canterbury Tales.* Do you know that story?"

Ellie replied dryly, "Why don't you go ahead and refresh my memory?"

As Walt was about to begin his tale, Stumpy appeared on the deck rail and launched himself across to the table, where he sprawled out, breathless from beating a hasty retreat from his temporary perch. "The hero returns!" Walt joked.

"My story has a hero too," he continued. "You might be surprised to find out who it is, however. Anyway, an elderly widow was scraping a living out of a small farmstead, making do with the bare necessities; she grew her own vegetables and tended her animals, which included three sows, three cows, a sheep named Maude, and the usual array of barn cats and yard dogs. Unlike many nowadays, the widow lived a simple, frugal life, and she was content with what little she had—no Starbucks or fancy French restaurants for her—though, of course, this was back in the fourteenth century, when the English were involved in the Hundred Years' War *against* the French, so haute cuisine was verboten, so to speak.

"The widow's yard was fenced with palings, pointed sticks set close together, and surrounded by a ditch that would have seemed like the moat of a castle except that it was, and always had been, dry. Within the little kingdom of this yard lived the woman's flock of chickens, overseen by the great Lord Chanticleer, a rooster whose voice was more rich than a church organ and whose sense of time was as refined as that of the finest church organist. The widow needed no clock because Chanticleer was so precise in his crowing that he might have been a chronologist measuring the degrees of the sun's movement through the sky. Come to think of it, perhaps that's exactly what his instincts allowed him to do. Every hour—or every fifteen degrees that the sun passed through the sky—Chanticleer would crow, and oh, what a glorious sound he would make! And what a handsome appearance our hero had as well! His comb was as red as a supermodel's lips and crenellated like the turrets of a castle; the rest of his body was also beautiful, with his jet-black bill, his legs and toes blue as a cloudless sky, his lily-white talons, and his feathers like burnished gold. When they heard his remarkably regular challenges ringing out from within the fortress he had vowed to defend, everyone—farm animals and humans alike—acknowledged him as the brave and peerless defender of his demesne. He was more than just a warrior too; he was a warrior philosopher—well read and always seeking to extend his knowledge. He was like a cross between Mel Gibson in *Braveheart* and Stephen Hawking, just with feathers . . . well, maybe more like a cross between Tom Brady and Nietzsche . . . well, I don't actually know what he was like a cross between, but he was pretty hot stuff.

"And much he had to defend too! In his charge and available for his pleasure were seven hens, his paramours and ladies gay, all similar in color to their lord. The one, however, with the loveliest colors around her throat was his favorite, Lady Pertelote, the most elegant, gracious, well-mannered, and courteous chicken that anyone could imagine, and he was as devoted to her as any human knight could be to his ladylove; he had worshipped her, and she him, ever since she was a mere chick one week old. Each day at dawn, the two would intertwine their lovely fowl voices—I said *fowl*, not *foul*!—in an ecstatically harmonized greeting to the sun, and never did strife of the sort that assails ignoble lovers ever ruffle their feathers. Each was the other's all, and no harsh words had ever passed between them.

"When the events of this story occurred, animals could still talk, and early one morning, as Chanticleer sat on his accustomed nightly perch in the rafters of the little cottage's kitchen, pretty Pertelote beside him and his other wives ranked around him, the handsome rooster began moaning and groaning like a human sleeper troubled by a dream. Pertelote nudged him with her feathered hip and said, 'Oh, my lord and love, what is wrong? Aren't you ashamed to be making such a din when we females so badly need our beauty sleep?'

"The well-bred rooster replied, 'Dearest darling, never fear. But I must say my heart is still fluttering from a terrifying dream I just had! Perhaps the dream will prove prophetic and save me from a predicted predicament! Perhaps it will save me from imprisonment or exile from my home, each a fate worse than death. Let me tell you of that dream, my treasure! I dreamed that as I was patrolling our yard, a doglike creature of the canine persuasion came toward me as if to lay hold of my body and carry me off. Its color was reddish-gold, like a blazing fire, except for its tail and ears, which were tipped with black; its snout was pointed, and above it burned two hungry eyes. And you wonder why I cried out in my sleep!'

"Chanticleer's favorite wife turned her own eyes to the shaken rooster and said, 'For shame! And you call yourself the cock of the walk! How could I ever have fallen for a coward, and how will I ever sustain the ignominy that goes with having a husband who is nothing more than a chicken? If only my feathers were white, I'd tear out four of them right now and hand them to you as a token of your cowardice! Don't you know what women want more than anything? I'll tell you: They want husbands who are courageous, wise, munificent, and dependable—not cheapskates or idiots or someone who faints at the sight of a weapon, but not boastful macho manure-heads either! How can you have a beard if you're not a real man? As that great educational philosopher Elder Blodget would say, "Suck it up!" How can you be afraid of a mere dream? Don't you know that taking dreams seriously is mere foolishness? Dreams are just a result of overeating, of poor digestion, and gas—nothing more. You're just suffering from a chemical imbalance. Don't you remember that the great Roman statesman and orator Cato said, "Pay no attention to dreams"?'

"'Now, my husband,' she continued, 'when we fly down from the rafters, you must take a laxative and purge your system. Since we don't have a CVS or even an apothecary to consult in the near vicinity, just let *me* advise you about what herbs will work best in relieving your distress, which is purely physical in its cause and not in the least a forewarning of any sort. Content yourself with a light diet for a few days. Let's go over here to the herb bed, and I'll find you some spurge and hellebore and buckthorn to help you cleanse your digestive tract, and you'll feel better in a flush . . . I mean, a flash.'

"The rooster, however, drew himself up with great dignity and, thrusting out his delicately colored chest feathers, replied, 'My dear, I thank you for your . . . informative lecture, but for all that Cato may have disapproved of dreams, a thousand other authorities warn us to pay careful heed to the dire warnings they convey. Besides, experience provides the proof that dreams *are* auguries and portents and bodings and presages, harbingers, and foretellings for those who are wise enough to respect their prognostications and vaticinations. I could tell you hundreds of old stories and present you with as many contemporary accounts of dreams that have proven true—like the one I overheard the parson telling our mistress about two travelers awaiting a propitious wind to begin a sea voyage; when the wind changed in their favor, both went to bed joyful that they could depart in the morning. During the night, however, one traveler dreamed that a man came to his bedside and told him that the ship would be cast upon the rocks and swallowed by the sea, a disaster of titanic proportions, but the other man laughed at his fears and said, "No mere dream will keep me from sailing after I've had to wait this long! Stay here like a mindless monkey or a fretful chicken if you like, but my time is too valuable to waste further." Although the dreamer remained ashore, the other man ignored the warning and boarded the ship, but when the ship was nearing its destination, winds blew it upon the rocks of the coastline, and all aboard were drowned. Would you have me ignore a divinely sent premonition? Would you give me a dressing-down and call me chicken when I deserve instead the title of sage? Phooey to you! If you think me not sage, you can stuff it! Haven't you heard of the prophetic dreams of Saint Kenelm and Scipio and of Daniel and Joseph in the Bible?'

"'You call dreams prophetic,' Pertelote replied. 'I call them pathetic!' She clucked and flapped in contempt.

"Chanticleer continued. 'Would you laugh at the dream of Hector's wife, Andromache, who warned her husband that he would die in battle that day and tried to dissuade him from taking the field? With dawn so near, I have no time to retell such a long tale, but I will say this much: It was that same day that Achilles slew the great hero and then dragged him around the walls of Troy in shame and disgrace! I know that Hector was a mere king's son and not a true sovereign like myself, ruling a massive empire like mine, but discretion is and must always be the better part of valor. I do, after all, have a kingdom to defend, and who will do it if some flaming canine carries me off to my doom? Duty calls me now to march out into my yard, so I will conclude by saying two things: First, though I will face my responsibilities, I declare that my dream *is* a true prophecy and foretells very real danger to my regal self. Second . . . I can't stand laxatives. They taste yucky, and they make me want to barf, so screw them! Yuck! Patooey!'

"The courtly cock shifted gears then as he looked again at his paramour's feathery shapeliness, and other urges kicked in. 'Let's change the subject, shall we, and find a more . . . pleasurable line of conversation. You know, my dear, God has been merciful and kind to me in at least one way, for you are my treasure. When I see the beauty of your face, especially those gorgeous red circles around your eyes, all my fears die, and I can think of . . . only one thing. Oh, as the Bible says, "*Mulier est hominis confusio.*" Since you don't know Latin, let me translate: "Woman is the only source of man's joy and contentment." Oh, my darling, when I feel your feathered side next to mine on our nightly roost, I curse the narrowness of our perch, for my desire for you is overwhelming, and I yearn to mount you there and then. Oh, blast it! You make me so happy that I defy all dreams and visions. Won't you fly down to the yard now, so I can . . . *show* you how I feel about you?'"

Walt interrupted the story here to comment. "An accurate translation of that Latin phrase, by the way, is the exact opposite of what Chanticleer says. The passage actually means, 'Woman is man's ruin and confusion,' but I've never been completely certain whether Chanticleer's Latin is faulty, and *he* is misunderstanding the quote, or whether he's simply condescending to his wife with conscious irony, knowing he can shut her up this way.

"In any case," Walt continued, "the flock all flew down from the rafters and out to the yard, with Chanticleer leading the way, and commenced their morning feeding, all observing, of course, the pecking order consistent with the ideals of their feudal society. . . . I said, their *feudal* society, not their *futile* society. Chanticleer had put his fears aside and now strode and strutted across the yard like a regal prince or the sternest of lions, clucking to his wives when he found a grain of corn, watching complacently as they ran to him at his command. Before 6:00 a.m. arrived, he had feathered the fair Pertelote twenty times and trod her just as often, so virile and vigorous was he.

"But the rooster's dream was no mere phantom produced by constipation, and as Almighty Providence had foreordained, a sly, black-souled fox had that night broken through the hedge and was now lying in the yard among the cabbages, awaiting his opportunity like a foul assassin—that time, I said *foul*, not *fowl*. Oh, he was a second Judas, another Ganelon, a new Sinon, like the Greek whose treachery brought down the walls of Ilium! Oh, Chanticleer, I don't know if everything that happens happens of necessity! I don't understand the distinction between 'simple necessity' and 'conditional necessity.' I'm no Augustine, no Boethius, no Bishop Bradwardine! I don't know whether your big problem, rooster, is listening to the advice of a woman, just as Adam did in the Garden of Eden, or whether your own lust or your self-obsessed pomposity or your cocksure and willful disregard of your own instincts is what brings you down. But let me finish my story!

"As the pretty Pertelote immersed herself in a morning dust bath and the rooster's other wives laid themselves out in the sun like a certain gray squirrel we know trying to work on his tan, Chanticleer's eye fell on a butterfly in the cabbages, and just as he was about to reach out to latch on to that lepidopterous snack, he found himself suddenly face-to-face with the creature from his nightmare. He stretched out his neck and in panicked but still mellifluous tones, cried '*Cuck, cuck, cuck*!' Though he had never seen a fox before, instinct helped him to recognize his natural enemy and told him to flee, and he was about to flap away when the fox spoke up.

"'Oh, *mon bon ami*, do not hasten away from me, your friend Reynard ze fox, a sojourn*eur* newly return-ed from ze continent and in need of coun-*sel* from a longtime resident of zis country in order to—how do you say?—refreshen my *mémoire* of ze customs here. I am no dastardly espy, come to perform ze treachery upon you. *Non, non, mon ami*, I was simply mesmeriz-ed by ze beauty of your sin*ging* and drawn here to your fortification by your deep and manly voice. Ze last time I was in zis vicinity, it was your own fazzere who serenaded me and zen welcom-ed me into zis magnificent residence. Oh, how he could sing, just like ze angels in ze Heaven! And ze sound of your voice carri-ed me back, for I had never sought zat anyone could make ze melody like his—how do you say?—equivalent, but, oh, my dear sir, you have perhaps surpass-ed even your fazzere! Oh, please, sing again! You remind me of your dear fazzere and of your mozzere, too, both of whom were kind enough also to visit my own dwell*ing*, to my great satisfaction, when last I frequented zis area. Do you make-a your song as your fazzere did, by shutting your eyes tight, standing on ze tippies of your toes, and stretching out your long and *très* elegant neck? Oh, I beg of you to show me again how you make ze beautiful melody so that I may re*vel* in ze family resemblance!'

"Suckered in by the fox's clever flattery but suspecting nothing, Chanticleer flapped his wings, stood on his tiptoes, and extended his neck with his eyes screwed tight shut, and in that instant, before he could even begin his proud though tuneless crowing, Reynard grabbed him by the throat, slung him over his back like a sack of groceries, and dashed toward the woods. You might have expected Venus, the goddess of love, to have better protected so devoted a lover as the royal rooster, especially since these events occurred on a Friday, the day holy to Venus. But no, Fate is ineluctable, and the stars must have been aligned against the gallant cock. Perhaps it was even Friday the thirteenth!

"When Lady Pertelote and the other hens saw what had happened, they cried out in lamentation louder than the Trojan women in the *Aeneid* when Ilium fell and the bloodthirsty Pyrrhus grabbed King Priam by his beard and thrust his sword into the aged man's flesh. Lady Pertelote cried loudest of all, louder even than the senators' wives when Nero burned Rome and their innocent husbands died, louder even than Hasdrubal's wife when the Romans killed her husband and put Carthage to the torch, upon which she bravely threw herself into the flames and perished. There is no tragedy like a barnyard tragedy!

"When the widow heard the uproar, she came running, shrieking, 'I see you, thief!' at the top of her lungs; the hired man emerged from the barn, also hollering, and the dogs streaked after them, barking out their vows of death to the fox as if they were the very hounds of hell. Soon, all the other animals joined the chase—cows, sows, Maude the sheep, and even the cats, all adding their voices to the chaos.

"But Fortune, that meretricious vixen, would spin her wheel once again, overturning the triumph of the once-favored Brother Reynard, for the rooster, bouncing along on the fox's back as they neared the forest's edge, gathered the wit and strength to say, 'Ho, ho, you foxy fellow, now you're home free, and you deserve to celebrate. If I were you, I'd turn back and holler, "Na na na boo boo! You'll never catch me, you mentally deficient peasants! In another second I'll be in the woods, enjoying a fowl-tasting meal! You'll have to settle for eating . . . *my dust!*"' (I should interrupt to clarify that he said *fowl*-tasting, not *foul*-tasting!) Anyway, though Reynard was not the master of English idioms that Chanticleer was, the fox did like the idea of voicing his superiority over his pursuers, so he opened his mouth to commence a string of Frenchified insults. (I said *Frenchified*, not *French-fried*!) In that instant, however, the great hero, Chanticleer, broke free from his assailant's clutches and flew up into a basswood tree . . . a lot like this one we're sitting under today.

"The outfoxed fox's response was to call out, 'Oh, but you must not take eet so perso*nal*, my dear Chanticleer! Please forgive me if my actions seem-ed to you—how do you say?—imperti*nent*. You see, *mon ami*, I had heard zat ze widow of ze house did have intention to knock of you upon ze head and flang you into ze cooking pot, and I knew I must act wiz ze quickness to espirit you away to safe-e-ty. You must come down now so zat I can explain to you my plan further, *vraiment*!'

"'Oh no you don't!' the rooster exclaimed. 'Fool me once, shame on you. Fool me twice, shame on me. I'm not a com*plete* featherbrain, you know. Damn you and me both, but damn me most of all if I listen to your flattery again! I have learned an important lesson: Anyone who willfully keeps his eyes shut when they should be open wide deserves whatever he gets!'

"'*Non*,' said the fox, 'it is *moi* who have learn-ed ze lesson today, and it is zat anyone who blither-blathers when he should be keeping ze mouth *shut* deserves whatever *he* gets!' Moments later, his black-tipped tail disappeared into the shade of the woods."

Walt sat back in his chair as the breeze off the river riffled the leaves of the basswood. "Well, Ellie, I leave it to you to decide if Lady Pertelote would have been happier to have her husband earn eternal fame by dying a hero or if she was happy enough to have him alive through cleverness rather than courage. You know, we hear people all the time telling others, 'Don't be chicken,' but I think this story is one case where it would be appropriate to tell the chickens, 'Don't be *human*.' I'm not sure that wishing human nature on anyone, even humans, would necessarily be a kindness."

In the course of the story, the rabbits had in their grazing moved across the grass and close to the deck. Doodle and her ducklings had also advanced farther up the riverbank onto the grass nearby. Stumpy, his courage apparently restored by a rest and some lunch, slipped off the table and hopped carefully over toward the two groups. When he was a few feet away, the gray rabbit known as Duck Bunny hopped curiously toward him, causing an intimidated Stumpy to take several steps backward. When Doodle, the mallard mother, saw those movements, she put her bill down and, as she had done earlier, again charged at the squirrel. Immediately, that tailless paragon sprinted back toward the humans and, once again, leaped onto the table; this time, he climbed Walt's shirtfront to the man's shoulder and paused only briefly before continuing right up onto the top of his roommate's porkpie.

Ellie was laughing so hard she could barely speak. "Well, Walt, your story raised doubts about whether that rooster was the hero he believed himself to be, but I'm not so sure we'll be changing Stumpy's name anytime soon to Hercules or Theseus or even Luke Skywalker. Maybe we should just call him Rocky the Fleeing Squirrel!"

32

Stumpy and the Blueberry Bonanza

JULY 18, 2012

Some hazy days last week trumpeted the arrival of summer in all its humid glory out at Kibbee Pond, where, at the cozy cabin along the shore, Walt Walthers and his furry friend Stumpy the stub-tailed gray squirrel began planning their strategies for beating the persistent muggy heat that seemed to be putting down its roots. The octogenarian weather watcher, always so dapper in his red suspenders and his omnipresent porkpie hat, is also a consummate professional, so he is always up-to-date on the long-range and more immediate forecasts; years of observation and interest, chronicled in his daily logs, allow him to see meteorological patterns emerging when big-name forecasters prove shortsighted. I should warn you that he has convinced himself recently that we're in for some hot stuff over the next couple of months.

One of Walt's strategies for coping with sizzling days is to shift from his characteristic hot coffee to iced coffee, though even on the hottest days, he'll still sometimes pour out a mug of fresh-brewed hot java. He knows, however, that a slight change can sometimes make a big difference, so one morning last week, he made his first glass of iced coffee this season. Although his late wife, Annie, used to drink her coffee at room temperature pretty much year-round, Walt enjoys using actual ice to cool his caffeinated beverages even further; to that end, he keeps a cube-filled plastic bucket in his freezer. Last week, when he made himself a cold drink, he brought an ice cube out onto the pondside deck for Stumpy.

"What do you think, Stumperoo? You want to sample this baby and cool yourself off?" Walt slid the ice cube across the deck toward his bucktoothed friend.

The squirrel, always curious and alert, jumped back quickly as the cube skidded his way but then stepped forward to sniff at the unfamiliar substance. "Go ahead and lick it, if you like," Walt said, "or maybe you can pick it up and try biting off a piece."

Stumpy batted the cube twice or thrice with his front paws, following it the few inches it would slide and swatting it again. When he tired of that game, however, he sniffed again at the ice where it was beginning to melt onto the boards and then—after three tries—grasped it with both paws. After three or four seconds, however, he dropped the cube and began shaking his paws as if some sensation in them, presumably the burn and numbness of extreme cold, had surprised him. Given the rodent's persistent and occasionally vengeful nature, Walt was *not* surprised to see his rascally roommate pick up the ice cube in his front paws again and begin nibbling determinedly at it; while he would occasionally set the object of his appetite down for a few seconds and shake the melted water off his paws, Stumpy continued to gnaw at the cube, and it continued to dwindle in size. At one point, he rolled onto his back and, holding the frozen delicacy above his head, continued to indulge himself with his *agua coolatta.* Suddenly, however, he stopped, dropped the cube, turned over unsteadily, and rose to his four feet; then, staggering slightly, he walked a few steps away. Walt thought he recognized the symptoms of brain freeze. "Oh, hey, buddy," he chuckled, "enough's enough, I think. You're not exactly an arctic animal, regardless of those animated *Ice Age* movies that include Scrat the prehistoric squirrel. Besides, you wouldn't want to end up like him. Doesn't he keep getting his nuts frozen into some glacier or other? Give it a rest, and just sit for a minute."

By the time Walt and Stumpy's new friend George the chipmunk appeared a few minutes later, his cheeks puffed full of seeds or nuts to store in one of his secret caches, the larger rodent had recovered and chattered a greeting. The ice cube—or the part of it Stumpy had not devoured—was now merely a pool of water, and George skirted it as he approached Walt's boots where the kindly elder sat at the deck table. "Well, Ge-e-e-o-o-orge, I guess I won't offer you an ice cube, seeing how the last one affected your buddy there, but how'd you feel about a bite of this blueberry muffin?" So saying, the charitable geezer set a small portion of the baked delicacy next to his left boot, where George quickly gathered the confection into his paws and began nibbling, seeming especially to savor the indigo berries embedded in the dough.

Walt chuckled and said, "Can't say as I blame you for your enthusiasm. We're at the height of the berry season, as I suspect you well know from your own foraging, and I've had good luck picking lately. Stump and I take along a plastic container when we embark on our morning cruises, and most mornings, we stop at one or another of the islands to do a little picking, maybe just a half hour or so, so as not to spoil our enjoyment of the routine by overdoing it. Even if we come back with only a couple of cups, I don't worry because they accumulate surprisingly fast. I just keep a plastic container in the refrigerator until it's full; then we either eat them or cook with them as we need them, or we freeze them when the container is full. I usually end up with a healthy stock for the winter in the freezer, and, boy, do those muffins taste good in February or March, when spring and summer seem too far away even to hope for!"

While Walt was waxing rhapsodic about blueberries and berry picking, George was cleaning up the crumbs from the deck boards; when he was done, he sat up on his haunches and continued listening to Walt, his bright eyes trying to ascertain whether any more of the muffin remained on the plate.

"Now, I wonder," Walt said. "Is begging innate or learned behavior? Did Stumpy play the big brother and teach you his techniques, or does this skill just come naturally to you? Unfortunately, the muffin is gone, but I suspect I'll have another one tomorrow morning if you want to come back. And if you like blueberries as much as you seem to, you could always join us on our morning cruise and eat your fill out at the islands. You know, little guy, this is the time of year when everyone else seems to see only green, but I always see a touch of blue in that green every July as the berry season arrives. I love that blue, and when things get steamy or scorching in mid-July, I just tell myself that the sun is helping the berries ripen up." Walt would have agreed that the conditions were definitely steamy at times last week.

Of course, the pines and hardwoods along the shore where the cabin perches provide regular shade that's helpful in counteracting the heat, and a gentle breeze often wafts off the water to add further natural cooling; somehow, the cabin and its shoreline never seem to succumb to the swelter when it settles in and holds sway over the rest of the area. Still, another technique Walt employs to cool off in the muggy weather is bathing, and the beach near his dock is one pleasant and convenient spot for him to have a splash when the temperature gets oppressive. Thus, a long-standing routine from past summers emerged again last week for the cabin-dwelling codger: a morning swim. Whether he ambled down to the sand near his dock and entered the water there or changed into his trunks before his early-morning outing with Stumpy in Nelly the boat so they could stop out at a sandy-beached cove on one of the islands, Walt found himself cherishing the leisurely time easing into the shallows and stroking casually out deep enough to let his legs dangle down as he trod water with his arms. "I suppose the boys would say I was taking too big a risk swimming by myself," he said to his gray-furred sidekick one morning, referring to his three sons, who all live too far away to keep as close an eye on their dad as they would like.

Stumpy, by the way, does not join Walt in the water by choice, even though he has demonstrated mastery of the squirrelly paddle in the past on a number of occasions. At home he usually hops out onto the dock so that he can be near Walt when the aquatically inclined codger is indulging in a cooling plunge; he knows he can trust Walt not to splash him intentionally. An added benefit to his placing himself on the dock is that he is then at eye level with his human roommate, a state he can achieve otherwise only by climbing up to his friend's shoulder, and under the latter circumstances, the two companions are really too close to focus clearly on each other. Stumpy does favor eye contact when Walt is telling him a story or just chattering away at him.

Out at the island cove, however, Stumpy hops ashore from Nelly where Walt moors her to the shoreline, and then the bandy-legged rascal explores the insular half acre of dry ground, climbing trees, digging around fallen logs, and foraging for nuts and berries; more than once, he's come chittering back to lead Walt to a particularly heavy-laden blueberry bush so they can do some picking there before they depart. Occasionally, the gray-furred Argonaut will stretch out on a sun-washed rock along the shoreline and bask while Walt's dip proceeds. One morning last week, Walt saw his mammalian friend lean from his rock perch and reach with one paw toward the shallows beneath the rock, where minnows were schooling. The squirrel would dip his claw tips into the water, and the minnows would rise curiously toward the disturbance. Stumpy continued the teasing game for several minutes, giving Walt the inspiration for a similar game of his own.

Out there at the island cove, although Stumpy won't join Walt in the water when he engages in his natatory pursuits, the geezer is not alone. Most days, a small group of full-grown bluegill sunfish show up when his movements disturb the water, and when he stands up on the sandy bottom, those kibbies come closer to investigate the nature of the intruder in their territory, hovering in the water a couple of feet away as if waiting for further evidence of the stranger's identity before taking action, individually or collectively. After watching Stumpy's game with the minnows last week, Walt decided to experiment with the bluegills, to see if the playful, ludic spirit inhabited larger members of the finny tribe as well. Nearly chest-deep in the cooling medium, he began wiggling his toes in the sand. The hovering sunfish did not take long to notice this new distraction, with one advancing to within a few inches of his twitching digits as Walt watched from above. Drifting a bit closer, then pushing backwards with its dorsal fins and gliding away, the kibbie seemed in no hurry to make a further move, but when another fish slid up closer, the first decided to take the bull by the horns—or the duffer by the digit—and nipped at Walt's right index toe before darting back.

"Okay," Walt said, "one-nothing, fish. But two can play at this game." As the fish came forward again, the man adjusted his balance onto his left leg and timed the raising of his right foot so that he lightly touched the underside of his opponent. "One-one!" he exclaimed. "Bring it on, fish! You've met your match now."

The bluegills had clumped as their interest in the proceedings grew, but now Walt expected at least the first one to flee, violated by human contact. Instead, the first fish slipped slowly forward again, and once again, Walt raised his foot to make contact. Now a second fish drew closer, and Walt reached up casually with his left foot and touched that one. He was giggling as his enjoyment of the game welled up, and the fish seemed emboldened rather than discouraged by the movements of his feet; they even seemed to like the touching. Perhaps they *were* playing along. Walt tried a variation on the game, this time wiggling his fingers, and that effort brought his adversaries even closer to his eyes; the fish, however, also seemed more wary of his hands than they were of his feet, so, soon, he went back to the bipedal edition of the game, losing himself in it and staying in the water for nearly a half hour. When he finally looked at his fingertips, he could only laugh at how wrinkled they were. "You know, Stump," he called to the squirrel on his rock, "my fingers haven't been wrinkled this prunelike since I was a little kid!" Stumpy, however, had tired of his own game and was snoozing on his granite mattress. "Well," Walt said, "maybe I'll have to tell George about my adventure when I get back. *He* might be able to keep his eyes open long enough to listen."

Walt hadn't seen his buddy Todd Jormonen for a week or more, so he called the handyman last Thursday and invited his friend over for a berry-picking outing the next day. "Throw in your trunks if you like, and we can stop out at the islands for a swim; we're bound to get a little toasty."

"Am I allowed to bring a blindfold?" Todd replied, laughing. "I'm not sure I'm ready for the sight of you half naked and thrashing around like a walrus in the shallows."

Walt chuckled, too, and replied, "As John Lennon would say, 'Goo-goo-ga-joob!'"

"Wow!" Todd said, "a Beatles reference! Impressive for someone born in the seventeenth century!" You see, Todd and Walt like to give each other a hard time. For that matter, Todd likes to rib Stumpy as well.

The next morning, around 7:30, Todd's black Ford F-250 pickup pulled into the driveway, gravel crunching, as Walt was finishing his first glass of iced coffee. Stumpy had been lounging on the deck rail in the already-warm sun, and George had, true to form, shown up as soon as man and squirrel had occupied the deck, maybe having even been there for some time before; the industrious striped youngster had completed two or three more seed-and-nut-hauling trips before resuming the previous day's begging posture at his elderly host's feet, and there he still sat, full of muffin hopes and dreams, until Todd climbed out of the truck cab. Stumpy, on the other hand, had roused himself quickly when he recognized the vehicle, hopping down to the deck and then actually slipping and scrabbling with his claws in his anxiousness to accelerate toward the new arrival.

"How's the old Jormenator running these days?" Walt asked, referring to the big black pickup, as Todd knelt and extended his left arm so Stumpy could jump up and climb to his shoulder, where he nuzzled the laughing man's ear.

"Hey, cut it out! That tickles, you verminous swamp rat!" Todd giggled at Stumpy. Then he turned back to Walt. "She's running fine now, thanks to Anthony down the road. I had him tune her up last week at Andy Martin's garage in Groton. He seems to know his stuff." Anthony is, of course, Anthony Riggetti, husband of Amy, father of Tony, and now, like the rest of his family, dear friend of his neighbors up the road, "the two swinging bachelors," as Walt likes to call Stumpy and himself.

"Coffee and muffin before we cast off for ports unknown?" Walt asked. "Our new friend here has developed a passion for my sour cream–blueberry muffins, so you'd be smart to have one before the insatiable varmint scoffs them all down." George had scuttled behind Walt's cherry tomato pots on the deck when the truck door had first opened, but he had emerged again quickly and was once more sitting upright on the deck to Walt's left and Todd's right.

"Sounds great, old-timer," Todd said, kneeling down, "but who is this little fellow? Is he an escaped convict with that striped outfit?"

"No," said Walt, "that's Ge-e-e-o-o-orge. I don't believe he has done time in the penitentiary. Until recently, I theorize, he led a cloistered life up in Chip Monastery, but I'm not sure that, technically, we can call him a chip-*monk* anymore. He seems to have abandoned his vows of poverty and obedience since his arrival here. Don't know about his vow of chastity 'cause these ground squirrel types are pretty secretive about their sex lives. I'm surprised he didn't run off at your arrival, though, because he's not used to company yet. Hasn't even come out for the Riggettis, though Tony was especially interested in meeting him. Maybe you and George can get better acquainted while I go in for your muffin and the coffee.

Hey, I'll bet he can sense instinctively that you're . . . special." That comment produced a smirk from Todd.

While Walt was gone, Todd, with mock seriousness, asked the chipmunk a series of questions—"You married? Got any kids? How about those Red Sox, huh?" He got no answers, however, though he hadn't really expected any. As an extension of the joke, Todd then asked Stumpy to translate for him. "Hey, Stump, in rodent lingo how do you say, 'Hey, good-looking, come here often?'" The gray squirrel had climbed off his friend's shoulder and was seated on the table in front of him now but seemed disinclined to get involved in a jest at George's expense.

Shortly after Stumpy changed perches, however, the smaller animal, almost as if he found Todd's voice hypnotic, made his way up over Walt's empty chair and onto the table, stopping next to Stumpy, sitting up on his haunches, and studying Todd while the handyman continued his gentle banter. When Walt returned with coffee for his friend and a plate of muffins, Todd was still talking to his striped auditor, and George was still listening in rapt adoration. Stumpy sat quietly on the table next to his chipmunk amigo.

Walt chuckled and said, "Looks like we may have to start calling you the Pied Piper of Kibbee Pond given the fascination you seem to hold for the rodent population around here. What's going on? What's your secret?"

"I don't know," Todd said. "The little guy just seems to find my conversation stimulating."

"Well, maybe 'soporific' would be a more accurate term," Walt said.

"No, no, he's *listening*, not going to sleep. Well, maybe *Stumpy* is dozing a little, but George isn't."

"Uh-oh," Walt said, "don't tell Lynn after all these years of marriage, but it looks as though at last you've found your true soulmate!"

"Well, you've got *your* special bond with Stumpy. . . ." Todd said, his voice trailing off.

"I bet you can seal the deal by sharing your muffin with your new kindred spirit. What were the terms Plato used—*psyche* and *epipsyche*? Twin souls, separated at birth, who search all their lives for each other . . . and here you two are, lucky enough to have met while you're both still young and beautiful."

"Don't listen to his sarcasm, George. Spiritual brotherhood transcends cynicism. Have a piece of muffin. You want one, too, Stumpy? The heck with your diet, right? This is a special occasion, when Damon meets Pythias!"

When the snack was done, the octogenarian host and his somewhat younger guest—Todd is the old high school friend of Walt's son Larkin—made their way down to Nelly, the rowboat, at the dock. Stumpy wasn't about to be left behind, especially if blueberry picking was involved, and since each man had brought a plastic gallon tub to pick into, the gray-furred scavenger interpreted the data correctly and scampered along with them, hopping into Nelly and then jumping from seat to seat to the bow. George followed the trio to the dock, but when Walt was about to pull the starter cord on the three-horsepower Johnson outboard that propels Nelly, the striped creature was still standing beside the boat.

"Here's the real test of your bond," Walt said, half seriously. "His one other boating trip was a bit traumatic; he and Stumpy got cast adrift on two wooden candle boats back around the solstice, and as a master of understatement, I'll say that I don't think he's a . . . committed mariner."

No sooner were those words out of Walt's mouth, however, than with a quiet *chit*, George darted across the aluminum dock and appeared on the bow seat next to Stumpy. "My word!" Walt said.

"Let's see," Todd said, obviously pleased. "We'll make Stumpy the commodore and George the coxswain. Of course, the coxswain won't have any official duties unless the motor breaks down and we have to row."

"Heaven forbid!" Walt said.

Thus, another crew member joined the S.S. Nelly that morning. Stumpy was kind enough to ride next to George instead of taking his accustomed post out on the wooden pulpit that Walt had built for him the previous summer, a structure that extends out from the bow over the water so Stumpy can enjoy the breeze and spray even more fully. In addition, Todd spent much of the trip out to the islands talking to his new friend, mostly nonsensical chatter designed to keep the unseasoned sailor calm.

When Walt slipped Nelly through the channel that runs between two of the larger islands, he called out, "Look at the kingbirds up ahead," and everyone watched as two white-bellied birds dropped from their perches in the pine boughs, each snatching a damselfly out of the air. One of them even buzzed close to Nelly, and Todd said, "Hey, Walt, I thought you told me that the bluegills liked to play tag, not the kingbirds. These guys almost seem to be playing chicken with us too . . . if a kingbird can be a chicken."

"Well," Walt said, "kingbirds are very territorial, and they will come after a boat when they have an active nest going. I've even seen them get zealous about guarding a particularly fruitful area of blueberry bushes." That comment sent Stumpy out onto the pulpit after all, where he put his paws up on the top rail as if daring the kingbirds to make a pass at him, a warrior squirrel, defending *his* territory.

They stopped at a number of islands to take full advantage of the variety of bushes and berries available—colors from smoky blue to near black, sizes from tiny elderberry on up to super-sized black raspberry. Stumpy showed George how to jump from the gunwale onto an overhanging tree branch, and the two would explore the ground of the island, large or small, as if they planned to plant a flag and claim the territory for their own rodent kingdom; sometimes they would climb into bushes or partway up trees, but the latter activity came more naturally to Stumpy than to George. Walt and Todd stayed aboard Nelly at all the islands in the early going because picking was easy from where they sat, and Nelly is very maneuverable. Although Walt and Todd would lose themselves for a few minutes in the pleasures and satisfactions of berry picking—which Walt theorizes is actually a genetically encoded instinct harking back to the hunting-and-gathering days of early man—they tried to move on to a new location every few minutes. Stumpy and George spent some of their time picking, too, but like six-year-old Tony Riggetti, they tended to eat what they picked. However, at one of the last islands they visited, George came ashore with both cheeks bulging and insisted on discharging his harvest into Todd's plastic container. Walt tried to contain his chortles. "If you're really lucky, maybe he already partially digested them before disgorging! Save you some time and strain later on. I'm getting the impression ol' George is willing to adopt you, Todd."

Walt had saved his favorite island for last, wanting Todd to have a crack at a game of tag with his scaled and gilled playmates the sunfish. Sliding Nelly gently up onto the crescent of sand at the cove, Walt released Stumpy with his customary "That'll do, squirrel!" The gray fur ball launched himself from the pulpit onto the shore, and George soon followed suit, with one look back over his shoulder at Todd. "They'll explore up under the pines for a while, I suspect," Walt said as Todd and he pulled off the T-shirts they had worn over their bathing trunks. "Now you get a chance to try your skill against the oh-so-quick Kibbee Pond Kibbie Cadre."

As Walt had suspected, Todd enjoyed being in the cooling water after the inevitable solar exposure that came with blueberry picking in some locations, but the younger man also engaged in piscine play with great enthusiasm. Deep enough in the water to achieve a degree of weightlessness but still able to watch what was happening below the surface, Todd was soon concentrating, lunging, and laughing with obvious pleasure.

"How many touches have you gotten?" Walt asked.

"Four so far," was the reply. "How about you?"

"About the same," Walt said. They were standing ten or twelve feet apart.

"You know, I can remember doing something like this when I was little. I just hadn't thought about doing it again until now. Thanks."

By the time the two men had had their fill of the game, a half hour had passed, although to them it seemed a few short minutes. The two rodents had been watching from the rocks on the shoreline for a while, ready to get back into Nelly and continue their cruise. Both men were glowing from the sensation of having recaptured a piece of their youth, and they were uncharacteristically quiet as Walt guided Nelly through the channel between two larger islands, the same spot where they had encountered the kingbirds on their way out.

The birds were still there, and both seemed miffed that the boat was returning to violate their territory again and—even worse—presumably to steal more of their precious berries. Each made a pass at Nelly as she putted through. As if watching the tag game with the fish had inspired him, Stumpy balanced himself with his front paws on the gunwale near the bow, waited until one of the kingbirds began another swoop, and leaped up as if trying to make contact with his head on the bird's underside. When his feathered antagonist swerved out of the line of fire, Stumpy landed back on the gunwale, swaying momentarily as he regained his balance. "Hey! Enough of that!" Walt shouted, but like a little brother who has to imitate whatever his older sibling does, George was now up on the gunwale, eying the other kingbird as it chirped and stooped. Unfortunately, limited shipboard experience made George's sea legs suspect, and although he was able to make an awkward jump in the general direction of the winged watchdog, his landing was even more awkward; although he scrabbled at the edge of the gunwale for a moment or two, he couldn't keep himself from pitching overboard.

Although Walt cut the engine quickly, Nelly had shot past the striped flounderer, and without any hesitation, Todd leaped into the water, leaving the boat pitching a bit. Soon, he was treading water at the stern, George perched on top of his head, and Walt was lifting the soaked rodent aboard. In the shallows at the nearest island, Todd climbed back in, too, and George spent the rest of the ride back to the dock cuddling in Todd's lap.

Another round of sour cream–blueberry muffins seemed in order when the foursome returned to shore. George sat on the table next to Todd's plate, where his rescuer could stroke his striped back, and he, the rescued, could stare up worshipfully. Laughing as he set down the plate of muffins, Walt said, "You know, Todd, maybe they should bring back that old lifesaving show, *Baywatch*, and you could have a starring role. Why not take the stage name of David Hassle-Free? In any case, I don't want to hear any more wisecracks about *my* ability to attract animals! You've definitely turned out to be a chip-magnet."

Todd just glanced up at Walt and smiled. Then he said, "I guess I'll have to come back soon for another visit."

"I'm pretty sure George would like that," Walt said, then added, with a good-natured laugh, "and Stumpy and I may be able to endure your company, at least for a little while . . . and as long as you don't scoff down all the muffins!"

33

Stumpy and the Dregs

SEPTEMBER 26, 2012

Out at Kibbee Pond, autumn is beginning to make its presence known, and although many people find the change from summer to fall depressing, Walt Walthers welcomes autumn's presence, since the autumn always brings with it presents aplenty. Perhaps because he is a professional weather watcher, the octogenarian pond dweller remains sensitive to the details of each season's advance and decline, and for him the ripeness of autumn is a special gift. Not only is fall, as the poet John Keats put it, "Season of mists and mellow fruitfulness," the time of harvest for fruits and berries and vegetables of all sorts, but it is also the time for country fairs and bird migrations and church bake sales (including the annual pie-baking contest down at the Church of Our Savior Lurks in West Groton, a contest that Walt always enters and has frequently won). All of those things qualify in Walt's mind as autumn's "presents," and as far as he can tell, his roommate and constant companion, Stumpy the stub-tailed gray squirrel, also finds the season a bearer of well-appreciated gifts. In Stumpy's case, though, seeds and nuts, in all their cornu*copious* abundance, are the primary reasons to appreciate the arrival of fall.

Every September, the rambunctious rascal is almost beside himself with enthusiasm for the *thunk* of the green shells of hickory nuts pelting the forest floor in the vicinity of the two roommates' cabin on Kibbee Pond Road, and he will happily spend an hour gnawing at one of those shells to work his way toward the savory nutmeat at the center. In addition, he's more than happy to carry a pine cone to the deck railing and spend fifteen minutes or more stripping it down to its stalk, scoffing the seeds tucked inside the flanges and then leaving the spine like some abandoned wishbone from a roast chicken. Like the greedy epicure he is, the gray-furred bandit has also learned how to climb the stalks of Walt's sunflowers until they bend back down to the ground like the ice-covered birch trees in Robert Frost's poem; once he has subdued them, he can at his leisure raid the seeds from the flowers' heads, leaving them literally downtrodden as if he were some despot despoiling his own kingdom.

Last week, Walt stepped out onto the deck one morning after a quick check of the forecast and of his phone messages. When he had gone inside a few minutes earlier, he had left Stumpy scrounging around the pine needles just above the shoreline, and now, when the silver-haired squirrel-tamer came back outside, he found his buddy in an unusual posture—sitting back against the rail like a person, hind legs sprawled and white belly exposed as he held the last bits of a cone in his front paws and pulled away the remaining pieces. All around him on the rail and on the deck below was the detritus of his recent efforts, the reddish pieces of pine cone looking like toenails torn from woodland trolls; some leftover acorn caps lay there as well with the hunks of a hickory nut husk from the day before. The breeze off the pond slightly riffled the fine gray hairs on the squirrel's shoulders as he sat, apparently abandoned to surfeit and repletion.

Walt could only laugh. "You make me think of that Keats poem 'To Autumn,' as if you were an embodiment of the season itself! How does that second stanza go?

> Who hath not seen thee oft amid thy store?
> Sometimes whoever seeks abroad may find
> Thee sitting careless on a granary floor,
> Thy hair soft-lifted by the winnowing wind;
> Or on a half-reap'd furrow sound asleep,
> Drows'd with the fume of poppies, while thy hook
> Spares the next swath and all its twinèd flowers . . .

Hey, not bad remembering for an old duffer, huh? There you sit, as if it were your responsibility to 'fill all fruit with ripeness to the core; / To swell the gourd, and plump the hazel shells / With a sweet kernel . . .' Who knew you were such an important personage in the seasonal scheme? Lord Stumpy, His Autumnal Reverence!" As usual, when the tone of Walt's voice makes clear that he is joshing, Stumpy ignored his human companion.

"Well, you can sit there all day," Walt laughed, "musing over bees seeking the late flowers and thinking of the mourning gnats and singing hedge-crickets and twittering swallows, even contemplating the oozing cider the way Keats did, but I'm going for my morning boat cruise!" Those words did spark a response from the lounging creature, who was off the deck rail and halfway down to the dock before Walt even had a chance to laugh.

Once Walt had cast off and Stumpy had climbed out to the end of the bow pulpit that Walt had built for him in a previous summer, the elderly skipper cranked up the ancient three-horsepower Johnson outboard and turned Nelly, his ten-foot skiff, toward the swamp at the northern end of the pond, hoping for yet another encounter with Ralph, the great blue heron, a spindle-legged frog stalker who had been frequenting the lily pad–festooned shallows on a schedule that seemed to match that of the two roommates' morning jaunt. Also essential to their recent outings had been "conversations" with Vanderbilt, a cormorant who claimed a tree stump far out in the water near the opening into the swamp; there, he sat nervously as Nelly putted past, occasionally flexing his legs or adding another coat of whitewash to the stump, whose surface already showed clear evidence of his excretory capacities. As Walt steered just close enough to avoid spooking the fish eater, he would regale the bird with jolly comments about the weather or other small talk and joking banter: "Nice day for perch . . . if you can muster the energy to get *off* your perch!" or "Are the hornpout biting today . . . or are *you* biting the hornpout?" With great dignity, Stumpy, in the bow, would simply look in the opposite direction as if to suggest that Walt was only his chauffeur and he would himself never stoop to such sad attempts at humor. For his part, Vanderbilt ignored Walt's comments, and as soon as Nelly was a safe distance past, he would once again spread his wings to dry in the sun so he could be ready soon for another dive in quest of a midmorning snack.

This particular morning, however, which was by the way last Saturday, the shipmates found neither Ralph nor Vanderbilt ensconced in their usual spots in the swamp. With disappointment beginning to register, Walt was about to swing Nelly's bow back to the east when suddenly, directly in front of them, something fell out of the sky and hit the water with a splash. Almost immediately, Walt could make out a complicated corkscrew wing motion as the white breast of an osprey emerged from the foam; the bird helicoptered up and swung back toward a huge white pine that stood watch along the shoreline. Landing on a branch some forty feet up, the sea hawk perched, its talons clutching the branch but also clinging to some kind of fish that it had struck; as it sat, it emitted a whistling *scree* that seemed designed to discourage the invading boat from getting any closer.

"Well," Walt said, "I'm not surprised that ol' Ralph and Vanderbilt have vacated the premises. I imagine any kind of raptor would make them feel less than secure. Still, I'm glad we got to see this fella catch himself a tasty tidbit. Let's leave him to eat it in peace." After tipping his porkpie hat at the bird, Walt eased Nelly's bow around to the east, and the mariners continued their cruise, with Walt noting once again the irony of how the ubiquitous blueberry bushes always turned the color of cranberries in the fall. Although water temperatures had not dropped precipitously with the cooler nights recently, the observant codger saw that waterweeds had already begun dying back in the shallows. The arrival of the fall equinox did mark some noteworthy changes after all.

Before lunch, Walt and Stumpy also set off on their daily walk in the woods near the cabin, designed, as Walt always said, "to work up a bit of an appetite." As they strolled along under the canopy of still-pendant leaves, the aged forest connoisseur savored the jewel-like quality of light. "It's like being inside some kind of chartreuse glass globe," he said as Stumpy scampered ahead of him, pausing to sniff at chipmunk holes and particularly pungent mushrooms, from which he took the occasional nibble. As they continued through the hardwoods, Walt noticed a few yellow leaves scattered on the path and recognized that most were birch, with a smattering of maple and chestnut leaves thrown in; he realized that in a few short weeks, Stumpy and he would be walking on a thick carpet made of the foliage that was for now still over their heads. At a leisurely pace, the pair continued to the big field that marked their usual turnaround.

The path there opens into that field near a stone marker defining the point at which the towns of Shirley, Lunenburg, and Townsend come together, and Walt likes to sit on a boulder there in the shade before continuing out into the field a short distance. On this trip he paused under some maples from which wild grapevines were suspended and pointed out to his squirrel companion the fallen fruits that still littered the ground. "Don't you be sampling any of those, Stump. They've been sitting there awhile, and they'll be fermented enough to get you tipsy. I don't want to have to deal with a snockered squirrel!" The gray-furred rascal sniffed with interest but soon turned his attention instead to a low spot in the grass that Walt knew was a dust bath for the local turkey tribe. In the adjacent grass lay a perfect tail feather whose quill Walt tucked into his hatband, intending to add his new treasure to the collection he kept back at the cabin. His wife, Annie, had been particularly fond of wild gobblers and their feathers, and he had continued to honor her preference for well over twenty years now.

Lunch and a short nap in the sun and breeze were next on the agenda before the weekend's big social occasion—a trip across town to Todd Jormonen's house on Shagbark Drive for a casual concert late in the afternoon, a cookout, and a wide-screen viewing in the evening of the Michigan–Notre Dame football game. Because Walt had grown up in Michigan before transplanting himself to New England, he retained some old loyalties to the maize-and-blue, and as it turned out, Todd was himself an emigrant Michigander, one more element that had cemented his bond with Walt many years earlier. Todd's wife, Lynn, was not a Michigoose, being instead New Hampshire born and raised, but what was good for her gander Todd was good for her, too, at least as far as football went. Their children had, not surprisingly, grown up as Wolverine fans as well, and although many other Michigan followers would have considered Ohio State their archrivals, the Jormonens happily embraced a rivalry with Notre Dame, although the reasons were somewhat obscure. I will, however, attempt an explanation.

Todd's parents, when they were first married right after World War II, had lived in southern Michigan, a short distance from South Bend, Indiana, and the Notre Dame campus. In those days, the Fighting Irish were a football powerhouse, their fans as brash and arrogant as New York Yankee baseball fans, and an oft-repeated family legend held that, with a typically American love of the underdog, Todd's folks had attended Notre Dame games and cheered loudly for whoever the visiting team happened to be. When the opponent was Michigan, Grammy and Grampy Jormonen became even more vocal, of course, and somehow that family tradition had been passed down to at least two more generations, even when they had to watch the games on television in New England.

When Walt and Stumpy pulled into Todd's driveway in Lulu, Walt's green 1960 Chevy pickup, Todd's younger son, Merle, greeted them outside the garage, wearing his blue Michigan sweatshirt with the bright yellow *M* on the front. "Come on in, you guys," Merle called. "George knows something is up but can't quite figure out what. Dad and I have been trying to get in the mood for the game by singing the Michigan fight song really loud, and the little guy seems a bit freaked out. He'll be happy to see Stumpy, though, and you, Walt, as familiar faces in the midst of the madness."

George is, of course, the young chipmunk, once resident at the Kibbee Pond cabin, whose heart earlier in the summer Todd's voice and kindly attention won over. What you may not know is that a few short weeks ago, the mutual affection between that striped rapscallion and Todd caused George to change his place of abode; after one particular visit from the amiable handyman, the smitten chipmunk followed Todd back to and then *into* his truck for the ride across town. Since early August, then, George has called Shagbark Drive home, having quickly won Lynn's heart and even the tolerance of the Jormonens' two aging springer spaniels; he has also become, of course, a big favorite with Todd and Lynn's grandchildren, who visit frequently.

"What are you up to out here?" Walt asked as Merle shook his hand.

"Well," replied the young man, a tall and handsome blond in his mid-twenties, "I'm setting up the charcoal grill for cooking later, but I started a new batch of my coffee stout today, so I'm also tidying up and putting my brewing equipment away. Earlier, I decanted some rice wine and rhubarb wine, stuff that has been fermenting since July, and I also have to get rid of those dregs before we serenade you." As you may remember, Merle plays in his father's band,

Grace and Danger, which also includes Walt's neighbor Amy Riggetti on vocals. As you also may remember, he is a skilled brewer, hoping someday to own a brewpub.

"You got any of your magical elixirs for me to sample tonight?" Walt asked.

"Sure," the younger man laughed, "if nothing else, I always try to have a batch of Old Lady Nutjob ready, the brown ale I named for Mom."

"Ooh," Walt said, "I'd drive at least 5.3 miles for a glass of that nectar!" (That's the distance from Kibbee Pond to Shagbark Drive.) "I've just got to cut myself off at a small tipple, though, because I'm the designated driver." He pointed at the squirrel, who had hopped right out of the truck and was now sniffing around the big glass carboy that Merle had just toted to the near corner of the garage. "This guy said he'd cover for me if I got snockered, but he has trouble reaching any of the foot pedals, and he always grinds the gears when he shifts, so I guess I have to limit my imbibition."

"Hey, Stumpy, old buddy!" Merle laughed, watching as the curious fur ball continued to eye the carboy. "You're going to have to show me some legal ID before I can serve you any of that, you know. I'm pretty sure your roommate is old enough to sample some safely, but you're gonna get me charged with corrupting a minor if you're not careful!"

Chuckling, Walt said, "Come on, pal. Leave the boozing to the experts! Let's head in and see if we can find your buddy George." Happily, the tailless squirrel scooted across to his roommate, then scrambled up his pantleg and shirtsleeve to perch on the kindly coot's right shoulder.

"Any of your siblings around today?" Walt asked.

"No," Merle said, "they wanted to be here, Arthel in particular, but his wife, Doreen, is expecting another baby in a week or so, and they worried the excitement might be too much for her."

"Too bad," Walt said as he continued through the breezeway that connects the garage to the main part of the house. Rapping on the door but not waiting for a response, he stepped into the kitchen of the long ranch house and just had time to register a smiling Lynn at the counter, pushing back a wing of her ash-blond hair, before a reddish-brown blur that seemed to have black-and-white racing stripes down its sides rocketed along the countertop toward him. The streaking creature launched itself from that surface onto the perpendicular plane of the man's right arm, sticking the landing like a gold medal–winning gymnast, and Stumpy leaned down from his perch to sniff noses with his friend George. In the next instant, the chipmunk darted up Walt's arm and under the white belly of his mammalian cousin, who jumped straight up; his movement dislodged Walt's omnipresent porkpie hat, which fell to the floor as the gladiators continued their fond tussling.

"Careful, you two!" Walt exclaimed. "If you don't show a little discretion, you'll—" But his comment had come too late, as the wrestlers tumbled from the geezer's shoulder onto a platter of sliced tomatoes on the kitchen table, sending the fruit flying as they themselves fell to the tile floor in a revolving ball of multicolored fur. "Enough!" Walt said, trying to make his voice convey authority despite his amusement at the irrepressible joy of the animal friends' greeting.

Lynn was laughing, too, as she reached for the paper towels. "At least the platter didn't get shattered," she said. "I don't know about you, but disciplining young children these days seems a lot more complicated than I remembered."

"Amen!" Walt answered, as Todd emerged from the hallway that ran the length of the house and led back to the bedrooms.

"Hey!" Todd said as he came closer. "Did you bring that puddle-swilling pond rat with you just to turn my house upside down? Don't you folks from the south of town have any respect for the polite and cultivated lifestyle we try to live up here in the center of civilization? But I see I must beg your pardon: You have at least removed your hat indoors, a major step forward for a backwards, backwoods rat catcher like you. Wonders will never cease! Next thing you know, you'll even start excusing yourself when you burp!" Grinning, the middle-aged handyman bent down to retrieve the porkpie, and then his right hand reached for Walt's, shaking it vigorously as his left hand held the hat to the side. "Shall I hang this thing up, Captain Neanderthal, or are you afraid we'll steal it?"

"To-odd!" Lynn said. "Is that any way to speak to a guest and a dear friend?"

Walt just laughed and said, "Thanks, Lynn, but we express our affection for each other in—shall we say—indirect ways. I just hope his way of showing his love for you isn't offering to hold your chair for you at supper and then pulling it out as you sit down!"

Once George and Stumpy had settled down a little, and Lynn had fixed Walt a cup of tea, Todd and Merle fetched their instruments to play Walt and Stumpy their arrangements of a few new tunes they had worked up, with Merle on guitar and his father playing the old Gibson mandolin that Stumpy has always loved. A year or so earlier, Walt had even started calling his musician friend the Pied Picker because Todd seemed to have the power to mesmerize the tailless rodent with his playing; somehow, the codger had not been surprised this summer when the young chipmunk had also responded to Todd's "animal magnetism," though this time, it was Todd's speaking voice that had possessed "charms to soothe the savage breast." Well, maybe that phrase from William Congreve is inappropriate here because "savage" is just about the last adjective anyone would apply to George. Nevertheless, Todd did seem to have personal qualities that drew the two once-wild creatures to him. Of course, the two springer spaniels, Yaz and Pudge, were equally fond of their master, but certain high notes, especially on the mandolin, seemed to hurt their ears, and Todd had learned to let them out into the yard when he was practicing or when the band was rehearsing; he'd leave the door ajar so they could return at their leisure.

The impromptu concert in the living room began with a rollicking version of Leroy Carr and Scrapper Blackwell's "Sloppy Drunk Blues," as Merle approximated the barrelhouse rumbling of a piano on the bass strings, and Todd played over the top. From there, they covered Mississippi Joe Callicott's "France Chance" and Sleepy John Estes's "Diving Duck Blues" while the two furry groupies sat rapt on the floor at the musicians' feet, and Walt tapped his foot in rhythm. When Todd pulled out what looked like a glass test tube and slid it onto the little finger of his left hand, Stumpy climbed up onto Walt's lap for a closer view, and George soon followed suit so that he stood on Walt's left thigh while Stumpy stretched out on his right. "This is what I was telling you about last week," Todd said, and the duo launched into their new arrangement of Mississippi John Hurt's "Hey, Honey, Right Away," with Todd playing bottleneck mandolin à la Sam Bush. Shortly thereafter, Lynn led in Dr. Brad

Schmidt, the fiddling veterinarian, who was a sometime member of the band. When Todd had called earlier in the week, Brad had accepted the invitation to join in for a while, knowing he would be returning late in the afternoon from judging a 4-H livestock competition in Ashby; as a Notre Dame fan, however, he had turned down the part of the invitation that included dinner and the football game, figuring he'd be safer at home than among a bunch of rabid Wolverines. As things turned out, however, he would be back before the game ended.

Dinner was a cookout, with Todd serving the old family recipe for beef shish kebob, which he prepared on the grill after the concert, while Merle poured out glasses of his Old Lady Nutjob brown ale. Although Walt rarely drank, he knew better than to pass up some of Merle's tasty brew, and he savored his glassful, parceling it out in sips over an hour while also discouraging Stumpy, who kept trying to slip his nose into the glass for a taste. "Now, come on, Stump," the silver-haired coot laughed. "I don't want to have to carry you home or listen to you slur your way through 'Ninety-Nine Bottles of Beer on the Wall'!" The squirrel seemed slightly miffed at that comment and hop-hop-pause-hopped off to join George in exploring some of the other parts of the house.

Yaz and Pudge were content just to lie quietly under the table, now that they had found their way back into the dining room with all the people. They had learned from years of experience to have faith in the manna from heaven that would occasionally fall from the table to the floor; along with some accidental droppings, on this night Walt even purposely handed each dog a small bite of his steak. At one point, Todd jokingly reprimanded his elderly friend, saying, "Hey, don't feed those chowhounds anything! They're getting so fat and lazy that they barely manage to fetch my newspaper in from the front lawn in the morning, and they used to take pride in alternating days for bringing it in. I've been wondering lately if I could train George to do it for me, especially if these two are going to turn into fur rugs."

The feast ended with dessert: a shoofly pie that Walt had baked and brought, and it drew moans of approval from everyone after their first bites and then again several more times before the plates were clean.

Game time was shortly after eight, but it didn't take long for the contest to turn to sour grapes. Maybe the Michigan quarterback mistook the Notre Dame home navy jerseys for the Wolverine home maize and blue, but in any case, he started throwing interceptions with depressing regularity. Although the Notre Dame offense proved inept, the home team did put up enough points to maintain a narrow lead at halftime, and the fans at Shagbark Drive did not have a lot to cheer about. Just as the teams were taking the field for the second half, however, something took those fans' eyes away from the game.

Walt had just experienced a tiny visceral tingle, realizing that, caught up in the game and the conversation, he had not thought to check on Stumpy for some time. He was just about to say something to that effect when George came scampering, if someone can scamper in super-slow motion, into the living room. As he passed that day's newspaper where it sat, as yet unread and still in its plastic wrapper next to Lynn's seat, the chipmunk stopped abruptly and turned, his bottom tipping forward and upward at the sudden shift in momentum and his nose bumping into the rolled tube of *The Boston Globe.* Having recognized the object in front of him, he, with some difficulty, straddled it with all four legs; then, shifting his position and stumbling over the object, he began opening his mouth and trying to get a grip on the paper but succeeded only in tearing a flap in the plastic covering. As the humans watched in mystification, George bit into the exposed newsprint and pulled upward, but the tube, at least twice as long as the chipmunk, did not respond. When several more tugs gave him no better purchase on the object, George tried nosing under it as if he could root it up into the air and onto his back, and that was the moment when Walt realized that the chipmunk might be trying to fetch the paper to his beloved master. But Walt also realized that something was not right with George.

At the moment of those realizations, Walt saw more movement near the door to the kitchen, the direction from which George had emerged moments before. To the kindly geezer's dismay, a staggering Stumpy then lunged into the room, his legs wobbling and then collapsing underneath him. When the squirrel tried again to stand up, he could only weave feebly and tumble down again, and Walt's heart climbed into his throat. "Stump, what's going on?" he asked, rising from his seat and crossing the room; he could think of only two options: that his roommate was having a stroke or seizure or that he had gotten into something toxic.

As it turned out, Walt's second guess was closer to correct, but perhaps *toxic* is not the precise word needed here. *Intoxicating* would be more accurate, because as Merle was quick to remember, he had not covered the rice and rhubarb wine dregs he had tossed onto the family compost heap, and the two mischievous rodents, as a quick whiff of the breath of each disclosed, had in their explorations come upon the temptation and succumbed to their tippling urges. In fact, bits of fermenting rhubarb were still stuffed into George's bulging chipmunk cheeks. Walt wondered later if Stumpy had taken offense at his earlier refusal to share his ale; he also wondered if one of the furry friends had taken the initiative and if the other had then succumbed to peer pressure. Somehow, he was pretty certain that Stumpy had been the instigator.

A quick phone call brought Dr. Brad back to the house, though curiosity more than concern motivated him. "I've never seen a chipmunk or a squirrel falling down drunk, and I couldn't miss out on this!" he said as he entered the house, this time carrying his medical satchel rather than his fiddle case. "I'm confident, though," he continued, "that their situation is like that of an adolescent kid or any other inebriated human: They need mainly to sleep it off and to stay hydrated. Have you got any animal crates?"

"We've got a couple of cat carriers downstairs," Lynn replied.

"Perfect!" Dr. Brad replied. "Bring 'em up. Any eyedroppers?"

The answer was again yes, and when the fiddling veterinarian left the house this time, Walt and Todd both had their potted pals in their laps, with the groggy critters on their backs, accepting water from the droppers. Though both of the boozers had been agitated and confused initially, the humans had calmed them with gentle, single-fingered stroking, and soon, they were both dozing. As Walt and Todd sat side by side with their soused sidekicks sucking at the eyedroppers, the gentle-hearted handyman said quietly to his wife, "This takes me back to the days when Merle and the others were little, and we used to spend quiet time like this with a bottle of formula."

Lynn just smiled, but Walt said, with equal quietness, "Takes me back too."

A little later, each furry tippler would go in his own crate, and as Walt carried the still-spifflicated but snoozing Stumpy out to Lulu for their trip back to the pond, he would say, "I guess I will be driving home tonight!" Both men would be up every couple of hours the rest of the night until morning, going through several rounds of the rehydrating routine. By midday, however, both Stumpy and George would recover their equilibrium.

The next afternoon, as man and squirrel relaxed in the sun on the deck, Walt joked a little more. "You know, ol' Stumpster, when you used to ride in the cart as I picked up leaves and branches, I never expected you'd have to go 'on the wagon' in another sense. Maybe the next time you want to get a buzz on, you should just sit on top of the blender. I don't want to have to put you on a twelve-step program, and I'd rather have you *on* the table than *under* it!" Though Stumpy had long before learned to ignore Walt's jokes, the silence this time was even more profound than usual.

Walt, however, just pressed on. "Hey, remember how I quoted Keats for you the other day? Maybe I should have gone with his 'Ode on Melancholy' instead: 'No, no, go not to Lethe!' Then again, I'm pretty sure you would have ignored any warning I could have given you. You *did* get blotto, and you *did* travel down that mythological river, though I doubt you remember much about the trip. Hey! Come to think of it, maybe Keats's 'Ode to a Nightingale' would have worked even better:

> My heart aches, and a drowsy numbness pains
> My sense, as though of hemlock I had drunk,
> Or emptied some dull opiate to the drains
> One minute past, and Lethe-wards had sunk . . .

"Ah, the joys of being well-read! Oh, I'm sorry, buddy. Did I raise my voice a little too much? You know, when I used to watch you sprawled precariously along the rail of our deck, I never thought that the phrase 'hang over' would apply to you in a second sense." He chuckled a moment but then stopped. "I guess it's only funny, though, because you and George are okay after all. You did have us worried for a while, you know."

After a moment, though, Walt's relief at seeing his buddy recovering made his elation irrepressible again. "Hey," he said, "maybe a name change would be appropriate. Instead of Stumpy, what do you think of my calling you Stinko the squirrel?" Stumpy just turned carefully on the rail so his back was toward Walt and then tried to cover his ears with his front paws.

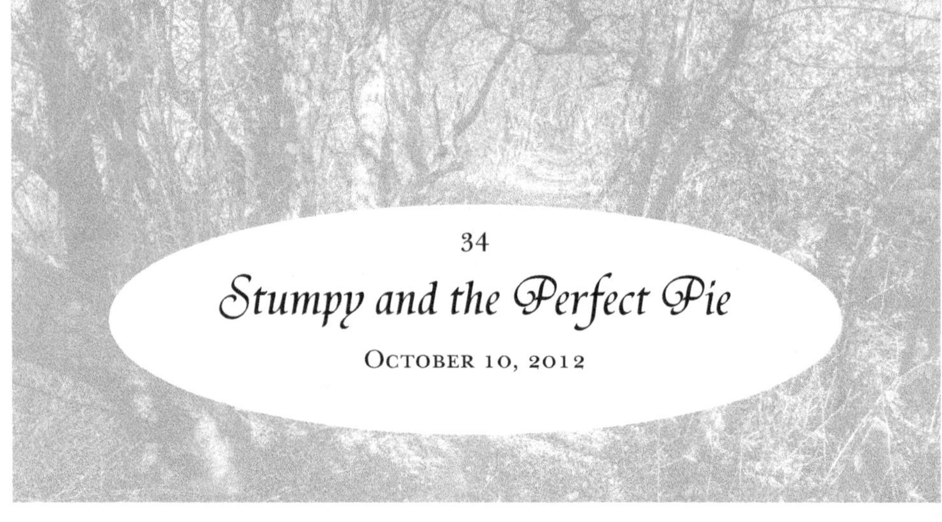

34

Stumpy and the Perfect Pie

October 10, 2012

Not many people think of October as the mating season, but as a result of the events of last week, Walt Walthers, the octogenarian weather watcher who lives out at Kibbee Pond in Townsend, is beginning to wonder if global warming or some other alteration of the natural order has wrought strange changes in the reproductive behavior of older female humans. Although October has always been one of Walt's favorite months, he has been thinking about reining in his enthusiasm for the leaf-peeping season, just in case future Octobers should hold more of the drama that took place over the last few days.

Of course, the week wasn't all bad. As always, the companionship of Walt's roommate and buddy, Stumpy the stub-tailed gray squirrel, provided a source of stability and joy, especially now that Walt is sure that the rodent rapscallion has recovered safely after tippling the dregs from some rhubarb wine a couple of weeks back; knowing that Stumpy will not, in fact, have to enroll in a twelve-step program as a recovering alcoholic has been a substantial relief to Walt. The two have continued their early-morning cruises out on the pond in the skiff, Nelly, with the skipper getting the most out of the ancient three-horsepower Johnson outboard that powers the craft; he knows how to feather the choke and understands how to ease the throttle up or down at just the right moments so that their trip remains pleasantly smooth even on windy days and in choppy water. Last week, however, featured a stretch of cloudy or even rainy days when the water remained as placid as a farm pond at sunset, and the duo's outings were especially peaceful then. In addition, as the damp, gray days continued, the changing foliage along the shoreline and beyond somehow blazed all the more brightly, with the pond mirroring those colors with a clarity that sometimes felt disorienting.

As Stumpy leaned out from the pulpit at Nelly's bow and Walt scanned the sights from his seat in the stern, they noticed some familiar personalities who heightened the voyagers' enjoyment of their outings. For instance, both Ralph, the great blue heron, and Vanderbilt, the cormorant, continued to fish in predictable areas so that Walt was able to address both of them in passing, usually with his characteristic humor: "So, Ralph, do you have any suggestions for what I should do when I get a frog in my throat?" or "Hey, Vandy, have you ever tried a *dill* pickerel?" The cormorant, originally given, as the boat approached, to taking flight with his legs running several steps and thus leaving a trail of splashes as he lifted across the surface of the pond, had with practice become more comfortable about the intrusions upon his privacy; in more recent days, therefore, he had remained perched on the protruding stump near the opening into the swamp, occasionally flexing his legs from nervousness and greeting Walt and Stumpy with yet another squirt of whitewash. Of course, Walt always had some sort of comment: "Well, I *have* heard people say, 'If you have a big gun, shoot it'" or "I was hoping for a *twenty*-one-gun salute, but I guess that'll have to do." As always, Stumpy paid little attention, or actually tried to ignore Walt's wisecracks, just as children try to ignore the embarrassing words or actions of their parents.

New sightings of unexpected visitors rewarded them too. One morning, for instance, Walt pointed out to his rodent sidekick three ravens frisking and circling above the trees to the north of the swamp; he shut down the motor, and the two full-time pond residents watched as one of the visiting birds would dive, and another would ride an accelerating air current almost like a surfer catching the curl on a monster wave. Occasionally, one flier would make a dart at one of the others, but soon, their circles took them farther and farther away, then finally out of sight altogether, though Walt's eyes still tried to convince him that the birds might be hovering even now just on the edge of his vision. Another morning, as they were rounding one of the larger islands, an osprey gave a whistling complaint and dropped from one of the tall pines there to stroke off toward the western shore; as it passed a spit of trees that protruded from that island, another osprey cried and, like a lightning bolt, flashed from the tree and flew off to the *south.* As Nelly rounded the same spit, a third fish hawk passed overhead back toward the still-rising sun. "Huh," Walt said, "I don't know much about migration patterns for osprey, but I didn't think they traveled in a flock. Could it just be a coincidence that they showed up here together today? I should ask Jerry Woodley when I see him." Jerry is, of course, Walt's friend who teaches ornithology and chemistry at Laurel Academy in nearby Groton, though Jerry has said he'll be hanging up his whiteboard markers after this year. Reminded of his fellow wildlife enthusiast, Walt mused, "Maybe I can get him out here more often after he's retired."

Sometimes as well, the two cabinmates observed the recurring signs of seasonal change that Walt, as a professional weather watcher, had been waiting for, many too subtle to register completely with just one day's passage. Nevertheless, one day last week, Walt realized that the majority of deciduous leaves along the shoreline had turned at least partially yellow, and after some wind and rain over the weekend, he registered that the pond's surface sported a growing profusion of fallen leaves. Those realizations jolted him into a consciousness that more dramatic changes will occur all too quickly now, as the trees disrobe teasingly before our eyes.

Of course, among the positive elements in Walt's October has been his ongoing friendship with the Riggetti family, who live just down the hill from the cabin on Kibbee Pond Road, and last Wednesday, after Walt and Stumpy had waved goodbye to seven-year-old Tony Riggetti, who had just boarded the monstrous yellow school bus for another day of first grade, Tony's young mother, Amy, had invited Walt in for coffee. Nothing was unusual about that event, since the two had a cup together virtually every morning that Amy was not working at Ayer Hair, a salon in the neighboring town. However, Amy's sudden shy quietness did surprise Walt. As Stumpy crunched at one of the plain cashews Amy had given him, the kindly duffer looked at her across the kitchen table and said, "Is something wrong, kiddo?"

Amy smiled and looked down at the table. "No, everything's fine . . . very good, in fact. It's just that I have some news to tell you, but I'm strangely embarrassed." Walt raised his eyebrows but said nothing. "You see," she said, looking up again, "I'm pregnant."

"Oh, Amy!" he said, his inquisitive smirk of a moment before broadening fully into a wholehearted smile. "What wonderful news! I almost said, 'How did *that* happen?' but a question like that could have led to further awkwardness. I remember telling my father-in-law when Annie was first pregnant with Ross, 'It's a dirty, thankless job, but someone has to do it.' I guess I don't always show the best judgment at times of intense happiness. Does Tony know yet?"

"Not yet," the now-beaming woman replied. "We plan to tell him tonight when Anthony gets back from the garage."

"Do you know whether it's a boy or a girl?"

"No," she said, "we decided we'd enjoy being surprised again, the way we were with Tony. It just means we have to have two sets of names ready."

"Oh, I can help with that," Walt joked. "How about Frederick for a boy and Elizabeth for a girl? That way, they could be Freddie and Betty Riggetti."

"Oh, Walt," Amy said, laughing. "But I guess it's true we do have to think about the possible repercussions of our name choices. My due date is in late May, though, so we have plenty of time to decide."

"Well," Walt said, "there's a joke in there somewhere. Something like: It's good to know that sometime in the next few months, we can expect an upturn in the stork market."

Another positive element in Walt and Stumpy's October was the news that their friend Todd Jormonen, the snowplow operator and handyman who frequently drops by the cabin to do odd jobs—or at least to enjoy coffee, baked goods, and conversation—would be taking his wife, Lynn, to Portsmouth, New Hampshire, for a weekend at the Atlantic shore, where they had spent a fair amount of time in the early days of their courtship. The only catch was that they could not take their adopted pet, George the chipmunk, with them, and Todd had suggested that George might be most happy spending that time back at his old digs; George had, of course, originally been a pond dweller, too, having made Walt and Stumpy's acquaintance while traversing their deck and caching nuts early in the summer, and Walt knew that Stumpy would enjoy having his protégé back for a lengthy visit. Although George had become snockered with Stumpy after feasting on rhubarb wine dregs two weeks ago, Walt wasn't worried about a repeat performance; that the two irrepressible personalities would get into some mischief was inevitable, but the silver-haired rodent handler felt certain he was up to the challenge. Circumstances would not prove him wrong, exactly, but they did drive home the perils of overconfidence.

I mentioned before that this October has bewildered Walt because he doesn't normally think of autumn as the mating season, so perhaps I should explain that comment. Doing so may require a little background, however. It occurs to me as well that autumn is hunting season and that Walt might have made more sense of the events that follow in this chapter if he had focused more on predatory than amatory motivations.

For several years, Walt has participated in a pie-baking contest at the Church of Our Savior Lurks in West Groton, where he still attends occasional services, particularly near Christmas and Easter. In the weeks leading up to Thanksgiving, the ladies affiliated with the church sponsor the contest, and participating has usually been a pleasant change of pace and a distraction for the silver-haired pastry chef, especially in the days before Stumpy took up his abode at the cabin. Furthermore, the culinarily-inclined coot has won first prize three times, most recently two years ago, although last year, the prodigious appetite of Big Bruno, the gargantuan Labrador retriever that belongs to his friend Arlene Tosh, cost him his blue ribbon. You'll have to check the archives to get that full story. I will say, though, that Walt took the loss in stride, with a humility that surprised no one who knows him well.

A couple of weeks ago, the phone rang out at the cabin, and when he answered, Walt recognized the voice of Louise Barnes, a perennial contender and occasional winner in the baking contest. "Walter, is that you? I think this connection may be bad; I can barely make out your voice." Louise has difficulties with her hearing, though she has never acknowledged those difficulties, and she has acquired some fame for the predictable consistency with which her response to another person's comment is "What?" When the other party in the conversation adjusts his or her speaking volume up,

Louise is equally consistent in responding, "You know, you don't have to shout!" Rumor has it that when her husband died ten years ago, Louise did not notice for several hours; her explanation was, "Well, you know, Herb always was soft-spoken."

The purpose for her call became clear quickly; at least Louise was not one to mince words. "Walter, we're having a church bake sale on October 6, and we've decided to use the occasion to publicize this year's Thanksgiving pie-baking contest. It'll be something of a warm-up for the big event. Everyone thinks that you should be involved, and I'm calling to ask you to contribute your best effort to the sale; that way, we can sell individual slices made by the perennial front-runners and create some suspense and excitement in anticipation of November."

"I could be persuaded," Walt said. "I suppose you'll make something with your world-famous meringue."

"Now, Walter," Louise replied, "I'm sorry that you think I'm haranguing you, but I thought you were a generous, community-minded individual—"

"Louise," Walt said, laughing genially and raising his voice a notch, "I'll *do* it!"

"Well, now, Walter, I wish you'd said so in the first place, and, you know, you don't have to shout. I can hear you just fine now. It must have been a bad connection. Must have something to do with that blasted Unitil utilities company. Of course, maybe you're out of practice dealing with the fair sex, living out there in that cabin without a woman's touch, surrounded by those wild animals you like so much and thinking that you have to yell at a gentle heart just the way you do at a savage beast. Why, I imagine you have forgotten how pleasant it is to have someone to talk quietly with . . . and to cook with. You know, maybe we should pool our expertise and work on some recipes together. I'm sure that with your flair for unusual flavor combinations and my meringue, no one else's creations could compare."

"You're probably right," Walt replied, trying to modulate his voice into the audible range for Louise without being obvious, "but I wouldn't want to have an unfair advantage over the other competitors. I like to emphasize trust in my relationships, and I don't believe in scrimping on that."

"Now, Walter," Louise replied, "I have the highest regard for your crust, and I wouldn't dream of crimping it for you if you wanted to do it for yourself. I'm good at compromising."

Walt could almost feel her batting her eyes on the other end of the line and raised his voice another notch, feeling a bit like a sparrow trapped in conversation with a hungry cat. "Well, thank you for calling, Louise. I'll come up with something original and bring it over Saturday morning. When should I arrive?"

"Oh, don't be silly, Walter," the woman said. "Of course you'll be alive! At our age we have to think positively, you know. Goodbye now."

During the phone call, Stumpy had climbed onto the table in front of Walt's recliner and had been nosing about, scrounging for crumbs without much luck. Walt looked at the squirrel and shook his head. "I wonder if anyone's ever tried to tell her she needs hearing aids. I suppose if they have, she just hasn't noticed . . . or she's assumed that they're talking about something else. Talking with her is like trying to take penny candy from an octopus, though I don't even know if octopi like candy, so maybe they wouldn't want to hang on to it. . . . Oh well."

In reality, Walt was happy to have an excuse to do some baking, especially with autumn flaring up outside. Each fall, he still remembers how his mother's apple pies would smell as they sat cooling on the counter and how, when he came home from school, he would quickly dig into his homework so he could listen later to the World Series on the radio while savoring a slice of pie. Leaves changing color, the baseball season's final games, sweet fruit and a fresh, buttery crust . . . Some associations never die, nor do we want them to.

Baking often reminds him of his mother but also of his wife, Annie, who had welcomed his taking on the role of dessert fixer and muffin maker while she prepared elaborate main courses; he still likes to say that the family ate like kings and queens and princes when the three boys were growing up. Sometimes, he and Annie had conspired together in making bread, and she had suggested one or two subtle touches that were now a permanent part of his anadama bread recipe, a favorite he prepares at least once a month.

When Stumpy went outside to indulge in a tree-climbing romp with his siblings Burwell and Lansdowne, Walt followed, sitting on the deck in his cushioned chair. He had decided then that when the time came, he would try out a new idea he had had: a vanilla rum walnut pie in his whole-wheat crust.

When Friday of last week rolled around, Walt made sure he did his baking in the morning. He knew that Todd and Lynn would be arriving around 3:00 to drop George off, and he wanted the pies cooked and tucked safely away where no rodent had ever gone before. He suspected that together, George and Stumpy could get into more trouble than they were likely to concoct separately, and he figured any precautions he could think of would be wise. Thus, he put each pie in a covered plastic container, and then he placed them in the cupboard, where they balanced securely on top of stacked plates. Walt had made two of the vanilla rum walnut beauties, the slightly less perfect one to be a gift to the Riggettis, who had invited the elderly gent and his two furry compadres down for supper that night. Walt doubted the wisdom of accepting the invitation and feared that bringing both the critters along could have wild consequences, but Amy and Tony had designed the dinner as a celebration of Tony's coming siblinghood, a situation about which the youngster had proven enthusiastic. As things turned out, both chipmunk and squirrel were on their best behavior, proving (probably to Tony's disappointment) to be charming but calm company.

At the Riggettis', the furry visitors had enjoyed climbing into the structures Tony built for them on the floor from his extensive array of wooden blocks, many of them interesting shapes and sizes that Walt had cut from the end pieces and leftovers of his woodworking projects, but although the two rodents were well-behaved during the visit, they also seemed genuinely sleepy by the time the trio got back to the cabin. Todd had brought along the wool watch cap that George likes to sleep in, and Walt had hung it from a nail so that it rested lightly on the mattress on which he and Stumpy always sleep. Walt was happy to get to bed at ten o'clock, a bit earlier than usual, but after all, he had the bake sale to attend the next morning.

Walt had eventually found out that the sale would start at nine inside the church, and consequently, he had planned to arrive a few minutes early to help with cutting and displaying the pies. George and Stumpy had sensed an adventure from Walt's preparations at the cabin, and both were happy to jump into Lulu, Walt's green '60 Chevy pickup, for their weekend outing. George followed the Stumpster's example and rode most of the way to West Groton on the back of the truck's bench seat, which both seemed to agree afforded the best view. Walt would have liked to strap them in in some way, but he had decided earlier in the week that borrowing Todd's cat carriers was overkill. Walt wasn't convinced that his passengers paid any attention to the now almost universal yellow of the hardwood leaves along the roadside, but he enjoyed what he knew was likely to be a short-lived display of natural pulchritude, with the trees seeming almost like supermodels on a runway as the three travelers drove past.

A greeting committee awaited them—or, more correctly, awaited Walt—just inside the front door of the church. Louise was there, of course, but so was Maureen Ripley, the third of their triumvirate, whose members had won the Thanksgiving pie contest ten of the last eleven years. Three times a widow, Maureen was no less obvious in her flirtatious designs on Walt than Louise was, as her thick cloud of expensive French perfume attested, but though she was noted for the flakiness of her piecrust, she was not flaky in any other sense, and her second noteworthy attribute, the steeliness of her stare, soon came into play. When Louise greeted the porkpie hat–wearing pond dweller with a wheedling "Walter, darling, so good to see you," Maureen's stare focused its spike directly on the other woman's forehead, and Walt thought for a moment that the three-time widow might actually have a hammer in her hand to drive that spike home.

In the next split second, before Louise could say or do more, Maureen stepped between her and Walt, clamping her hand onto the wary man's forearm and drawing close, trying to hold his gaze with the Vise-Grip of her own eyes. Walt was carrying the plastic container with the carefully crafted masterpiece inside—the other pie had been a huge success at the previous night's dinner—and he was unable to pull away, but as Maureen noticed only too late, he also carried his two rodent bodyguards on his shoulders, one on either side. As the musky cloud of scent drew closer, Stumpy drew back and, without warning, sneezed—"*Ps-s-shew*!"—then beat a hasty retreat down Walt's back to the floor, his striped partner following suit. The two hid behind Walt's legs, glad to have something solid between them and the excessively fragrant woman.

"It's not contagious, is it?" Maureen muttered, trying to pin the squirrel to the floor with that spike-like gaze; Walt's legs, however, kept her from striking either animal with the metal darts of her glare. "I've heard there's some kind of . . . *rat* flu making the rounds in Asia somewhere."

"Oh, no, ma'am," Walt answered, trying to laugh off the awkwardness. "The little fellow's just got a hypersensitive nose. Comes in handy when I'm measuring spices. He's good at telling me just when to stop. I always used to overdo the cinnamon in my apple pie until the Stumpster here moved in. I'd have left him and his buddy in the car, except that I promised my friend I'd babysit little George there and keep a close eye on him."

"Well, aren't they cute!" Louise said, trying to gain an advantage as she again stepped forward. Leaning down, she extended her index finger toward Stumpy and said, "*Kitchy, kitchy, koo,*" careful not, however, to get too close. Encouraged by what he took as a sincere gesture of interest and friendliness, the gray-furred charmer hopped forward, but Louise took three quick steps backward, saying, "Oh, my! Look at those big front teeth! They look very sharp."

"Here, Stump," Walt said. "Maybe you and George had better keep a low profile. Come on back up on my shoulder."

Walt's pie was one of ten on display once he got it out of the container, sliced it, and left it on one of the two folding tables placed in the back of the church. The other bakers were standing and chatting or sitting in the pews and conversing while Louise and Maureen from their metal chairs took charge of manning the display and welcoming prospective customers. Walt guided Stumpy and George over to the stairway that led up to the choir loft and organ room, thinking that they could explore upstairs without causing any problems, and he could keep an adequate eye on them without having to strain. However, as the two explorers climbed those stairs, Walt noticed his relatively new friend Officer Irv Stickler of the Lunenburg Police Force across the nave on the other side of the church, and the amiable duffer without thinking walked over to greet his sometime lunch guest. As he did so, he could feel the gaze of both women on his back. Ignoring them, he greeted Officer Irv with a wisecrack that brought from the rotund policeman his unmistakably resonant belly laugh. At that moment, an ominous sensation rippled through Walt's belly.

Apparently planning to walk over herself and reclaim Walt's attention, Maureen stood up from the table and stepped out from behind it. However, halfway up the staircase, Stumpy had heard the distinctive rumble of the law officer's laugh and recognized it. With George scampering behind, little legs moving so fast that he looked like a racing-striped millipede, Stumpy put the pedal to the metal himself and tore down the steps and across the back of the church, passing like a cannon shot right under Maureen's foot as she started toward her prey. At the sight of first one and then a second rodent zipping past her at full speed, she gave a little shriek and stepped involuntarily backward, tripping on the molding of the entryway and sitting down on the table . . . right on top of Louise's mocha-chip meringue pie.

"Oh, you scheming hussy!" Louise shrieked as she stood up. "Look what you've done! You were planning this all along!"

"Oh no I wasn't, you platinum slut!" Maureen retorted. "How dare you accuse me?"

"Slut, am I?" Louise said, looking down at the table and locating Maureen's perfectly sliced chocolate–peanut butter custard pie, which she then picked up and deliberately smooshed into her rival's face.

Stumpy, followed by George, who seemed to be playing the role of tagalong little brother today, had scooted up Officer Irv's pantleg to his shoulder and was nuzzling his friend's cheek when the hullabaloo broke out behind them. If Irv had not been out of uniform, it's likely that both rodents would have tried to hide under his patrolman's hat, but in the absence of that port in this particular storm, they opted for the even more familiar location of *Walt*'s shoulders, launching themselves in quick succession onto the mortified elder, who was staring at the evolving cat-and-food fight at the table. It looked as though hair pulling might be the next phase.

"You know, Walt," Officer Irv said, "I don't claim to know a lot about women, but I get the feeling you'd be wise to beat a hasty retreat before they both decide a third party—who shall for the moment remain nameless—is actually to blame. Hell hath no fury like a woman hit with a pie . . . unless it's one who's *sat* in a pie in her best dress. I'd suggest we head on outside, and you can fire up that chariot of yours and get while the getting is good. Make sense to you?"

Walt stared only a moment more in disbelief before the gist of Irv's wisdom sank in. "Oh, geez," he said as he put one hand on each of his furry epaulettes and strode hastily to the exit.

Looking bewildered, Stumpy and George stayed on the truck seat itself for the whole ride back to the pond, as if they figured it was safest to lie—or, at least, sit—as low as possible. Walt kept glancing into the rearview mirror and, with varying degrees of success, tried to resist the temptation to tromp on the accelerator. "Women!" he said, with yet another look behind. "I doubt I'll understand them as long as I live!"

35

Stumpy and the Noodleheads

NOVEMBER 14, 2012

It was a dark and, well, stormy night last Wednesday when Winter Storm Artemis blew into the Northeast on the coattails of Hurricane Sammy. I know hurricanes don't have coattails as such, and the image of a storm even wearing any kind of clothing is, I guess, a contradiction in terms, but what I mean to say is that the two storms hit the region in all too close proximity to each other. Once again, however, out at Kibbee Pond, Walt Walthers, the octogenarian weather watcher, and his faithful rodent sidekick, Stumpy the caudally impaired gray squirrel, lucked out in not losing power even during the hardest part of the blow, which left two inches of snow, of all things, on the ground when our heroes awoke Thursday morning.

"What's that white stuff on the ground out there, Stump?" Walt asked with transparent innocence. "Somebody spill a big bag of powdered sugar and forget to clean it up?"

As usual, the squirrel played deaf to Walt's joking irony, although he did sneak a look out the window from the kitchen counter.

"I suppose now that snow is on the ground," Walt continued, "you're going to want me to get out the toboggan so we can go sliding over on Shagbark Hill. You know, I haven't even dug out your scarf and mittens yet, so you'll have to be a little patient while I look through the drawers for them."

Again, Stumpy ignored his silver-haired roommate.

"All right," Walt said. "I give up. I guess I can't get a rise out of you this morning. Did you want to go out and see how Burwell and Lansdowne are doing after a bracing night in their treetop lairs?"

This time, Stumpy went to the door, as Walt had thought he might. The gray-furred bandit, for all his mischievous ways and all his adaptation to human companionship, continues to exhibit devotion to two of his wild siblings who live in the forest that spills into part of Walt's twenty-acre lot. More and more, those two have also grown accustomed to the presence of Walt and his other human guests, like the Riggetti family in the little Cape down the road and Todd Jormonen, the snowplow driver and handyman who remains one of Walt's dearest friends and who back in the summer adopted Stumpy's rodent protégé, George the chipmunk. In fact, in the aftermath of Hurricane Sammy, Lansdowne and Burwell had joined George and Stumpy in jumping from the cabin roof into a huge pile of leaves that Todd had blown next to the structure.

When Walt opened the door last Thursday morning, Stumpy scampered off across the deck and scooted up one of the big pines, and Walt realized that, especially with new wet snow on the ground, passage might be easier for his buddy through the upper branches of the trees than along the slushy ground. Walt chuckled, "Count on a gentleman of leisure like the Stumpster to find a way to waste as little energy as possible!"

Only five minutes after the bucktoothed rapscallion had set out on his quest to find his brothers, Walt heard a vehicle pull into the driveway, and a quick glance confirmed his suspicion that he was hearing Todd Jormonen's Ford F-250, outfitted with its bright yellow snowplow. The younger man, however, didn't attempt to plow the inch or two of snow out on the gravel, instead pulling up close to the deck, getting out of the cab, and hoisting George the chipmunk to his shoulder before turning to the bed of the truck and extracting a snow shovel. By the time the parka-wearing handyman had turned back toward the cabin, Walt had stepped onto the deck in his work boots, and now he greeted the new arrival with the first volley in their usual round of insults. "Hey, buddy, don't you respect private property? Can't you see the sign there that reads 'No Trespassing: Prosecutors will be violated'? Don't they teach you to read over there in *West* Townsend?"

"Oh, listen to that, George," Todd said loudly to the chipmunk on his shoulder. "This guy doesn't appreciate a charitable act when two generous souls from the far side of town, the civilized side of town, travel all this way to keep him from getting his arrogant feet wet and cold. What's this world coming to? It's like a little old lady turning down a generous Boy Scout who only wants to help her across the road!"

"Oh yeah?" Walt said. "What if that little old lady doesn't want to cross the road? I'll bet you and that striped seed stealer would force her to anyway and then probably lead her out right in front of a tractor trailer! Some Boy Scouts you guys'll turn out to be! And by the way, you look like something out of a cartoon where the guy has an angel on one shoulder and a devil on the other, except you seem to be getting lopsided advice from only one shoulder. That can't be good."

"Oh yeah?" Todd said, trying not to laugh. "Where's the buck-toothed demon that usually offers you advice from *your* shoulder? Did he decide that you weren't listening anyway and run off to try to help somebody who *would* listen?"

"Maybe he saw your truck coming," Walt retorted, "and ran off so he wouldn't have to listen to you make these incredible claims of benevolence when you're really here just to set a new Guinness world record for pastries devoured in five minutes."

"Well . . . maybe-e-e," Todd said, dropping the pretense of hostility. "What kind of pastry do you have? And does fresh-brewed coffee go with it?" By this time, he had crossed the driveway, and George had hopped from Todd's left shoulder to Walt's right as the men reached out to shake hands with each other.

"Well, hi there, little fella!" Walt laughed as the striped rascal nibbled at his ear just under the brim of his omnipresent porkpie hat.

"We figured we'd come by and clear that deck off for you, and you're right: We also figured we might be able to bum a muffin or something else tasty while we were here. Right, George?"

The chipmunk was obviously looking around for Stumpy, but he was fond of the gentle geezer as well, and he seemed to know that a treat awaited him inside the cabin, so he wasn't upset at the squirrel's temporary absence. Walt smiled as he said, "If you're bound and determined to win your snow-shoveling merit badge this morning, why don't you get to it? Your warm-blooded epaulette here can come in and help me brew the java. But you know, before we go in, are you any good at whistling—you know, the fingers-in-the-corners-of-your-mouth, end-of-the-workday factory kind of whistle? Amy can do that, and it gets great results from the rodent population around here." He was referring to Amy Riggetti, the young mother who lives down the hill with Anthony, her husband, and Tony, their seven-year-old son; Amy has been known to call back all three of the squirrel siblings with one high-decibel blast. "My own whistle," Walt continued, "just isn't as impressive as it used to be."

"Can't help you there," Todd said, shaking his head. "I can whistle a tune pretty well, and I like to do that, but I've just never gotten the knack of the other kind. Lynn can do it, and she uses it to get Pudge and Yaz back in when they've fallen asleep in the sun or wandered off in the yard." Lynn is, of course, Todd's wife, and Pudge and Yaz are the couple's elderly springer spaniels, who are surprisingly fond of their adoptive brother, George.

"Wait a minute," Walt said. "I've got an idea!"

"Oh, Lord help us!" Todd snorted. "Weren't you the guy who invented a ninth tentacle for the octopus and who wanted to build your cabin from the roof down?"

"Oh, ye of little faith!" Walt said, stepping across the slushy deck to the wooden post along the pondside rail from which hung his bird feeders. Todd watched as the elderly man reached up to detach a metal wand that dangled from a nail and then began ringing a triangular dinner gong that also hung from the post. The loud but musical sound echoed under the tall shoreline pines.

"That figures!" Todd laughed. "The dinner gong always works for me, and from what I've seen, that nut-hauling goofball roommate of yours loves his chow too."

And sure enough, a few moments later, the two humans could see a commotion up in the pine boughs to the northwest as if a concentrated but high-powered breeze or maybe a gray-furred lightning bolt were passing through and headed in their direction. Soon, Stumpy was barreling headfirst down the nearest big pine and then, since his cabinmate's shoulder was already occupied, zipping up Todd's pantleg to *his* shoulder for a quick nuzzle before heading back down to the ground for a rendezvous with his pouch-cheeked cousin. The two furred compatriots were soon rolling around on the slushy deck in playful abandon.

"Okay," Walt said decisively after a minute or two of watching the cavorting antics, "you two come in with me and help me stir up some grub while Mr. Wonderful plies his shoveling trade out here. Thanks, Todd. It was thoughtful of you to come."

A few minutes later, the humans were on their second cups of coffee as a batch of carrot-raisin muffins came steaming out of the oven. Without warning, Walt commenced a new direction of conversation in a manner that Todd recognized as a prelude to a competition.

"Well," the playful fogy said, "I still wonder how you can stand to live over there on the other side of the tracks in *West* Townsend. Everybody here in Townsend proper knows that folks over there are a bunch of knuckleheaded bone brains. Why, I remember a story about one of the founding fathers of West Townsend from many years ago, this shoemaker named Nick Noodle, who had heard story after story about life in the big city, Fitchburg, and really wanted to see the wonders of Fitchburg, the City of Light, for himself. Finally, one day after his children had all gone to sleep, Nick, sounding a little like Mortimer Snerd, said to his wife, 'Norah, I can't wait any longer. All my life I've heard about Fitchburg, yup, yup, with its grand houses and endless shops and skyscrapers, and I must go there before I get too old!'

"Well, Norah was upset but couldn't dissuade her husband, who had the typical tenacity of West Townsenders, who can't let go of a bad idea once they've gotten ahold of it. 'Everyone says that Fitchburg is one of the wonders of the world,' Nick Noodle said earnestly, 'and besides, yup, yup, I'll bring you all presents!'

"*That* idea appealed to Norah, so the next morning, she prepared a lunch for her husband to take with him, and Nick Noodle set off for the wondrous city of Fitchburg. After walking for an hour or so, however, Nick felt the pangs of hunger, and passing by a stream, he found a shady spot to sit down; there, he took out the peanut butter and jellyfish sandwich that Norah had made for him. When he finished eating, he was so comfortable that he didn't want to get up yet, and he said to himself, 'Fitchburg isn't going anywhere, nope, nope, and it'll still be there if I take a little nap right now. Besides, that way, I'll be more alert when I get there, yup, yup, and I can take in even more of the wonders.' So saying, he took off his boots and arranged his knapsack as a pillow for his feet (he was from West Townsend after all, so he didn't grasp a sophisticated concept like the proper use of a pillow). In that instant, though, he had a moment of self-awareness, the sort of thing that is, I might add, rare for residents of West Townsend. 'What if I wake up and forget which direction I'm going in? I might never get to Fitchburg that way, nope, nope!'

"A moment later, he said, 'I know! I'll take off my boots and leave them with the toes pointed toward Fitchburg, that center of culture, yup, yup, and that way, I can't go wrong! Toes toward the wonders of Fitchburg, heels toward home in West Townsend! Ingenious, yup, yup!'

"Of course, what Nick Noodle didn't count on was that while he was snoozing, a cart loaded with tree branches came by, and a dragging branch turned his boots exactly 180 degrees. When he woke up, he saw his boots and remembered the stroke of brilliance that had galvanized him before his nap. 'Now I know which way to go to see that amazing metropolis, Fitchburg! I can't believe sometimes how smart I am, yup, yup!' And he set off, unaware that he was actually heading for home in West Townsend, not for the happening hub called Fitchburg.

"As he arrived a bit later at the edge of a settlement, he was surprised by how much the outskirts of Fitchburg resembled the outskirts of his beloved West Townsend. He saw the same ramshackle dwellings, the same piles of junk in everyone's yard, the same abandoned cars housing chickens or just standing as markers of the homeowners' rank in the pecking order. You see, then as now, the number of abandoned cars in one's yard was the most essential factor in determining social rank in West Townsend. Mud everywhere, the aroma of manure everywhere—Nick Noodle felt right at home, and he thought, Wow! This Fitchburg really is a magical place, yup, yup, the sort of place where everyone feels at home immediately even if he's never been here before! As he walked along and took in all the familiar sights, he sighed and said, 'What a marvelous place, the one place in the world where no one ever could get lost, nope, nope! The perfect city, Fitchburg!'

As he spoke, however, he saw what appeared to be his friend Norbert Ninny step out onto the porch of the house he was passing by. After only a brief moment of hesitation and confusion, though, he began to comprehend the real situation. 'Oh-h-h,' Nick Noodle said, 'Fitchburg is such a magical place that even the people look exactly the same as those back in West Townsend!'

"As he continued on his way toward the center of town, Nick Noodle decided to test just how much like his beloved hometown the miraculous big city could be, and he turned down a side street in the direction of where his own house would have been back in West Townsend. Sure enough! There was a house just like his own, with four children playing in the yard and looking just like his own Ned, Nelly, Nat, and Nick Jr. As he stood and stared with his jaw hanging down, a woman exactly resembling his beloved Norah stepped outside to call the children in for dinner. 'Come in, my darlings. I've made a delicious stone soup!' At that moment, however, she noticed the man standing and staring and called out to him, 'Oh, Nick, you're home! Come and join us!'

"Nick Noodle hesitated a moment and then understood. 'Good heavens! The people here not only look like the ones in West Townsend; they also have the same names, yup, yup!' Now, however, he had to worry that the Fitchburg Nick Noodle would come home while he was himself enjoying dinner with the people who thought *he* was their husband and father. Either that, or soon, somebody else in Fitchburg would recognize him as an impostor.

"However, nothing like that happened that night or the next night or the next night after that. In fact, nothing like that has happened ever since, year after year, and as far as Nick Noodle knows, he is living still in Fitchburg with his mistaken Fitchburg family, afraid to leave and head back to West Townsend because he still hasn't bought his family there the presents he promised to bring back with him, and he thinks the real Norah will be angry at him."

Walt looked expressionlessly at Todd on the other side of the kitchen table.

"Hm-m-m," the poker-faced handyman replied. "Reminds me of a story I heard about another guy from West Townsend, except that this guy made his fortune in some business dealings with the dunderheads who live in Townsend center. He was a horse-cart driver who'd fallen on some hard times and was down to his last horse, but he knew the reputation for thickness of the folks in Townsend proper, so he hooked up his horse and drove over to the center of town, where he pulled up next to the Honeycomb Farms convenience store. There, he scattered a few gold coins, the last of all his money, on the ground between Snowball the horse's hooves, and when people passed by, he started to pick the coins up.

"'Did you drop your money, mister, yup, yup?' the Townsenders asked.

"'Oh no,' Wes Whiskers answered (that was the name of the guy from West Townsend), 'I didn't drop it. My horse here lets fly with a few gold pieces every time he sneezes.'

"Well, the Townsenders, thick as rouge on an aging elephant, desperately wanted that horse, and when the people convinced the mayor to buy Snowball for the town, Wes went home with a hundred gold pieces in his pocket. Of course, the Townsenders caught on eventually, because even after the horse had sneezed fifty times over the next couple of weeks, it never showered down gold coins or silver coins or even copper ones.

"Wes Whiskers looked out the window of his house in West Townsend one day the next month and saw a crowd of agitated Townsenders coming his way, with the mayor and the sheriff at their head. Immediately, he turned to his wife and said, 'My dear, I'm going to take one of our two black cats out into the forest. You keep the other one with you, and when these Townsenders get here, tell the cat to fetch me, and then let it go.'

"When the crowd arrived, the mayor immediately asked, 'Where is that cheater Wes Whiskers? He owes us money, yup, yup.'

"'Oh,' the wife replied, 'he's gone into the woods to chop wood. Let me send the cat to fetch him. Fetch, puss,' she said, releasing the cat, which fled from the crowd.

"A minute or two later, Wes emerged from the trees, carrying a black cat under his arm, as the mayor, the sheriff, and all the rest of the Townsenders looked on in amazement. 'All right,' the mayor said, 'we'll forgive you for cheating us on the horse if you let us have that messenger cat. We'll even pay you a bit more money . . . yup, yup.'

"Wes Whiskers looked distraught. 'But do you have any idea how much time and effort I've put into training this animal? I couldn't part with it for less than two hundred gold coins.'

"'Sold!' shouted the mayor, and the sheriff took the cat under his arm as the crowd turned back for the town center. Once there, they decided to call a meeting of the town council to decide whether they should feed the cat in the morning or at night, but when they sent Puss out with the message for the council members, they got no response, even when the next morning came. They even had to look for the cat itself, which seemed nowhere in the vicinity of Townsend center. Finally, the sheriff and four other men made the walk out to Wes's place in West Townsend, where they saw the black cat stretched out in the sun on the woodpile.

"But Wes had spotted them, too, out the window and said to his wife, 'Lie down, my dear, and pretend to be dead. When I tap you three times on the forehead with this turnip, sit up as if you were returning from the dead.'

"When the furious Townsenders pounded on the door, Wes opened it, his hair disheveled and tears running down his cheeks. 'Oh, my poor wife has just dropped down dead! Whatever shall I do?' The Townsenders were taken aback, and Wes clapped his hand to his forehead. 'Oh, I almost forgot! I can use the magic turnip! That will bring her back!' Reaching over to the counter, he picked up a turnip and *tap, tap, tap,* he touched it three times to her forehead, whereupon the woman groaned and sat up.

"'Oh, Wesley,' she said, 'I've seen such wondrous sights! A glorious flock of angels descended and was carrying me up to heaven, and then there came a flash of light, and I was back here!'

"'All right,' the sheriff said, 'sell us the magic turnip, yup, yup, and we'll give you three hundred gold coins.'

"'Oh no, I couldn't,' Wes said. 'It's a family heirloom, and my wife is prone to accidents of all sorts. I really need it.'

"Finally, though, the sheriff gave him five hundred gold coins, and the men went back to the center of Townsend, with the sheriff cradling the turnip very carefully. The next day, the sheriff called all the Townsenders together at the Town Hall, right there behind Clyde's Diner, and—thick as a hippopotamus omelet—he hit his wife over the head with a wooden mallet so that she fell down dead.

Everyone gasped, but the sheriff said, 'Don't worry, nope, nope!' Pulling out the turnip, he tapped the dead woman three times on the forehead with it . . . but nothing happened. Once again, Wes Whiskers had bamboozled the nincompoops of Townsend center.

"By the way," Todd said, interrupting his own narrative, "as a resident of Townsend center, you probably don't know the origin of the word 'nincompoop.'"

Walt sighed and said, "Enlighten me, O Omniscient One."

"Well," the smirking handyman said, "the term derives from the Latin *non compos mentis*, regularly applied to people from your part of town. It means, as you probably don't realize, 'lacking control or mastery over one's mind,' or 'not possessing a sound mind.' You might be more familiar with the vernacular equivalents—you know, people saying that folks from your part of town have a leak in their think tank. Or their belts don't go through all the loops. Or their elevator is stuck between floors. Or they have room-temperature IQs; in fact, a paramecium could outscore them on an IQ test. To use nautical metaphors you might like, they don't have both oars in the water, and they aren't tied too tightly to the pier. In short, they have minds like steel . . . sieves! And to top it off, they have delusions of adequacy.

"But now back to my story, since I see such linguistic niceties are beyond your comprehension. . . .

"This time, after Wes's latest deception, a huge crowd advanced on his house, and the Townsenders took him prisoner. The mayor shouted, 'You'll pay for cheating us! We're going to drown you . . . yup, yup!' and the sheriff threw Wes into a big burlap sack. Then they all began dragging him down to Townsend Harbor to cast the bag into the water. Without a weather watcher's sense of the seasons, however, they had forgotten that it was winter, and the pond by the Cooperage was frozen over. Thus, they had to go back to their homes for picks and axes and sledges so they could break through the ice. They left Wes with only one man to guard the bag, and that man was a typical Townsender: Distracted by the big icicles melting on the eaves of the Cooperage, he simply hadn't been listening to his instructions.

"Soon, Wes started calling out, 'You can't make me! I don't want to do it!'

"The inattentive guard became curious. 'What can't they make you do, yup, yup? And who's they, uh huh?'

"The muffled voice came back from inside the burlap sack. 'They want me to be the richest man in Townsend, and I don't want to do it. They put me in this sack, and when they come back, they're going to force me to take all kinds of money that I don't want.'

"'Well,' the Townsender said slyly, 'if you don't want to do it, I could do it for you, yup, yup.'

"Wes tied the man in the sack and hurried home, where he gathered his wife and all their money and moved out of West Townsend to Leominster, knowing he'd be safe there. He did, however, return to Townsend center one summer many years later, thinking no one would be bright enough to recognize him. To his surprise, he was dragged immediately before the mayor and the sheriff and the town council, who demanded to know how he had gotten out of the sack.

"'It was a miracle!' Wes said with the typical quick thinking of a West Townsender. 'As I sank to the bottom of the harbor, angels swam to me, opened the sack, and took me out. They fed me with ambrosia and nectar and showed me, there under the water, a storehouse full of gold, silver, and diamonds, and from it they gave me many gifts to take home with me. But I was recently robbed by a clever thief, so I came back today to try to find the storehouse again. If you'd just let me get into the pond. . . .'

"But the Townsenders were not going to be fooled again, and they all wanted to take Wes's place and find the angels' storehouse full of treasure. As Wes walked quietly away, they held an impromptu council meeting, at which they determined that the mayor and the sheriff, as the ones who had done the most for the town, should be allowed the honor of fetching home the treasure. Everyone cheered as two young football players threw the sacks containing the mayor and sheriff into the water to bring back not only gold, silver, and diamonds, but also the angels' own nectar and ambrosia. Unfortunately, forty years later, they're still waiting for the mayor and sheriff to resurface, and a few of the townspeople are beginning to think that their leading citizens have made off with the treasure for themselves. Even so, they remain proud of their heritage as residents of Townsend center . . . yup, yup."

Todd smiled at Walt, and the silver-haired gentleman nodded back. "Good thing that guy moved out of West Townsend," Walt quipped. "He might have raised the average IQ to dangerous levels and cost you guys your federal subsidy for stupidity. Care for another muffin?"

Both Stumpy and George looked hopeful that Walt was asking them that question. "At least," Todd said, "the animal residents of the two areas are, clearly, not subject to any mental impairment based on where they live. Don't they make you wonder just how much they understand of what we're saying?"

Walt laughed. "Not as much as I wonder how much you understand of what I'm saying!"

"Ouch!" Todd said, grinning. "Hey! I have an idea. You know those old 'Yo' Mama' jokes? Maybe we could start a round of 'Yo' Rodent' jokes. You know, 'Yo' rodent is so dumb, he thinks the Kentucky Derby is a hat!'"

"You mean, like '*Yo'* rodent is so dumb, he got fired from the M&M factory for throwing out all the *W*s'?"

"Yeah? Well, yo' rodent is so *ugly*, you take him everywhere so you won't have to kiss him goodbye!"

"And yo' rodent is so ugly, when he went to the beauty shop, it took three hours . . . and that was just for an estimate!"

"Didn't you say," Todd asked coyly, "that Stumpy was watching his weight on doctor's orders? Well, yo' rodent is so fat, when he goes to an all-you-can-eat buffet, they have to install speed bumps!"

"Yeah? I've seen those chubby cheeks on George, you know, and yo' rodent's so fat, when he ran away, they had to use all four sides of the milk carton!"

"Yeah? Well, yo' rodent's so fat, his graduation picture was an aerial photograph!"

"Yeah? And yo' rodent's so fat, he eats Wheat *Thicks*!"

While the rodents in question looked on in disbelief, the barrage of insults continued over the next several minutes, like a parade of colorful floats that seems to go on and on and on. Nevertheless, men of Walt's and Todd's generations don't always find it easy to acknowledge in straightforward language the depth of their affection for each other, and for these two, this perverse but entertaining method of communication works quite well. As their delighted laughter at their improvisations continued, Stumpy and George could easily feel behind the superficially aggressive words all the love the men chose not to state directly. Never underestimate the emotional understanding of a fur-covered creature.

As Todd and George piled into the pickup cab an hour or so later, Todd said, “We may never agree about which is better, West Townsend or Townsend center, but at least neither of us has to live in Lunenburg!”

“Yeah,” Walt replied. “I just don’t think I could handle living with a bunch of loonies!”

36

Stumpy and the Upper Crust

NOVEMBER 21, 2012

The mergansers are back out at Kibbee Pond, and when those personable ducks show up each November, Walt Walthers, the octogenarian weather watcher who lives in a cozy cabin on the shore of the pond, always feels as if old friends have returned for a welcome visit. Not that mergansers of any sort let Walt get very close, but he and his rambunctious rodent roommate, Stumpy the tailless gray squirrel, still enjoy going out on the water each morning in Nelly, the skiff, for their daily jaunt, and while out on the water, they enjoy getting as close as possible to the pond's feathered visitors. However, although a raft of those divers may hold their ground briefly as Nelly approaches, they soon beat the retreat and take flight. The mergansers, whether the larger common type or the smaller and jauntier hooded variety, insist on flying off in a huff if Walt steers too close. A huff is, for you non-birders, the name of a particular flight formation popular among waterbirds . . . or at least I *think* that's where that phrase comes from. The elderly skipper does keep Nelly's ancient three-horsepower Johnson outboard finely tuned, so that the motor emits sounds hardly louder than a kitten's purr; the mergansers, nevertheless, have sensitive ears and perhaps distrust anything that sounds even remotely catlike, as the purring Johnson certainly does.

By the way, despite their names, nothing is veiled or deceitful about the *hooded* mergansers; no, nor is anything *common* about either of the merganser types in the sense of their being ill-bred or uncouth; they are perfectly respectable citizens of the natural world and outright ornaments at the pond. Like Walt, an individual merganser will occasionally talk to itself, but the sound is never as abrasive as the nasal outbursts of mallards; besides, the elderly duffer finds the muttering of birds companionable. Walt loves to look out on the pond and see sunlight flashing off the white on the male mergansers' heads and sides, and he finds the females of both types, with their rust-colored heads and cowlick-like crests, completely charming. If Walt sees the best in these birds, I would have to say that I see both Walt and Stumpy in a similar glowing light, even though sterling character and the best of intentions don't always keep the two roommates out of awkward situations, as we will see once again this week.

I mentioned going off in a huff a few moments ago, and over the last couple of weeks, Walt has been preoccupied with thoughts of two human females who went off in a huff the last time he encountered them. As a prelude to the annual pie-baking competition that takes place just before Thanksgiving every year at the Church of Our Savior Lurks in West Groton, Louise Barnes and Maureen Ripley arranged a pie-tasting back in early October. Louise and Maureen are perennial contenders in the competition itself, as is Walt, but the two women in recent years have made it clear that they are rivals as well for the porkpie-hatted codger's amatory attentions . . . or at least that was the case until the October pie-tasting. At that event, circumstances—in the shape of Stumpy and his protégé, George the chipmunk—conspired to draw down upon Walt the wrath of the two widows. You see, the two scampering rodents startled Maureen, who sat down in a meringue-topped confection created by Louise, who then picked up Maureen's custard-based creation and smooshed it into the other woman's face. Acting on some good advice from a friend who was in attendance, Walt fled the scene with his two partners in crime, and from that time until the competition this past weekend, he had seen and heard nothing from either of the women and had studiously avoided initiating face-to-face contact himself. However, because the kindhearted geezer felt guilty about his role in the melee, he had the following week carefully composed brief notes of apology and had mailed them to the two women, who he suspected felt he was primarily responsible for their mortification. The messages were the same:

Dear Louise (or Maureen, depending on the recipient, and, believe me, he was careful to address each note precisely!),

I am deeply sorry for my role in the recent incident at the church, but I'd like to assure you that neither of my furred companions intended any harm. By the way, your pie certainly looked delicious; I wish I had had a chance to sample a piece.

Respectfully and regretfully,
Walt Walthers

As he composed those notes, Walt had muttered a little to himself, not unlike a lone merganser out on the pond, saying things like, "I'll never understand women . . . at least not women like those two."

The disconcerted elder was about to voice his doubts about whether the two women in question were actually human and whether their behavior might be better explained by likening them to females of the canine species, when he looked up to find that Stumpy, uncharacteristically, had been staring at him. You see, usually when Walt addresses comments to his fur-faced roommate, the squirrel simply ignores him, especially when the comments have a bantering tone. Given Stumpy's perverse side, however, it probably makes sense that he would pay attention to Walt only when Walt would prefer he didn't, as was the case at that particular moment.

"Sorry, Stump," the elderly gent had said. "I guess I'm not at my best right now. I don't like feeling the need to apologize for something I didn't think I was responsible for in the first place. Sometimes, though, you have to do what you can to keep the peace or, in this case, try to restore it."

Walt must not have realized that his notes of apology were going against the old adage "Don't poke the bear" or that in trying to clear the air, he was actually just stirring up a hornets' nest. I don't know if either of those metaphors works precisely, but I figured they were both more appropriate than saying Walt was waving a red flag at a bull, given the gender of the two antagonists he was dealing with.

Fortunately, the phone rang a moment later, and Walt's long-time friend and sometime sweetheart Arlene Tosh was calling to invite him to lunch at Bangkok Gardens, the Thai restaurant in Lunenburg. I say "sometime sweetheart" because the two had dated very briefly in high school, but each had eventually married quite happily elsewhere; their friendship has endured, nevertheless, rekindling strongly in the last year and a half, while Stumpy has also become pals with Arlene's gargantuan yellow Labrador retriever, Big Bruno. Last year, that Leviathan-sized pooch may have spoiled Walt's chances of winning the pie-baking contest for a second straight time when the dog had, in an unsupervised moment, gobbled down the exquisite confection Walt planned to enter. Nevertheless, the silver-haired codger had held no grudge; instead, he had taken the incident as yet another warning against complacency and excessive pride.

"Arlene!" Walt had exclaimed when he picked up the phone two weeks ago. "I can't tell you how good it is to hear the voice of a woman I can understand!"

"Well, Walt," the congenial widow had replied, "I think that might be just about the nicest compliment you've ever given me. And by the way, it's nice to hear *your* voice too. I was thinking that it was about time for us to pay a visit to our friend Fai."

The Fai she mentioned is the hostess at the Thai restaurant and its owner as well, and Walt is almost as enthusiastic as Arlene about Fai and the food and atmosphere at Bangkok Gardens; his enthusiasm comes partially from his taste buds but even more from loyalty to Stumpy, whom Fai allows the humans to sneak into the restaurant if they arrive at a quiet time. Big Bruno is just too big to conceal, so he has to wait out in Arlene's Volvo or in Lulu, Walt's '60 Chevy pickup, depending on which vehicle they bring; the humongous beast barely fits into the cab of Lulu with the others, though, so they usually rely on the Volvo. The agreement with Fai is that Arlene will tuck Stumpy into her purse if other customers come in, but when business is slow, Fai is happy to let the gray-furred epicure enjoy his egg roll on his own plate right on the tabletop. Kindhearted as she is, she usually sends something tasty out to the slavering Labrador as well. Aware of the privilege and grateful for the preferential treatment, the Stumpster is always on his best behavior at Bangkok

Gardens. Furthermore, his curiosity about the tropical fish in the nearby tanks and his solicitous concern for their welfare always entertain the hostess. "Yes, Mr. Squirrel," she will say, "I know the fish would like to eat, but I have to serve people first! Then I can give food to the fish."

Of course, Walt may be paying indirectly for Fai's indulgence of Stumpy. The hostess continues to tease him with accusations of satyriasis, for no good reason that Walt is aware of. Personally, I suspect her sense of irony is primarily responsible, given Walt's gentlemanly propriety and choirboy-like good intentions; in other words, Fai just likes to stir him up and see him flustered. Whenever Walt enters the restaurant, therefore, the hostess is ready with raised eyebrows and comments for Arlene like, "Oh, you're back. It's nice to see *you.* But you brought the dirty old man again. You'd better keep an eye on him!" Waggling a finger at the gentle-natured geezer, she will chide him, "You just sit there and behave, dirty old man!"

Walt initially protested against the unjust label but has since learned to improvise and play along. Now, he'll respond with comments like: "You've got me pegged, all right, ma'am. I'm just coming from my appointment with the sex therapist now. She told me that Thai cookery has aphrodisiac properties, though, so you'd better be careful."

During this most recent lunch with Fai, which took place a little over a week ago, Walt came up with an idea for coping with the upcoming pie-baking contest, which was becoming even more of an obsession for him this year because of the retribution he feared from Louise and Maureen for the wrongs they perceived he had inflicted on them. Normally, the competition does preoccupy him for at least two weeks before the actual date; he has, after all, won the title three times in the last thirteen years. Usually, though, he spends the time leading up to the contest trying new recipes and providing samples to his friends in exchange for feedback he can use to refine his creations. This year, he had found himself thinking less about what to make and worrying more about if and how he could survive the occasion, convinced as he was that two strong-willed women would be simmering in resentment and hungering for revenge. Had he known they would actually be plotting *together* against him, he might have been even more concerned.

"Maybe you could help me, Arlene," Walt had said as he held a steaming forkful of chicken pad Thai and let it cool; his idea for a solution had just risen above the horizon, as welcome as the orange ball of the sun climbing above the trees on a morning after several days of rain. "Officer Irv offered to go with me as my bodyguard, but it might work even better if I took you, and, you know, we gave them the impression that we were . . . a couple."

"Why, Walter Walthers!" Arlene said before taking a sip of her Thai iced tea and batting her eyes at him ironically. "Are you telling me that we're not already going steady? And why would you turn down such a generous offer from Officer Irv? Could it be that you secretly have designs on *me* as your . . . 'bodyguard'? Ooh, and do we get to smooch a lot in front of everybody?" I should mention here, by the way, that Officer Irv is Irv Stickler, the Lunenburg policeman who counseled Walt to beat a hasty retreat from the cat-and-food fight that broke out at the church in October; the patrolman first became friendly with the pond dwellers back in June, when he had rescued Stumpy from the roof of the gazebo at an outdoor concert while the policeman was on patrol in the center of his town. The squirrel, who suffers from a thunder-and-lightning phobia, had panicked and bolted, so to speak, when a large truck had struck a nearby pothole with a noise like one of Zeus's fiery flashes.

At the restaurant Walt had become a little flustered with Arlene's teasing him about his intentions toward her so soon after Fai had yet again teased him about his supposedly insatiable libido, and he found himself tongue-tied. He wiped his mouth with his napkin and then wrung that cloth silently with both hands.

"Oh, Walt," a laughing Arlene had said after only a moment's hesitation, "we've been friends too long for you to have to worry about any romantic nonsense coming between us. I'm not some scarlet woman, you know."

"I know you're not a scarlet woman," the jumpy geezer had replied, "but I'm feeling a bit yellow at the moment. You see, those two women will probably be green with envy of any female companion I bring, so I'm probably putting us both at risk, and we may end up . . . black and blue."

Arlene giggled. "Walt, you truly are a . . . colorful character. But I'm willing to take the risk of a little hair pulling or mudslinging for the privilege of accompanying you. It can't be as bad as you fear, and besides, who knows? You might win the contest again, and then you'll be . . . in the pink. But just to be prepared for the worst, maybe you'd better wear your brown trousers." Walt was able to laugh in recognition of the allusion to one of his favorite jokes, but he was still not feeling comfortable or secure about the upcoming contest. As Officer Irv had said back in October, "Hell hath no fury like a woman hit with a pie . . . unless it's one who's *sat* in a pie in her best dress." And I might add, "Unless it's *two* women scorned who have teamed up together."

"Oh, Heavens to Betsy, Walt," Arlene said, laughing as she used one of her characteristic expressions, "everything will be fine. Surely, those women can't be as vindictive as you fear. People aren't like that in real life. You haven't been watching those soap operas again, have you? I'm sure you're exaggerating, and things will work out just fine." Even in the early years of their friendship, Walt had realized that Arlene had a penchant for thinking positively and giving other people the benefit of the doubt. She often made comments like, "Oh, the sky seems to be brightening over there; I'll bet the bad weather's almost over," even when his own objective and experienced weather watcher's eye assured him that the worst of the blow was yet to come. He wondered if she was simply falling into that old predictable pattern of positivity now or if she was accessing some more trustworthy sort of intuition.

When the phone rang a day or two later, the ensuing conversation did little to assuage Walt's anxiety. The caller this time was Edith Bagshaw, a member of the board of governors at the Church of Our Savior Lurks and one of the longtime organizers of the pie-baking competition. A few weeks earlier, she had called with her annual reminder of the upcoming contest, a courtesy she paid to all the regular contestants, although she also posted open invitations online and on the bulletin board at the Four Leaf Farm Store in the center of West Groton. As someone who had been friendly with both Walt and his wife when Annie was still alive, however, Edith was now making a second call of a slightly different nature.

"Walt," Edith said, "I don't want to alarm you, but I'm afraid Louise and Maureen have lodged a protest against your participation in the contest this year, claiming that you sought to cause them public embarrassment at the pie-tasting last month in order to create bias against them in the upcoming event. *I* know the charge is ridiculous, and I'm pretty sure they do, too, but I worry that they may be scheming against you in other, less obvious ways. Until recently, they could hardly bear to speak to each other, and now they seem inseparable. The organizing committee has no intention of discouraging you from entering, but I wanted, as a friend, to warn you that you might face some . . . unpleasantness."

After thanking Edith for her concern, Walt had immediately phoned Arlene, his "bodyguard" for the contest. The word "unpleasantness" had particularly reminded him of his obligation to the positive-thinking widow, because the two of them had recently worked out what she called "an unpleasantness scale" for when Walt wanted to recommend a book or movie to her. "It's not too . . . unpleasant, is it, Walt?" she would ask. "On a scale of one to ten, how much unpleasantness would you say is involved?" Unpleasantness for her involves primarily acts of violence and cruelty, especially harm to animals or children. She is, after all, determined to maintain her optimism as much as possible, and terrorist acts or serial killings do not bolster the faith in essential human goodness to which she clings. After his talk with Edith, Walt wanted to be sure Arlene knew that she might be walking into some of the very unpleasantness from which he usually tried to protect her.

"Oh, Heavens to Betsy, Walt," she had said when he told her his news, "I really don't believe that these women can be capable of anything all that . . . unpleasant."

"Well, you're a kindhearted, generous, and forgiving person," Walt had replied. "You wouldn't understand. I'd love to have your company and moral support, but I want you to know what you might be getting into."

"Now, Walt, how could I back out when you've been saying so many nice things about me lately? Are you sure you're not just flirting with me after all? You're not going to surprise me with an engagement ring, are you?" The mischievous woman couldn't help breaking out into giggles as she voiced her last question.

"Okay, okay," Walt said, "maybe nothing horrible is going to happen, but my past observation of those women makes me uneasy now, and my intuition tells me they're capable of retribution on a

Shakespearean level. They remind me of the witches in *Macbeth* concocting something, or maybe even of Goneril and Regan in *King Lear.*"

"Oh, Heavens to . . ." Arlene caught herself and started again. "All right, let's just say that I don't share your low expectations. Time will tell if your cynical view is correct. Now, tell me: What are you planning on making for your entry?"

The culinarily-inclined codger spoke with genuine enthusiasm: "I'm trying a new recipe for what I call an Upper Crust Apple Pie. It starts with my whole-wheat crust on the bottom with sliced apples, cinnamon, and a little apricot brandy layered in; then I add a mock middle crust made of butter, brown sugar, cinnamon, flour, and oatmeal, so it's like a regular crumble topping. But then comes the tricky part! I layer in a cream cheese, cheddar, and cottage cheese mixture, and finally, I add the whole-wheat *upper* crust! I've tested it out on Amy, Anthony, and Tony Riggetti, the family down the road, and they said they thought it might be my best yet! I plan to make a backup or two, so if you do come, I should have one to give you as a thank-you for your support."

As last Saturday and the competition approached, Walt concentrated on his baking and tried to put Louise and Maureen out of his mind. He has never been a competitive person, though he did enjoy the acknowledgment of his skill that came on the three occasions when he won the contest; above all, however, he takes joy in the baking itself and in watching the pleasure of the people who eat his baked goods. "Something primal and deeply satisfying in that," he told Stumpy on Friday as he was preparing the cheese mixture for the final pie he was making, which also happened to be the one he took with him to the competition the next morning.

Arlene arrived at 9:00 Saturday morning so that Stumpy and Big Bruno could have a little time to play before they all headed off to West Groton around 10:45. As usual, the elephantine Lab had a tennis ball tucked back into his cavernous cheek, and as usual, he made the mistaken assumption that Walt would want to throw it for him to retrieve. "You know I like you, big fella, but I admit a strong and perhaps irrational aversion to objects first coated in slimy dog saliva and then dipped into gritty sand. Why don't you talk to the Stumpster and see if you can convince him to play that digging game you guys enjoy?" The dog had been standing at Walt's feet on the shore near the dock, looking from the ball up to Walt's face, then back down to the ball, up to Walt's face, down to the ball, and so on, but Stumpy took his cue from Walt, pouncing at the ball and beginning to dig at the sand on which it sat. Immediately, Big Bruno began a similar action from the opposite side of the orb, except that the mammoth mutt flung about ten times the sand that Stumpy did, and Walt, who was directly in the line of fire, had to duck out of the way. "Hey, you big goofball," he said, laughing, "didn't your mom tell you I already had enough dirt-slinging of a different sort to worry about?"

When the time to leave for the church came, they took Arlene's Volvo. Big Bruno was slightly damp still from the swim that both humans knew better than to try to deter him from taking, and he could sit in the back seat while the humans stayed dry in front; besides, while the other three went inside for the pie-tasting, he could be comfortable on his blanket in the car. The tennis ball was again safely ensconced in his cheek, so he was content and would remain so; for further consolation, Stumpy made a point of riding to West Groton with him in the back, where they both looked out the side window like small children counting cows on a long trip.

Outside the church, the contingent from Kibbee Pond encountered two familiar faces and a couple of new ones. First, Walt introduced Arlene to the Reverend Captain Tommy Hawthorne, and Tommy introduced both of the elders to his two adopted sons, four-year-old Jack and five-year-old David, whom he and Sarah Knightley, his wife, had recently brought back from an orphanage in Ethiopia. The boys stared wide-eyed at Stumpy, where that gray ball of fur sat on Walt's shoulder, bobbing his head at them in a friendly manner; Walt bent over and extended his arm toward the boys, and the squirrel slipped down to where Jack and David tentatively stroked his head, smiling shyly. "I'll bet you've never seen anything quite like him before," Walt said, smiling. Turning back to Tommy, he pointed at the plastic cake tin in the younger man's hand and said, "Hey, are you entering the competition, too, this year? We need some more male competitors."

Tommy, who is a captain in the Groton Fire Department, an EMT, and an ordained minister in the Church of Spiritual Humanism (like Walt), and on top of all that is the admissions director at nearby Laurel Academy, answered, "Yes, I am. I'm already sleep-deprived enough to last the rest of my life, but I wanted the boys to get the full flavor of Thanksgiving, so I made a maple pumpkin pie in honor of their arrival."

"Well done!" Walt said. "I wish you good luck in the competition too. Maybe you'll end up with even more to celebrate."

The other familiar face that Walt and his companions encountered was Officer Irv Stickler himself, who, true to his word, had come to offer his services. Giving one of his patented deep, rolling laughs, the policeman said, "You know me: Stickler by name, stickler by nature! I like to follow through on my duties and commitments. Right now, though, I feel a bit like a prizefighter's manager, getting ready to send him into the ring against the reigning world's champion. 'Bob and weave, son; bob and weave!'"

Walt laughed, too, and said, "Actually, I feel like Gary Cooper in *High Noon*, gearing up for the big gunfight. I've got my Grace Kelly with me"—he put his hand on Arlene's shoulder—"and I did deputize Stumpy this morning, so he can cover my back if the Miller gang tries anything nefarious. Of course, I don't know if a porkpie is as intimidating as a Stetson." He adjusted his omnipresent porkpie hat at a rakish angle down over his forehead.

"I see what you mean," the jovial policeman laughed. "I guess I'll stick around, though," Irv said. "Bound to be entertaining one way or another."

The format for the pie tasting is simple. Each competitor displays her or his creation on one of the tables set up in the fairly substantial vestibule of the church, having sliced it and placed one piece on a plate so the interior is also visible. Meanwhile, all the onlookers circulate through to admire the pies before the judges finally step forward to sample the contestants' wares.

As Walt entered the church, with Arlene on his arm and Stumpy on his shoulder, Louise Barnes and Maureen Ripley stood on either side of the entryway to the nave, behind the tables on which some pies were already displayed; the women looked a bit like life-size bookends based on some classical sculptures of the Gorgon sisters. At least, that's what Walt was thinking; Arlene's thoughts may have been more generous. Maureen's steely stare was very much in evidence and directed itself at the just-entering trio. Walt felt somewhat reassured that her glare had not immediately petrified him. The usually vociferous, if hard of hearing, Louise was atypically silent, at first staring openmouthed at the attractive woman on Walt's arm, then turning away to fuss with the coconut caramel meringue pie she had prepared for the contest. Arlene made a point of drawing closer to Walt, leaning in as if to whisper in his ear, and Walt decided then to take the bull by the horns even if it also meant stirring up the hornets' nest *and* poking the bear. He set his pie down on the table in an open space next to Louise's and turned to his competitor. "Louise, I'd like you to meet my friend Arlene."

The hard of hearing woman nodded coldly, nose in the air, and said, "We all could use a friend to lean on."

"No, Louise," Walt said, raising his voice slightly. "Her *name* is Arlene."

"You don't have to shout," the other woman replied primly.

"And Maureen," Walt continued, "I'd like you to meet Arlene as well."

"I bet you would," the three-time widow smirked, her eyes darting steel spikes at both the newcomers while Stumpy on Walt's shoulder perch shrank back behind Walt's head to get out of the path of those ocular projectiles. Maureen maintained a stiff-backed regality as she leaned back against the doorframe.

"There should be a law against rats being allowed in a church," the woman muttered as, Medusa-like, she recalculated altitude and range for another firing.

"Actually, Stumpy is a very clean animal," Walt replied, "and he spends a great deal of time grooming himself, even more than many cats I've known. More than many women too."

"He really is quite charming," Arlene added, smiling as she reached out to stroke the squirrel's nose but drawing glares from both of the Gorgon sisters; she refused, however, their summons to petrification. "Intelligent too," she added with another warm smile. Both women looked icily at Arlene but said nothing more.

Recognizing that neither Maureen nor Louise was ready to abandon her hostility, Walt focused on cutting his pie and arranging a piece on the plate provided for him. Then he led Arlene over to the far corner of the vestibule to chat with Officer Irv, onto whose shoulder Stumpy happily clambered.

Events came to the sort of head Walt had feared a few minutes later when he heard Maureen exclaim, "Oh my God! Look at that! How disgusting! There are droppings from that . . . *rat* in the man's pie!"

In the hubbub that ensued, Walt worked his way back to the table on which his pie sat next to Louise's, and he saw, on the plate on which his once-carefully composed slice sat, a garnish of small, dark pellets spilling out from the crust onto the white China surface. He recognized immediately, of course, that the droppings were not Stumpy's, as they clearly came from a smaller animal and looked indisputably like the excretions of a house or deer mouse, common to the cupboards of many homes.

Walt said nothing as Edith Bagshaw intervened. As a member of the church's board of governors and the longtime organizer of the pie-baking event, she also serves as chief judge. Not quite five feet tall, Edith nevertheless radiates authority, and Walt knew from her earlier phone call that she was aware that sabotage was involved. "Louise . . . Maureen," Edith said, her voice quavering slightly with controlled anger, "this is a pretty transparent attempt to discredit and disqualify Walt, and I think it would be best if you removed your entries from the competition. I can't allow this sort of thing."

"What are you talking about?" Maureen hissed, her steely glare attempting its transformational power on the shorter woman, who simply stared back and said, "Maureen, I am a fossil already, so staring at me that way is not going to turn me to stone. Louise, what's going on here?" She spoke this last question in a slightly louder voice and with careful enunciation.

"You can't prove anything," the other culprit said, "and you don't have to raise your voice to me either!"

"How did those droppings get there?" the chief judge persisted. "Stumpy has been on the policeman's shoulder for the last fifteen minutes, and he never came near this table."

"I'm going to take my pie and go home!" Maureen hissed, and she turned first to pick up her purse from the floor. Stumpy, however, with a preternatural understanding, launched himself from

Irv's shoulder onto the table and then onto the floor, where he bowled into Maureen's bag. As the bag toppled over, a plastic pill bottle fell out, and its cover rolled away as its remaining contents spilled onto the floor of the vestibule. Several people gasped as they recognized more of the mouse droppings that had been strewn across Walt's Upper Crust Apple Pie.

When Louise saw the spillage, she blurted, "It was all *her* idea! I told her it would never work!"

In the ensuing hullabaloo, the ever-competent Edith Bagshaw stepped up once again to restore calm. Maureen and Louise both beat the retreat and left in a huff—I think a Huff may, after all, be some kind of compact foreign car, but I could be wrong. Upon their departure, Edith did the judicious thing; since Walt's pie had lost considerable appeal with its added ingredients, Edith regretfully disqualified him along with the two dropping-sprinklers and confined the competition to the remaining entrants. When the dust cleared, Tommy Hawthorne walked away with this year's title.

After congratulating Tommy, Walt walked his companion back out toward her Volvo. As they approached the car, Arlene said quietly, "Heavens to Betsy, Walt! You were right. Those women are unpleasant. In fact, on my scale, they go from 'unpleasant' to downright 'upsetting'!"

Officer Irv gave a rolling chuckle as he strode beside them, Stumpy again on his shoulder. "What will you two do now?" he asked.

"Maybe we'll have some lunch and take in a movie," Walt said, looking at Arlene, who nodded approval.

"Good idea," the big patrolman asked. "What'll you see?"

"I'm not sure," Walt said, "but isn't this week the opening for *Life of. . . Pi*?"

37

Stumpy and the Budding Bard

December 19, 2012

Even with the holiday season closing in, not all that much is changing out at Kibbee Pond for Walt Walthers, the elderly weather watcher who lives out there in his snug cabin, or for his rascally rodent roommate, Stumpy the stub-tailed gray squirrel. Because temperatures have been dipping, the duo has felt a strong urge to persist in some of their favorite autumn activities while time still allows. For instance, they continue to make time for a morning jaunt around the pond in Nelly, the skiff, with Walt at the helm of the three-horsepower Johnson outboard. He keeps that motor so finely tuned that even aboard the craft in mid-voyage, you might wonder if the sound you hear is some large domestic cat purring on the shoreline or some gigantic flying insect defying the seasons to cruise, copter-like, over the water itself. Of course, neither feline nor bug is responsible; it's just the ancient Johnson contentedly doing its duty in pushing the boat gently along.

Some cold nights recently have led to a skim of ice that appears around the outside edges of the pond in the morning, starting in the coves and inlets and arcing outward; out on the more open stretches, on some days, wafer-thin frozen rafts drift across broad areas, and when Walt sees those dull, opaque sheets ahead of Nelly, he calmly steers away. He could pretend the skiff is an icebreaker, like the ones he served on as a Coast Guardsman in the North Atlantic in World War II, because the ice is too thin at this point to damage Nelly's hull. Nevertheless, the elderly skipper anthropomorphizes his craft and can't bear the thought of treating her roughly in any consciously chosen way, any more than he could contemplate cruelty toward the fur-faced rascal who lives inside the cabin with him. He realizes that those floating sheets of ice will soon lock away from him some parts of the pond, even if a substantial snowstorm does not come along to end the boating season entirely in one big blast of arctic air; he also realizes that, one morning soon, even without a big storm, he may awaken to see ice stretched across the entirety of the pond's surface in front of the cabin. He plans to keep an eye on the forecast, and if a storm of any size is coming, he'll get his neighbors down the road, Anthony, Amy, and Tony Riggetti, to help him roll Nelly up onto the shore, where he can secure a tarp over her as she settles into her winter hibernation.

If the approach of winter always brings a slowdown in the good-hearted geezer's activity, it affects his rodent companion as well. Although Stumpy does not retire into a hollow oak or treetop nest shaped from dried leaves, as many of his squirrel brethren do for stretches of the freezing weather, the gray-furred Skeezix, like his roommate, is content to spend more of his time indoors; he likes supervising Walt's projects, but you might also find him simply curled up in slumber on the couch or balanced on the rafter over the woodstove, dozing. In recent winters, Walt has occupied himself with patient, step-by-step focus on his woodworking, as he fashions lamp tables and bookcases, fold-down desks and upright coat racks, magazine holders and original inventions like his combination television-stand-and-plant-stand. Recent winters have also focused the competent coot's attention on his stamp collection, his metal casting, his model-boat building, and of course his garden planning and seed ordering for the coming spring and summer. These days, however, in contrast with the past few winters, Walt's primary project has involved writing, a relatively new activity for him, though a logical extension of his experience as a storyteller. The inspiration came to him after the Thanksgiving feast that he and his lady friend Arlene Tosh had hosted for a group of their friends; after the moans of pleasure evoked by the pies Walt had baked for dessert, Arlene had asked him the distracting question, "Have you ever thought about writing a little cookbook?" She had gone on to suggest that the dough-loving duffer's expertise at designing new flavor combinations for pies made those confections and other favorite baked goods a logical focus for the text. In the spontaneous inspiration of that moment, Walt had embraced Arlene's suggestion. Eventually, he also expanded it.

"What do you think," Walt had said after their guests had left, "of my adding some background to each recipe—you know, a story about how the recipe came to be or how it connects to my family history? For instance, did I ever tell you that the first pie I ever baked got raided by my neighbor's pet crow? The darn thing flitted down from a maple tree and pecked away at my creation where it sat cooling on the sill of a window my mother had left open for that purpose. By the time I noticed, that fool bird had ripped open over a third of the surface of that pie, gorging on the cooked apples and blueberries inside it. I'd heard of blackbirds being baked in a pie before, but not of big black birds stealing crust and pie filling. Of course, I had always admired that bird and envied Tommy Fleming, my neighbor; he had earned Midnight's loyalty by rescuing him and nursing him when the feathered trickster had been struck by a car. Tommy even taught Midnight to say a few words, chief among them, 'Beer!'—a word he would croak out any time someone opened the refrigerator."

Walt had laughed then, his excitement and growing inspiration leaving Arlene no chance to get an oar back into the conversational waters. "Of course, I guess you could say I have a Midnight of my own now. And if you were to ask me whether I'd rather have had a crow as a pet when I was younger or have the ol' Stumpster here now, in my advanced age, I wouldn't hesitate in answering. I'd rather have a pi-rate like this swashbuckling squirrel than a pie *thief* like that crow any day, and besides, I value the company even more now than I would have back in those earlier days. Of course, I value your company greatly too," he had added, reaching across the bench seat to pat the attractive widow's hand. Stumpy was curled up in her lap, already snoring as if he were a lumberjack with a chainsaw going after a hefty oak. Arlene's smile was wide with amusement and affection.

The daily routine of the two cabin dwellers—as I said before—has not altered all that much recently, except that Walt sets aside a chunk of time each morning to labor away at his opus. The roommates' early mornings still include that pond cruise and at least a short walk in the woods that stretch across much of Walt's twenty-acre property. The stoic elder realizes that winter weather could soon make the path under the pines treacherous to tread, but he does have some alternative plans: Stumpy and he often walk along Kibbee Pond Road out to where it meets Gold Crest Road, turning in one direction or another at the T depending on their moods. More often, though, they head right, toward the center of Lunenburg and past the house of Walt's friend Byron Ford, the painter, even occasionally stopping in to see Byron's latest canvas and to indulge in some conversation with a fellow artist, unaccustomed as Walt is to thinking of himself as such. Recently, Walt got his friend talking about his creative process. The painter, who likes to work *en plein air*, said that he takes most of his inspiration from the natural world. He said he walks every day in the woods, hills, and fields, trying to empty his mind until his eyes catch some play of light that infuses a scene with what feels to him like a divine effulgence; then he sets up his portable easel, takes out his brushes and watercolors, and lets the light and air flow through his body and hands. When things are right, Byron said, he works quickly, with almost no conscious thought; years of practice allow him to respond instinctively to what he sees outside himself, and he said the painting seems to flow from inside him like a brook bubbling over a course of stones in a shaded forest. No surprise then that so many of his paintings take as their subject the play of light on water.

Not every day is suitable for a walk outside, however, so on days when the weather conspires to keep him indoors, Walt has yet another exercise option in the Bottomless Basement beneath the cabin: a treadmill near his woodworking bench. By the way, he calls it the Bottomless Basement because it is bigger on the inside than it appears on the outside, with several areas for various activities—from a woodworking shop to storage shelves for Walt's canned vegetables, fruits, and pickles; from a small library with several bookshelves, a comfortable chair, and a reading light to an exercise spot, equipped for both the healthy-living codger and his furry roommate. In that last-mentioned area, beside the treadmill and on that woodworking bench, sits a large guinea pig exercise wheel that Walt reclaimed from the dump a while back courtesy of his friend Flippo Byrd, who supervises the landfill and has a good eye for still-useful discards. Often when conditions force the fitness-conscious geezer to retire to the cellar for some exercise, Stumpy will join him there on his wheel. "I don't know whether we're getting anywhere," Walt will say to his nimble-footed companion, "but at least we can get our circulation going somewhere! And that helps me get my creative juices flowing too!" Walt has found that the rhythm of walking, whether indoors or out, complements the rhythm of his thinking, and a spontaneous flow of language and ideas often follows his exercise period; for that reason, he likes to sit down and write soon after his daily walk.

Other activities fill the kindly elder's days as well, some of them seeming at first to have little to do with his creative process. Of course, Walt has come to realize that virtually everything he does eventually connects in some way to his writing. For instance, although the town's trash pickup service sends a truck out to Kibbee Pond each week, and although the ecologically responsible coot does recycle religiously, Walt and Stumpy also make a trip to the dump at least twice a month throughout the year, occasionally taking over a bag of trash but making the trip even when they have nothing to leave behind. They do, nevertheless, regularly return home with some treasure they've stumbled upon or with something that Flippo has set aside with them in mind. Stumpy's exercise wheel is just one example, as is the hinged metal storage bin in which Walt now keeps his seed and cracked corn for feeding the wild birds. The trip, however, has social and creative functions as well.

When the two pond dwellers make a jaunt to the dump, which involves a twenty-minute drive diagonally to the farthest corner of the town, Walt always stops along the way at Clyde's Diner in Townsend center. There, he buys the landfill operator a cup of coffee with cream and two sugars, Flippo's preferred beverage. Originally, Walt would just bring along a thermos full of his own brew, preferring it himself to anything store-bought, but he quickly learned that, dependent as the dump attendant may be on caffeine to get through his day, he also has a fondness for Styrofoam cups, which he assembles into amazing sculptures reflecting characters from Greek and Norse mythology. Of course, Flippo also employs Styrofoam packing forms, the ones in which many electronics companies ship their products, and whatever other plastic discards suit the particular work he envisions; he claims that he can often "see" a particular sculpture in his head just from glimpsing one or two bits of plastic refuse. The end products are difficult to describe but eerily effective. For instance, Walt has often marveled at Flippo's representations of Odin and Theseus, the latter capturing both the hero's dauntless courage and his inconstant affection, primarily through the angle of one eyebrow. Still, some of the works are disconcerting. For example, Stumpy has never been comfortable around the cow-sized sculpture of Cerberus, the three-headed dog that guards the entrance to Hades in classical legend. In fact, even the usually brave and tolerant octogenarian Walt claims that the hellhound's eyes seem to follow him around the shed where Flippo keeps his artwork; he says that he always feels a bit relieved to get back out into the open spaces and that he might not feel so comfortable about visiting his friend if that particular sculpture stood at the gates of the dump itself.

Since Walt has started to take writing seriously, he has become interested in the routines and methods that all his artistic friends employ, and he considers the dump supervisor every bit as much of a dedicated artist as Byron Ford. Once, when Walt asked Flippo how long he had needed to conceive and produce his twelve-foot-high representation of Yggdrasil, the world tree from Norse myth, the landfill supervisor had rubbed his hands on the front of his forest-green work shirt and had then pushed back the brim of his matching cap. "Don't know," he had muttered, then looked down and away from the curious duffer. "I lose myself in the work sometimes . . . lose track of time . . . don't even sleep until a certain detail is just right, and then I'll curl up on the glider there"—nodding toward a plastic-covered, metal-framed remnant of the 1950s—"and sleep until I wake . . . and then go back to the work again. Get in trouble with the board of selectmen sometimes when somebody complains they needed help unloading some appliance and I wasn't handy. Can't help it, though . . . an idea just takes hold, that picture in my head, and I have to follow it where it leads. . . . This thing"—he nodded toward the tree sculpture—"is based on the big ash tree that used to stand in front of my parents' house. At least until the town drunk in those days, Curtis Surtaine, set it on fire, claiming there were poisonous snakes crawling in the branches. It was like the end of the world for me, losing that tree. I used to climb in it when I was a whippersnapper, and I was still only thirteen when it burned. I tried to bring it back with this sculpture, but it's still gone, I know that. . . ." He had looked at Stumpy then and said, "At least Ratatosk there made it out alive, even if the fire did claim his tail. . . ." Walt had had to wait until he was home to go online and learn that Ratatosk was the swift-mouthed gossiping squirrel the Norsemen believed resided in Yggdrasil, carrying messages and insults between the eagle in the tree's tops and the dragon at its roots. The budding writer had wondered then once again how closely the artistic temperament and the capacity for inspiration might be linked to psychological imbalances; as the eternal optimist, however, he was happy to have picked up a new nickname to apply to his bucktoothed companion.

Walt's creative process is somewhat more mundane than Flippo's and a bit more like Byron Ford's. For the porkpie-hatted duffer, walking and exercise are vital elements in preparation for his daily writing, while consistency of effort and self-discipline seem to be the keys for the progress he is making as the weeks go by. After the morning walk, whether it occurs indoors or outdoors, he sits down at the kitchen table with a handful of freshly sharpened No. 2 pencils and a lined yellow legal pad; then, from about nine o'clock until noon, he will continue the previous day's labor. One trick he has learned is to end at a point when he knows what he wants to say next; that way, starting up the next day is relatively easy, and he can regain momentum quickly. Because ideas usually start flowing during his morning walk, he has also learned to carry a small spiral notebook with him then so he can jot down points before he forgets them.

Last week, Walt felt the urge to get to the dump and visit with Flippo again, and he invited seven-year-old Tony Riggetti to accompany the human elder and his squirrel sidekick to the landfill. Thus, on Tuesday afternoon, as soon as Ellie Wentworth's yellow school bus had dropped the youngster off at his house just down the hill from "the two swinging bachelors' pad," as Walt occasionally refers to the cabin, the silver-haired treasure hunter hustled the excited squirt into the cab of Lulu, where he fastened the lad's seat belt and invited Stumpy into the little shaver's lap. With enthusiastic waves to Amy, the boy's mother, the trio departed.

"We'll just stop at Dunkin' Donuts on the way, since Clyde's has already closed for the day," Walt explained to Tony. "I want to get Flippo his traditional coffee, and you might like a hot chocolate. I'm *not* going to get Stumpy another latte, even if it's decaf; last time he had one, he kept me awake most of the night since he couldn't get to sleep. And the time before that, he couldn't wait for it to cool, so the little rascal burned his mouth. Then I had to listen to him complain the whole rest of the trip. And you know how he chatters on when he's feeling querulous!"

Tony giggled.

As Walt steered Lulu through the gates leading into the landfill, they could all see Flippo standing outside his "office," a corrugated metal shed that abuts the five or six dumpsters into which townspeople unload their recycling; that office is the same building whose entrance the sculpture of Cerberus guards, and since it houses another dozen or so of Flippo's creations, Walt thinks of it as his friend's studio. Lulu crunched to a halt on the gravel outside the shed, and Flippo, a short, wiry man, ran his left hand over his salt-and-pepper beard as he raised his right hand shoulder-high in greeting. Walt recognized the nervous habit in his reclusive friend from frequent past visits.

"Hi, Mr. Flippo!" Tony called as he launched himself from the slippery bench seat, out the pickup door, and onto the ground, laughing as he landed and then turned back to offer his arm for Stumpy to clamber onto. "Thank you for sending those things to me with Mr. Walt." The dump attendant, wearing a battered green parka over his green work uniform, tipped his also-green cap at the seven-year-old. I should mention that ever since Walt and Stumpy had brought Tony along on one of their previous visits, Flippo had been keeping his eyes open for any discards he thought might appeal to the first grader. Among the items he had found and sent back with Walt were a bag of green plastic soldiers, a dozen or more of the ceramic animals originally enclosed in boxes of Red Rose tea bags, and a plastic tub nearly full of Lego pieces he had accumulated over the years, from older blue and red and yellow ones to those from more recent sets. From Tony's point of view, the Lego pieces that had stood out the most were two medieval knights and figures of Darth Vader and Harry Potter, and Walt got the sense that

Tony's imagination could come up with any number of play scenarios growing out of that unusual combination of characters. He was also realizing that what Tony did with the Lego figures was a lot like what he himself did as a storyteller when he was mixing and matching motifs and story elements; it was also like what he was doing these days as a writer in putting recipes together with anecdotes about his family and snatches of myth and folktale. More and more these days, as he writes, he is sensing that an artist's acts of creation are full of the elements of play that fill a child's life too.

"Come see what I've done!" Flippo said quietly as he shook first Tony's hand and then Walt's and then turned to open the shed door for his visitors. As the trio walked past the sculpture of Cerberus, Stumpy zipped from Tony's right shoulder to his left and peeked timidly around the back of the boy's head at the Styrofoam monster that loomed by the entrance; he seemed to want to keep as much distance as possible between that infernal watchdog and himself. Flippo laughed and asked, "Where are your insults now, Ratatosk?"

Walt defended his roommate. "Well, now, friend, that particular creation of yours intimidates *me* a little too. Stumpy's not usually bothered by dogs, but one with three heads . . . well, that's a bit too many teeth to ignore, I'd say." Before they moved on from Yggdrasil, the world tree dominating the center of the shed, Walt paused to explain the Ratatosk reference to Tony. Then the elderly aesthete saw a new creation in the back corner. "Oh my!" he said with an intake of breath.

Flippo was standing, looking shyly down, next to an eight-foot-tall sculpture that Walt recognized immediately, especially from its giant hammer, as Thor, the Norse god of thunder. "Every time an electrical storm descends on me here," Flippo said, "I think how much safer I'd feel if the god of thunder himself were with me . . . so I made this. Now I don't have to worry about being struck by lightning ever again."

"Well," Walt responded, "I wouldn't want to get hit with that hammer. The head of it looks a little bit like a plastic beverage keg of some sort."

"That's exactly what it is, " Flippo said, smiling shyly.

On the way back to the pond a half hour or so later, both Walt and Tony were smiling themselves because of their finds from the dump. Flippo had set aside a bag of cat's-eye marbles for the first grader and had steered Walt toward a nearly perfect wooden screen door, with which, come spring, he would be able to replace the old one at the cabin; too many mosquitoes and midges had found their way into the living area the previous summer, thanks to some tears in the screening on the other door.

As the trio pulled back onto Route 119 in West Townsend, Tony spoke up. "Mr. Walt, who is Thor?"

"Well," Walt replied, "as Flippo said, he was the Norse god of thunder, and our day of the week Thursday was named after him: Thor's day. I haven't noticed over the years that Thursdays have been any rainier than the other days of the week, but Thor was said to bring on storms, and he could crush mountains with his great hammer, Mjolnir. His archenemy was a huge dragon-like sea serpent, Jörmungandr—no relation, though, to our friend Todd Jormonen, even though the names sound a bit alike.

"Now, I've been using that word 'Norse,' so I should tell you that Norsemen is basically another name for the Vikings, those restless and violent people from northern Europe; 'Norse' basically means 'north.' You've got a Lego Viking ship, don't you?"

Tony nodded. "Yes, Mr. Walt."

"Well, the Vikings, or the Norsemen, traveled far in their graceful ships, looking for new lands to conquer and treasures to raid. Many say that they voyaged to the New World long before southern Europeans like Columbus, even though a lot of folks still say that Columbus discovered America. They had a large pantheon—that is to say, they had a big bunch of gods they worshipped—but among them, Thor was famous for his strength and using that strength to protect humans, so he was one of the Vikings' favorites.

"There's an old story about Thor you might like. It seems he loved fishing and was quite the fisherman, though I don't think he ever fished here at Kibbee Pond. He was probably a pretty interesting guy, so I'm sure I would have enjoyed taking him out in Nelly, though it could be that the old three-horsepower Johnson outboard motor wouldn't have been powerful or flashy enough for his taste. Now that I think of it, sometimes even Stumpy complains that we don't go fast enough when we're out on the water.

"Anyway, I mentioned before the rivalry between Thor and

Jörmungandr, who was the offspring of a giantess and Loki, another god and an untrustworthy trickster. The father god, Odin, threw the monstrous Jörmungandr into the sea, where he grew so big that he could wrap his snakelike body around the entire earth and still put his tail into his mouth; the Vikings believed that if he ever lets go, the world will end, but I guess that part doesn't really apply in the story I'm trying to get to.

"In any case, Thor had made plans to go out fishing with this giant he knew named Hymir, and he laid in supplies for the outing—you know, nine or ten bags of chips, some beef jerky, a few pickled eggs, and about twenty six-packs of beer, to wash it all down with. I don't know whether he had some special propulsion system on his boat or if he had to put up with Hymir complaining that they weren't going fast enough; I suspect, though, that if he heard any moaning whatsoever, Thor would have just bopped that giant over the head with Mjolnir. Before they left, Hymir told Thor he wouldn't share any of his bait with the thunder god, so Thor turned around and cut off the head of one of Hymir's oxen to use instead. As I said, you really don't want to get Thor angry.

"Well, Hymir said, 'Thor, I know a great fishing spot off one stretch of shoreline. I get a dozen or more flounder there every time I go out.' You know, Tony, flounder are flat fish that live on the bottom of the ocean, much in demand with chefs and those who favor haute cuisine. Thor, however, wasn't big on delicate delicacies, but he *was* big on whales, which are big themselves, and sure enough, he caught two, one each time he put that ox head into the water. 'This is getting boring,' he said to Hymir. 'Let's go out deeper, where the really big ones are.'

"But Hymir said, 'Oh, Thor, I really don't think you want to do that. Out there, you might hook into Jörmungandr—you know, the Midgard serpent—and he's one nasty piece of work.'

"Well, old Thor liked a challenge, and he didn't like anybody telling him he couldn't do something, so Hymir's words just convinced him to go looking for that scaly monster, no matter what. He dragged out of the hold of his ship a huge metal cable with a gigantic hook at the end, impaled the ox's head on the hook, and threw his bait and line overboard. This was in the days before plastic bobbers like the ones you and your dad use were even invented, so that cable went straight down toward the bottom, and it was only a matter of moments before Jörmungandr grabbed on.

"For several hours, Thor tugged on his end of the line, pulling that cable in ever so gradually until, finally, he was face-to-face with the ugly monster. Now, Jörmungandr had the unsanitary habit of drooling blood and poison, and the sight of his unsavory salivation made Hymir turn as white as a newly bleached bedsheet (and since he was a giant, that sheet would have had to be even bigger than a king-sized sheet, or even an emperor-sized sheet). As Thor was reaching for his hammer to finish off that scaly slime-factory of a sea serpent, Hymir found a spare battle axe and with one blow severed the metal cable. After the Midgard serpent made his escape by diving back into the ocean depths, Thor called Hymir just about every bad name in the book, but Hymir offered him the last beer. Impressed with that act of generosity, the god of thunder forgave the giant, and they headed back in to shore. I think that fishing trip was the first time anyone ever came back and used that immortal phrase, 'You should have seen the one that got away!'

"Now, the Vikings believed that Thor and Jörmungandr would meet up again, but it wouldn't be until Ragnarok, the end of the world. Then, the deadly serpent would come out of the sea to contaminate the whole sky with his toxic drool; in a last stand, the god of thunder would face the monster and slay him with his great hammer. Then Thor would take nine steps and fall down dead, succumbing at last to the serpent's poison."

Walt was just pulling Lulu back into the cabin's driveway as he finished the story. When he glanced over at Tony, the silver-haired tale spinner saw Stumpy leaning back in the boy's lap, his eyes even wider than the first grader's. "Oh, now," Walt said hurriedly, "don't either of you take that story too seriously. Those Norsemen took a pretty dark view of things, and I don't want anyone having nightmares. Let's go inside, and I'll tell you another fishing story. I'm pretty sure I never told either of you about the time I went ice fishing and caught ten pounds of ice. Almost drowned trying to cook it!"

As the trio got out of the cab in the driveway, a crow was cawing from the top of one of the tall pines that line the pond's shore in front of the cabin. With the raucous call clanging like some unmusical metal bell, Stumpy sprinted to the deck, launched himself from the deck rail onto the trunk of the evergreen giant, and raced up the gnarled bark. In a few moments, Walt could hear churring and chattering in counterpoint to the black sentinel's cries. When the affronted crow flew off shortly thereafter, the squirrel slipped back down from the treetops and began chattering at Walt from a head-height branch; both of the humans were standing mystified by the kitchen door.

Laughing in sudden recognition, though, Walt offered an explanation. "Darned if he didn't find the perfect excuse for some role-playing! He heard that crow name-calling up there and remembered the eagle at the top of Yggdrasil, the world tree, so he went up to exchange insults, Viking-style. Now, I suspect, he's pretending that I'm the dragon at the root of the tree. And I thought *I* had an overactive imagination! Come on, ol' Ratatosk. Let's go inside now. I want to tell you guys that fishing story I promised you."

38

Stumpy and the Blossoming Romance

MARCH 10, 2013

"April is the cruelest month," T. S. Eliot says in "The Waste Land," but Walt Walthers, the elderly weather watcher who lives out at Kibbee Pond in Townsend, has occasionally offered a corrective to Eliot's position; Walt thinks that we start "breeding lilacs out of dead land" and "mixing memory and desire" even earlier in the year. If April is a cruel month, Walt says, then March can be downright sadistic, and never more so than when she dumps a big snowstorm on a populace hoping for some sign of spring. If Eliot claims that:

> Winter kept us warm, covering
> Earth in forgetful snow, feeding
> A little life with dried tubers. . . .

. . . Walt is skeptical, at best, well aware that despite the insulation that a layer of snow can provide, the shrill and chill winds still penetrate the siding of a cabin in the dying months of the season. He doesn't think that the snow ever fully forgets its mission, which involves more of snuffing than of feeding life; besides, he's never been a big fan of dried tubers, even when sautéed in fresh creamery butter. And this year, March in its early stages decided to be as perverse as possible; first, it teased the residents of the Northeast by dumping another foot and a half of snow on them, and then it marched out vernal temperatures for several days and turned the pristine, if suffocating, snow into rivers of mud. As the third month of the year bore on, colder temperatures returned, and several more snowfalls tortured various parts of New England. March, a perverse as well as cruel month!

If March is a difficult month, however, at least Walt can take comfort in the companionship of his longtime cabinmate and sidekick, Stumpy the stub-tailed gray squirrel. Although the gray-furred rascal has lived with Walt for three years now, many of the little fellow's natural instincts remain intact, and as Walt has been bracing himself to endure the cruel trials of March, Stumpy has been emerging more and more from his winter doldrums. Although squirrels do not formally hibernate, the Stumpster did slow down a bit through the bleakness of January and February; nevertheless, the little fellow shows great sensitivity to the lengthening days and to the different slant of light that appears as the spring equinox approaches, and Walt noticed that with the arrival of March, his roommate was spending more and more time outside, even on the coldest days, looking for spots to bask in the sun. The wild squirrels in the neighborhood, most notably Stumpy's siblings Burwell and Lansdowne, also increased their activity in the weeks leading up to the equinox, putting in regular appearances at Walt's bird feeders as well as romping and playing chase-the-tail through the tops of the pines that line the pond's frozen shore.

Losing an hour to daylight saving time has always seemed a mixed blessing to Walt, since gaining an hour of daylight at the end of the day is not always adequate compensation for the thick cloak of darkness that once again awaits him when he rises at 5:30; after reveling in earlier and earlier sunrises, waking again in darkness seems like plunging back into winter. Nevertheless, as a professional weather watcher, Walt can easily remind himself that dawn creeps backward more and more noticeably as the March days lengthen.

Compensations of other sorts bring hope, too, particularly the changes in birdsong and the arrivals of a slightly different clientele at the bird feeders. For many years, a pair of Carolina wrens has nested in the vicinity of the cabin, and although Walt had been seeing a single wren off and on throughout the late winter, it was only in the aftermath of the time change that he glimpsed both male and female perched together on his suet feeder on the deck. A pair of cardinals had been dining daily with him as well over the past few months, but only in March did they begin that loud and slightly comical calling that signals the surging of springtime hormones. Walt has often thought the male cardinal's call sounds a bit like a child's slide whistle—loud and insistent but not exactly musical, though certainly endearing. The wrens are not likely to earn slots in the Mormon Tabernacle Choir either; nevertheless, their distinctive cries of "Wheat-eater, wheat-eater, wheat-eater!" evoke warmer weather even if they don't match the exquisite beauty of the wood thrush's flutelike trills. As an experienced birder, Walt knows, of course, that he can't expect to hear thrush song—a favorite of his late wife, Annie—until substantially later in the year. Decades of living have taught Walt the virtues of patience, and decades of weather watching have taught him that wishing can't hurry the seasons.

Thus, news in mid-March of yet another approaching winter storm did not surprise the suspender-wearing octogenarian, and he decided he would build some plans around the event. Initial forecasts called for three to six inches for the area around Kibbee Pond, but some irregularities in the continental wind patterns made Walt suspicious; even a day or two in advance of the storm's arrival, he thought the area might get belted with even more precipitation than others were predicting, so he decided that the best way simultaneously to defy and respect the weather was to organize some festivities. Since the slow-moving event seemed likely to start Thursday morning and continue through Friday evening, Walt decided to invite friends in two tiers: For lunch Thursday, he would see if he could tempt his lady friend Arlene Tosh to journey down from central New Hampshire and take in an early lunch at Bangkok Gardens, the Thai restaurant in Lunenburg where the couple, and Stumpy, are now regulars; then for a late-afternoon smorgasbord Friday, he would invite his neighbors down the road, the Riggetti family, and his snowplow-driving buddy Todd Jormonen.

Walt and Arlene have been seeing each other at least once a week through the winter, and those who know Walt well—especially Amy Riggetti, the young mother who has grown particularly close to Walt in the past two years—sense that the couple's long-standing friendship is evolving, in ways of which the couple themselves might not yet be fully aware. Friends since high school, both Walt and Arlene lost their spouses some time ago and have learned to function comfortably on their own, but Amy recognizes that both have found together on the shores of the pond something they had been missing by themselves.

Something of a tomboy throughout her life, Arlene is content in warmer weather to putt around the pond in Walt's rowboat Nelly, sometimes even convincing the jovial coot to let her man the three-horsepower Johnson outboard motor that powers that pond-worthy craft. She is nearly as interested in birds and turtles and other forms of wildlife as is her former classmate, often arriving for a visit with several new stories about the deer and bears that populate the wooded acres of her home. Walking the forest paths near the cabin and sharing coffee are also pastimes of which the attractive widow is fond, and the other male in her life, Big Bruno, the elephantine yellow Lab, far-famed for his good nature, his uncontrollable appetite for unsavory substances, and his copious drool, has long been a boon companion to Stumpy. Unlike some residents of New England, Arlene is comfortable driving in snow, and Walt knew that his invitation might be all the more attractive for her because of the potential challenge of negotiating slippery roads. Age is making her, if anything, more daring than she was in her youth. What Amy, another woman, sensed that Walt did not was that Arlene would welcome being snowed in with her chivalrous admirer; women do sometimes know better than men what the men want and are too timid to admit. As Arlene has said to the plaid-shirted geezer more than once, "You know, Walter Walthers, sometimes you are a bit slow." A teasing smile always accompanies that comment.

Walt hates presumption more than just about anything else, so when he called Arlene a couple of days before the storm's projected arrival, he said, "Now, if you have other plans or the weather forecast makes you nervous, please feel free to say no. We can always get together after the roads are cleared."

Arlene's response revealed her usual blend of irony and playful suggestiveness. "Walt," she said, "I'm sure I'll be fine. The Volvo has all-wheel drive, and besides, you know how much I enjoy fishtailing and doing doughnuts. I'll be sure to pack my toothbrush, too, in case we get—you know—snowed in." He could hear the teasing edge in her voice and realized once again how much she enjoyed making him sound prudish. Although her own behavior was beyond reproach, Arlene was good at reminding him that some things are more important than mere propriety.

By the time the silver Volvo pulled into the driveway Thursday morning at 11:00, the snow had begun, and almost an inch coated the ground. Arlene's tire tracks were the only thing to violate the pristine surface until Big Bruno leaped from the back seat to bound toward Walt and Stumpy. The squirrel had begun scratching at the window over the kitchen counter as soon as he saw the familiar vehicle pull in, and now he dashed at his gargantuan friend, then swerved right at the last moment so that the tan fleabag skidded on the slippery ground as he tried to react. Although Big Bruno ended up tilting onto his nose like some cartoon character, he lost none of his high spirits and soon righted himself to scoot back to greet the gray-furred bandit, who had reversed course out of concern. Before either Walt or Arlene could say anything, the huge canine was on his back, nipping playfully at the rodent, who was dancing merrily on his barrel-like chest.

In the next breath, Stumpy had skittered off toward the Volvo with Big Bruno again in hot pursuit, but the squirrel slipped under the vehicle, whereas the dog had to accelerate down the side of the car, his rear legs almost skidding out from under him as he tried to negotiate the turn to meet his buddy on the other side. Walt and Arlene could see nothing for a second or two, but then Stumpy reappeared, weaving back and forth as he rushed toward the watching humans; the dog rounded the front bumper in pursuit, the proverbial mountain coming to Muhammad, and for a moment, Walt feared a collision with that avalanching land mass, suspecting that Stumpy would scurry up his pants leg and that Big Bruno's brakes might not have received servicing recently. Nevertheless, the thundering beast seemed to recognize the danger himself and went into a slide, not unlike a baseball player trying to touch home plate while avoiding the catcher's tag; he ended on his right side to the right of Walt's feet, while Stumpy, having defied his roommate's expectations by circling around behind Arlene, darted back in concern to sniff at his friend's snout. Big Bruno's eyes were closed, and he lay still until Stumpy was in reach of his tongue; then that pink entity snaked out of the dog's mouth to slurp a track of drool across both of the squirrel's gray-furred cheeks and the bridge of his nose. "Ooh!" Walt said, chuckling. "He slimed you . . . and he gets the last laugh. I may need to give the big oaf a bit more credit."

Inside the cabin, the two animal friends continued cavorting, but with a bit more reserve, both because of their surroundings and because of the fatigue factor they were beginning to experience. The two human friends sat near the woodstove and conversed; because Arlene's visits had become so regular, Walt had moved another comfortable chair up from the Bottomless Basement and set it next to his recliner, at an angle that allowed each to see the other as the conversation spun along. Forgetful of time as Arlene's company always makes him, Walt did remember after a few minutes that they had an outing planned and reluctantly said, "Well, if we're going, I guess we'd better *get* going."

Glancing at her watch, Arlene laughed and said, "Time does fly when I'm with you, but I don't intend to miss out on some of Fai's pad prik king. Are you driving, or am I?"

With his somewhat outmoded manners, Walt was nevertheless determined to do the driving, especially since Arlene had already traveled down from New Hampshire. Besides, he had followed the lead of his friend Todd, the snowplow driver, and added some extra weight over the rear axle in the bed of Lulu, his green 1960 Chevy pickup, in the form of two blue plastic brewer's tubs filled with sand; the improved traction made him all the more confident on greasy roads. Of course, the limited size of Lulu's cab meant that Big Bruno would have to stay at the cabin, but tuckered out from his romp with the resident rodent, he would sleep while the others were gone, and Walt was too smart to leave any kind of food out on the counters for the insatiable pooch to scrounge. While Walt was sure that the dog would have loved to join them at Bangkok Gardens, he was simply too large to conceal in Arlene's purse, especially since the understanding with Fai, the restaurant's owner and hostess, was that Stumpy would retire to the purse if any other patrons arrived; although Arlene was partial to large totes, the squirrel already placed a strain on her handbag's capacity, and though Big Bruno's spirit would certainly be willing, his flesh was weak . . . or, rather, his flesh was too substantial to conceal in that manner. Thus the elephantine woofer had to resign himself to a long snooze.

Normally, the ride to the restaurant takes about fifteen minutes, but few cars were out on the roads that morning, and even with Walt's customarily cautious driving (after all, he was once a driver's ed instructor), the diners needed only a couple of minutes more than usual to reach their destination. No other vehicles were in the parking lot, but Arlene urged Stumpy into her bag anyway, just to be safe. "Just push the hand lotion and my compact aside if you need to, Stumpy," she said as the squirrel scooched his fanny around a little to get more comfortable. "But don't go trying out my lipstick. That particular shade just wouldn't go with your complexion."

Walt was chuckling as he came around to help his guest with the door. "Makeup on a squirrel, eh? Maybe that's how red squirrels got red: too much rouge and an unsteady hand with the lipstick!"

Fai was waiting for them inside the door with her customary feigned disapproval for Walt. "Oh, the dirty old man comes back again and brings the attractive younger woman. You'd better be careful," she said to Arlene. "The dirty old man may be looking for a trophy wife!"

"Now then, Fai," Walt countered, "my mantel is already covered with my antique kerosene lamp collection. Besides, you're the one who deserves the trophies, what with how delicious your food is."

"Oh, I might learn to like the dirty old man yet," Fai said, laughing.

"Well now, don't like him *too* much," Arlene said. "I have designs on him myself." As usually happens when the two women team up to tease him, Walt fell into an embarrassed silence.

"Is Hamsterface with you?" the slight, dark-haired woman asked, peering toward Arlene's bag. On cue, Stumpy thrust his whiskered chops out through the mouth of the purse and bobbed his head at the younger woman. "Oh, yes, I see he wants his spring roll now!"

Because Walt, Arlene, and Stumpy were the only customers, the always-ravenous rodent was able to enjoy his complimentary spring roll on the tabletop as the three humans conversed. Vat, the chef and Fai's husband, had come out from the kitchen to say hello and to take their order directly.

By the time their food came out a few minutes later, Stumpy had finished his snack, and Fai asked permission to give him a tour of the dining room. "Of course," Walt said. "He's always fascinated by tropical fish, and I'm sure he'd like to see your tanks close up." As soon as she made her offer, the squirrel eagerly climbed Fai's arm to her left shoulder, where he sat like a dull-colored and featherless parrot.

The restaurant has three ten-gallon aquariums in various corners of its cozy dining room, each with a few fish and some elegant landscaping. One tank features guppies and mollies with a sunken treasure chest as a bubbler, the second is occupied by three personable goldfish who cruise among the columns of some Roman ruins, and in the third swim a variety of large and small catfish that often tuck themselves under and behind the artfully arranged rocks that Fai herself collected from the woods behind the restaurant, washed and soaked, and then placed within to form underwater grottoes and caves. At the guppy tank, where they stopped first, Fai established the pattern of kneeling so that both her eyes and Stumpy's were on the same level as the piscine inhabitants. The furry sightseer nodded his head and chattered softly in appreciation. At their next stop, the goldfish tank, Stumpy leaned forward as the goggle-eyed inhabitants pressed against the glass; they seemed almost as good as the squirrel at begging. "No spring roll for you!" Fai laughed, wagging her finger at the orange koi that continued to stare longingly at the human and rodent faces gazing back into the aquarium.

The catfish tank is clearly Fai's favorite, and she saved it for last to show Stumpy. As the pair turned from the goldfish tank toward that final habitat, Walt paused between bites of steaming chicken pad Thai to say, "Stumpy is a big fan of catfish. He's made friends with an *Otocinclus* at one of the elementary schools where we go to tell stories, so I'm sure he'd like an introduction to all of the residents of that tank."

Fai had been chattering happily in Thai to the squirrel as she carried him around, but now she paused to say, "*Finding Nemo* is partly right: These fish are friends, not food. . . . Other fish are good to eat, but not these!" Stumpy chattered excitedly as a large brown catfish swam languidly out of one of the rock caves and began poking in the gravel along the front wall of the tank.

When the phone rang with a takeout order, Fai warned Walt and Arlene that Stumpy might need to slip into *his* cave briefly when the customer arrived, and that's just what the furry bandit did about fifteen minutes later, when a middle-aged woman came in, shaking off snow, to pay for her order. Unfortunately, when Stumpy had scrabbled back into the purse, he had inadvertently knocked the cover off Arlene's compact, and as he huddled in concealment, the powdered makeup affected his sensitive nose. Just as the parka-clad, heavyset customer was turning from the counter, brown paper bags in hand, Stumpy let out a "*Ya-shew-w-w!*" Thinking quickly, Walt said, "Bless you!" and patted Arlene's arm, but the bag-carrying customer stared at Arlene's bag suspiciously and then raised her eyes inquiringly to Arlene's face.

"I know," Arlene giggled, putting a hand to her mouth. "Isn't it strange? My father was a ventriloquist, and when I was quite young, he taught me to throw my voice. Somehow as I got older, though, I could no longer do it consciously, and instead, for some reason, whenever I sneezed, the sound always seemed to come from somewhere or someone else. I grew out of that, too, eventually, but every once in a while, I do it again. Strange, isn't it?" She smiled warmly at the other woman, who simply humphed and went out the door.

No sooner had the door closed again than Arlene and Fai broke out in gales of laughter, gales stronger than the storm that was now blowing persistent snow against the windows of the restaurant. Walt soon joined in chuckling, and Stumpy, dusted with powder and somewhat abashed, crawled out of Arlene's purse and back onto the tabletop.

"Not my favorite customer," Fai said, wiping her eyes. "She's always complaining. Hamsterface got her good!"

"I'm just glad we didn't get you in trouble with the health inspector," Walt said.

"Oh, Mr. Squirrel is always welcome. You too," Fai said, nodding at Walt and Arlene.

Two inches or more of snow had fallen by the time the trio left the restaurant, and the wipers worked nonstop as Lulu made her way back toward Kibbee Pond. Stumpy was snoring in Arlene's lap, and Walt drove in uncharacteristic silence.

"Is something wrong?" Arlene asked finally.

"Well, the snow is piling up, and the plows aren't out in force yet. Roads are pretty slick. I'm a little concerned about your drive back up to Contoocook, even with that expert Swedish engineering in your Wol-Wo. . . ."

"Why, Walt Walthers," the attractive widow replied, "are you trying to suggest that I should spend the night with you? What kind of girl do you take me for? You ply me with delicious Thai food and witty conversation, but all along, you're planning to take advantage of me!"

Walt's face had gone as red as if it were a sweltering summer day rather than a snowy, late-winter one. "B-but I . . ."

"Oh, you men are all alike! There's only one thing you're interested in, no matter how virtuous a girl tries to be. My mother warned me about you when she first laid eyes on you back in 1939! 'Watch out for that one,' she said, 'all sad eyes and sweet talk. Don't let him fool you! It may take him decades, but he'll get what he wants from you before he's done.'" But with that comment, Arlene could maintain the facade no longer, and her bell-like laugh rang out in Lulu's cab. "Oh, Walt, I'd be happy to spend the night. I'm too old to care what anyone thinks, and I promise *I* won't take advantage of *you.* Still, I'm pretty sure anyone with sense would say this should have happened long ago; we enjoy each other's company too much to pretend otherwise."

"Did your mother really say that about me?" Walt asked.

Arlene broke into laughter again. "My mother told me that the best kind of man thinks more about others and their needs than about his own wishes, and she might well have had you in mind when she said that, but she never had a bad word for you, that's for sure. And don't worry: I'm not trying to move in permanently. I just think it would be nice to sit quietly with you in the evening after dinner and to have you as a trusted companion through the night. Big Bruno fills the bill admirably in many senses, but his conversation is limited . . . and he's not very good at hugging."

Walt said, "Well, you can have the bed, and I can sleep on the couch. . . ."

"Don't be silly," the woman said, reaching over to pat his arm. "There's room for both of us in the bed, and if you like, you can emulate one of those knights from Arthurian legend and put your sword between us. Or maybe you could use that old wooden canoe paddle you keep in Nelly. But I don't see the need. I trust you, and, besides, I've always said that the best part about sleeping with someone is *sleeping* with someone. You've become very dear to me, Walt Walthers."

Walt took his eyes off the road long enough to glance over at Arlene, tip his porkpie hat, and say, "As are you to me, Arlene Tosh."

Perhaps March is not always such a cruel month after all.

And, by the way, when the Riggettis and Todd Jormonen arrived for their dinner with Walt the next day, no one was surprised or disappointed to find Arlene still there. Her presence seemed the most natural thing in the world, especially to Amy Riggetti, for whom the older woman's presence at the side of her dear friend was a consummation for which she had devoutly wished.

39

Stumpy and the New Arrival(s)

June 12, 2013

Walt Walthers has been on the planet long enough to know that most things in life run in cycles and that if you wait patiently and occupy yourself with other meaningful activities, whatever it is you're waiting for may well come back around again. He was reminded of that hope-filled principle recently when four days of late-May rain gave way to a glorious sunny Sunday morning, whose light breeze felt like a gesture beckoning the octogenarian cabin dweller to venture into the woods for a morning walk. Somehow that breeze made him feel that around some bend in the path, beneath the greenery of the burgeoning spring leaves, amidst the rushing babble of some tiny stream swollen into song, he would stumble onto a realization that he had encountered thirty or fifty or seventy years before, a realization that had since slipped away, returning only on mornings like this one, mornings spread out in time like a map he still has not learned to follow. He wondered whether he might, if he rushed out now, round that bend and see his son Larkin as a six-year-old, walking beside him with a fishing pole in his hand and the whole world before him, or whether he might look up at the sound of a bark and see his childhood companion Friday, the collie-cross mutt, racing up the path toward him, fresh from a round of tormenting the local chipmunks and in turn being tormented by them, or whether he might even find himself walking hand in hand with his wife, Annie, gone now these twenty-five years, on their way to some weekend picnic in some other corner of New England. Even without such fantastical intrusions of magic, however, the morning would still have drawn him out, especially with its treasure of birdsong filling the air. Even from the cabin deck, the octogenarian ornithologist could distinguish the swirling metallic song of a veery, the flutelike trillings of a wood thrush (Annie's favorite), and the insistent *teacher-teacher-teacher* of an ovenbird . . . or maybe it was two or three ovenbirds. Perhaps his stretch of woods supports more than a one-room avian schoolhouse.

Walt has read passages that compare such mornings to "newly minted coins," but the mercenary tone of that expression has always seemed inappropriate to him. After all, the fresh smells and clear air left behind by such cleansing have a value beyond any currency, and no one could hope to possess or control them, instead simply to savor them while they last. Walt has also long wondered about the concept of "spending" time. He does see time as having immense value, and he knows that time is easy to waste, but even though he is well into his eighties now, all the time that stretches away behind him does not diminish the value of the moments that still remain ahead. Furthermore, a glorious, sun-swaddled morning at Kibbee Pond, with the wind riffling the water and diamonds of light spangling those riffles, seems almost to carry a person outside time entirely, back to some elemental essence of existence. And the morning's measure-defying value became all the more clear on May 26 this year, when he turned his head where he sat savoring his second cup of coffee and saw his longtime companion and friend Stumpy the stub-tailed gray squirrel soaking up the sun on the deck rail.

Stumpy is, of course, more than willing to accompany Walt on a leisurely stroll through the sun-dappled woods and perhaps even happier to join the silver-haired skipper on a jaunt out onto the pond itself in Nelly, Walt's skiff. Nelly sports a wooden pulpit that Walt constructed two summers ago so his furry roommate could hang even farther out over the water as the three-horsepower Johnson outboard motor pushes the craft gently along. Walt long ago noticed that the rambunctious rodent enjoys taking on the breeze and spray head-on, and he suspects that if he cared to purchase a more powerful motor to propel Nelly, Stumpy would be ecstatic about the wind's attempts to push his cheeks back. Walt can picture the squirrel with his buckteeth bared and cheeks quivering, almost like the dewlaps of a bloodhound riding in a car with its head out the window, except that squirrels, of course, have no such massive caruncular growths. Maybe Stumpy's buddy George the chipmunk, with his species' propensity for storing nuts and seeds in their cheeks, could, were his pouches empty, do some dramatic flapping in the breeze, but the tighter-lipped Stumpy is ill-equipped for that endeavor. If an accident some years back had not severed the rodent's tail near its base, that plume-like appendage might well have done some serious whipping and waving under such conditions; it would at least have made an efficient telltale to indicate wind direction, but Walt has his suspicions that it might even have served as a sail in case the Johnson had stalled or run out of gas.

Stumpy's tail, however, is gone forever, and—frankly—the little guy doesn't seem to miss it. He retains near-perfect balance for racing along deck rails and tree branches, and he regularly hangs by his rear feet while stripping pine cones of their seeds. When he happens to fall overboard during one of the roommates' boat excursions, the absence of his tail actually seems to make him a faster and more efficient swimmer, and while Walt thinks the little fellow might miss his tail during naps in colder weather, when he might like to wrap it, doglike, around himself and use the tip to cover his nose, the sympathetic geezer knows that these days, the squirrel does not have to brave the cold on his own; he can simply come inside the cabin and warm up next to the woodstove or avail himself of other options, like the lap of one of his human friends or the woolen watch cap that Walt keeps at his bedside for his buddy to curl up in.

And speaking of Stumpy's human friends, this may be a good time to mention some changes that have occurred since we last visited with our pond-dwelling protagonists. First of all, Walt and Stumpy have acquired a fairly regular third roommate: Arlene Tosh, the attractive widow who has been the elderly weather watcher's near-lifelong friend, going back even before their high school days, when Walt had an unrequited crush on the young goddess who has aged so gracefully in the subsequent years. Arlene, I say, has moved into the cabin on a more or less permanent basis, although on this sun-and-wind-polished gem of a morning, she was spending a few days back at her house in central New Hampshire, where she has more room to entertain guests. On this particular occasion, the guests were her daughter Hadley, her granddaughter Jamie, and her one-year-old great-granddaughter Paisley, who had all flown in from Minnesota for the early-summer visit that is a family tradition, though the family gathering was extending itself now for the first time to include a fourth generation.

Walt and Stumpy had entertained the four females for lunch a day or two earlier, during the hot spell, and they had all enjoyed sitting on his dock and dangling their feet in the water, where the bluegills could nibble their toes. Having just learned to walk in the last month or so, Paisley still moves with that lurching step reminiscent of the Frankenstein monster, but she had endeared herself to Walt when she first arrived at the cabin by staggering up to him as soon as her mother set her down and then raising both arms in an obvious indication that she wanted the kind-hearted geezer to lift her up. As soon as he had done so, she began pointing at various objects as if to command him to move her closer to them, and he had spent a few minutes narrating the contents of the main room of the cabin: "Oil lamp . . . that's an old-fashioned coffee grinder . . . wooden beam . . . that's my feather collection . . . the big one is from a great blue heron . . . and that's my porkpie hat. Would you like to try it on?"

Arlene was almost beside herself trying to control her giggles as she watched toddler and duffer together. "I can just about imagine you now, back when you were carrying Ross or Larkin or Gavin around. Could they wrap you around their fingers as easily as this little one is doing?"

"I guess they could," Walt replied, "but you may be forgetting that I never had a *girl* of my own to carry around, and I turn to putty in the hands of the females of the species. You know how I feel about my granddaughters and my daughters-in-law . . . and I don't notice *you* ever having much trouble getting me to do what you want either."

"Cha!" Arlene replied, while both Hadley and Jamie smiled.

After lunch, Jamie had donned a bathing suit and carried Paisley down to the sandy shoreline adjacent to the dock. The elders were all content to watch from the dock as mother and daughter splashed in the shallows, but once the two of them began digging in the sand and constructing something like a sandcastle, Stumpy had to get closer and supervise, chattering occasionally as Jamie dumped a plastic bucket of damp sand to shape a tower. The furry foreman, however, kept a bit of distance between the little girl and himself, having had his stump tweaked at lunchtime when he tried to examine the finger foods spread on the tray of Paisley's high chair. His good nature overcame his hesitancy, however, when Walt said, "Say, Paisley, I bet the Stumpster will be willing to go inside your castle if your mom makes an opening big enough for him. Just tell him he can rule over your kingdom as your consort, and his delusions of grandeur will make him toss caution to the wind!" The comment, of course, was intended more for his adult audience than for the yearling.

Walt was right about the rodent's willingness to join in, of course, and everyone enjoyed seeing King Stumpy approach with his characteristic hop-hop-pause-hop gait and then perch himself on the throne Jamie had fashioned from a handful of stones. As the squirrel sat back on his haunches and emulated what he must have considered a regal posture, Walt chuckled and said, "Uh-oh! Looks as though I'll have to send to Buckingham Palace and see if the queen has an old unused crown she can lend us. Summon the servants to bring out a platter of honey-roasted cashews in the meantime!"

Let me pause to reassure any of you who may have noticed the absence of another regular visitor to the pond, Arlene's gargantuan yellow Lab, Big Bruno, who has become another fairly regular roommate for Stumpy and Walt; after all, past stories have suggested that Arlene rarely goes anywhere without her canine companion, that preternaturally large "Drooler of My Heart," as she sometimes calls him in honor of the New Orleans singer Irma Thomas. However, much to his buddy Stumpy's disappointment, this time she had left Big Big at home, concerned that his enthusiastic tennis ball chasing might lead to his inadvertently knocking Paisley over. She wanted to be sure that the younger human generations had a chance to enjoy the water, and she didn't want to risk anyone being washed away by the tidal waves that the dog's leaps into the pond usually produce.

Don't be concerned about Big Bruno being lonely up there in New Hampshire, either, though. Even Walt, who likes to joke about the gigantic pooch having limited brain power, little self-restraint, but a hefty need for attention, has noted the gentle giant's reveling in occasional times of peaceful solitude and contemplation; the burly beast is, in fact, not unlike Ferdinand the bull in his love for sitting quietly in the sun and sniffing flowers. Walt has watched him some days sitting on the sandy plateau above the pond's shoreline and staring off into space, nostrils gently twitching as he savors who knows what daydream-inducing scents on the air. The empathetic geezer, fond of meditation himself, theorizes that in a former life the brontosaur-sized canine might have been a monk or maybe a yogi or maybe even one of the earliest Dalai Lamas. Arlene's New Hampshire house has a huge fenced yard and a saber-toothed-tiger-sized cat flap, allowing the dog to roam freely indoors or out, and Walt thinks that Big Bruno sees his occasional returns there now as welcome spiritual retreats. . . . It must be added, however, that the pooch is always happy to get back to the pond, returning refreshed, with energy and enthusiasm as massive as his physical dimensions.

But we return now to that later sun-and-wind-caressed morning, when the "two swinging bachelors"—as Walt likes to call his roommate and himself—were luxuriating in the Eden-like perfection of the weather, sans Arlene and Big Bruno. On that occasion, Stumpy was showing few signs of pretensions to royalty as he sprawled in a particularly undignified way on the deck rail. "Sorry to disturb you, old buddy," Walt said, "but I can't resist the urge to wander through the woods for a while and then take a jaunt in Nelly, just the two of us, like in the old days. What d'you say?"

A bit of drool dribbled from the corner of the squirrel's mouth as he lifted his head slightly, and Walt realized that the nap and the sun's warmth had figuratively put more cobwebs into his roommate's head than ever literally appear in the cabin, even down in the Bottomless Basement, where Walt actually encourages spiders to live and build their gossamer castles.

"Aw, you can stay here if you like, Stump," Walt said. "You look very comfortable." The squirrel, however, had already sat up on his haunches and was wiping at his face with his front paws, as if he had in fact become tangled in some large arachnid's woven creation. In another few seconds, though, he stretched up tall with his paws in a prayerful posture and bobbed his head three or four times. "Okay, then," the octogenarian animal lover said. "Ready when you are!"

While nothing very remarkable occurred on their walk under the pines and oaks, the two strollers did notice that several lady's slippers were now in evidence, even though some of the earlier wildflowers were dying back—starflower and bird-on-the-wing and false lily of the valley. At one point, Walt commented on the profusion of blossoms just starting to show on the mountain laurel bushes that lined the trail for several stretches. "Wonder if we're gonna have a laurel blizzard this year? I remember a few years back when I'd get confused out here; there were so many of those white blossoms opened up that I'd think maybe it was really February, not June, and we'd had some kind of big snowstorm without my even noticing. That's how unreal those blossoms seemed."

The cruise in Nelly exposed the two crewmates to more of the sun and the steady breeze, so that they were warmed and cooled simultaneously as Nelly putted across the ruffled surface of the pond. Once they had left the dock, Stumpy hopped out onto his pulpit, leaning into the wind for ten minutes or more until the inevitable effects of fresh air and sunlight kicked in; Walt could tell the bobtailed wonder was getting drowsy again as the squirrel's upright posture began to relax, and his chin, which he had been thrusting purposefully into the spray and air currents, began to droop. Just before Stumpy surrendered to the pull of his own soporific gravity, Walt called out excitedly, "Hey, look, old Stumpster! There goes Ralph!" About fifty yards in front of them, a great blue heron had taken wing from the shallows under an ice-weakened leaning birch, and the bird was now winging from east to west just off Nelly's bow. "First time I've seen Ralphie this year!" Walt finished. Although Stumpy had mustered the energy to glance at the long-legged frog hunter ahead, his gray-furred body soon slumped to the deck, and before long, he was on his back on the pulpit, splayed like some kind of mammalian roadkill. Over the quiet purr of Nelly's well-tuned three-horse Johnson motor and the steady press of the breeze, Walt fancied he could hear his friend's breathing deepen to his characteristic snore.

On a morning as beautiful and long-anticipated as that one, Walt was in no hurry to return to the shore, so even with his first mate awash in slumber, he continued his cruise, poking up into coves he usually passes by, causing painted turtles to dive from logs, enduring flyovers by tree swallows that left the upper branches of snags to sail and swoop past like paper airplanes, even startling a beaver at one point, which slapped the water once with its tail before disappearing beneath the surface. Savoring the spring air and the approach of summer, the elderly skipper circled several of the islands in Kibbee Pond, looking for the orioles that, despite the brightness of their coloration, he could hear but not see. He peered as well into the small group of cormorants that perched on one stony spit, hoping to spot Vanderbilt, another avian compatriot that, like Ralph, had wintered elsewhere. Walt knew that the previous summer Vanderbilt had kept himself apart from the sometimes large flock of cormorants that, like teenagers on a city street corner, had hung out on that spit, so the silver-haired skipper did not expect to find the feathered loner in this group now; he assumed that like Big Bruno and Walt himself, the diving bird had a need for regular stretches of solitude. Still, he looked forward to seeing a familiar beak again and to calling out comments and questions to the skilled diver when he would at last find him, perched and drying his wings in the sun.

Stumpy slept through it all, and now, Walt knew he wasn't imagining that he could hear the squirrel's snore; he was certain that no one's chainsaw was cutting down trees along the shoreline, and that was the only other sound that came even close to approximating the racket whenever the gray-furred rascal was sawing wood of his own. From the stern, where he handled the Johnson, the porkpie hat–wearing duffer could see his friend's white belly, turned up toward the open sky, and he could make out the two buckteeth that Stumpy's cheeks had fallen back to expose. In his relaxed state, the reclining rodent looked more like a corpse than a living creature. Laughing, Walt called out, "Come on, Stump! Wake up! I don't want anyone to see us from the shore and think that I've been harpooning baby walruses. I could get into big trouble with Greenpeace that way!"

If Walt's joke didn't awaken the squirrel, Nelly's gentle nudge against the aluminum dock did, and the squirrel shot into wakefulness like a dart penetrating the cork of the bull's-eye on the dartboard. His engines fired almost before his eyes opened, and he achieved liftoff only a second or more later, leaping from pulpit to Nelly's middle seat and onto the dock in one nearly continuous motion, then whooshing up the hill to the deck like a cork released from a wine bottle. A chuckling Walt said, "Hm-m-m. He must think it's time for his midmorning snack! Guess I could use a few cashews and dried cherries myself."

With Arlene still away, the next thing on the duo's docket for that sunny Sunday, the day before Memorial Day, was a visit to an outdoor concert in West Groton featuring the band Grace and Danger. Not only does the core of that band include Walt's great friend Todd Jormonen, the snowplow driver and handyman who spends a substantial portion of his free time at the cabin on Kibbee Pond, but it also includes Todd's son Merle; furthermore, the lead singer is Walt and Stumpy's dear friend and closest neighbor, Amy Riggetti, who lives in a little Cape just down the hill on Kibbee Pond Road from Walt and Stumpy's abode with her husband, Anthony, and their seven-year-old son, Tony.

Early in this story, I mentioned some changes that have occurred among Stumpy's human friends, singling out Arlene Tosh's semi-permanent status as a resident at the cabin. Now I should mention that a second change was impending for the family of Amy Riggetti, who on that beautiful late spring day was in the thirty-seventh week of her second pregnancy. Although both Walt and Anthony had counseled her to curtail her activities with the band until the child was born, Amy—not usually headstrong—had refused, saying, "'Curtail'? I don't believe in *cur-tailing* things. It sounds like something you'd do to a vicious dog or maybe like what happened to poor Stumpy! No *cur-tailing* for me! And if I have to walk around with this bowling ball under my blouse, I think I have the right to make some choices for myself. Besides, I need an excuse to sing these days, just to make me feel like a human being and not somebody's prize broodmare." Walt had forgotten the emotional conviction with which expectant women often speak, and Anthony, husband to this pregnant woman, knowing better than to say anything more, adopted a meek expression.

Thus it was that Amy continued to rehearse with the band at least once a week, though she found that projecting her voice was a substantially greater challenge when she was sitting down, a circumstance dictated by the balance issues that her ever-expanding belly created. However, she had absolutely refused to cancel or even postpone this pre–Memorial Day concert, saying, "How did the Lakota Sioux warriors put it? 'It's a good day to die'? I'd say, 'It's a good day to give birth!' If nothing else, maybe I can induce an early labor and get this torment over with sooner. I want to put a human face and a gender and a name to this watermelon!" I should mention that Amy and Anthony opted not to hear any prediction based on prenatal tests, preferring to be surprised by the child's sex at birth. "As long as the fetus is healthy," Amy had said, "I don't care whether we have a girl or a boy. Knowing in advance would be like having somebody tell you beforehand what's inside your best-ever Christmas present. Some suspense is worth enduring, and some surprises are worth being patient about. Still, I *am* getting a little sick of waiting for Santa to arrive." Although Walt didn't say anything, he had observed that, as her child's birth date drew near, Amy's usually soft-spoken and calmly persevering manner had undergone some changes.

The first part of the plan on May 26 was for Walt and Stumpy to drive to The Square in West Groton, what other people might have called the local baseball "diamond." However, in addition to hosting the concert, The Square is also the venue where the much-loved Squannacook Squealing Squirrels play their Rosehip League home baseball games, and people in the area are very fond of alliteration; therefore, the name has stuck, and the Squannacook Squealing Squirrels play at The Square. Walt calls the arrangement fair . . . and square. With the concert scheduled to start around 4:30 and with various local groups selling a wide variety of foods and drinks and desserts, Walt planned to arrive a bit early, help the band set up, and commandeer Tony for a walkabout to scope out the snack options. Having helped Stumpy into his yarn harness back at the cabin, Walt parked Lulu, the octogenarian's 1960 Chevrolet pickup, then attached his quadruple-strength yarn lead to the Stumpster's harness and made his way into the ballpark. With the remarkable rodent perched on his shoulder, the silver-haired gentleman, tipping his porkpie to anyone the unusual pair encountered, strolled toward the visitors' dugout, where a bandstand had been erected. From some distance away, Walt could see Anthony's tall form, and as the cabin dwellers drew closer, he could make out the winged cat tattoo on the young man's left biceps; a moment later, they both spotted Tony, sitting on the arm of a wooden Adirondack chair, within which Amy was ensconced. Walt kept a firm grip on Stumpy's lead, knowing how excitable the little guy can get in public places and not knowing how many people might have dogs with them.

Of course, the other little guy, Tony, got excited at the sight of his two friends and propelled himself off the chair arm to hit the ground running. "Look out, Tony! Here he comes!" Walt said, because he could feel his mammalian epaulette tensing to jump. And jump the gray-furred bandit did, though the beaming seven-year-old was ready for him and turned to one side so his own anatomical landing strip was directly in line with the flight path of the leaping acorn eater.

"Stumpy!" the tyke shouted as the squirrel touched down and then reached around from the boy's shoulder to grasp the youngster's cheek with his front paws and nibble at the tip of Tony's nose. "Mr. Walt!" he continued, spinning his body to present his hand to Walt for a high five.

"Gee whiz!" Walt exclaimed. "An onlooker would think you hadn't seen us for months, and you were just out in Nelly with us yesterday afternoon . . . but I'm glad to see you, too, and Stumpy has already spoken for himself. Let me say hi to your folks, and then maybe we can head off in quest of snacks. I think I smelled fried dough when I got out of Lulu."

"Yummo, Mr. Walt!" the boy said. "I'll share mine with Stumpy."

After shaking hands with a smiling Anthony, Walt turned to Amy and bowed. She was wearing a gorgeous purple caftan with gold embroidery. "I am yours to command, my queen," the elderly charmer said. "I like your throne, and I hope it's comfortable."

"Oh, Walt," Amy laughed. "I may never be able to get out of it again, the way the seat cants back."

"I thought I'd steal Tony for a minute and find some snack that's not good for either of us. Can I bring you guys back anything?" the old-timer asked.

"I'm fine for now," Anthony said. "What about you, sugar babe?"

"I would love a pint of Ben & Jerry's Coffee Heath Bar Crunch," Amy said, "but I don't think I could sing very well if I was stuffing ice cream into my mouth. Thank you anyway."

I'll pause here to acknowledge that you've known for some time what is going to happen in this story. Right? I don't want to be coy with you, but there still might be one or two rabbits I could pull out of my hat . . . well, not rabbits exactly, but . . . well, you'll see what I mean in a minute.

"Tony," Walt said, "let's go over and see if Todd wants anything while we're cruising the food stands. I'm sure Stumpy will want to see George as soon as possible too. Todd hasn't been out to the cabin in well over a week, and we've missed both of those guys." George, by the way, is the chipmunk who first lived near the Kibbee Pond cabin and was originally Stumpy and Walt's neighbor and sidekick. However, the striped creature later met and instantly became enamored of Todd, and the amiable handyman refused to let George's fondness go unrequited; thanks to the generous nature of Todd's wife, Lynn, George now lives at the Jormonen house on the other side of Townsend.

Todd was just taking his Gibson mandolin out of its case when the trio of visitors arrived. Seeing Walt, the smiling man said, "Oh, Lord, look what the cat dragged in . . . and then decided it didn't want after all." He grasped Walt's right hand with his own. "Congratulate me, old-timer! I'm a grandpa again!"

"Wait a minute," Walt said. "Not Arthel and Doreen again?" Todd shook his head at the reference to his older son and daughter-in-law, who have already given him three grandchildren. "Not Merle and Scrumper . . ." Walt's voice trailed off.

"Nah," Todd laughed, "they're not even married yet. No, it's not one of my human children."

"Not Pudge or Yaz . . ." Walt said, referring to Todd and Lynn's two elderly springer spaniels.

"Naw-w-w," Todd said. "Am I gonna have to tell you?" He paused as Walt raised his eyebrows expectantly. "It's George!"

"George!" Walt said. "That little villain with the convict stripes is a father? That rascal has been sowing some wild oats . . . planting some wild acorns . . . shelling some wild peanuts?"

"Not exactly," the younger man said, eyes twinkling. "George is not a father; George is a mother!"

Once the dust cleared, Todd explained that his chipmunk houseguest had given birth to four tiny munklets a week and a half earlier, a bit later in the year than chipmunks usually give birth, but as a live-indoors-mostly chipmunk, George may have experienced some readjustments to his, or I should say *her*, internal clock—maybe the equivalent of Rodent Savings Time. Todd and Lynn had noticed that George was sleeping more than usual and staying inside the woolen watch cap that hangs just above the headboard of their bed, but it wasn't until a few days of that uncharacteristic behavior had passed that they awoke one morning to the tiniest of squeaking noises and discovered four pink chippies inside the cap with their mom.

"I guess that explains why George didn't dash out to greet Stumpy when we came up, Mr. Todd," Tony said.

"Good thinking, T-man," the smiling musician said. "Say," he continued, turning with mock suspicion toward Walt, "you don't think your juvenile delinquent of a squirrel is the father, do you?"

"What are you saying?" Walt replied in mock horror. "That you wouldn't want to be related to me, even by marriage?" The two men laughed and clapped each other on the back while Stumpy watched from Tony's shoulder.

I could drag things out further here, adding some witty dialogue and building suspense with other distracting and delaying details, but as I said before, I don't want to be coy. Yes, Amy *did* go into labor in the midst of the band's performance, and yes, the baby *was* delivered in the ambulance by Walt's fireman and EMT friend, the Reverend Captain Tommy Hawthorne. But in fairness to Amy, I must say that her water broke only after she was well into the second set, having already earned thunderous applause for her rendition of "Why Don't You Do Right" and for a string-driven version of Aretha Franklin's "Chain of Fools." In fact, the natal action got underway at a convenient time: during a momentary break from the vocal portion of the program while Todd, Merle, Dr. Brad the fiddling veterinarian, and the rest of the band were playing one of Todd's own compositions, a waltz named for a beautiful area in Northern Vermont. True labor came on very quickly, but since the fire station is about two minutes from The Square, Tommy and his partner seemed to think the situation was less urgent than it proved to be. Their sense of timing was just a little off. At least Anthony could ride along in the ambulance and be present holding Amy's hand and encouraging her efforts when his daughter came into the world about two minutes down the road from Nashoba Hospital, and at least Amy's dear friends Walt and Stumpy were already watching Tony, who stayed with them for the rest of the concert. Todd's daughter June was able to fill in for Amy, as has long been the plan for Amy's enforced maternity leave from the band. As it turned out, Anthony called from the hospital as the last song was being played and invited Walt and Stumpy to bring Tony into the ward to see his new sister.

Had the baby been a boy, Anthony and Amy were planning to name him Walthers—Walthy, for short, in honor of their sage and beloved neighbor, but they had been having trouble figuring out how to acknowledge the kindly geezer in a girl's name. They had already decided to follow a family tradition for a daughter's first name, Isabella, but fortunately, the circumstances of Amy's labor suggested a nearly perfect middle name. Thus, the newest resident of Kibbee Pond Road bears the slightly musical moniker Isabella Waltz Riggetti.

40

Stumpy and the Telescope

June 19, 2013

The magical nights of late spring and early summer feed an appetite that seems to defy satiation, and who better to attest to that truth than someone who has been on the planet for more than eighty years? As Walt Walthers, the veteran weather watcher, would agree, hardly anyone can get enough of mild temperatures, gentle sun, and cool breezes, especially after long stretches of heavy rain, when shoes and socks seem perpetually wet and in need of changing. Of course, Walt knows that, without the rain, the jewel-like greenness of mid-June would dull and fade prematurely, but he still contends that in spring and early summer, our deepest hunger focuses on two things: wind-crisped, sun-laden days and clear nights when the stars seem to swoon close to the earth, when the insect calls still sound fresh after several months of silence, and when the air seems tense with the possibility that a moon might any moment make an appearance. Out at Kibbee Pond, where the moon likes to sneak up over the opposite shore from Walt's snug cabin and then stare longingly at its reflection on the water, these nights seem to supply yet another thread weaving together all the years of Walt's long existence in this world he loves so much; each fine evening seems to connect with myriad others in a tangled pattern that the thoughtful geezer still can't fully tease out, no matter how much time he spends staring at the moon and stars or discussing the issue with his now almost permanent housemate, the lovely widow Arlene Tosh. Of course, his other two housemates, Stumpy the caudally impaired gray squirrel and Big Bruno, Arlene's yellow Lab with the gentle soul but elephantine body, do not take part in those discussions, because although they may listen with some interest, they do, after all, lack the capacity for human speech.

When the perfect evenings returned last weekend after prolonged sogginess, Walt and Arlene found themselves drawn to the deck of the cabin, where the view of the pond in the angled sunlight of dusk's approach more than compensated for the occasional mosquito that ignored Arlene's citronella candles and buzzed inquiry in their ears. Stumpy, of course, has proven a mosquito hunter of near-legendary skill, snatching individual kamikaze skeeters from the air with one dexterous front paw and then popping them into his mouth for a bit of supplemental protein; as a consequence, Arlene is unable to tell for certain if her candles are making a significant difference or if the gray-furred epicure is the one keeping the area safe for non-arthropodan democracy. Whatever the case, human and animal housemates alike have come to look forward to an extended session of sitting as twilight falls and as insect and toad calls begin to replace the diurnal birdsong.

To that end, Walt and Arlene have made a couple of adjustments to their living arrangements; first, they have agreed to move the target time for supper back an hour to 5:30, and second, Walt has brought up from the Bottomless Basement and placed on the deck a much-traveled aluminum glider, on which Arlene and he can sit together and rock quietly as they watch ducks and herons winging past on their way to their own nighttime safe havens. If the urge strikes, Arlene can lean her head on Walt's shoulder, or he can take her hand in his as they rock. The glider seat even has sufficient space for Stumpy to join them on one side or in the middle, although these days, the two happy and affectionate elders don't leave much room between them for him to squeeze into; consequently, he is more likely to climb into Arlene's lap and, in that comfortable location, slip into the wood-sawing rhythms of the stertorous. Big Bruno, of course, doesn't fit on the glider even when it is otherwise empty, but lying at the feet of his humans contents him, especially if some part of his body is touching the foot or leg of one of them; through some strange freak of nature, the gigantic canine does not emit snores anywhere near as loud as those of his more diminutive gray-furred companion, a fact that remains a standing joke between the woman with the bell-like laugh and the kindly codger she has chosen as her consort. Unless some unusual event intrudes, the quartet is likely to sit quietly for an hour or more on the deck as night begins its advance and the stars blink again into existence above the water's mirror. Well, come to think of it, I'm not sure "sitting quietly" is ever an accurate term to use for anyone in proximity to Stumpy's snoring.

Occasional conversational exchanges occur between Walt and Arlene, but their thread tends to meander and eventually lose itself again. Walt might say something like, "You know, if there really are divine presences above, this is the kind of night on which they would be wise to leave the celestial existence behind; they very well might choose to descend and take on human form so they can drink up all this perfection—short-lived as it might seem to them, given their constant proximity to the eternal."

Arlene might reply with a quiet "What makes you so sure *I* haven't already done just that? What if I've just been sitting around waiting for you to recognize my divinity? What would you do in that case?"

"Hm-m-m," Walt might reply. "Would a deity say yes to a second slice of peanut butter pie? Would that offer impress a celestial being? It tasted pretty heavenly to me."

"*Some* divinities may be monitoring their caloric intake," Arlene might reply, with a smirk barely visible in the growing darkness. Then she might squeeze his hand as the two lapse back into satisfied silence.

As June has pressed past its halfway point, nightfall has brought the return of one group of welcome visitors, and some might argue that their origins *are* celestial. With the glider positioned thoughtfully—and how else would Walt position it, given his love of these quiet evenings with Arlene?—the sitters can not only see the wind-kissed riffles of the pond's surface, but peripherally, they can also glimpse the shadows that deepen to utter darkness along the edge of the woods that border the cabin's yard. One night last week, as Stumpy was producing neat stacks of cordwood in Arlene's lap and Big Bruno was lying contentedly with his massive head on Walt's left foot, the porkpie hat–wearing geezer gave a quiet "Hmm-m! They're back!" and pointed toward the nearly invisible tree line. There, a tiny light would wink on and then wink off before another light, a few feet to one side and higher up, would do the same. As the two observers smiled at each other, they noticed more of the fireflies spread out along the tree line and nearer at hand.

Walt chuckled and said, "I used to tell my boys that fireflies were fairies, searching for gold that they had hidden long before. Somehow they'd forgotten its precise location, but because they didn't want humans or anyone else to find it, they could search only at night. They came equipped with special bioluminescent lanterns with glowworms inside, and the fairies would fly up and down and all about, looking for any familiar landmarks that might help them remember where they'd put that gold. Come to think of it, that sounds a little bit like me when I buy a bunch of chocolate bars and try to stash them away where the Stumpster can't find them. So if you notice anything unusual in my sock drawer, don't be alarmed. Sometimes I'll stick a Hershey bar in a rolled-up pair of calf-high dress Argyles, just to throw the furred wonder off track." In the gloaming Walt raised his argentine eyebrows at his attractive companion. "Gosh, I hope he really *is* sound asleep right now. Otherwise, I may have given away an important secret, all for the sake of better communication with you!"

"Found 'em already," Arlene whispered with a giggle. By the way, when I said, "argentine eyebrows," I meant that Walt's hair has grayed to silver, even on his eyebrows, not that he hails from South America. His nationality, by the by, is mostly German, not Argentinian, though he does admire the writings of Jorge Luis Borges.

"You know," Walt continued, "I do know one or two stories about how fireflies came to be."

"I'd be surprised if you didn't," Arlene replied, turning to look the unassuming polymath in the eye. "You know one or two stories about just about everything. Why don't you tell me one of those firefly tales?"

"Well, I may have to tell you more than one," the no-longer-drowsy octogenarian said. "There's a Filipino tale and a Japanese one, in both of which fireflies prove to be the tears of supernatural beings who have descended to earth to help people but then fall in love; they're forced, though, to return to the heavens and separate forever from the humans they love. The transformed tears are reminders to the forgetful humans of that love and of the spiritual and intellectual illumination the spirits have brought. I guess they're also a way of suggesting that even though a gulf separates the living and the eternal, some connections remain and light our way to a higher truth.

"There's also a Native American trickster tale that explains how fireflies came to be. It starts with a little star nicknamed Dim Bulb who is envious of his sisters, all of whom are parts of various constellations and therefore important in the grand scheme of things; as a result, however, they have no time to play with him. In his sadness at his own insignificance and loneliness, the little star keeps forgetting to shine—hence his name.

"One night when her own need to shine full upon the earth distracts his grandmother, the Moon, Dim Bulb slips away and drifts closer to the earth, where he sees animals of all kinds playing in the moonlight. When his hope of companionship draws him closer to the animals, Squirrel, the great trickster, notices him and calls out to him. I should mention that I'm taking some liberties with the story, Arlene, changing some species names, though not exactly to protect the innocent, as they used to say in those police dramas in the fifties. I think you'll see, though, that the shoe still fits.

"Well, Stumpy—I mean Squirrel—sees this little star and thinks, Hey, I've never tasted a star before. I bet they qualify as a rare delicacy. And you know by now what a squirrel's appetite is like. So, anyway, Squirrel calls out, 'Hi there, little guy! Would you like to come down and play with us? I can teach you our special dance!' And before you know it, Dim Bulb has let himself be drawn right down to the earth's surface, where Stumpy—um, Squirrel—grabs him and scoffs him down just as quickly as some women I know scoff down peanut butter pie. Stuck inside Squirrel's stomach, the little star is so frightened that he doesn't know what to do; given his track record and name, of course, it just doesn't occur to him to try shining or twinkling the way any other star might have done. Instead, he just hunkers down like Jonah in the whale, blubbering and feeling sorry for himself. Did you like that whale joke? *Blubbering*? I can work in more, you know. That one wasn't just a fluke." Arlene just looked at him in silence, raising one eyebrow.

"Okay, we'll just move along. In the meantime, the Moon has realized that her little grandson is missing, and she sends out a search party of comets. However, they see no sign of Dim Bulb because he is, as usual, still languishing in his misfortune and lying inert inside his devourer. Nevertheless, when Squirrel sees the comets in the sky, he realizes just how much trouble he'll be in if he gets caught, and a sense of guilt and a fear of impending punishment well up within him. He starts scampering about, looking, without luck, for a hiding place. Squirrel's panic increases when, suddenly, the tricky rascal's whole body begins to light up! Dim Bulb, at long last, has finally realized that he can be his own beacon and distress signal simply by doing what should have come naturally all along: shining and twinkling. Inside Squirrel, that little star strains and squirms, like a toddler filling his diaper, and soon his irrepressible star nature is shining forth, and his host, panicked at the thought of celestial revenge as he glows like the Rockefeller Center Christmas tree, coughs away like a cat with a fur ball, then reaches his paw down his throat, gags, and spits up that little lump of light.

"Anyway, the story of Dim Bulb's abduction spreads quickly across the heavens as the comets do their job as messengers and CNN reporters (CNN is the Celestial News Network). Soon, the little star's relatives are all massing to teach Squirrel a lesson, the Clouds calling to the Thunderbirds and everyone together summoning up a huge lightning storm. Old Squirrelly can run, but he can't hide, and a well-aimed lightning bolt—shades of Zeus in Greek mythology—strikes the rascal's tail and sets it on fire. Mortification of all mortifications, he has to jump into Kibbee Pond, or some other similar body of water, to put out the fire, though he is too late to save his plume-like appendage. Among other things, you see, this is a story about why squirrels don't have tails. . . . Oh, wait, that's just Stumpy. Hmm-m.

"Well, anyway, Squirrel's wiles have brought Dim Bulb to earth, and although he wants with all his heart to return to the heavens, the Earth Mother—and by the Earth Mother, Arlene, I mean the original Earth Mother, not you, though the term fits you well too—anyway, the Earth Mother tells Dim Bulb that if she releases her gravity to let him return to the sky, all living things will be drawn off into space as well, and life on earth will end. Thus, the little star will have to live on earth from now on. As consolation, the Earth Mother and his grandmother the Moon agree to let Dim Bulb change into a flying insect so that he can visit the sky even if he can't return all the way to the heavens and be with his family; in addition, they allow him to shine and twinkle still by giving him a minuscule star in his abdomen, knowing that he will never again forget to shine. And that's the story of how fireflies came to be.

"Oh, and in case you hadn't noticed, the story also explains why squirrels are afraid of thunder, a characteristic the old Stumpster here has amply demonstrated in the past. Thus, like most good stories, this one has more than one function." As he finished, Walt smiled at the Earth Mother–cum–celestial visitor next to him in her human form.

"Okay, Professor," the woman responded, the bell-like tinkling of her laugh ringing out. "Where can I sign up for the full course of lectures?" Then she leaned over and kissed him on the cheek. When she did, Big Bruno shifted positions at their feet and let out a sleepy moan.

That reminds me. Some of you may be wondering about how difficult the adjustment to a new home has been for Big Bruno. In fact, the gargantuan canine has always felt comfortable at Kibbee Pond, and given his love for the water, he may actually prefer living where a convenient splash is just a few steps from his front door. *No,* you might say, *I know Labrador retrievers love water. What I was really asking was, How well has the dog adjusted to sharing his mistress with Walt, especially since he had her all to himself for most of his life?* Well, the answer is simple: Big Bruno, or Big Big, as Arlene often calls him, with his big heart, has mastered one of the most important principles in life. He understands that living creatures do not have to dole love out sparingly because they do not possess a merely finite amount of it; instead, paradoxically, the amount of love they can give grows greater with each little bit they give away. Thus, giving love freely to Arlene has left the dog with plenty more for Walt and Stumpy, who have been inspired to return the favor, a circumstance which has made Big Bruno feel all the more loved himself. Besides, Arlene's love for Walt and Stumpy has not taken away from what she feels for and shows to her pooch; if anything, what she feels for her new housemates simply deepens what she feels for her faithful canine companion.

Down the hill from the cabin, however, seven-year-old Tony Riggetti has been going through some big adjustments that may yet prove difficult; so far, though, he's been doing just fine since the arrival of his new sister, Isabella Waltz Riggetti (whose middle name is a tribute to the family's cherished friend and neighbor). Izzie, as Tony and his parents, Anthony and Amy, have been calling their newest family member, has not deprived Tony of any of his parents' affection, even if late-night feedings and the constant responsibilities of an infant presence have left both young parents tired. Besides, Tony has a second home up the road at the cabin, where he is always welcome. And Walt and Arlene have made a point over the last two weeks of taking their young neighbor on special outings, inviting him up for frequent meals, and even hosting him for some sleepovers, which have been occasions for celebration for Stumpy and Big Bruno as well. After all, a dog needs a boy—and a squirrel does too—on a regular basis.

Thus it was that last weekend, Tony joined Walt, Arlene, and their beasts on the deck one lovely evening. Earlier in the day, Walt had ventured downstairs in the cabin to the Bottomless Basement, which is larger on the inside than it appears to be on the outside, and, after moving some boxes and storage crates around, had come back upstairs carrying a rectangular wooden box. With the moon half full and the clear nights seeming to draw the stars closer and closer, Walt thought that Tony might enjoy looking through his telescope, a holdover from the childhoods of his three sons, who had enjoyed camping and watching the stars in the backyard at their old house.

"Okay," Walt said as he helped Tony get the lens adjusted, "see what you can see on the moon's surface, and then we'll take a closer look at some of the constellations too. Maybe we can do some research soon and try to match them up with the appropriate Greek myths. See the Big Dipper up there? They call it that because of the cup there and then the handle that extends back. Of course, some people call it *Ursa Major* instead of the Big Dipper. That Latin phrase means the "Great Bear," though I've always thought the stars together look more like a squirrel than a bear—you know, with that dipper handle being a long, flag-like tail, something a bear doesn't have. When you get done looking, I can, if you like, tell you a Native American story about how the Big Dipper came to be in the sky."

A few minutes later, the two older humans were comfortably ensconced on their glider while Tony was settling back into the small wooden rocking chair that Walt had built for him in the Bottomless Basement during the winter. Stumpy was in the boy's lap, and Big Bruno was settling down with his head on their guest's foot.

"You know how I always tell you what my dad used to say to me?" Walt asked the youngster.

"Sure, Mr. Walt," Tony said. "He always said we shouldn't complain about the weather because there's nothing we can do to change it."

"Correctamundo, pal! But this story is about a great hero who *did* do something about the weather. You see, way back, in the time before things as we know them now were locked into the way they must now remain, the world was a very cold place, and the animals around here had to live with constant snow and ice; in the woods, no birds sang. One day, when Squirrel came back to his nest in a big pine tree, his young son said, 'Pops, I'm cold. I wish we didn't have to huddle together for warmth all day long, and I wish we could find food more easily, because I'm always hungry. You always say you're an important person, and you have powerful friends. Can't you do something to make it warmer?'

"Squirrel, a devilishly handsome creature with a long and shapely tail"—at those words, Stumpy sat up in Tony's lap and began to listen carefully—"yes, devilishly handsome with that full-bodied plume the color of woodsmoke . . . I say, Squirrel blushed at his son's words and hurried away again, mumbling, 'I'll see what I can do. . . .'

"A proud creature, Squirrel had always thought of himself as a good provider and a supportive father, but now he didn't know what to think. He climbed higher in the pine and then crossed over on a branch to another tree and then over on another branch to a third tree, where he sat with his back pressed against the trunk. If he hadn't been a fully grown adult, I would have said he was pouting. Fortunately, though, he realized that there *was* something that he could try, and after he had sat in solitude and deep thought for a few minutes, his plan began to take shape.

"'I'll gather some of my strongest, most resourceful friends,' Squirrel said out loud, 'and I'll take them to the Holy Mountain, where the lower world almost reaches to the land of the sky. The

People Above, who live in the sky, have kept all the warm weather for themselves, and maybe if we can find a way into their land, we can bring back some of that warmth.' After that brainstorm, Squirrel hurried back to his home and announced a feast, to which he invited all his friends; there, he told them of his plan, and three of the bravest and strongest agreed to come with him—Fisher, Otter, and Bear.

"Slogging through the deep snow of the forest took a long time, and they had to cover themselves with snow at night for insulation against the bitter cold. Climbing the Holy Mountain exhausted them further, but they pressed on, and at noon of the third day, they reached the summit. 'Let us give thanks to the Spirit Who Rules,' Squirrel said, and they all bowed their heads.

"'What do we do now?' Bear asked. He was big and strong but not the brightest bulb in the closet.

"'We have to break through the skin of the sky. We'll have to jump up and try to crack it open,' Squirrel answered. 'Who wants to go first?'

"'I'll try,' Otter said, but although a tiny crack appeared in the firmament when he bashed into it, he did not break through. Instead, he tumbled back, landing on his belly, and before he could stop himself, he was sliding all the way back down the mountain. That's how otters came to build slides for their own enjoyment.

"'I'll try next,' Fisher said, but although he made a mighty leap, he simply conked his noggin and knocked himself out without widening the crack.

"'Why don't you go next?' Squirrel said to Bear. 'You're definitely the strongest among us.' And this time, Bear broke through into the land of the sky, a beautiful green land, where the sun shone and vegetables, fruits, and flowers all grew. Fisher was still unconscious, but Squirrel followed his big friend by leaping up and grabbing onto the lip of the hole Bear had made.

Although they saw no people, the two heroes heard birds singing and saw many beautiful houses. Inside the houses were cages full of birds of all different kinds, and Bear and Squirrel immediately released them so that the winged singers flew through the hole down into the world below. 'Good prey for a great hunter like me,' Bear boasted. And thus we have birds in the world now.

"'Quick!' Squirrel said. 'We must make that hole bigger so the warm air can reach our world and make it green too.' Elated by their success so far, the two creatures bit with their teeth and dug with their claws so that the opening grew ever larger. As they looked down, they could see the snow melting and the plants coming to life. 'We've done it!' Bear shouted.

"Just then, however, the People Above came out of their houses and, recognizing what was happening, raced toward the invaders, bows in their hands. 'I'm getting out of here!' Bear shouted, diving into the hole. However, knowing that he had to make the hole so big that the People Above could never again close it fully, Squirrel kept digging and biting and slashing until the angry natives were almost on top of him. Enough warmth had already escaped to ensure that the world would be warm for half the year. Then, knowing that the hole would become permanent if he stalled for time, the brave adventurer shouted a boast to antagonize his antagonists: 'I am Squirrel, the great and mighty ruler of the lower world! I have stolen warmth and life and sent them to my world! Catch me if you can, you fools!' Then he turned and ran to the highest tree in the land of the sky, climbing branch to branch as the People Above gathered around below, drawing arrows from their quivers.

"Like other great heroes, Squirrel had special powers, one of which was imperviousness to injury, except for one spot right at the base of his tail. It was like his Achilles' heel, except it was at the base of his tail instead of on his foot. Though he stood tall and defiant for a long time, an arrow finally hit that one vulnerable spot, and Squirrel plummeted from the tree. He never did, however, hit the earth. Because he was acting for the good of all creatures in the world, the Spirit Who Rules decided to break his fall and place him in the sky as one of the constellations; that way, we who live below can always remember Squirrel's bravery and treat his descendants with respect."

In the darkness on the deck, Tony's jaw was hanging down as Walt finished: "So while some people call that cluster of stars the Big Dipper and others call it the Great Bear, *I* call it the Heavenly Squirrel. Every year, he makes his journey across the sky. When the arrow hits him in the winter, he turns over on his back, but when spring approaches, he rights himself and sets out on his journey all over again so he can once more bring warm weather to us all here below."

"Wow!" Tony said. "So the Heavenly Squirrel is one of Stumpy's relatives?"

"You could say that," Walt replied. "I thought about trying to pretend that the People Above's arrow was the reason Stumpy lost his tail, but I guess that wouldn't have made much sense. Like that constellation, most squirrels do have tails, after all. And even though this one without a tail woke up long enough to hear the story, I suspect that, now, he's about ready to call it a night. Why don't you head on in, too, Tone? You can brush your teeth and get your pajamas on, and once you're comfy in the cot, Ms. Arlene and I'll say good night."

The smiling woman spoke then from her seat on the glider. "Maybe before you go to sleep, Mr. Walt will even be willing to tell you the squirrel story he told me the other night. You can learn a little more about what Stumpy's ancestors were like."

The tailless squirrel was already headed for the kitchen door; having heard a reference to toothbrushing, he figured he might get a chance to snitch some toothpaste from the tube, one of his favorite tricks to pull. Tony quickly followed his rodent pal. "Just don't let Stumpy con you into giving him a squirt of toothpaste to lick off the counter," Walt warned. Over his gray-furred shoulder, Stumpy shot his roommate what seemed to be a dirty look.

Big Bruno was sitting up now, looking a little groggy after sleeping through the tale of the Heavenly Squirrel's exploits and clearly ready to stagger soon to his dog bed indoors. Arlene reached down to pat his enormous head. "Walt," she said, "you remember how I suggested you write the cookbook you've been working on?"

"Ye-e-e-s," the wary duffer replied.

"Well, I have another suggestion. Why not write a collection of trickster tales from around the world, but substitute Squirrel for Brer Rabbit and Anansi and Jabutí and all those other characters? You could work on that one at the same time as the cookbook, alternating days or something."

"Hm-m-m," Walt said. "Sounds promising. But what are you going to do while I'm spending all my time slaving away over my creations?"

"Oh," the laughing woman replied, "I don't know. Maybe I'll just sit out here under the stars and thank my lucky squirrels that I found you!"

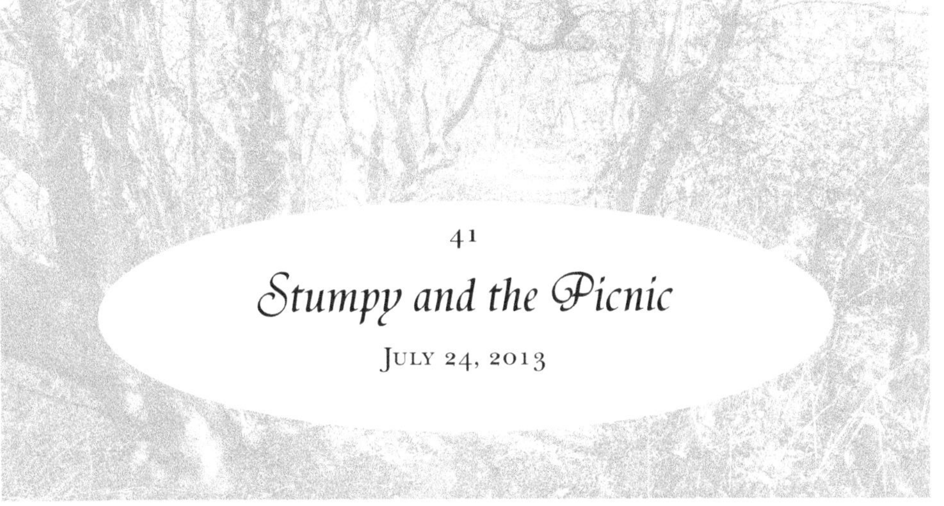

41

Stumpy and the Picnic

July 24, 2013

Out at Kibbee Pond, sultry summer conditions have prevailed recently, and even when the overcast keeps the sun at bay, moving around outside has felt like trying to walk while submerged in warm water. Of course, Walt Walthers, the octogenarian weather watcher who lives in a comfortable cabin out there, has enough years under his belt to know that despite our arrogant egocentricity, we humans can't shape the weather to our liking, and—besides—his professional experience reinforces the idea that if we can't change the circumstances we live in, sometimes we have to change our attitudes and behavior. Accepting an inescapable reality is sometimes the first step toward reclaiming control over our lives. I believe some popular cliché exists about lemons and the beverages that people can make from them, and while Walt is not fond of clichés, he does like lemonade, with the way the sweet and the sour interpenetrate each other. He agrees with the basic sentiment that sometimes we have to make virtue of necessity, as the Roman writer Boethius would say, and simply seek out the positive elements in a negative situation.

Walt is lucky in many ways, one of them being that his housemates are no more prone to pointless complaining than he is. For instance, Arlene Tosh, the striking widow and former classmate of his who lives almost full-time at the cabin now, refuses to let steamy conditions dampen her enthusiasm for time spent with Walt, even if the humidity does literally dampen her clothing on some occasions; she remains just as eager for their morning boat rides as she was the first time her silver-haired consort took her out in Nelly, the dependable skiff with the quiet-running three-horsepower Johnson outboard, and she continues to rave about the flavor of the vegetables that come from Walt's gardens, claiming that they are even tastier than the ones she grows herself at her house in central New Hampshire. Furthermore, as much as she adores her preternaturally large yellow Lab Big Bruno, she has become equally fond of Walt's faithful rodent sidekick Stumpy the squirrel, who has been spending even more time lately in her lap than in his *longtime* roommate's. As she puts it, "Here at Kibbee Pond, I get two for the price of one: two adoring animal companions, both of whom seem to think that I'm the Queen of the Universe. Now that I think of it, though, you, Walter, qualify as a third adoring animal, so maybe I'm actually getting a three-fer! Peel me a grape and fan me a bit faster, will you, my pet?"

Of course, living next to a well-shaded pond is in itself a consolation in hot weather for a philosophical bloke like Walt . . . and it would be for most other folks too. The silver-haired geezer appreciates the cool breeze that seems to come off the water even when the temperature has ramped itself up. Furthermore, if the humidity is settling in already as Arlene and he sip their coffee in the early morning, and if the sun is seeming a little too intense up on the deck, the clever coot can break out the short-legged aluminum folding chairs that he keeps in the tiny lean-to near the dock and set them up in the shallows so that Arlene and he can plunk themselves down in a comfortable, semiaquatic state. If the omnipresent sunfish drift in close to investigate and even begin nibbling at the humans' toes or the fine hairs on their legs, the elders can amuse themselves by playing tag with their finny neighbors, trying to nudge them before they nibble. It doesn't take a lot to amuse Walt, a quality that makes him pleasant company even in weather that makes most people miserable.

As you might have guessed, the two housemates rarely go out the cabin door without the dog and the squirrel tagging along. That huge drool factory Big Bruno is always looking for a chance to get into the pond, and when the angle of light is right in the mornings, he likes to cruise up and down the shoreline, belly-deep or deeper in the water, wading with his head tilted at an angle so he can see beneath the surface; that massive skull turns systematically back and forth, left and right, and every once in a while, he will plunge his snoot or even his whole head into the depths, tail wagging feverishly. Sometimes, too, he'll suddenly change direction, eyes focused and tail whipping, to double back on his course as if in pursuit of an evasive quarry. The first time Walt saw the gargantuan canine in the midst of these maneuvers, he turned to Arlene with a grin on his face. "Is that crazy mutt fishing?" he asked.

"Well, of course he is!" the woman replied, her hazel eyes smiling. "Big Big is a creature of many talents."

"Has he ever caught anything that way?"

"Well, no, not that I've ever seen," Arlene said, "but don't you claim that you like to go fishing although you don't even bait the hook anymore? The pleasures of fishing are countless, and some of the greatest ones have nothing to do with whether you catch anything, as you've told me yourself."

"Hm-m," Walt said. "I can't argue with that logic, but I also can't claim that his technique is very subtle, even if it is somewhat entertaining. Maybe we should get him a conventional rod and reel and even a porkpie hat of his own to keep the sun out of his eyes during his piscatorial pursuits." Walt, of course, considers himself to have committed a fashion faux pas if he steps out the cabin door without his own porkpie firmly in place on his head.

While the other three companions are cooling themselves by placing some or all of their body parts in the pond, Stumpy usually takes a more conservative approach, employing his typical hop-hop-pause-hop gait as he nears the shoreline, then bending down to take a quick drink before turning to rummage among the bushes around the bases of the big pines. If he has luck locating some blueberries, he'll help himself to a snack, then return to the shore to dip his front paws into the water, like a small child at the ocean trying to accustom himself to the ankle-ache-inducing water before taking the plunge. Stumpy, however, rarely chooses to immerse himself, even in the hottest weather; although he is not averse to swimming (and is a surprisingly fast and efficient swimmer when he does get in the water), he sees no need to compete with his new housemate, the natatorially inclined pooch. In fact, he seems glad that Big Bruno takes on himself all the pressure to amuse the humans with his cavortings in the water, thus relieving Stumpy from any aquatic obligation. Besides, even if he does need to cool down, the squirrel is often in the line of fire when Big Bruno finally gets around to shaking. No, puttering on the shoreline is more Stumpy's style these days, though he does remember his crazy youth, when a similarly crazy Big Bruno lived for nothing more than to run and leap off the dock in pursuit of tennis balls and when the squirrel himself—inadvertently and then purposely—rode the gigantic dog's back like a scuba-diving buckaroo on more than one occasion. Seeing his three friends indulging themselves along the water's edge these days, however, sometimes inspires the gray-furred rodent to take a philosophical viewpoint not unlike that which Walt often evinces, seeking out a grander perspective from the upper branches of the magnificent white pines that surround the cabin; sprawled in the shaded heights, he can keep an eye on his friends but also play sentinel with his view of the whole pond and a good angle backwards on Kibbee Pond Road and any visitors that may wend their way toward the cabin.

One day last week, while Big Bruno was fishing and Walt and Arlene were drinking coffee and sitting with their feet in the water, some visitors did arrive, and from his lookout in the pine, Stumpy recognized the black pickup immediately. As a measure of his excitement, the gray-furred watcher was down the rough-barked tree almost as quickly as a firefighter might slide down the pole at the station on her way to an emergency call. Spurring the Stumpster on in his precipitous descent was his affection for the driver of the truck and for that driver's usual striped companion. He had, of course, immediately recognized the black Ford F-250 that belongs to Todd Jormonen, the middle-aged snowplow driver and handyman who has long been Walt and Stumpy's boon companion, and the squirrel knows well that, as in the nursery rhyme, wherever Todd goes, his sidekick, George the chipmunk, is sure to follow. Like Mary's little lamb, Todd's little chipmunk exhibits deep devotion to her human companion, but unlike a sheep, a creature that flocks and follows instinctively, George most definitely has a mind of her own and has *chosen* the object of her affection rather than simply imprinting on him.

Of course, Walt had named George, and the chipmunk had gone to live with Todd, long before either human realized that

"George" was a misnomer because George herself was a *miss*, no more nor less; back in the spring she had unexpectedly given birth to four little munklets in the wool watch cap that Todd's wife, Lynn, keeps tacked slightly above their headboard, where George has slept since she first arrived at the Jormonens' last summer. The human couple has happily supported the unwed mother and has quickly adjusted their thinking about her gender, though they haven't changed her name. After the births, George raised her litter and weaned them quickly, having already dug an extensive burrow with a labyrinth of tunnels outside the Jormonen residence; from that burrow, the young chipmunks now emerge regularly to greet their human family and any visitors. They have been surprisingly responsive to Lynn's basic training, but then a shelled peanut is a powerful bargaining tool when you're dealing with ground or tree squirrels. Walt knows that principle from his years with Stumpy.

As is usually the case, Stumpy and George greeted each other that morning with great enthusiasm and little restraint, the chipmunk launching herself from the truck seat as soon as Todd got the pickup door open, and the squirrel barreling across the gravel driveway like a freight train at full throttle. Despite the apparent inevitability of an injurious collision, however, the two rodents proved themselves nimble enough to avoid disaster, and when the actual contact came, it seemed like something as skillfully choreographed as a performance on *Dancing With the Stars* or *America's Got Talent*, though I don't think any of the onlookers for this hoedown would have made comparisons to the Bolshoi Ballet or the Alvin Ailey Dance Theater. Funny how absence makes the heart grow fonder—was it Henry Fonda or Jane Fonda who originated that expression? It is an expression that Walt is kinda fonda, although, as I said before, he doesn't generally like clichés. In any case, the enforced separation brought on by the birth of George's stripe-wearing progeny seems to have *re*inforced and perhaps even deepened the furred friends' affection for each other. Just as Walt and Todd have discovered much that they have in common despite their age difference, Stumpy and George seem to view themselves now as kindred creatures despite their gender and species difference, particularly in the way both interweave their adaptations to the human world with their identities as residents of the natural world.

Todd, a friendly faced fellow in his early sixties with a thoroughly gray beard and a New Hampshire Fisher Cats cap on his head, shouted down the hill to the water, “Better get up here quick, old-timer. Your pet piranha is trying to maul my innocent young ward, and I don’t want to take matters into my own hands. I might have to stuff the rascal into my pocket and let him eat honey-roasted cashews until he explodes.”

Having stood up at the sound of the truck’s approach, Walt was already climbing toward the deck, and from there, he spoke his retort: “What is this, a prison break? Or did you just snatch that vicious beast of yours off a local chain gang? For crying out loud, she’s still wearing her striped convict’s pajamas!”

By the time Walt had finished his joking accusation of criminality and moral turpitude, he was stepping off the deck, right arm outstretched, and the smiling men were soon shaking hands in the midst of their chuckling. At that moment, the two rodents, who had been happily continuing their tussle, broke free of each other, and each one made a dash for the other’s master, Stumpy leaping from the ground to Todd’s outstretched arm but George pulling up short at Walt’s feet, baffled by his bathing trunks because she normally just scrambles up the pantlegs of his usual chino work trousers. When Walt bent over and offered her his cupped palm, though, the chipmunk hopped in, and he raised her to his shoulder, from where she put her front paws on his cheek to nuzzle at his ear. Meanwhile, Stumpy had draped himself around Todd’s neck like a furry boa fashion accessory while the handyman dug into his pocket to pull out the leguminous delicacies to which he had alluded earlier. He handed a cashew over to George after feeding two to Stumpy.

From the other side of the truck came a woman’s amused voice: “I swear those two critters are bigger moochers than Pudge and Yaz ever have been. And you two encourage them with your own antics. How is anybody else going to earn their affection with you two bribing them all the time?” The speaker was Lynn, Todd’s tall, ash-blond wife, who had gotten quietly out of the passenger’s side of the truck while the rest of the hullabaloo was going on. “Imagine how happy your lives would be if you just treated the women you claim to be devoted to with as much indulgence as you show to these, your wayward children!” She stopped her mock tirade as Big Bruno snuffed happily up to her, licked her kneecaps, and began pushing at her shapely shorts-clad legs with his massive head; when Lynn reached down to pat the big dog's rump, his front end collapsed at her feet, and he began swinging his bottom back and forth in the air and groaning happily as the woman continued her ministrations. "I guess I haven't lost my touch after all," Lynn continued, "even if those two lazy springer spaniels of mine don't even get up to greet me anymore; they just lie there and, if I'm lucky, flap their tails a little against the floorboards. About as enthusiastic as my husband!"

"Now, my gorgeous darling," Todd countered, "you exaggerate. I wag my fanny at you all the time, and I even go out to the mailbox to fetch your morning paper. Isn't that devotion?"

"Yes, and I'd be a totally happy woman," the laughing wife replied, "if you didn't shed so much and I could finally get you housebroken." The big dog was now flat on his back in the gravel, gyrating and panting in a state close to ecstasy. "Gee whiz, Walt," she continued, "you'd think from this greeting that your critters didn't even know we were coming for the picnic today."

"Oh," Walt said, "well, maybe, just maybe, accidentally on purpose, we forgot to tell them."

By this time, Arlene had also crossed the deck, and now the elegant widow was hugging Lynn, who laughingly called her attention to her elephantine pet rolling in the gravel, tongue lolling and tail thrashing, looking up at both women as if Cupid's arrow or maybe two of Cupid's arrows had just pierced his breast.

"Yes," Arlene said, "we thought we'd experiment and see whether surprise would increase the critters' excitement at your arrival. Besides, we feared that if we told them in advance, they would keep staring out the windows and whining until you arrived—or at least Big Big would keep whining—and he, of course, still hasn't learned the difference between today and tomorrow, so he certainly doesn't understand the pleasures of anticipation."

"I know what you mean," Lynn replied. "We asked George yesterday evening if she wanted to go see Stumpy for a picnic today, and she kept poking us all night, hoping it was time to get up and leave."

I didn't warn you readers, either, but I hope you can forgive me. Walt and Todd had for some time been wanting to take the women for an outing to one of their favorite islands, and the steady run of hot weather had convinced them that coupling a picnic with a splash at what Walt called the Swimming Place could supply a pleasing respite from the steamy weather. Thus, they had finalized the menu the day before on the phone and had agreed to set out around ten in the morning. While Walt and Arlene led the way in Nelly, Todd and Lynn would follow in Walt's metal canoe, Tippy Tyler 2. Upon hearing the canoe's name that morning, Todd chuckled and asked, "What happened to Tippy Tyler 1?"

"Oh, there was no Tippy Tyler 1," Walt replied. "I just thought it would be funny to pun on that 1840 Whig Party campaign song, 'Tippecanoe and Tyler Too.'"

"I see," Todd said, trying not to give Walt the satisfaction of laughing, though not fully succeeding, "but just how tippy is this canoe?"

"Well, I've never tipped it over except on purpose," Walt said. "I know how unbalanced you are, though, so I can't make any promises. Lynn, just make sure you're wearing a life vest with this maniac at the helm."

"Are you kidding?" Lynn said. "Just getting in that pickup with him, I say seven Hail Marys and cross myself before fastening the seat belt and checking it twice. Getting in a boat with him, let alone a tippy canoe, will confirm that I have some sort of subconscious death wish."

The plan was straightforward. While Todd and Lynn paddled the canoe, with Stumpy and George accompanying them, Walt and Arlene would putt along in Nelly, putting to the test all the hours of Big Bruno's training over the last two months. In case I haven't already told you, most mornings before their longer boat outing to explore the pond, the two elderly cabin dwellers have invited the gargantuan pooch into Nelly for a short jaunt along the shoreline close in; given his bulk, the possibility that Big Big might capsize the skiff with one ill-timed and unplanned lunge had kept the captain and his second-in-command from venturing out onto the pond proper while the dinosaur-sized dog was aboard. This morning, however, was a chance for the water-loving retriever to extend his seafaring range and join the outing to the largest of the islands. Arlene knew that her canine compatriot would be disconsolate if they left him behind on an occasion this special, one which might prove to be the biggest social event on the summer's calendar; thus, Walt and she had decided to brave the potentially soggy consequences and offer this possibly premature invitation to the motel-sized mutt.

For most of the year, the fire engine red–hulled Tippy Tyler 2 lies inverted under a row of hemlocks just up from Walt's dock, so the effort to turn her over and slide her into the water was minimal. The silver-haired skipper and trip leader had brought down two extra life vests for his human guests as well as two paddles. Big Bruno, of course, loves the water, and as a Labrador retriever with the breed's legendary buoyancy, he seemed unlikely to need a life preserver of any sort; both Stumpy and George were already seasoned veterans as boaters, though Walt did supply one cushion for each of them in the canoe, as much to provide a comfortable seat during the ride, however, as to prepare in case he heard a shout of "Rodents overboard!"

For the picnic itself, Walt had prepared a batch of his chicken salad with green grapes and scallions and a sour cream and Dijon mustard dressing, a longtime summer favorite among his friends, especially when served with his own lettuce and fresh cherry tomatoes, and Lynn had fixed a green bean and kale salad from her own garden. To top off the meal, Arlene had cooked a batch of gluten-free lemon-blueberry muffins sweetened with a little maple syrup and had also labored over her world-famous homemade lemon-lime-ade. With his usual claim that he was too good-looking to labor over a hot stove, Todd had said instead of food he would bring his adored-everywhere sunny disposition and his mandolin, in its special waterproof bag; that way, he claimed, "I can brighten everyone's day with my smile and my plectral prestidigitations." Lynn simply groaned at her husband's comments. Of course, Walt had packed some honey-roasted cashews as a treat for Stumpy and George and some peanut butter–flavored dog biscuits for Big Bruno.

With the main cooler loaded into the stern of Nelly, where Walt could keep it secure while operating his beloved and now-antique Johnson motor, the party loaded themselves into their vessels for a leisurely cruise around the pond before seeking out the spot they had chosen for their lunch and splash. Part of the fun for Walt was pointing out his bird friends when they came upon them. As they paddled and putted up into the swamp to the north of the cabin, he called a greeting to Ralph, the great blue heron with whom Walt has been communing for the last couple of summers and who was doing some of his step-freeze-and-strike style of fishing in the shallows. "Hey, Ralph, care to come over and meet Todd, Lynn, and Big Bruno? You know the rest of us already, I think." The bird's only response, however, was to turn his crooked pipe-cleaner neck toward them for a moment before going back to his slow stalking. A bit later, as they approached the big island where they were to picnic, Walt also pointed out Vanderbilt, the cormorant who, for reasons not discerned as yet by the silver-haired naturalist, seeks out solitude instead of congregating with the other seven or eight members of his species that frequent the pond and hang out on fallen logs like a group of teenaged humans on a street corner.

As if he had been promised a barrel of dog biscuits as a reward for staying still while in Nelly (and for all I know, Arlene could have made just such a promise), Big Bruno held himself nearly as steady as a statue during the half hour or so required for their slow-moving tour, shifting only his head to peer at various highlights along the way. A delighted Arlene crooned praise at her pet from time to time. "Oh, what a good Big Big! He's Mommy's good boy!" Walt, of course, rolled his eyes in the direction of the canoe as she spoke since the woman's back was toward him, but Arlene realized what was happening anyway. "I know what you're doing, Walter Walthers," she said more than once. "I used to tell my daughter I had eyes in the back of my head, and she believed me. Now maybe you will too!"

On board the canoe, George and Stumpy were decidedly worse-behaved than their canine counterpart. Like small children drunk on the excitement of a special event, they tussled and wrestled under the seats of the craft and even raced along the gunwales, heedless of warnings from both Todd and Lynn, who were also busying themselves with paddling; with the woman in the bow and her husband manning the stern, the central part of Tippy Tyler 2 was open space for the rodent rascals' romping. The tailless squirrel even proved oblivious to the chastising comments of his longtime housemate, who called out such gentle reprimands as "Hey, ol' Stumpster, why don't you settle down? You don't want Todd and Lynn to think you're a malfeasant, do you?"

Before the misbehavior had frayed anyone's nerves too much, the quartet of humans pulled their crafts up onto the sand of the crescent-shaped patch of the island beach where they planned to lunch; then they unloaded the cooler and the blankets and the folding short-legged chairs they had brought along in the bow of the skiff so the group could lounge in the cooling water. Out on the island, a persistent breeze penetrated the pines and oaks, sweeping from the north side to the south, where the picnickers were establishing their site, so that the shade and the movement of the air were already counteracting the muggy heat the voyagers were seeking to escape. Of course, stepping even ankle-deep into the pond had further mitigating effects, and those who chose to immerse themselves completely found further refreshment in the time before lunch. Big Bruno was among those who went whole hog, even swimming out along the adjacent spit of land with its line of trees and blueberry bushes, as if hoping to discover a new world and plant a flag claiming it for the future generations of dogdom. While Walt and Todd stood waist-deep in the shallows, playing foot tag with the bluegills residing there and watching the tawny battleship of a dog steam out on his explorations, Arlene and Lynn took a plastic container each and wandered up onto the island, soon finding a wealth of blueberry bushes that the cedar waxwings and other avian fruit lovers had not yet harvested; Stumpy and George went along with the women, still galvanized by the occasion and seeming to have made a compact to race each other up to the lowest branch of each sizable tree they encountered, sometimes going straight up but other times going around and around as if using their bellies to paint the stripes on a barber's pole.

Lunch came an hour or so later, and the rambunctious rodents slowed down enough to scoff some blueberries, some grapes from the chicken salad, and as many of the honey-roasted cashews as the humans would give them, then begging for still more. Shaking his head, Walt said, "No more for now, you bandits! Between the fruit and the cashews, you're probably already on enough of a sugar high to last you until bedtime and even beyond. Why don't you just go explore some more and see if you can burn off some of that energy?"

With a chorus of *chit*s and squeaks, the two furred tornadoes spun away from the blankets spread in the shade. Big Bruno, now in his seventh year and tuckered out from his extended aquatic excursions, snored on one of the blankets with his horse-sized head at Arlene's feet. He was content to let the younger animals amuse the others with their antics, and he still seemed a bit groggy when the time came to reload the boats and head back to the mainland. Todd's mandolin playing had apparently enhanced the depth of the big dog's dozing.

With Nelly purring quietly, the gigantic retriever placidly resumed his position amidships, sitting between Arlene's legs and facing forward, tongue lolling as the Jormonens' canoe kept pace a few feet to port. Not far out from the Swimming Place, however, his bucktoothed counterparts on the canoe resumed their misbehavior, galloping and gallivanting from stem to stern and finally running without warning straight up Lynn's back so that she dropped her paddle into the drink.

"Now, Stumpy, you cut that out!" Walt shouted. "You're embarrassing me in front of my friends."

At the uncharacteristic sternness in Walt's voice, Big Bruno stood up with a lurch and a deep bark—*oof!*—launching himself at the starboard gunwale of Tippy Tyler 2, which seemed more than happy to live up to its name as the canine Godzilla arrived. Even if Lynn had not been leaning out the same side to fetch back her paddle, the weight of the dog would probably have been sufficient to overturn the canoe, but with the woman's already awkward position, Tyler proved all too tippy, and the four passengers and the high-flying pooch all ended up in the water. Somehow, Nelly did not capsize after the dog's leap, though she did rock back and forth for some time. Fortunately, both Todd and Lynn were laughing when their heads broke back through the surface.

"Man overboard!" Walt called, intending the slight delay to underscore the humor of the situation.

"Yeah, or *woman* overboard!" Lynn sputtered as she tried to catch her breath.

"Well, we could try 'chipmunk overboard' or 'squirrel overboard' or even 'dog overboard' if we wanted," Arlene quipped.

"Arlene," Todd said, laughing, "maybe we should say 'elephant overboard!' That was like a scene out of *Dumbo,* and I believe I can now accurately say that I *have* seen an elephant fly . . . or at least the canine equivalent."

Still laughing, Lynn said, "I was just about to say we needed to throw a bucket of cold water on those two rodent scalawags when Big Big provided the bucket. . . ."

". . . or at least the canine equivalent," the floating couple said in unison.

The massive yellow Lab also provided the canine equivalent of a Coast Guard rescue boat—not unlike those that both Walt and Todd had manned in their different eras in that service—and the big dog cruised up to first George and then Stumpy, dipping his snout so each drowned rat could clamber up onto the fur-covered deck behind his brow ridges, where they huddled, looking suitably chastened, until the dog strode up onto the sand of the island they had just left. After lying down so that his bedraggled passengers could disembark easily, the colossal beast stood up again and shook onto them all the water his coat had absorbed while he was swimming.

"Well done, big guy!" Walt shouted as he pulled Nelly up to the bow of Tippy Tyler 2 and attached a rope so he could tow the water-filled craft ashore. There, dumping it out would be easier than attempting some other maneuver on the pond's surface. Todd and Lynn had already waded ashore, whereupon the embarrassed squirrel and chipmunk crawled closer to make their abject apologies. The humans were all trying not to laugh at the obvious contrition the guilt-ridden rodents were displaying.

Moments later, as Todd and Walt rolled the canoe onto its side and the water poured back out of the bilge and into the pond again, the octogenarian skipper pushed back his omnipresent porkpie and chuckled. "I can't decide whether bringing Big Bruno was a mistake or exactly the right thing to do. Those two weren't about to listen to us, you see, and it took a pachydermal pooch attempting to fly to snap them out of their naughty behavior. I suspect there'll be peace in the valley for a while now, though." As if to prove the truth of that statement, each of the soaked cashew chompers slunk up to the feet of its beloved human, clearly craving forgiveness. Each man stooped down to pick up the culprit in his care; Walt cuddled Stumpy to his chest, and Todd did the same with George.

"Parenthood isn't easy," Todd said, trying to conceal his amusement from the animals.

"What do you mean, you whippersnapper?" Walt said. "Imagine what it's like at my age!"

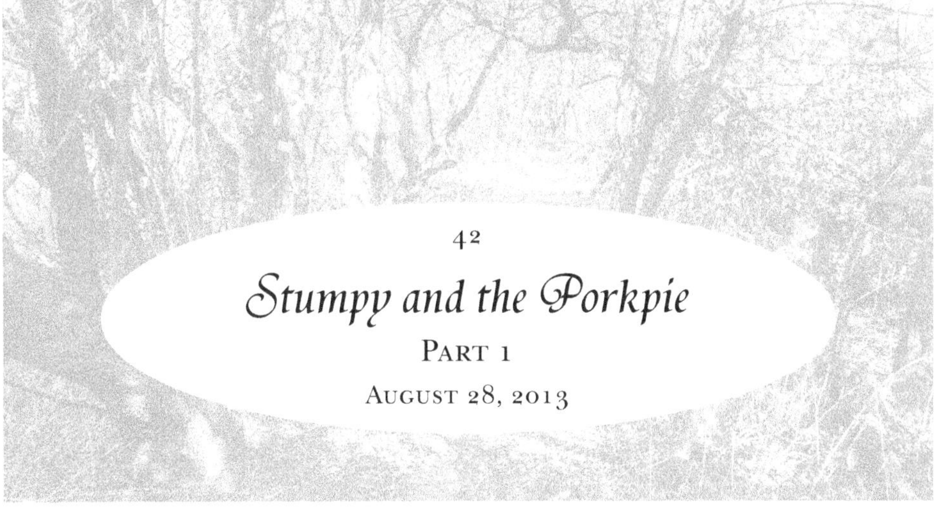

42
Stumpy and the Porkpie
Part 1
August 28, 2013

Certain objects have taken on iconic status in American culture or even world culture: Robin Hood's bow, Charlie Chaplin's cane, the Lone Ranger's mask. However, in day-to-day life, we also associate ordinary individuals with trademark items: your mother and her cooking apron with the embroidered flowers, your favorite teacher and his sweater vest, your uncle Ernie and his Swiss Army knife. Walt Walthers, the elderly weather watcher who lives out at Kibbee Pond with his trusted cohort and chief partner in crime, Stumpy the stub-tailed gray squirrel, hardly qualifies as ordinary in *my* opinion, but he, too, ordinary or not, would hardly seem himself to most people without his trademark: his easily recognized and omnipresent porkpie hat. At some point in all the stories I've told you about Walt, the porkpie has come up, and while on some occasions he will substitute another kind of headgear or even go entirely hatless, that hat is a kind of trademark or landmark or signpost or at least reliable indicator by which travelers who've never laid eyes on Walt might nevertheless recognize that they have arrived at Kibbee Pond, that fabled location for the legendary Walt and Stumpy's exploits.

Well, Kibbee Pond isn't *exactly* fabled, except inasmuch as it provides a location where animal characters often act as if they were human and where sometimes simple truths do emerge by the story's end about the benefits of compassion, openness to wonder, and so forth. It does, in those senses, seem an appropriate setting for a fable. Walt and Stumpy aren't exactly legendary, either, especially inasmuch as they are not characters in ancient stories. They might, however, to someone's way of thinking, deserve—on moral and ethical grounds—to be as famous as those more obviously and traditionally heroic figures who appear in the legends of King Arthur and Sigurd and Charlemagne or any other noble-born champions of traditional cultures. The stories about Walt and Stumpy might even have greater credibility than those other, more-heralded tales—perhaps because the man and his loyal squirrel seem more down-to-earth and ordinary than Odysseus or Gilgamesh or biblical figures like Moses. No, Walt and Stumpy have no pretensions to greatness, but they are in many ways big fish in their small pond—well, Kibbee Pond isn't exactly small as bodies of fresh water bearing the appellation "pond" go, but I think you know what I mean. It's no Atlantic Ocean, and it isn't even Lake Winnipesaukee. Of course, for that matter, the old codger and his furry companion are technically mammals and not fish, but again, you know what I mean. Navigating through this English language with all the mines and torpedoes provided by clichés and idioms and double meanings is never easy.

Yes, Walt has been wearing his porkpie for a long time, and few living people remember a time when that headgear was not a regular part of his habiliments. Of course, dead people probably have an even smaller chance of remembering a hatless Walt, since, as I understand things, they're not likely to remember *anything.* All I meant was that some people who are now dead *were* around when our octogenarian hero first donned his characteristic noggin shader, so, if they were still alive, they might be able to remember the story and possibly even supply some further details. Of course, given the nature of stories and the unreliability of human memory, the presence of a second raconteur might lead to a *Rashomon*-like moment, in which alternative versions of the same story existed, with each teller firmly convinced that his or her version was the only accurate one. So, maybe we're just as well off with only one person telling the story. But I'm not quite ready to tell that story yet, and I'll probably let Walt himself tell it when the time comes. So let's just pause now to consider some other issues.

Why *is* the porkpie so indelibly associated with Walt Walthers, you might ask. Regular visitors to Kibbee Pond will, of course, remember several moments when the hat has played an important role in the experiences of our pond-dwelling friends. For instance, there was the time when Walt and Stumpy took then six-year-old Tony Riggetti, their nearest neighbor, who still lives down the hill from them with his mom, Amy, and dad, Anthony, off for a ride in his green '60 Chevy pickup, Lulu. Even though Tony is now approaching the ripe old age of eight, he still remembers with great fondness how Walt parked Lulu at a turnoff on a back dirt road across town and took the lad and Stumpy for an exploratory walk up a shaded path on a sunny mid-August day. "Wow!" Walt said as they disembarked from the truck. "I haven't been up here since Annie was still alive." (Annie, as you know, was Walt's wife and the mother of his three sons; she died back in the mid-1980s.) "We used to come up here pretty regularly for a pre-sunset walk on summer evenings," Walt continued, "and bring the dogs with us. At that point, we had three: Rufus, Tea, and Firefly, all littermates and all named collectively for a character Groucho played in a Marx Brothers movie. Ever see any Marx Brothers movies, Tony?" When the youngster shook his head no, Walt continued, "Well, you just might like them. Even if the wordplay gets too fast for you, the slapstick and horseplay will probably still be worth a giggle or two or even a gaggle of guffaws . . . if there is any such thing."

"Are there a lot of horses in those movies, Mister Walt?" the wide-eyed boy asked.

"Oh," Walt said with a chuckle, "when I said 'horseplay,' I didn't mean that they were literally playing with horses. It's just an expression that means they do a lot of roughhousing in the movies and engage in a good deal of tomfoolery too. . . . Oh, but I can tell by your expression that those terms don't make much sense to you either, and I can't say as I blame you for not following them. We grown-ups do a lot of figurative talking without even realizing that what we're saying can be taken a whole different way. 'Roughhousing' and 'horseplay' both mean the same thing: just being rough and wild in how you play, pushing and shoving or wrestling . . . you know, not thinking about the things you might break so that you end up knocking over a lamp or dropping a plate so that it shatters on the floor—the kind of rough playing you probably shouldn't do inside a house—hence, 'roughhousing.' 'Horseplay' is what some people call horsing around—again, being rougher than people ought to be, like horses forgetting where they are and bucking and kicking or charging around indoors. No actual horses are involved in horseplay, though. And 'slapstick' is the kind of comedy in which people are clumsy, often on purpose, and end up in embarrassing situations—bumping into each other and falling down, breaking things, and making themselves look silly. The Marx Brothers do that sort of thing pretty often, though they don't seem to get embarrassed by much of anything."

The boy still looked a bit perplexed. "What's a guf-flaw, Mr. Walt?"

By this time, the two humans had gotten about halfway up the shaded, two-rut path they were following under the rows of big sugar maples that lined both sides of the way. Walt could see the crest of the hill, where another path ran left at a right angle to the first, with a stone wall and another line of sugar maples marking its course. "Well," Walt said, "a guffaw is a kind of laugh, usually loud and obtrusive, even obnoxious. I hadn't thought of it as a *flaw* before, but you may have a point there: A guffaw can be rather crude. Hey, let's take a left up here and explore along the ridgeline. There's a pretty cool field up there where Annie and I had picnics once or twice."

And there, in that mid-August field, while following the flight of a yellow swallowtail butterfly, Walt spotted a large clump of blackberry bushes in the shade along the tree line bordering the path. Many of the dark purple fruit were as big as cherry tomatoes, and oldster and youngster smacked their lips, emitting loud *mmm-m-ms* as they gobbled the first few each. "Doesn't each berry look almost like a miniature cluster of wild grapes?" Walt said as he reached for another berry.

By this time, Stumpy, whom Walt had allowed to wander off on his own to explore the trees and check for fallen hickory nuts, had seen the two humans engaged in what seemed to his rodent's sharp eyesight suspicious behavior; with catlike curiosity, he descended from the branches and hopped through some now-browning ferns to stand up inquiringly at Walt's feet. "Hey, Stump," the silver-haired forager said, reaching down with a particularly plump berry in his hand, "try this." Holding his treasure with both paws, the squirrel turned the orb over several times before finding just the right spot for his first bite; when two or three more speedy chomps had dispatched that fruit, the gray-furred bandit was once again begging at his roommate's feet.

"I don't think I've ever seen bigger, juicier blackberries than these," Walt said in between bites of his own. "They'd be perfect for a pie or even blackberry roly-poly, my mother's favorite. Ever had blackberry roly-poly, Tony?"

The boy, whose lips were taking on an ever-redder hue as the fruit juice dribbled from tongue to chin, mumbled, "No. What's that?"

"Well," Walt said, "it's a dessert. What you do is, you take a bunch of blackberries and put them in a pan with some sugar, cinnamon, and a little water, and then you cook them for fifteen minutes or so. Then you make a batch of baking-powder biscuits and a bowlful of hard sauce, which consists of some confectioner's sugar, a little rum to moisten it, and some nutmeg to sprinkle on top. You spoon the blackberry stew, which you've thickened with some corn starch, onto the opened biscuits and smear the hard sauce on top. It's a little like strawberry shortcake but bolder in flavor. But you say you've never had any, so we'll have to change that situation when we get home! Let's see. How are we gonna get these babies home?"

And of course, he didn't have to meditate long on the problem before coming up with the obvious solution: the porkpie. You probably thought I had forgotten that I was talking about the porkpie and had just gotten carried away with telling another story, but I assure you: There *is* a method to my madness, at least once in a while. Walt could not stand, of course, to leave those beautiful berries behind, especially after promising Tony some roly-poly, so he took off the porkpie, and the two friends set about filling it with the ripe and succulent berries. When they got back to the cabin and measured their treasure, they found that the hat held just over four cups. Of course, if any of you are fans of blackberries, you know that they would not have made the trip back to the truck and then back to the pond without leaving signs of their presence on their container. Thus, for several months Walt's porkpie sported telltale stains that leaked through the khaki fabric from inside, where the berries had bled. From the outside, the brim of Walt's chapeau looked as if it had a dark red hatband, and splotches of a similar color showed elsewhere on the crown, on both sides.

This story leads us, of course, to a recurring question, or a series of related questions that people often ask about this legendary lid. The basic question is this: Is the porkpie Walt wears the only porkpie he has ever owned? Some variations from Google include: How many porkpies has Walt owned? How often does Walt replace his porkpie? Has Walt's porkpie changed in significant ways over the years?

Just as Batman's mask undergoes periodic updates and even major makeovers, both in the comics and in the movies, so Walt's porkpie has gone through some evolution over the years. The short answer is that Walt has had several different porkpies, and he always keeps a spare one in his closet in the cabin. Rumor has it, he may even have an extra tucked away behind the bench seat in the cab of Lulu.

You might also be asking what else Walt has carried in his porkpie over the years, and—of course—I'm sure you want to know how long he's been wearing a porkpie. Let me focus on the first question for a moment. Some of you will remember hearing about the time Walt attended a minor league baseball game in Manchester, New Hampshire, and awed the crowd there by catching a foul ball in his porkpie—without thinking, as the ball was arcing toward his seat along the third-base line, just snatching off his headpiece by the front brim, rotating it slightly, and snagging the jetting hunk of horsehide without even the slightest flinch. Well, all right, he didn't *carry* the ball home in his hat; he held it proudly in his hand all the way back to the parking lot, but he did catch it with the porkpie, and for a moment or two, the hat did serve as a container of sorts for that ball.

Of course, Walt has used that omnipresent haberdasher's creation to carry other objects and substances over the years, from other fruit like apples and peaches picked in various orchards to tomatoes and beans he has picked in his own gardens on occasions when he forgot to take out his picking basket, from the geometrically patterned red-and-yellow fallen leaves of sassafras trees to injured birds and even small animals, as on the occasion when he discovered a baby porcupine wandering in the middle of Warren Road and let the youngster crawl into the porkpie so he could ferry it off into the woods on the far side of the road. He has used the hat to collect donations after a benefit concert at the gazebo in the center of Lunenburg and has allowed people to choose the winning numbers at various raffles from inside the fabled headpiece.

Speaking about what Walt has carried in the porkpie, however, has reminded me of some events that occurred well before Stumpy came to light up the octogenarian's life, going back in fact more than twenty years to the time shortly after the death of his beloved Annie. We all know about Walt's devotion to Annie, and we've seen over the last couple of years how his long-standing friendship with Arlene Tosh has deepened into a January-January love relationship, but I've never spoken of another relationship that was once very important to our modest hero, and since we're talking about the porkpie's history and about the times Walt has used it to carry various things and even about how many porkpies he has had over the years, perhaps this is an appropriate time to mention Leela Haven, a name that might already be familiar to some of you as one of the more famous former residents of the Kibbee Pond area.

In part as an expression of his grief as a brand new widower, Walt made an impulsive decision back in the mid-1980s: Since his three sons were all grown and established elsewhere, he would sell the house in which he had raised his family and lived with Annie and use that money to buy twenty acres at Kibbee Pond; on that land he would build the cabin where he now lives, having made an arrangement with his mechanic friend Andy Martin to camp in a tent at Andy's house in Groton until the cabin was ready. In those days, before he had installed his dock or bought Nelly, his skiff, which now is powered by his ancient but still reliable Johnson three-horse outboard motor, Walt had purchased a used kayak to explore the pond. Still largely undeveloped even now, Kibbee Pond in those days felt even more wild, and despite proximity to the heavily populated Beech Tree Lake in neighboring Lunenburg, the pond's shores sported only a handful of structures, of which Walt suspected his cabin might be the only full-time residence. Paddling was for him both exercise and meditation, as he mourned his loss and contemplated other major changes in his life. One day, however, his explorations provided a revelation.

As Walt drew his craft around a small wooded point, he saw a woman on the shore, tall and lithe as a sapling in a slight breeze. In fact, his first impression was that he was looking at some natural feature of the landscape, until she straightened further to gaze back at him from thirty yards away. As a reflex, he tipped his porkpie—yes, he was wearing his porkpie even in those long-ago days—and then, with more conscious thought, he called out, "Pardon my intrusion! I hadn't thought to encounter any other humans this morning." As the woman faced him directly, he found justification for his first impression: She wore a cream-colored shirt with khaki shorts, and her waist-length ash-blond hair was tied back behind her head so that as she stood there, straight and supple, she resembled a young birch tree with its leaves turning gold in the fall.

The woman held his gaze as she replied, "Nor had I."

"I'm Walt Walthers," the paddler said. "Live in a cabin over by the swamp." He inclined his head to the northwest.

"Leela Haven," the woman said quietly, her voice carrying across the water. "I live back up here." Her head turned slightly toward the woods behind her. "I guess we're neighbors, of a sort. Probably see you again." She nodded as she turned and strode, a full bucket in hand, back among the trees.

From that point on, Walt made an early-morning paddle part of his ritual, hoping to see Leela again, often encountering her on what he eventually learned was her dawn jaunt to the shore to fetch water for coffee. Several weeks passed, with Walt, whenever he did see the woman, calling hello and offering information about the wildlife he had seen on his excursions around the pond. That quiet, patient approach proved the best way, as it turned out, to pique her interest and gradually wear down her natural inclination to suspicion and detachment. Perhaps it didn't hurt that he tipped his porkpie each time before he sculled away.

The morning finally came when, after several innocuous conversations across the water about mink and snapping turtles and otters, Leela called back, "Care for a cup of coffee? I'll have it brewing in about three minutes."

That's when Walt first got to see her shack, even smaller and in some ways more basic than his cabin; it was also when he got to see Leela up close for the first time. After pulling his kayak up on the beach, he followed a barely discernible path up through the oaks and maples that came right down to the water, and paused to take in the structure about a hundred feet back in the woods; it looked square and no more than twenty-five feet on each side. Stepping up onto the covered front porch and rapping at the screen door centered between two windows that faced back toward the lake, Walt removed his porkpie and stepped through into the interior when the woman said, "Come on in." As his eyes adjusted to the dimness, he took in the stone fireplace along the back wall and the full bookshelves that lined every other available space. The ceiling went up to the peak of the roof, with a central exposed beam running left to right, and the single front room had windows on three sides. As his eyes adjusted, Walt made out, above the windows on both sides in the triangular areas beneath the rafters, two murals, the one on the left featuring an osprey hovering over an expanse of water that reflected the sky among its lily pads and blossoms, the one on the right depicting a great blue heron stalking its prey along a swampy shoreline beneath big white pines and hardwoods. A stunned "Oh-h-h . . ." was all he could manage to say as he stood unconsciously squeezing the hat in his hands.

Leela laughed as she turned from the stove in the far corner on the osprey side of the room. In the soft electric light there, Walt realized that she was not a young woman—though she was deceptively youthful in appearance and even manner—perhaps as old as forty but likely somewhat younger, but in any case still twenty-plus years his junior. Although her skin was smooth enough for a twenty-year-old, her eyes, in their blend of boldness and guardedness, gave her experience away. "They came out nicely, I think," she said, nodding toward the osprey above her and then the heron on the opposite wall. "I have trouble with the wings of birds in flight, but I got this one pretty nearly right."

In the conversation that ensued, Walt learned that Leela was not only an accomplished painter in oil, acrylic, and watercolor, but also a writer and photographer; both murals were actually based on photos she had taken. She had been living in the cottage, which Walt could no longer think of as a "shack," for almost a year and planned to stay at least until she finished two manuscripts she was working on, one a prose meditation on living alone in the woods and the other a collection of poems. Occasionally, for more subsistence money, she would sub as a science teacher in the local schools, but she preferred having her time free for her writing and art and for her long rambles in the woods and along the shore that provided much of the inspiration and rumination for her other work. In a clearing not far from the cottage, she maintained several garden patches that provided vegetables for canning and freezing so that most of the food she ate she had also grown. After many more coffee conversations, at her cottage and at his cabin, Walt learned that Leela had suffered a broken heart in her graduate-school days and had since forsworn love, dedicating herself to her research, creative activities, and self-sufficiency.

Of course, the widower, for all the pains of his grief, fell half in love with the beautiful younger woman, a circumstance that brought on some pangs of guilt when he thought of Annie, but he also realized that Leela's companionship was helping him to heal. When he had the time, he would join the graceful blonde on an occasional ramble in the woods. She was, in fact, the main inspiration for his decision to buy Nelly, the skiff, so he could squire Leela around the pond and cover the water more quickly and thoroughly than was possible in her canoe, though they made their share of expeditions in that craft as well. If you've been wondering what role the porkpie plays in this part of the story, we've reached the point where I can make that matter more clear.

As the two companions wandered through the woods, they would find objects that Leela wanted to take back to the cabin for further examination, and the porkpie worked admirably as a vessel of conveyance that did minimal damage to even delicate materials. Birds' eggs, wildflowers and leaves of trees and shrubs, mushrooms and lichen, feathers and snake skins, even occasional living creatures (efts, frogs, an injured mole, beetles, praying mantises, a walking stick) found their way into the hat for the trip back to the cottage; there, Leela could draw them or photograph them at leisure or, in the case of berries and other fruit or fungi and herbs, cook with them. She was also, as Walt soon learned, a licensed wildlife rehabilitator, and over the two years they spent as friends, fellow woods walkers, pond explorers, and—gradually—confidantes, Walt's porkpie carried to Leela several baby birds, including a young wood duck he found dashing through the tall grass in a field far from water, as well as a batch of field mice orphaned by a lawn mower, and a number of other creatures. In fairness, the wood duckling, which Walt nicknamed Bungee because of its prodigious jumping and bouncing abilities, required a cardboard box for delivery because it refused to sit quietly in the hat, but Walt did start out trying to confine the boisterous young bird to his chapeau.

Later, after Leela had left, Walt realized that his time with her had been a great gift from the universe that allowed him to rediscover the joy he had always taken in living and in the natural world. Sometimes in the early days of their time together, he wondered if the woman might be an embodiment of some natural principle—a dryad or nymph—but her story, as he learned it, made clear that she was a vulnerable though strong human being and not someone to deify, tempting as he found it in his smitten state. When, through the public libraries in the area, she had begun a program of nature walks and talks, as well as some lectures on topics like "Newts and Efts" and "The Turtles of the Townsend Area," Walt had volunteered to assist her—though his hat didn't come into play much in those circumstances, except as he tipped it when introducing himself to the participants.

Well, actually, it did play a substantial role on one occasion, when a small group of adults signed up for a special pond cruise Leela was leading. She had two middle-aged women riding in her canoe with her while Walt was chaperoning an elderly husband and wife in Nelly. As the two craft pressed through the lily pads into the swamp, Leela pointed out a painted turtle sunning itself on a protruding stump; when she lamented not being able to turn the turtle over so her guests could examine its plastron, Walt jazzed the Johnson motor a bit, swung Nelly's bow toward the stump, and then, in one fluid movement, reached up to the porkpie, grasped it by the brim with the thumb and first two fingers of his right hand, and flung it like a Frisbee. Spiraling slowly, the hat arced and then dropped directly onto the basking reptile, which had barely begun to register alarm at the closeness of the boats. With another spurt of speed, Walt pulled the boat alongside the stump, grabbing hat and turtle before the creature was able to struggle out from under its dark prison. For the rest of their time together, that moment remained a frequent topic of conversation, with Leela joking that the throw was merely lucky and Walt contending that he had been practicing all his life for just such a moment.

Walt realized that Leela's departure had always been inevitable when she completed her manuscripts and both were accepted for publication. Higginbottom & Stearns snatched up the nonfiction work, *Hermit Woman at the Pond,* and Stone Mountain Press put out the volume of poetry, *Sky-Woven Water, Wind-Wefted Sky,* shortly thereafter. Before the dust had settled and before Walt registered that dust was even flying, Leela had accepted her dream job, writing, photographing, painting, and traveling for *National Geographic.*

Her first assignment came quickly, and their parting was understated: a final dinner, with Leela bequeathing Walt her red metal canoe and asking him to check on the cottage occasionally. The years since Annie's death had given the widower time to polish his stoic facade; he gave the younger woman a final hug, kissed her on the forehead, smiled, and then stepped back toward the door of the cottage. Pausing there, however, he turned to face the woman with her supple, tree-like form; reaching up, he removed his porkpie and, across the ten feet that separated them, tossed it with a gentle spin and arc so that it landed perfectly positioned on Leela's golden hair. For the next few years, whenever Leela's pieces in the magazine included a photo of her, she was wearing the hat that Walt had left with her when he returned to the cabin that last night. Postcards from various distant parts of the world still arrive at the cabin every year or two.

It occurs to me that I haven't yet gotten to the story of how Walt began wearing porkpies in the first place, and I've also sidestepped some of the other questions I implied I would be answering. I apologize, and I'll plan to make it all up to you in the near future, maybe even next week. I may have mentioned that many people have theories about the origins of the legendary hat, but Walt has told the true story to only one person, his dear friend Amy Riggetti from down the road. Actually, the theories may be more intriguing than the truth, but I'll let you judge for yourself when the time comes. And if you resent that you have to wait to hear a story that Amy already knows, I'll just mention that Walt has not told anyone, even Amy, the story of his infatuation with Leela, so the score balances out somewhat at this point. Sheesh! Who would have thought a simple hat would prove so complicated to explain!

43

Stumpy and the Porkpie

Part 2

September 4, 2013

Many objects have taken on deep symbolic importance in our culture, from the Statue of Liberty to the Twinkie, from the Green Monster at Fenway Park to the TV dinner, from Mount Rushmore to the Big Mac . . . wait a minute! I knew I should have had something to eat before sitting down to write tonight . . . but to return to my point, we all know that a great variety of items and a whole bunch of stuff have taken on much more emotional significance for us as Americans and especially as individual humans than their intrinsic value might suggest. After all, even the magnificent Grand Canyon is just a sort of hole in the ground, and Niagara Falls is just some water under a bridge . . . well, actually, I guess the river is too wide there for any bridge to span it, but you get the idea: We inflate the importance of things for our own purposes, creating a mythology and perpetuating our sense of wonder, sometimes over what might seem unremarkable to others.

Hats are a good case in point, an issue we began to explore last week. Don't you know somebody who is attached to an old baseball cap, even though it's covered with dirt and stains and its color has faded, and even the embroidered logo on it has been torn off or become almost unrecognizable? Obviously, that cap would have little resale value . . . well, unless its owner happened to have become famous or been elected president or elevated to some other prestigious role. Still, its associations and history give it great value to its owner. Sometimes, too, as we saw last week, some specific hats have become icons, and while Walt Walthers's porkpie may seem an insignificant example, his circle of friends and admirers might have trouble recognizing him if he were not wearing the trademark topper; after all, Arlene Tosh, the lovely widow who has moved into Walt's cabin on Kibbee Pond on an almost full-time basis, sometimes does have to remind him to remove the aforementioned head covering even after he has gotten into bed for the night, so attached, both figuratively and literally, is the octogenarian weather watcher to his cranial lid.

And of course, you can think of many famous hats from legend and history: the green, feathered cap of Robin Hood (at least if you're a fan of Michael Curtiz's film with Errol Flynn in the title role); the bowler hats of Stan Laurel and Oliver Hardy (or the bowler of Charlie Chaplin, for that matter); the fedora of Sam Spade (as portrayed by Bogie); the bathing cap of Esther Williams; that sideways-sitting monstrosity that Napoleon Bonaparte wore to battle; Abraham Lincoln's stovepipe hat (or, for that matter, that ridiculously tall top hat that Colin Firth wore as Mr. Darcy in the A&E film of *Pride and Prejudice* that made him a star—you know, the one that was so tall its top kept getting cropped out of nearly every shot—quite the distraction!). Consider as well Che Guevara's beret; the John B. Stetson hats associated with Gene Autry, Roy Rogers, John Wayne, and other cowboy stars; Sherlock Holmes's deerstalker with the earflaps and double brims; the sombrero sometimes associated with Pancho Villa; and the fez (or tarboosh) that Sydney Greenstreet wears in *Casablanca* (or is that too obscure?). How about Daniel Boone's coonskin cap or the plaid atrocities that football coaches like Bear Bryant and Tom Landry and Paul Brown used to wear? Or the Pope's miter, that tall, white ceremonial headdress that gets handed down from pontiff to pontiff? Even though I've already mentioned the fedora once, Walt and others would insist that I mention it again in the context of Indiana Jones, with whom many people may associate that hat even more closely than his leather jacket or whip. Even the porkpie hat, which in its inexpensive Sears, Roebuck incarnation is Walt's favorite, also reminds many people of other figures as well: the silent film comedian Buster Keaton and musicians like Lester Young, Tom Waits, and Mississippi John Hurt (the latter being a great favorite of Walt's good friend Todd Jormonen, the snowplow driver and handyman).

Last week, I set out to encapsulate the history of Walt's porkpie but found that the hat is so omnipresent in Walt's life and so obtrusive in his personal history that I barely scratched the surface in the episode. . . . Well, I didn't literally scratch the surface of Walt's hat; I just mean that after nine single-spaced pages, I still had barely made a dent in the mystique of that chapeau. . . . Well, again, I didn't make a dent in the hat literally; I didn't touch it at all, and I respect Walt too much to even consider folding the brim down from a different angle or adding a hatband or feather. No, my hat is off to Walt. . . . Well, again, not literally off, mainly because I don't usually wear a hat while I'm writing, but I suspect you know what I mean. Anyway, I hope that tonight, I will be able to tell you about the origins of Walt's porkpie, even including some of the speculation in which his friends have engaged on that topic over the years.

Before I get to those stories, however, I want to clarify what I mean when I say "porkpie hat." In fact, Walt's hat is a kind of cross between a classic porkpie and a fedora, so I sometimes wonder why he doesn't refer to it as a "fedorkpie." While its crown is not particularly tall, it is flat like that of a porkpie; on the other hand, the brim is relatively shallow, more like that of a fedora. Walt achieves his distinctive look by leaving the back of the brim turned up but the front tipped down; the result is jaunty without being insolent, and the khaki fabric he prefers is neither expensive nor flashy. If he wants to impress someone as a sharp dresser, he emphasizes, instead of his headgear, the bright-red suspenders that are also a regular part of his wardrobe. In addition, he has occasionally tucked a bird feather into the hat's brim as a slight ornament, favoring a two-inch black-and-white downy woodpecker feather, though he has substituted a slightly longer blue jay feather for some especially festive occasions, like Arlene's recent birthday party.

Someone at that festive gathering on August 14 made the mistake of asking Walt why he wears a porkpie. What that inquisitive interlocutor really meant to ask was why the dapper geezer wears a porkpie instead of another style of hat. The crafty codger, however, is—as his friends will tell you—a manipulator of language from way back, and he does insist on some exactitude in the phrasing his acquaintances choose. On the occasion of that slightly careless question, Walt simply smiled and said, "To keep the sun out of my eyes and the rain off my head." You have to be careful to say what you mean around Walt Walthers, or you can end up in one of those chicken-crossing-the-road moments!

But why a porkpie and when did Walt first start wearing one? Well, before I address those questions directly, I want to give you an update on the activities that have been taking place at Kibbee Pond over the last month or so. In contrast with the situation in recent years, *this* August started off as an unseasonably cool month, and in the first couple of weeks, leading up to Arlene's birthday celebration near the midpoint, a breeze seemed to have taken up permanent residence out on the water so that even if the temperature rose to slightly uncomfortable levels, Walt, Arlene, and Stumpy, the stub-tailed gray squirrel who remains Walt's steadfast sidekick (or is it the other way around?), could find some moving air and refreshment by cruising around the pond in Nelly, Walt's skiff. From Nelly's bow protrudes a wooden pulpit that Walt constructed for his gray-furred first mate two summers ago, when he realized how much Stumpy enjoys flapping his jowls in the wind created by the boat's passage and bathing in whatever spray the boat's ancient three-horsepower Johnson outboard can produce; thus, Stumpy always assumes the role of lookout and navigator on his catwalk—or would it be a rodent walk?

These days, Arlene assumes her position on the second seat, amidships, while Walt sits in the stern to handle the tiller on the soft-purring motor; he takes great pride in keeping that outboard as finely tuned as a violin in a first-class orchestra. In the course of late July and early August, the elderly human couple persisted in their efforts to acclimate Arlene's dog, Big Bruno, to boat rides as well, with great success, despite the awkward incident on the picnic back in July; then, you might remember, some tomfoolery by Stumpy and his partner in crime, George the chipmunk, galvanized that elephantine yellow Lab into leaping from Nelly and capsizing the canoe occupied by the rambunctious rodents and by Todd Jormonen and his wife, Lynn. These days, Big Bruno sits happily astern of the Stumpster's pulpit and between Arlene's legs, where she can keep him calm with an occasional pat. His tongue lolls like a pink eel, and his regular panting registers his contentment at being with his mistress rather than back at the cabin, where leaving him behind was the regular procedure just a month or so ago. These days, the gargantuan pooch sometimes even *chooses* to stay home for a mid-morning nap rather than join the crew for their voyage, though usually only if an early-morning ramble in the woods with his cabin-mates has tuckered him out. Sometimes the wild chipmunks out there seem to shriek and flash under his nose just to agitate the poor beast and drive him into frantic diving after their striped flanks, digging at their tunnels, and barking loudly in his frustration. Arlene commented to Walt just the other day, "It amazes me that the poor dog distinguishes between these wild hooligans and George, whom he loves almost as much as he does Stumpy. I guess there's just so much taunting that even a sweet-natured galumpher like Big Big can put up with."

With a weather watcher's fine eye for changes in the climate and waterscape, Walt has noticed recently telltale signs of the shifting seasons. In the third week of August, the breeze that had seemed committed to perpetual companionship with the pond skittered off capriciously, fickly following some new impulse, and the water's surface, constantly riffling before, now went glassy, mirroring the sky so that as Nelly putted through the occasional patch of lily pads, she seemed also to be soaring across that firmament. If Walt hadn't occasionally reminded himself that the clouds being penetrated by the skiff's prow were water rather than air, he might have become dizzy. Had he fallen overboard from vertigo, would he have gotten wet or continued freefalling into the heavens? When he asked Arlene that question, she just laughed and patted the happily panting Big Bruno.

Walt also noticed how the vegetation in and around the pond was changing. Whereas the three colors of water lilies had been present for more than two months, the lily pads themselves were showing signs of wear, with insects and who knows what else having chewed holes in their leaves. In the slanting light of early mornings in August, the silver-haired skipper also noted the arrival of two other flowering aquatic plants. One shot its blossoms an inch or two above the surface of the pond, and those blossoms were a pinkish purple, with two petals, a bonnet-like top and a flounced lower jaw; in the middle was what looked like a marigold-yellow mouth. Although the blossoms were only about a quarter-inch tall, their rich, powdery aroma wafted in the air above them, even with the nonexistent wind. The second plant sent single stringlike stalks up from the bottom, and when those stalks were about two feet from the light at the pond's surface, each one corkscrewed crazily until the end of the stalk lay limply on the surface, having brought a tiny, white orchid-like flower to the light; with the morning brightness cutting through the still water, Walt could see hundreds of the stalks curled like the thinnest fettuccini but motionless in their straining toward those tiny flowers and pollination. Walt didn't know the name of either plant but recognized them as representatives of summer's movement toward the plenty of harvest time.

Some mornings as Nelly cruised in near silence above her own reflection with bright sun overhead and only fair-weather clouds in sight, Walt and Arlene would see pockmarks all around them on the surface tension of the pond, as if rain were starting to fall and the droplets had not yet gathered momentum. Although the first time Walt saw the pocking, he reached out the palm of his right hand as if feeling for raindrops, he soon realized what he was seeing and laughed heartily. "Look more closely, Arlene," he said to the woman on her seat in front of him. "Can you see them?"

Arlene laughed then, too, and said, "They're tiny, and there are hundreds—no, thousands—of them if you look around."

"Must be that the water striders have had a recent hatching," Walt said as he watched the countless small insects careen and dart across the glistening plane, their legs pressing down as they changed direction, each time creating the visible pocking of the water that the elderly voyageurs had noticed.

Besides the newly noticed insect arrivals, a larger avian visitor made a big impression in August too—though more a figurative impression than the literal ones that the tiny dancers produced on the surface of the pond. A bald eagle was appearing with some regularity at the pond, sometimes soaring high above like a feathered barn, the sun catching the whiteness of its head and tail; at other times, it perched in the tops of tall pines on the biggest of the islands, where crows and smaller birds would take turns mobbing it or where ospreys would strafe its perch five or six times before continuing on their way. As Walt and Arlene watched smaller birds tormenting the eagle, the silver-haired Shakespeare lover commented, "Some people say that the eagle is the monarch of all the birds, but these subjects certainly don't treat this king with much respect. They make me think of those lines from *Henry IV, Part 2*:

> Canst thou, O partial sleep, give thy repose
> To the wet sea-boy in an hour so rude,
> And in the calmest and most stillest night,
> With all appliances and means to boot,
> Deny it to a king? Then happy low, lie down!
> Uneasy lies the head that wears a crown.

"That poor eagle looks as though he'd give his kingdom for a horse that could carry him far away from here right now . . . or am I getting my history plays confused?"

Many mornings, too, the boaters found, floating on the placid water, a myriad of small Canada goose feathers, suggesting that the resident flocks had been preening in preparation for their impending migration. "It's almost as if somebody had a big old-fashioned pillow fight out here before we arrived," Walt chuckled the first time they noticed. Each subsequent time they saw the drifting down, he would comment, "Those naughty kids have been bashing the pillows again! And you wonder why we can't have nice things around here!"

But I've strayed rather far from the subject of Walt's porkpie, so maybe I'd better get that issue back into clear focus. This past weekend was Labor Day weekend, the traditional end to summer, and Walt and Arlene had invited a number of friends for a cookout on Sunday afternoon, their guests including the Riggetti family from just down Kibbee Pond Road—almost eight-year-old Tony and his parents, Amy (one of Walt's dearest friends) and Anthony (the former soldier turned real estate agent and car mechanic), and Tony's infant sister, Isabella. Also attending were Todd Jormonen and his wife, Lynn, and of course their rodent companion and Stumpy's compatriot, George the chipmunk. Rounding out the company (in more ways than one) was Officer Irv Stickler, the rotund and good-natured Lunenburg policeman who has become a regular visitor at the cabin. Stumpy and George had scampered off to play along the shoreline, and the human group was relaxing on the deck over a tasty meal of barbecued chicken, fresh beans and corn from Walt's garden, and Arlene's trademark potato salad with bacon, cheddar, dill pickles, and mustard, when the topic of Walt's hat came up again. Much joking speculation resulted about where it came from and under what circumstances the sharp-dressing codger had started wearing the characteristic cranial covering.

In fact, Walt's buddy Todd was the one to raise the question again. When the charcoal fire happened to flare up, the octogenarian grill jockey removed the porkpie and used it to fan down the flames before returning the dapper cap to its favored perch on top of his head. "So, come on, you cantankerous old-timer, why don't you finally clear up the mystery?" Todd said. "Where did your first porkpie come from, and why did you start wearing it?"

"Well, now," Walt replied, "wasn't curiosity the sin that undid Adam and Eve and thus forced all of humanity into a world of imperfection? Don't you think some secrets deserve to be kept? And besides, how are you going to react if the answer doesn't live up to your exalted expectations? No, I don't yet feel the need to tell that story to the world."

"Well, I have a theory," Officer Irv said, his bulky frame clad for this festive occasion in Bermuda shorts and a flowered Hawaiian shirt, size XXXL. "Given what we all know about Walt's character and generosity, I suspect that his first porkpie was some kind of award early in his life for charitable acts or a selfless gesture of some sort. You know, he was driving down some country road late at night and saw a disabled car on the shoulder. For the driver, who was some sophisticated city type in fancy dress, young Walter Walthers changed that tire or refilled that radiator or fixed that carburetor, and in gratitude the city slicker gave him his own natty hat, which ever since has been a mark of distinction, especially out here in the sticks . . . which Townsend *is*, compared to an urban center like, say, Lunenburg."

Walt was chuckling as Arlene replied, "I don't know, Irv. I've known Walt since elementary school, and he never wore the porkpie until sometime after the war. I know for certain that the first porkpie came sometime after high school, when we lost touch for a while."

"Well, that would feed into *my* theory," Todd said, with his usual mischievous twinkle in his eye. "Everybody knows that, like me, Walt is a former Coast Guardsman . . . though I'd better make clear that his service preceded mine by a *substantial* amount of time. You started in the Coast Guard, what, Walt, back in the Revolutionary War?"

"Yeah, that's just about right," Walt said, managing to keep a straight face.

"Anyway," Todd continued, "after many months of Heavy Weather Coxswain Walt manning surfboat teams and tending lighthouses and such, World War II came along, and Walt, as a seasoned and wily veteran, was tapped for a new security detail. Not many people know about this even now, but a group of the finest Guardsmen was chosen for espionage work and sent behind Nazi lines throughout Europe. You see, nobody expected *Coast* Guardsmen to be that far inland in a foreign country, so it was the perfect cover. Walt learned to speak French, German, Russian, and Norwegian as part of his training, and like his compatriots in the Undercover Inland Brigade (as these seamen/spies were called), he was issued the unofficial uniform: a trench coat and a porkpie hat. When the war ended and Walt left the service, government officials allowed him to retain the porkpie in gratitude for his vigilance and bravery in protecting the interests of his country. He's worn that darned hat ever since."

"Wow!" Tony said, his eyes wide. "Is that the true story, Mr. Walt?"

"No," Walt said quickly, "not exactly. Kind of flattering, though."

"Well, I have a theory, then, too," Anthony said. "Walt's a big football fan, and since he grew up in the Midwest, I'm guessing he followed the Cleveland Browns when Paul Brown was their coach. You know, Paul Brown always wore those hideous plaid hats that were a bit like Walt's in shape, so maybe he started wearing them as a devoted Browns fan, in tribute to their great coach."

"I don't know," Todd said. "Bear Bryant and Tom Landry and even Vince Lombardi wore similar, if not quite so garish, modified fedoras, and I don't get the sense that Walt has any special fondness for the Browns or the Cowboys or for the University of Alabama, for that matter . . . though he has professed some admiration for the Packers. We-e-e-ell, I'm still skeptical. . . ."

"Gee," Tony said quietly, "when I first met Mr. Walt, I used to misunderstand some of the things he said, and I didn't hear '*porkpie* hat.' What I thought he said made me think of Davy Crockett and his coonskin cap . . . you know, a hat made from the fur of a raccoon? I thought maybe he had made a hat out of one of those prickly, quill-covered animals because I thought he said he was wearing a '*porcupine* hat.'"

"You stick with that idea," Todd said, raising his eyebrows. "I think we all get the point . . . or points!" He looked at the almost eight-year-old and said, "You see, Tony, that's a little bit of porcupine humor. Stick? Points? Quills?" Tony was already laughing.

"One more possibility you might not have considered," Anthony said, drawing up his six-foot-five frame in his chair and leaning forward conspiratorially, "is that the porkpie might be a carryover from some job he had growing up . . . you know, like if he worked at a particularly posh pharmacy as a soda jerk, and the owner insisted on his workers wearing classy head coverings, partly for sanitary purposes and partly for making a fashion statement. 'Yes, madam, and would you like nuts and a cherry on top of that? We have a fresh shipment of Maraschinos just in from Dalmatia, and some pistachios that came in from Lebanon just the other day. They would make a delightful garnish for your hot fudge sundae.'" Everyone, including Walt, was laughing as Anthony finished.

Regaining his poker face, Walt said, "You might be a bit closer than the others, but that's not it either."

As I've mentioned before, only one person at that gathering had heard the true story, and as I've also said before, the truth may be less dramatic than the fictional versions. Back in the days while Anthony was still in the military service in Afghanistan and before Arlene became a regular resident at the cabin, the kindly geezer had been visiting with Amy one morning after Tony had climbed on the school bus for kindergarten, and over coffee, the young wife had mentioned how she always enjoyed looking up and seeing the porkpie headed down the road toward her house. "Is it a family tradition?" she had asked then. "How did you get started wearing a porkpie?"

The naturalness of the question elicited, for once, a straightforward answer from Walt. "No," he said, "no one in my family that I know of ever wore a porkpie, but when I first started working for the town road crew back after the war, an older fellow was the crew chief, and he was a kind of mentor to me, not just in the work but in a lot of other areas too. His name was Ed French, and he always wore a porkpie on the job . . . well, unless we had to do something that required safety helmets. I was a young man starting a family with Annie, and I looked up to him, with good reason. He knew a lot about all kinds of practical matters, not just highway maintenance stuff, and although he had a gruff exterior, once you penetrated it, his heart was unadulterated gold. For instance, he came by our new place one weekend when we were starting out and helped me build a brick outdoor fireplace so I could barbecue and look out over the mountains as I cooked. He also volunteered to help me put up a line of post-and-rail fence, then counseled me on planning a shed and pitched in on erecting it.

"Ed was quiet most of the time and an incredibly hard worker, but every once in a while, he would pause to lean on his rake and tell a story, and over the time we worked together, a lot of water passed over the dam for us. We grew into a deep and comfortable friendship, a bit like a father-son connection but more relaxed, and we could talk about virtually anything, without artificial shyness. When he finally retired, he literally passed on his porkpie to me, and I wore it proudly for a long time as a badge of honor until Annie finally convinced me to go to Sears and buy a new one. She urged me to save Ed's hat, though, and it's still here, in a box down in the Bottomless Basement.

"When Ed died, he left a space that's been hard to fill, and wearing the hat has been a way of perpetuating his memory and reminding me of the kind of man I want to be, the kind of man he was. I don't tell the story to many people, though I'm not sure why. Guess I'm a bit shy about sharing my love and respect for him with other people. Maybe I'll get over it someday."

Amy had said, "I suspect a lot of folks out there want to be the kind of man *you* are too. I know Tony, for one, wants a porkpie of his own someday."

This weekend, after Walt's friends had tried out their theories about the hat, Amy, holding the sleeping Isabella with one hand, leaned over and put her other hand on her elderly friend's arm. Softly into his near ear, she said, "I'm sure Ed wouldn't mind your telling them the story too." And that's just what Walt did.

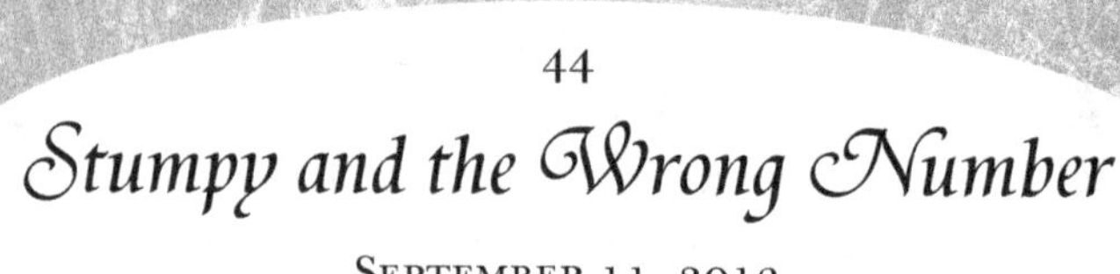

44
Stumpy and the Wrong Number

SEPTEMBER 11, 2013

September is a hectic time for many people, with the start again of school and the feeling that the more leisurely times of summer have evaporated. Out at Kibbee Pond in Townsend, Walt Walthers, the elderly weather watcher who resides in a cozy cabin under the big pines along the shore, feels something of that hastening of life's pace, but he tries to maintain a philosopher's detachment from the artificial urgency that modern life can impose. Perhaps it's easier for him to draw some deep breaths and slow his thinking down because of where he lives; the surrounding natural beauty reminds him regularly of what is truly important. Perhaps even more important for keeping him balanced are the companions with whom he shares that more thoughtfully paced world: Arlene Tosh, the attractive widow who now makes the cabin her almost-constant home; Arlene's king-sized drool factory, the yellow Lab Big Bruno; and of course, Stumpy the stub-tailed gray squirrel, who has been Walt's right-paw rodent for over three years now. "Right-paw rodent" is the proper term, isn't it? I mean, "right-hand man" doesn't quite seem to apply here.

Each morning, Walt and Arlene are up with the sun, not because either has pressing obligations, but because they choose not to waste one of the most beautiful times of day. Of course, Walt would have a difficult time telling you what time of day is the most beautiful at the pond or which is his favorite, questions that his good friend Amy Riggetti asked him last week while he stood with her, waiting for the school bus outside the Riggettis' house, which is just down the hill on Kibbee Pond Road from Walt's cabin. Amy was holding Isabella, her four-month-old daughter, and Stumpy and Tony, her soon-to-be eight-year-old son, were engaged in a spirited game of hide-and-seek under the ashes and oaks and maples that line the road. I say "under," but Stumpy was spending a good deal of his time dashing up *into* the trees and chattering playful insults at Tony from branches above his head. As soon as Tony would call out a laughing reproach—"That's not fair, Stumpy. I can't climb like you"—the bobtailed wonder would streak back down the trunk and dart past the youngster's feet like a furry cannonball racing down a sharp incline.

"Amy," Walt had said, pausing to push up his omnipresent pork-pie hat from his forehead and then adjust it back into place at its characteristic rakish angle, "I couldn't pick a favorite time of day or season of the year at this place. I think whatever time of day or season of the year it happens to be is my favorite right at that moment. There certainly is a lot to recommend early September, though: The summer isn't yet over, but our sense that it's winding down makes the pleasant weather seem all the more precious; the start of school means that I get to go back to more regular storytelling at the schools around the area; the apples, especially the tastiest tarter kinds, are coming into season; the hawks and songbirds are beginning their migration and the insects are shouting every evening; and besides, I get to walk down here in the morning and wait for the bus with you guys before going back up to my place for another cup of coffee with Arlene on the deck. And by the way, you girls"—he nodded at Isabella, who was smiling back up at him—"are welcome to come join us if you like. How does Izzy take her java? Cream and two sugars?" Amy chuckled, knowing that Walt's question, like so much that he says, was rhetorical.

"Oh, that's another great thing about this time of day at this time of year," the kindly octogenarian continued. "The cool nights mean that we can choose on a day-to-day basis between iced coffee and hot coffee. Now, I haven't really answered the second question, about what time of day is my favorite, but I do have to say that waking up to find Arlene still here goes a long way toward making dawn the best. Of course, I could also make a case for early morning, when we walk in the woods, or a bit later, when we take Nelly out for a spin around the pond (Nelly is Walt's ten-foot skiff, powered by the legendary three-horse Johnson outboard). I'm also fond of lunchtime, when we often watch part of an old black-and-white movie or a newer foreign film. And late afternoon, when Arlene and I conspire to prepare our dinner, is pretty special too. Of course, I'm still ignoring the part of the question about the most beautiful time of day or year, but I don't think I could choose an answer there either. This place just offers too much to look at any time."

If I've given the impression that no urgency enters into Walt's existence at the pond, I've misled you somewhat, because as summer winds down and the gardens become even more prolific in their output, Arlene and he have their hands full with putting up vegetables for the winter. This year, the beans have been particularly prolific, seeming to favor the cooler-than-usual temperatures in the region; whereas they had seemed to be dying back early in the month, the plants, both the bush beans and the pole bean varieties, have undergone a resurgence in the last couple of weeks. Having planted twenty different kinds of tomatoes, cherry and full-size, Walt has been inundated with the red, orange, yellow, and green globes as well. As he explained to Arlene just the other day, "Having all these varieties of tomatoes"—by the way, he says "to-may-toes," and she says "to-mah-toes"—"always makes me feel as if Christmas has come a little early. Not only do we get the presents of all these delicious fruits, but the plants also look a little like Christmas trees with all these 'ornaments' of different colors hanging from their branches."

Walt grows some of his tomatoes out in one of his larger garden beds near the tree line, but he also tends several varieties in big plastic pots on the deck. Stumpy and his buddy George the chipmunk—originally a resident of the pond's vicinity and a cherry tomato thief extraordinaire, but now a better-behaved member of the family of Todd Jormonen, Walt's dear friend the snowplow driver and handyman—both rodents, I say, have mastered the fine art of begging for tomatoes underneath the Sun Gold cherry plants that Walt keeps near the kitchen door. Whenever Todd brings his striped companion by in the late summer, she sits up on her haunches next to her favored pot, front paws held together as if she were praying, and rolls her sad eyes at the kindly codger. "She *is* hopeful, isn't she?" Walt will say before reaching up to pluck a yellowish orange orb and then bending over to offer it to the now well-mannered rodent. Of course, Stumpy insists on having a treat as well. Then the two will set off to see what acorns and other nuts they can find under the hardwoods that coexist with the pines around the cabin. Although George prefers to explore from a terrestrially based perspective, Stumpy can sometimes lure her up into the trees, especially if his siblings Burwell and Lansdowne happen to be in the area. Then the four bucktoothed acquaintances play rodent games like Chase, Squeak, and Squawk up and down the trunks and among the lower boughs, usually where Todd, Walt, Arlene, and Big Bruno can watch from the deck.

Putting up tomatoes for the winter is part of what lends some urgency to these late summer days for Walt, as I mentioned before, and recently, Arlene and he have been stewing and canning tomatoes but also refining things still further by making several batches of Walt's famous spaghetti sauce, adding onions, peppers, garlic, fresh herbs, and other seasonings to the tomato stock and then filling the quart Mason jars with the magical elixir that will allow them to taste the freshness of summer throughout the cold months as well. And I've barely mentioned the beans—yellow and green bush varieties as well as several pole beans. Properly frozen (and Walt has mastered several important secrets of freezing beans over the decades), the bush beans retain most of the flavor and snap that make them so wonderful when they are fresh, and although the silver-haired connoisseur likes nothing better than to shell beans fresh off the pole, several of his pole bean varieties, with their range of flavors and textures, are just as good for freezing unshelled in their pods as are the bush types. He simply picks them while the husks are still green and the seeds are still small. You can well imagine that the process of picking, snapping, and freezing beans eats up—so to speak—a good chunk of time for Walt at this moment of the year; nevertheless, he loves to see the plastic containers of summer's bounty fill up the big freezer down in the cabin's Bottomless Basement.

As a professional weather watcher, Walt feels an obligation to his clients, even when beans and tomatoes are inundating his residence and crying out to be preserved, so every morning, he continues to prepare and send out a meteorological forecast and report. As something of a traditionalist and someone who absorbed his family's values of politeness and concern for others, not to mention a good businessman, he does feel compelled to pick up the telephone when it rings (he still has a landline, by the way). In case he can't get there, he does also have an answering machine, but he doesn't like for people who want to speak directly with him to get a recording. Thus, even though he hates dealing with solicitors, he makes every effort to answer whenever his phone rings, even if he has a bunch of sterilized canning jars to remove from boiling water. You can imagine, however, that the ill-timed ringing of his phone can produce some consternation on his part, and though he tries always to keep cursing to a minimum, some colorful language can result if a caller's timing proves inconvenient.

One afternoon last week, just as a batch of jars of stewed tomatoes were ready to come out of the bath, the phone rang, and as Arlene giggled at the look on Walt's face, he burst out in a string of what, for him, qualify as curses. "Dad gummit, and consarn it all! Why do people have to call at a time like this! Toad-spotted, tundra-dwelling, tadpole-faced dimwits are what they must be to call right now! Of all the guldurned, blame-fool things to do!" Arlene thought more steam might be coming out of her consort's ears than was whistling from the boiling water in the canning pan.

Nevertheless, despite his disgruntlement, Walt pulled the thermal mittens off his hands and reached over onto his equipment table for the receiver. "Hello," he said, having drawn a deep breath and trying hard to remove any trace of annoyance from his voice.

"Yes, Carlos needs grooming. Do you have any openings today?" a female voice replied.

"I beg your pardon?" the mystified oldster said.

"Do you have any grooming openings today?" the woman repeated.

"I'm sorry, ma'am, but were you trying to reach the weather-watching services of Walt Walthers? We don't do grooming of any sort, not even seeding clouds for rain. We just report the forecast for upcoming meteorological events."

"Well, I have a long-haired male cat who needs to lose some fur balls, and this is the number I have for the new Townsend Veterinary Services' office." The woman's voice was beginning to register the annoyance Walt had tried to stifle in his a few moments before.

"Could I ask, please, what number you're calling?" Walt said.

"597-6577." The voice definitely qualified as huffy now.

"Well, that *is* the number you've reached," Walt said, "but it's been *my* number for about twenty-five years now. I'm not a veterinarian, and as far as I know, nobody's changed this number recently. Is it possible that someone gave you the wrong number?"

The woman snorted, then said, "I wrote it down from a flyer I received, so I don't see how it can be wrong."

"Well, that is frustrating," Walt said. "Could I suggest checking the flyer again or maybe calling directory assistance? They should be able to help you."

"I just want to get my cat groomed," the voice said, sounding as if it were emerging from between gritted teeth, "and as soon as possible. Can you tell me if they have any openings today?"

"Well," Walt said, "I didn't even know there was a new vet in town, and I haven't had any contact with the office there, so I really can't tell you how busy they are. Wish I could, but I'm afraid I can't. I take my critters to Dr. Brad Schmidt, the fiddling veterinarian over in Pepperell, but I can't tell you whether *they* have any openings today either."

"Well, what did I call you for, then?" the voice said. Walt was sure the receiver slammed down right after those words, and he was pretty sure it slammed down hard.

"Wrong number, eh?" Arlene said as Walt turned back to the stove, shaking his head.

"*She* wasn't convinced of that. By the end, she seemed to think that I had somehow blocked the number she was trying to reach or maybe had hijacked her call. Wanted to get her cat groomed at some new vet in town but had dialed this number."

A bit later in the day, the phone rang again. Walt and Arlene had just finished lunch and were about to take Stumpy and Big Bruno outside to keep the humans company while they picked red raspberries from the line of bushes the fruit-loving cabin dweller had planted about five years earlier along the tree line at the edge of the woods. The gargantuan dog was sitting immediately in front of the door, wagging his tail as if it were an out-of-control metronome of almost deadly proportions, and Stumpy was above the dog on the kitchen counter, scrabbling with his front paws at the doorknob, as if uncounted earlier efforts had not convinced him that the knob was just too big and slippery for him to get the necessary purchase to turn and open on his own. Both creatures are, you see, inordinately fond of raspberries, and they know that their human companions will share any overripe fruit with them; neither one cares that the dripping berry juice will soon leave them looking more like blood-sated carnivores than sweet-tempered beggars with a berry addiction.

This time, when Walt picked up the phone, he heard a male voice. "Is this Townsend Veterinary Services?" that voice asked.

"No, it isn't," Walt said. "May I ask what number you're dialing?"

"Why do you need to know that? I got hold of you, didn't I? You know what number you're at, don't you?" The man's voice sounded suspicious.

"Well, yes, I do," Walt said, "but I had another wrong number earlier in the day, and I'm trying to get to the bottom of what's going on."

"What makes you think *I* dialed wrong?" the voice said, its pitch rising. "Maybe you just picked up at the wrong time!"

At a loss for a response, Walt at first managed only to clear his throat. Then he raised his eyebrows and gently shook his head before saying, calmly, "Could I ask you again, please, what number you were dialing?"

"Well, 597-6755, of course. Isn't that the number I reached?" The tiniest hint of doubt had entered the voice.

"No, it's not," Walt said. "You're off by a couple of digits."

"What do you mean?" the voice asked, and Walt could imagine the man narrowing his eyes as he asked the question, edging closer to outrage once again.

"Well, you've reached 597-6577, not 6755," Walt replied. "You see? The last three numbers are out of sequence."

"Huh," the voice said. "You suppose the operator punched it in wrong?"

"Did you have the operator place the call in the first place, or did you dial it yourself?" Walt asked.

The voice huffed and then said dismissively, "I dialed it myself."

Walt tried to keep the irony out of his voice. "I can only suggest hanging up and dialing again."

"Harumph!" the voice said, and Walt was pretty sure that another receiver slammed down just then, or at least that a finger jabbed none too gently at a cell phone to turn it off.

"Let's pick some berries!" the silver-haired sage said, shaking his head. "The crazies can just leave messages if they can't wait for us to do our hunting-and-gathering bit for today." From their reactions, the gyrating Big Bruno and the chattering Stumpy, both of whom were still hovering near the door, liked Walt's solution. Both of them were hoping for a bounty of those overripe berries and thinking that some perfectly ripe ones might come their way too.

Of course, when they came in from the raspberry picking a half hour or so later, some messages awaited Walt. While Arlene began transferring the berries to plastic containers for freezing, and dog and squirrel sat at her feet looking hopeful and maybe even expectant, Walt pushed the playback button on the answering machine. The electronic voice said, "You have three new messages."

Walt's reaction was "Oh, boy . . ."

First up was a woman's voice: "Mr. Frisky won't stop scratching, and his nose is starting to look raw. I'd like to know if you can recommend some kind of salve or ointment to help or if I need to bring him in to see the doctor. I'll call back later."

"Phew!" Walt said. "At least she didn't ask us to call her back."

Next was another woman's voice: "I just want to know if Sweet Pea's prescription is ready to pick up. Could you please call me back at 597-8822? Thanks."

"Huh," Walt responded, looking at Arlene. "I think that's Muriel Peabody's number. I wonder if she's got a new cat. Then again, maybe Sweet Pea is one of those potbellied pigs I hear are getting popular."

"I lived with a pig for a little while once," Arlene said mischievously, "and no, it wasn't my husband, Bill. As a 4-H project, our daughter Hadley raised a piglet in a pen we built in the field behind our house. The pig's name was Chopper, and she was very intelligent, but Hadley finally gave her away to a friend who lived on a farm and had some other pigs to keep her company."

"I see," Walt said, smiling, his finger having pressed the pause button on the answering machine when Arlene had started speaking. "All right, let's hear this last one."

This time, the voice was male. "Hi, uh, I'm calling to see if you people can recommend a treatment for a flea infestation—uh, nothing too expensive, I hope. We brought a new puppy home from the pound, and, well, now we're all scratching nonstop, and my wife is about ready to shoot me for suggesting we get a dog. I hope you can help. I'll call back later."

"Poor guy!" Walt said, shaking his head. "I don't envy him that situation. He needs to get that pup into a bath and lather it up with some flea soap and, at the same time, throw out all the bedding. Maybe they've got some sprays for carpets and rugs now that would help too. I'm glad Big Bruno didn't give the ol' Stumpster a case of flea-itis when you guys started sticking around here!"

Arlene was about to respond when the phone rang again. Walt picked up the receiver, winking at Arlene. "Townsend Veterinary Services," he said. "How can we help you?" He had pressed a button and put the phone on speaker so Arlene could listen in.

A youthful-sounding woman spoke. "I think it's time to neuter Bilbo. He tried to attack Aragorn again this morning."

"Yes," Walt said, "that would do it for me too. How old is he?"

"He's three."

"Hmm," Walt said, "and I'm guessing he's not actually a hobbit?"

"No, he's a cat," the woman said.

"Ah-h-h!" Walt said. "I was going to say, we've never neutered a hobbit before, but now I guess we won't be getting a chance after all." Arlene was frowning and shaking her head at Walt but also trying to hold back her giggles.

Walt got her message. "Ma'am?" he said. "I'm sorry, but I'm afraid I've misled you. You've reached the wrong number, like a number of other people recently, and this isn't Townsend Veterinary Services after all."

"Oh, I'm sorry . . ." the woman said, and then after a slight pause, "but why did you say it was, then?"

"Not a very good reason," Walt said, trying to sound sincere in his contrition. "We've gotten several wrong numbers just this morning, apparently because our number is so close to that of the new vet. But I must apologize once again. It wasn't kind or compassionate of me to play that joke on you. I can say from experience, though, that it probably *is* wise to get Bilbo neutered; as male cats get older, they do have a tendency to act on their substantial testosterone levels, being aggressive with other animals and even biting their humans. I hope the real vet can help you. And again, I apologize."

"That's all right," the woman said. "I can understand your frustration. I'll try dialing more carefully."

"Good luck, and sorry again," Walt said, hanging up. He turned to Arlene. "That's what I get for trying to be a wise guy. She was a perfectly nice person with a legitimate concern, and I made sport of her. I'm glad she has a forgiving nature."

Before Arlene could respond, though, the phone rang again. Having left the speaker phone option on, Walt answered, "Hello?"

A male voice sniffled and said, "I'm looking to euthanize Bitsy."

Walt whistled softly. "I sure hope Bitsy isn't your wife!"

"No, she isn't," the man said. "She's one of my hamsters, and she's been hiding herself away and sleeping all the time lately."

"I'm sorry, sir," Walt said. "That was just a little attempt at humor there on my part, but probably not at all appropriate. I need to tell you that you've reached the wrong number, as I'm assuming you were trying to reach the new Townsend Veterinary Services' office."

"You're not the doctor?" the man asked.

"No, I'm not," Walt replied, "but I do know a little about hamsters, and while I don't want to give you false hope, if Bitsy is a female, the symptoms sound as though she could be pregnant. You might not be losing your pet but gaining several more. I hope I'm right, but you'll need to talk to the real doctor to be sure. Good luck with that."

Over the next several days, the calls continued to come in from time to time, with both of the octogenarian cabin dwellers amazed that so many people could be dyslexic or abysmally lazy in their dialing habits. Whether he picked up the call or let the machine answer, Walt came to view each wrong number as something like the Joke of the Day, and he did refuse for the moment to erase a few particularly amusing or ironic messages, such as "Hi! I need a shave and a shampoo. Can you call me back?" Walt found that one particularly funny, both because he wasn't sure if the caller thought he had reached a vet or a barber and also because the potentially shaggy fellow didn't leave a return number.

Perhaps the easily amused codger's favorite live call came late last week, when the phone rang late in the morning. A harried male voice said, "I need to talk to the doctor. Burl is having a kitten."

"Literally?" Walt said.

"Yes."

"Well, that's exciting. Congratulations."

"Yeah, thanks, but Burl is *supposed* to be a boy."

"I see," Walt said quietly. "But I think I should tell you that you've reached a wrong number. This isn't the Townsend Veterinary Services."

"You're not the doctor?" the man said.

"Ah, no, I'm not," Walt said.

"What are you, then, a vet tech?"

"No, this isn't the vet's office. I suspect that in your excitement, you pushed the buttons in a different sequence from what you intended."

"Well, can you get the doctor for me? I don't understand how a male cat can be having kittens, and I need to know what to do. Do you think he'd make a house call?"

"I'm sorry," Walt said. "I can't get the doctor because he isn't here. This is a private residence, not the vet's office."

"I don't get it," the man said. "Why do you have the same number as the vet?"

"It's not exactly the same; it's just pretty close," Walt said, but before he could explain further, the caller interrupted.

"Well, why would you *want* a number so close to that of a vet's office? It seems irresponsible of you, especially when people like me have emergencies and need to talk to somebody with medical expertise. I mean, isn't that against the law, to masquerade as a doctor?"

"I'm sorry you think I'm an impostor trying to take advantage of you," Walt said, trying not to laugh as the misunderstanding seemed to be deepening despite his efforts to clear things up. "I'd suggest dialing again, sir—carefully this time—and I wish you good luck with Burl and her offspring. Goodbye now."

When the phone rings these days, Walt isn't quite sure whether he feels more excitement at the possibility of comic drama or apprehension over the chance of more unwarranted recriminations.

Recently, he looked at Arlene, his blue eyes wistful, and asked, "Do you think I should get a new phone number?"

"Why ever would you do that?" the woman said with a chuckle.

"Well, when someone calls and thinks I'm the doctor, I feel like an impostor. You know . . . they're looking for help, and I can't give it to them. And on top of that, there's the matter of the belligerence that some of them show even though they're the ones who dialed wrong."

Arlene's bell-like laughter once again dusted the air with a music like that of spring peeper frogs in April. "Walt Walthers, you handle the calls perfectly well, and most of the time, you seem to find them amusing. You're never rude or short-tempered in your responses. Why not just relax and go with the flow? You've got some great stories to tell now, thanks to the Townsend Veterinary Services and all their would-be clients. Maybe you'll get still more, and you can collect them in yet another book. You could call it *All Crank Callers Great and Small* or *The Doctor Is Not In* or something like that."

"I'll have to think it over," Walt started to say, just as the phone rang again.

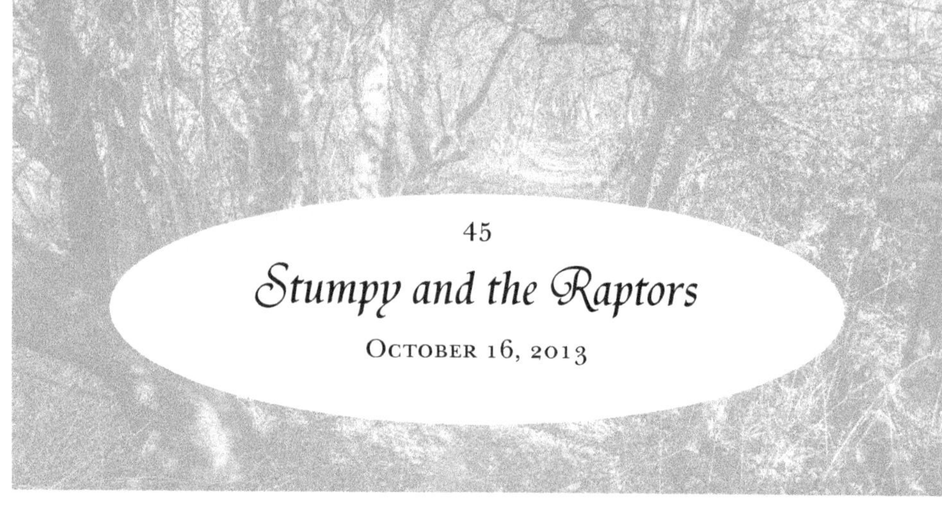

45
Stumpy and the Raptors

October 16, 2013

The first weeks of October always have magic for Walt Walthers, the octogenarian weather watcher who lives out at Kibbee Pond. Of course, living with that rambunctious rodent, Stumpy the stub-tailed gray squirrel, is a constant source of magic in his life, but the turn toward winter that occurs sometime during October transforms how Walt sees the world around him, casting a spell that makes him more aware of the fleetness of time's passage at the same time that it makes him appreciate, paradoxically, time's endless repetitions.

This October is different from Octobers in the recent past, however, because in addition to Stumpy's faithful presence, Walt has the benefit of daily human companionship, too, in the form of Arlene Tosh, the attractive widow who now resides almost full-time at the cozy cabin with the two "previously swinging bachelors," as Walt, in Arlene's presence, teasingly refers to Stumpy and himself. Human and especially female companionship has had a magic of its own for Walt, especially after his twenty-five years of living by himself since the death of his wife, Annie. "Now I feel almost human again," he has said on a number of occasions in Arlene's presence, sometimes continuing, "not that Stumpy's company has necessarily left me feeling *less* than human, but there was a stretch of time before your arrival when I did run naked through the woods at night and try to hide my valuables in hollow trees. Would you call that animal behavior, exactly? Just sounds like a fella letting his hair down a little, if you ask me."

One part of October's ongoing magic for Walt is the annual

raptor migration, and he spends a lot of time throughout late September and October out on the deck above the pond with his binoculars, watching for visitors to wing past or settle into a cruising circle overhead; in fact, since his buddy Todd Jormonen and his neighbor Anthony Riggetti helped him build a screen house closer to the water, Walt has divided his hawk-watching time between the two locations. The kitchen deck is closer to the coffeepot, but the screen house has a better angle on the open sky above the water, and from there in recent weeks, he has spotted harriers and Cooper's hawks, broad wings and redtails, kestrels, and even a goshawk. With the pleasantly warm weather we've had—a bit unseasonal, the experienced weather watcher would tell you—Arlene has frequently joined the silver-haired avian enthusiast, and she has, in fact, made several choice sightings herself. Although Walt feigns chagrin when Arlene's eagle eye beats his, he actually takes pride in his consort's skill, marveling that he has attracted two nearly perfect partners in his lifetime (never for long forgetting his departed wife, Annie). And speaking of eagle eyes, the two elders have seen a baldy once or twice, no surprise since at least one of those magnificent birds had appeared several times during the past summer, fishing the waters of the pond and trying to evade the mobbing tactics of various smaller birds in the tall pines.

Of course, Walt and Arlene—and Stumpy and Big Bruno, Arlene's furry leviathan of a yellow Labrador retriever, whom Walt claims is big enough to retrieve all of Labrador if only he had the chance—continue their daily outings on the pond in Nelly, the porkpie-hatted commodore's wooden skiff, which an ancient but soft-purring Johnson three-horse outboard propels. Only when winter temperatures are about to lock Kibbee Pond under a shell of ice will Walt enlist his friends' help and pull Nelly up on the shore, turning her over and covering her with a tarpaulin until March (he hopes) or early April brings the melt.

A week or so ago, Arlene traveled back to her house in New Hampshire for a brief stay while she interviewed prospective tenants—her plan is to move into the cabin full-time and add her longtime home to the list of rental properties from which she draws her monthly income. For that trip, she took Big Bruno with her. As she readied her silver Volvo for departure, she had said, "I'm sure he'd be happy to stay with you, Walt, but I'd like his company while I'm away. Besides, he'll get a chance to splash in his favorite brook up there, and you and Stumpy can go back to your rowdy and raucous bachelor ways for the time being—you know, soliciting those fast women and even faster lady squirrels over in Lunenburg, staying up late playing poker and smoking cigars, blasting your Duke Ellington tapes on the stereo, and generally making nuisances of yourselves. Not at all the sort of thing I'd want my Big Big to get involved with! And just remember: If you get carried away, I won't be around to bail you out when the po-po lock you up!"

Of course, Walt and even Stumpy are nowhere near as wild as Arlene's joking comments suggested, and while the once-wild rodent may have contemplated some high-spirited shenanigans, the multitalented human was looking forward to devoting his time to several projects, including his memoir of life at Kibbee Pond (which also manages to squeeze in some of his favorite recipes) and the collection of traditional trickster tales he is reworking to feature a mischievous tailless gray squirrel as the central figure. In addition to his writing, however, Walt welcomed the chance to work on the Christmas present he had planned for Arlene: a handmade cherry wood dresser, designed to fit into the wall space beneath one of the windows near their bed.

The first morning Arlene was gone, Walt and Stumpy loaded themselves into Walt's 1960 Chevy pickup, Lulu, for a jaunt into the neighboring town of Groton, where the Paradise Bakery had recently opened its doors. Referring to the outing as a search-and-sample mission, the octogenarian gastronome, who is an accomplished baker himself, intended to purchase a variety of items so as to have a full report ready for Arlene upon her return from the Far North, as the playful codger teasingly calls central New Hampshire. Knowing that his female companion enjoys the occasional croissant but having so far avoided trying to prepare those buttery delicacies himself, he made sure to bring back both an almond croissant and a chocolate-hazelnut one.

The new bakery is a short distance from the campus of Laurel Academy, where Walt has befriended a number of teachers over the years, including Michael Swift, the science department chair who conducted some of his dragonfly research with Walt and Stumpy out on Kibbee Pond a couple of summers back, and Jerry Woodley, the now-retired chemistry teacher who still lives in Groton and occasionally bicycles out to the cabin for coffee and conversation. On this particular morning, however, as Walt came out of the bakery with his croissants in a paper bag, he saw a different familiar form strolling down the sidewalk toward him—a tall, broad-shouldered, elderly form that, though stooping ever so slightly, still bore the hint of a military demeanor. The eyes in that large bald head with its prominent brows were turned up toward the still-colorful maples along the sidewalk, but as an avid bird-watcher himself, Walt recognized that the shifting movements of the man's head meant that he was scanning the branches for feathered rather than leafy beauty. As those eyes refocused on the walkway in front of them, they took in Walt, and a smile spread across the craggy features of Ben Brazier, former head of Laurel Academy, who now resides in Connecticut.

"Walt Walthers!" the bass voice rumbled as the large man, solid as a granite house foundation, reached out his hand toward the porkpie-hatted octogenarian.

"Ben," Walt said, grasping the hand held toward him and smiling up into the other's rheumy eyes. "Back for a trustees' meeting?"

"Exactly," Ben replied, "but everyone keeps telling me about this new bakery, and I slipped away to look for myself. It's a good excuse, too, to walk downtown, something I haven't done for more years than I care to admit. What brings you to town?"

Walt laughed at the irony. "I had to try out this new bakery too. Maybe I'll stroll back that way with you and catch up. Stumpy won't mind sitting in the truck a bit longer, though I wish I could bring him in."

"How is that rascal?" Ben asked.

"I'd say fat and saucy," Walt chuckled, "but with the diet he's on, the 'fat' part doesn't really apply . . . unless he gets addicted to these croissants. The 'saucy' part remains essential to his character, of course. You, as a dog lover, might appreciate that he's living now with a big yellow Lab, not unlike the black Labs you've had over the years, and while most of the dogs I've known would have considered that arrangement as sleeping with the enemy, Big Bruno doesn't seem to have an aggressive bone in his body. He has never chased Stumpy, and I'd swear that the two of them have conspired together, especially recently, in their begging routines—sort of a good cop, bad cop alternating of roles. You know, one is really obnoxious about it one day while the other shows admirable restraint and earns praise, but then they switch roles completely the next day. And then again, some days, it's like a tag team bout; one stares at the plate and leans in close for two minutes while the other sits back, apparently indifferent, and then, as if some whistle too high-pitched for human ears to detect has blown, the other shoulders his way in so the first can take a breather. I swear the psychology of nonhuman mammals is far more complex than most people think."

By this time, the two men had made their way back into the bakery, and soon, they were sitting down with coffee at a table to continue their conversation.

"I've witnessed some strange animal friendships too," Ben said. "Did I ever tell you about my black Lab Nanny and her chicken? I guess we named her well, because when my boys were young, Ben Jr. raised a chick as part of a science project, and Nanny ended up adopting it. When the chick was little, the thing started climbing up between her forepaws and huddling in against her chest as if she was some kind of heat lamp, and that led Ben Jr. to name it Rotisserie—rather an ironic name for a young chicken, I would say. Anyway, as the darned thing grew bigger, it would climb up on top of Nanny and gently groom her back with its beak. I don't think Nanny had fleas or ticks; I think the bird was just being affectionate or maybe proprietary. We had intended to give Rotisserie away to a farmer on the other side of town, but the attachment between those two was so strong, we ended up building a pen and a little coop out behind Williams House, which was at that time the head's residence on campus. Those two spent some portion of nearly every day together for several years."

Walt laughed. "Yes, I'm curious to see what happens when the cold weather arrives. Is the Stumpster going to take his naps on the dog bed with Big Bruno, or will he still take his usual spot on the beam up over the woodstove?"

The conversation turned soon to birds and the fall migration, and Ben introduced the topic of raptors. "I had some help while mowing my fields last week. Three red-tailed hawks thought I was serving them up a smorgasbord and hung around for the two hours or so that it took me to finish. Sometimes they'd be circling overhead, sometimes they'd be perched in branches along the edge of the tree line, and sometimes they'd be hopping about on the ground, ready to snatch up whatever voles and mice the cutting uncovered. At one point, the tractor started a rabbit, and one of the hawks swooped down after it, making a lunge just as the rabbit dove into a tangle of briars at the wood's edge. The redtail had a bit of trouble extricating itself, it was going so fast, but it managed to back out, looking disappointed, with its feathers literally ruffled."

Walt stepped in then to tell Ben about a strange sequence of events that had occurred on one of his morning cruises a day or two before. "We'd already cruised through the swamp up in the northeast corner of the pond and then had turned back out toward the complex of islands closer to the far eastern shore—no big plans, just looking to see what we could see. Stumpy was up on his pulpit, scouting the route as he usually does. As Nelly's bow swung back around the east side of the little island, I noticed a mourning dove, with that characteristic pointed tail, flying across the water and landing on the branch of a dead tree above the lily pads that cluster near the island's shore. A moment later, in what seemed like a coincidence at the time, I spotted, a short distance off the starboard bow, a dove feather floating on the pond's surface; it had that white tip and dark edge that contrast with the sandy tan along the leading edge. As I was smiling at the coincidence, my eye caught another dove feather parachuting down directly ahead, spiraling like a maple seed and weighted by a small mass of apparent down at its stem. Before that oddity could fully register in my brain, I found himself in a shower of feathers, large and small, some of which fell directly into the bottom of Nelly and others of which landed in the water on either side of the skiff. It was like a miniature blizzard erupting in beautiful Indian summer weather. The feathers aroused my suspicions, though, and I looked up, recalling having heard a *scree* call a bit earlier that had put me in mind of an osprey. Well, there, tightening a circle overhead, was a small hawk with its long accipiter's tail fanning out. As soon as my mind registered that it was a sharp-shinned hawk, I realized that that migrating raptor must have struck a dove just overhead a few moments before. As I put the evidence together in the next moment, however, I suspected that the dove had in fact made a getaway, since I had heard no splash. Besides, given the rain of feathers directly above me, any dove corpse falling from the sky might well have struck me in the head. And I'm sure that a sharpy couldn't carry a dove off on the wing; they must weigh just about the same amount. I admit, I couldn't help hoping the best for the dove, although I do understand how the natural world works, and I do sympathize with disappointed predators as well as with their prey."

"Well," Ben said, "sharpies do love mourning doves. From what I've seen, they turn up their noses at the other birds when there's a chance of snagging a squab dinner. When I go out to my feeders and find piles of dove feathers—and that happens with some regularity—then I know a sharpy has been around. People used to call merlins pigeon hawks, so I guess we could call sharpies dove hawks if we wanted to. But, say," Ben continued, "did I ever tell you about what I saw two Novembers ago when I was visiting a friend who lives on the Hudson River not far from Saratoga?"

"No," Walt said. "Another raptor at work?"

"Yes," Ben said. "I happened to be standing in the living room by a sliding door that looks out on the river, just watching a wicked wind whipping frigid air across from the west. Suddenly, two large birds came streaking downstream, from my right to my left, perhaps eight feet above the water. My first impression was that they were of the same size and species, and my second impression was that the trailing bird was an osprey, because its head was white but also seemed to have a dark stripe across the eye. Somehow, though, as they swept past, I realized that the second bird was a bald eagle and that it was pursuing the other and gaining with powerful wing strokes. Before any of that really had soaked in, the eagle struck the other bird from behind and above, and the first bird tumbled immediately into the water. I remember now the impression that the first bird had a dark head, and given its size and what I saw later, I believe now that it was a Canada goose."

"Good Lord!" Walt said under his breath.

"The eagle bent back against the wind and hung over the prey bird for a moment, and I could see the one in the water lift its head weakly before the eagle dropped onto the river and finished it off, apparently by riding on the goose's body while holding its head underwater. I was stunned at what I had seen, feeling a mix of wonder and pity, but then, I couldn't believe my eyes or, rather, the binoculars that I had grabbed to try for a better view. Still in the river and fighting the raging wind, the eagle had gripped the corpse with its talons and now, floating in the water, was starting to *row*—with its wings—toward the shore of an island about thirty yards away. To get there, it had to paddle against a steady and bitter wind. But by the time I had thrown on a coat and hat and gotten outside to the bank of the river, that eagle had already dragged its prey up onto the island. With its beak, it soon commenced to pluck the feathers, which at first blew out onto the water in clouds like the seeds from shaken milkweed pods. Pretty soon, all I could make of the corpse from that distance was a pile of cream-colored down. For the next hour or so, the eagle came and went, but I had to leave shortly thereafter and didn't get a sense for how many visits it needed to polish off its meal or how long that persistent diner took to finish, if it did. I've heard that other eagles sometimes will contest a corpse if they come along. The whole incident was awesome . . . in the correct sense of that word."

"I should think so," Walt said reverently.

"On a lighter note," Ben said, "have you seen any ospreys of late?"

"Yes," Walt replied, "but only irregularly now, so late in the migration season. One particular branch on a white pine near my dock seems to be a favorite perch for them throughout the year—convenient for me because it gives me regular opportunities to watch them when they're taking a breather from fishing. Of course, they're still fishing while they're sitting there, keeping those eagle eyes—or, rather, hawk eyes—peeled for piscine prey."

"Hey," Ben said, "you did know, didn't you, that ospreys always carry the fish they've caught with the fish's heads facing forward?"

"No, but come to think of it," Walt answered, "I've never seen them carry a fish any other way."

"Yes," Ben continued, "if they've initially grasped it crossways or backwards, they'll actually flip the fish into the air and then catch it again with the head facing in the proper direction. They carry prey with one foot gripping the forward part of the fish's body and the other gripping behind. It's all about creating the optimal aerodynamic conditions. After all, it can't be easy to stay in the air when you're carrying a bass that weighs almost as much as you do!"

Walt laughed. "I can just imagine the fish playing it cool and saying, 'Oh, thanks, pal! Now I can see where we're headed. Oh, and by the way, I see a bunch of my buddies over there by that fallen tree. Would you mind dropping me off somewhere in their vicinity? It would be very thoughtful of you.'"

Ben laughed too. "I hadn't ever considered comparing raptors to taxi drivers, but I have seen ospreys drop fish they've caught, so maybe they are dropping them off. Wonder what they charge for their fares?"

The conversation continued for another few minutes before Walt and Ben said an affectionate goodbye, with the former head strolling back toward campus and the octogenarian weather watcher returning to Lulu and an impatient Stumpy. Miffed as he always is at being left out of any social gathering, the gray-furred manipulator spent much of the rest of the morning in a pout. On the ride back to the pond, for instance, he sat on the back of the bench seat as far over toward the passenger's side window as he could get; there, he refused to respond to Walt's good-natured comments as the green pickup climbed the hill into Townsend and wound around on the back roads toward home. Instead, he stared out the window with his back turned toward his roommate. After a few minutes, Walt felt compelled to apologize again.

"Oh, come on, Stump! I'm sorry you had to sit in the truck that long, but I didn't plan on meeting Ben, and the bakery is a new and busy spot right on Main Street. I didn't want to stir up trouble for them with the health inspectors, especially since they don't even know us yet. It's not like Bangkok Gardens or the Brookside, where we're regulars. And even at those places, I didn't just boldly carry you in the first time."

Stumpy, however, was having none of Walt's logic. Clearly, to the squirrel's mind, the duffer's arguments were mere rationalizations, and besides, Walt hadn't even offered him a nibble from the croissants, which to his sensitive rodent's nose were plenty fragrant even inside their paper bag.

Walt did remedy that last mistake as soon as the two roommates arrived back at the cabin, supplying his fuming friend with a slice off one tip of each of the confections. Even that gesture, however, did not appease the stubborn squirrel, who was capable, like a three-year-old human, of holding a grudge for some time. When his gray-furred companion had finished his portion of pastry, Walt watched with some amusement as Stumpy scouted the tabletop for further crumbs and then, reminding himself that he was supposed to look betrayed and miserable, slumped to the floor; there, looking as downcast as a downy woodpecker when the suet container is empty, he drew a deep sigh and, like an exhausted salmon on the last leg of its long journey upriver to spawn and die, dragged himself dejectedly to the couch, where he curled up with his back to his human roommate.

Fighting back chuckles at the melodramatic performance, Walt retired to the Bottomless Basement to put a final coat of silicone sealant on the bathroom cabinet he had built for his neighbors, Anthony, Amy, Tony, and Isabella Riggetti. He was proud of the design, his own invention, especially of what he called the cathedral doors, their tall rectangular shapes cut out with two centered arcs, each coming together in a point at the top; the shape emulated that of the tall windows in many of the churches he had attended over the decades. As usual, he had signed his work with his trademark, using a woodburning tool and just seven smooth strokes to shape a tailless squirrel, then carefully adding the lettering, which read "Smiling Squirrel Manufacturing." Applying the sealant to his creation took only a half hour of Walt's patient, unhurried work; as he always says, "A job worth doing is worth doing well, and patience is a high virtue" (I think that last part may be a quote from Chaucer). After cleaning his brush, the creative coot busied himself with an inventory of the supplies in the shop, adding a few items to the shopping list he keeps on the pegboard above his main worktable.

Just as Walt was putting his broom back into its place after a quick sweep of the area, he heard a pattering on the concrete, and he was not surprised when he turned back to see his mammalian roommate sitting upright on the worktable, front paws held in a posture that could have indicated either prayer, entreaty, or repentance.

"Well, hello there," the woodworking geezer said, careful to keep his voice neutral so as not to betray his amusement at Stumpy's change of mood, just in case his roommate was still feeling miffed. "Hey, I just realized that I'll need some more wood screws if I am going to assemble the drawers for Arlene's dresser." Walt paused, then continued, "I figured maybe we could ride down to Apple Orchard Hardware and visit with Sam for a bit if you're in the mood. He might have gotten in some of those special-cut wide pine boards I like too." Walt knows that Stumpy is partial to the small dog biscuits that Sam keeps behind the counter, though the perceptive cabin dweller has always suspected that what the sociable squirrel likes even better is the attention he always gets from Sam, his staff, and the motley crew of regular customers. More familiar faces always seem to drift in while the man and squirrel are lingering in conversation.

Walt might have expected Stumpy to respond by chattering in excitement or even leaping from the workbench onto his human companion's shoulder, but as prone to sudden mood shifts as the bucktoothed brigand can be, Walt has also experienced the squirrel's pensive side. Given Stumpy's simple and subdued head bob, the perceptive geezer theorized that his friend was probably feeling some embarrassment about his earlier pouting. Thus, when Stumpy reached out both front paws toward him, the doting duffer stepped forward and reached out his right arm so the supplicant could climb to his shoulder and make his apology with a gentle cheek nibble.

"I'm glad you're in a better mood," the silver-haired animal lover said. "You *are* capable at times of being a little sulky, and you know what I always say: 'The best use for a little sulky is to harness a little horse to it and drive that little sulky into town!' Well, I don't know if I *always* say that, but I might have said it a time or two before. I may have put the cart before the horse with that last remark, so I guess I'd better rein in my enthusiasm. Otherwise, I might end up taking the bit in my teeth and running with it. Oh, too late! No use *stall*ing for time! I've already gotten started on a run of puns, and as you know, ol' Stumpster, there's no use . . . locking the stable door after the horse has already gotten out! Oh, and I can see what you're thinking, so don't even think about calling me *un*stable!"

With that last remark, the two friends headed back up the stairs and out to the shed, where their—ahem!—chariot awaited them.

46

Stumpy and the Autumn Bonfire

October 23, 2013

The weather has continued to be mild out at Kibbee Pond in mid-October this year, and Walt Walthers, the elderly weather watcher who lives out there in his snug pondside cabin with his somewhat-domesticated rodent roommate, Stumpy the tailless gray squirrel, has had no complaints. Well, perhaps I can't say that he has had *no* complaints, but he certainly hasn't complained about the weather, and he certainly hasn't complained about the Red Sox as they have continued their postseason success. In fact, Walt has recently suggested to his childhood sweetheart and now nearly constant cabinmate Arlene Tosh that she consider renaming her ginormous yellow Lab, Big Bruno, in honor of the Sox slugger David Ortiz. "Can't we just try calling him Big Puppy and see if the name feels right? You never know if the team might need that sort of intangible psychic support to get to the World Series."

Arlene was understandably skeptical of Walt's logic but replied, "You're welcome to call him that if you like. After all, it's better than some of the names you've called him at other times, and it does fit. He *is* a big puppy! If you don't mind, though, I'll stick to using his given name or one of the nicknames *I've* chosen, like Big Big or Tater Tot. Fair enough?"

One of the reasons that Walt's friendship with Arlene has persisted across the decades and has now even deepened into mutual love is that both are excellent at compromising; each recognizes what is most important and thinks first of the other's happiness, so Walt had no trouble laughing and agreeing to Arlene's more-than-reasonable proposal.

You may remember, though, that toward the middle of the month, both Arlene and Big Bruno departed for the attractive widow's house in central New Hampshire, a house which she has been readying for rental. Part of her purpose was to meet some prospective tenants, and another part was to say goodbye to the place where she raised her family and lived for many years with her beloved husband, Bill. Her decision to move into the cabin full-time she has not made in haste, and Walt himself understands the emotional complexities of balancing past and current loves; after all, he remains devoted to the memory of his wife, Annie, whom he lost to cancer some twenty-five years ago. Walt knows, however, that love comes from opening the heart, not from locking it down around one object of affection. He has often said that love is not quantifiable or subject to mathematical reduction, and raising three sons and caring for many animal companions over the years has taught him a vital paradox: that a person's capacity for love expands as he gives that love away. Like a natural spring or an ever-replenished pitcher of wine, love will well up in us no matter how much has already run out.

However, with Arlene gone for a few days, Walt and Stumpy reveled, at least initially, in their sense of having returned to the good old days of their "bachelors' freedom," as the mischievous octogenarian had jokingly commented to Arlene on the night before her departure. Arlene had simply laughed and responded, "Yes, your ball and chain must be chafing you something awful." She was nevertheless sensitive to how her presence had modified the two friends' mode of living and realized that her taking a little time away with her faithful canine companion would only make man and squirrel more appreciative of Big Bruno's and her companionship when they did return. "Just don't get too wild in celebrating your release from bondage," she said. "I don't want the first thing I have to do when I get back home to the pond to be bailing you two out of the hoosegow!"

The reality was, of course, that after only a day or two, Walt and Stumpy were feeling the absence of the woman and dog enough to be slightly lonely by suppertime, when darkness was starting to cloak the cabin. Thus, one night a few days ago, Walt decided to change their routine a little.

"It's a mild evening, old pal," the clever codger said to Stumpy. "What do you say to a moonlight putt around the pond?"

Without hesitating, the gray-furred rapscallion scooted up onto the kitchen counter and started scratching at the edge of the kitchen door.

"I'll take that as a yes," Walt chuckled. "Let me get my coat."

The colors of sunset were lingering in the sky when the roommates pushed off from the dock around 6:15, but the almost-full moon had already climbed above the trees to the east. Only the lightest of breezes stirred, and it did so only occasionally, so that the purring of the three-horse Johnson motor was the only sound disturbing the stillness, if anyone could consider a sound so somnolent to be disturbing. Stumpy had hopped up to his usual lookout post on the wooden pulpit Walt had long ago made for him and attached to Nelly's bow, and Walt noticed that the squirrel seemed to be leaning out over the rail as if trying to watch his reflection on the glassy surface of the pond. Walt considered making a joke and chastising his companion for mirror-gazing; he even thought about mock-lecturing him on the dangers of narcissism. The kindly duffer, however, knows that Stumpy in the late fall slips into contemplation as quickly as he does himself, and with darkness lowering around them, he suspected that the squirrel was missing Arlene and Big Bruno as much as he was. Thus he simply said, "It's just like a mirror tonight, isn't it, pal? Pretty cool, I'd say. Did you see the moon peeking over the pines?" A moment after Stumpy's eyes tipped up toward that gleaming globe, the pensive passenger looked back at Nelly's skipper and bobbed his head twice.

The first leg of their jaunt took the two-man crew and their craft up into the swamp north of the cabin, where Ralph the great blue heron was still lurking in the dusk. Walt called out, "Yo, Ralphie! How minny mannows . . . I mean, how many minnows have you managed to manhandle and maneuver into your maw this magnificent evening?" The long-necked bog walker's only response was to hunker down and then lift off into flight, his course bending in an arc away from the cruising skiff. "Oh, come on," Walt hollered. "You're no fun! Sorry to disturb you, though!"

The two mariners had cruised back out into the central part of the pond and were just making the bend back to port to enter the next section beyond that dogleg when Stumpy stiffened from the reverie into which the outboard's song on this darkling cruise had put him. As soon as he heard the squirrel's low chirring above the motor's purr, Walt knew that his friend had sensed something unusual ahead, and he leaned forward to peer into the gloom along the shoreline. When Nelly had cleared the point, Stumpy upgraded his vocalizations to outright chattering; he would look ahead, then turn back toward the stern, bobbing his head as his excitement spilled out. On the eastern shore, almost directly underneath the yellow face of the moon and in a spot where a small clapboard camp had sat for as long as Walt could remember, he recognized the flaring of a bonfire. Although he had never met the owner of the lot, he realized in that moment that he was about to do so.

The sentinel in the bow grew quiet as the distance shortened between the craft and the shore, and from Walt's seat in the stern, the elderly skipper could make out a figure in the flickering tides of light around the bonfire, as it walked to and from the pyre, apparently fetching and adding fuel. Out of courtesy and in order to give the person on the shore some advanced warning of their approach, Walt reached beneath the stern seat and pulled out his flashlight, then turned it on and beamed a few flashes toward the shore. "I won't bother trying any Morse Code right now, Stump," he said. "Besides, 'We come in peace' or 'Take me to your leader' would sound too much like a bad science-fiction movie . . . even if I had time to spell out all those letters."

As Nelly approached the small wooden dock that was familiar to both the voyagers from past jaunts around the pond, they saw, for the first time, a human figure actually standing on that structure. Before they could make out the person's features, Walt and Stumpy heard a female voice calling out across the water: "Now what have I conjured with my magical, end-of-the-autumn signal fire? Are you supernatural entities or just curious residents of the natural world?"

"More the latter than the former," Walt called back, laughing as he cut the engine. "We're your neighbors from the other side of the pond!" When Nelly's port side nudged the dock, he reached out to grab a metal piling, then continued. "I'm Walt Walthers, and my harpooner riding up there in the bow is Stumpy the squirrel. In all our time here, we've never seen any signs of residency or even activity on your lot, so it was a bit of a surprise to spot your fire."

In the dusk the woman also laughed, then said, "It's no wonder, since I haven't been here myself for many years! In fact, I hate to think how many. My name is Eve Wood . . . well, actually, it's Evening Wood, but most people just call me Eve. Why don't you step on out if you like and come up to the fire? It's a bit nippy out here now that the sun is down."

"Thanks, but we don't want to intrude," Walt said.

"You won't be intruding," the woman replied. "I welcome the company, especially since you're not some sort of otherworldly entities. Funny how the falling dark can work on the imagination!"

Walt chuckled. "Just let me tie Nelly off here on your dock cleats, and we'll follow you." He hoisted Stumpy onto his shoulder as he often does when circumstances are unfamiliar.

As Eve led the way up the dock in the dusk, Walt could see that she was tall and slim, and although he had been unable to make out her features with much precision in the still-swelling dark, he estimated from her athletic stride and the relaxed confidence in her voice that she was in her late twenties or early thirties. She continued to talk as they approached the hissing and crackling fire, from which an occasional strand of sparks rose like summer lightning bugs drifting up through the pine boughs overhead. "My grandfather bought this lot and built a camp on it well before I was born, back, in fact, when he was a young man, and he used to bring my dad here for fishing trips when Dad was a 'squirt,' as he put it. I came up only once while Grandpa was still alive and just a couple more times with Dad while I was still little. I remember very little of what it was like then, except for the sounds of the nuthatches *feemp*-ing in the trees and the water lapping the shore when I woke up . . . and maybe the smell of bacon frying. When I unlocked the door to the camp earlier today, I was surprised that I didn't have more visual memories of the inside. In any case, except for one oil lamp on the mantel over the woodstove, nothing in the place looked familiar to me, yet at the same time, it felt in some odd way like home, or at least like a home I had been yearning for without knowing it."

"That's the way I feel about my cabin," Walt commented, "or I should say, the way I *felt* about it even when I first moved in. It's not fancy or big—in those senses, a lot like your cottage here—but I've been living in the place for over twenty-five years now. I built it when I lost my wife to cancer and just couldn't stand the thought of staying in the house where we had raised our boys together. My friends and family thought I was being rash, but I knew I had made the right choice as soon as I moved in."

By this time, the two humans had walked up to a stone-ringed firepit where the fire Stumpy had noticed from the water was blazing; for the moment, the squirrel remained on his friend's shoulder. From the aromatic clouds of smoke and the sputtering sparks, Walt could tell that the fuel included a healthy portion of pine and hemlock branches. The flames cast light up under overhanging pine branches while creating shadows across the faces of both Eve and her elderly neighbor. Walt could make out the windows of the small structure farther back from the water.

"If I may ask," the kindly elder said, "what brings you back to this spot after such a long time away?"

In the firelight Eve's face had a timeless quality with its high cheekbones and full lips, and Walt revised his estimate of her age; he thought she must be closer to forty or even older. She raised her eyes to his in the flickering light, then looked down again at the flames; she gestured to a wooden bench close to the stone ring and sat down herself on a large rock a few feet away.

"A promise I made to my grandfather years ago and again to my dad a short while ago. Neither wanted me to let go of this place, because it meant something special to them, and they knew it was special to me as well. I remember Grandpa saying, 'You may roam far, but you can always come back here and find me. I'll be in the pines as they sough in the wind and in the nuthatches as they scuttle up and down. And you'll be here too—some precious part of you that you thought you had lost.' It sounds silly, I know, but that's the way Grandpa spoke sometimes—like life was full of mystery and wonder. . . ." She glanced at Walt across the fire.

"You mean it isn't?" Walt said, laughing. "I suspect I would have liked your grandfather. *I* find plenty of mystery and wonder around here . . . like this little guy here on my shoulder." Stumpy took that line as a cue to clamber down from his perch and begin exploring the pine needle–strewn clearing.

Eve laughed too. "Yes, where I live now, not a whole lot of folks have pet squirrels!"

"Well," Walt chuckled, "I'm not sure Stumpy thinks of himself as *my* pet . . . more the other way around . . . but where *do* you live now?"

"Ah-h-h," she said, "New York. I'm in publishing and have been for a long time. A far cry from this place, I'm afraid."

"I imagine so," Walt said, "but I suspect it's full of wonders and mysteries of its own."

"That it is," Eve said, "but sometimes it's hard to appreciate them with the pace of my life. I think that's why my dad reminded me that this place was still here, even though he hadn't been back himself for some time. I needed to pause for a little cheese in the midst of the rat race, as he put it."

"Your dad sounds like a man after my own heart too," Walt said. By this time, Stumpy had made his way around the fire and, with his typical hop-hop-pause-hop gait, was tentatively approaching Eve. "I should warn you," Walt added. "It looks as though he wants to say hello. If you don't object, you can hold out your arm, and he'll climb up to your shoulder. He's such a rogue, he may even try to give you a kiss." Which is exactly what the gray-furred Casanova did, eliciting girlish giggles from the sophisticated, big-city editor.

After Stumpy had finished his greeting and had settled onto Eve's shoulder, Walt continued, "I'm surprised I haven't seen your dad here at some point. We take an excursion around the pond almost every day, though we usually do it during the daylight hours instead of in the evening."

Eve spoke softly. "We lost Dad last year, and for some time before that, he wasn't getting here much. He hadn't been here for three or four years because of ill health, and even before that, his visits were infrequent. Still, he held on to the place, he said because it had magical memories for him, both of the times spent here with Grandpa when he was young and of the times he brought me here. I vowed I would come back and try to recapture some of that magic, for his sake, though I was skeptical that anything would happen. Now that I'm here, though, I can feel the magic working on me, too, clearing some of the cobwebs and letting me see things I'd forgotten were there. I built the fire, I guess, because I wanted to conjure more of that magic if I could. A late-summer bonfire to signal the end of the season was something Dad always talked about as a tradition he loved here with Grandpa, and I half-believed when I built this fire that I could bring them both back. The funny thing is that, right on cue, you two arrived as the darkness was thickening." She paused. Stumpy leaned over and rubbed against her cheek with his own.

Walt smiled and after a moment said quietly, "That's us. *Semper paratus*—the old Coast Guard motto: 'always ready.' Something made me come out for a moonlight cruise tonight, maybe the last one before the cold weather clamps down on us. Otherwise, from our lot up near the swamp, I would never have seen your fire, and we might have missed out on this evening's particular magic, the chance to make a new acquaintance. How long will you be sticking around?"

In the flickering of the autumn flames, Eve's face looked up again toward Walt. "I've taken two weeks off from work, but I hadn't planned on staying here for more than a night or two. I've gotten used to being surrounded by people, even though we city folks don't look at each other's faces when we're walking in crowds; I may have been hungering to get away, but I also figured that the solitude here at the pond might be too much for me."

"Huh," Walt said. "When I first came, I craved solitude, and I still need some time alone every day . . . but I've found that some regular good companionship is also essential as a balance to that silence and introspection. Truth is, Stumpy and I were both feeling a bit lonesome when we cast off tonight, and the light of your fire was a welcome sight. Right, Stump?"

The squirrel pushed the top of his head against the woman's cheek as she giggled. "Something tells me," Eve said, "that the two of you are capable of providing 'regular good companionship' for other folks . . . and each other."

"Well," Walt said, "you're welcome to come over to the cabin tomorrow for lunch, if you like, and try out our hospitality. I made a pot of split pea soup today and can throw together some savory muffins to go with it. You can drive over if you like, or we can come and pick you up in Nelly. I'm just sorry that Arlene isn't back yet." He noticed Eve's raised eyebrows. "Oh, Arlene is my better half . . . or my consort . . . or my partner. . . . You know, I'm not sure exactly what to call her. Maybe 'true companion' is as good a title as I can come up with. We've been friends since high school, somewhere back in Revolutionary times, and we've reconnected in the last year or so. She should be back in another day or two, so if you stick around, you'll have a chance to meet her too."

Thus it was that a moonlight cruise and a chance encounter led to a special friendship for Walt and Arlene. The next morning around 11:00, Walt and Stumpy untethered Nelly, and the two crewmates motored across the tranquil pond, which mirrored on its surface the mustards, rusts, and olives of the remaining foliage on the maples, oaks, and pines along the shore and on the islands. In the morning light, Eve's age remained hard to pinpoint, but as the three new acquaintances headed back to Walt's cabin, her comments made clear that she had been reading and editing manuscripts for some twenty-five or more years. With Nelly putting past the Horseshoe, a small inlet where in his quest for food Ralph the heron often strolls the shallows or freezes in a pose like an artist's model, Eve was saying, "From what you mentioned last night, I'm guessing I started my current job just about the time you built your cabin here. I can't help but think that Kibbee Pond is the kind of place where many writers could find their muse."

"Well," Walt said sheepishly, "it took me quite a while, but I've been doing a little writing myself recently. It was Arlene's idea originally, but now I find that the day doesn't feel right if I haven't spent at least a few minutes at my desk." Nelly was now slipping toward the aluminum dock on the shore below Walt's cabin.

"I hope you'll tell me more," Eve said as the wooden skiff gently nudged the metal of the landing.

That's just what Walt did over lunch, though he apologized several times for dragging his guest back into a conversation so much like what she must face at work every day. At his first apology, however, Eve just laughed and said, "Editing is like writing. If you love what you do, you never stop doing it, and there's no constraint involved. In fact, the only constraint comes from making yourself *not* do what comes naturally; that's why I don't take a lot of vacations. I love to read and to find out what others have to say, and I love helping people with something to say both say it more effectively and find an audience. So quit fighting me, and tell me what you've been writing." Her gray-gold eyes smiled above the rim of her coffee cup.

Shyly, Walt told her about the first of his two main projects: the cookbook containing his favorite recipes for muffins, pies, and other dishes, the recipes introduced with and accompanied by reminiscences of raising a family and living with various pets and animal guests. "It's a real hybrid of several genres, I'm afraid, but it's held together by my love of the seasons and my love of animals . . . and my love of baking, in particular."

"What's the second project?" Eve asked, raising a spoonful of soup to her mouth.

"That one grows out of my experiences with telling stories at schools and elsewhere over the last couple of years. Since Stumpy goes with me to all my tale-telling sessions, it occurred to me that I could make him the protagonist of a lot of the old trickster tales from various cultures, just adapting them to a New England setting and the local cast of critters. If other parts of the world have Anansi the spider or Beep Beep the Road Runner or clever frogs or mischievous monkeys, I figured I could glorify the old Stumpster here by retelling old stories my way and by coming up with some new ones. It's one of those projects that feels like it could go on forever; I mean, once you tap into what I call the Well of Story, its waters keep bubbling up spontaneously all around you."

"I'm pretty much immersed in that same well, so I know what you mean," Eve said, laughing. "I've learned that there are many different ways to tell stories, and one of the things I like about Smalley & Black, where I work, is that we remain open to material that's hard to buttonhole, manuscripts that bend and combine genres." Stumpy was sitting on the table about equidistant between Walt and Eve but facing the woman, seeming to take in her every word with rapt attention; he even seemed to have forgotten that a few moments earlier, his focus had been on trying to keep his begging subtle enough to avoid a reprimand from Walt. His roommate would only remind him that he had already enjoyed an appropriately sized portion of one ham, cheddar, and salsa muffin. Now, however, from his look of concentration, the gray-furred rascal seemed to be anticipating Eve's next words, maybe even trying to conjure them from her mouth.

"Walt," the woman said as she smiled at the squirrel, "would you happen to have your manuscripts in a form I could borrow and read through? Something tells me that they may well have captured some of the magic of this special place, and you'd honor me by letting me have a look. Perhaps you want to keep your work private, but you'd give me a good excuse to extend my stay long enough to meet Arlene. And," she added, eyes smiling yet again, "you might be providing me with the publishing discovery of the decade."

An embarrassed Walt was, nevertheless, happy to oblige the big-city editor, and Eve did in fact remain at the cottage across the pond for the next several days, meeting Arlene when Walt's true companion returned the next day and joining the elderly couple for lunch or dinner each of the remaining days of her vacation. By the time she left again for New York, she had annotated Walt's manuscripts with reactions and suggestions and had talked him through some of the revisions she thought would make both works publishable. One last cruise in Nelly followed a lunch of spicy barbecue hamburger on homemade yeast rolls with green bean vinaigrette salad, and Eve waved fondly at her new friends from her dock as Walt steered the skiff back across the mirrored surface of the autumn water. Stumpy even left his privileged perch on the pulpit to join Walt on the stern seat and then to climb all the way up over the skipper's shoulder and onto his ubiquitous porkpie hat, as if to prolong his view of their new friend.

"I think he'd be waving if he knew how," Arlene said to Walt.

"I'm pretty sure we'll see her again, and with some regularity," the kindly duffer replied.

As Nelly putted back into their dock and Walt cut the quiet purr of the three-horse Johnson, the elderly man said wistfully, "I wonder how much longer it will be before we have to take both the boat and the dock out of the water for the winter. It's been a warm fall, but things can turn quickly around here; the pond can glaze over with ice after just a couple of frigid nights."

"I'm not worried," Arlene answered, laughing at Stumpy as he scampered up the shore and toward the deck, as if remembering some rash promise one of the humans had made about a snack when they got home or, from a more generous perspective, as if he were just anxious to get back to his buddy Big Bruno, for whom there had been no room in Nelly this time. Arlene continued, "You've got plenty of firewood stacked, plenty of vegetables put up, and plenty of baked goods tucked away in the freezer. I don't much care what the weather does now that I know I'm going to be here with you regardless. The time I spent at the house up north just made me realize that I do my real living here these days. Even after all those years in that New Hampshire house, it is this cabin now, with you and Stumpy and Big Bruno in it, that feels like home to me."

"You'll get no argument there," Walt said. "It feels like home to me too."

AFTERWORD

The Origins of Stumpy the Squirrel

I GREW UP WITH stories both read and told to me. As soon as I could read for myself, books became my near-constant companions, and I lived inside their pages even more fully than outside them. More subtle but still powerful in their effect were the family stories that my parents, especially my mother, told. Sometimes I was the intended audience, but often, I overheard stories intended for other, more adult audiences. A personal mythology emerged, its elements mingling, from all these different kinds of stories.

When my parents died in 2008, first my mother and then six months later my father, I lost my direct connection to parts of my family's past, and I realized that my memory of many of those stories was imperfect. I had yet another loss to mourn.

The mythology remained, however, and slowly, I realized that I needed to reconstruct it or even reinvent it for myself. I had received stories for a long time, but now I wanted to make them and give them away, build them in the way that humans have always built stories: as a means of consoling themselves and others and as a means of understanding death and other kinds of loss in a world where nearly everything passes away, most of it quickly, or at least more quickly than we are ever really ready for.

In 2011, at the age of sixty, I was living a lifelong fantasy: I had begun to host a radio show on the station sponsored by the private high school where I taught English. Part of the fun in realizing that dream was inventing sponsors for the program and thus ironically crafting an illusion (which no one, including myself, was expected to believe): that the station was bigtime radio, and I was a professional announcer. I enjoyed playing further with the persona I had created for myself in the classroom: Doc Haman, serious about literature and its ambiguities but also enamored of humor and irony. One week, in preparing for the show and writing commercials for nonexistent products and businesses, I came up with an idea for a mock public service announcement as a subtle, tongue-in-cheek joke: I would urge listeners to sign up for the "weather-watching" service run by an octogenarian retiree who lived in a cabin at a fictional pond with his tailless pet gray squirrel. The weather watcher had the alliterative appellation of Walt Walthers, and his companion was Stumpy. My intent was to urge listeners to support the financially challenged fogy by subscribing to his daily weather reports, which Walt would record and send out over the phone. I thought my announcement would be a one-time thing or perhaps a recurring but brief gag. I guess I fooled myself.

The inspiration for the characters of Walt and Stumpy was a true story I remember my dad repeating to my sister, my mom, and me when I was six or seven years old. We had lived briefly in a summer cottage (which we called a "camp") on a small pond in central New Hampshire before the house that was being constructed for us was ready to move into. While we were at the pond, my parents had initiated my sister and me into the delights of feeding the local chipmunks shell-on peanuts; the big excitement was that, with patience, we could gradually convince the chipmunks to take the peanuts out of our hands, and thus we could gain a close look at them as they tucked their treasures into their cheeks. If I remember correctly, they could, almost unbelievably, fit three or even four peanuts into their mouths at the same time. One day, however, Dad told us the sad story of an elderly widower who had cultivated a similar symbiosis with a young chipmunk; so tame and so enthusiastic did the young animal become about receiving its treats that one day it climbed the screen door to the house and leaped onto the man as he emerged to feed it. Startled, the man lost his balance and fell over, landing on and crushing the intended recipient of his charity. Dad pressed no moral onto the story and, I think, shared it simply out of his own horrified wonderment. The story, nevertheless, had stayed with me for more than half a century when it reemerged, ready for an on-air transformation. My version, however, had some important differences. For one, the animal I chose was a gray squirrel; for another and even more important one, my animal did not lose its life, just most of its tail.

Something happened as I read the public service announcement on the air. I realized that I wasn't ready to let those characters go and that comic possibilities existed in extending their tale further, so to speak. Thus, for the following week's program, I wrote a tall tale that involved the territorial Stumpy getting sprayed in a confrontation with a skunk; to deal with the odor, Walt used the dog owner's time-honored method of applying tomato juice to the squirrel's fur, but he did so by convincing the trusting Stumpy to nap in a puddle of that deodorizing liquid left in a glass pan on the dormant stove top. Unrealistic hilarity ensued (or I hope it did) when a visiting social worker mistook Walt for a starving pauper and the sleeping squirrel for Walt's supper, laid out to marinate; she fled when the apparently dead creature came back to life.

Between that week's story and the next one, I realized that I had stumbled across characters who struck far deeper resonances in me than I had expected. When my parents died, my wife and I had used part of our inheritance from them to buy a small cottage on a local lake, and the place we had chosen reminded me strongly of that childhood camp on Rolfe Pond. By the time I started broadcasting my show, *The Doctor Is In*, I had, like E. B. White, reestablished emotional connections with fresh water and was kayaking every day that the weather allowed; often while at The Lake (the places I love take on an archetypal quality for me, so I tend to capitalize my names for them), I thought of my parents, convinced that they would have enjoyed being there with me. Sometime shortly after conceiving of Walt and Stumpy, I realized that Walt's real inspiration had not been that chipmunk-slaying widower but instead was my dad, and I wanted to write more stories, both to learn about Walt as a person and to keep my father alive.

Seeing Dad in Walt led to some important principles that wove through the eighty or more stories that followed. First of all, nobody would die at the fictional Kibbee Pond, and certain characters would not even age; eventually, the stories hinted that Walt might even be reversing the flow of time, becoming more spry physically and mentally, as well as revealing a vague spiritual kinship with the shamans of indigenous peoples. I needed the stories to carry a not-always-subtle element of fantasy and wish fulfillment, and I was aware that I would at times pass inevitably into sentimentalism, though I hoped that irony and humor would help me avoid outright bathos.

A second principle emerged: that the seasons would ground the stories, with many episodes beginning with a leisurely trip around the pond in Walt's wooden skiff, Nelly, and each of them alluding to the actual weather during the week when I was writing. The weather often influenced or even determined the plot of that week's episode, and the characters paid close attention to the appearances and disappearances, and the arrivals and departures of the native wildlife, particularly the birds.

The third principle involved the close relationship between the imagined characters and real people. Walt's grounding in my father is one example, but most of the other characters had some connection with one or more of my friends or family members. (I'll interrupt here to acknowledge that Walt's sartorial splendor—porkpie hat, chinos, and suspenders—derived not from my dad's habits of dress but from those of a second father figure I admired as I was growing up, Bernie Stearns, my sister's longtime companion, who passed away a few months after Dad. Walt's capacity for banter is also akin to Bernie's.) As another example of real-life correspondences, Arlene Tosh first appeared as a version of my mother-in-law but soon took on traits of a close college friend and eventually evolved into a variation on my wife. Amy Riggetti, the young woman who, with her kindergartener son, Tony, moves into the house down the road from Walt's cabin, originally seemed the exception to this third principle, because she seemed to spring fully formed from the Zeus-like brow of my inspiration; with time, however, as a model mother, she reflected many of my own mother's behaviors, perhaps most consciously Mom's tendency to sing standards from the Great American Songbook while cleaning the house and doing other domestic chores. Although I did not base Amy on a real person, she prefigured the entrance of a real person into my life: My daughter-in-law Ashley married my second son and lived in our lake cottage with him and her young son, now my grandson, Kyren, for several months not long before my radio show ended. However, I had not yet met Ashley when Amy came on the fictional scene. Relatively late in the radio show's tenure, the return of Amy's husband, Anthony, from duty in Afghanistan gave me the chance to share with him some of the characteristics of my son Locke, Ashley's husband. In a further irony, the birth of Tony's sister, Isabella, occurred well before the birth of my granddaughter Paisley, Locke and Ashley's first daughter. Those real people, though they entered my life after I had created and lived with their fictional parallels, have nevertheless had some influence on how, in later stories, I have conceived of Amy, Tony, and Isabella. Also, as I write more stories in the future, Anthony and Amy's family will probably reflect subsequent additions to the real-life Hamans.

From another real person, one with whom I had little direct contact, came one of my favorite characters, Todd Jormonen; his original was the son of a high school classmate of mine, a young man who tended to my parents' landscaping and snowplowing late in their lives. Because I met the original Todd only once, all I really knew of him was his concern and kindness in helping my "folks" (as my dad would say); in a nod to verisimilitude, I did invent a Finnish last name for my fictional character to parallel the real-life individual. Nevertheless, the fictional Todd was older than the real one—my age in fact; as the stories continued, I saw myself more and more in him, though I should also admit that his practical and musical skills are abilities I lack but deeply wish I possessed.

When I read that first story on the air, I realized that it was slightly off in tone. The broad nature of the humor was just about right, and subsequent stories often included Twainian exaggerations in plot, but another basic principle was slowly shaping itself in my consciousness: I wanted the stories to avoid satire and mockery (except, of course, as an inverted expression of the love and appreciation the characters felt for each other, as in Walt and Todd's constant banter). I wanted the audience to laugh *with* the characters but not *at* them, and gradually I realized that I wanted to redeem the characters, even if they initially made mistakes or judged others harshly. Despite a few exceptions (the pie-baking widows, Louise Barnes and Maureen Ripley, come to mind), I sought to create characters I liked being around. When I first started writing Officer Irv Stickler, for instance, I thought he would be bossy and officious, an unkind caricature of a small-town police officer; however, before the draft of the story in which Officer Irv first appeared was complete, he had revealed more than two dimensions, actually becoming the "hero" when Stumpy suffers a panic attack. Sometimes fictional characters take over their own lives and exhibit behaviors independent of their creator's intentions.

In creating the characters and their world, I was trying to pay homage to the self-deprecating approach my dad took to life and relationships, and thus I imagined the environs of Kibbee Pond as having some of the traits of Shakespeare's Forest of Arden in *As You Like It*, a place where people mostly lived by the principle that Orlando expresses in the play: "I will chide no breather in this world but myself, against whom I know most faults." Arden is a "green world" where self-realizations and transformations take place and where many of the restrictions of everyday life have evaporated. Similarly, Kibbee Pond has its own magic, its characters growing and undergoing subtle metamorphoses in this pastoral setting. A bigger metamorphosis, however, occurred in my own understanding of Walt and myself as the stories continued to come out of me over those two and a half years on the radio.

Walt is always open to the exterior beauties of the natural world, but he keeps his mind and heart open as well to the interior beauty of the people around him. At first, I conceived of him as something akin to a holy hermit, living by himself and needing little company beyond that of Stumpy, much as my dad seemed to me at times in his final months, without my mother, although he was also without the equivalent of Stumpy. I think Stumpy was my way of trying indirectly to give Dad a special companion he lacked, just as the squirrel fills a void for Walt. Within the stories, however, Stumpy does something more, though I had not originally expected or intended him to do so: He nevertheless proves to be a magnet drawing other companions to Walt. To my conscious surprise (though my subconscious may well have understood something that my conscious mind had missed), Walt becomes a wise elder, a mentor, even a guru for some of the other characters (Tony, in particular), as well as a cherished friend for virtually all of the others. Relatively early in the stories, that empty world of the holy hermit begins to fill up, with other animals and other humans, though Walt never loses his holy qualities.

Maybe the biggest metamorphosis for me lay in the deepening understanding that came, with time, of how the stories reflected my own emotional needs. After my parents' deaths, I felt isolated in my grief; my wife's sometimes-difficult relationship with her parents left me wondering if she understood the depth of my loss, and I drew more into myself. Buying our lake cottage gave me hope that she and I would spend time there together, relaxing into a return of intimate companionship with the last of our sons off to college. However, the big ice storm in December 2008, with its lengthy power outage that came only four months after we bought the cottage, forced my wife to spend twelve straight nights alone there while I stayed at the main house, each of us trying to keep pipes thawed and functioning. Feeding the woodstove there in the frequent snowstorms and sleeping alone while also returning to the main house each day to cook meals on the fireplace hearth gave her an understandable aversion to the lake house that she has still not gotten over. Thus, my newfound love of kayaking and my attachment to the cottage put me in a position similar to Walt's: spending appreciable chunks of time by myself on the water, on the shore, and in the cottage, as well as projecting personalities and names onto the wildlife I encountered as I paddled around the lake. A real-life Stumpy did appear outside the cottage for a couple of years, but she remained wild and kept her distance from me. Thus, most of the time I spent at the lake I spent in isolation from other humans.

One of the wondrous things about writing is that sometimes you write the story, and sometimes it writes you. In fact, most of the time, the story *is* writing you, or at least the process of writing is transforming you in ways you can't recognize in the short term. Gradually, in the radio stories, more and more characters came into Walt's orbit, and the first important arrival seems now to have been a fortuitous gift reflecting the way that the world (or maybe our own imagination) sometimes gives us what we need before we know we need it. When Walt and Stumpy were still in their fictional infancy, my wife and I were investing in rental properties, and our son Locke, the real estate agent, took us to see several houses. While my wife was touring one particular house, my son and I were talking in the yard outside when a young boy sidled up to us through the tall grass, seemingly out of nowhere (though he must have lived next door).

A strange and amusing conversation ensued in which I misheard his name, calling him "Timmy" several times before he corrected me: His name was actually Tommy. In that moment I felt myself slipping into Walt's character, willing myself to try out what I thought would be his approach to a similar situation. Thus, instead of apologizing and walking away as I might normally have done, I decided to draw Tommy out more by gentle teasing: I said he still looked like a Timmy to me and asked if it would be all right if I called him Timmy anyway. Part of my inspiration there, though, was still my dad, who regaled my sister and me throughout our childhood with stories about his younger days with his best friend, "Uncle" Charlie to us. When they shared an apartment as single men immediately after World War II, they had joked regularly with a young boy who lived nearby, insisting on calling him George though he kept protesting, "My name ain't George!" The older men's behavior in Dad's story, however, had always seemed more condescending to me than felt comfortable for Walt, so when that kindly elder first meets Tony Riggetti in the radio story, some grandfatherly concern tempers his playfulness; furthermore, I realized that Tony needed to stand up for himself, so while his naivete often shows through in malapropisms and misunderstandings, he also quickly catches on to Walt's sense of humor and is able to play his own pleasant tricks on the oldster. I didn't want characters or the audience laughing at Tony's expense; I wanted his natural intelligence and good nature both to come through, reflecting and complementing similar qualities in Walt, much as Walt and Todd are near doppelgängers, though of different ages.

Over the decades I've known my wife, she has often reminded me that all the characters in a dream are, in some way, the dreamer herself or himself; similarly, writing the Stumpy stories has reminded me that every character in a piece of fiction is the author, reflecting hopes, fears, desires, and traits of that creator figure. Thus, not long into my radio days, I realized that Walt was more than just a variation of my father; he was also a version of me, or at least of the me I wanted and still want to become. Early on, I even contemplated having a T-shirt made whose lettering would read "What Would Walt Do?" I never did because the slogan seemed vaguely sacrilegious and felt too much like a private joke; offending others or condescending to faithful Christians was never my desire. Nevertheless, almost as if Walt were my grandfather, who was the voice of my conscience in childhood dreams, I sometimes wondered if that fictional character would approve of decisions I was making and actions I was taking; because Walt *is* me in certain senses, conjuring his deep-lying values and beliefs granted me greater access to my own. In other senses, Todd is also the me I wish I were: pragmatic and handy, skilled at music, good at solving real-world problems. On the other hand, he shares my loyalty, generosity, and love of humor and language and music.

Because of the regularity of the radio show, I felt pressure to produce a story each week to read on the air, but partway into the first year, I stumbled across a couple of ways to ease some of that pressure: first, having Walt tell myths and folktales to Tony and others of the regular cast of characters and, second, having Walt go into the local schools on occasion as a storyteller. These approaches allowed me to incorporate more or less ready-made story lines into some weeks' episodes, thus saving time, although recasting those stories in the characters' vernacular phrasing and shaping them to fit the events in Walt and Stumpy's world took time and effort too; nevertheless, taking such a tack eased some of the strain on my creativity. Since nearly all the episodes included details about the current weather and seasonal activities of local wildlife, Native American myths and folktales from other parts of the world often made appropriate tie-ins with what was happening at Kibbee Pond during that particular week in the year. Sometimes, an actual sighting during my daily kayak outings on the real Hickory Hills Lake would inspire an episode but also connect with a traditional tale (or more than one), as with episodes like "Stumpy and the Mosquitoes," "Stumpy and the Swan," and "Stumpy and the Raptors." Other times, a traditional story was already in my mind, and I shaped the natural details to create a fitting setting for that story. I also proved capable of inventing myths and explanations of my own.

Tall tales are a particularly American form of story and one I've loved for as long as I can remember, and the basic premise of my series of stories pushes the boundaries of credibility as tall tales do: a gray squirrel who takes on the traits of more conventional pets like dogs and cats, seems to understand and respond to what humans say to him, and engages in actions that require considerable suspension of disbelief on the audience's part. He has something in common with Lassie (or Bob and Ray's Tippy the Wonder Dog), with trickster characters like Anansi and Brer Rabbit, with the too-numerous-to-count animal helpers of fairy tales, and with the speaking, humanlike animals of fables like Aesop's (though I never actually allow Stumpy to speak). One of my favorite episodes, "Stumpy, the Meat Wagon, and Squiffy the Trout," was just an excuse to have Walt and Todd exchange a couple of the tall tales I love best, each adapted to its teller and the specific circumstances (a concept I borrowed from Chaucer's *Canterbury Tales*). From my own experiences as a storyteller, I have embraced the idea that stories fall into a limited number of patterns or actual plots (as in Christopher Booker's *The Seven Basic Plots*) and are composed of individual motifs that can combine and recombine in almost infinite variations (as in Stith Thompson's *The Folktale*); thus, no story is precisely "new." However, personalizing stories by changing and adding details or by giving the teller a distinctive voice helps to make those stories the teller's own. Shakespeare borrowed and adapted stories from other sources in nearly every one of his plays, and writers constantly reshape Greek myths and Bible stories for their own purposes. Why can't I retell *Moby-Dick* with Walt as a beneficent Ahab and Stumpy as a cross between Ishmael, Starbuck, and Queequeg?

Journey and quest stories have fascinated me throughout my life, and Walt and Stumpy's daily outings in Nelly the skiff bear some resemblance to those basic plot patterns or even to Joseph Campbell's version of the "hero's journey": the characters go away from home (though not very far and over a similar course each time), they observe new and, to them, exciting creatures or events (though by most standards those "new" sightings are mundane, related to a predictable natural cycle), and they return home with a "boon" for their people (though Walt and Stumpy's boons are usually simple reports of the beauties and mysteries of the not-especially-exotic natural world around them).

Looking back on the writing process, I can now see that the plot pattern of one particular work of literature emerges at the heart of the stories as they form a larger whole detailing Walt's emotional growth; more importantly and wondrously, that same plot pattern describes what happened to me as a person over the years I wrote the individual stories. Never did I consciously intend for the stories to parallel the plot of Homer's *Odyssey,* but some similarities seem important now. Odysseus leaves Ithaca for ten years of war in Troy, followed by ten years of circuitous wandering; as he attempts to return home, he faces trials and temptations but persists in his desire to reunite with Penelope and the son he has known as an infant, though only briefly. Walt has lost Annie, his wife, to cancer twenty or so years in the past but still seems unbalanced by that loss as the stories begin; he lives in isolation, although Stumpy's arrival begins Walt's reconnection with the world beyond the cabin, both its natural and its human elements, and that reconnection begins his own journey home.

Initially, I understood Walt as sad but uncomplaining and thus heroic; I admired his endurance and his loyalty to his own Penelope, though he had no way to return to her except in poignant memories. Through those qualities, however, I had unintentionally made him a static character, in some senses dead himself, living only in the past. Walt, however, fought back—understandably—against me, recovering his will to live by tending and then adopting Stumpy and by letting Stumpy draw him out again into the world. His eye attuned now to perceiving beauty and joy and to sharing them, Walt found he was putting himself in the way of more and more characters who seemed to stumble into his life, starting with Tony and Amy, his new human family, who were followed by many others, most importantly Todd and Arlene. George the chipmunk and Big Bruno the dog expanded his family into the animal world as well.

In some ways Walt Walthers has written me as much as I have written him. He came into my life when I most needed him, a dark time of depression and apparent isolation; he refused to fall into the stoicism and victimhood for which I seemed to have shaped him, and he carried me with him on the course we both needed. Writing these stories has helped and shaped me, I am certain, in more ways than I have recognized even now. The stories have brought both Walt and me home.

ACKNOWLEDGMENTS

ALTHOUGH WRITING IS lonely work, envisioning an audience lightens the load, and when I originally composed these stories to read on my radio show, I could easily picture a particular audience I had in mind: a group of close friends ranging in age from their late twenties to their late sixties—adults who retained a childlike delight in the humor of little things and everyday life and who could appreciate irony, playful language, and comic subtleties. Those people were the ones listening to my show—or at least parts of it—with some regularity: Colin Igoe, Eileene Stergiou, Jerry Boucher, and Jerry and Sharon Wooding. I was a household name in their homes even if nowhere else, so I owe them gratitude for keeping me from working in a vacuum and for supplying the encouragement of valued friends. All of them have appeared in some form in my Stumpy stories, and each deserves much more acknowledgment.

My colleague Peter Hazzard and Matt Bosselait, the student manager of WRLA at Lawrence Academy in Groton, showed me the ropes of broadcasting and patiently walked me through how to handle the CD players, microphones, and other equipment in the little room that was our broadcast booth. Pete encouraged me by saying that I had the perfect face for radio. Thanks to them and to the student hosts whose shows kept the station vibrant for the time I was on the air. Thanks also to John Bishop, who kept me going when Pete stepped down, and to Connor Melvin, who took over as station manager after Matt graduated. Without WRLA and my supporters there, I would never have fulfilled the lifelong dream of hosting my own radio show, and without my show, Stumpy would never have come into the world.

While I'm talking about radio-related matters, I should mention that Garrison Keillor and his Prairie Home Companion were inspirations for me when I designed my own show. I knew that I wanted to mix music with made-up sponsors, much as Mr. Keillor did on his show, but I did not even dream at the start that I would also be able to produce a twenty-minute story to read nearly every week for two and a half years.

Of course, what you are reading is a book, rather than a radio show, and I owe tremendous thanks to the people at Small Batch Books, who have believed in this book more than I initially allowed myself to. Trisha Thompson, my editor, has guided me through the various stages of publication, and Allison Gillis, my copy editor, kept track of recurring details in the stories with precision and navigated the intricacies of grammar, punctuation, and fact-checking; she also offered many excellent suggestions for adjustments, major and minor, along the way. Wolcott Gibbs offered this advice to editors: "Try to preserve an author's style if he is an author and has a style." Trisha and Allison have flattered me by treating me like an author with a style of his own; dealing with my idiosyncrasies as a writer can't have been easy, and I am grateful for their help and support. I owe thanks also to Mary Wirth, whose cover and interior designs have created a more visually beautiful book than I imagined possible, and to the rest of the publishing staff in Amherst. My gratitude goes as well to Sharon Wooding for enthusiastically introducing me to Small Batch in the first place.

My dear friend, the late Jerry Wooding, taught me to say thank you to my dogs after each walk, and it seems appropriate here to thank not only Jerry for forty years of friendship but also all the animals in my life for their companionship and love; Stumpy is a composite of the dozens of dogs and cats who have lived with me from childhood to geezerhood, as well as the other critters, domestic and wild, with whom I have connected over the years. My world would be cold and empty without those furred, feathered, and even finned fellow sojourners.

Special thanks I owe as well to Jerry Boucher, my college roommate and godfather to two of my sons, for ongoing hilarity even in the face of ill health. It is a blessing—though others might say a curse—to have found in my youth another person whose sense of humor parallels mine so closely.

And, of course, my love and thanks go to my family. Though physically gone now for many years, my parents stay with me through the stories I tell and my ongoing desire to emulate them in many other ways. Now my sister, Cara, remains to keep alive the familiar and forgotten tales from our childhood together. My three sons—Muir, Locke, and Tristan—inspired me to share stories with them as my parents had done with me, but they also gave me an excuse to tell stories at their schools as they grew up and even to design and teach a storytelling class at my own school, which they all eventually attended. Now my grandchildren—Kyren, Paisley, Henley, Wren, Ryley, and Torben (and, I hope, more to come)—have given me inspiration to continue telling stories and to publish a book that they may eventually enjoy. They love stories already, and with luck, they will all become storytellers too.

Finally, where would Stumpy, Walt, or I be without the love and support of my wife, Lee? She endured the drain of time and energy that the radio show caused and now has become the driving force behind the publication of these stories. Not only that, but she contributed the beautiful watercolor portrait of Stumpy that graces the cover of this book, a portrait that captures the fur-faced rascal's personality in the whimsical but knowing expression on his face. She even was able to imagine his appearance before the accident that claimed his tail! She appears in various manifestations throughout this book and remains the celestial body around which I orbit, the moon that draws my tides, the star that guides my voyage . . . too clichéd? Then, as Stumpy might say (if he were not a squirrel of few words), she is the most treasured nut in my cache. Or, as Walt might say (being more articulate than Stumpy and I are), she is my shelter when dark clouds advance and chilly winds conjure whitecaps on Kibbee Pond, my haven of warmth and sunlight even in winter, my lee shore where the breezes almost always blow gently. Besides, she is at the heart, in every sense, of the ongoing story that I love best: our life together.

SOURCES FOR STORIES WITHIN THE STORIES

Many of these Stumpy stories include my adaptations of traditional tales. Most of those tales I've known for years, and many of them I've personalized and retold in storytelling sessions over the past four decades. What follows is my attempt to acknowledge the sources in which I first encountered those stories, although my records and memories are in some cases hazy.

Arlene's account in "Stumpy and the Snapper" of her childhood fishing and turtle-racing escapades with Roger came from a story told by my mother-in-law, Irene Muir. Thanks, Nana, for helping me get this whole adventure started!

Is it necessary to say that Herman Melville's *Moby-Dick* lurks beneath the surface in "Stumpy and the Bluegills"? Probably not.

For one piece of "Stumpy and the Toothpaste," I owe a debt of gratitude to Russell Peck, my mentor and dissertation director, to whom in fact I owe more debts of gratitude than I can enumerate. The Lightning Loins story that Walt tells came from Russell years ago when he was reminiscing about his youth in Wyoming. The actual body part has been changed to protect propriety and the innocent reader.

"Stumpy and the Kindergarten Class" contains three stories. The first, "The Golden Tree," which Walt tells to Amy and Tony on their way back from their "river shoes" outing, I encountered in Howard Schwartz's *Elijah's Violin and Other Jewish Fairy Tales* (Harper & Row, 1985). Tony's confused synopsis of the version of Theseus and the Minotaur that Ms. Aristea has told his kindergarten class is the second story in the episode, and while many sources recount the tale, this is my chance to mention Anne Terry White's magical collection, *The Golden Treasury of Myths and Legends* (Golden Press, 1959), a Christmas gift my Auntie Joanie chose for me the year I turned nine and a book that introduced me not only to Theseus but also to Orpheus, Daedalus, Oedipus, Beowulf, Tristram and Iseult, and characters from a number of other tales that have enriched my life ever since. The illustrations by Alice and Martin Provensen added to the magic. Not something I could outgrow, my battered copy even now graces the bookshelves in my study, a reminder that old stories renew themselves with each retelling and that keeping those stories alive in new, personalized versions is an honorable and important task. The third story, "Why Dogs Hate Cats," which Walt tells to the class, appears in many forms, but I believe I first encountered it in Julius Lester's *The Knee-High Man and Other Tales* (Dial Books for Young Readers, 1972).

Walt's own version of the Theseus myth informs "Stumpy and the Birthday Celebration," in which the cordial coot reveals his fascination with labyrinths and mazes, a longtime interest of mine as well.

The insane misdirections of love in Shakespeare's *A Midsummer Night's Dream* were in my mind as I recounted the love quadrangle in "Stumpy and the Love Affair." I'm not sure you needed to know that, but there it is.

"Stumpy and the Gobblers" contains Walt's enthusiastic version of "The Firebird, the Horse of Power, and the Princess Vasilissa," which I originally encountered in Joanna Cole's *Best-Loved Folktales of the World* (Anchor Press/Doubleday, 1982), the first text I ordered for students in my storytelling class at Lawrence Academy. Arthur Ransome's *Old Peter's Russian Tales* was Cole's immediate source, though Aleksandr Afanas'ev was presumably the ultimate wellspring for Ransome's version.

In "Stumpy and the Return to School," Walt adapts "Jack and the Widow's Cloth" from Duncan Williamson's *Fireside Tales of the Traveller Children* (Canongate Publishing Limited, 1983), a source to which I return in "Stumpy and the Swan." Williamson's Scottish stories have a special appeal for me, and I had great fun embellishing this one in its new geographical location.

When our three boys were growing up, they all loved "The Seawife and the Crone" with its several false endings, and though it's a long and somewhat convoluted story, I was convinced that Shel, Mac, and Hammy's fourth-grade class would gobble it up too: in "Stumpy, the Seawitch, and the Hag," they do. I found the story long ago in *Alan Garner's Book of British Fairy Tales* (Harper Collins Publishers, 1988); Garner had adapted the story from J. F. Campbell's *Popular Tales of the West Highlands* (London: 1890/3).

Walt's retelling of "One Hairball" from Carol Kendall and Yaowen Li's *Sweet and Sour: Tales from China* causes Tony much hilarity in "Stumpy and the Fur Ball," primarily because of the unfamiliar vocabulary Walt uses.

For the version of the Inuit myth of Qivioq in "Stumpy and the Magic of Kibbee Pond," I am indebted to James Houston's *Kiviok's Magic Journey: An Eskimo Legend* (Atheneum, 1973). The quest of one spouse to reclaim another is a theme that has fascinated me for decades, with the Orpheus myth and the happier, Middle English poem *Sir Orfeo* helping me define for myself the complex distances and barriers in married life as well as its intimacies.

Perhaps the most fun I had in writing any of these stories came from assembling the two main pieces of "Stumpy, the Meatwagon, and Squiffy the Trout." "Big as a Cow" in Alvin Schwartz's *Fat Man in a Fur Coat and Other Bear Stories* (Farrar, Straus and Giroux, 1984) gave me an outline for Walt's account of Orsino the bear. Todd's Squiffy tale derives from "The Trained Trout," Ed Grant's whopper in *The Tame Trout and Other Fairy Tales,* recounted by Francis I. Maule (Maine Woods and Woodsman Printing, 1904); the story is one treasure I found in Catherine Peck's *QPB Treasury of North American Folktales* (The Philip Lief Group, 1998).

"Stumpy and the Mosquitoes" features three stories, starting with Walt's adaptation of a Tlingit myth, "How Mosquitoes Came to Be," included in Richard Erdoes and Alfonso Ortiz's *American Indian Myths and Legends* (Pantheon Books, 1984). Next the eloquent geezer adapts "The Killer Mosquitoes," from *Cajun Folktales* by J. J. Reneaux (August House Publishers, 1992), which I also found in Catherine Peck's *QPB Treasury of North American Folktales.* Walt shows his playfulness in this tale by mimicking three accents. Finally, his version of "Brer Rabbit Goes Courting" owes much to its source: Julius Lester's *The Tales of Uncle Remus: The Adventures of Brer Rabbit* (Dial Books, 1987).

"Stumpy and the Buried Treasure" includes Walt's retelling of an old English tale, "The Peddler of Swaffham," which I encountered in Jane Yolen's *Favorite Folktales From Around the World* (Pantheon Books, 1986). In the Fall 2004 issue of *Parabola (The Seeker),* Madronna Holden provides an analysis of the Russian folktale to which Walt alludes earlier in this chapter; the article is entitled "Go 'I Know Not Where': Tracking the Trackless." At the end of the chapter, Walt alludes to a French tale about a farmer's sons; a version of that story appears as "The Farmer and His Sons" in the Winter 1994 issue of *Parabola (Hidden Treasure).*

Duncan Williamson was again my source in "Stumpy and the Swan"; the arrival of a mute swan on the lake where I kayak every day inspired me to adapt "The Hunchback and the Swan," from *Fireside Tales of the Traveller Children,* with an array of animals appropriate for New England.

In "Stumpy and the Graduation Speech," Walt retells another story from Howard Schwartz's *Elijah's Violin,* "The Golden Mountain," which I myself have enjoyed retelling for several young audiences. It seems especially appropriate for a graduation ceremony.

Two stories play off each other in "Stumpy and the First Night of Summer," both dealing with spouses who become separated from each other. "Diccon and Elfrida," from Ellin Greene's *Midsummer Magic: A Garland of Stories, Charms, and Recipes,* ends less happily than the Maori tale of Ruarangi, which comes from Jane Yolen's collection, *The Fairies' Ring: A Book of Fairy Stories and Poems* (Dutton Children's Books, 1999). Anthony wisely recognizes that Walt is playing a role similar to that of the tohunga. By the way, Greene's book, with its combination of recipes, poems, and stories, is the kind of book that Walt himself eventually writes. It contains the recipe for the Destiny Cakes that appear in "Stumpy and the First Night of Summer," a recipe that my wife, sons, and I used for our own solstice celebrations.

In "Stumpy and the Rodent Regatta," Walt tells his squirrel friend a version of "Chipmunk and Bear," collected by Joseph Bruchac in *Iroquois Stories: Heroes and Heroines·Monsters and Magic* (The Crossing Press, 1985), where I originally encountered the tale.

Later, Bruchac and his son James produced a delightful illustrated children's version, *How Chipmunk Got His Stripes* (Puffin Books, 2001), which I recently discovered.

"Stumpy and the Vulpine Thief" incorporates my Modern English translation of Chaucer's "Nun's Priest's Tale" from *The Canterbury Tales*; my version itself incorporates many additional details that I hoped would amplify the humor (though it's amazingly presumptuous to try to amplify Chaucer's humor). I chose to emphasize the relation between Chaucer's fox and the traditional medieval trickster Reynard by giving the vulpine thief an overblown French accent. By the way, I heartily recommend Anne Louise Avery's recent retelling/translation of *Reynard the Fox,* which adds many comic details to the stories drawn from the Middle Dutch version set in Flanders.

The stories that Walt and Todd exchange about the foolish residents of the two parts of Townsend fit well into the traditions of noodlehead tales, but I don't recall their specific sources. Isaac Bashevis Singer's stories about the fools of Chelm in his *Stories for Children* (Farrar, Straus and Giroux, 1984) and other books have a great deal in common with those told in "Stumpy and the Noodleheads," but stories about fools and noodles are popular throughout the world, I guess because foolishness knows no boundaries.

The story of Thor and Jörmungandr that Walt retells in "Stumpy and the Budding Bard" takes me back to my childhood, but not to a specific retelling of the tale. Since I wrote this chapter, Neil Gaiman has recounted the legend in his *Norse Mythology* (W. W. Norton & Company, 2017). Gaiman is always worth reading.

Once again, the specific source for the Dim Bulb story in "Stumpy and the Telescope" evades my recollection, though the tale has a Native American origin, as does the story of the four animals who steal warmth from the People Above; that second story appears in Michael J. Caduto and Joseph Bruchac's *Keepers of the Earth: Native American Stories and Environmental Activities for Children* (Fulcrum Inc., 1988) as "How Fisher Went to the Skyland: The Origin of the Big Dipper." Walt's adaptation of the story, of course, involves giving Squirrel the lead role and relegating Fisher to a subordinate position. No amount of Googling "firefly origin myth" has proven helpful in prodding my shamefully impaired memory in locating the other story's source; Dim Bulb may be an appropriate nickname for me too.

"Stumpy and the Raptors" gave me a chance to pay homage to Ben Williams, the headmaster who hired me at Lawrence Academy, where I spent thirty-six years teaching English and growing as a human being. On one of his returns to campus for a trustee meeting, Ben and I met and conversed at a new bakery in Groton; most of the individual stories in this chapter came out of that conversation with a man I deeply admire. For verity's sake, I will add that the story I put into Ben's mouth about an eagle killing a Canada goose and rowing it across the Hudson was not one he told me; that event I witnessed myself while visiting my sister in Fort Edward, New York. Unbelievable as it may seem, the story is true.

ABOUT THE AUTHOR

MARK HAMAN, called Doc for decades by his students, has never had a pet squirrel but, boy, would he love one like Stumpy! Doc earned a B.A. from the University of New Hampshire in English Literature and an MA and a PhD from the University of Rochester, with his dissertation focused on Middle English literature. He taught writing and literature at Rochester and colleges in New Hampshire before settling in to a long career teaching English and coaching basketball, soccer, and lacrosse at Lawrence Academy in Groton, Massachusetts. Now retired, he divides his time among three locations: a house in Townsend, Massachusetts, a cottage on Hickory Hills Lake in nearby Lunenburg, and the family farm in Wilton, New Hampshire. His best days include walking in the woods with the dogs, communing with the cats, kayaking, baking, watching birds and other wildlife, reading, writing, playing with grandchildren, and annoying his wife with puns and bad jokes.

CPSIA information can be obtained
at www.ICGtesting.com
Printed in the USA
JSHW031622210622
27249JS00001B/2

9 781951 568245